A NOVEL BY

ALISON McLEAY

NEW YORK/LONDON/TORONTO/SYDNEY/TOKYO/SINGAPORE

Passage Home

SIMON AND SCHUSTER

SIMON AND SCHUSTER
SIMON & SCHUSTER BUILDING
ROCKEFELLER CENTER
1230 AVENUE OF THE AMERICAS
NEW YORK, NEW YORK 10020

DESIGNED BY EVE METZ
MANUFACTURED IN THE UNITED STATES OF AMERICA

1   3   5   7   9   10   8   6   4   2

LIBRARY OF CONGRESS CATALOGING IN PUBLICATION DATA
MCLEAY, ALISON.
PASSAGE HOME: A NOVEL/BY ALISON MCLEAY.
P.   CM.
I. TITLE.
PR6063.C55P37   1990
823'.914—DC20   90-30069
CIP
ISBN 0-671-69299-2

PART ONE

The Island

1

"The Hunter and the Ploughman—you can't have them both, and that's the tragedy of it."

That's how he said it, and I can even tell you when—at nearly eleven o'clock on the 21st of June, in the year 1827—because I wrote it all down next morning in big childish letters, and the yellowed paper is still safe between the pages of my Bible.

I thought he was only talking about the stars: it never ceased to amaze me, the ease with which he could reach up to the Heavens and create birds and beasts and demigods from that rustling host of light.

I'd asked him about Orion, the Hunter of the starry skies and the only constellation I'd heard of in my almost-eight years. He smiled as if I'd mentioned an old friend—that lop-sided, whimsical smile which brought a pale warmth to his gray eyes—and then shook his head.

"The Hunter and his dogs are long gone, far below the horizon. But if you look there—follow where I point—you'll see the Ploughman still up above us, chasing them across the firmament. That big star, Arcturus, is the Ploughman's knee, and just in front of him is his plough. Do you see how he's tearing a furrow through the darkness for the planting of new stars?"

I said I did, which was very nearly true. All I wanted was for Adam Gaunt to go on talking, to go on conjuring magic from the night sky.

"The Hunter and the Ploughman," he repeated thoughtfully. "Round and round they go, always in the same order—first the Hunter, then the farmer after him. The Hunter can never escape— but then, the farmer has never yet caught up with him. There's always been an open space ahead."

It was all he ever asked, that open space stretching into the distance, beckoning him on. And in the beginning, it seemed to all of us that the planet was limitless, there on the threshold of the New World in the third decade of a new century.

But the Ploughman and his kind were moving over the face of it even then, breaking the earth to their use, covering it in bricks and mortar, throwing up houses and roads and mills. For good or ill, the tide could not be turned once it had started to flow.

That's what he meant, *You can't have them both,* though I was too young to understand it at the time. In those days I wanted only the Hunter, and wanted him for myself alone. What if his eyes were fixed on the horizon and the passion of his heart was all for the virgin wilderness? I can still remember, those long years ago, sitting in the darkness on a grassy bank in the scrubland behind our house at Crow Cove, drawn as near to him as I could be without actually touching, while my world turned upside-down with exquisite slowness and a carpet of stars spread itself for me to walk on in heart-stopping grandeur, only provided Adam Gaunt should be at my side.

How simple it seemed at that moment! As simple as that last, innocent summer of my childhood, before the sear leaves of longing, jealousy and despair brought it abruptly to a close. As ever, my mother was at the root of it; yet she and my wretched father, and Frank Ellis, Watches Smoke, Crazy Kate, my blundering, romantic Aunt Grace, poor Jonas and the rest of the mighty Olivers—and, yes, Adam Gaunt in spite of himself—all of them contributed their share to the woman I am now. Though I am more than the sum of those parts. I am, myself, a limitless horizon: I know it for sure now because *he* said so.

It was fitting that he should have come to us out of the eye of a tempest, the worst storm to hit the island of Newfoundland in half a century. Afterward, twenty-three graves scarred the cleared land beyond the village, marked by twenty-three plain wooden boards, most of them bearing no more than the date, *17th May, 1827.*

Adam Gaunt was not among the dead. Fate or one of his own wild gods preserved him against all the odds, though a time was to come when I could wish with all my heart that he had perished with the rest.

———

In Crow Cove the uproar began quietly enough with a stiff breeze from the sea and a piling-up of clouds out over the gray expanse of

Conception Bay. Wind was no novelty to us on our northern island, and I took no notice of the change in the weather until I saw Jacob Birch's wife glance out from the doorway of her house across the ruffled water of the inlet, and quickly cross herself. I knew Captain Birch's schooner *May* was fishing far out on the Banks, and wasn't expected to return to Crow Cove until August, when her holds were filled. Until then, Catherine Birch could only watch the skies and wait with the other wives.

Her gesture made me curious, and for the rest of the afternoon I hung about the front windows of our house, looking out over the rooftops of the village to the cove beyond, searching for signs of the storm which was on its way.

It was easy enough to slip out after supper, as I often did now that the daylight lingered. No one in that household took any interest in the whereabouts of a plain, dark child of nearly eight years who preferred searching for partridge-nests in the scrub to playing with dolls like other girls of her age.

I made my way cautiously round the end of the house, glancing automatically toward the nearest window. In a corner of the parlor a pool of lamplight contained an upright chair and a huge old desk where my mother's head was bent over spidery columns of figures from the store accounts. My father—my father was off somewhere in the village as usual, not to return until well after dark, unnaturally cheerful, his breath reeking of brandy when he insisted on bending to kiss me. Edward and Maria had already been carried off to bed; only I had escaped.

A few freezing drops were starting to fall, the vanguard of the rain-squalls, as I let myself out of the garden gate on to the stony track which wound down the slope toward the village. Behind me, beyond the scrubland which began just after the house, the dark firs of the forest edge were beginning to shiver and lash their sinuous tops. Half-buried on the hillside, the wooden houses of Crow Cove seemed to hug the land, squat and snug, a window here and there already lamplit in the gusty twilight.

There wasn't a soul about as I dawdled through the village toward the lower cluster of houses near the shore. The wind was snatching at my hair now, snaking damp strands across my brow as I halted for a moment to slip off my horrible, heavy shoes and leave them on a flat stone by the roadside to be collected later. For once, blessedly, there was no one to see me.

Except that I had forgotten my mother's own personal spy. When

I glanced toward the low wooden verandah of the store, a pale oval
behind the nearest window confirmed that Susan Vinegar, my mother's assistant, was at her usual post, overseeing the comings and
goings of the village. No doubt Susannah Dean would be told next
morning that her wayward daughter had been seen, shoeless and in
a cotton shift like a village child, wandering by the shore, and I
would be soundly beaten for my disobedience. Again.

There was no point in turning back: the damage was done, and
there was still that eerie, blustery evening to be enjoyed before the
price of my mischief had to be paid. Wriggling my bare toes in the
soft dust, I rambled on down the steep track, following where it
curved past the store to skirt a huddle of houses and the meeting-
hall which also did duty as a schoolroom. After that the path seemed
to lose heart, and dissolved into a wide area of trampled ground
bordered by the coarse, tufted grass of the raised beach and the
terraces of fish-flakes, the drying-racks which proclaimed the principal business of Crow Cove.

By the time I reached the shore, rank upon rank of toothed waves
were already driving into the narrow inlet which gave our village its
name. Every few seconds, a plume of spray would spurt up between
the weedy planks of the jetty as the sea boiled, rumbling and sullen,
among the piles which supported it, sending tongues of fizzing foam
far out along the shingle beach.

While I watched, the wind seemed to unleash its malice in a sudden explosion of power. Furious gusts began to race in from the sea,
hurling rain-squalls before them to rattle on the shingle, and when
the wind drew breath, the rain attacked in earnest, plastering my
thin shift to my shoulders and sending me scurrying back toward the
steep road leading to my home. I was wet through, but I was also
afraid.

Rivulets of water were already coursing down the deep ruts of the
hill track, binding the dust into mud. Head down and unheeding, I
dashed on past the flat stone where I'd left my shoes, splashing up
the slope to our garden gate. I'd reached the sanctuary of my little
attic room before I remembered my bare feet—and only then because I suddenly thought of the warty old toad which lived under
the wayside stone, no doubt reveling in the sudden deluge. Now it
would be bread-and-water for me all week.

But late that night, as I lay in my bed under the rafters, listening
to the furious assault of the storm on the roof-shingles, events were

taking place which soon drove such matters as missing shoes out of my mother's mind. Out on the broad and maddened waters of Conception Bay, the American packet-ship *Adelaide Ross,* four days out of Boston, was drifting, rudderless and dismasted, toward the rocks of the southwestern shore. As the storm roared to its climax, the vessel broke her back at last on a grim saw-edge of stone, and the howl of the wind mingled with the shrieks of the helpless creatures aboard her. Just before dawn, the first bodies began to drift up on the shingle beach of Crow Cove.

———

"A woman an' child, Mrs. Dean—an' the babe tied to her own body with cord, true as I tell you! I daresay she thought to save the child as she saved herself, but they're laid out near the boatyard all the same, white an' dead, both of 'em."

I remember Susan Vinegar's eyes growing round as buttons in her freckled face as she told her tale. The storm had hardly blown itself out when a commotion at first light brought her running from her quarters at the back of the store, a woolen shawl thrown over her nightgown. Catherine Birch, sleepless at her window, had seen an ominous dark mass among the retreating surf on the shingle, bobbing and nudging at the shelving beach until at last the sea left it stranded among a skein of weed, a single pale, twisted limb now visible in the graying dawn.

Susan Vinegar had hurried to the beach with the others. Eighteen corpses were there, counting the infant tied to her mother's breast—four of them seamen by their dress, the rest travelers who'd found an untimely end to their journey. In silence, the bodies were carried up from the beach, straightened and smoothed by sea-worn hands, and laid on trestles in the meeting-hall to await decent burial. But the image of the drowned mother and child stayed to haunt Susan Vinegar and, as soon as she could, she scuttled up the hill from the village to relay the news in our parlor while the teakettle was still warm on the hearth.

"Eighteen of them—think of it! One of them an older man, right enough, by the whiteness of his beard, but the rest as young as you or I. . . . Just think of it!"

Susan Vinegar's shock of straw-colored hair stood out round her head, and her mouth with its gap-tooth hung open in wonder at the frailty of human existence.

"How unfortunate," my mother remarked politely, stirring her tea. "How very sad."

I remember staring at her then, expecting that any woman who'd felt her child's downy head butting at her knee must surely spare a thought for that desperate mother, frantically trying to preserve her baby's life, only to drown in the end with the infant's tiny body at her breast. But my mother was not made of the same stuff as other women. Once upon a time, perhaps—but not then.

"Tell me again," she said sharply, "this woman—the one with the child—did you say she was well-dressed?"

"Her gown was fine, certainly, though the sea had spoiled it. And there were gold rings in her ears."

"And on her fingers?"

"On her fingers, too, I think. I don't rightly remember."

I looked at my mother once more in disbelief. As I'd feared, there was a slyness in her expression, a subtle tightening of the muscles round her blue eyes which seemed to close in her thoughts behind the fair porcelain mask of her face. I knew that expression: as usual, Susannah Dean was debating how best to turn this unlooked-for event to her own advantage. The woman and child were dead and beyond help, but my mother and her own children might yet manage to benefit from their tragedy.

"The babe had a gold chain round her neck, I remember that," Susan Vinegar added after some thought.

"She'll not need it in the grave, I doubt. Best put it somewhere safe for now. And the rings. In case the family comes to claim them, you understand."

"Where, then?"

My mother pursed her lips, and tried to pretend that the problem required some consideration. "The store would be safest. In the cashbox. Or here in the house, perhaps. Out of charity, I'd be prepared to take care of them, and anything else that might be valuable."

I had to look away, a hot wave of shame rising to the roots of my hair.

"I'll tell Preacher what you say," Susan Vinegar agreed, as if robbing the dead was the most natural thing in the world.

Out of the corner of her eye, my mother caught sight of me, sidling to the door.

"And where do you think you're going, my girl? There'll be no school in the meeting-hall today, by all accounts, so you can go into the kitchen and help Liddy pluck a chicken for dinner. It's time you stopped this gallivanting round the village."

"You never know, dearie—we may get more of these poor souls washed up on the beach today, and it's hardly a sight for your eyes." Susan Vinegar managed a gap-toothed smile. "You stay here with Liddy till it's all over and done with."

To tell the truth, I wanted nothing to do with their shameful business. For once I was content to stay at home for the rest of the day, out in the yard with the one-legged crow which flopped at my heels and the blind kitten I'd rescued from the cow-man's bucket, or sitting on the scrubbed kitchen table, my legs swinging, discussing the day's dramas with Liddy, the maid-of-all-work.

Little by little, more news drifted up from the village. The wrecked ship was the *Adelaide Ross,* a well-known flyer; her bows still clung to the rocky ledge where she'd hit, though the next storm would break her up for sure, turning what was left of her hull to matchwood like the rest.

Another six bodies had been found on the beach at Crow Cove, one of them, it seemed, the vessel's master, and more corpses had been reported from different points on the shores of the bay. Only three souls had survived—one man plucked from the rocks near Brigus and another two washed up almost beyond help at the mouth of Crow Cove itself.

Then, in the evening, further news came. One of the inshore boats, searching the bay, had picked up two men and a woman from a mat of floating spars formed from the wreckage of a topmast. The woman was dead, her ribs crushed in, but the two men were still alive. One of them, certainly, was hardly expected to live: his left leg was gashed to the bone almost from knee to ankle, an infection had set in, and by the time he was brought ashore, the poor fellow was almost delirious with fever. The fishermen who found him were all for taking him to the meeting-hall straight away, and leaving him with the rest—he was a big man, and it would save a double journey. But in the end kinder counsel prevailed and the sick man was carried instead to the little cottage near the beach which was owned by the Widow Creran.

Mrs. Creran, midwife and nurse, was also conveniently the layer-out of corpses. For a while, she confessed later, she couldn't tell which of her skills would be soonest required. But the man, though fevered, clung ferociously to life, and the widow set to and cleaned the gaping wound while the patient muttered incoherent, broken phrases, sometimes in a language she didn't recognize, and stared wildly round her immaculate cottage as if it were Hell-mouth itself.

None of this, needless to say, interested my mother. At a time like that, Susannah Dean was less concerned with the living than with the dead. The woman and child were to be buried together, which meant that twenty-three lengths of store linen were required for winding-sheets and enough lumber for twenty-three coffins, the cost to be met by the community. Susan Vinegar, beside herself with excitement, provided constant bulletins on the injured man who raved in strange tongues in his narrow bed in the Widow Creran's house, but my mother simply made a note to put aside linen for another shroud. By all accounts, it would be needed.

———

Even then, I wanted him to get better. There had been enough dying, and I felt in a strange way that another life saved was some recompense for that poor woman and her little baby who'd never lived to see the safety of the shore.

I was standing alone in the garden early in the morning of the next day but one when I noticed the stout midwife climbing slowly up the hill from the village, short of breath, her skirts hitched up in her massive red hands to negotiate the steep slope. When she saw me, Mrs. Creran paused at the side of the path to catch her breath.

"Faith, when you're my age, child, you'll find such hills as this grow steeper every day! And not so long ago, I could fly up it like a bird!"

When she saw my face, she laughed. "In a manner of speakin', young Rachel, in a manner of speakin'. Even my magical powers ain't strong enough for such witchery, if that's what you're thinkin'!"

It was exactly what had gone through my head, the tales which were spread in the village about Mrs. Creran's mysterious potions and cures. But how had *she* known it?

"Are you looking for Ma? I mean *Mamma.*"

"Not I—it isn't your mother that brings me up the hill, don't you fret. I need some nice young ivy leaves for a poultice for a poor man's leg, and a few bits of centaury for a fever infusion." She coughed, and spat into the dusty verge. "With all this cutting of firewood, I've to go further away from the village every time."

"I've heard Susan Vinegar speak about the man. Will he get better, do you think?"

"If the fever goes down, then he may have a chance, poor fellow. If not—well, I shall end by laying him out, that's all."

This was disappointing news. "I wonder if there's a special sailor's Heaven, where he'd be with his friends."

"Oh, he's no sailor, m'dear—not he. Another man saved from the packet-ship told Preacher he was one of the passengers—an' a gentleman, I'd say, by his clothes an' his manner of speakin'. When he's talkin' plain English, that is. Why, I've even had bits of Latin out of him—'least, that's what the Preacher calls it—but most of the time it's nothing at all you'd recognize.

"Preacher's been through the leather bag he had with him—to see who he is, you understand, in case we have to make a headboard for the grave. There were letters addressed to a bank in Liverpool in England an' a mess of other papers too, but at least we're sure of his name now. Mr. Adam Gaunt—that's what he calls himself." Mrs. Creran straightened her back and glanced briefly down the hill toward her own little house among the huddle of pitched roofs. "I wish I was as sure that he'll live."

When I repeated this conversation to my mother later, she simply shrugged and made a face. The wind had torn down the cowshed at the back of the house and lifted a large patch of shingles off the roof of the store, so she had plenty to occupy her mind without the uncertain fate of a castaway.

"If there's a way of keeping him alive, I daresay Mrs. Creran will know it," she remarked briskly, "though if the Flanagan woman's baby comes early he may find himself without a nurse. Don't slouch like that, Rachel—your shoulders are quite hunched. And where are your shoes, for any sake? Heaven knows, I'm justly punished for all the things I said when I discovered I was carrying you! I never longed for you, Rachel, as a mother should for her firstborn, and you've turned out every bit as plain and self-willed as I expected. Why couldn't you have been more like Maria? She's the kind of daughter I hoped for!" Maria, three years old, had red-gold hair, a passion for pretty dresses and the fastidious manners of a *grande dame*.

"If you were even a little . . . *pleasing* . . ."

It was the same every time. When she noticed me, it was always to criticize, to resent my existence. I can see her now, her eyes hard and narrow in that doll-like face, shaking her head with a little hiss of perplexity that such an ordinary, unfathomable child should have crept, unwanted, from her womb. But her scrutiny never lasted long: there were always better things to do, and she never believed in wasting time.

I must confess that I too forgot about the sick man in the Widow Creran's house for another three days.

After that, no more drowned bodies were washed up on the shingle beach, though I couldn't help looking round apprehensively whenever I wandered along its weed-strewn length, half in fear, half in curiosity lest a pallid, waxen face should gaze sightlessly out from one of the great drifts of flotsam piled high on the shore. The gale had ripped out a line of fish-flakes, hurling the spindly piles and plank flooring down into the turbulent water of the cove, and the sea had responded by flinging the debris back, far up the beach, to lie in company with shattered spars and burst crates washed from the wreck of the *Adelaide Ross,* and the strange, strong-smelling corpses of deep-sea fish churned up from the abyss by the turmoil of the storm.

It was amid this disordered line of wreckage that I first noticed the bird. Its back was pale gray, its head and body rounded and white, too large somehow for the short black legs which hopped and scrambled among the weed-strands. Its wings were almost completely blue-gray except for the tips, which were black—I could see as much because the bird trailed one wing and thrashed the other in panic at my approach.

Without going nearer, I squatted down on my heels and waited for the bird to settle. It was a seabird, obviously, with webbed toes and a yellow bill like a gull; yet I couldn't remember having seen one quite like it before. I assumed it must be one of those wanderers which spend their lives far out at sea, only coming to land to nest on some inaccessible cliff or when forced ashore, injured, like this one.

The bird had grown quiet, cornered next to the shell of a burst water-cask, and was watching me sharply from first one bright brown eye and then the other. Slowly and gently, I leaned forward until with a final lunge, avoiding the sharp yellow beak, I managed to take firm hold of it, folding its injured wing to its side as gently as I could.

For the next few moments the bird continued to twist its head in an attempt to peck at the hands which imprisoned it. Then all of a sudden it lay still, and I could feel its heart thumping desperately against my fingers.

There was something seriously amiss with its wing, that was clear, otherwise it would have flown off as soon as I tried to approach. I'd already nursed several birds in my own distant, weedy corner of the kitchen yard—an orphan owlet I'd found behind the cowshed, a brood of partridge chicks, and my flapping, one-legged crow—but I was afraid that this stranded seabird might be beyond my well-intentioned help. If I was right and its wing was broken, should I splint it with twigs or strap it to the bird's side and hope for the best? And if that wasn't its only injury, what then?

Holding the bird carefully against my chest, I looked round for help. But I was alone on the beach—most of the able-bodied men of the village were out in the cleared land, digging graves for the last of the people from the *Adelaide Ross,* and there was no one to give me advice. No doubt they'd only have told me to leave the bird to fend for itself, in any case, to live or to die as God should decide.

But I'd never entirely trusted God with His own creation, and I knew instinctively that I needed to speak to someone of similarly heretic views. By chance, my eye fell on the shingled roof of the midwife's house a hundred yards away. Mrs. Creran would know what to do. Even the Preacher had admitted that the widow's cures were sometimes "beyond understanding"—I'd heard him say as much to my mother—and some folk in the village were prepared to go further than that in their account of her powers. Mrs. Creran knew the names of all the flowers and plants that grew round the bay, and made use of them as she pleased. Certainly, she would be able to tell what was the matter with the bird I'd found.

The widow's door opened directly on to the earthen track, and my confidence began to ebb as I drew nearer. To encounter Mrs. Creran out in the open, in broad daylight, was one thing; to walk trustingly over that dangerous doorstep was quite another.

Holding the injured bird before me like a talisman of safety, I halted in front of the wind-scarred door, and found it ajar. Goodness only knew how often I'd been told to knock at doors before entering, in the English manner—but how could I knock at a door which wasn't even shut, while keeping a firm grip on an agitated seabird?

With one elbow, I pushed the door further open and called out, "Mrs. Creran!" in a voice which only trembled a little. There was no answer from the shadows beyond.

"Mrs. Creran?" I tried again. "It's me—Rachel Dean. May I come in?"

Once again, only the faint echo of my own voice answered. I began to consider retreat, but the seabird's renewed struggling made me determined to try one last time. If the midwife had been called out during the night, she might well be dozing now before the fire, oblivious to my small voice at her door.

Greatly daring, I made my way into her dim, bitter-smelling house, into the room which was parlor, kitchen and everything else save a bedroom. There were two proper bedrooms, I knew—one for the widow and another in the loft for her two fishermen sons, away at sea until the end of the season.

But there was no one in the chair before the stone hearth, and no one in the room at all, though knitting-pins and wool lay abandoned on the whitened deal table, the row of stitches half-finished as if the work had been flung down in haste. It followed that Mrs. Creran must be somewhere nearby, and since the door of the bedroom beyond stood open, I crossed the kitchen, still clasping the struggling bird to my chest, and rudely peered in.

————

A man lay in the old wooden bed, motionless against a pile of pillows, his eyes closed. His face had that strange mustard pallor which marks skin weathered by long exposure to the sun, but drained of life—and for an awful moment I remembered the drowned corpses on the shingle beach, and wondered if Mrs. Creran's patient had died after all. But this man was breathing, his chest rising and falling steadily under the whitework coverlet, his feet stirring under the blankets a good way down the bed.

For the life of me, I couldn't draw back. I simply stared, fascinated. So this was the sick man saved from the wreck of the *Adelaide Ross!* Nothing so glamorous as a real castaway had ever entered my life before. Yet the man seemed quite old—at least as old as my mother, who would be twenty-six that year—and not even handsome, with his prominent nose and tawny hair the color of wild grasses in autumn.

At that moment the seabird, despairing of its struggles, let out a loud squawk. The eyes of the man in the white bed flew open— savage gray eyes, gray as slate—and turned to survey me where I stood, transfixed with dread in the doorway.

For a moment he said nothing, but simply looked at me, trembling there like a fool with the angry, screeching bird in my arms.

"Bring it here, then."

I was taken aback. Most grown-ups began with, "What have you got there, child?" and followed it up with orders to remove *at once* whatever horrid, slimy creature I'd brought into the house.

"I beg your pardon . . . I didn't mean to waken you. I thought Mrs. Creran might be here."

"Well, since you have wakened me, let's have a look at this bird of yours. I suppose he's injured, or you'd never have caught him." As I watched, the sick man turned with an effort on to his side. His voice was low but perfectly steady, though his accent fell strangely on my ears.

Reluctantly, I took a couple of steps toward the bed, unable to resist the stare of those compelling gray eyes.

"I don't even know what kind of bird it is," I admitted.

"A kittiwake, by the look of him, though I've heard him called a *tarrock* by sailors. By rights he should be far out at sea, catching fish. He must have been blown ashore by the storm—much as I was." The man smiled ruefully, and I began to think he looked less stern than before. "What's the matter with him?"

I had to confess that I didn't know that either. "But he holds out his wing in an odd way, and I think it might be broken."

The sick man—Adam Gaunt, the widow had called him—reached out to take the bird from my grasp. The kittiwake, unused to being handled, tried at once to thrash its long wings, only to have them trapped securely to its sides, and soon it lay quiet, seduced in some subtle way by the calm, assured touch of the man who held it. I watched enviously as he gently spread out the injured wing, probing it slowly with his fingertips.

"I reckon you're right—it's broken. See—just there, near his body." He folded the wing back carefully against the bird's side, and absently stroked the soft white plumage of its head. The bird made no further attempt to struggle, but nestled calmly, its head drawn in, apparently mesmerized by the soothing passage of lean brown fingers over its feathers.

"Poor creature—I doubt if you did him a kindness in rescuing him today."

"Why's that?" I too was mesmerized.

"Well . . . he's bound to die in the end. He'd have gone a little sooner if you'd left him where he was, that's all."

"But I'm going to look after him, and make him well!" My indignation left no room for self-doubt.

"And what do you know about doctoring birds, Miss Whatever-Your-Name-Is?"

"My name is Rachel Dean. And you are Mr. Gaunt, so they say in the village. And I know a good deal about birds: I have a crow of my very own, and a baby owl which takes food from my hand. And I mean to make this bird well again, too!"

"Do you indeed?" For a moment the stranger looked amused. Then he glanced down at the kittiwake in his hands, and his smile faded.

"This bird isn't like your tame crow, you know. He's wild. He's a wanderer. You can't expect him to sit on your windowsill forever, waiting to be fed. Even if you mend his wing, he'll probably never fly again—he'll never be able to soar out over the sea, and feel the wind lift him—"

"At least he'll be *alive!* Surely that's better than nothing!"

"Do you really think so? How would you like to be condemned to hop around a few square yards of dusty earth—a prisoner—when you're used to being as free as the ocean?" The gray eyes fixed me steadily once more and I was helpless to look away.

"The best thing—the kindest thing you could do would be to wring his neck now, and have done with him."

I stared at the injured man, appalled.

"If you can't bring yourself to do it, then I'll do it for you. It'll all be over in a second or two."

"*No!*" I found my voice at last. "I won't let you kill him! You're hateful—give me back my bird!" The spell shattered, I lunged forward and snatched back the startled kittiwake before it could protest.

"And what's all this shoutin' about, may I ask?" boomed a voice from the kitchen behind me. "Rachel Dean! Shame upon you! Whatever d'you think you're doing, coming into my house an' bothering poor Mr. Gaunt, an' him greatly in need of his rest?" The bulky figure of the midwife filled the doorway, her hands on her hips.

"I never meant to disturb him, truly I didn't." Guiltily, I clasped the illicit bird to my chest. "The door was open, and I was looking for you—"

"I was fetched an hour since to look over Maud Flanagan in case her baby was coming early, but it was all a fuss over nothin'. She'll still be waiting this time next week, if I'm not mistaken. But that's by the way. You've no right to go botherin' a sick man."

"No harm done," Adam Gaunt interposed quietly. "We've been having an interesting talk about what's to become of this injured bird. Miss Dean here thinks she can mend its broken wing as good as new."

"She might, at that," pronounced the midwife thoughtfully. "She has a way with wild creatures, I'll admit."

"Ah."

I was conscious—physically conscious—of his sharp gaze passing over me like a caressing hand. Then he sighed, and lay back wearily against his pillows. "See what you can do, then, Miss Dean," he conceded, "and I wish you well. But promise me one thing—" He was waiting for my agreement, but I still didn't trust him. "Promise me you'll bring the bird back in a few days' time, so that I can see how it's faring."

I hesitated, but only for a second. "Very well. Since you ask."

"Thank you."

"Now come along out of here, young Rachel, and leave Mr. Gaunt to sleep." Briskly, the midwife steered me and my burden out of the sickroom. "He's not well enough yet for visiting, poor man, though I daresay you've given him something more to think about than his aching leg, which is all to the good. Now—let's see what we're going to do about this gull of yours."

———

I said nothing at all to my mother about my meeting with the injured man in the midwife's house. I always shrank from the prospect of confiding in her in any case, but now some sixth sense made me particularly careful to guard my words. I knew she'd never notice the new addition to my collection of stray creatures in the kitchen yard; provided I was quiet and out of my mother's sight, I could do pretty well as I pleased. If I chose to spend my time among a menagerie of mangy, flea-ridden animals, so be it. No doubt my mother felt it was marginally better than forming unsuitable friendships with children from the village.

As things turned out, I waited four days before returning to Mrs. Creran's house with the bandaged kittiwake, both wings now bound firmly to its sides. For the first two of those days the bird had absolutely refused to eat and its feathers had soon become so staring and dull and its eyes so sunken that I feared it would die after all. Then suddenly the kittiwake appeared to make up its mind to live, snatching ravenously at the fish-scraps I begged for it from the boats at the jetty and leaving my fingers torn and raw. By the fourth day I was confident enough of its health to return with it to the village. The bird would live, at least: whether it would fly again was another matter.

This time Adam Gaunt was sitting in a chair by the bed, dressed in a shirt and trousers belonging to one of the widow's sons, the trousers too short by a good six inches. His injured leg was propped up on a stool, thickly wadded in bandages, but he looked less of an invalid than before and strangely feral in that small room, like some vivid forest animal which had wandered by chance into the neighborhood of men.

Yet the wildness was tempered when he smiled as Mrs. Creran ushered me into the room, and soon I was startled to find myself telling this quiet stranger all about my one-legged crow and my blind kitten, my orphan owlet and the fat old toad under the flat stone by the road—all the creatures of my own private world.

I even told him of the time I'd taken the toad home and hidden it in my sister Maria's bed.

"She's five," I told him in explanation, "and she's so *good* it's awful. When she saw the toad she screamed and screamed until she went purple, and she had to sleep in Liddy's bed for the rest of the week. I was beaten for it—but it was worth a beating just to see her!"

"Who beat you? Was it your father?"

"No. Mamma has a special cane." I remember frowning then, and wondering how to explain that my father simply didn't count, that it was my mother alone who held sway over the household at the top of the hill.

"We hardly ever see Papa. He comes home very late at night and lies in bed till nearly noon. Then he goes out. He doesn't think I know where he goes, but I do. . . . He and Mamma have rows about it, sometimes, when he comes back."

"Your father must be Joseph Dean, then. The small, dark man with the big moustache? Mrs. Creran pointed him out to me one day as he passed the house."

"Yes." It was a fair description: my father was slim and dark like me, and we had the same eyes and skin. I often wondered if that was one of the reasons my mother despised me so much, as if even when my father was out of the house she could still see him standing there

in me, with his soft brown eyes, his soft pink lips, and the great soft
dusky moustache which he seemed to imagine made up for his lack
of inches.

But I didn't want to discuss my father. There had been another
row that morning, just before I snatched up the bird and fled down
the hill to the midwife's house and to Adam Gaunt. My mother had
stamped into the big bedroom overlooking the garden at eleven
o'clock, slamming the door behind her, but I was sitting quietly with
a book on the stairs, and I'd had no difficulty in hearing what was
said. *Drunken pig!* my mother shouted. *Wastrel!* and many other
things I didn't understand, though her anger and frustration were
plain enough to hear. Shortly afterward, my father rose from bed,
dressed himself as neatly as ever, and set off without a word toward
the village. I remember deciding to be in bed and asleep, the blankets
pulled over my head, before he returned that night.

The house was an unhappy place in those days, and it was usually
a relief to have somewhere else to go. For the next three weeks I
visited the invalid nearly every day, sometimes with the bird, sometimes not, but in spite of all my resolutions to the contrary, I always
seemed to be the one who spoke while Adam Gaunt listened. He
said very little about his own history, except to tell me he was English, as my parents were, but born in Norfolk, while my parents
had come out from Liverpool. He'd traveled to America seven years
before—to the half-explored wilderness of the Rocky Mountains—
and had been returning home on the *Adelaide Ross* when she was
wrecked. As soon as he could travel, he said, he would make his way
to St. John's, the colony's capital, and from there continue his journey to England. *As soon as he could travel:* how I began to hate
those words!

One day I arrived to find him on his feet, swinging himself over
the short distance between the bed and the window, then the window and the chair, then back to the bed again, round and round in
the little room, driving himself as pitilessly as if the room were a
cage.

"'Tis such a small house," Mrs. Creran said mournfully, "and no
doubt less than he's used to. I wish there was somewhere for him to
go, where there was more space—and books too. He's read almost
everythin' Preacher could find for him."

There was indeed somewhere for him to go—though not, perhaps,
exactly what she'd planned—and curiously enough, it all came about

because of Susan Vinegar. I say *curiously* because Susan Vinegar was seldom the cause of any of life's great upheavals, only a witness to them: in this case, however, she was solely and entirely to blame.

If Adam Gaunt was bored with Crow Cove, Susan Vinegar, for her part, had long since ceased to take an interest in his welfare—from the day it became obvious that he would live. For Susan was a connoisseur of doom. Her own life offered so little drama that she leaped upon the misfortunes of others like a terrier on a bone, and was always disappointed when they fell short of real tragedy. Sneeze near Susan Vinegar, and the whole village would shortly inquire after your chill; take to your bed with the quinsy, and she would have a hat looked out for the funeral. As a result, she had entirely dismissed the convalescent Mr. Gaunt from her mind until one particular morning when she spied him at the widow's door, leaning motionless against the worn doorpost, surveying the dawn face of the village with his thoughtful gaze. For several long minutes Susan Vinegar was distracted from her work.

"Preacher's wife says Ma Creran's a witch," she remarked pensively to my mother later in the store. "She says that man's leg should've gone bad on him, but the old woman fixed it with leaves an' bits of ground-up bugs an' I don't know all what. Preacher's wife reckons the Devil must tell her what plants to use, an' she picks them at night, when there's a full moon."

I was sitting on the flour barrel at the time, and I heard my mother snort in disbelief, but Susan Vinegar remained unrepentant.

"She's not coming near me if I get sick, that's for sure."

"Not unless you want to recover," my mother commented dryly, counting out nails from a sack. "If you fall ill and Mrs. Creran comes to take care of you, just thank the Lord she knows as much as she does. Devils and full moons indeed! And while I remember—has the Preacher's wife paid us what she owes from last month yet?"

Susan Vinegar fetched the ledger, but returned to her subject.

"Tell you what, though . . . that Mr. Gaunt—now, he's the kind of man that'd do me just fine. He's not bad-looking now he's well again, an' he's an educated man, you can tell he's had book-learning. I bet there'd be plenty of hearts broke if he'd really gone down with the *Adelaide Ross*. He's got that look . . . you know."

Susan Vinegar wriggled her bony shoulders and swirled her hands about, trying to describe the indescribable. "But I don't suppose he'd give me a second glance—more's the pity."

I saw my mother look up from the bag of nails, her fingers stilled, digesting this information.

"When did you say you saw him?"

"Early morning. Now he's on his feet—with a stick, of course— he's got into the habit of standing at the widow's door for a while at sunup, just looking down the road toward the cove. I did hear Ma Creran's hoping someone else'll take him in till he's better—someone with a bit more room to spare. It must be hard, having a man like that cooped up in her little cottage." And Susan Vinegar wriggled again, and sighed.

Next morning my mother came late to breakfast, her cheeks flushed and her shoes damp with dew, and afterward in the garden I noticed the same preoccupied expression on her face that I'd seen in the store. The same—yet different. Now there was a firmness to Susannah Dean's dainty mouth which I knew of old. I'd last seen it on the morning after the storm which wrecked the *Adelaide Ross* and washed the drowned woman and her child up on the shingle beach—the baby with the costly chain round her neck. *I want,* it said. *And I will have.*

"If anyone asks for me," she declared a short time later, "I shall be in the village, at Mrs. Creran's house. There's a matter I have to discuss with her."

She was going to visit *him.* I knew it. And at that instant a wisdom as old as woman herself began to settle in my almost-eight-year-old heart.

Until that moment it had never occurred to me that other eyes might see my mother differently from my own. Looking back now, that seems strange. But then, the world of a child is full of certainties: it's the adult world which contains doubt and indecision.

Occasionally I'd noticed fishermen in the store glance up from the purchase of a knife or a piece of tobacco with frank admiration in their faces—and had thought them ridiculous. Why, Susannah Dean was *my mother! Old. Married. There* . . . just as the house was *there,* or the village . . .

Yet I remember making a valiant attempt that day to view my mother with a stranger's eye, and what I saw disturbed me.

Not so long before, in the bitter days, my mother had been cold, red-eyed and silent, a woman with rough hands and untidy hair who was often to be found sitting on the chopping-stump behind the store, staring with frigid dislike at the village of Crow Cove. That was in the first years after we moved there from St. John's, after it had finally become plain, even to my father, that his clockmaking venture—the rosy prospect which had brought the newlyweds to Newfoundland from Liverpool—had only made us paupers.

"Your Ma was a lady at home, see," Susan Vinegar had confided once unexpectedly. "'Least, she told me her Pa had a clockmaking business of his own, with journeymen an' apprentices an' such like. I suppose they thought St. John's would be a fine place to set up, bein' a growin' settlement with ships comin' regular. Trouble was, so many folk are off fishin' they've no need of fancy watches. My Pa jes' looks to the sun an' waits till his belly rumbles, so he says!"

Susan Vinegar had been engaged as maid during the first heady, confident days in St. John's, and at last, with weeks of wages owing, had loyally stuck by the family during their humiliating removal to Crow Cove.

Andrew MacDonald, owner of one of the biggest warehouses on the St. John's waterfront, had been our other mainstay in those days. Almost alone among my parents' new acquaintances, Andrew MacDonald and his ample wife, Christian, had continued to call on them after their clothes became shabby and their faces pinched with making do. Perhaps remembering their own early days in the colony, the MacDonalds searched for a means of saving the family—for I had been born by then—from certain destitution. Clockmaking was out of the question, as Andrew gently tried to explain to my father. Perhaps, though, Joseph and Susannah would be prepared to take charge of a new store he had decided to set up in Crow Cove, on the shores of Conception Bay? The accommodation would only amount to two rooms at the back of the building—but then, if the store did well . . .

"Your Pa was fair put out by that," Susan Vinegar recalled. "I can still see him coming back to the house, an' your Ma asking *Well? Well?* an' him saying *The impudence of the man! To think of a craftsman of my skills and training, reduced to serving behind the counter of a tuppeny-ha'penny trading shack in the wilderness!* He'd always a proper opinion of himself, your Pa."

Soon after this, I'm told, I fell ill, and needed medicine and good food. My mother, her jaw set and her eyes hard, had paid a visit of her own to the merchant's offices in the harbor, and as a result of it the offer of the storekeeper's job was repeated.

"Take it," she instructed my father, and this time, startled by the expression on the face of his fierce little wife, Joseph Dean did as he was told.

There had followed the first dreadful years of exile, when the three of us and Susan Vinegar existed in the two little rooms behind the store where Edward, and later Maria, were born. Then the store began to flourish, as my mother had been determined it should, and our family prospered along with it. People no longer looked to Harbour Grace, the larger town along the west side of the bay, for their financial dealings. My mother learned to give credit—or to refuse it —to her best advantage, and my father, taken aback by his wife's unsuspected cleverness with money, was reduced to the role of book-keeper in her ingenious schemes.

The fishermen were notoriously prodigal with their money, but their wives were not. Before long, Susannah Dean had invented a burial society for the community, and a means whereby the fisher families could save against the cost of a daughter's dowry at marriageable age. Noticing the number of sheep beginning to dot the newly cleared land round the villages of the bay, she encouraged the neighborhood wives to spin and dye the wool at home instead of sending it to St. John's, and to knit up jerseys and other garments. Naturally, she became their agent, dispatching the products of their industry to St. John's aboard the returning MacDonalds' schooner which supplied the store, fixing the sales, and awarding herself a handsome commission. Soon we were able to abandon the two rooms behind the store to Susan Vinegar and move to a sprawling, dilapidated wooden house at the top of the slope overlooking the village, which became our property when a family of local fisherfolk took to rum and defaulted on their debts. My mother had made sure there was always plenty of rum on the shelves of the store.

To his great joy my father suddenly found himself a person of consequence in Crow Cove, flattered to be asked his opinion on all sorts of matters he knew nothing whatever about. Every day, in his fashionable nipped-in coat and his high starched collar, he paraded down to the harbor to join the village men who met there to set the world to rights. Politely, they asked my father what he thought of the weather, of the prospects for the fishing, and of the Irish Question—but it was to my mother they went for their loans. The store was still Andrew MacDonald's property, but all the other activities which clustered round it and used it as a headquarters were entirely my mother's own. And as our fortunes improved, it was noticeable that little Mrs. Dean began to bloom once more.

Young as I was, I recognized the change in her, and with it a restlessness which the passing months had only increased. Now, on that awful day, I watched gravely as she pinned a jaunty straw hat to the top of her piled, copper-brown hair, pinched her cheeks, picked up the basket of eggs which was her excuse for sick-visiting, and set off for the garden gate, humming a little tune under her breath. Her eyes were clear glass-blue, bright with speculation, and my heart sank to the depths of my lonely soul.

2

Next day Adam Gaunt moved into our house at the top of the hill.

"*No!* It isn't fair! You shan't have him! He's *My* friend, and you shan't have him!"

I remember shouting it out, almost beside myself with anger and betrayal as soon as I heard the news. The announcement hadn't even been intended for me. I'd overheard my mother tell Liddy to prepare a room for the new arrival, and I don't think she was even aware of my presence in the parlor until I made my sudden, outraged protest. I can still remember her swinging round to look at me, amazed at this passionate outburst from her normally taciturn daughter.

"If he's your friend, then you should be pleased he's coming to stay with us," she sneered, and then, as anger overwhelmed her, she fairly yelled at me, "How dare you speak to me like that! It's none of your business what I do or who comes to stay in this house. Go to your room at once, and stay there until I send for you!"

That was when I threw the candlestick. It was there, at my hand, and I simply picked it up from the parlor table and threw it at her. It missed by a mile, of course, and very nearly hit Liddy, waiting nearby with a tray. Then everything began to happen extremely fast, and within seconds, it seemed, I was bent over a chair while my mother inflicted several painful cuts with her nasty, whippy cane.

I didn't care. The hurt of the thrashing was nothing compared to the agony of seeing my secret friend—my first real friend, the first adult who'd spoken to me as if I had thoughts and feelings worth consideration—enticed away to my mother's world of grown-ups.

On the face of it she was right. I should have been delighted to have him living with us, sleeping under the same roof in our second-best bed, the one with a pine post at each corner and a mattress stuffed with feathers from my mother's own geese. But I knew that

Susannah Dean had never performed a single charitable act in her life, and if she'd decided to install Adam Gaunt in the empty room at the back of the house it was only because she was bored, and meant to monopolize his attention.

Soon he'd have no time for me at all—of that I was certain. My mother could be utterly charming when it suited her, and knew exactly how to dress to show off her soft, rounded body. With such a captivating hostess to amuse him all day, why on earth should Adam Gaunt bother himself with a plain, hero-worshiping child?

My father, of course, was never consulted about his new lodger. My mother was the power in our land, and she didn't believe in wasting time.

And so Adam Gaunt moved in among us, and after a day or two it began to seem quite normal to find him limping slowly along the neat paths of our garden, forcing the torn and wasted muscles of his injured leg to resume their work. When the pain of walking became unbearable he would lie down with a book in the tufted grass under one of the apple trees, a long, still shadow which melted into the pattern of light and shade as if he'd dissolved entirely into the summer greenness.

My father hardly appeared to notice Mr. Gaunt. Yet you could never be sure. It was easy to write off Joseph Dean as a worthless fool, a man who'd hardly worked for his living since the collapse of his cherished clockmaking enterprise, and who was content to live off the resourcefulness of his wife. That was certainly my mother's opinion; yet he'd once been a man with dreams and ambitions like any of us, dreams which he'd seen dissolve into impotent disappointment. I think my mother in her brusqueness often missed little give-away gestures and sounds which should have warned her that my father couldn't always be bought off with a new silk handkerchief and a bottle of good brandy.

In truth, the humiliation of it all had become more than he could bear, and some three weeks after Adam came to stay with us I was an accidental witness to the dreadful scene which exposed the last pretense of my parents' disastrous marriage.

As usual, Edward, Maria and I had eaten our supper in the kitchen with Liddy before being packed off to bed. Maria, who always did what was expected of her, quickly fell asleep, but I lay for a long time listening to her faint breathing and the brilliant chorus of song with which the birds were marking the fading daylight. For some reason sleep would not come that night, and since there was still enough light in the room to read by, I hopped out of bed and pattered downstairs to fetch the half-finished book I'd left on the parlor windowsill.

Normally at that hour my parents would still have been in the dining room, finishing their own meal. I'd counted on that being so, and as I reached the turn of the stairs I was reassured to see the glow of candlelight seeping from the dining-room doorway.

Then on the next step I froze. Ahead of me, the front door of the house swung open with a squeal of hinges to reveal my father, an hour and a half late for supper, his coat slung over one shoulder, negotiating the shallow step with the intense concentration of a man treading through a snake pit.

I knew where he'd been. One of the fishermen—Thomas, his name was—had set up a still at the back of the boatyard where he made his own liquor, call it poteen or moonshine or what you will. I'd followed my father there once, just to see where he went in such a guilty hurry, and I knew he was a frequent visitor. But he'd never come home in this condition before, and I drew back swiftly into the shadows to see what would happen next.

———

Shutting the front door behind him with elaborate care, my father steered himself unsteadily toward the dining room, feeling his way delicately along the wall. My mother and Adam Gaunt had waited for him, minute by dreadful minute, and although I crept like a mouse to a point on the stairs where I could see into the room, I had no need to set eyes on my mother to imagine the expression on her face when the prodigal returned. She said nothing, but watched her husband in utter disgust as he dropped into his usual chair at the head of the board with a little sigh of achievement and a smug smile at the poor fools on either side who didn't share his alcoholic secret.

My mother signaled to Liddy to bring in the first dishes of the meal, which had been kept hot in the bake-oven to the point of ruin. The salmon, brought fresh and firm that morning from a river two miles away, was poached to a mush, and the pastry on the turkey pie had become brown and brittle. I heard my mother say, "It wasn't meant to be like this," and cast apologetic eyes toward Adam Gaunt, sitting opposite her but with his broad back to me.

My father leaned across and stabbed his finger on the shiny wood of the table by her plate. "Time you had words with that Liddy, my girl," he declared. "How often have I told you to keep the servants up to the mark, or they'll take liberties? Look at that pie! Black! Ruined! It won't do, Mrs. Dean—you'll have to speak to Liddy tomorrow."

He'd emphasized each word with a flourish of the big serving spoon, and now he made an attempt to shovel a fair portion of the burned pie out of its dish and on to his plate, only to dump most of it on the table, where a pool of gravy began to collect and coagulate on the polished surface.

For a while there was silence while he crammed his mouth with the remains of the pie. My mother ate little, and quickly, as if anxious to get the meal over with before anything worse could occur.

"Wine!" demanded my father suddenly, banging the table with the flat of his hand until the dishes rattled. "Wine!"

"You've had enough!" snapped my mother, goaded to the breaking point.

"Oho!" I saw the drunkard's black, shiny little eyes slide across to contemplate his wife. "*Enough?* Is that your—" he struggled with the word—"your *o-pinion,* my dear wife? My dear, penny-pinching little wife?" He glared about him, wiping his mouth on his coat-sleeve, until his roving stare finally came to rest on Adam Gaunt.

"Never marry a mean woman," he muttered sullenly. "Bad mistake." Then a new thought struck him. "Though I could've been worse off. D'you know—I nearly married her sister? Her sister!" My father began to chortle with mirth at the very idea.

This was a real nugget of information. I'd occasionally heard my mother speak of my Aunt Grace, now married to a sea captain in Liverpool, but of course I'd never met her, and I'd often wondered what she looked like. Now it seemed as if my father was about to satisfy my curiosity.

"Oh, dear," he sniggered, "that woman was such a fright. Seven feet tall, and a long yellow face like a donkey. And she laughed just like a donkey, too!" My father gave a loud bray, and subsided for a moment in muddled hiccups.

"Joseph—go to bed," said my mother coldly, more steel in her voice than I'd ever heard.

"What d'you reckon?" Ignoring his wife, my father turned again to his guest. "Did I pick the right one? The miser or the fright? What d'you say?"

I could see my mother's face clearly from my perch on the stairs, and when she looked at my father, sprawled there in his chair, there was nothing in it but loathing and contempt for the man she'd married. Abruptly she rose to her feet.

"I have some things to see to in the kitchen," she said quietly, "and then I shall go to bed. Goodnight, Mr. Gaunt."

Pushing back her chair, she walked behind my father without giving him so much as a glance, and then on down the near side of the table toward the door leading to the kitchen. As she passed behind Adam Gaunt's chair she reached out swiftly and fastened the fingers of one hand hard into the muscles of his shoulder. There could be no mistaking the pressure, but he never moved, nor gave any sign that he'd noticed, and in a moment she was gone, my father's voice echoing coarsely after her, "You warm the bed, Susannah! I promise you won't have long to wait!"

In another moment, they would come out of the dining room. Hopelessly confused by what I'd seen, I scrambled from my corner and flew up the darkened stairs to my bed.

———

And yet, strangely enough, by next day everything appeared to be back to normal. My mother presided calmly over breakfast, went into the kitchen to give Liddy her instructions as usual, and then put on her hat and walked down to the store for a conference with Susan Vinegar. Adam Gaunt patrolled the garden paths as he always did and my delinquent father lay in bed until midday before vanishing into the village on one of his secretive errands.

It was all very baffling. I was certain my mother and father must have had words of some kind over the dreadful scene of the previous evening, yet there had been no shouting or slamming of doors, no white, shocked faces or sulking mouths. I sensed that this time my father had offended beyond all hope of pardon: he'd committed the ultimate sin in my mother's book by making her look ridiculous and pathetic, and she'd never forgive him for it. Worse, I was sure she would try to pay him back for his offense in some way. My mother's self-respect would demand it—and the continuing bland serenity of the household was far more sinister than any noisy quarrel would have been.

As I'd feared, my mother spent a great deal of time in Adam Gaunt's company, often sitting with him in the garden on dry, fine summer days, or, as his leg improved, taking an unhurried stroll at his side across the scrubland behind the house as far as the forest edge. They made a handsome couple, Adam with his height and spare, supple body walking next to Susannah's smooth roundness, the morning sun shining on her mass of copper-brown hair. I sometimes heard them laughing together, and noticed a careless gaiety in my mother's voice which I'd never heard before. It was all so unfair, unfair, unfair.

Certainly Adam still found some time to spend with me. Every evening he made a point of coming out to the kitchen yard to watch me feed the ravenous kittiwake, which had learned to accept potatoes and cheese in addition to its usual diet of fish and small crabs. It was some time before I dared to unbind its wings, and then I watched in silent agony as the bird spread them wide and tried unsuccessfully to flap itself into the air.

At least the broken bone had healed. Adam examined it for me, and once more I watched, fascinated, as his long-jointed fingers caressed the kittiwake's plumage, sinking into the plump, oily feathers with hypnotic sureness. We were his slaves, the bird and I, seduced and enraptured by his company. I simply wanted to be with him, that was all. With him, and without my mother.

In a desperate attempt to please, I'd done my best to improve my appearance. I began to comb my straggling dark hair every morning, copying Maria and her red-gold waves; I forced myself to endure the dreadful shoes I'd been given, and occasionally allowed Liddy to bully me into a dress. One day I even filched hair-ribbons from my sister and appeared downstairs with my hair tied up in what I hoped were bewitching ringlets. I can still remember the look on Adam Gaunt's face when I promenaded into the garden with my ribbon-bound tresses, sweeping a stray lock back from my brow with the same artless gesture Maria had practiced to perfection.

"What on earth have you got in your hair?" he inquired, amazed. "Was that Liddy's idea?"

"No—mine."

He must have seen my face fall, because he immediately tried to salvage the situation. "It's—most unusual."

"You think it's silly, don't you."

"Not at all." He closed his book with a snap. "But if you want to come with me to look for that otter slide by the creek, I suggest you take it all out again. You'll scare every otter on the island with your finery."

"The otter slide! Oh, can we? Can we go and look for it?" My fingers were already tearing the ribbons out of my hair.

"As soon as you like. And I noticed a squirrel's nest in the big fir tree near the forest path this morning. I'll show you where, if you want."

We found the otter slide quite easily because Adam knew exactly where to look for it on the steep bank of the creek, almost as if he could become an otter himself and think as an otter would think. It was partly inborn talent and partly skill learned and practiced in the Norfolk fenlands of his birth, where he'd hunted wildfowl from childhood until the day he left for America.

I discovered why he'd been reluctant to tell me how he earned his living there. The Rocky Mountains were still chiefly the preserve of the native Indians—the Blackfeet and the Shoshone and their kin— but in recent years the region had been explored and opened up by white men looking for a new kind of wealth: animal skins, especially beaver for the hats of fashionable gentlemen in London and New York. Looking for work, Adam had made his way to St. Louis, that enterprising city at the junction of the Missouri River and the mighty Mississippi, and had seen an advertisement placed in a newspaper there by a man named Ashley who was looking for young men of resource and determination to join an expedition into the mountains. For two years, and then for another three after General Ashley's expedition was over, Adam had roamed the vast ranges of the Rockies either alone or with small bands of trappers, gathering beaver pelts, bear skins and buffalo robes for the traders of St. Louis.

I made him tell me how beaver were trapped, and I was very, very sorry for the beaver whose wonderful fur condemned him to a painful, waterlogged death in some mountain stream. At least the bears had a chance of escaping the hunter's gun, and there were some satisfying tales of trappers being mauled to death or badly injured by their infuriated victims. But the beaver were no match for these cunning men who learned their habits and lured them to their deaths with their own enticing scent.

Yet I don't remember blaming Adam for the slaughter. In his own way he loved the wild creatures of the world he lived in as much as I did, and if I blamed anyone, I blamed the foolish city gentlemen who thought that the beaver's skin looked better on their heads than on the beaver. Besides—I was convinced in those days that anything Adam did must be honorable and fair, and I was sure that if he had a reason for killing any living creature, then the hairy goat-footed gods of the woods and the rivers would forgive him.

As the summer passed he taught me something of woodcraft. I learned how to creep up on nodding moorhens before they could run to water, cocking up their white tails and diving out of sight among the reedy shallows. With Adam as my tutor I discovered how to slide into the edge of a pool, quiet as a fish, and work silently to leeward of sitting birds without disturbing them. And then, late one night, sitting on that grassy bank amid the straggling hillside scrub, he taught me the names of the constellations of stars overhead, and told me for the first time about Orion the Hunter and the Ploughman who pursued him.

"What would happen to the Hunter, if the Ploughman ever caught up with him?" I wanted to know.

"I've no idea. I sometimes wonder what *will* happen to hunters like me when the earth is covered with fields and cities, and there isn't a single wild corner left."

"But surely that could never happen! The world is so huge. . . . There must be room for everybody."

"You'd think so, wouldn't you? Yet there's never quite room enough. Do you read your Bible?"

"The Preacher tells us Bible stories in school."

"Do you know the one about Jacob and Esau? About Jacob, the farmer, stealing the inheritance of his brother Esau, the hunter? It's true, you see—the farmer envies his brother's birthright, and in the end he'll find a way of cheating him of it. The sad thing is that the hunter likes the world just as it is, just as it was made in the beginning, but the farmer and the townsman who come after him want to change it all with roads and warehouses and mills."

"But can't the Hunter and the Ploughman agree to divide the world between them?" I asked with childish logic, and was puzzled when he shook his head.

"You can't have both. One or the other must win the battle in the end." And with that he stood up, dusted the grass from his clothes, and added, "It's time we went back to the house. Your mother will think I've run off with you."

I thought at the time it was an odd choice of words.

———

In principle he was right. My mother resented not only that evening but every single moment Adam spent with me. She began to leave

the day-to-day business of the store more and more to Susan Vinegar
in order to stay at home with him, and as soon as my daily lessons
in the meeting-hall were over she invented errands to take me to the
farthest ends of the village, simply to keep me occupied.

"Rachel—take this note to Sylvestre Marin at the boatyard. . . .
Take these goose feathers to Mrs. Creran . . . this book to the
Preacher, with my compliments. . . ." The list was endless. And I,
poor wretch, used to run all the way to the village and then run back
in order to finish the task and still have my quarter-hour's consultation with Adam over the progress of our mutual charge, the kittiwake.

For some reason this daily ceremony of feeding the bird annoyed
my mother more than anything, probably because she knew that I
looked forward to it so much and also because Adam always set
aside time for it, no matter what she herself had planned. The kittiwake's progress was important to us both, and as the summer weeks
passed we began to think there was a real chance that our grounded
bird might fly again one day. Once it had started to feed we tried to
encourage it to beat its wings by holding the best morsels of fish just
out of its reach, and forcing it to flap a few inches off the ground to
reach them. Gradually, its strength and confidence seemed to be
returning, although I imagined that its final departure was still some
time away.

I was mistaken—utterly mistaken—in that belief. One day at the
end of August I came back from my morning lesson in the village,
stripped off my shoes and went out to the kitchen yard to inspect my
old friends. The blind kitten was there, and came mewing up to my
legs as soon as she heard my soft step; the one-legged crow flapped
down from the roof-ridge as usual; but when I went to the box we'd
fixed up as a shelter for the kittiwake, it was empty. The bird had
gone.

I looked round the yard. There was no sign of its white and gray
feathers anywhere, and nothing to be seen of it near the cowshed
either. I called, but there was no reply.

Assuming that suddenly, from nowhere, the kittiwake had found
the strength and the will to fly away from us, I dashed into the house
to tell Adam what had happened. My mother was in the hall, waiting
at the foot of the stairs.

"Ah, Rachel. I was just coming to look for you. I want you to run
down to the village for me—"

"But I must find Adam! There's something I simply must tell him!"

"*Mr. Gaunt.* And whatever it is, you can tell him later."

"But it's important!" And to prove how important my news really was, I added, "The kittiwake's gone! Flown off! All of a sudden!"

"Ah yes. The bird."

She could have left it at that, left me in my excitement to imagine that my careful nursing had been successful, and that a fully restored kittiwake had soared off to join its fellows out at sea. But my mother could never resist savoring the last sweet drop of her victories.

"You're wrong about your bird. There's nothing to bother Mr. Gaunt about after all, since it didn't leave of its own accord. Dirty, noisy thing! And in my kitchen yard! I gave the Birch boy threepence to take it down to the headland and throw it over the cliff. I should imagine that taught it to fly quickly enough!"

I couldn't believe my ears. It had never entered my head that my mother would do such a thing. And it had never entered Adam's head either; I could tell that from the look on his face as he came out of the parlor in time to hear her last few words.

"Adam! I didn't realize—"

"Did I hear aright? Did you just tell Rachel you'd paid some boy to throw her bird over the cliff?"

"And what if I did? It's my house, and I'll do as I please."

"I can't believe you'd be so cruel. And to your own daughter."

His eyes were pale with anger, and his face looked as if it had been carved from stone. And he was saying all the things I wanted to say, but couldn't.

"Oh, Adam—" My mother assumed her sweetest and most winning manner. "It was only an old bird."

She reached out a playful hand to touch his arm, but he shrugged her off and, without another word, strode angrily into the garden.

She'd already forgotten me. With a look of sudden concern, she ran into the garden after Adam, and the door shut behind them both.

I sat on the headland for a long time that afternoon, watching the seabirds wheeling and diving out over the bay, and wondering if by some miracle my kittiwake was among them. There was no bedraggled bundle of white and gray feathers on the rocks below the cliff, certainly, but that meant nothing. If the bird had been pounded helplessly against the jagged ledges by the sea, the ebbing tide would have carried the remains far out to where the spiraling gulls could make a feast of them. No—the kittiwake had gone. My bird. And I lay on the headland until the heat went out of the sun, and cried as if my heart would break.

It was nearly midnight, I should think, by the time I'd cried myself to a standstill over the bird, and over Adam, and over my own loneliness. Maria had long since gone to sleep after complaining pettishly about my noisy sobs, and I was about to put out the last stub of my illicit candle when I heard a gentle knock at the door. As I watched, it eased open a fraction, and Adam himself looked in.

"Still awake?" he whispered. "Somehow, I thought you might be. May I come in?"

"Of course."

He came into the room, treading with deliberate care, then sat down on the edge of the bed, which gave a loud creak. The noise was so ridiculous that we both grinned, stifling our mirth at once as Maria stirred in her sleep.

"I'm glad you're still awake. I wanted to talk to you. To say how sorry I was about the kittiwake."

"It wasn't your fault."

He gave me a penetrating look, and then his eyes slid away. "Perhaps it was."

"But how could it possibly have been?"

He shook his head sadly, as if the true state of affairs was too complex to explain. "Let's just say some things which should have been said were held back for too long." He smiled ruefully. "But they've been said now."

There was no answer I could make. I had no idea what he was talking about.

"I shouldn't have stayed so long in this house. Once I realized—well, I shouldn't have stayed, that's all. Still—that isn't why I'm here. I have something for you. Perhaps it'll make up a little for the loss of the kittiwake. Lean forward."

I bent my head toward him and he looped something round my neck. When I looked down I saw it was an amulet on a leather thong, a circle of reddish stone inlaid with the tiny stylized shapes of animals in a paler material, forming an endless procession round the central hole.

"Do you remember asking me about the Indian tribes in the mountains? Well, I found this today in the bag I brought with me from the ship. It used to belong to an Indian woman I knew, but it was made long before she was born. Even she couldn't tell me how old it was, or how many people had owned it. But you seemed interested in the Indians, and I thought you might like to have it."

"To *keep*? Forever? Oh, Adam, it's beautiful!" I flung my arms round his neck with delight.

"Call it an early birthday present, since I'll be far away from Crow Cove by the time your birthday arrives."

"You're going away on the September schooner?" It seemed unthinkable. The schooner was expected in the next ten days, and I could hardly believe that when it left for St. John's it would carry Adam away with it. The subject of his leaving had been raised before, but my mother had always refused to discuss it, on the grounds that his leg wasn't sufficiently healed for the long journey to England.

"I always told you I'd go when my leg was well again. Well, now it is, and it's time I was on my way."

I looked down at the amulet, and a question formed in my mind.

"The Indian woman who owned this. The woman you knew. Who was she?"

"She was an Oglala Sioux woman, and very pretty. Tahtokay was her name." He hesitated for a moment, and then added, "She was my wife."

My jaw must have dropped. I'd never thought of him as married, and certainly not to anything so exotic as an Indian woman. "Where is she now, your wife? What does she look like? Is she going to England with you?"

"She died, Rachel. Having a baby. There was nothing anyone could do for her, or for the child. Do you understand that?"

I nodded. A woman in Brigus had died in the same way the previous summer, and at least I was old enough to know roughly how babies were born, even if I'd no idea how they were made. I remember feeling dreadfully, desperately sorry for Adam, but I just didn't know the proper words to say. Now that I knew its story I was staggered by the generosity of his gift.

"I'll take very good care of it, I promise. For ever and ever."

He smiled. "Just *forever* will do."

———

And so in the end it all dissolved into rancor and conflict. That was always how it went with my mother: if she was given her own way in everything our lives were undisturbed, the horizon unclouded, but if there was something she wanted yet couldn't have, all the spite and malice inside her seemed to pour out on whoever was closest. I didn't know why she and Adam had quarreled, yet for the week which remained until the MacDonalds' schooner called to replenish the stock in our store, the two of them barely exchanged a word, stalking round one another, stiff-legged, like cats, each watching the other with hot, baleful eyes. I was furious with my mother for bringing it to this. She was the one who'd wanted Adam Gaunt to stay with us in the first place, and now, it seemed, she could hardly bear to see him in her home.

From the moment he gave it to me, I wore his amulet everywhere —but out of sight, inside my shift, next to my skin. I even wore it in bed at night, and that's where my sharp-eyed mother noticed it, though why she should have been in our bedroom in the middle of the night I can't imagine. Normally it was Liddy who came to us if we ever had nightmares.

Next morning she demanded to know where the strange ornament had come from, and without thinking. . . . No—that's not entirely honest. The truth is that I was in seventh Heaven that Adam should have given the amulet to me and not to my mother, and I couldn't resist making her jealous. So I told her quite candidly the story of the circular charm, and simply to show her that she didn't know *all* there was to know, I added that it had belonged to Adam's dead Indian wife.

The effect on my mother was devastating, a hundred times more satisfactory than I'd expected. It was almost as if I'd struck her.

"His *Indian* wife?" she whispered at last. "He has . . . with an *Indian?*"

I couldn't understand what all the fuss was about. Then I remembered that four years earlier, she'd seen a wretched group of three Beothuck Indian females, the last of their race, captured somewhere in the north of our island and brought to St. John's for the people to stare at. They reminded her, my mother had said, of the slaves she'd sometimes seen as a child being sold in front of the Liverpool Customs House—not because of their appearance, but because of the lifeless expression on their faces. The women had stared about them with the same look of blank incomprehension the slaves had worn, but their skin was lighter than the negroes' had been, and instead of cropped, woolly heads they'd had long, dark hair which fell in oily tangles to their shoulders. They were no taller than she was herself, but in spite of the cotton shifts they'd been compelled to wear they seemed strongly built and sturdy, as befitted creatures who'd been hunted like wolves by the white men.

I could imagine my mother staring at the Beothuck women with no more embarrassment than she would have felt in examining a team of horses. They were female, obviously enough, with prominent breasts, and they gave off a strong, musky smell which pervaded the room where they were confined. But were they human or animal? That was the question. Did anything finer than the most basic urges pass through those dark heads?

She never forgot what happened next. The nearest woman—presumably resenting the intensity of the inspection—raised her head and stared at my mother with an expression of such implacable hatred that for a moment she knew real fear. Then the woman spat, deliberately and accurately, leaving a trail of spittle on the hem of my mother's dress. One of the attendants leaped forward to cuff the culprit, but at least my mother had discovered the answer to the question which had puzzled her. Despite their almost human appearance, the Indians were animals after all, squalid and bestial, and the island was well rid of them.

Now I realized that her flesh fairly crawled at the thought of having any contact with such degraded creatures. She looked quite ill, though I couldn't see why. It was surely Adam's own business whom he chose to marry. He wasn't asking my mother to have anything to do with the woman, was he? In any case, I was sure that anyone Adam loved would be quite angelic, and he'd already told me his wife had been pretty.

At any rate, by the time the schooner had arrived in Crow Cove and finished unloading all the lumber and nails, coffee and tea, soap and candles and dried peas and leather it had brought up for the store, my mother could hardly bring herself to say a civil word to Adam Gaunt. The atmosphere in the house was dreadful, and it was almost a relief when the schooner's skipper sent up to say he was anxious to set sail for St. John's right away.

My father had already bolted to his lair in the village, and so only my mother and we three children took part in the awkward, perfunctory ceremony of leave-taking at the garden gate. I'd said my piece in private the day before, and no one else seemed to have anything to add but the barest of farewells. Then suddenly he was off, swinging away down the hill with hardly a trace of a limp, and turning back once to wave. I was convinced I'd never see him again, and I felt sadder and emptier than I'd ever felt before.

For a long time afterward my mother waited near the garden gate, watching the little schooner cleverly haul itself out of the mouth of the cove and into the vastness of Conception Bay, where it dwindled slowly to a perfect miniature before dropping out of sight over the horizon.

And that, I thought, was the last we'd see of Adam Gaunt.

3

Adam Gaunt's departure from Crow Cove marked the start of a great period of change in our lives. All at once, from the narrow, confined spaces of our village on the shores of Conception Bay my horizons began to widen, and went on widening until they encompassed people and places I could never have dreamed of in a thousand years beside the shingle beach of Crow Cove. So much seemed to happen in a short space of time, as if one new experience followed another with hardly a moment to draw breath between them. But of course it wasn't like that at all, though in the seven years which were to pass before I left the island for good, I changed from a child into a half-made woman, through all the perplexing and painful stages of that process.

On the face of it, it's hard to see what Adam Gaunt could have had to do with the whirlwind of events which overtook our family as soon as he left us. Yet I'm sure he was partly responsible for it, if only because my mother, who for a whole summer had been distracted from her self-imposed task of making her family financially secure, flung herself with renewed obsession into the business of making money as soon as he'd vanished from her sight. The Mac-Donalds' schooner had hardly left for St. John's when she turned once more to wringing every penny from her various schemes, and before many weeks had passed she'd hit on the venture which was to bring about the most sweeping change in our circumstances.

By now the fisher families for some distance round the bay shore treated my mother almost as a bank. When catches were poor she allowed them credit at the store, bringing in profitable business which might otherwise have gone to Harbour Grace; out of loyalty when times were good they still came to her for provisions. If a man wanted to borrow she would take his boat and fishing gear as collateral; sometimes she contributed to the building of a new boat in return for a share of its profits. And always, until the MacDonalds' schooner made its monthly visit to the village, she had the use of Andrew MacDonald's store profits to invest for herself. Provided the proper amount was sent off to St. John's with the returning schooner, the merchant could hardly object.

Before long, my mother had saved enough money to outfit a sealer of her own which was sent off in the spring to hunt among the ice floes drifting south with their cargo of Harps and Bedlemers. Everyone agreed she had the Devil's own luck with that sealing schooner, which always came home safe and sound, loaded with valuable pelts, though every year there were one or two vessels which went out and didn't return. This loss of life—and of boats—could cripple a small village, just as the loss of an inshore fishing boat was a major tragedy for the family which owned it.

My mother knew that in the great shipping cities of the world such as her own childhood home of Liverpool, ship-owners took out insurance against the loss of a vessel or any damage it might suffer in the course of trading. Why shouldn't the owners of fishing boats and sealing schooners be able to do the same? They might not be able to afford the huge premiums paid by the owners of barks and full-riggers, but at the same time their boats were comparatively small and easy to replace.

She began in a modest way that year by offering to indemnify the other owners of boats she already had a share in. For a certain regular sum they could be sure that if the boat was wrecked or damaged Susannah Dean would replace it or its fishing gear at no further cost to themselves. If the men were reluctant to accept her offer, my mother consulted the wives who waited at home for their absent husbands and sons, and the money was always paid over. After all, surely it was a small outlay in return for the new measure of security in their lives. . . .

Word spread, and the owners of boats in which my mother had no share at all began to approach her. She was careful at first to keep the level of risk within bounds, unsure of how much she should charge in premiums, but as the notion of boat insurance grew in popularity she was able to raise the level of premiums to amazing levels without discouraging business. The benevolent summer of '28 set her venture firmly on its feet; all round the island the weather seemed to bring nothing but gentle breezes, and the sea treated the Conception Bay boats with unusual kindness.

By the end of that year my mother's sights were set further afield. Surely what was working so well in Conception Bay would work on a larger scale elsewhere—say, in the capital, St. John's?

This was how we came to spend the greatest part of each year in St. John's, first of all in a rented house in Duckworth Street and then later, as our fortunes surged ahead, in a new house of considerable size built specially for us on the outskirts of the city.

My mother had another motive for wishing to be free of Crow Cove. My father was now spending so much of his time at the secret still behind the boatyard that he'd become a positive embarrassment to the family, and the shame of having the town drunk for a husband was more than my mother could bear.

And yet in May of that year—1828—her fourth child was born, and I supposed that my mother and father had somehow patched up the shreds of their marriage for a time at least. Reuben Dean, my younger brother, was born in Crow Cove on the 6th of May in the pine bed with the goose-feather mattress which had once been Adam Gaunt's. The Widow Creran was fetched in the dog-cart and arrived to find the baby well on its way, my father in the parlor with a bottle of brandy, and Susan Vinegar ministering anxiously to my toiling mother.

From my post at the door I saw the midwife take a swift glance to see how matters stood, and nod with satisfaction.

"Now, you just keep that up, my lamb, and we'll have you delivered in no time. Susan, put another pillow under her back. And now, Mrs. Dean, if you'll do that once more for me, we may well have the head. And after that it's no bother, is it?"

The door was shut firmly in my face, and we all waited outside for the baby's first cry.

———

The child was thin and long-limbed, with fair down on his head. Mrs. Creran washed and wrapped him, cooing over the beauty of his tiny, wrinkled form, and then summoned Joseph and the rest of us to inspect the new addition to our family. I remember my father peering unsteadily at the infant lying in my mother's arms and trying to avoid breathing neat spirit over the midwife.

"You're sure there's nothing the matter with him?"

"Nary a thing!" cried the widow indignantly. "He's quite perfect, the mite. Why should anything be amiss with him? Why, the good

Lord has given you a fine-looking boy this time, and no mistake! You've a beautiful son there, Mr. Dean."

"So it would seem," replied my father morosely, hiccuping in the baby's face.

In time, my new brother turned out to be dark-haired like his mother and father, though his eyes were neither blue like Susannah's nor brown like Joseph's, but settled down to a kind of shifting gray and a direct gaze which hinted that he already knew who we all were and how we were related to him. Immediately I preferred him to Edward and Maria, who were so unlike me in personality, and I'm sure I spent more time with him than my mother did, certainly after the first few weeks of his life. In the course of the move to St. John's we acquired a proper nursemaid to take charge of us all, and as soon as she could, my mother relinquished the baby to the nurse's arms and returned to her great mission of making money.

The Deans' presence in the city of St. John's was marked by the opening of a modest office in Water Street, the long thoroughfare running behind the warehouses of the harbor which, when my parents first arrived in Newfoundland, had simply been known as the "Lower Path." At first, business arrived in a trickle, but within a year—after the affair of the *Guide Us*—the trickle had turned into a flood. I have no difficulty in remembering the name of the boat because its effect on our fortunes was so great.

The *Guide Us* was a small inshore fishing boat from a village not far from Crow Cove, swamped by a wave while rounding the point at the mouth of her home creek, loaded down with herring. Two of the men aboard her were picked up out of the water, but the third was feared drowned until, after considerable searching, he was miraculously discovered, more dead than alive, cast up on a rocky ledge some distance away from the scene of the capsizing.

His story took up three columns in the *Gazette,* and made much of the fact that although the *Guide Us*—now at the bottom of the sea—had originally been insured by Crow Cove Mutual Aid Society, the premiums had recently been allowed to lapse, and the boat's owners expected to have no claim.

Much as my mother hated to part with money, instinct told her this was no time to stick to the letter of an agreement. Making sure the *Gazette* was informed of the Society's great generosity, she met the claim in full.

"When God has seen fit to spare a man's life," ran a quotation in the *Gazette* attributed to Mr. Joseph Dean of the Crow Cove Society, "it's surely a sign to us that we should restore his livelihood." My mother had labored for two days on those words, hunting for the correct note of pious thrift. I knew it irked her to have to pretend that *Mr. Joseph Dean* was in charge when all he did was to sign whatever was presented to him by his tireless wife. But this was St. John's, not Crow Cove, and if the law held that a wife was her husband's chattel, then this was how it must appear. And so in the same edition of the *Gazette*, Mr. Dean was praised to the skies for his open-handed charity to the unfortunate men of the *Guide Us*.

The astonished fishermen spread their tale all over the peninsula, and a queue formed at the door of the office in St. John's. Before winter could tighten its grip on the bay, a grapnel-crew was sent out to raise what was left of the *Guide Us* from the sandy seabed at the mouth of the creek and convey it to the boatyard in Crow Cove. In spring it was launched again, trim and well-found, and my mother leased it to some fishermen from Point de Grave whose own boat had been wrecked not long before.

By now the lawyers were suggesting it was time to turn the fledgling insurance venture into a public company with directors and stockholders, however much my mother hated to lose control of its activities.

"The risk is too great," they warned her. "Think of a hurricane! Think of a tidal wave! You must share the risk even if it means sharing the profits."

A curious magic had begun to work its spell among the boat-owners of first the east and then the south and southwest coasts of the island. A paper certificate from the Crow Cove Mutual Aid Society became like a talisman of safety at sea. Somehow the notion spread that to be outside the comforting circle of an insurance policy was to invite wreck and disaster. For every boat-owner who took out insurance and bragged of it later, two more looked long and hard at their own insecure profession and, as often as not, presented themselves next day before one of my mother's newly appointed agents. Out of this sudden surge of business the Avalon and Crow Cove Marine Insurance Company was born.

Anyone who expected my mother to pause after this and rest on her substantial income was totally mistaken. What good was money if it wasn't laid out to make more? Once again my mother looked round for ways of investing her profits. In those days, of course, I knew nothing of what went on outside the walls of our house, but as I grew older I heard rumors of her business dealings—and eventually the whole story—from people who were in a position to know the truth.

In her pursuit of profit she spared no one, including her friend Andrew MacDonald, that good-hearted man who'd saved our family from the consequences of my father's folly. I only knew him as "Uncle Andrew," a genial bear who arrived with pockets full of humbugs and small wooden toys whenever he visited our house in St. John's, but in city offices he had a reputation for being a shrewd, plain-speaking businessman whose word was every bit as good as other men's paper contracts.

My mother had turned his store in Crow Cove into a thriving concern, certainly, but before long it had begun to irritate her to see the fruits of her hard work paid over to another person, even if that person was Andrew MacDonald. Soon after we were established in St. John's she went to Uncle Andrew and informed him bluntly that she wanted to buy his store, one of several she intended to acquire in the outlying communities. If he wouldn't sell, she would open up in opposition and simply put him out of business. On the other hand, if they could come to a suitable agreement she would continue to buy stock from him for all her trading posts—provided, of course, that his prices remained competitive.

I think perhaps Uncle Andrew already suspected he'd made a rod for his own back when he set my mother up in business in Crow Cove. At any rate, he sold her the store, and though his visits to our house became markedly fewer after that, he continued to take an interest in the lives of the younger members of the family, something for which I was to be profoundly grateful a few years later.

Along with the store, Andrew MacDonald offered my mother a piece of advice which, after some consideration, she decided to take.

"Remember," he said, "that even now the businessmen of St. John's still believe it's *Joseph* Dean who's the moving force behind these schemes of yours, since you've always used his name. They'll find out the truth soon enough, I don't doubt. But in the meantime, swallow your pride and let them go on thinking what they please, for two reasons. Firstly, men are prepared to see another man succeed, but they'll close ranks against a woman, and you'll find it hard to deal with them. Secondly, think of your marriage and your children. For the sake of your children, take care, Susannah. Joseph must go on as head of the family, or you'll leave him with nothing."

The plain truth was that every day it mattered less to my mother whether my father felt himself head of the Dean family or not. But the opinion of outsiders was a different matter. For the sake of appearances she'd prized him away from his grog-swilling cronies in Crow Cove, and she was too shrewd not to recognize the truth of Andrew MacDonald's warning about the business community of St. John's. After several days' hesitation, she instructed the lawyers who were drawing up the details of her new company to insert the name "Joseph Dean" after the words "General Manager."

My father was both pleased and flattered to find his name on the official documents. Best of all, the title appeared to carry a handsome salary but no specific duties except an occasional visit to be bowed to and fawned over by the eager young man in charge. At home in the evenings, full of brandy, my father signed whatever he was told to sign, sometimes falling asleep with his head on the paper, so that my mother's version of *Joseph Dean* quickly became more legible than his own.

As soon as she began to feel more secure, my mother bought a plot of land for her own use, a site just beyond the city boundary, sheltered from the westerly blasts by a stand of fir trees. This was the place she had chosen for our new home, a house built of local stone, not lavish enough to attract envious notice but solidly respectable, with spacious grounds round it and a wide avenue for the use of a carriage in summer and a sleigh in winter.

The contractor who built it had more experience putting up the huge warehouses which lined the waterfront at St. John's than of house building, and forever afterward our house had more the look of a Gothic fish-store than a gracious residence, but the addition of a classical portico over the main door and a fine brass weathervane twirling on the roof succeeded in giving it at least an appearance of grandeur. To my relief, however, there was no question of giving up the house in Crow Cove, which would remain our summer residence. The Deans had arrived.

There was one final scheme which remained to be put into effect, though like the men of the St. John's commercial world I knew nothing at all about it at the time. One day, without fanfare or announcement of any kind, a Relief Association opened its offices in an unfashionable part of the city, ostensibly to see to the welfare of the deserving poor, but in reality, so it was whispered, to lend money at staggering rates to any needy wretch who could provide security. The ownership of the Association was shrouded in mystery, and my mother took care never to visit its offices or be seen with its staff. But the loan business put her huge profits from the insurance company to work, and the rates she charged ensured that those who came to her were desperate people who'd had every other door in St. John's slammed in their faces. Not one of them dared object to her conditions.

Andrew MacDonald once told me he thought my mother had forgotten what it was like to be poor, but I don't believe that was true.

To my mother, poverty was like some shameful, disfiguring disease which had scarred her for life, and she could never forget it. She didn't forget, and she didn't forgive. I think she meant to be revenged on the whole city of St. John's for making her suffer.

———

Even I found little to like about St. John's. Brought up on the open hillside of Crow Cove I found the steep streets and crowded buildings of the city hideously confining, and the stiff shoes and billowing pinafore I was forced to wear all day were pure torture. Edward, on the other hand, loved the horses and carriages, and so did Maria, who could spend all day dreaming of *fichus* and frilled Indian muslin, of turquoise beads and fur muffs, and of having an elegant beau to squire her round town. I was the odd one out. The nursemaid despaired of me: my attempts to embroider dainty handkerchiefs ended in crumples and knots, my long dark hair refused to curl, and all I ever wanted to do during boring city days was to hide myself in a corner with a book.

All winter, I longed for the summer and our return to Crow Cove. My dreams were all of the dusty hillside and the cool, blue-green forest with its birds and animals, and sometimes during the tedious winter months I would take out the Indian woman's amulet and rub its smoothness between my fingers as if, like summoning the Genie of the Ring, I could make Adam Gaunt come back to us once more. My mother had never mentioned his name since he left us, and I assumed she'd forgotten him. But I hadn't; and I could still feel his presence in the long summer hours at Crow Cove.

Every day there was precious to me now, and I hated to waste a minute of it lying in bed after the sun had risen. Each morning I rose early and left the house by the kitchen door, pausing to gaze down the slope to the familiar, huddled rooftops of the village, each with its straight stem of gray smoke winding up against the dark water of the inlet as the cooking fires were lit. Two or three gulls were always wheeling overhead, searching for fish-heads by the jetty, and the mingled scents of wood smoke, sea-salt and the lavender bushes by the path which brushed against my legs as I passed seemed fresh and clear and cool. Another winter in the city stretched ahead but those Crow Cove mornings lay like a fragrant salve on the rawness of my spirit.

I was ten years old in September, and I remember that summer as the last in which I was allowed to run gloriously wild in the scrub-land at the forest edge of Crow Cove. I'd never taken any interest in dolls or in playing "house" with the village girls, but I could climb trees or throw homemade spears as well as any of the neighborhood boys, and by this time I'd won grudging acceptance in their noisy, brawling pack. In fact, from the rear there was little to distinguish me from a boy except for my long hair. My mother's essential round-ness of form seemed to have passed me by, and my bony shoulders and slim hips were more of my father's mold.

As the warm days of summer rushed past there was one place above all which we loved, a natural pool of deep black water hol-lowed out where the creek disgorged into the apex of the cove, cool water which glittered invitingly at the end of a hot, dusty day. That was where I learned to swim and also to dive, plunging with the careless confidence of youth from the grass-tufted rocks which over-hung the pool into the sudden silence of its clear water.

And that was where my mother found me one day, splashing naked like the rest, and furiously dragged me home, still damp and dripping, to my little bedroom under the eaves.

"What were you doing, down there at the creek?" she demanded to know.

"Swimming."

"Just swimming?"

I shrugged. "What else can you do at a swimming hole?"

My mother gave me a searching look. "Did any of the boys try to . . . touch you?"

"*Touch* me?" This was a novel idea. "Why would they want to touch me?"

"Just as long as they didn't, that's all." And my mother swept grimly out of the room, locking the door behind her.

She must have made her plans that very day, because by the time we returned to St. John's at the end of August, a governess had been appointed to take charge of Edward, Maria and me instead of the harassed nurse who'd looked after us until then and who still had charge of Reuben.

The governess's name was Miss Penrose, and she was small and pleasant and something of a bluestocking, and although we tended to take advantage of her good nature we became quite fond of her during the sixteen months she stayed with us. But she was, as I said, small and sweet and intellectual, and before long Miss Penrose was "walking out" with a local Anglican clergyman and was about to become Mrs. West.

For obvious reasons, her successor was a middle-aged, rather dog-like German widow—something of a rarity on the island—who believed that anything which could be learned was capable of being learned by rote. Our constant chanting filled the house with noise, drove my mother to distraction, and resulted in the eventual dismissal of the indignant Frau.

After that my mother felt she required a governess of a different stamp. Edward, being a boy, would have his education seen to in due course, while Maria and I, as girls, needed only to make sense of milliners' bills and the descent of the British monarchs. We didn't require teaching so much as *watching*.

In the event my mother succeeding in killing more than one bird with her well-aimed stone.

The truth was that despite all her efforts in prizing my father loose from a set of dangerous friends in Crow Cove, she only seemed to have flung him into worse company in town. It was astonishing how quickly he'd smelled out the dens where uninhibited drinking and gambling were to be had even in that hard-working community.

For days on end—sometimes even for weeks—we all imagined he'd grown tired of these dismal dungeons in the alleys of Water Street, where the fetid stink of rum and pipe-smoke drifted out into the highway. During these periods he'd appear sober every evening and be studiously civil to my mother and to the servants, a model husband and father. Then all at once he'd stumble home in the early hours of the morning, penniless and reeking of spirits, loudly abusive to my mother when she rose from her bed, candle in hand, to investigate the cause of the noise.

He no longer bothered to hide his sprees from us children. Drunk, he sneered at my mother's reproaches and demanded more money for his entertainment; sober again he was abject and pathetically repentant, but just as disgusting. Even if she no longer cared about the effect on his health, my mother was deeply pained by the fact that the whole of St. John's buzzed with news of her husband's riotous ways.

For the good of the insurance company she had Joseph's name struck out as general manager on the grounds of ill-health, and instead engineered the appointment of the young man who'd actually carried out his duties since the company was formed. My father protested feebly, knowing he was wasting his time, and then crawled off to drown his disappointment in second-class rum.

He never had to look far for female company. If he'd started up a quiet liaison somewhere in St. John's my mother would no doubt have turned a blind eye to it, but rampant whoring in the lowest haunts of the city was another matter. It was almost as if my father had set out to shame his family as publicly as he could.

As always, my mother's chief spy was Susan Vinegar, who'd followed us to town and was staying with her widowed mother while she did her best to capture the affections of the young man promoted to general manager of the insurance company. To her delight, her efforts had soon paid off in the form of long Sunday walks by the seashore and eventually in what Susan called an "understanding" between them. One day—it had solemnly been agreed—Miss Susan Vinegar would take her place as the general manager's wife and helpmeet.

I wasn't surprised by her success. With my mother's help Susan now cut a modish figure, her rebellious hair almost tamed into a chignon, her skirts raised to precisely the new ankle length over white openwork stockings and dainty white shoes, her knees kept primly together when she sat on a drawing-room chair. But nothing could be done with the gap-tooth, and Susan Vinegar's grin always tended to resemble a hole in a fence.

Transformed though she was, Susan was as quick with the tattle of St. John's as she'd ever been with the gossip of Crow Cove, and regularly brought home tales of gold earrings and India shawls flaunted by the rouged ladies of the waterfront—presents from my amorous father—of window-smashing and ale-drinking contests financed by him, and of a hideous afternoon when, in full view of a large crowd, Joseph Dean and his cronies set out to see which of them, on a bellyful of wine, could piss farthest from the Court House steps.

Two days later a huge fisherman called Theo moved into our home, and before long my father, missing from his usual dens in town, was seen enjoying healthful walks on the snow-girt Barrens with his massive warder at his heels. Even when he went to town with my mother in the carriage or in the sleigh, Theo went too, and plodded doggedly after them as they made their calls, covered in umbrellas and parcels like a human hat-rack.

However, in the spring of 1832 my mother managed to solve two of her most vexing problems at a single stroke. And that stroke was Florence Sutter.

———

We all waited at the top of the stairwell, Edward, Maria, Reuben and I, to see what she would be like. The staircase rose through the center of the house, square and iron-bound, and since we'd been forbidden to come down to the hall we rushed to the topmost rail as soon as we heard the bell clang at the front door, and peered down to the distant rectangle of tiles below.

She was due at three, and at two minutes before the hour the sonorous gonging of the bell announced her arrival. All we could see of her from above, however, was the top of a pale blue satin hat with a chimney-pot crown topped by a riot of flowers and a coquettish white feather. Somewhere below it was a rustling pale blue pelisse of many capes and black-gloved hands clutching an ineffectual blue umbrella which she handed disdainfully to the servant who ushered her into the drawing room to receive her instructions.

We discovered later that as a source of refinement and genteel conversation, Florence Sutter was hardly more qualified than the hulking, silent Theo. But the jaunty white feather in her hat proclaimed that her ambitions soared above the slate-pencil and the English Grammar. She'd come to Newfoundland in the firm belief that St. John's was the kind of place where a resourceful woman might overcome default of rank, and make something of herself. In the meantime, for a modest sum she was prepared to let my mother make a jailer of her.

When summer came again and we moved back to Crow Cove, Miss Sutter came too, lodging with a respectable family in the village since there was no room for her at the top of the hill. In spite of the fine weather we had lessons every day, followed by grisly open-air drawing classes and tedious rambles at the edge of the cultivated land to pick wild flowers for pressing. I was bored to death, but

Miss Sutter's sharp brown eye was upon me, and there was no escape.

Miss Sutter's eye took in other things that summer—especially anything which could be turned to her advantage. She was quite pretty in a common sort of way, with a fluff of fair curls arranged *à la girafe* from a knot on the top of her head, and curious dark eyebrows which met in a sprinkling of hairs on the bridge of her nose, and which instantly made us all suspect that her hair was bleached.

Inevitably, she and Susan Vinegar loathed each other on sight, and it was Susan who told me, many years later, those parts of the governess's story which had escaped me at the time. For Florence Sutter was, in Susan's book, a silly woman, and silly in the worst possible way—she imagined herself far more cunning than she actually was.

Always in pursuit of her private plans, little Florence examined every part of our household and made her own assessment of its inner workings. My father was happy to help her and since, thanks to Theo, he was then leading a blameless if unexciting life, Miss Sutter came to believe that the saintly Mr. Dean toiled unceasingly for the benefit of his ungrateful family and that his shrewish wife did no more than spend his hard-earned wealth.

How sad it was to find a man so good, so misunderstood, and . . . so rich! My father's tales of woe produced a rush of sympathy in Miss Sutter's tender breast, and my father, bored by his imprisonment, opened like a flower to the gentle understanding of little Florence, imagining himself truly appreciated at last.

Soon we were astounded to find Papa taking an interest in schoolroom matters, dropping in at all hours of the day to see how work was progressing. Miss Sutter would smile shyly and show him our copybooks or our flower drawings with trembling hands; the book would slip, my father and she would both reach for it, and somehow fingers would become accidentally entwined, giving rise to more blushes and smiles. Often, out for a decorous walk in the garden, we would come upon my father sniffing at rose bushes or doing something equally unlikely. Straightening up with an exclamation of surprise, he would insist on escorting us from that moment, going on ahead with Miss Sutter while his children rambled mutinously in the rear.

As far as we were concerned, Florence Sutter was a downright nuisance, but apparently to my mother she was a considerable and unexpected asset. Before long, sly glances over the breakfast table, urgent whispers and footsteps pattering past her door in the middle of the night made her certain that a full-blown affair was in progress. No doubt the little governess thought she'd been amazingly astute. Joseph Dean was a wealthy man, and he obviously adored her. Even if there was little chance of his ever divorcing his vixenish wife and installing Miss Sutter as the new Mrs. Dean, who could tell what benefits might not come Florence's way?

And while the governess continued to charm him, my father stayed away from his drinking dens in town and the need for secrecy kept him on his best behavior at home. Theo was no longer needed; my mother could hand over his responsibilities to Miss Sutter, thus saving a good wage and three very large meals a day. It was all utterly, entirely satisfactory.

As children, we were only aware of a period of unusual domestic calm in the house since Miss Sutter's arrival. I say *children*, but in fact I was twelve years old when she came, and thirteen that September—older than my years in some ways, and yet woefully ignorant in others. My brother Edward was ten just before Christmas, and the following year my mother decided it would soon be time for his formal education to begin. As befitted a young gentleman, he was to have a tutor; the only problem was to find a suitably qualified person.

In those days Uncle Andrew MacDonald and his wife still visited us occasionally and, although his relations with my mother were now somewhat cool, Uncle Andrew was genuinely fond of us children. When he heard that my mother was looking for a capable tutor for Edward, he suggested a young man he thought would be ideal for the position.

"John Francis Ellis," he announced solemnly. "A lad after my own heart. You'd be hard put to find a finer fellow in the whole of St. John's, wouldn't you say, wife?" At his side, Christian MacDonald nodded her wholehearted agreement.

"His father was my good friend," Andrew MacDonald continued, "and the boy had two years at university in the United States before the old man died, and there was no more money to pay for his studies. There were debts, you see. Oh, I offered to give him what he needed, but he wouldn't hear of it. Not a word. He'd pay his own way, he said, and that was the end of it. But you should write to his professors, Susannah—they'll tell you what kind of scholar he was. Brilliant—and only nineteen! He's a rare man for his books, is young Ellis. Just exactly what you need for Edward. Ach, I'm persuaded they'll get along just fine."

And that was how Francis Ellis joined our household in St. John's —suddenly, out of the blue in early 1834, just as he was to turn up again and again in my life in the future, carrying the seeds of calamity with him every time.

4

He was a dark young man, darker even than my father, with a romantic bluish pallor to his skin and that Celtic blackness of hair which in the thirties becomes suddenly, dazzlingly white. His hands, too, were small and pale, and altogether he cut a dashing figure in that prosaic, no-nonsense city, with his elegant coat and carelessly tied cravat, and his air of melancholy, world-weary cynicism.

Edward was enchanted by his new tutor and at once started to copy all Francis Ellis's gestures, from his habit of putting a hand to his forehead while he considered some complex thought to the languid way in which he threw himself down on a chair. Even Miss Sutter began to simper at the new arrival over the breakfast teacups under the very eye of my jealous father, and my sister Maria declared herself hopelessly in love with him at once.

"How terrible to be an orphan!" she exclaimed with all the passion of her ten years. "How Mr. Ellis must have suffered after his father died and left him all alone to make his own way in the world! It's one of the saddest things I ever heard."

"But his mother is still alive," I reminded her. "Uncle Andrew told me she lives near the end of Duckworth Street with her other four children, though their new house is so small that she's quite pleased to have Francis living with us. So he's hardly alone in the world."

"I don't care," Maria insisted stubbornly. "It isn't the same. You can see from his face that he needs peace and beauty around him, not some poky little hole in Duckworth Street full of shouting children. I don't expect Uncle Andrew would understand that—all he ever thinks of is money, like Mamma, and his great, dull warehouses in the harbor. Say what you like, I think Mr. Ellis is by far the most interesting person who's come to see us for years and years. Have you seen his embroidered braces? And the little brass links that fasten his trousers under his shoes? Oh, Rachel—do you suppose he writes poetry? Oh—I do hope so!"

I found it hard to share her enthusiasm. From the little I'd seen of him, Francis Ellis had seemed altogether too self-assured for my taste, still bathed in the smooth gloss of his two years at Yale University, subtle and clever. I was sure he regarded my sister and me as silly, chattering girls hardly worth a second glance. In any case, Mr. Ellis had been engaged as Edward's tutor, and I doubted if we'd see much of him beyond mealtimes.

The truth was that I didn't know how to make the bright, captivating conversation which was expected of young ladies on the verge of entering polite society. I saw very few people of my own age, and those I did meet were hardly the kind of bosom friends with whom I could discuss matters of the heart. My mother had never forgotten being "dropped" by the modest circle in which she'd moved when the clockmaking venture failed, and now she insisted on a place among the very best society in St. John's, and even there thought only a few people good enough for her notice.

It was well enough known in St. John's that the Deans had hauled themselves up from nothing at all, but that only made my mother's victory sweeter. If the governor's wife received an invitation to Mrs. Dean's reception, the governor's wife duly appeared in our drawing room at the appointed time, since my mother was now a person of consequence. I daresay it was amusing to be bowed out of the haberdasher's or the milliner's all the way to our carriage, but I can't remember knowing one person of either sex with whom I could laugh about it later.

I'd never had much in common with Edward or Maria. Edward, very much the boy, was still going through his phase of despising everything feminine, and to try to confide in Maria was to risk having my confidences repeated word for word to my mother. Reuben, on the other hand, was a thinker, a secret worrier who spent hours brooding over the state of the world as it seemed to his six-year-old eyes, and trying to make sense of it. He was a kindly child and a good listener, even when he didn't entirely understand what I was trying to tell him, and I think I loved Reuben more than any other member of my family. He was certainly the only one I loved without reservation, and he was probably the only one who truly loved me.

No doubt I was hard to love at that time. By my fourteenth birthday I'd taken to spending hours walking alone in the big gardens round our house in St. John's, especially since my knowledge of history and geography was now embarrassingly better than Miss

Sutter's, and she was delighted to have me out of the schoolroom. I now had a bedroom of my own where I could read my books in peace, though sometimes I just sat at the dressing-table, staring at my altered image in the looking-glass and wondering what sort of woman was this enigmatic stranger who gazed back at me.

My face had grown finer with the passing years as my body lost some of its angularity, but it was obvious that I would never have my mother's voluptuous curves. My shoulders still stood out squarely under the lightest covering of flesh, my breasts were hardly formed, and even my best brown silk dress with its wide, gathered sleeves and narrow waist failed to give me the shapeliness I longed for. I'd taken to parting my hair in a "V" in the center of my brow like a solemn, dark cap, and sometimes when I walked near a mirror and caught sight of myself unexpectedly, it was as if a nun were passing one of those little windows through which the outside world can communicate with the peace of the cloister.

Miss Nose-in-her-Book—that's what Francis Ellis called me the first time he discovered me on my favorite wooden bench in the garden, tucked away in a quiet loop of the big yew hedge which sheltered my mother's roses. Autumn had set in swiftly that year; the first yellow splashes had hardly marked the trees before the tints of red and gold spread quickly from branch to branch, banishing the last heady lees of summer. The mountain ashes, burdened with berries, had no sooner blushed dark crimson than they were turned into burning bushes of fiery carmine, their branches flickering like flames in the first chill winds of the year.

"It's too cold, surely, to read in the garden now?" Francis promptly joined me on the bench without waiting for an invitation, lounging elegantly across its high back and peeling spars.

"This seat is very sheltered. And I like the peace of the garden."

"Which is a polite way of telling me you don't need my company, is that so?" Yet he didn't seem at all contrite, and made no move to leave. On the contrary, he settled himself comfortably next to me, and tried to identify the volume on my lap.

"You're a great reader, Miss Dean—you always seem to be absorbed in some book or other. What is it this time?"

It was Young's *Night Thoughts on Life, Death and Immortality,* and I held it up for him to see.

"Hah . . . ! That labored stuff!"

"You don't think much of it?" To tell the truth, I'd found the blank verse hard and depressing to read. But Miss Sutter had insisted I study the piece, and to avoid a scolding I'd attempted to read enough to answer her questions later in the day.

"I think it's dreary rubbish, and bad poetry into the bargain," Francis Ellis declared firmly. "Apart from a few clever lines he was lucky enough to stumble on. 'Procrastination is the thief of time.' That's good, I'll admit. But it's a very small jewel in a mountain of very tedious clay."

He moved imaginary spectacles down his nose and frowned at me over the top of them in imitation of one of his professors, and I laughed in spite of myself.

"That's better! I knew you couldn't possibly be such a serious young lady as you looked. Take my word for it—speaking as a poet myself—this verse of Young's is miserable nonsense, a travesty of real feeling. If he missed his wife half as much as he claims, he'd never have written such trash. Surely this isn't the sort of thing you usually read?"

"No . . . not usually. Not from choice. Sometimes I read novels. Mrs. Radcliffe, or Anne Porter. Though my mother doesn't really approve of them."

"Novels, indeed? Knights in armor rescuing their fair ladies from dismal castles or riding with them through haunted forests. . . . That kind of thing?"

It was almost precisely that kind of thing, but I resented his patronizing tone.

"Not exactly."

"But a good deal better than *Night Thoughts?*"

"I prefer them."

"Then you must lend me one of your novels, and I'll judge it for myself."

I gaped at him. "*You?* You don't read novels!"

"Then perhaps it's time I started," he suggested smoothly, "since you rate these books so highly. You're going to broaden my education for me, Miss Dean, I'm sure of it. One should never be afraid to try a new experience, don't you think?"

———

"He does write poetry," I told Maria that evening. "At least, he says he does, though I haven't seen any of it yet."

"I *told* you!" crowed my sister triumphantly, bouncing joyously on her bed. She snatched up the bolster and hugged it to her chest. "Oh, Rachel, you can see it in his eyes! He's just so—"

"Too perfect by half, if you ask me."

"So *romantic,* I was going to say. Don't you just *adore* romantic men?"

"I don't know any romantic men," I persisted. "Come to think of it, apart from Edward and Papa, I don't know any men at all."

"Oh, but you do! I should say you know Mr. Ellis, if he comes borrowing books from you! Rachel, you're so lucky . . . I wish I had a book he could borrow, but I don't suppose he'd want Flaxman's *English Grammar* or my *History of England.*"

"I don't imagine for a single moment he wants *Outcast of the Forest* either. Goodness knows why he asked me for it. He was probably just trying to prove what a broad-minded man he is—as if I'd be impressed by that!"

"Oh, but Rachel, if he doesn't want the book, and was only asking for it to impress you . . . then that's even better, don't you see?"

"No, I don't see."

"Good gracious, you are a goose sometimes! Mr. Ellis must like you! Why else should he ask for a book he doesn't want and doesn't intend to read, unless it was simply for the pleasure of being with you, and talking to you?"

"But that's nonsense! What on earth could he want with me?"

"Rachel, sometimes I think you *try* to be stupid! Mr. Ellis—Francis—" she added with a sigh—"is probably passionately in love with you! Perhaps he fell in love with you on the very first day he came here, and has been screwing up his courage to come and speak to you ever since."

"Maria, I've never heard such silliness! I'm sure Mr. Ellis has no time at all for fourteen-year-old girls, least of all girls who spend all day alone reading books."

"But that's exactly the kind of woman he'd find irresistible! You're so pale and quiet, and you think a lot—and he's only nineteen himself, I know that because I heard Uncle Andrew tell Mamma."

Mention of my mother stifled the conversation at once. For two pins Maria would rush to Mamma and pour out all her crazy theories about the new tutor and her elder sister. I began to wish I'd never mentioned Francis Ellis in the first place.

"Now listen to me, Maria," I said severely, "your imagination is running away with you as usual. Mr. Ellis has merely asked to borrow a book, that's all. I shall give it to him tomorrow, and I don't suppose we'll exchange another two words between now and Christmas. Is that quite clear?"

"I still think you should be nicer to him. At least let him hope."

"*Maria!*"

"Oh, very well! Ignore him, if that's what you want! But I think you're horrid and heartless, all the same. He'll be inconsolable—just you wait and see."

I had a sudden vision of Francis Ellis lounging next to me on the garden seat, a little half-smile twisting up the corners of his mouth, his blue eyes alight with sly amusement at my expense, and decided I'd seldom seen a man look less heartbroken. Whatever had prompted his sudden interest in my modest collection of novels, I doubted very much if it was unrequited love.

Yet he took the book, brought it back three days later, and even seemed to have read it.

"A little fantastic in places, perhaps, but none the worse for that. After all, coincidences do happen. Life has a habit of playing strange tricks on us when we least expect it."

I was surprised by his favorable verdict, to say the least, and absolutely stunned when he insisted on borrowing another of my books, and a third one after that was finished.

"I think you must have a wobbling table in your room, Mr. Ellis," I suggested gravely when he returned it to me in the garden.

"Why's that, Miss Dean?"

"You keep taking my books to wedge the leg. I can't think why else you might want them."

He laughed at that—quite genuinely—and shook his head. Then he sat down next to me with a great sigh.

"You don't think much of me, Miss Dean, do you? You're still afraid I'll make fun of your precious romances."

"I can't believe you spent two years at Yale University simply learning to read novels. You must have discovered something there better than knights-errant and damsels in distress."

"But what could be better than romance? Or better than fantasy or imagination? Good gracious, Miss Dean, it's only our higher feelings that raise us above pigs or geese! Once we forget how to weep over a sad story or laugh at a clever one, we'll be no better than brute beasts."

I stole a look at him out of the corner of my eye, quite certain he was teasing me. To my surprise he seemed perfectly serious. He was leaning toward me on the bench, his arm along the high wooden back, his gaze fixed intently upon me.

"Have you never shed a tear over one of these tales of yours? Be honest, Miss Dean."

"Well . . . Perhaps once or twice."

"Of course you have! Because your heart is still simple and good, and not made shallow by the cruelty of the world. You can still be moved to tears by a well-told story. I'd give a great deal to share such innocence as yours."

"Why on earth should you want to cry over a stupid novel?"

"Because I'm a poet, and a poet should be open to all sorts of feelings and emotions. The greatest poets have always known the depths of misery, but also the most sublime heights of ecstasy. One or the other—anything between those extremes is commonplace rhyme—mere doggerel. This stuff—" he snatched Collins's *Ode to Liberty* from my hand—"this stuff is an apology for good poetry!"

"I'm afraid I haven't read much recent poetry. Almost none, in fact. So I'm not in a position to judge whether it's good or bad."

"You aren't acquainted with the works of Shelley? Or Lord Byron? Or William Wordsworth?"

"Not at all. Miss Sutter has never encouraged it."

"Amazing!" He gave me a curious glance. "How very surprising. Well now, Miss Dean, I see that we can open up a trade here. You can supply me with your very interesting novels, and I shall show you how poetry is written. My poetry! Here's Fate at work, just as we said: I was obviously destined to come into your life at this time, and open your eyes to the beauty of verse. We can have long, intellectual discussions—just the two of us—"

"Oh, I don't think that would be possible—"

"In the garden, or somewhere in the house if it's cold. Oh—I can show you *so much*—"

"Miss Sutter would never allow it!"

"Forget Miss Sutter!"

"But my mother would be furious."

"Forget your mother! I'm offering you grandeur beyond your wildest dreams! Isn't that enough for you?"

"It's hardly . . . It's just that . . ."

"Ahhh . . ." He breathed a long sigh. "You don't trust me, Miss Dean. That's the truth, isn't it?"

"I can't imagine why you should think that."

"I don't think it. I know it. You look at me with those great shining eyes of yours, and I can feel the mistrust and suspicion in your heart. You have beautiful eyes, by the way, do you know that?"

This took my breath away. I wasn't able to utter a word.

"You seem surprised. Has no one ever told you before. I'm sure there must be a young man somewhere in St. John's who would die for a glance from those eyes of yours. Several young men, perhaps."

"Mr. Ellis—please!" I was sure there must be a cleverer, more sophisticated response to his compliments but I didn't know of one. He'd confused me so much I simply wished he would stop talking in that way.

"Ah—there I go, I've offended you again! And I meant what I said in all sincerity, believe me. You're a beautiful, graceful, sensitive young woman, and there's no denying it, whatever you may say. I just find it strange that I seem to be the first man to notice it."

"I—I must go into the house now, Mr. Ellis. Miss Sutter will be expecting me in the schoolroom. Excuse me."

"Your book, Miss Dean."

"Oh, yes. Thank you."

He held out the volume, but as I reached out to take it, deftly trapped my fingers under his own.

"You won't avoid me in future, will you, Rachel? I'd be most unhappy if you did. I feel we have so much in common—so much to share."

I felt my face begin to burn at his use of my given name. It was as much as I could do to murmur some kind of disclaimer, snatch the book and my hand away from him by force, and fly back to the sanctuary of the house.

———

I didn't dare to tell Maria, and Reuben wouldn't have understood, or been much help if he had. Miss Sutter—roguish, flirtatious Miss Sutter—would have shrieked with pious horror, and gone straight to my mother. And that left no one at all who would listen to my difficulties and then offer the advice I needed. There was no one even to tell me if well-brought-up young ladies were supposed to sit complacently while strange men paid them outrageous compliments on their eyes or their figures; and after that . . . what?

I avoided him. What else could I do?

Yet he was determined not to be avoided. When I went to my favorite corner of the garden with a book, he was there, waiting. When I left the drawing room to go upstairs I'd find him on the second-floor landing, leaning innocently over the balustrade, apparently lost in thought. In addition I began to find notes—lines of poetry, mainly, left where he thought I'd be sure to come across them, in books or in the pocket of my velvet mantle if I'd left it in the hall on my way in from the garden. Lines of poetry he said he'd written for me.

The verses were undeniably good, and I was impressed in spite of my unease. I was—he assured me—a source of inspiration for him. Through knowing me, his writing was better than ever before; words and phrases were coming to him unbidden, rushing into his mind in a great, voluptuous flood . . . Thanks to me. Always thanks to me. And to prove his sincerity, he left me more and more samples of his work.

At first they were innocuous enough, observations on the coming of winter and the lonely life of a friendless man. Sometimes they were funny—barbed remarks about the inconstancy of women when their sweethearts were true. Then, after three or four weeks, the tone changed. One day, in my work-basket, I found:

> Know this: what'er my future fate,
> Shall joy or woe my steps await,
> Tempted by love, by storms beset,
> Thine image I can ne'er forget.

I thought it was exquisite: after much soul-searching I told him so.

"However do you think of such things?"

He smiled sadly. "When I think of you, Rachel, the words just seem to come into my head. *You* are exquisite—and the poetry simply confirms it." There was nothing but candor in his blue, blue eyes as he lifted my hand to his lips and kissed it.

No one noticed what was going on between us, neither the whispered conversations in shadowy corners nor the passing of furtive notes. Gradually, my suspicions faded away before his obvious sincerity and the dreadful anguish he seemed to experience whenever his poetic muse deserted him. I was flattered, too, at being able to help him, however humbly, in the creation of his wonderful verses. Francis Ellis, without a doubt, was a genius, and one day the whole world would know it. In the meantime he was mine alone.

And no one knew. Miss Sutter was too taken up with my demanding father and the care of Maria and Reuben to have much time left
to keep watch over me, and my mother already had her hands full
with other matters, otherwise I'm sure she would have realized something was afoot.

In fact, in her own devious, skillful way, my mother was also
having to deal with the male of the species, in the shape of the
colony's new Representative Assembly, whose first session had been
opened two years earlier by His Excellency the Governor to a nine-
teen-gun salute from the fort. My mother had resisted the Assembly
to the last. For a start, she disapproved of any change which simply
encouraged a crowd of men to bicker among themselves to no purpose at all for hours on end. In addition, she'd invested a great deal
of time and money in getting on good terms with the members of the
island's Legislative Council, who'd been the sole governing body
until then.

The principal difference was that the Council members were appointed while the assemblymen were elected by the people and in-
cluded various ranting fellows of suspiciously liberal views who
might one day make Newfoundland a less pleasant place to carry on
profitable businesses like the Relief Association. My mother was
afraid that once the colony became used to the idea of voting for its
government, the growing feud between the Council and the Assembly would become an entrenched war between the classes. The large
Irish element in the population was already threatening trouble, and
the next Assembly elections might provoke all sorts of unrest in the
community. Who could tell what might happen? Riots and demon-
strations? Fighting in the streets?

Quietly, and without any fuss, my mother began to reduce the
family investment in the Avalon and Crow Cove Insurance Company. The company was no longer tied to marine insurance; life and
property were insured too in great quantity, and it hadn't escaped
my mother's notice that the majority of the houses in St. John's and
the outlying towns were built of wood. If rioting broke out in the
capital, a single rebel with a flaming torch could wipe out a year of
company profits. It was high time to look overseas for investment
and lay out money in London and New York instead of in risky
Newfoundland. And when Henry Winton, outspoken editor of *The
Public Ledger,* was waylaid one night near Harbour Grace and had
his ears cut off by Carbonear's Irish surgeon, Dr. Molloy, my mother
was convinced her instincts were right.

Normally, with my mother so occupied by business matters, the eagle-eyed Susan Vinegar would have kept her informed of any suspicious goings-on at home. But for once, as luck would have it, Susan too was temporarily distracted from her spying duties.

One morning, out of the blue, a frost-bitten office boy arrived from town to inquire whether Mrs. Dean knew if the general manager of the insurance company would be reporting for duty that day. He was nowhere to be found at his lodgings, and no one at the office had seen him since dinner time the previous day. Papers required to be signed . . . and funds which should have been available in the office safe appeared to have been removed . . . a considerable sum, in fact, was missing.

It took my mother less than a second to realize that her protégé had bolted, and that several thousand pounds of company money had vanished along with him. My father immediately began to prance about, crowing I-told-you-so, and It-wouldn't-have-happened-if-you'd-listened-to-me, but by this time Susan Vinegar was having shrieking hysterics in a corner of the dining room over the lost love of her life and the discovery of his true, shameful nature. Racked by horrible whooping sobs, she slumped in a mahogany carver, her head lolling from side to side, for all the world like a rag doll in a fit. My furious, exasperated mother was trying to hold a bottle of salts to Susan's nose; Miss Sutter was rubbing her hand; my father hovered smugly behind Miss Sutter, and even Maria and Reuben had run downstairs to see what all the noise was about. Only Edward was missing, visiting a tailor in town, and his absence left Francis Ellis at leisure to materialize at my elbow on the fringe of the drama.

"For Heaven's sake come out into the garden. I can't bear all this noise."

I followed him to the glass-paned doors and stepped out into the rose garden. The shouting and weeping in the dining room had become embarrassing, and I was glad to be out in the clear, sunlit frosty air, with the gravel paths ringing hard under my shoes. I was sorry for Susan Vinegar, but not for my mother. Many people in St. John's would say it was no more than she deserved—and in any case, the loss was a small one, and shared among many stockholders.

"Down here. To the bench by the hedge."

It was the bench where Francis had first found me toiling through
Night Thoughts, and perhaps because I remembered that first meeting so vividly I realized how much his manner toward me had
changed since those early days. He was still sure of himself, secure
in his own dashing good looks, but there was a boyish sincerity in
his face when he looked at me now, and sometimes his voice actually
seemed to tremble with the force of his feelings.

As soon as we were alone that day, he took my hand and enclosed
it in his own. When he released it, there was a folded scrap of paper
in my palm.

"I was going to slip this into the book you left in the drawing
room last night, but I hoped I might see you before then. Read it,
and then tell me what you think. It suddenly came to me yesterday,
all at once—yet I feel it's one of the best things I've ever done."

I gazed at the verse on the paper.

> Deep in my soul that tender secret dwells,
> Lonely and lost to light for evermore,
> Save when to thine my heart responsive swells,
> Then trembles into silence as before.

"Oh, Francis! It's so beautiful! One day, when everyone reads your
poetry, I shall be so proud to have known you."

"Read it again—every word of it is the bare truth. We belong
together, you and I. And when my poetry is published one day,
everyone will know that you were my inspiration. That the verses
were written for you alone, out of the love you inspired in me."

"It's more than I ever dreamed of."

"You'll see—I'll do better yet! With you there before me, I'll write
some of the greatest poetry the world has ever seen."

I couldn't speak. It was glorious almost beyond belief.

"But there's one thing you must promise me, Rachel. That you'll
never desert me. You must never leave me or send me away, because
I couldn't bear it. I need you more than you can imagine."

"Oh, I won't—ever."

"Then kiss me. Kiss me to seal the promise. Now, before someone
comes."

I'd never kissed a man before. Except Papa, and those were swift
duty-kisses at bedtime which more often than not were sound rather
than substance.

This one wasn't. I don't know what I'd expected, if anything, but the sudden urgent pressure of his lips on mine, warm and frighteningly alive, was quite shocking at first, and then strangely exciting as he pulled me tightly against him and I felt his tongue moving between my parted lips . . . I broke away then, convinced that even love must have its limits.

"Rachel!" His face was full of reproach. "I thought you understood! I thought you cared for me, and yet now I find you don't love me after all." There was unbearable despair in his voice. "Not as I love you. Rachel—I would *die* for you, and yet you're so cold toward me."

"That isn't true! It's just that I'm not sure . . . I don't know what I should . . ."

What would the heroine of one of my novels have done? Pledged undying love? What was this *love* in any case? I'd never said I loved him: I was bewildered by the magnificence of his poetry and by his own declarations of love, but I wanted to tell him the truth, and the truth was that I wasn't sure. I was confused, overwhelmed, all at sea . . .

His expression had softened again.

"My poor, sweet, innocent Rachel—of course you're not sure. How could you be? It's wrong of me to expect you to know your own mind when we have to keep up these hole-in-the-corner meetings. How can we ever really talk to one another about what's important between us? And how can I persuade you to trust me, if we don't?"

"I don't know," I repeated miserably, aware only of having let him down in some indefinable way. I was a feeble, ignorant child, unfit to be the object of such devotion.

"Listen—I have an idea. Your father and mother are going into St. John's this afternoon to deal with the mess at the office. Florence—Miss Sutter—won't miss a chance of touring the shops. Edward's riding; and I don't think we need worry about old Susan Vinegar spying on us for a while. Come for a walk with me, then, away from the house, and we'll have a proper chance to talk."

"But do you think—"

"Rachel—my love—there's so much I want to say to you! Please! Just a walk, that's all. Where's the harm in that?"

Where indeed was the harm in it? How could I be so heartless as to refuse?

At three o'clock the sleigh rolled off to St. John's, bearing my
parents, Miss Sutter and my sister Maria, who'd successfully pleaded
to be allowed to go too. Edward disappeared on his favorite horse
to ride over to the house of a friend several miles away. Reuben—I
have no idea where Reuben was, except that he was off on some
ploy of his own, and nowhere to be seen.

At three-fifteen Francis Ellis and I let ourselves out of the glass
doors which led to the snowy rose garden, and set off on our walk.

———

We didn't go as far as I'd expected. For twenty minutes we strolled
under the bare branches of the frosty trees, arm-in-arm once we were
out of sight of the house, and stopped once for a brief, decorous kiss
behind a huge laurel beside the path. For the rest of the time Francis
talked, repeating again and again how precious I was to him, how
he would lay down his life for my sake, and how swiftly he would
die of a broken heart if I ever deserted him. I was his inspiration; I
was each succeeding beat of his heart; he asked only to spend the
rest of his days in cherishing and protecting me.

To my surprise, at the end of twenty minutes I found myself back
at the side of the house, facing the glass-paned doors to the breakfast
room out of which we'd come such a short time before.

"It's cold out here, and you're such a delicate young thing." Francis drew my mantle closer round my shoulders by means of reaching
an arm round my back. "I think perhaps we should go in."

So this was the end of our romantic stroll! I was disappointed, but
allowed myself to be ushered into the breakfast room as he suggested. The house was utterly quiet; not even a distant footstep
disturbed the hush.

"Excellent. This fire's been kept up all day. Here—let me take
that."

He reached out, and slipped the mantle from my shoulders, dropping it on a nearby chair.

"Now come and sit here beside me. No—on this sofa. Rachel, I
thought we were friends . . . I hoped perhaps after all we've said . . ."

I moved across the room to his side, and his face brightened.

"That's better."

We sat next to one another on my mother's Grecian sofa with its
striped upholstery, and Francis talked again. I couldn't tell you what
he said; I was only aware of his arm sliding reassuringly round me,
and of his voice talking on and on while I began to relax, so much

so that when he pulled me against him and kissed me I wasn't as surprised as before. In fact, I wasn't surprised at all, and managed to kiss him back with something approaching enthusiasm. Was this what it was like to be in love? The tenderness of it, the touching and the closeness, was something I'd never experienced before, and for the first time in my life I felt wanted and secure.

He began to kiss my hair, and my ears and my neck, and I felt his hand traveling down my back, pressing me close to him. So *this* was love, I thought to myself. I remember thinking it over and over again, as he went on kissing me. . . . And then he was rummaging about at my skirt, and his breath was coming in sort of gasps, and all of a sudden I felt his hand running up the inside of my leg under my petticoats—and of course, in those days we didn't wear drawers, which were still considered very fast—and suddenly there was the warmth of his hand between my legs, and his fingers . . . oh, my goodness, his fingers . . . and I was so startled, I shrieked out loud.

It was only a little shriek, and Francis clapped his hand over my mouth at once—but it was enough to attract the attention of someone in the passage outside, and to bring whoever was passing to the breakfast room door.

How was I to know that my mother would leave a vital document on the desk in her study, remember it halfway to St. John's and insist on turning back to fetch it?

But that was what she'd done. And now, attracted by the sudden faint sound, she stood framed in the breakfast-room doorway, an expression of horror and outrage on her face that I shall never forget if I live to be a hundred.

"Ellis!" She fairly spat the name. "You *vermin!* I brought you into my home—trusted you with my children—and *this* is what you get up to as soon as my back is turned!"

Francis had rolled to the floor in fright, and now stumbled to his feet, clawing at his clothes and trying to smooth his rumpled black hair. Suddenly he looked rather pathetic, as if all the suave sophistication had been drained out of him by my mother's arrival. I waited for my ardent hero to tell her all the things he had told me—that he loved me, and would always love me, that he couldn't live without me—that I was dearer to him than life itself.

Except that he didn't do anything of the kind. He tried to dodge nimbly out of the door into the passage, but my mother blocked his way without any trouble.

"Go on! Run! Run if you can! Rats like you never have the decency to stand their ground." My mother stared at Francis Ellis with limitless contempt, as if he were less than an insect in her path. "You loathsome wretch! Get out of my sight, and get out of my house! Don't bother to pack your bags—whatever dross you brought will be sent after you. Just think yourself lucky to get away from here in one piece!"

She moved aside to allow him to leave, and then at the last minute placed her arm across the doorway and her furious face close to his.

"I have friends—as I'm sure you understand—who'd be glad to show you what happens to young men who take advantage of foolish girls. Though I don't suppose your sort ever learn. But remember this—*Mister* Ellis . . ." She fixed him with a hard, vicious stare. "Only three of us know of this afternoon's escapade. You know—I know—and that baggage of a daughter of mine won't be allowed to forget it. If I hear *one word* of it outside these four walls, I promise you'll regret it. Is that clear? My advice to you is to leave St. John's right away—leave the colony altogether—otherwise you'll find life very difficult for you in future."

I saw Francis clench his fists until they were white. Trapped in the room, he'd straightened up; he was breathing quickly, desperation lending him courage. Now, surely, he would speak—to defend our love, to tell my mother he'd no intention of leaving, unless he could take me with him . . .

"Oh, I'll go," he was saying. "Don't worry—I can find ten better than your daughter, any day of the week. Women whose families didn't start off as paupers in the streets of St. John's!"

I saw my mother throw her head back, and the sudden gleam of her teeth.

"My father could have bought and sold you without noticing it!" Francis flung the words at her. "You're trash, Mrs. Dean, common trash. Sell your daughter where you can—I've no use for her!"

My mother had let her arm fall to her side, and suddenly Francis had gone—leaving the echo of his viciousness to stoke the fires of my mother's fury.

Now she looked at me as though I were dirt underfoot.

"Pull your skirts down, slut, and get to your room! I'll deal with you later."

———

She left me there for the rest of the afternoon, locked in my bedroom, staring out over the frosted garden as the daylight faded, taking with it all my rosy, romantic dreams. The interrogation, when it came, was deeply unpleasant—all the more so because of my humiliation at seeing Francis Ellis, my dashing, poetic cavalier, transformed in seconds to a sneering coward.

My mother's main object was to find out exactly what had taken place between us, and how often. My ignorance was so complete and so obvious that even she recognized the truth of the matter before long, and concluded that no real damage had been done.

"No thanks to you, you baggage," she commented sourly. "You're your father's daughter, all right. I should never have taken my eyes off you. If I hadn't come back when I did—"

"What? What if you hadn't come back?"

"Never mind *what*. Just be grateful I did come back."

"But Francis promised he loved me! He *promised!*"

"You poor fool! Ellis and his kind never love anyone but themselves. If you weren't so stupid, you'd have known his romantic nonsense for what it was—a pack of lies to deceive silly girls into ruining themselves. I should have realized what sort of man he was as soon as I set eyes on him! But no—I invited him into my home, paid him to teach my son—and all the time, he was scheming to get his dirty hands on my daughter."

I must have looked more than usually blank at that, because she shook her head and made a frustrated little noise, as if she were dealing with a complete imbecile.

"If I thought I could beat some sense into you, Miss, that's exactly what I'd do. But I'm beginning to think you're too foolish even for that. The sooner you're well married and off my hands, the better. Perhaps a husband will be able to deal with your surliness and stupidity better than I can. And you can forget all this silliness about *love*. You'll marry the man I choose for you, like a decent, well-brought-up girl, and think yourself lucky you're still in a position to get a good husband. No doubt if I left you to it, you'd run off with some pathetic good-for-nothing, like one of those mangy animals you used to collect at Crow Cove! Did you imagine for a moment I'd let you throw yourself away on some penniless student, even if he *had* been willing to marry you—which he wasn't?"

My mother stared at me, wondering if I really appreciated how close I'd come to ruining the future she'd planned for me. Then her eyes narrowed in that closed-up, acquisitive look I knew so well.

"It's time you understood, Miss: I've spent a great deal of money on you in the last fifteen years—invested it, if you like—and I mean to make some use of you before I'm done. There are one or two young men in St. John's who could be very useful to me as a future son-in-law—young Horwood the lawyer, for instance, or the Cormack boy—and I see no reason at all why you shouldn't be as well off married to either of them as to any other man. Considerably better, I shouldn't wonder. So I've no intention of letting you spoil your chances by behaving like a trollop in the meantime. Do you understand?"

I understood. At least—for the very first time I understood what my future was to be if my mother was allowed to have her way.

"Very well. From now on, there'll be no wandering about in the garden on your own. You can help in the schoolroom if you've nothing else to do. Let's see if Miss Sutter can do the work she was hired to do for a change, instead of letting you moon over a worthless student. I would send her packing too, if it didn't mean the whole of St. John's getting to hear of this."

But of course, she didn't send Miss Sutter away; the governess was altogether too useful in keeping my father at home. Miss Sutter was simply told that Francis Ellis had been sacked for "pestering" me, and that in future she'd better keep a far closer eye on her eldest charge. All of which made Miss Sutter take a violent dislike to me, so that I was hardly allowed to stir outside the house without her, and had to sit in the schoolroom writing endless lists of dead kings or covering wretched little placemats with drawn-thread work and crocheted lace.

Then one day in February I was summoned to my mother's study to find her considering a letter which lay before her on the desk. Even sideways-on, I recognized the untidy, angular writing which criss-crossed it in both directions, using every inch of precious paper. My mother and her sister Grace had never been particularly close, but I knew they corresponded from time to time, though the letters had grown less frequent since my maternal grandparents had died in Liverpool a few years before.

"Read this," my mother instructed, holding the page out to me.

My Dear Susannah, [I read.] Your letter with its seasonal greetings has only just reached me. How unreliable the mails still are! Of course, all of us here wish you and your family good fortune in this new year, though from your account of present circumstances, you seem to be managing well enough. But then, you always did, my dear.

Children are a burden, are they not! Even though my sweet Harry is so remarkably amiable in temper, and so remarkably intelligent, sometimes I find he quite tires me out. You have all my sympathy regarding Rachel. It must be doubly hard to raise a young woman to any cultivation at all in such a remote settlement as you have chosen to inhabit, where the opportunities for instruction in feminine arts can be few indeed. No doubt her defects of temper arise from this cause, and not from any inherited willfulness. At least, I hope it may be so.

I have spoken with my dear husband about the arrangement you propose, and he is quite willing to undertake Rachel's care for two years, here in Liverpool. I would be prepared to introduce her to my own admirable circle of acquaintances, provided always she is fit for it, and to have her instructed in music and art as you suggest. It would be hard, in all charity, to let her suffer from her mother's wish to live in the wilderness, beyond the reach of any good society, deprived of the countless benefits my own darling Harry enjoys.

I notice you say she would be amply provided for from Papa's legacy in the bank here. I should, of course, need your warrant to draw on it as I saw fit for her clothes, etc. Bringing a young woman into society these days is not *cheap*.

There was more in the same vein—a catalogue of the wonders of my aunt's house in Liverpool and the useful arts I could learn there, for all the world as if Aunt Grace's terraced house in Leghorn Street was an academy for young ladies.

"Well?" My mother was waiting for a reaction.

"You aren't really sending me to England?"

"You'll sail next month. Dr. West and his wife—who was Miss Penrose, you remember—are going back to England to visit his father, the bishop, and I've arranged for you to travel with them. Grace has only one child and a large house; she has plenty of room for you, and plenty of time to keep you out of mischief. Perhaps in a couple of years she'll manage to send you back a lady, with some idea of how a lady ought to behave. Heaven knows, it's more than I've been able to do."

"But I don't want to go to Liverpool! I want to stay here, in St. John's, and go back to Crow Cove next summer!"

"We shan't be going to Crow Cove in the summer. I'm closing up the house there. It was always a shabby old place in any case." My mother met my brimming eyes defiantly. "And tears won't help you. I've decided that the sooner you're away from this island the better. Two years in Liverpool will do you nothing but good. And by the time you come back, I'll have settled on a husband for you. With a dowry such as yours, I should think any young man would be glad of the chance to take you off my hands."

Two years, and then a life sentence, all for listening to the honeyed words of a poet. There was no possible reprieve, and no pardon. I was packed off, bag and baggage, like some nameless parcel thrust into the hands of Dr. and Mrs. West, bound for Liverpool. Apart from my clothes, I had little of my life in Newfoundland to take with me, beyond Reuben's tears wet on my cheeks, and the Indian woman's amulet, my last link with Crow Cove and with the distant, faded memory of Adam Gaunt.

All I had of Francis Ellis was a confused image of black hair, warm lips, and a bewildering, humiliating transformation. For the three weeks of our ocean passage I could think of nothing else; when the other passengers crowded to the ship's rail to gaze at a westward-bound vessel, all towering white sails and flying foam, I brooded alone by the saloon door; when fiddles were brought out for dancing I preferred the peace of our cabin. All the wonders of my first ocean voyage passed me by like a dream—roaring wind and drenched decks, magical calms on a twilight sea, all the color and bustle of shipboard life. In spite of everything my mother had said, I still found it impossible to make sense of all that had happened between Francis and myself, and I'd saved every last scrap of his wonderful poetry, hidden away the timeless lines I'd inspired to weep over in secret. Yet I was destined to lose even those.

On the twentieth day of our voyage, walking on the windswept deck of the *Athena*, I discovered in my pocket one of Francis Ellis's verses, crumpled and overlooked.

> You were a form of life and light,
> That, seen, became a part of sight;
> And rose, where'er I turned mine eye,
> The Morning-star of Memory!

Tears pricked my eyes, to be whipped away at once by the breeze. Kindly little Mrs. West peered at the paper over my shoulder, and smiled.

"I didn't know you were a reader of Lord Byron's work," she remarked. "It's from *The Giaour*, isn't it? Except that it's not quite accurate. It should be '*She* was a form of life and light,' I believe. Oh, I do think Lord Byron's poetry is so romantic, don't you?"

I nodded. I couldn't speak. Instead, I stood on that tilting deck and vowed never, ever, to trust another man as long as I lived. I suppose my mother would have said I'd begun my education at last. It was just as well she couldn't have foreseen who was to complete it.

5

"You're Joseph Dean's child—there's no doubt of that."

Those were the first words she spoke to me: not *Welcome to Liverpool*, or *Rachel, my dear,* or anything of that sort. Aunt Grace Fuller simply stood back a yard on that Liverpool quay, tilted her long head to one side, stared at me, and said without any preamble, "You're Joseph Dean's child." Then she nodded, apparently quite content with her discovery, and began fussing with the long ribbons of her bonnet and her great fringed shawl.

I knew I resembled my father in many ways—dark hair, dark eyes, slimness of build—but I was surprised all the same to find that my Aunt Grace remembered her sister's husband so exactly after the passage of more than fifteen years.

"And how is your mother?" Aunt Grace inclined her cheek, indicating that I should kiss it.

"She is very well, thank you."

"And your father?"

"He's in good health, Aunt Grace."

"Hmmm." She pursed her lips for a moment. "Are these boxes yours? And the valise? Very well, they can go to the carriage. No doubt the rest will be sent up to Leghorn Street, if the labels haven't been torn off by some clumsy sailor. This way."

A small carriage with a single horse waited on the quayside. Without another word, my aunt gathered her skirts to climb aboard, I scrambled up after her, and the red-faced groom loaded my modest luggage at the rear. With a violent lurch the carriage set off, making a laborious turn on the cobbles before rolling away through the streets of the city which was to be my home for the next two years. Still my aunt said nothing, but clung grimly to the embroidered tassel beside her seat, staring out at the tall, sooty buildings which seemed to surround us as far as the eye could see.

I saw little of the city that day; I was too taken up with secretly examining Aunt Grace Fuller, whose word would regulate my life until the day came for her to put me aboard ship once more and send me back, perfected, to my mother.

The two sisters had never been particularly close, so that the only account I'd ever had of my aunt had come from my father during that dreadful, drunken supper at Crow Cove when I crouched on the stairs in silent horror, listening to the ramblings of his pent-up malice. "A fright," he'd called her then. "Seven feet tall, with a long yellow face." And for a long time after that my Liverpool aunt had invaded my dreams in the guise of an ogress, skinny and malevolent.

She was tall, it was true—taller than might be thought decent in a woman, with the calm, long-jawed features and dun-colored mane of a patiently waiting horse. I knew Aunt Grace was three years older than my mother, which made her thirty-seven to my mother's thirty-four, and now that I saw her in the flesh it was easy to picture the two sisters together as girls, Grace plain, mouse-haired and angular, almost as if she'd been designed as a foil for my mother's pink and white brilliance and vivid red-brown hair.

Aunt Grace leaned toward me in the carriage, interrupting my inspection. Fascinated, I watched the feathers on her tall bonnet wag to and fro as she spoke.

"Can't see much of your mother in you at all. Neither looks nor figure. You're Joseph's daughter, there's no getting round it. My sister was already carrying you when they left from the docks here in '19, but your mother and father wouldn't wait for the birth—not they. They were in such a hurry to get to Newfoundland and make their fortunes right off." Aunt Grace gave a disapproving snort and turned back to the window without losing the thread of her discourse.

"Always in a hurry, your mother. Whatever took her fancy, she must have it then and there. Then and there! Look out, here's Leghorn Street."

The Fullers' house was built of mellow brick like its neighbors, standing as solidly in line as part of a cliff-face, very weighty and permanent compared to the jumbled wooden buildings I'd known in St. John's. This was no nailed-up, fish-reeking colony half a world away across an ocean. The houses of Liverpool announced that here was a city which could point to its ancestry in the Domesday Book, which had a royal charter to prove its worth and a great deal of money in the bank. Here in Liverpool King William was more than just a face on a coin—these citizens could look to a flesh-and-blood king who walked and talked and sat on his throne to rule over them.

This was the city in which my own grandfather, James Allen, had built up his watch manufactury, raised two daughters from a brood of eight babies, and died before I could know him. To my surprise I felt a small flame of anticipation kindle inside me. In this city things *happened*. In spite of myself, I became quite lighthearted.

"Of course, Captain Fuller won't be home for a couple of months yet," Aunt Grace told me later. "He's away more than I'd like on that ship of his, but then, Oliver's can't seem to manage without him. Many's the time I've heard old Captain John Oliver say *If only I had ten like Tom Fuller.* . . . He's dead now, of course, Captain John, and the sons aren't a patch on the old man. What they'd do without my husband I dread to think."

My aunt adored the Captain, whose ship, the Oliver vessel *Spartacus,* was presently reckoned to be somewhere in the West Indies, loading a cargo of sugar and whatever additional items her master thought he could trade on his own account. This extra source of income was one of the benefits allowed by the Oliver Line to its senior masters, and Captain Fuller had used it well, keeping his wife in considerable comfort in Liverpool while he sailed his ship to and fro across the North and South Atlantic.

And of course, there was the baby. As soon as I set foot in the house I was rushed to the nursery to admire little Harry, the miraculous infant of my aunt's letters, hardly more than a year old, but already, I was told, showing signs of amazing sagacity. He seemed to me very much like a normal baby, a little like Reuben had been at that age, burbling contentedly in his nurse's arms. But Aunt Grace had borne him after eleven childless years of marriage, and she was convinced he'd made up for his late arrival by vast intelligence and wondrous strength.

But to praise Harry was to win his mother's heart. As we went downstairs again she began to smile on me at last, and patted my hand for all the world as if I was a favorite niece she'd known since birth.

———

After the first few days of my stay in Liverpool I became accustomed to the routine of the Fullers' house. Breakfast was at eight o'clock sharp, sherry and biscuits were taken in the drawing room at eleven, and then, because my aunt had decided that a late dinner-hour was a sign of good breeding, tea was served at two in the afternoon to stave off the pangs of starvation. After dinner came more tea at nine, fifteen minutes of prayers for which the servants gathered in the dining room in a shuffling line, and then a swift peck on the cheek before we all went upstairs to bed.

For her part, as she became used to my presence in the house Aunt Grace lost much of her stiff reserve. She seemed glad of someone to talk to in the Captain's absence, and spoke to me quite often about her own childhood and the home in which she and my mother had grown up. I'd heard none of it before. My mother had never volunteered more than the barest facts of her life in Liverpool, and then grudgingly, as if they concerned a stranger in a distant land. The old Susannah Allen had been left behind in England when a quite different woman had quit her home and family to take up a new life in Newfoundland.

Gradually Aunt Grace told me more and more, as she began to discover I didn't necessarily take my mother's part in everything.

"Of course," she declared suddenly one evening over dinner, "I suppose you know that I was the one who was supposed to marry Joseph Dean, and not your mother."

I made a great effort to look astonished—and I must have succeeded, since she continued at once, "No? Well, to be honest, I'm not surprised. It isn't something a mother would tell her daughter, after all. Susannah would keep that little tale to herself."

For a moment Aunt Grace eyed me speculatively.

"Do you know—in spite of everything, I like you, Rachel. I didn't expect to—I'll admit that straight out. But as I've said before, there's a great deal of your father in you, and you're certainly a sweeter-tempered soul than my sister ever was. But I never thought I'd take to you, because by rights you oughtn't to have come into the world at all. That's why I was perhaps a little . . . strange with you at first." She sighed, and looked down at her plate. "You see, Joseph Dean was to have been my husband, not Susannah's. Your grandfather had it all planned—Joseph and myself—but she took him from me in spite of that, and you might as well know it."

For a moment I felt as if I should apologize for my mother's deceit; yet I was hardly to blame for the accident of my birth. In the end I just sat mutely on my chair, my food growing cold in front of me, unable to think of a word to say.

Fortunately there was no need for an answer. Aunt Grace, having set herself to tell the tale, rambled on without any encouragement from me. She remembered it all in great detail—every harrowing moment of it—in spite of the years that had passed, her marriage to Tom Fuller and the birth of their son. There was such resentment in her voice and such a bitter gleam in her eye that I wondered at times how much of her story was true and how much had been magnified by her own hurt pride. Yet I knew my mother of old, and as Aunt Grace described the events leading up to my parents' marriage I found it all too easy to believe her.

"The Allen Girls," they'd been called then. Miss Allen and Miss Susannah Allen, daughters of a respected watchmaker in a good way of business, no longer living over the manufactury in Dale Street but residing respectably in a terraced house a little distance away, looked after by a cook, a maid and a footboy who cleaned the boots and answered the door. I could easily imagine Grace at the age of twenty, her long, bony fingers as red as if they had been stained with raspberry juice, sliding breakneck into spinsterhood and a lifetime of good works. And there beside her was my mother, a sparkling seventeen-year-old, pretty as sugar-icing, sweet enough for the confectioner's window, doing exactly as she pleased and yet basking in universal adoration.

"There were just the two girls, you see, and no son to take over the business. That was your grandfather's great sorrow. Daughters are all very well: you settle a little money on them and marry them off. But here was the watchmaking business, growing busier all the time, keeping a crowd of apprentices and journeymen in work—and yet without a son to take it over, the effort was all for nothing." Aunt Grace leaned forward significantly. "And then Joseph Dean came along."

Joseph Dean had been my grandfather's apprentice, but long before his indentures were over it was clear he'd a natural talent for mending clocks and watches. In his hands the tiny pivots and balances and scape-wheels flew into place as if by magic. For Joseph alone the delicate ships' chronometers clicked and whirled like things possessed. And he didn't overlook profit: it had been Joseph, not his master, who'd thought of buying good steel for turret-clock springs from the local sawmaker at half the price the springmaker asked. Certainly, by the end of his apprenticeship Joseph Dean was already a master of his craft, and at last James Allen saw a way of safeguarding the future of his business and of his spinster elder daughter at one and the same time. Joseph, the watchmaking wizard, would marry Grace Allen and in due course would fall heir to the assets and reputation of *James Allen, Clockmaker*.

It was an ideal solution to a difficult problem. Fortunately there was no need to worry about Susannah's prospects. His younger daughter had already attracted the attention of several wealthy merchants' sons and could be counted on to make a good marriage when the time came.

"He'd a standing invitation, had Joseph, to come to us on Sunday evenings." My aunt's voice grew grim. "Nine o'clock . . . tea in the parlor with Father reading from his book of sermons and Mother doing her wool-work, and Susannah and me fiddling with pressed flowers or something of that sort. I always poured; Mother had inflammation of the joints in those days and couldn't lift the tea-kettle."

Aunt Grace smiled suddenly. "Does your father still have a moustache and side-whiskers?"

"Oh, yes. Ever since I can remember."

"Well, that's when he grew them first. When he started calling at the house. It made him look ever so trim, but a bit foreign, being so dark."

I could imagine the scene: my father, matured all at once from a gawky, pale youth into a slim young man in his best clothes; my mother, her blue eyes flicking sharply from face to face; Aunt Grace, blushing and mumbling, knocking the silver strainer awkwardly against the rim of each teacup as she tried to make proper drawing-room conversation.

. . . How damp the summer had been! Perhaps the autumn would be finer, however. A shower must certainly be due—perhaps more drenching than the last—or then again, not so drenching. . . .

And all the time, the talk tiptoeing round the great, gaping chasm in the center of the conversation—would Joseph Dean take Grace Allen, or no? Was a bargain to be concluded, or wasn't it?

"He used to tug at that moustache, I remember, whenever something bothered him. Father said he looked like an Italian organ-grinder, and Susannah laughed and agreed with him. She did, the deceitful hussy! That was what really hurt, the way she kept it a secret between the two of them until it was all settled. *That's* what pained me most, Rachel—the slyness of it. You've no idea how badly it hurt me. What had I ever done to deserve that?"

No doubt my father had been flattered at first by the wide-eyed coquetry of the younger Miss Allen, the shared, sidelong glances and the furtive brush of soft fingers passing teacups. Pretty Susannah had been noticed by the gentry, and now here she was, flirting with her father's recent apprentice in a way which made the blood race in his veins. It would have taken a far stronger man than Joseph Dean to pledge devotion to her plainer, older sister.

"She was always finding excuses to run down to the shop or the manufactury. Either Father had left his spectacles behind, or Mother had a message for him or something of that sort. But she went at a time when she was sure of finding Joseph alone, working at his bench, though I was too blind to notice her cleverness. Poor fool— he thought she was interested in his work! Can you imagine that? Susannah, interested in watch-arbors and escapements and so forth! She was never interested in anything but herself, my fine sister."

Herself, perhaps . . . and her sister's intended husband. I could imagine my mother, standing admiringly at Joseph's shoulder, watching him piece together the delicate mechanism of some French clock, pressing near enough in her eagerness to start his heart beating like a three-hundredweight pendulum bob. That, at the time, had been her real interest: the thudding, vulnerable heart of Joseph Dean, all but promised to her sister.

By all accounts, my mother set out to haunt the poor man, emerging suddenly from the milliner's as he returned from the docks, dropping her cluster of dainty parcels in surprise, her hands fluttering like pale, agitated moths before the softly rounded bosom of her best afternoon dress. What could the poor fellow do but hold first the parcels and then later a dear little kid-gloved hand?

And so it was Susannah Allen, not Grace, who became Mrs. Joseph Dean, and who, after a decent interval, discovered she was carrying his child. Grandfather Allen had agreed to the marriage with a heavy heart. For poor Grace—poor, lanky, *diligent* Grace— was still without a husband, while her younger sister had hardly made the brilliant match he'd hoped for.

"So he didn't give them the business," concluded my aunt with satisfaction. "Though I daresay Susannah thought it was Joseph's by right. He reckoned, Father did, that Joseph had got all that was coming to him, so he settled a portion on Susannah and told them that if Joseph wanted to go on as an assistant in the manufactury, that was well enough, but if he wanted a place of his own he'd best go off and start one for himself. That's how the notion of Newfoundland came about. Newfoundland! They knew no more of the place than the name, and only that because Joseph had got talking to some ship's captain in the docks! Still—off they went, and you not yet born. She was quite put out, you know, when she knew there was a baby coming."

That came as no surprise. My mother had told me—often—how much she'd resented my inopportune birth.

"She never says much in her letters, but I can tell they've had their troubles. There never were any clocks and watches, were there? And no fine shop in St. John's? No—I thought not. Oh, they're well enough off now, I daresay—but I'd still like to know how it's been done. Though she was always good with money, my sister. Not to spend, you understand; just to *have*. That's why we were so astonished when she took up with Joseph instead of some rich merchant's boy."

Aunt Grace tapped her index finger on the table. "But she isn't content, all the same. Whatever she says, I know better. And what's more, she'll never be content. Not her: not even if she owns the whole of Newfoundland one day. If I weren't a Christian, I'd say it serves her right for what she did to me—except that I know it's just her nature, and not a punishment. *Want, want, want*—no matter whether a thing is yours or mine, she has to have it, straight off. And woe betide anyone who gets in her way."

"But you're so happy with Captain Fuller now. Perhaps it was all for the best in the end."

Aunt Grace straightened her back and looked away. "*Now,* maybe so. But I'll never forget the pain or the shame of everyone knowing, and the fingers pointing in church, and the pitying smiles. . . . That isn't something you can push aside like a bad dream, and especially now you've come to me with Joseph's eyes and Joseph's face—almost as if Susannah sent you on purpose to remind me of it all again."

For an awful moment I thought she was about to burst into tears. Then she gulped, sucked in her long upper lip for a second, and pronounced with an air of finality, "One day she'll know what it's like. One day, Susannah will know too."

———

But for the present my aunt was able to enjoy a minor revenge in spending a great deal of my mother's money on me. Horrified to discover I didn't sing or play any instrument, she engaged a fashionable singing-master to rehearse my scales and give me lessons on the pianoforte. Discovering I sketched a little, she called in Miss Rose, a local flower painter, for a weekly lesson in watercolor painting and the drawing of the clothed female form. But best of all as far as my aunt was concerned were our shopping trips in the carriage to mantuamakers and haberdashers, milliners and corsetières, where large sums of my mother's money could be laid out in filling her daughter's wardrobe.

She meant it kindly, I know. And because almost no one since Adam Gaunt had taken an honest interest in my happiness, I was sincerely grateful for her concern. The problem was that whatever the current fashion might be, my tastes were simple, and my aunt's were not. Aunt Grace believed that however fussy a gown might be, it could only be improved by the addition of sashes, ruffles, silk net mittens, feathers, folding fans, boas, posies and dangling chains. No lady could be seen in summer without a white silk parasol, lined with pink. No lady could be seen in winter without an ermine muff. The wearing of a scarf called for a cameo pin to fasten it and a piece of ruched muslin to complete the effect. A morning call meant a white silk bonnet with a lancer feather and veil; dinner meant a French cap trimmed with a garland of forget-me-nots. And so on, ad infinitum. Within two months I couldn't believe there were so many Bird of Paradise feathers in the world, so much rice straw, so much striped Pekin or Amy Robsart satin.

And yet it was all wasted, so my aunt swore, quite *wasted*, on a young lady who was so . . . so . . . *flat*. Aunt Grace's gesture indicated exactly where the deficiency occurred. Flat. Flat *here*.

There was some truth in what she said. I'd often secretly compared my own small breasts with my mother's ample bosom and been puzzled by my boyish figure. No doubt large, heavy breasts would have looked freakish on my slender body, but somehow at each dress-fitting I was made subtly aware that the ladies who stitched these promenade dresses and evening gowns considered me a poor advertisement for their skill.

At last one of them went so far as to cluck her teeth in despair: the young lady had nothing—nothing, Madame—to fill out the charming bodice of her gown, though her waist was enviably small and her skin good. It was such a pity. . . . Could dear Mrs. Fuller perhaps arrange for proper corsets to be worn?

An elegant Frenchwoman with a discreet workroom in the city

constructed long drawstring corsets which were miracles of whalebone and lace. Under her direction I was installed, the laces were
threaded and pulled very tight, and *Voilà, Mademoiselle!* my modest
breasts were cunningly molded and supported in the most bewitching way.

"It is *necessaire,* of course, Mademoiselle, to 'ave zem made to fit
you *exactement.*"

"I understand," I gasped, for the lacing was very tight indeed. Yet
the effect was undeniably dramatic. I gasped again when I heard the
price: but *Il faut souffrir pour être belle, n'est-ce pas?*—it was one
of the few pieces of French I knew.

By the time Captain Tom Fuller returned to Leghorn Street in
August, I'd already become what my aunt described as "present-
able." I suspect the Captain had been afraid of discovering a spoiled
brat or a simpering child, since he seemed visibly relieved to find me
a normal young woman—a little quiet perhaps, but very anxious to
please. And Aunt Grace more than filled any silences which descended over the dinner table.

I liked Uncle Thomas Fuller from the start. His presence in the
house was like a salty sea breeze, and it was hard to hear his gusty
laugh without feeling compelled to join in. Tom Fuller had married
my aunt when she was twenty-four years of age and whisked her
away from her lonely crochet in the Allens' parlor to a fine house of
her own—or almost her own, for the Captain's old mother had
shared it with them for the first few years of their marriage, the
single thorn in my aunt's new garden of roses.

When it suited him, Uncle Tom could act the bluff old sea-dog to
perfection. But in reality the loud laugh, weather-worn face and solid
outline concealed a shrewd and active mind, and I began to understand why Captain Fuller and the *Spartacus* were spoken of with
respect in any port they visited.

I couldn't help comparing Uncle Tom Fuller with my father. Here
was a man who'd spent his life in the profession he loved, using his
skills to the full: how different might my father have been, had the
fishermen of Newfoundland stood in greater need of watches and
clocks?

"Stranded like a whale on a sandbar," was Captain Fuller's verdict
on my life in Liverpool. "Stuck here in the house with only an old
woman and a baby for company—you need taking out a bit, where
there's young folk to talk to."

Certainly, I hadn't met many young people of my own age. Doro-thy Austin, the doctor's daughter, shared the same singing-master and a liking for novels; Hester Clark and her younger sister lived a little way down Leghorn Street, and often visited us; but with the two Austin boys and Hester's brother Philip I had very little to do. I knew I'd made a fool of myself over Francis Ellis and I was now lastingly suspicious of young men. I never seemed to be able to find anything to say to them, and I'm sure they thought me cold and distant.

Aunt Grace called me "trustworthy." "I *had* thought you might be a trifle fast, my dear, being raised in such an outlandish place, but I can see I have no fears in that respect. You behave entirely as a young lady should. I've never had a moment's anxiety over you. If anything, perhaps you're a little too . . . *reserved* at times. You'll want a husband one day, you know!" And she wagged a roguish finger at me.

But I didn't want a husband. I certainly didn't want to be hurled unwillingly into a loveless marriage simply to seal some business alliance of my mother's. Yet as I began to feel more and more like a sheep being fattened for the sacrificial altar, Aunt Grace pressed on with her efforts to turn me into an exemplary bride.

She wasn't always successful. Despite endless lessons, I never mas-tered the pianoforte, and though Signor di Angelo praised my singing voice as almost fit for the concert platform, he scolded me endlessly for not working at my scales as I should. And I didn't speak French —though Aunt Grace considered this unnecessary: who, after all, wished to converse with a quarrelsome nation reeking of garlic and cognac?

But I could certainly paint a little, and to prove it I'd produced a sketch of baby Harry which my aunt insisted she'd have recognized at once. All in all, progress had been made. In September 1836 I would reach the age of seventeen, and sometime the following year Aunt Grace planned to restore me to my mother as a shining tribute to her care.

I tried not to think about that return to Newfoundland. It was true that I longed to see Reuben once more—my grown-up, eight-year-old brother—but without our home in Crow Cove there was very little to draw me back to my distant island. It would only be a matter of time before my mother married me off to some man of her own choosing, a lawyer or a banker who could be drawn into her financial web for the greater glory of the Deans. Thousands of young women faced exactly the same future, yet the thought of being the reluctant wife of some loud, oafish, rich young man made my flesh crawl. I wanted to put off my return for as long as possible.

So far, thank Heavens, Mamma hadn't mentioned the subject in the letters she'd written to Aunt Grace, but on the rare occasions when a letter arrived I waited anxiously for a summons. Aunt Grace would open the packet with grim precision, slitting the seal with her tortoiseshell knife as an anatomist might open a cadaver. Several tense minutes would pass while she scanned the contents through the eyeglass which hung on a chain at her waist; then, reassured at last, she'd read out with relish the parts which interested her most.

In this way I learned that Edward had yearned for an army commission, but had been persuaded to give it up in favor of the family business. My sister Maria was turning into a beauty, and except for her light hair was the image of her mother at that age—"Fiddlesticks!" snorted my aunt, pouncing on the boast at once, "Susannah always had a great opinion of herself."

Reuben was . . . just Reuben, entirely his own man. And exactly as my mother had predicted, there had been political unrest in St. John's and the towns of the Newfoundland coast as the assemblymen tried to wrest control of the colony from the Legislative Council.

In Newfoundland, of course, the example of the United States of America, Land of the Free, where every man was as good as his neighbor if not considerably better, was always under our noses. With this vision before them, at least half the population of Newfoundland was bent on having the entire legislature put itself up for election—Assembly, Legislative Council, governor and all. My mother shuddered at the very idea. It was just as well she couldn't see the state of things in England, where the Municipal Corporation Act had put Dissenters and candle-manufacturers on the Bench and hatters and apothecaries into the council-chamber.

But now that I'd seen for myself, I could understand how it had all come about. Locked away on my northern island, I'd had no inkling of the sheer, unstoppable creative energy which had gripped the teeming cities of Britain, where the needs of one industry immediately became the business of another. Cotton must be spun and woven; steam machinery was devised to do the work. The machinery had to be built; iron and steel were hammered and cast into shape.

In fact, if anything brought home to me the urgency with which this country was moving ahead, it was the tide of metal which lapped over it in its headlong rush. In Newfoundland iron came to us by sea along with everything from leather to linen, and was used sparingly. But here in England it was put to every conceivable use—far beyond the machines which clanked and roared in the mills. Water pipes, gas pipes, gutters, gratings and gasometers were made of it; roofs and their delicate supporting pillars and arches were cast from it; bridges were built of it, from huge chasm-leaping spans to cobweb footbridges over canals; and now the rails and railway trucks which hurtled across the land were made of it too.

The iron founders needed coal, and the cotton manufacturers needed coal to raise steam for the machines the ironfounders had made. And the coal was dug and thrown into iron trucks to run on iron rails. And all the time raw cotton flooded into our port of Liverpool while spun cotton yarn and cotton piece-goods flowed out —every year enough of it to pay twice over for the exports of the entire Russian Empire.

Yet Captain Fuller, that champion of Free Trade, wanted more. He prayed, he said, for a day when American corn would be allowed into the country unhindered and British goods would flood untaxed into American markets. Then the waters of the Mersey would be black with the hulls of ships, and Liverpool docks would extend as far as the eye could see.

It was all building and planning, this new world of mine, and I found it thrilling. The thought of being shut up once more in St. John's after a glimpse of the exciting life to be lived elsewhere was too dreadful to contemplate, and I began to agree with my aunt's verdict on my old home. As she laid down my mother's letter at last and let her eyeglass fall on its chain, she would look at me and snort with contempt.

"It sounds a wretched place to live. Wouldn't do for me at all. Poor Joseph. A wretched place to live."

———

It had been a particularly fine late August afternoon, ruined by a persistent young man who'd walked with us in the park, talking about nothing but horses until I knew everything there was to know about coarse heads and grass sickness and the various parts of a driving-harness. By the time we reached Leghorn Street once more my head was aching, and when Captain Fuller met us in the hall with the news that there would be company for dinner, I begged him at once to excuse me. A tray brought up to my room and a cool bed with the curtains drawn was all I asked at that moment.

"Oh, Rachel! Not tonight, of all nights! These people are particular friends of yours, I believe—Andrew MacDonald and his wife, and some acquaintance of theirs, just landed in Liverpool from the Boston packet. Oh, I could've warned them not to sail on the *Borealis!* She rolls like a pig in a mudhole, and that Yankee pirate Taylor couldn't lay a course across a bathtub. But never mind! They did sail in her, and a lumpy ride they had of it. Next time, I daresay, they'll pick a good British vessel. Anyhow—they're coming here at six, which your aunt insists is the fashionable time for dinner. I can't believe you don't want to be there."

The prospect of seeing Andrew MacDonald again cheered me up at once. I hadn't even been allowed to say goodbye to the Mac-Donalds before leaving St. John's, since my mother had taken it into her head that the disastrous arrival of Francis Ellis in our home had been Andrew MacDonald's revenge for the forced sale of his store, and she refused point-blank to let me visit him again. But somehow the MacDonalds had found out where I was staying in Liverpool and had called as soon as they arrived in the city. I was so excited by the unexpected treat that it didn't even cross my mind to wonder who their "acquaintance" might be. It was only when I rustled downstairs in my newest full-skirted dinner dress of flowered green silk that I discovered the identity of the friend they'd brought with them.

6

I couldn't have blamed him for not recognizing me. He'd last seen me nine years earlier, a dreamy child in a percale frock who scorned a sunbonnet and threw off her shoes whenever she could get away with it. Now here was a young woman of almost seventeen, as near a fashion-plate as my aunt could contrive, pale shoulders set off by the low bodice of my dress and a fall of blond lace, and dark hair looped up into a knot on top of my head, entwined with moss-roses. He glanced at me as I entered the room, just as any man would look at an unknown young woman. Then as Andrew and Christian MacDonald came forward to embrace me, I saw the first doubt enter his face, and a puzzled look came into those gray eyes I remembered so well. *Ah, Adam Gaunt,* I thought, *where is that child with her injured seabird now?*

He'd changed very little. The web of lines round his eyes had deepened and the bones of his face stood out more starkly—that was all. Otherwise he was the same tall, spare, brown magician who'd found me a squirrel's nest in the trees at Crow Cove, and taught me the names of the patterns of stars overhead.

"D'ye see who we found, Rachel," Christian MacDonald exclaimed, "crossing from America on the *Borealis?* Mr. Gaunt, who stayed with you after the shipwreck in the bay—it must have been in '27. Gracious, you were only a child then! Do you remember him?"

As if I could have forgotten! Though as she spoke the words I had a sudden fear that he might have forgotten me.

"Miss Rachel Dean . . . I can hardly believe it." He studied me for a moment at a polite distance. "I was expecting—well, someone about *so* high, with an owl on her shoulder and a blind kitten following at her heels! Which only goes to show what tricks our memories can play on us."

Somewhere beyond him, I could hear Andrew MacDonald telling Aunt Grace and the Captain about the wreck of the *Adelaide Ross* and Adam Gaunt's rescue.

"How is your leg now?" I managed to ask. "I hope it's better."

"Oh, perfectly healed, Miss Dean, I assure you." He still seemed at a loss to know how to treat me. "And you're Susannah's child . . . I find that hard to comprehend."

Across the room I noticed my aunt regarding us with a bright, inquisitive stare. She'd caught the words *Susannah's child:* not *Mrs. Dean's child,* or even *Joseph and Susannah's child,* and I knew she wouldn't rest until she'd found out as much as I could tell her of that summer's stay.

"Three and a half months sick, Mr. Gaunt!" she exclaimed. "That must have been a dreadful injury! I'd no idea my sister was such a patient nurse."

He swung round to face her. "Not so dreadful, Mrs. Fuller. Simply a torn leg. I was fortunate to find an excellent nurse in the village who made up medicines and poultices. Mrs. Dean simply gave me somewhere to stay until I was better, and I'm indebted to her for her kindness."

I saw Aunt Grace set her face in a suitable smile. *Kindness* wasn't a word she often associated with her sister.

I can't remember much of what was said over dinner, except an awful moment when Andrew MacDonald, thinner and grayer than I remembered him, began to speak about his protégé Francis Ellis. For a second I thought he knew the whole sordid story and was about to reveal it.

"I'll never understand why your mother took against the lad," he remarked to my relief. "Whatever she said to him, he left the island at once, and set off back to the States as fast as he could travel. I did hear he'd opened a school in some little town beyond the Mississippi, out in the wild country."

It was enough to know Francis Ellis was far away, out of my life; and my attention began to wander while Andrew MacDonald held forth on the present state of affairs in Newfoundland. I was more interested in watching Adam Gaunt out of the corner of my eye and wondering where his wanderlust had taken him in the nine years which had passed since he strode off down the hill to the waiting schooner. He might only have been gone a week, for all he'd changed —and when later in the drawing room he sat down next to me, it was with the same loose-jointed ease I remembered so well, bone and sinew moving together in perfect harmony and economy of action, giving him that strange quality of stillness which had always marked him out.

Captain Fuller had grown bored with Andrew MacDonald's direful prophecies about the Irish in St. John's. Scenting a good tale, he steered the conversation in exactly the direction I longed for. Was it true, he wanted to know, that Mr. Gaunt had quite recently come from the Rocky Mountains, where water was said to boil from the ground like steam from a kettle?

It was true: and there were indeed hot springs, and other places where a black, tarry substance oozed from the earth for the relief of the trappers' rheumatic joints. Little by little, urged on by the Captain, Adam talked of the places he'd seen. The Bighorn Mountains —the Wind River Range—Jackson's Hole—the Sweetwater and Popo Agie rivers—bullboats and roast crow—horses and men—I listened, enraptured, to the magical words and to that familiar, beloved voice. Cotton mills and gasometers became commonplace as he spoke: here was a world I'd never dreamed might exist.

"You eat *crows?*" cried Aunt Grace suddenly, no doubt thinking of her well-stocked larder.

"Not from choice, Mrs. Fuller, believe me. The meat's too rank for me, but sometimes it's that or go hungry. I've eaten boiled moccasin-sole when I had to. Moccasins are shoes," he added in explanation.

"You've eaten your *shoes?*" I could hardly believe such privation.

"Only once, in the winter." He laughed at my astonishment. "And I don't recommend it. Moose, now—that's gamey, but better eating. And buffalo—fat cow-buffalo can be as good as the best venison you've ever tasted."

I tried hard to imagine this soft-spoken man in his good dark kersey coat dressed in a fringed suit of skins, following some mountain trail with his gun and his pack-mule. I noticed he wore long boots, American-fashion, and I saw my aunt's eyebrows rise in disapproval of the eccentric footwear stretched out on her Oriental carpet.

Uncle Tom, a connoisseur of strange places, was eager to hear more.

"They say there are wolves, and bears and savage Indians in those mountains."

"There are. All three. But we've agreed to treat one another with respect, for the most part. Though I'm not always sure about the Indians. Some of them I count as friends—as for the others, well, it's often best not to make their acquaintance if you can avoid it."

"Please excuse me for a moment—"

The word *Indian* had awakened a memory. It took me no more than a few minutes to run upstairs to my room and fetch the red stone amulet Adam had given me just before leaving Crow Cove. Down in the drawing room I held it up for him to see, turning slowly on its loop of elk-hide, intricate and barbaric, the inlaid animals chasing one another round its rim as they'd done for countless generations.

I could see from his face that the sight of it reminded him of more than a single summer in Crow Cove—perhaps of the Indian woman who'd worn it and then died giving birth to his child. But after a second he smiled as if it was a thing of no consequence, and said lightly, "I'm surprised you've kept it for long. I doubt if it will ever be the height of fashion."

"Of course I kept it! I wouldn't dream of parting with it."

I hadn't meant to sound so sharp, but I was hurt by his offhand manner: I'd treasured his gift, just as I'd promised.

But while the MacDonalds and my uncle and aunt inspected the amulet, I was aware of Adam Gaunt examining me just as curiously, as if I were something entirely new and unexpected. If he was searching for a glimpse of the child who'd tied ribbons in her hair in an effort to please him, and wept when her tame seabird was thrown over a cliff . . . then I feared he'd find very little of her remaining.

"It must be wonderful to be free to go where you please." I felt myself flush with excitement under his scrutiny. "Everything I do seems to be decided for me."

"That's because you have friends who care about you, and want to keep you from harm."

"But don't you have friends like that?"

"No one who'd care if I went missing. That's the price of the freedom you envy so much. I've no one to say *don't go*—but no one to notice I've gone, either. If I died somewhere in the mountains I'd be forgotten as soon as the snow had covered my footsteps."

"But that's so sad! Doesn't it make you unhappy?"

"Sometimes it does—when I find myself by a warm fire in good company. But not for long."

"Mr. Gaunt!" called my aunt from her place by the table, "I hear you're to be in Liverpool for some weeks."

"That's so, Mrs. Fuller. The MacDonalds are bound for Kilmarnock, I understand, but Liverpool will serve me as well as anywhere."

"And you've taken a room in a hotel?" My aunt uttered the word *hotel* as she might have said *thieves' kitchen*. "Well then, since by all accounts you're an old friend of my sister's . . . you must call on us here as often as you wish. Even if I'm not at home, I'm sure Rachel will always be pleased to see you. Isn't that so, my dear?"

Instantly, I assured him it was so.

———

"Oh—this is too much! How dare she say such things to me, when I've done no more than carry out her wishes? It's too much! Too much!"

I'd feared the worst when the letter arrived, directed in my mother's bold, vehement script to *Mrs. Thomas Fuller, 16 Leghorn Street, Liverpool, England.* Any day now I expected to be summoned back to St. John's, and my heart sank when I saw my aunt fling down her eyeglass with a furious cry after reading no more than a few lines. My first despairing thought was that my mother had demanded my immediate return to Newfoundland, destroying the happiness which had come into my life in the few weeks since Adam Gaunt's arrival in Liverpool. He'd called on us often, and though my aunt could never quite overcome her suspicion of a man who wore long boots with a frock coat, the Captain had enjoyed his company almost as much as I did.

But my mother's letter said nothing about my return to St. John's. It was a short, spiteful note to my aunt, hard on the heels of her last letter and written in the white heat of anger and resentment. Perhaps if the Captain had still been at home he might have prevented Aunt Grace from planning a mischievous revenge. But he'd sailed off on the *Spartacus* a few days before, and my aunt had nothing left to occupy her mind but righteous indignation and a determination to pay her sister back for every hurtful word.

It wasn't until many years later that I discovered all the domestic disasters which had made my mother write so viciously to her sister. Chief among them, though, was a paper from her Liverpool bank, detailing how much of Grandfather Allen's legacy my aunt had spent

on me—far more than my mother had intended to "invest" in turning her daughter into marriageable material. She'd written to Aunt
Grace at once, in terms almost scorching enough to melt the seal.

> Moderation? Restraint? Why—you don't know the meaning of the
> word! Almost a thousand guineas spent in eighteen months! And you
> call that *a small outlay*. . . . Does that husband of yours earn nothing
> at all, so that you support your entire household at my expense? I
> can't think how else you've managed to get through so much.

"The wretch!" cried Aunt Grace in a passion. "How can she say
such terrible things? I *told* her there would be expenses! I did warn
her!"

Yet there was worse to come. My wrathful mother had aimed her
barbs precisely where she knew they would hurt.

> I should have known [she sneered] that you wouldn't resist the temp-
> tation of spending someone else's money on tawdry finery and trin-
> kets. No doubt I'll find Rachel dressed up like a scarecrow in whatever
> vulgar nonsense has caught your eye since I foolishly agreed to pay
> for your whims! Grace—you are a blockhead!

My aunt was sniffing into her handkerchief, but the tears in her eyes
were tears of vexation, not sorrow. Once more she'd been treated
unjustly by her sister; but this time she was determined to cause my
mother some pain in return.

I truly believe Aunt Grace never intended to hurt me by her scheming—only to provoke my mother. While I stayed in her house I'd
become genuinely fond of her and in her own haphazard, awkward
way I think she returned the affection. But in my aunt's mind I was
"trustworthy": I was the obedient niece who never caused her a
moment's anxiety, indifferent to the society of young men, my heart
secure against flattery or good looks until (in Aunt Grace's view of
the world) the gallant hero fated to become my perfect lover would
arrive with a fanfare of trumpets and a polite proposal of marriage.

There could be no possible harm, then, in stirring up a little devil-
ment to annoy my mother. And while my mother had always seemed
the more Machiavellian of the two, there's no doubt that Aunt
Grace, for all her girlish frills and ridiculous feathers, was cunning
enough to pick out a chink in her sister's defenses. Certain remarks
had been made which had roused her curiosity, and all at once Aunt

Grace decided that I should have an admirer for her to boast of to my mother.

"Don't think that because Captain Fuller's away you're not welcome here," she told Adam Gaunt with much playful finger-wagging. "I'd miss you now if you stayed away, and I'm certain poor Rachel would be quite desolate."

Both of us stared at her in surprise. It was no more than the truth: I would indeed have been desolate, but fortunately Adam's visits to Leghorn Street had become such an established part of his daily routine that the Captain's departure had made no difference at all. As autumn turned into winter he continued to call, closing the front door behind him on some cold, blustery afternoon and stretching out comfortably in the big rosewood chair before the fire, the heels of his top-boots resting on the brass fender and his mind filled with an image of early summer in the high mountain passes he'd left behind.

I loved those afternoons. He would talk to me then of the sights and sounds and smells of the wilderness—of the scent of the pines and the wild peppermint leaves crushed under his horse's hooves, of the wine-sweet streams and the cobalt gentian among the rocks, of the seven-foot grizzly bears and their bumbling cubs, and everywhere the livid green fuzz of new spring growth.

"And the stars, Adam—do you still watch the stars?"

"Ah, the stars you see in the mountains are different from all the rest. . . . The night sky there is the darkest blue imaginable—not velvet or oppressive, but clear and deep like the mountain streams, a sky you can stare and stare into, listening to the mass of stars rustle and shimmer in the furthest distance . . . just as if the universe were turning over thoughts in the depths of its mind. And when it rises, the moon's so beautiful it hurts your eyes, like a glimpse of eternity too fine for us mortals to see."

And I gazed at the stilted, sooty lilacs crowded beyond my aunt's Liverpool window, and began to long for this land of his which I'd never seen. It was almost as if he was offering it to me; and somehow my feelings for Adam became mixed up with my image of the wilderness, so that they were one and the same. Adam himself was an unknown tract of savage splendor, drawing me to him and to his own fugitive, untameable ways. I wanted to soar on the wings of his siren-song, far above the filthy city streets and the grime-spewing chimneys. My whole mind was suffused with the scent of pinewoods and the winking of a multitude of stars, and all at once I began to make sense of that strange starlit night in the scrubland when Adam showed me the endless struggle in the Heavens between the Hunter and the Ploughman . . . and laid the whole grandeur of Creation at my feet. The truth was so obvious that it made me laugh out loud. For the first time in my life I was hopelessly, irresistibly, exultantly in love.

Quite unaware of my newfound rapture, Aunt Grace continued to smile upon me in her absentminded fashion, and encouraged Adam to visit the house as much as he pleased. We were often alone together while my aunt paid duty-calls on her friends. She could see no possible impropriety in it: if Adam had been twenty, or twenty-one —well, that might have been different—but at thirty-five he was only three years younger than she was herself.

Strangely enough, in spite of all the time we'd spent together, Adam's age was almost all I knew about him. His past was as trackless as the mountains he'd lived among for so many years, and whenever I tried to ask him about it I'd find the conversation diverted before long to another subject. I began to understand that in his own mind Adam stood alone, not at the tail of some ancestral army which had created him. His virtues and his faults were all his own, take him or leave him, praise or blame.

One thing I learned from a chance remark—that his family name had descended from a fourteenth-century mercenary knight, Roger of Ghent, hired from Flanders to fight Henry Bolingbroke's battles; and I remember thinking how stunningly grand it all sounded, like a page from a history book. As far as I was concerned my own ancestry began with Grandfather Allen, and I couldn't help wondering how Adam could know so much about his great-great-great-however-manygrandfathers ago. "My father spoke of it once . . ." he began, and then deftly turned the conversation to other matters before I could ask any more questions.

I didn't care. I'd discovered one definite fact at last, and after that I carried a picture of him in my mind, dressed in heroic armor, Adam's face superimposed on a painting of Saint Michael which had hung in our schoolroom in St. John's.

————

He was careful never to make himself the hero of his tales, but I always supplied that element for myself. It was so different from anything I'd ever known—these stories of the great rendezvous each year in the mountains, when the trappers would come to barter their furs for provisions and whisky brought up on the traders' mule-train, and meet together in a great encampment of white men and Indians for a month of horse-racing and drinking and swapping of yarns. *Shoshone, Flatheads, Nez Percés* . . . even the names of the tribes were strange and exotic, as glamorous to my ears as any of Captain Fuller's tales of Montevideo or the China Sea, and I could never hear enough. It was all I asked—to be near him, to hear his voice and to see him smile. Beyond that I hadn't begun to consider.

Then one frosty afternoon when we'd been sitting by the fire as usual, discussing the perils of blizzards in the mountains, an idle remark of my own led to the utter destruction of my peace of mind.

"For all its hardship," I said, "I expect you'll always miss the Rocky Mountains, now you've come home. I'm sure I should."

"Home?" He considered the word as if it came from a foreign language. "If I have a home at all, it's more likely to be across the Atlantic Ocean than here in England. If *home* means a place of peace and contentment, then mine is somewhere on the slopes of the Wind River Mountains, with the sun in my face and a rifle in my hand. Here in England, I'm only a visitor nowadays. And not even that for much longer, if everything goes as it should."

A great chasm yawned black at my feet, and I tottered desperately on its edge as the bedrock of my happiness crumbled rapidly into the void.

"You're not going back to America?"

"I am indeed, and quite shortly. My business here is almost done. I've called on all the people I came to see, and now I've only to arrange my passage."

He said it with casual satisfaction, quite unaware of the overwhelming despair which was sweeping me into the abyss of forsaken love. Never again to see him stand, lost in thought, before the drawing-room fire; never again to feel his gray, appraising glance upon me, or to know the fluttering of the heart which his arrival in the house always caused in me—it was too much to bear, too cruel.

"I'll never see you again. You'll never come back here, I know it." For what was left for me after he'd gone but a dismal Atlantic voyage with a prison at the end of it? I was more miserable than I would have believed possible, yet Adam didn't seem to notice. He even tried to tease me about my unhappiness.

"You'll forget all about me in two weeks. Buy a new parasol and a pair of gloves, and you'll soon put me out of your mind."

"You think of me as a silly girl, don't you? You've never forgotten that seven-year-old child you saw in Crow Cove! I've grown up, Adam—I'm a woman now."

"And a pretty one too, if I may say so."

"*Don't* tease me! I deserve better than that."

The laughter fled abruptly from his face.

"I'm sorry. I wasn't aware of treating you like a child, or of treating you as anything except—a younger sister, perhaps. Someone to listen to my stories and wave me off at the quayside when I sail away again on my travels. Was that such a mistake?"

He rose to leave, and panic swept over me.

"Oh, please don't go. I didn't mean to offend you."

"I've stayed too long as it is, and tired you out."

"Oh, no—you mustn't go away on my account. My aunt expects you to dine with us, I'm sure. It's just that . . . I didn't expect you to leave England again so soon. Your news was very sudden, that's all."

I saw him frown and hesitate, wondering what to do for the best.

"You must stay. Forget my silliness. Please."

"Oh, very well. It's impossible to refuse you anything when you look at me with those great, shining eyes, Rachel. See what power you have, you little child-woman? You have me in the palm of your hand."

———

"Rachel dear," remarked my aunt thoughtfully that evening as we sipped our late-night tea, "I do hope you aren't getting to be *fond* of Mr. Gaunt. I don't mean fond of him as an old friend—which I know he is, of course. I mean. . . . Well, it's just that I saw the way you looked at him over dinner tonight, and it crossed my mind to wonder. . . . But no. You're a sensible girl. I'm sure I imagined it all. I did imagine it, didn't I, Rachel?"

"Yes, Aunt Grace."

"Of course I did. As I say, you're a sensible girl. And Mr. Gaunt —however good-looking he may be, and I wouldn't disagree with that—is not a suitable person for you to be getting fond of. Not at all suitable."

"No, Aunt Grace."

"You see, dear, there are men who might one day be marriageable

—a few, very few—and there are the rest, the impossible ones. In time you'll learn the difference, and learn not to waste your affections on the wrong sort. Of course, I blame myself. I've left you together too much."

"Oh, no, Aunt Grace!"

"I have, though. You're still very young and impressionable, Rachel. You don't know what *devils* men can be." Aunt Grace sucked her long teeth and shook her head gloomily over this somber truth. "And that one—Adam Gaunt—is the kind of man that's forever on the move, always wandering off somewhere, leaving broken hearts behind. Believe me, I've seen his sort before; some of the Captain's friends are just the same. Here today, gone tomorrow. Nothing and no one can keep them in one place."

"Uncle Tom's not like that."

"No, he isn't. His mother saw to that, God rest her soul. But Adam Gaunt is, and I'm afraid you'll be made unhappy when he sails off again, back to his American mountains. If I thought it would do any good I'd tell him to stay away from this house in future, for whatever time he has left in England."

"Oh, please, Aunt Grace—you mustn't do that! Please!"

"I don't suppose it would help. You'd only be miserable now instead of miserable later. And he'll be gone from here soon enough, I daresay, without my interference. Otherwise I'd speak to him about it, you may be sure."

"I couldn't bear that."

"You can rest easy, since I've made up my mind not to say anything. Though whether it's what the Captain would do if he were here, I can't say. No doubt Mr. Gaunt thinks it's all very fine to have a young girl of seventeen mooning over him—yes, mooning, Rachel —when he knows he'll be safely over the Mersey bar in a short while. But it's hardly a kindness to you. Men can be devils, Rachel, I warn you."

Was Adam a devil, as my aunt said? Suppose she was right, and he did know of my feelings for him. . . . He'd never forbidden me to think of him in that way, or shortened his visits to us in Leghorn Street. Could this possibly mean he cared for me as I did for him? The mere idea of it sent my senses reeling.

"At any rate," my aunt was saying, "from now on, when he comes to call, you'll oblige me by having Harry and his nurse down in the drawing room if I'm not at home. I won't have you left alone with

Mr. Gaunt; I'm not saying he'd try to take advantage of you, mind, but I don't believe you're quite as trustworthy now as you were before. Not from any fault of your own, but young girls get strange ideas sometimes, when their heads are upset."

And with that Aunt Grace went to bed, convinced she'd dealt with the problem once and for all.

Besides—it had always been part of her grand plan, her great mischief, to throw Adam Gaunt and myself together, and even if her scheme had rather run away with itself she still saw no reason to hold back now from the principal part of it. The very next day she sat down to write a letter to my mother in St. John's and, when she'd finished it to her own satisfaction, she showed me what she'd written, smirking over her little triumph.

"Read it, my dear," she urged, "and tell me what your mother will think of it."

I picked up the paper, and read the part she indicated.

Our dearest Rachel [it began] has recently been the object of the most flattering attentions from a gentleman of comfortable means and good appearance, recently returned from America, where he has been engaged in the fur trade.

I write to you, sister, to know your mind on the question of further acquaintance, since although there is some little difference in age, I am convinced Rachel is by no means averse to his company, nor he to hers. His name is Mr. Adam Gaunt. . . .

"Well?" demanded my aunt. "What do you think?"

I thought of the day I'd watched my mother pin on her straw hat to walk down to the village and carry off Adam Gaunt from the Widow Creran's house; I thought of their walks together up the forest road, and of the seabird she'd had hurled from the cliff so that Adam would spend less time in my company, and the quarrel we'd had when I threw the candlestick and tried to claim Adam for my own.

And I shuddered at the memory, and tried not to think of it any more.

7

I was adrift on a sea of confusion, one minute uplifted by wild joy and the next plunged into the depths of misery, quite unable to control either mood. Most of the time I daydreamed about Adam or lay at night in my narrow white bed re-creating him, greedily, piece by piece, in my imagination. Every morning I dressed myself to please him, chose jewelry and put up my hair for him, just in case he should call. In church on Sunday my thoughts wandered so far from the service that I completely forgot to kneel for a prayer until the soft clump of a multitude of hassocks reminded me I was the only one still standing.

I returned to my novels, spending hours over Mrs. Radcliffe's *Mysteries of Udolpho* and Scott's *Ivanhoe* and *Quentin Durward*. What was I now but the Lady Rowena, shut up by the Templar in Front-de-Boeuf's castle, kept by force from the man I loved?

Aunt Grace constantly reproached me for picking at my food.

"If you're ill, child, you should go to bed."

"I'm not ill, Aunt Grace." Then, after a pause, "And I'm not a child any longer."

"No, my dear, I suppose not." *And you're not sick either, unless it's lovesick.* She never spoke the words, but I could tell what she was thinking, and whom she blamed for my troubles. No doubt she began to wish at the same time that she'd never offered me bed and board in Liverpool. Here I was, outwardly meek and obedient but still possessed of a fair portion of my mother's willfulness and that rebellious pout—no more than a slight bulge of the lower lip— which my aunt remembered so well.

She saw to it that I was never alone with Adam now, afraid of what I might say to him in my present besotted state. I loathed her for her care of me, for her constant presence in the room, settled four-square beside the fire, scratching at some hideous piece of wool-work as she smiled and nodded her way through the conversation.

Adam didn't seem to mind her chaperonage, but he called less often now and kept his visits brief and inconsequential. It drove me mad to think of the three of us sitting there, solemnly discussing the weather or the king's health when all the time my heart was beating crazily for love of him and the remaining minutes of his time in England were ticking, ticking away. Soon he'd be gone, sailing away again to America, and soon afterward I'd be aboard ship myself, summoned home in disgrace by my furious mother. For that would be the result of Aunt Grace's letter—a demand for my instant return, far away from sight or sound of the troublesome Adam Gaunt.

Then not long before Adam was due to sail, Aunt Grace caught a feverish chill in a drafty church pew during (she insisted) an overlong sermon. She promptly took to her bed, and next day I found myself packed off unwillingly in her place to pay a duty-call on an elderly Allen relative who could on no account be left unvisited.

I pleaded in vain to be allowed to go in a day or two's time: though the weather was fair it might change, and in any case—though I didn't say so—I had a feeling Adam might call, for once giving me a chance of speaking to him alone, without the brooding presence of my aunt. But Aunt Grace had anticipated my plan. I was to visit Great-aunt Allen, and that was that.

I set off across the city in watery sunshine, but within a few hours a hailstorm was slicing the gathering gloom into freezing ribbons, turning the streets into treacherous, glistening traps for unwary travelers.

There could be no question of spending the night at Great-aunt Allen's. For one thing she'd no room for me, and for another, the old lady could never have borne the disturbance. Despite the weather, my aunt's carriage would be sent to fetch me back, but with Captain Fuller at sea and Aunt Grace confined to bed by her chill there was no one but the cook to go with it as escort. In the end, the problem was solved when Adam Gaunt arrived at that moment in Leghorn Street, rivulets of water sluicing from his greatcoat, and volunteered to set off at once in the jolting gloom of the carriage to carry me home.

———

I couldn't believe my good fortune. To my great, soaring joy I found myself at last legitimately alone with Adam in the shadowy carriage as it swayed and skidded through the city on its return journey to Leghorn Street. I'd spent a long afternoon humoring the whims of the deaf great-aunt, and I knew my eyes were ringed with blue smudges of fatigue. But my tiredness no longer mattered. Adam was there, and as the vehicle lurched round the street corners, throwing me painfully from side to side against the buttoned upholstery, he even slipped an arm round my shoulders to steady me against the uneven motion.

It was wonderful to be able to relax against him, luxuriating in his strong, solid presence and the damp roughness of his greatcoat against my cheek. I gave a long, blissful sigh of pure contentment—which Adam took for a yawn, since he murmured, "You're tired," and continued to hold me against him in the swaying dimness of the carriage.

How I wished that ride could last forever, and not just as far as Leghorn Street . . . But time was short, and however seductive the silence and closeness of the carriage might be, there was a matter which had to be put into words.

"Adam," I began, "do you know yet when you'll sail?"

"On the nineteenth, I'm told."

"So soon? And today's the sixth. That's only . . . thirteen days away. I hadn't realized there was so little time left."

I felt Adam stir uncomfortably in his seat, and when he spoke his voice sounded unnaturally cheerful.

"Spring will be here before you know it. I'll disappear with the winter, and you'll soon forget that either of us existed."

"But winter will be back again within a year, and you won't."

"Oh, you never know . . . Perhaps I'll miss that fetching smile of yours, and come running back to Liverpool just in time to see you married off to some dashing young fellow who owns half of Cheshire and drives his cabriolet at breakneck speed round the park."

"*Will* you miss me, Adam? Will you really?"

A violent swing of the carriage tipped us both unceremoniously to one side and gave him a few seconds to think of a safe reply.

"Of course I'll miss you. And your aunt, and peaceful afternoons in front of the fire . . . and good cooking, too. There are no oyster pies or sugared almonds where I'm going, I promise you."

I couldn't believe he was being so offhand with me. And it was all a pretense—as false as the genial note in his voice or the sudden interest he'd taken in the toes of his boots.

"Oh, Adam, that isn't what I asked you! I meant will you miss *me*. Not the tables and chairs in the drawing room or your wretched oysters! What I mean is . . . Will you sometimes think of me again—

in the mountains or wherever you're going? Think of me, and perhaps wonder what I'm doing—or whether I'm thinking of you?"

"Well, of course. There are bound to be times like that—late at night, probably, lying beside a campfire in the darkness. And I'll get to thinking of places I've seen and people I've known, and wonder what's happened to them all since I saw them last." He glanced down at me in sudden, genuine affection.

"I'll always want to know what becomes of you, little one. Perhaps you can write to me in St. Louis, care of the fur company, and give me all your news. I'll get your letter in the end."

That was all he would offer, and he turned his head as he finished speaking, and stared out of the window at the sleet-spattered street.

"Adam—"

"Mmmmm?"

"Take me with you."

I heard him give a nervous laugh: he must have thought I was teasing him.

"I mean it, Adam. You could take me with you to America if you wanted to—you know you could. My mother doesn't care what happens to me. My father's only interested in the next bottle, and Aunt Grace would be pleased to have me off her hands. None of them care about me the least bit. You're the only one who's ever treated me as if I had a mind and a soul of my own, worthy of any notice."

"Rachel—"

"I'd make you a good wife, Adam." In my eagerness, I twisted round and took hold of the breast of his coat. "I'm not afraid of discomfort, or lack of company. I'm stronger than I look—truly I am—and I promise to do whatever you tell me, and go where I'm told. I wouldn't be a burden to you. And I can cook . . . a little. I used to help the cook in our house in St. John's when I was small. Oh, Adam, *please*. You must take me to America! I can't bear it here without you. You're my whole life—the only person who matters to me."

He frowned, and leaned away from me, withdrawing the arm which had supported my shoulders.

"I was afraid something like this was going through your head. You don't know what you're saying, Rachel. This is foolishness."

His voice was suddenly so cold that I was startled. Nevertheless, I pressed on with my case.

"Why is it foolish?"

"Because you're too young to leave home, and you'd regret it five minutes after you'd gone. You couldn't possibly live in the kind of places I'm bound for—even if I were prepared to take you."

"Missionaries' wives have traveled through the mountains—you told me that yourself."

"Passed *through,* that's all. And it was a hard road, by any standards."

"Then I could live somewhere on the Plains, and you could come back to me every winter."

"That's a ridiculous idea. Rachel, you're too young to leave home, and that's an end of it."

"I've already left home, you may remember—such as it was. And as for my age, my mother was very little older when she went out to Newfoundland with my father."

Mention of my mother only seemed to make him crosser.

"Yes, your mother married young. Too young, to my way of thinking. Do you really think she has a happy marriage as a result of it?"

"But I'm not my mother. And you're worth a thousand of my wretched father, Adam."

Whatever I'd said, it dissolved what little was left of his patience.

"Rachel, there's no point in discussing the matter any more. If I'd known you were thinking of such a thing, I'd have put a stop to it far sooner. Yes, you're a delightful, accomplished girl—a woman, if you like; one day you'll make some lucky man a wonderful wife. But not me. For one thing, hasn't it occurred to you that if I needed a wife, I'd have had one by now?"

What occurred to me was that he was being deliberately brutal, trampling relentlessly on my dreams in order to show me how impractical they were.

"For all sorts of reasons," he added, "you must forget this nonsense. Put it all behind you, wave me off at the quayside like a sensible young woman, and let's part as friends at least."

There was nothing more I could say. I sat shocked and silent at his side until the carriage rumbled at last to a halt at my aunt's door when, without waiting to be handed down from it, I scrambled to the slushy ground and raced away from him, up the steps to the house.

———

For three long, tedious days I saw nothing of Adam. Numb with loneliness, I sat in the deserted drawing room, pretending to sew but in reality forcing my mind to relive every moment of our argument in the sleet-lashed carriage, wondering what else I might have said to convince him of my overwhelming, agonizing love. *Too young:* he'd always come back to the same theme. I was only seventeen, and too young. But too young for what? Too young to know my own mind? Too young to create a home for us both in whatever out-of-the-way corner he might choose?

At eighteen my mother was already a young wife in a distant land with a baby to care for, and I knew the Newfoundland fishermen's daughters often married a year or two younger than that and went to setting up home. So I wasn't too young for homemaking. But how could I convince Adam he was wrong, if he wouldn't come to see me any more?

For three days I brooded in the shadowed, silent house, where the deep wool rugs soaked up every footstep and only the ticking of innumerable clocks clicked away Adam's last few days in Liverpool. I was left entirely to myself, since although my aunt's chill was better, she still spent most of her time in bed or dozing in an armchair before the blazing fire kept up in her bedroom hearth.

Too young. Still, in Adam's mind, the child in the cotton shift who ran wild at Crow Cove with her animals and birds. Too young to be married. Too young to be a wife.

Too young for . . . Not in Francis Ellis's estimation, I wasn't. Even after two years, a wave of shame swept over me when I remembered that afternoon in the breakfast room in St. John's—not because of what had happened between us, but because of my dreadful, humiliating ignorance. He must have thought me a complete fool, a stupid, trusting girl with no more idea of the facts of life than a dog knows of algebra.

Not that I'd discovered much more in the two years which followed. In spite of Francis Ellis I still knew hardly anything of whatever went on in private between men and women, and life with Aunt Grace wasn't likely to enlighten me on the subject. One or two clues had come my way, such as the fact that it had something to do with the monthly bleeding and with the *marriage bed*—always referred to by my mother's women-friends in specially hushed tones accompanied by significant nods. The result of it all was the arrival of babies at intervals after a marriage had taken place. Ducks paired off, and there were eggs. Girls became married women, and there were babies. But how exactly it came about, no one had ever seen fit to explain to me.

When God finds out two people are married, the kindly cook in the house in St. John's had told me once, *he sends them babies to look after. It's as simple as that.*

But what about Bella Rooney, an older girl at the school in Crow Cove, who'd suddenly vanished from class one day and never returned? Everyone said she'd been delivered of a little boy a few months later, yet she'd had no husband, or I would have known of it. Had God made a mistake, then, in sending Bella a baby? The cook became confused. *God doesn't make mistakes, Miss Rachel. If there was a mistake, then it was Bella Rooney who made it.* And she would say no more, leaving me with a muddled impression of the unhappy Bella accidentally deceiving God as to her marital state. For a long time afterward I lived in dread of unwittingly following her example, and always reminded God at the end of my nightly prayers that I was still absolutely single and not even thinking of being married.

I was no longer so naïve. Thanks to Francis Ellis, Bella Rooney's mistake had nearly been mine. Yet the mechanics of the act still defeated me, and I was ashamed of my ignorance.

My mother might have told me if I'd asked, but with a sneer and unkind remarks about my innocence which I couldn't have borne. Aunt Grace, as I've said, was no help. Little Harry had descended from Paradise to Leghorn Street on a pink cloud as far as she was concerned, though generally the common run of babies were apt to be found under gooseberry bushes. Aunt Grace was so genteel she couldn't even mention the *w . . . r cl . . . t* without silently miming the words.

I was seventeen, and I didn't know what I thought I ought to have known. And I was sure Adam sensed my ignorance of these facts, and thought me a child because of it. Too young. Too young to be able to give him whatever a woman should.

My humiliation was made worse by the turmoil which Adam's presence invariably created inside me. When he was there I became suddenly clumsy and tongue-tied, unable to eat or drink because of the huge, pulsing knot in my stomach, each untouched plate at dinner only drawing attention to my confusion.

I found myself studying him as I'd never looked at a man before, drawing pleasure from his height, his broad shoulders and the regularity of his features in exactly the same way I'd once run tingling fingers through the silky fur of my mother's sable muff, reveling in the sensation of soft hairs rippling against my skin. The same impulse made me want to reach out to touch Adam, to brush my fingers against the place at the back of his neck where his hair crinkled into tiny curls, to skim the delicate rim of an ear or the tight, pale line of his cheekbone.

He invaded my dreams at night now, closer and more intimate than ever by day, until I began to imagine naked skin sliding under my fingertips and his breath lingering warm on my cheek . . . and I would wake again in the darkened room, my heart thumping great drumbeats against my ribs, wondering why such a fierceness of longing could not be seen, a white iridescence like the spectral fire of marsh-gas, hovering over me where I lay. And yet I was too young —not yet a grown woman—and because of that he stayed away from the house, and left me to my despair.

———————

After breakfast on the fourth day of my vigil I went as usual to my aunt's bedroom to ask after her health—by now walking and speaking like an automaton. I found Aunt Grace in excellent spirits, sitting up in bed in a blue worsted dressing-gown, curl-papers sprouting at her temples from her ruched cambric nightcap, an empty breakfast tray indicating how well she'd eaten.

As I crossed the room toward the bed she let out a little giggling shriek of embarrassment and tried feebly to gather up a cataract of snowy lace and pink silk ribbons which lay across the coverlet.

"A new dress, Aunt Grace?" I was puzzled by her frantic attempts to hide it. Normally she was eager to show off anything the dressmaker had delivered as soon as it arrived.

"Well—not exactly a *dress,* dear." Aunt Grace teased out a tiny, extravagant corner for my benefit. "Not a dress, in so many words. It's . . . a nightgown. Now do you see?"

"Oh. Of course." Though there was no *of course* about it. My modest white cotton nightgowns cost six shillings and fourpence, covered me from neck to ankle, and were something to sleep in. This sumptuous creation of my aunt's must have cost at least ten guineas: it was pin-tucked and scalloped and piped, all in the finest cambric, flounced with an edging of lace and fastened by huge bows of pink ribbon. It looked more like a ballgown than a nightgown; a peignoir perhaps, or a *robe de chambre.*

"It's French," Aunt Grace whispered significantly, as if that ex-plained everything. And in a sudden rush of confidence she held up the fantastic garment for me to admire. "They're all the rage in Paris, so the Captain says. Well—you know what the French are like. But isn't it beautiful? Isn't it the most delicate, the most elegant night-gown you've ever seen?"

I agreed with her at once. I'd never seen anything remotely like it, and the idea of my aunt, that churchgoing paragon, wearing such a piece of French frivolity was amazing indeed. I couldn't help won-dering what her neighbor in the next pew would think if he knew that the plain woman in decent gray praying loudly beside him had recently climbed out of such a wanton garment.

My aunt seemed torn between sharing her pleasure in her new purchase and the suspicion that she shouldn't be sharing it with a young woman of seventeen quite innocent in the ways of the world. To my amazement she turned suddenly girlish and coy.

"I dread to think what your mother would say if she knew I'd shown you this." Aunt Grace's bony fingers picked at the ribboned yoke. "You must never tell her, Rachel, I beg of you. She'd wonder what on earth I was thinking of. But the nightgown is *so* beauti-ful . . ." She stroked its lacy folds. "I couldn't resist letting you peek at it."

She waited for me to say something in its praise.

"It'll be warm, at any rate." I was vaguely aware that I hadn't chosen well, since my aunt looked up at me in surprise, opening and shutting her mouth like a landed fish.

"Oh . . . very warm," she agreed after a moment. "Very warm." Then she seemed to feel that some explanation was called for, and blundered on, "It's the Captain, you see, my dear. When he comes back from these long voyages he likes to see me looking . . . nice. It pleases him, you understand. He likes . . . frills and feminine non-sense such as this. For myself, of course, I wouldn't dream of it, but a woman's duty is to please her husband. That's what the Bible tells us, after all."

In spite of many years' study of holy scripture I'd never yet noticed a reference to extravagant lace nightgowns, but my aunt doubtless knew better. *A woman's duty is to please her husband.* In bed, pre-sumably, since that was where nightgowns were worn. Something my aunt had said struck a chord in my mind, and I searched for words to frame a question. There was so much I wanted to ask, but

I knew Aunt Grace would only be scandalized by my boldness and would pack me off at once to my own room to purge my mind until I was once more fit for her company.

Instead, I tried to approach the subject obliquely—subtly—in a manner which only suggested innocent curiosity.

"Does a man . . ." I began hesitantly, seeing her eyebrows rise. ". . . Does a man *love* his wife more when she takes such trouble?" It wasn't really what I wanted to know, but it was enough to shock Aunt Grace.

"There! I knew I should never have shown it to you! Unmarried young ladies, my dear, have no need to ask such things. You'll find out in God's good time, I've no doubt, if you lead a blameless life and say your prayers every night without fail."

Then my aunt tittered again, and her severity collapsed. Picking up the nightgown, she hugged its marvelous flounces to her spare bosom and smiled smugly down at herself. Then she wagged a warning finger in my direction.

"One day, Rachel, you'll have a husband of your own, and you'll discover that sometimes a man likes a little pretty nonsense waiting for him at home. There isn't a man born who doesn't appreciate a few frills, believe me. And that's all I shall say on the subject, however much you may ask, my lady!"

Folding the lacy cascades of the nightgown with a knowing smile, Aunt Grace hopped out of bed to lay it reverently in the top drawer of her huge mahogany wardrobe.

For the rest of that long, empty day I was left to think about what I'd learned. Aunt Grace, afraid of a relapse, kept to her room, leaving me to my hours of solitude in the drawing room, afraid even to go upstairs to play with Harry in the nursery in case Adam should call and no one come to find me.

I was too disturbed to read. Instead I sat with my crumpled piece of embroidery where I could watch the street outside and the steps leading up to the front door, trying by sheer willpower to make that familiar tall figure materialize beyond the area railings and walk steadily toward the house. But late afternoon came, and he'd still not arrived.

By seven in the evening I'd come to a great decision, and to mark it I laid down my stitching at last, burying my needle deep in the linen fabric. Please God I should never see those three embroidered roses again.

In spite of the coldness of the night, the courtyard of Adam's hotel was crowded when I arrived, thronged with men who'd gathered in groups to chat and smoke cigars. Postboys lounged grandly round the archway, flicking their whips and drawing admiring glances from a scattering of ragged children. Porters in leather aprons dragged trunks noisily across the flagged court, and here and there a pale-faced woman in a bright shawl strolled among the throng, exchanging winks or nudges with old acquaintances.

I was unfamiliar with the ways of hotels: I'd no idea what to do next, but at last I noticed a man in a black waistcoat and shirtsleeves leaning against the wall under one of the flaring lamps, a stained clay pipe thrust into the corner of his mouth. He seemed utterly unconcerned by the milling caps and beaver hats and greatcoats, the squeal of the hand-carts and the mist of hot breath rising up around the lamps. He was so entirely at ease, scratching his unshaven chin as he solemnly regarded the scene before him, that after watching him for a few moments I decided he must be one of the hotel servants.

"I'm Mrs. Gaunt," I announced as confidently as I could. "I'd arranged to meet my husband here, but the London coach was late, and he may not be expecting me now until tomorrow."

The man prized himself slowly off the wall and looked me cautiously up and down. But any suspicion in his mind was lulled by the sight of my quietly expensive clothes and the matronly portmanteau I'd brought with me. After a second's hesitation he went so far as to remove the pipe from his mouth.

"Mr. Gaunt, Ma'am? He didn't tell us to look out for you, certainly, but I daresay he didn't expect you to come at this hour. In fact, I'm sure I saw Mr. Gaunt go out, Ma'am, not above an hour ago. He gen'rally does about this time, but I should think he'll be back afore long." The man gestured to a pillared doorway nearby. "The girl will take you up to his room."

I'd counted on Adam's being away from the hotel. I'd long since absorbed every detail of his daily routine, but I held my breath all the same as the servant-girl knocked at the door of his room, and only let it out in a long sigh when there was no answering voice from inside and the door was thrown open for me to enter as if I'd a perfect right to be there. In my relief at the success of the first part of my plan I even managed to thank the maid before walking firmly into the room and dropping the latch into place at my back.

It was eight o'clock when I arrived at the hotel, expecting Adam to return in half an hour or so. But at eleven I was still waiting.

In the meantime, by the light of the fire blazing in the grate and a branched candelabrum I'd lit when I arrived, I'd had ample time to memorize every scratch and score on the round rosewood table in the center of the room, every twist of the fire-dogs, every sagging stitch in the chair-seats of that once elegant apartment.

Two of Adam's books lay on the cupboard next to the bed and another on the washstand nearby. The poems of Catullus in Latin, and another book full of strange symbols which I took to be Greek: I touched them gently as if the leather covers might still be warm from his hand. But there was little else to indicate whose room it might be, except for a battered leather valise in one corner and a shirt thrown hastily over the back of one of the chairs.

I waited. And as the hours passed with no more than distant noise from the yard and the clump of heavy boots in a room overhead, I peered into the empty clothespress and poked the fire again and again. I even gingerly examined the dusty hangings of the bed—remembering my aunt's remarks on the insect life to be found in city hotels. But there was no more than the first tentative guy-ropes of a spider's web and a pocket of withered flies in a fold of the flowered brocade.

I didn't want any more time to think. In the drawing room at Leghorn Street I'd thought and thought until my brain was dizzy: at last I'd made up my mind, and I was afraid that as the blank hours passed my resolve would weaken. Though it never did. Even when every passing minute made my crime more unpardonable, I never considered retreat. At eight I could have changed my mind and bolted back to a frosty welcome in Leghorn Street; at eleven—and later—I'd gone beyond the possibility of salvation. I caught sight of myself in the spotted mirror above the washstand, and almost gasped in fright. For a second in the shadows I saw my mother's face, set and determined, the eyes glowing with an unearthly light.

Countless pairs of feet had tramped past the door by the time I heard Adam's distinctive step approaching. The footfalls grew louder until he halted in the corridor outside; just beyond the pool of light round the fire I saw a gleam of metal as the brass handle turned slowly in his hand with the faintest of clicks. Then the door swung open, and there was no longer any going back.

Adam hesitated in the doorway, puzzled by the unexpected candle-light.

"Who's there?" I saw him shade his eyes with his hand, but a sudden panic gripped me, stifling speech.

"God in Heaven! Rachel—is that you?"

I'd known it was unfair of me, but it was all I could think of at the time; and I was desperate—desperate to convince him that I would make the perfect wife, that I could be everything a man might desire in a woman, if he would only give me a chance. I'd taken the nightgown, the monstrous nightgown in all its frilled white lace and pink ribbons, from my aunt's wardrobe while she dozed after dinner, and brought it with me in my borrowed portmanteau. It was too big for me in every way, and far too long, but I'd put it on nevertheless, combed out my hair in dark waves over my shoulders, and perched myself on the end of the huge posted and canopied bed in what I hoped was a languid and alluring pose.

What else could I have done? If the nightgown made Aunt Grace a vision of loveliness in the Captain's eyes, might it not do the same for me? All I wanted was to be irresistible, and no longer too young.

I don't know what I expected Adam to do, but it wasn't to stare at me in amazement from the doorway as if the ceiling of his room had just fallen in. I jumped to my feet, ruining the effect, realized what I'd done, and tried—too late—to smooth down the thousand flounces of the nightgown which had somehow become wound round my legs, threatening to engulf me at any minute.

Still he said nothing, but stood, astounded, just over the threshold. Then after a moment he seemed to remember that the door stood open, providing a fine spectacle for any passerby; without taking his eyes from me he kicked the door shut behind him, and leaned back against it with a weary sigh. I tried hard to read his thoughts from the expression on his face: annoyance, certainly—and compassion —and yes, affection too. Of that I was certain.

"You have courage, I'll give you that," he said at last, taking a step forward into the room. Then he seemed to lose patience with me, and his voice became hard.

"Rachel—what in God's name are you doing here? Have you gone completely mad?"

I was so startled by his anger that I took a couple of quick steps backward, stood on the hem of the nightgown and sat down smartly as I collided with the end of the big, high bed. This wasn't at all what

I'd intended. My plans had become vague at this point, dissolving into a romantic mist of joyful reunion, followed by . . . whatever was supposed to take place. But instead of sweeping me up into his arms, Adam had begun to interrogate me like a silly child caught in some act of disobedience.

"I had to see you, Adam. You wouldn't come to the house—what was I to do?"

"I've had no time for social calls. You must have realized that."

"I thought perhaps, after our quarrel that night . . ." I didn't dare to finish the sentence.

"Yes, I admit that had something to do with it. After I realized what you were thinking of . . . Well, I thought I'd better leave you alone to come to your senses. Unfortunately that doesn't seem to have happened. But Rachel—coming here alone in the middle of the night? What on earth put this mischief into your head?"

I could feel hot tears pricking my eyes, but I was determined not to cry.

"I can't believe you'd be so stupid! Still—there's no time to deal with that now. We have to find a way of getting you out of this mess you've contrived. Who else knows you're here? It's almost midnight, but it might still be possible to take you back to Leghorn Street without anyone finding out where you've been."

"It's too late for that. The servants will know I've gone by now. Aunt Grace was asleep, but I left her a note."

"Your aunt won't be anxious to tell anyone."

"No, I don't suppose she will, since I'm now a 'fallen woman' in her eyes. But the servants will talk, and the people in the hotel here have seen me. The story will get out, one way or another. I am, as they say, thoroughly compromised. Perhaps if you'd come back sooner . . . But not at this hour."

I spoke bitterly, but I knew I'd only myself to blame for my disgrace. My splendid plan had gone disastrously astray—that was all. I'd been stupid to come. I'd made a fool of myself, and my evening's escapade would probably cost me dear in the future, though at that moment I didn't care what might happen next day or next year; all I could think of was that I'd now lost Adam for good, through my own stupidity.

Adam had moved to the window. He stood there, staring out, leaning stiff-armed against the wooden frame as if the answer to his problem might somehow be written across the night sky.

"Is this what you intended all along?" He didn't turn, as if he found it hard to look me in the eye and ask the question.

"Is this what you wanted—to risk ruining your life by this adventure, in the hope that I'd come to your rescue? Was this some kind of blackmail? Because if so, Rachel, you've chosen the wrong man for your little game, I promise you that."

The worn boards of the floor were mellow gold between my bare feet as I sat miserably on the end of the bed—too miserable even to resent such an unjust suspicion.

"That never occurred to me. Not for a second. Because I never thought you'd send me away. I only wanted you to realize I'm a woman now, not the child you remember. A woman, Adam! A woman you could *love,* if you'd only give yourself a chance!"

I waited, but he said nothing.

"My aunt never leaves us alone for a moment these days, and I could never speak to you—and soon you'll be gone forever, and I can't even bear to think about that. And so I came . . . To be here when you came back. To prove I'm a woman, not a child any longer."

I heard a great sigh from the direction of the window, but still Adam didn't turn toward me, as if he couldn't look at me and say what had to be said.

"Rachel—you say you want me to treat you as a grown woman. Very well, let's be honest with one another. First of all, no matter what you may believe, I don't love you. Not in the way you want me to, at any rate. I doubt if I'm even capable of it."

"But you're fond of me, aren't you? I've seen it in your eyes, sometimes, when you smile at me. And that's enough, Adam, really. Perhaps it will grow into more in the future, if you let it."

"And secondly"—he went on, ignoring me—"I've no idea how I'll live when I reach St. Louis. In the last few years I've spent most of my time out in the wilds, living in places where there are no white women for hundreds of miles—nothing but Indians, animals and men that are little better than animals. I've been filthy most of the time, and cold and hungry at least some of the time. Even if you could stand living like that, I couldn't spare the hours to look after you. I'm sorry, but that's the truth."

"If it's so hard, then why do you do it?"

"It's the only life I know. And . . . well, there are other reasons I can't even begin to explain, because I don't understand them myself. But you can see, surely, that it's no life for a woman."

There was nothing I could say, and so I said nothing.

"And there's another thing you don't seem to have thought of before you came running down here tonight. What do you know about me?" He swung round to look at me at last. "Well? I stayed in your home once—almost ten years ago when you were a child. A shipwrecked man! That was my pedigree—no more than that. I could be a murderer or a thief for all you know. Who are my family? Perhaps I have a wife already, have you thought of that?"

A great stone turned over inside me. "But you said . . . You said *if you had needed a wife* . . . I understood you weren't married." My voice seemed to dwindle to a whisper. "Do you have a wife?"

"No, I don't. But you had no right to assume it." He gazed at me in perplexity. "Rachel—you were out of your mind to come here tonight like this! To trust yourself to a man you know nothing whatever about—"

"But I do! I know all I need to know about you!"

"No, Rachel, you don't. Great Heavens, you're only a girl! I'm eighteen years older than you, do you realize that?"

"What difference does it make? My singing-master has a pupil of my age who's just married a man even older with the blessing of her parents. *And* she has no love for him, because she told me so. Though everyone says it's a wonderful match."

"Dancing-masters . . . singing-masters . . . Oh, Rachel, what are we going to do with you?" Adam cast his eyes up to Heaven with a gesture of despair.

I watched him from the bed, leaning my flushed cheek against the coolness of one of the great carved posts, my arm encircling its turned knobs and spirals. The smooth-grained surface was silken to the touch, and my fingers followed the carving of their own accord, seeking out its swellings and hollows as if here, at least, was something solid and responsive in a world gone sadly adrift.

Adam's eyes followed the movement for a few seconds, and then he glanced away.

"Plenty of men would take what you're offering, and throw you out into the street next day."

"Would you do that?"

"Not to you. Don't ask me why."

"Why not to me?"

"Perhaps because I'm as big a fool as you are."

"But you do . . . want me?" I didn't even know the words. "You know what I mean."

"If you mean do I want to take you to bed right here and now, and put an end to that innocence shining in your face—then yes, God help me, I do. No doubt I'd be damned for it, but it makes no difference. Rachel—I wanted you from the first moment I saw you in your aunt's drawing room, even before the MacDonalds told me who you were. You've turned into a beautiful young woman, though I sometimes wonder if you realize it. And now—sitting there half-naked on my bed . . . What on earth do you expect? Of course I want you!"

I'd known it, somehow, even as he tried to seem cold toward me. I must have sensed it, not in my mind but in some deeper, less controllable part of me, and a wild joy began to flow through my veins like a warm tide, making my heart beat to a new rhythm.

"Then—"

"No. Not tonight. Not ever."

"But why not? Oh, Adam—why not?" I was on my feet now, taking a step toward him, all the longing I'd ever felt welling up in me like a desperate hunger for the man who stood not six feet away, staring at me as if I were an assassin coming for his life.

"Because the price is too high, Rachel! Because you want to chain yourself to me for the rest of your life and mine. We'd only make one another unhappy."

He thrust both hands into the pockets of his coat as I reached him, as if he didn't trust them to obey his will.

"I won't be a burden to you, Adam, I promise." I was near enough now to twine my fingers round the tiny buttons of his waistcoat.

"You don't understand what I'm talking about."

"I want to understand. About you—about everything. Don't you see—that's why I came here."

"Is that what this . . . nightgown . . . is all about?" Of its own accord, one of his hands escaped from its pocket and began, gently to disentangle a twisted pink ribbon at my throat.

"Is it quite hideous?"

"Hideous. Where on earth did you find it?" Somehow his left hand joined its fellow among the clustered ribbons which held the nightgown across my breasts.

"It's my aunt's. She bought it to wear for the Captain."

"And you took it. To wear for me."

"Yes."

For a long moment there was silence.

"Take it off."

That was all he said, and for a second I thought I'd misheard him. Then I looked down, and saw his long-jointed brown fingers enmeshed in the tangle of ribbons like sinewy jungle beasts in a net of silk. And I longed—oh, so much—to feel those hands caress me, strong and cool on the warmth of my flesh . . .

The nightgown slid easily from my shoulders, an ebbing wave of lace, as I reached up to him. His eyes were dark and opaque as he bent to kiss me, to hold me at last with the closeness of my dreams, arched against him like a drawn bow. Gloriously—unbearably—his fingers descended the downy cleft of my spine until Aunt Grace's nightgown finally slipped to the floor with a long, regretful sigh.

Now there was no shame in lying, naked and languid, in the shadows of the canopied bed, my arms flung out above my head, my hair spread like a dark stain in the light of the single guttering candle which remained. For the first time I discovered the pleasure of cool air on flushed skin—and of a body aching with a strange, blissful, unfocused yearning.

I'd never seen a grown man naked before. Until then my mind had fed only on the memory of the pale, quicksilver limbs of the boys at the swimming-hole, dappled like gangling fawns in the leafy sunlight of the overhanging trees. But this honey-colored man was something beyond imagining, and I delivered myself up to his strength with the gladness of a woman who knows she has won her war.

———

He loved me. He'd denied it, but I was sure of it, after that. How could he have behaved as he did, and not loved me?

And afterward, lying in the canopied gloom of that vast bed amid the scent of dead candles, I tried desperately to stay awake, not to lose a second of the luxury of his arms about me, the faint burned-wood smell of his skin and his quiet breathing.

Adam was awake, silent and staring at nothing, and I wondered vaguely what he was thinking. Perhaps he'd have told me in time. Perhaps he even tried to tell me—I can't remember. All I know is that I lost my battle against overwhelming drowsiness, and there, held safely against his side, I fell fast asleep.

8

On 17th March, 1837, the marriage service was read over us, Aunt Grace's permission being accepted *in loco parentis*.

"Permission" was hardly the word for it. My aunt had agreed to the match in guilty haste, almost fainting with relief when she discovered Adam was actually prepared to marry me and save the shreds of my ruined future. She'd been certain he would simply go on his way, leaving her to salvage the awful consequences of her meddling.

By the time she'd glanced at her pocket-watch on that fateful evening and realized I hadn't come to her room to share her evening prayers, it was already too late. My bed and my room were both empty, but on my pillow was a folded paper addressed to her, though there was no need for her to read it to know where I'd gone. She could guess that only too easily. I'd run off—shameless girl that I was—run off in my stolen finery to throw myself at a vagabond stranger.

By then it was eleven o'clock. What could be gained by going after me at that hour? The damage was already done, the act of folly no doubt committed. Why, oh why was Captain Fuller at sea, when my aunt needed him so badly?

She lay awake for the rest of that night, reproaching herself for having put the idea into my head in the first place, for having shown me the sinful nightgown, for having encouraged Adam Gaunt to visit the house for her own unworthy purposes . . . and a thousand other things she imagined had added to the disaster. When Adam and I returned to Leghorn Street next morning, Aunt Grace certainly looked as if she hadn't slept at all. She was in a great state of agitation, torn between a desire to scold me for what I'd done and guilt for her own part in my escapade.

We arrived later than we'd intended. The sheer strangeness—and the voluptuous joy—of waking up alongside Adam, of lying there naked and unwed while a manservant went impassively about his business of cleaning out the grate on the other side of the room . . . It was all so outrageously immoral that—well, in the end it was almost eleven o'clock before we rose from our huge posted bed, dressed hurriedly and set off to confront my aunt.

We were, after all, to be married. At least that was something—I was fortunate, wailed Aunt Grace, that any man wanted me after the way I'd behaved. No—she didn't want explanations or excuses. It was just as bad if nothing had taken place as if *the worst* had happened. My reputation had been in tatters from the moment I reached Adam's hotel—foolish, worthless girl. What would that refined young man Philip Clark think of me now?

And the foolish, worthless girl stood before her, radiantly happy, not caring one whit for anything Philip Clark might think. I was going to be Adam's wife, and he would take me with him to the United States of America: nothing and no one could spoil my blissful state that day.

Except that my aunt went on, and on. Adam came in for his share of the blame, though a good deal less than mine, and bore Aunt Grace's scolding for a while with great patience. Then without raising his voice at all he said, "What's done is done. I think we should leave it at that, don't you?"

And something in the way he spoke made my aunt decide she'd said enough, though I could tell she was only just getting into her stride.

I wanted to be married at once, as simply as possible, but Aunt Grace wouldn't hear of it. *That,* she said, would be as good as announcing that some immorality had taken place. And so I was married in blond lace and orange-blossom like the virgin I wasn't, with Adam in black at my side, very thoughtful and grave.

And all through the ceremony, my aunt claimed later, the crucified Christ above the altar seemed to gaze sternly down at her in silent rebuke for having tampered with the emotions of an innocent girl.

Her worst punishment was still to come. Somehow Aunt Grace would have to find words to explain the catastrophe in a letter to my mother, a task she was dreading. Thank Heavens her sister was far away across the Atlantic Ocean, unaware of the disaster Grace had brought about. . . .

Yet Adam and I had been man and wife for only four days and

were due to sail for America in another three when the *Minotaur,* with my mother aboard, reached Liverpool. My mother flew straight to Leghorn Street, where her imperious knocking at Aunt Grace's door brought a servant at a run to open up. My aunt, pausing in the hall to know who on earth was assaulting her door in such a manner, saw to her horror the small, fierce figure of her sister Susannah framed in the portal.

Seconds after the drawing-room door closed upon the two of them, the servants in the basement kitchen heard a shrill scream of fury echo through the house. Not a soul went to investigate, though when I arrived at the front door, quite unaware of the drama taking place inside, even the cook and the groom were standing white-faced in the hall, wondering whether someone should inquire if all was well with their mistress.

I'd gone to Leghorn Street with a porter from the hotel to collect the last of my trunks, leaving Adam to write a few necessary letters. I had no way of knowing that my mother had left St. John's almost as soon as she'd read her sister's letter and had crossed an ocean in the fastest available vessel in order to drag me home before my ill-conceived romance could go any further.

———

"Oh, Miss Rachel—Ma'am—thank goodness it's you—" The cook was almost in tears as she explained what had happened.

My first instinct was to turn tail and run as fast as I could back to Adam and safety. But what might have done for Rachel Dean would certainly not do for Mrs. Adam Gaunt. Sooner or later I would have to face my mother and hear her judgment on my crime; at least by confronting her now I would draw some of her anger from my unfortunate aunt. And all she could know was that I was married and happy—not how the marriage had come about. I could be grateful for that small mercy.

But when I made my way, unannounced, into the drawing room, one look at the expression on my mother's face told me she knew the whole story. To save herself from her sister's wrath, Aunt Grace had babbled it all out, everything that had happened since Adam Gaunt first set foot in her house a few months earlier. Now she was slumped, weeping bitterly, on a footstool in front of the hearth where my mother stood over her, fists clenched, almost as if she was about to strike her sister. As I rushed into the room she turned, furious at the interruption; and then a look of utter contempt came into her face as she saw who was the cause of the intrusion.

"You!" She stalked across the floor toward me. "You . . . *slut!*"

Her hand flashed out in a vicious slap, but I was too quick for her, and parried the blow. I heard a shriek from my aunt behind her.

"No, Susannah—you mustn't!"

"Don't you tell me what I mustn't do! Imbecile! If you'd told this —this little whore—what she *mustn't* do, instead of filling her head with a lot of nonsense about dresses and hats, things would never have come to such a pass!"

"Oh, Rachel, I'm so sorry!" wailed my aunt. "She made me tell her! I couldn't help it!"

"I understand, Aunt Grace. Don't be upset."

"Oh, yes, Grace, we all understand," mimicked my mother nastily. "Don't trouble your stupid head about it. My daughter's run off with a vagrant, thanks to you—but don't give it another thought."

Aunt Grace began to sob once more, her bony fingers holding a ridiculously tiny handkerchief to her eyes. Ignoring my mother, I went to her and knelt down at her side.

"Don't blame yourself, Aunt Grace. It wasn't your fault. How could you have known what I meant to do?"

"She should have locked you up!" hissed my mother. "She should have locked you in your room and made sure there was no way *that man* could speak to you, or write to you, or communicate with you at all. Adam Gaunt, of all men!" Her eyes glittered. "Your great hero! At Crow Cove you followed him round like a dog; I suppose when he found you here he only had to snap his fingers and—"

"That's unfair!"

"Is it? You're a poor, pathetic fool, Rachel. You'll always be the dupe of any clever man. I should have known, after your adventure with the Ellis boy, that you'd fall into bed with the first good-looking scoundrel to catch your eye."

"What adventure? What Ellis boy?" Aunt Grace looked up suddenly, her eyes red and round with surprise. "You never told me."

My mother ignored her completely.

"I came here as fast as I could travel to save you from your own folly. But what did I find? Rachel, the blushing bride! The bride with plenty to blush about, from what I hear!"

"I'm not ashamed of anything I've done. You can say whatever you like! If you'd been any kind of mother to me at all—"

My anger was rising to match hers. If she had ever—even once—shown me any genuine affection, I might have felt some guilt for having deceived her. But now, as Adam's wife, I was free of her control at last, and the knowledge dispelled the last of my fear. I could stare back into her face as fiercely as she glared at me.

"I was no more to you than one of your insurance policies! An investment! Something that might bring a decent return at the end of the day, if you struck a good bargain! Well, I'm no longer your chattel, to be disposed of as you please. I'm a married woman now, and I answer to my husband and no one else."

I expected some biting retort, but my mother remained silent, her face a mask. It was almost as if she'd mastered her rage, for her voice when she spoke was honey-smooth, but I knew from past experience that after the height of such a storm came a deceptive calm no less vicious and destructive.

"Well, well . . ." My mother drew back a pace and looked me slowly up and down. "So you're a fine married lady now, with your whalebone stays and your pretty gowns. Very fetching! And a paisley shawl . . . Quite the fashion, I see. And do you happen to remember who paid for it all, by any chance? Who was it gave you the money for everything, from the braid on your bonnet to the buttons on your shoes? Why, *I* did! Your cruel, heartless mother provided it all!" Suddenly her voice cut like a whiplash. "You were happy to make free with my money while it suited you, Miss. Did you think I intended to finance your love-making with a beggar?"

"Don't speak of—" I began, but she ignored me.

"You let me feed and clothe you—and all the time you were making up to that wastrel, that shiftless fortune-hunter, behind my back!"

"Adam's no fortune-hunter!"

"Oh, isn't he? I wonder . . . Let's see what he has to say to *this,* then! Since you saw fit to marry without my consent, Rachel, you may shift for yourself from now on. That's the first thing I have to tell you. From today I have no more interest in you. Your admirable husband bedded you fast enough—let him support you too from now on. If he thinks he's married a wealthy young wife, he's made a sad mistake. You'll have no more of my money to spend so freely."

"Adam knows I shall have very little."

"Very little! You'll have nothing at all! Not a single penny-piece! How d'you like that, dear daughter? You've nothing more than the clothes in your trunks and what you can raise by your own wits. That's the fate of girls who marry without their parents' permission."

"Would you ever have given your permission?" I demanded hotly.

"Agreed to your marrying Adam Gaunt? I'd have kept you locked up for the rest of your life sooner than see you with that man!"

"Susannah!" exclaimed my aunt, shocked. "How can you—"

This time both of us ignored her.

"You'd have married me off to some swaggering bully in St. John's," I shouted then, "simply to get free credit from his father's bank! Married me off, to be as miserable as you are. Well, you can keep your precious money, Mrs. Dean—I wouldn't touch it!"

I was on the point of losing my temper entirely. I wrenched at the gold chain round my neck, breaking the clasp in my passion, and threw it at her. It caught on one of the buttons of her dress, and swung there for a moment until my mother snatched it angrily away.

"I have Adam—and that's all I want!"

"So you have Adam, do you? Well, I wish you joy of your husband, *Mrs. Gaunt*—for as long as you can keep him. Without money, what use are you to him? He'll be sick of you inside twelve months, and he'll run off and leave you to go to the Devil. You needn't come sniveling to me when it happens, either."

"Adam would never do that. I know he wouldn't."

"You're sure of that, are you?" A grim smile lit her face. "Tell me then, since you know so much about this man you've chosen to marry . . . What is his father's name? Who are his family? Has he ever told you that?"

He hadn't, though we were four days married, and I was only too aware of the unanswered questions which remained between us. I'd kept reminding myself that it was Adam I'd married and not his family, and therefore it made no difference who his parents might have been. But he'd been so evasive that I couldn't stop thinking about the mystery. With her unerring instinct for any hint of weakness, my mother had pounced on my confusion.

"Adam told me he was born in Norfolk," I said defensively. "His father is—a Mr. Gaunt of Norfolk, I presume."

My mother hooted derisively. "He hasn't told you! I thought as much!"

"There's nothing more I need to know."

"Oh, but there is. You see, I made it my business to find out more about our shipwrecked friend after he stayed with us in Crow Cove that summer. I wrote letters to people in England who have ways of hunting out secrets. Shall I tell you what I know about him, this fine husband of yours?" Her eyes narrowed with malice. "Don't you want to know whether he was sired in the marriage-bed or in some farmer's haystack? Or by some passing gypsy who stopped to mend a pot and found a warm welcome in the kitchen?"

I should have said *No. I won't listen. I don't want to hear another word. Adam will tell me what he wants me to know,* but I couldn't utter a sound. Instead, I heard my aunt protesting feebly at her sister's forthrightness, and to my face, with unholy glee, my mother repeating a single word.

"A bastard. That's what your husband is. *A bastard.* Illegitimate."

"That's a lie! You couldn't have found that out!"

"Oh, yes, I could—because his father is the old earl of Wellborough, and noblemen's bastards are rather better known than the casual, run-of-the-mill sort of trash that other men father. *Gaunt* is the Wellboroughs' family name—which is as much as he got from them, by all accounts. His mother was some skivvy in the house, some slattern from the kitchen who caught his lordship's eye, I daresay—"

I'd heard enough.

"And what makes you think I'm proud of my own family?" I roared at her. "What do I have to boast about? A drunken father, and a mother who thinks of nothing but money! Just about fit company for the kitchen maid's bastard, wouldn't you say—Mother?"

By the fireside, my aunt gave a great wail.

"You ungrateful little viper!" My mother almost spat the words. "My hard work put food in your stomach and a roof over your head —and this is the way you thank me for it! One day you'll realize, my lady, that your fine romantic ideas of love don't count for the mud on your boots when you've nothing to eat and your children go in rags. The day you see a child of yours go hungry, you'll sing a different tune."

"Adam will never let that happen!"

"Oh, won't he? Unless he's long gone, leaving you in some wretched hole in the wilderness without a penny to your name. One of his red-skinned savages will take your place, and he'll be just as content. But of course, you know about his taste in women!"

"Get away from me! I've heard enough of your wicked lies!"

"Oh, never fear—you've set eyes on me for the last time. Since your family isn't good enough for you now . . . from today you *have* no family—no mother, no father, and no home under my roof. Don't come to St. John's—I'll turn you away. Don't write—I'll burn your letters. I hope I never have to look at your deceitful face again."

My mother took a deep breath. "I'd have seen you in your grave sooner than married to that man. Anyone but him! But since it's too late to undo what's been done, you're as good as dead to me now, Rachel. Remember that."

The door banged behind her, and she was gone.

———

When two hours had passed and I hadn't returned to the hotel, Adam came to Leghorn Street to find me.

That was the worst part—worse even than facing my mother or trying to comfort Aunt Grace after she'd gone. Because I'd found out Adam's secret, and I was hurt that he hadn't told me himself. If he'd said nothing, it could only be because he imagined I'd think less of him when I knew. And yet the more I thought about it all, the less it seemed to matter. I didn't care about his birth; I genuinely didn't care.

After all—if Adam hadn't married me as I'd hoped, I might already have been carrying his bastard child, bringing down shame on the head of a blameless baby. Why should Adam inherit the burden of his father's sins? But I still wished he'd told me, all the same, and my anxious efforts to hide what I knew only made my discomfort more obvious.

My aunt was upstairs, resting behind drawn curtains, and I was alone in the drawing room when Adam arrived.

He pulled me to him, there before the drawing-room fire, and I hid my face in his shoulder so that he couldn't see the guilt in my eyes. Somehow, in jumbled phrases and mixed-up sentences, I managed to give him an account of what my mother had said—her fury at my disobedience, her bitter abuse of my aunt, and her promise to cut me off entirely from my brothers and my sister. I'd been stunned by the immensity of her anger, and I found it hard to explain. A great pent-up hatred had been released that day—hatred of Adam as much as of me. Was my mother insane? Surely the harmless friendship they'd enjoyed in Crow Cove was long since forgotten: could she not give him up, even now?

Adam listened in silence to my muddled tale as I poured out what I could remember of her words . . . Everything but the part which concerned him most.

"She's left me with nothing, Adam. No settlement, no money—nothing at all."

"Did you expect anything else?"

"I thought, perhaps, when she'd grown accustomed to the idea . . ."

"She'll never accept you as my wife, I promise you. And she'll never forgive us for this—neither you nor me, as long as we live."

"Is it so awful to marry the man you love?"

"Not if you fall in love with the right man. If I were Governor of the Bank of England your mother might find room in her heart for me. But a penniless nobody is hardly her idea of the perfect match."

"But you aren't a nobody! You're—" I stopped, about to trespass on forbidden territory.

"What am I? What were you going to say?"

"Nothing. I've forgotten."

"No you haven't. What did your mother say about me?"

"Some nonsense about your being a beggar. . . ."

"And worse than that, I imagine."

"Other things too. But they were all lies."

"Such as?" His arms had tightened around me, and I could feel the tension in his body. "Rachel—your mother said something else about me, something which has made a difference between us. I can feel it. You're upset and unhappy, and I want to know what she said. Tell me."

"It was nothing important, Adam—honestly."

"Important enough to distress you, all the same."

"I'm not distressed."

"Look at me and say that."

"No . . . I can't."

"Look at me, Rachel."

"Adam—please!"

"I want to see your face."

With a finger under my chin he tilted my face up toward his own, and my last pretense was at an end.

"She found out . . . about your father. And your mother."

"Ah . . . that." He let out his breath in a long sigh. "You'll never make a liar, Rachel, you're far too honest for that."

"I'm sorry, Adam. I tried not to tell you."

"If anyone's sorry, it should be me. I ought to have been straight with you before we were married—I should have told you what sort of man you'd thrown yourself away on. I did mean to tell you everything—and then you looked up at me with those huge, worshiping eyes and I kept putting it off for another day. It isn't easy to be a hero, Rachel; you've no idea how hard it can be."

"Adam, I'm sorry," I said again. It was all I could think of.

"Sorry for me?"

"Sorry I found out this way."

"Oh."

"Adam—will you tell me now? Since it doesn't matter anymore. My mother said very little, except that you were—"

"A bastard."

"The son of the Earl of Wellborough. That was all. Please tell me the rest."

"Very well." He was looking over my head now, toward the narrow strip of sky beyond the drawing-room windows.

"My father's name is Henry Gaunt, as you've heard. My mother was a woman called Ann Rainey, the daughter of one of my father's tenants, and Lady Wellborough's maid. And there you have it—born on the wrong side of the blanket. A by-blow. A *natural son,* the history books would call me. But a bastard all the same."

"Adam, I'd love you if you were the son of the Devil himself, don't you know that?"

"Perhaps that's exactly what I am."

"You're the son of an earl and his countess's lady's-maid—and I think it's very romantic. It doesn't matter at all, believe me."

"Oh, my innocent love, it matters a great deal! At least, it does here in England, where a man's family is his fortune. But you're right —it makes no odds at all in America. Nobody there asks where you come from, or why. You'll meet all sorts of jailbirds and remittance men . . . perfect company for a well-brought-up young woman."

"Adam, you know what my parents' house was like. Papa was drinking by the time you stayed with us, and well . . . ."

For a moment the echo of my mother's physical presence haunted the room, not yet dissipated by time.

"Adam . . . do you ever see your father? Does he know of your life in America? You don't have to tell me if you don't want to. It's just that it seems strange to find an earl's son wandering in the mountains."

"I wasn't raised as an earl's son while Lady Wellborough was alive. That would never have done. And in any case, I've only spoken to my father twice in the last sixteen years. We've very little to say to one another, he and I.

"My mother's people brought me up until I was ten years old, running wild in the Fens with the other boys. Then the countess died, and suddenly everything changed. They'd always told me my father was dead—though I'm sure all the local people knew the truth. Then one day the earl arrived on his big black horse and dragged me off to his house, shouting that no son of his, however got, was going to turn into a ruffian if he could prevent it."

"How terrible for your mother!"

"My mother was humbly grateful, believe it or not. She thought it would be a fine thing to have a proper gentleman for a son. The earl had some idea of turning me into a churchman as a sop for his own sins, the old reprobate."

"You—a parson! How could he ever have imagined it!"

"Oh, he reckoned a good beating can work wonders. He shut me up in his library with a tutor to cram Latin and Greek into my head when all I wanted was to be off across those great, flat fenlands with the rest of the boys, stalking the wild geese and feeling the wind in my face.

"And so I ran away—I don't remember how often—and every time I was fetched back and beaten again. But each time I escaped, it was harder for them to find me, and little by little I learned to keep out of sight and stay quiet as a cat at a mousehole while they searched for me. Before long I knew every bush and every tuft of grass for miles around. I could move through the water of a fen, and the ducks wouldn't even turn their heads. That's how I learned the hunter's trade. My father can hardly blame me for following it now."

"Does he mind very much that you aren't a parson?"

"My father and your mother would make a good pair. He expects everyone to do as he wants, and when they don't he flies into a rage. He's a selfish old wretch, really."

"Then you must be like your mother. Will I ever meet her, do you think?"

"My mother's dead. She died four years ago, when I was in America. One of the reasons I came back was to go to Norfolk and see about a headstone. And to upset my half-brothers and sisters a little. They prefer to forget I exist."

"What did you do to upset them?"

Above my head, I heard Adam laugh.

"I suggested that, as the mother of a Gaunt, Ann Rainey ought to be buried in the Wellborough family vault. Brother Henry almost choked on his port at the thought of a lady's-maid among the bones of his ancestors. Not that I was serious—she was too good a woman to spend eternity among a gang of medieval cutthroats. Which is exactly what I told Henry."

"Oh, Adam!"

And we laughed together, and I was certain in that moment that there were no more secrets, and that I knew my husband's heart as well as I knew my own. Which shows that I was as blind and deaf in the sublimity of my love as I'd ever been in my childhood loneliness. I believed that the rest of my life would be spent in the security of Adam's arms, that one day my mother would relent and bless our marriage, and that America—free, hospitable America—would be our land of milk and honey. Oh, I believed it! And in my blissful, besotted state I looked forward eagerly to our arrival in New Orleans.

PART TWO
The Plain

9

Thirty years earlier, so Adam told me, the lands west of the Mississippi River were known as the *Outlands* because they lay beyond the boundary of familiar territory and there were strange tales about what might be found there. Unicorns and devils were said to live in the forests; there were Amazons and pygmies, gemstone cliffs and a mountain made entirely of salt; moreover the heat was too great and the cold too fierce for men to survive. And yet—the curiosity of the human race being what it is—white men gradually began to penetrate the untamed country beyond the Father of Waters, mapping and exploring, testing the land to see if it would provide them with a living.

Gradually the Outlands were forced to give up their secrets—first their wealth of game and furs, and then the produce of their soil. The plunderers were ruthless and determined, but the rewards were never easily won. The land left its mark on the invaders, printed on the skin by sun and wind, and on the soul by unrelenting hardship.

In the early days, the only way to survive in the western mountains was to live as the Indians did, to become part of the wilderness, a two-legged animal among the rest. Literature, law or religion existed only where a man had brought them with him, and few men saw the need. Most of them lived like the beasts of the field, killing and risking death for themselves with equal unconcern, sharing out their seed and their diseases among the Indian tribes, cheerfully content amid the blood and the dirt.

Thirty years had brought town life creeping into the Outlands, putting a veneer of decency on the rawness of daily existence. Churches and schools and barrooms appeared in the river bends as farms began to dot the valleys. All of a sudden men who'd lived without sight of another white face found themselves with neighbors and a broad highway passing their doors. Some of them approved of

the change, but many of them didn't, and packed up their few belongings to move off to a less populated part of the wilderness.

They were wise to leave; their presence would have made the
respectable townsfolk nervous. Jedediah Smith, who went like Adam
to the Rockies in 1822 and returned a philosopher, later wrote that
the mountains could make a man—if he survived—no better than
"a semi-savage" for the rest of his life.

That was the part of the story which Adam never explained to me,
perhaps because it came too close to his own inner fears to be spoken
of, or perhaps because he knew he'd already told me the essence of
it many years earlier:

"The Hunter and the Ploughman—you can't have them both, and
that's the tragedy of it."

And so we arrived in New Orleans, just as the earth of the Outlands was being scored all over by the parallel tracks of the plough.

———

"Rachel—do you understand what I've been saying to you?"

"Mmmm?" I was standing at the rail of the *Sarah C. Jones* as she
loitered off the strange stilt-town of Balize at the mouth of the Mississippi River, waiting for her pilot to come alongside, and I was too
taken up with staring at the ramshackle cluster of houses to pay
much attention to what Adam had said. To tell the truth, I'd been
rather taken aback at my first view of American soil. There was very
little to see on the flat, featureless mud-banks of the Mississippi
delta, where rafts of tree-trunks lay stranded amid clumps of dismal
bulrushes and the only items of interest were the white pelicans
picking about on the sandbars. Even the green-blue of the sea had
turned to a dull mustard color as we entered upon the silty waters of
the great river.

"Have you even listened to a word I've said?"

"Of course I have! You've been telling me—once again—how
different America will be from St. John's or from the life I led in
Liverpool. Adam, you've told me the same thing a hundred times
already."

"I wish I thought you believed me." He was leaning on the rail,
his back to the shore, regarding me thoughtfully.

"But I do believe you! I do realize everything will be new and
strange at first, but I'm not afraid of that, truly I'm not. You'll see—
I'll be the perfect wife, wherever we decide to settle . . . I've been a

good wife to you so far, haven't I?" And I slipped my hand into the crook of his arm and pressed close to him so that he should understand what I meant.

"I've no complaints." But he smiled all the same, and I knew I'd won my point.

For seven weeks there had been nothing to do aboard our ship but read, walk on deck, take our meals, and make love. And for the first time I'd had Adam entirely to myself. In Crow Cove there had been my mother, and in Liverpool Aunt Grace had constantly intruded; but our fellow passengers for New Orleans had turned out to be a dull crowd, and for once I'd found it easy to keep Adam's whole attention. Bored with the sea passage, he seemed amused by the idea of turning me into a sensualist and found me a willing pupil, until my naked flesh learned to glow, unbidden, at his touch, and my body cried out for more . . .

There was . . . how can I explain it? There was a seductive danger in his love making which never failed to thrill me, a dark, restless force within him which could be temporarily appeased with passion. I soon realized there was no possibility of tedium or predictability with Adam. He could be both tender and generous, intuitive and kind—yet sometimes I was even a little afraid of him.

But as our ship put the gray northern waters behind her and flew toward the warm south, those golden, languorous hours in Adam's arms taught me all the things I'd wanted to know. I could rouse him now with a glance or a touch, quicken him as he disturbed me, flood his senses with the ecstasy of total possession until we clung to one another—soundless and satiated. And whenever he returned to his somber warnings about the hardships of the life which awaited us, that's exactly what I did.

We stepped ashore in New Orleans on the 12th of May, 1837, and it was, as Adam had promised, like no city I'd ever seen before. The very essence of romance suffused the air with the scent of tropical plants. There was a lightheartedness about this Creole community far removed from the solid burgher brick of Liverpool, a brilliance mingled with a ravishing sense of elegant decay.

We spent three days in the city—no more, since the Yellow Fever season was about to begin—exploring the narrow, crowded French streets, with their rakish verandahs, cool amid leafy blue shadow, and the cobweb of wrought-iron balconies which clung with rusty claws to the old stucco walls.

And Sunday in New Orleans! There was no solemn Sabbath kept here: Sunday was a festival. Far from closing their doors, the coffeeshops were full of gossiping groups discussing the latest duels or poring over copies of one of the city's newspapers. The market buzzed with trade, and at night even the theaters were open, both the American and the French, crowded with fashionably dressed men and women.

Oh, it was different, all right—as different as possible from staid old Liverpool. New Orleans sparkled, flicked up her skirts and flirted with the handsome, dark-eyed Creole men. What other city would prohibit marriage to a quadroon woman, but establish a district where gentlemen could formally keep their lovely, olive-skinned mistresses?

Ah, yes—and in another way New Orleans brought home to me how different this new, adopted land was from anything I'd known before . . .

The difference waited there on the pier as I came ashore; it sat high on the boxes of elegant carriages, held horses at distinguished doors, followed fair-skinned masters and mistresses along the streets. In starched dresses and bright kerchiefs, it hurried to the Cathedral on Sunday morning, shoulder-to-shoulder with the black-clad Creole women. And it finally dawned on me with bewildering suddenness when I paid a call on an up-country planter's daughter in another room of the hotel and watched her calmly lace her stays while a black footman polished the lamp-brasses on her dressing-table not four yards away.

As far as Miss Doretta Duvalier was concerned, the man simply did not exist. Not as a thinking, breathing human being, at least. And because of that, a young woman driven to crimson blushes when she was discovered, stitching her trousseau, by a male cousin, thought nothing of parading herself half-dressed in front of a negro footman.

I knew all about Liverpool's part in the slave trade. Captain Fuller had often spoken of the Guineamen of his youth, those grim vessels which left the Mersey with their holds full of brass pans and copper bars, cutlasses and gold-laced hats, bound for the slave pens of Old Calabar and Whydah. There they loaded their black cargoes for the Middle Passage to the West Indies, those "flying houses" full of displaced men, women and children, the living merchandise which had built the wealth of an English city few of them would ever see.

England had long since turned its virtuous back on the slave trade, and the only negroes I'd seen in the Liverpool streets had been seamen from the docks, taut, muscular men who strode through the city with a swagger which declared they'd take on the king himself in a fair fight. Now I was confronted with the legacy of the "flying houses," and I was perplexed by it.

There were apparently free men of color in the city, too, but the slaves I saw in New Orleans were mostly domestic servants—"house niggers" as Miss Duvalier kindly explained—who seemed well fed and smartly clothed for the most part. I never saw one beaten or abused, but at the same time there was a puzzling general assumption that a large part of the population—the enslaved black part—had neither eyes to see what went on under their noses, nor ears to hear what was openly said about them, nor minds to resent this treatment. They simply fetched and carried and did as they were bid, as if that was the role of their race in the natural scheme of things.

In the end I tackled Adam on the subject. All I said was that the slaves I'd seen so far appeared content with their lot—yet I was amazed by the sudden savagery of his reaction.

"One human being *content* to be owned by another? *Content* to be dragged away from a mother or a child and sold to the highest bidder? Rachel, do you know what you're saying?"

"I only thought—"

"After three days in a slave state you've made up your mind, have you? Though you've seen nothing of the field-hands on the plantations? You've never seen those wretched creatures bought and sold, stripped in front of a leering crowd, their teeth examined as if they were so many horses! Did you know that in Maryland and Virginia they *breed* slaves to sell down here in the cotton-fields? Breed them like sheep, for a quick profit. 'Light skin—looks well in livery—buy him for the house. That big black one will do for the sugarcane. We'll get a few months' work out of him before he's too broken to be any use.' Are you trying to tell me that isn't an *obscenity?*"

"I didn't think . . ."

"No, you didn't think. Wait till you've used your eyes for a bit before you start forming any opinions. And if you can understand how these people survive at all, then explain it to me. I look at them, bent double in the fields while some bully-boy stands over them with a stock-whip, and I wonder where they find the strength to begin each day. Put irons on my legs, and I'd be dead in a week. To be bound, body and soul, to another human being—there can be nothing worse."

And Adam looked so grim at that moment that I was shocked by the demons I'd unwittingly released. For the first time I was glad that next day we were due to leave the heat and the cloying pleasures of New Orleans for the journey upriver to St. Louis.

———

The *Southern Rose* was a lofty side-wheeler, a queen among the great throng of vessels which crowded the levee, their tall chimneys poking up into the sky, the tiers of white-painted railings forming an endless frieze along the river bank. Upriver and below were the wharves where seagoing ships loaded the produce of the south or unloaded such exotic items as cutlery, coffee and wine; but the central section of the levee next the city was the domain of the great river steamers, the unchallenged aristocrats of the Mississippi.

We'd secured the ultimate luxury aboard the *Southern Rose,* a tiny cabin with two bunks, entirely painted white inside and with room for no more than a washstand with a pitcher and basin and a minute cupboard. It was even smaller than our shipboard quarters, but as soon as I saw it I forgave Adam for his lecture on slavery. Without the cabin we'd have been separated for much of the twelve-hundred-mile journey, since the custom on these riverboats was still for the ladies and gentlemen to inhabit two huge saloons, the ladies visiting the gentlemen's saloon only for meals. I was touched by Adam's thoughtfulness, though later I began to wonder if he was perhaps as anxious to avoid the company of blustering southern majors, New Orleans gamblers and swaggering Kentuckian horse-dealers as he was to spend his time with me.

Something was troubling him, I could tell—something more than our disagreement of the previous night. By now I was accustomed to his moods of preoccupation, but watching him there at the riverboat's rail, gazing out over the swarming bustle of the levee and seeing nothing of it, I longed to ask him what the matter was.

Instead, I tried to distract him from his worries. Above our heads, twin columns of sooty smoke plumed the funnels, and the air was hot with the tart smell of burning pinewood as the *Southern Rose* got up steam for her departure.

"It can't be long now, Adam. We'll soon be off."

"What did you say?"

"I said we must be about to cast off at any moment. Look, there's the mate in the bow, waiting for a signal! Oh, Heavens, I do wish those little boys wouldn't swing from the ropes . . . And such a crowd of steamers! How will we ever slide out past all these other boats?"

"I daresay the pilot knows his business." Adam glanced at his watch, and then a moment or two later absentmindedly consulted it again.

I couldn't bear the mystery any longer.

"Adam, something's troubling you, I know it. You've been deep in thought all morning, and you've hardly said a word. Please tell me what the matter is."

"It's nothing you need bother yourself about. A small problem which will be gone by the time we reach St. Louis. That's the truth, Rachel," he added as he saw me hesitate. "There's nothing to worry about. Now keep your eye on that big boat ahead, and see how our pilot pulls us out of here like a cork out of a bottle."

At exactly half-past four in the afternoon, with much ringing of bells and horrendous oaths from the mates, the *Southern Rose*'s great paddles began to thrash the water on either side of her shallow hull, backing the boat slowly out into the sunlit stream and clear of the pack of steamers still clinging to the bank. Shaving the curving line of craft so close that I expected any minute to hear the roar of a collision, the *Southern Rose* steadily picked up speed and began to leave the city of New Orleans behind her. Gradually the square tower of the Cathedral fell away from us, then the great dome and cupola of the St. Charles Hotel and the cluster of shipping at the levee. By the time we'd passed the looming brick warehouses at the upper end of town, the *Rose* was pushing along in fine style, the flag at her jackstaff stiff and snapping in the breeze.

We were afloat on the Mississippi—sluggish and dull by day, with tons of dun-colored mud caught in its toiling stream, but by evening a wide, shining expanse taking its color from the last of the sunlight and touching every gallery and pillar of our steamer with gold.

For a while above New Orleans we passed one sugar plantation after another, the fields of cane stretching back from the river to the dark cypress swamp beyond, cradling in their midst the tall white tower of the sugar mill and the pillared, tree-shaded mansion of the

planter. Timber huts stood in a big square behind the house or in
rows parallel to the river: these were the homes of the slaves, as
Adam was careful to point out to me whenever he thought I was
becoming carried away by the idyllic beauty of the scene.

But after a while the sugar and cotton plantations became fewer,
until for mile after mile the banks were either thick with impenetrable forest or thrown up in steep, bare bluffs. Sometimes there were
other steamers to see, tearing downriver in the strong current or
making heavier weather of the upriver passage than the powerful
Rose. Our foredeck was crowded with flatboat crews returning
upriver after leaving their craft in New Orleans, and the comments
of these seasoned river-men floated up to us on the deck above
whenever we passed another vessel.

"Look at the old *Seraphina!* Slow? Couldn't pull a shad off a
gridiron! Now, the *Falcon*—that's a fast boat, that is."

"A rattler, she is too. An' the sweetest thing to steer, so they say."

"'Bout here the *Carolina* sunk, wunnit? When her boilers went
up?"

"I allow it was, friend. Left the Cap'n in the barber's chair, with
his backside hangin' over nothin' at all. Dod-dern it, that was a boat!
Now, the ol' *Sunflower*—"

The experts could keep it up for hours on end.

One by one, the stops on the river slipped past: Baton Rouge,
Natchez on its flowery bluff, Helena, reputed haunt of horse-thieves
and counterfeiters, Memphis amid its forest, and all the rest. The air
here was less oppressive than in New Orleans, though the heat was
still intense and the mosquitoes just as troublesome. But I couldn't
forget that every hour on the river was bringing us nearer to the city
of St. Louis and to a decision on where we were to live. It was harder
now to sound cheerfully confident; and though Adam and I were as
close as ever in things of the flesh, I was dismayed to sense him
slipping away from me in spirit, his mind filled with matters he
wouldn't allow me to share.

At last I understood that I'd been so taken up with the notion of
arriving in America that I'd given little thought to what would come
afterward. I began to wish I hadn't made light of Adam's warnings
about the differences between my new life and the old. Now whenever I raised the subject of our future together he answered me
absently, as if the time for dreams was past and reality was upon us.
And I loved him—oh, I loved him, enough to walk through Hell at
his heels if that was where he wished us to go.

But after five days on the Mississippi we reached St. Louis, and I still knew nothing of what was in his mind.

At first sight, the bustle along the St. Louis levee was identical to that of New Orleans except that the big steamboats were fewer and the number of flatboats and keelboats greater. Together with ponderous, low-sided sailing craft called mackinaws, these small boats were the common currency of the upper Missouri and her tributaries, where the shallow waters were inhospitable to the lordly steamers.

We went at once to the City Hotel, but it was clear that Adam could hardly wait to disappear into the streets of St. Louis to pick up the threads of his past life. The city was still the capital of the fur trade and the headquarters of any organization involved in exploring the mountain ranges to the west, except for the British Hudson's Bay Company; if there was news to be had, it would be found in St. Louis.

I had no part in his business. I waited for him in our room, looking down from the window at the throng of passersby in the street outside, wondering where in all this busy nation was a place for Rachel Gaunt.

The news, when at last it came, was bad.

"There was no reason to worry you with this before, but you might as well know it all now," Adam announced bleakly, dropping into a chair with an air of finality. It had taken him barely an hour to confirm his worst suspicions. "There's been a crash—a financial crash involving the whole country—and by sheer bad luck we were still at sea when it started. The New York banks locked their doors ten days ago when the run began, and now banks all over the country have done the same thing. Depositors are shouting for gold, and the banks won't pay it."

This was hard to comprehend. Apart from the earliest days in Crow Cove—a time I could hardly remember—money had always been available to meet any particular need. I'd never heard of banks running out of money before, and I could only assume that someone had embezzled their funds.

"Paper!" Adam informed me. "That's what's at the bottom of it. Paper money issued by banks with hardly a dollar to their names. Huge loans to farmers with the deeds to worthless land as collateral. Paper I.O.U.s no one has any intention of repaying. Then when the government announced that land must be paid for in specie—gold and silver—the bottom dropped out of land speculation. President

Jackson demanded his gold back from the banks he'd lent it to, and *hoop-la!* the whole house of cards came tumbling down. The banks shut up shop in order to pay back the President, and suddenly all the paper's worth less than a bent cent."

"Does this mean we're poor, then? Have we no money at all?"

"We're not destitute, thank Heavens, but we'd better call a halt to all this high living—riverboat staterooms and so on. The money I put into state bonds has gone for good, as far as I can see. I doubt if they're even paying interest. What I left on deposit in the bank here should be safe enough—when I can get my hands on it in good, solid dollars. So much for paper! The banks can keep their paper from now on, and I'll stick to gold. You can melt it down, bend it, wear it or fill your teeth with it, and it's still worth its weight."

He thumped his fist on the arm of the chair in annoyance. "The damnable part of it is that if I'd been here in America instead of in England, I might have seen this collapse coming and done something to save my own skin."

"But if you had been here, my love, you'd have been off in the mountains and you'd have known nothing at all about it."

"That's true enough, I suppose. And *if only* will get us nowhere. I'll just have to set about earning us a living sooner than I expected, that's all."

Here at last was my chance. "I don't mind being poor, Adam—truly I don't." I knelt down by his chair and took his hand in mine. "Aunt Grace made sure I've more clothes than I know what to do with, and there's nothing else I need. Perhaps I could even find some work to do that would pay a little."

Adam withdrew his hand. "We're hardly in the workhouse yet," he said stiffly. "Which is just as well, since I don't suppose you can remember what it's like to have nothing. Many years ago, I came to this country without a cent and I was perfectly happy. If there's nothing to steal, you've no fear of thieves. But in those days I didn't have a wife to look after, and it isn't so easy for a woman—particularly one with small idea of keeping house."

"If I wasn't here you wouldn't give this crash a second thought. That's what you're saying." I'd been so anxious not to be a burden on him that the injustice of his remarks hurt me deeply, and in spite of my efforts to prevent it, my eyes began to prickle with involuntary tears. Adam relented at once.

"But you are here," he said softly, "and I wouldn't have it otherwise. I mean that, Squirrel."

"Really and truly?"

"Of course. And if you mean what you say about being a perfect wife, you can make a start tonight. We're invited to supper with the Fur King. See if you can work your charms on old Pierre—we need a few friends of his sort."

"Who's the Fur King? How can he help us?"

"Pierre La Fontaine and his partners own the biggest fur company west of St. Louis, and he tells me he's about to buy out the others and take it all for himself. He has a steamboat on the Missouri, company forts and trading-posts, warehouses here in the city and countless brigades of trappers working for him in the mountains. Since I gave up trapping myself, I've hired out to him a few times to take his traders into the mountains and his furs back to the city. No one can move in the Rockies without La Fontaine getting to hear of it. There are other companies in the business, but I'd put money on Pierre to hold out to the last."

"He must be a clever man."

"La Fontaine? Oh, he's clever, certainly. And a good deal more besides."

———

Until that evening I'd thought St. Louis a poor shadow of fascinating New Orleans. There had been a charming indolence about the southern city and a tawdry edge to its gaiety, but all I'd seen of St. Louis made me think it industrious and dull compared with the sparkle of its southern sister.

I'd reckoned, however, without the glories of the Fur King's palace, a magnificent limestone mansion overlooking the jostling city, a house more exotically splendid than any I'd ever seen.

Here, the house declared, was permanence. Here was wealth. Not a dollar had been spared in creating this monument to the influence of the La Fontaines.

Inside, waterfalls of crystal chandeliers cascaded from the ceilings, specially imported from Europe to set off the Italian marble statuary, the antique bronzes, the gleaming, pollarded candelabra sprouting from the gilt mirrors, and yard after yard of fine silk brocade looped up as curtains and hangings. A liveried black footman showed us into a drawing room as large as a park, dotted with handsome inlaid chairs and tables, every piece reflected in the highly polished lake of its black walnut floor.

The first La Fontaine might have cut down trees for a cabin—but his sons and grandsons had established an aristocracy of fur to vie with the sugar lords or the cotton barons as the nobility of this egalitarian land. Here the step from cabin to mansion was a short one, and a man could make it with the mud still wet on his boots. What kind of country, I wondered, allowed banks to bubble up and burst and an unlettered immigrant to found a dynasty? I was still gazing around me in amazement as I walked forward at Adam's side to be presented to the Fur King.

It was impossible for any man to live up to such a house, and even Pierre La Fontaine was dwarfed by the immensity of his home. I decided he must be in his late forties or perhaps a little older, shorter than Adam but vigorous in a way that a spider is vigorous, his black, wavy hair and dark eyes proclaiming his French descent as loudly as the impeccable cut of his clothes. I'd expected someone regal and distant, but the Fur King seemed disposed to charm, curious to see at first hand this specimen of English womanhood which had fallen in his way. He fixed me with a bright, amused glance and then bowed ceremoniously over my hand.

"*Enchanté,* Madame Gaunt. I've been most anxious to meet you, ever since Adam told us he'd brought a bride to the Missouri. So you are the young woman who has trapped the hunter! *La Chasseresse même!*"

I thought I detected a hint of sarcasm, too subtle for me to be certain. Meanwhile La Fontaine's birdlike black eyes were scanning every detail of my appearance. I might have been the pelt of some hapless animal offered to him for sale.

"*Parfaitement à l'Anglaise!*" he pronounced. "Do you speak French, Madame, by any chance? No? A pity: your husband speaks it well." He turned to Adam at my side. "*Mais, c'est un enfant, mon ami!*" This was accompanied by a smile and a shrug, and a little gesture of his hands. "*Chacun à son goût, n'est-ce pas?*"

The remark was lost on me, but the gesture, slight enough in itself, defined his meaning only too graphically, and the look of irritation on Adam's face confirmed it. I felt myself starting to blush like a fool, and decided I could easily hate Pierre La Fontaine.

It was all the more galling since I'd taken great pains to look well in the flowered silk gown in which Adam had first seen me at my aunt's house. I would have loved the dress for that alone, but I knew its colors flattered the paleness of my skin and its narrow waist made the most of my slender figure.

And I knew what would happen next. I'd been long enough in the United States to know that at social gatherings the men and women immediately separated into two groups at opposite ends of the room, not to meet again until refreshments were announced or it was time to go home. As Adam was absorbed into the group of men surrounding the Fur King, I found myself sitting with Madame La Fontaine, her sisters and her friends, and because I neither spoke French nor had attended the last St. Louis gumbo ball, I'd nothing at all to contribute to the conversation.

For some time I sat in silence, studying the lavish furnishings of the room and the expensive dresses around me. This was Paris fashion, or as near to it as could be contrived at several thousand miles' distance. Every button, every bow was in the latest style which St. Louis dollars could command. I began to reflect that life in America was, as Adam had warned, very different from my existence in Liverpool, though not at all in the way he'd described.

I was roused from my thoughts by the sound of Adam's voice nearby.

"The beaver trade's in trouble, Pierre," he was saying. "And there's no help for it. For one thing—who'd have thought, fifteen years ago, that a day might come when there were no beaver left in large parts of the mountains? We all thought the beaver was indestructible—and yet we've almost wiped the animal from the face of the earth. It isn't something I'm proud of."

"*Hélas* for the beaver! You must forgive me if I don't shed a tear. And I'm surprised to find you *si compatissant*—so sentimental—about a creature you've slain many thousands of times! You're the murderer of the beaver, Adam, not I. I simply sell the furs!"

"It's a fine distinction, Pierre. It's just as well the few beaver left up there don't have to rely on you for their survival."

"So now you intend to look after them, my friend! From assassin to savior, is that it? Like Saint Paul, you've suffered a conversion!"

I heard Adam laugh. "I'm no saint, Pierre. No—my guess is that silk will save the beaver. Bales of the stuff are pouring into Britain through London and Liverpool, enough to make hats for the whole population, and I imagine the story's the same all over Europe. A silk hat's lighter than a beaver, and cooler. They're fast coming into fashion, if what I saw in the streets is anything to go by."

"I've heard all this before. *Donc,* if the market falls still further and your friends, the beaver, are almost trapped out, I shall have to

make sure I have all the trade that remains, *n'est-ce pas?* That's only
sensible! And perhaps at the same time I shall invest in some other
enterprises too ... But I'm sure you're exaggerating, Adam. There
will always be a market for beaver, and for marten and fox too.
What lady doesn't feel more beautiful wrapped in furs?"

To my consternation, I heard the voices growing louder. Adam
and Pierre La Fontaine were approaching the corner where I sat,
trapped by a great bronze urn next to my chair.

"But we have an expert among us to give an opinion! Madame
Gaunt," he continued, swooping down to perch on the end of a
chaise longue opposite me, "your husband and I have a dispute
which only you can settle for us. We need the wise words of a clever
and beautiful lady."

He was annoyed with Adam, I knew, for having brought bad
news. And now the Fur King had noticed me sitting alone and silent
in my corner and had chosen me for his victim.

"Adam warns me, Madame, like a *prophète de malheure,* that
some day soon no one will want to buy my furs. And I've assured
him I know the female heart better than he does." La Fontaine
treated me to a glittering smile. "I've told him that ladies will always
wish to feel soft fur around them ... So now you must tell me: can
you really see a day, Madame Gaunt, when you would willingly give
up your fur pelisse, or your fur-trimmed hat?"

The Fur King fell silent, sitting on the very edge of the sofa and
fixing me with a sharp, bright eye and a tight little half-smile. *Let's
see what the little English bride will say now. Ten to one she'll blush
and stammer like the idiot she obviously is.*

I glanced at Adam for some hint of what I should say, but his face
was expressionless, giving me no help at all. I wanted above all to be
loyal to him and to take his side in the argument, but I knew that
would only give Pierre La Fontaine the victory he wanted. I took a
deep breath.

"Give up my furs, Monsieur? But of course!" I saw his eyes narrow by a fraction. "I give up my furs gladly ... every summer, when
the weather is hot. Would you have me roasted to death in sables,
or boiled alive in fox?"

The Fur King stared at me, and then laughed, and the tension
dissolved.

"Not only beautiful, but *adroite.*" Now his smile was fiercely
controlled, tucked up under his cheekbones without ever reaching
his eyes.

"Tell me then, Madame—what do you think of our *beau monde,* our smart society, here in St. Louis? How does it compare with what you are used to in England? I realize we must look a little primitive to European eyes, we men from the backwoods . . . But we make our own humble effort to be civilized, nevertheless."

With a casual gesture he indicated the vast drawing room, filled with elegant, expensively dressed men and women and the most costly furnishings. Pierre La Fontaine was fishing for a compliment, that was all: and I found myself disliking him even more.

"Oh, I think it's all very fine," I assured him innocently. "But tell me—are all these gentlemen really *fur-trappers?*"

"*Trappers? Juste ciel!* I should think not!" The Fur King looked at me incredulously for a moment, and then I saw a suspicion begin to dawn that I was teasing him.

"Madame, I am properly punished for—*quêter des compliments,* Adam, what is that?"

"Fishing, Pierre. Fishing."

"*Justement.*" He gave a little bow in my direction. "I don't know if you've met any of the trapping fraternity, but I assure you, you'll find none of them in my *salon.*"

"But Monsieur La Fontaine, my husband was once a trapper. So at least one of them is present tonight."

"Ah, Adam! But Adam is *différent.*" He gave the word its French pronunciation. "He's not like one of these wild animals—he is . . . *eh bien,* you must know what he is. And when you meet the real mountain trappers—if you ever meet them, Madame—you'll see what I mean. Good men, but savage beasts, most of them."

"But useful, Pierre," Adam's voice interposed quietly.

"*Mais oui!* Most useful!"

———

"I don't think much of your friend Monsieur La Fontaine," I remarked later in the hotel, sitting on the edge of the bed to peel off my white silk stockings. "He was a pleasant enough host, but all the same . . ."

"*Friend,* did you call him?" Adam, unraveling a knotted rope from a hide-wrapped bundle in the corner of the room, looked up in amazement. "Rachel, I have enemies I'd trust before Pierre La Fontaine! The man has no conscience whatsoever. Up in the mountains, his men have instructions to bribe anyone who'll take his money. He pays the Indians in watered spirits for their furs, and the white trappers too, if he can get away with it. I know for a fact that his men have set friendly Indians to attack other traders. There isn't a dirty trick invented that La Fontaine hasn't tried at some time or another, simply in order to get the whole mountain trade for himself. That's your gracious host for you. Still—talking with him tonight has given me a few ideas."

I'd been curious about the package which Adam had brought back that afternoon from one of the warehouses on the levee, and dropped to the floor without a word of explanation. Now that he'd freed the bundle from its time-stiffened knots and almost unrolled the length of soft hide, I leaned across the bed to see what it contained.

Something gleamed dully in the lamplight as its coverings were drawn off, and all at once I saw in Adam's hands the long metal barrel of a rifle, three feet of oiled iron bedded in a smooth hardwood stock, its double lock glinting with the sheen of satin as he turned it this way and that, examining it for any sign of damage. I watched his hand caress the molded curves of the stock with the eagerness of a lover, slipping automatically into the firing position as he sighted along the barrel. I found myself feeling irrationally jealous of the weapon as he stood it at last against the wall by the tall wooden bedstead. Why did it have to stay so near at hand? Were there bears in hotel bedrooms in St. Louis?

"It isn't loaded, is it, Adam?" The gun had only to fall sideways during the night to kill one or other of us with a shot through the head.

"Of course it isn't loaded! What do you take me for?" Adam glanced at me crossly. "And you'd better get used to the sight of it, because one way or another, that gun will have to earn our living. It's been a good friend to me often enough in the past, I can tell you. I bought it from the Hawkens here in St. Louis—oh, six or seven years ago now. Beautiful, isn't it?"

He sat down on the bed, hardly able to take his eyes from the gun, his iron mistress.

"I've made up my mind where we're headed, by the way," he added suddenly, as if suggesting the most casual picnic. "Something La Fontaine said gave me an idea. This run on the banks will bankrupt a lot of people—farmers especially—and I reckon they'll look round for new places to settle where there's land for the taking. They'll want to go through the mountains to somewhere like Oregon, with men who know the trails and the cutoffs—men like me.

The fur trade won't last much longer in the old way, whatever La Fontaine says, but Bill Sublette's already taken wagons into the mountains, which means it's possible to get them through South Pass to the other side. Perhaps one day we'll head for Oregon ourselves —but for now, we'll go as far as Independence, a few hundred miles upriver."

And that was that. The decision was made. The town of Independence, Missouri, was to be our new home.

10

"There ought to be room for us aboard the *St. Peters*."

That's what Adam had hoped: the *St. Peters* was the American Fur Company steamer which set out each spring on a passage to Fort Union, high on the upper Missouri. But by the time we were ready to leave St Louis the *St. Peters* had sailed, and in the end our trunks and boxes of household goods were loaded aboard another, smaller craft for the journey to Independence.

I wasn't, after all, to see the mountains. Adam had made that quite clear, pointing out to me on the map the vast expanse of prairie which lay between the township of Independence and the first foot-hills of the Rockies. Perhaps, one day, if he decided to take me to Oregon, I would see as much of the alkali plains and the mountain passes as I could ever wish. But in the meantime I was to stay in town and keep house.

"Just that?" I said, disappointed, thinking of the boredom of Leghorn Street. And I wondered why Adam sighed, but said nothing.

The river was low that summer, and our little stern-wheeler—hardly bigger than a tea-chest compared with the mighty *Southern Rose*—continually ran into shoal water on her way upstream. We traveled by day and tied up to the bank at night, not daring to risk running in the darkness into one of the huge fields of "snags" which lay across the river, sunken tree-limbs which could easily rip the hull out of our boat or tear off her churning paddles. This was an entirely different kind of river-boating from our stately progress up the Mississippi, with such frequent halts to drag tree-trunks out of our path or to sound the shallows from the boat's yawl that I began to wonder if we'd ever reach our destination.

The living accommodation, too, was far more spartan. Our meals consisted mainly of cornmeal in various forms, coffee, and whatever could be shot along the wooded banks of the river whenever we pulled in for fuel, the whole lot shoveled down in a few silent minutes at the long table in the common cabin before everyone dispersed again to light cigars and clay pipes out in the fresh air of the deck.

At night, when the last of the coffee and cornmeal had been swept from the board, a curtain was drawn across the end of the single large cabin, dividing off a small area for the use of the half-dozen women passengers aboard. We all lay down to sleep, nose to tail, rolled up in blankets on the narrow benches which had served as seats during the day, listening to the chorus of profanity and other horribly explicit sounds which drifted through from the far side of the curtain.

But at last, after six days and almost four hundred miles of adventures and delays, we came within sight of the landing for Independence, which, Adam explained, moved from place to place at the whim of the flooding Missouri River, always ending up a few miles distant from town.

Our steamer was expected. Knots of men waited at the landing to unload whatever the boat had brought, and my first thought was that I'd never seen such a startling-looking crew in all my life. Most of them were swarthy Mexicans, employees of one of the Santa Fe trading companies, but near them stood six or seven trappers, to judge by their skin tunics and their long guns—though I noticed that what I'd taken to be skin trousers turned out, when they bent down to pick up the bales of pelts at their feet, to be leggings such as the Indians wore, ending at mid-thigh and exposing sunburned buttocks to the gaze of one and all.

Beyond the trappers stood two figures so exotic in appearance that I was sure they must be wild Indians. They were dressed in what seemed to be rags of hide; long, wicked-looking knives were stuck through their belts, their hair was matted with some kind of orange substance, and there were streaks of the same stuff on their unsmiling faces.

"Adam—aren't those Indians?" I whispered, tugging at his sleeve.

"One is. T'other isn't, unless you count halfway Pawnee. That's High-Bear Lefèvre. Hey there, Lefèvre!" he shouted, and I saw the painted creature shade his eyes with a hand before suddenly grinning and lifting an arm in greeting.

"Adam, *mon ami!*"

For the first time I began to understand the truth of what Adam
had tried so often to tell me. Things *were* different out here.

———

My first sight of Independence, Jackson County, was even less reassuring. It seemed to me that day to be the most squalid, rough-hewn,
half-built, dust-girt cluster of dwellings ever to aspire to the name of
town. Independence had clearly not long passed the stage of being
an untidy hamlet of log cabins, and many of these were still to be
seen on the outskirts, but its importance as the jumping-off place for
traders headed southwest on the famous Santa Fe Trail was turning
it into a minor metropolis of clapboard buildings. Two or three of
these on the main street even had the word HOTEL paraded across
their walls in faded, wind-blasted paint, though from the look of the
buildings and the men lounging outside their chief business was that
of a grog-shop.

There were several stores near the central square, the biggest of
them labeled GENERAL STORE—*Prop. Titus Meadow,* and as our
hired wagon jolted along the wide, rutted roadway I counted at least
one barber's shop, though there was no sign that many of the men
who walked or rode past us had ever ventured through its doorway.
There was no bookstore and no haberdasher, but any number of
blacksmiths, wheelwrights and harness-makers to cater for the lumbering wagons of the Santa Fe traders. And that was all—we'd
passed the center of town almost before I realized it, and my heart
sank to my dust-caked boots to think that this dismal wallow was to
be our new home.

The immediate problem was to find somewhere to stay that night.
The rowdy hotels near the square were out of the question, and after
a little searching we found a small, unusually tidy clapboard house a
few yards back from the main street, where a handful of straggling
gray bushes were enclosed by a proper fence with a gate. In its neatly
curtained window was a sign which read "Rooms To Let," and I
hurried up the path like a traveler discovering an oasis in the desert.

The boardinghouse was as spotless inside as out, owned by
the widow of a preacher sent to the west three years earlier by the
Reformed Domestic Missionary and Bible Society to convert the
Indians of the upper river, only to die of yellow fever in Independence before starting his task. Mrs. Lizzie Fletcher, having sold up
and taken leave of her old life back east, had decided to stay where

the Lord had set her down, and had bought the house with the money her husband had saved for his ministry. The boardinghouse was both her livelihood and her mission: Godliness, she maintained, could be aspired to by all, but cleanliness—in such a place—was a vocation.

Mrs. Fletcher hardly seemed old, but her abundant brown hair was already well streaked with gray, and wisps of it continually escaped from the fat knot on top of her head to curl down about her eyes, giving her the anxious look of a bird in a thicket. As she spoke, her hands chased endlessly after these stray tendrils, twisting and twitching at them in a hopeless attempt to shoo them back into place. But there was something so comforting and decent about her that I began to warm to Lizzie Fletcher at once, and through her well-polished windows even the town of Independence began to look a little less hostile.

We stayed with Mrs. Fletcher for a fortnight while Adam looked for a house of our own. His requirements were precise: he wanted somewhere on the western edge of town, near the road which took trading caravans to their gathering-point for Santa Fe and trappers out toward the endless prairies, the North Platte River and the Rocky Mountains.

"Titus Meadow tells me the Nugent place is empty now," remarked Lizzie Fletcher one evening. "Old Man Nugent got so's he couldn't see too well and went off to live with his daughter in Cincinnati. The house isn't much, but it's on the west side of town, an' you could do something with it, I reckon."

She was right. The house wasn't much—a log cabin very nearly as big as Aunt Grace's drawing room with a huge stone chimney at one end and another small log-walled room built on beyond it as an afterthought. The pitched roof was made of a mixture of wood, turf and mud, baked as hard as iron in the drying wind which blew in from the prairie, and below it, over the larger of the two rooms, was a loft reached by a rickety ladder of rough poles.

"Adam!"

I had to call to him from the doorway; he'd gone to inspect a smaller, log-built shed at the side of the cabin which served as stable and store. "Adam—there are great holes in the wall of the back room! I can see straight through it!"

But when Adam emerged from the stable, I realized that he hadn't heard a word.

"This place should do for the present, don't you think? We'll get some shelter from the trees round about, and there's a stream just beyond that rock which should keep us supplied with water. We'll buy a couple of horses, but at a pinch we could walk into town."

"You haven't even been inside the cabin, Adam! The large room seems sound enough, but the small one is just made of rough logs with nothing between them."

Adam followed me into the little house, immediately making it seem smaller than ever. He gazed, unmoved, round the second room with its airy lattice of logs.

"We can sleep in here. The carpenter in town will soon knock a bedstead together for us."

"But look at the *holes!*"

"We won't be cold while the weather's warm. And by winter we'll have done something about the holes. You can whitewash the inside, if you want."

"I *don't* want it!" I muttered rebelliously, thinking of the clapboard houses near the square. "I want a proper home!"

Adam swung round, his face grim. "I warned you," he reminded me. "I warned you what it would be like, as honestly as I could. You promised you'd make the best of things, and I expect you to keep that promise."

Then, like the sun emerging from behind a cloud, his face cleared.

"Don't worry—you'll soon get used to this kind of life. Wait until we've moved in and put up some shelves—or got a fire going in the hearth and found a couple of chairs to sit on. It'll be as cozy as you could wish."

"I wonder."

"There's everything we need here, I promise you."

"There isn't—there doesn't seem to be—"

"Doesn't seem to be *what?*"

"Well . . . You know."

He took a deep breath. "Dammit, I'll dig you a hole out in the bushes there. In the meantime"—he indicated the vastness of the country beyond our door—"use Missouri."

———

"A *servant?*" echoed Lizzie Fletcher two days before we were due to move into the Nugent place. "You won't find any servants in these parts, Mrs. Gaunt! Slaves, sure enough, poor devils. But no self-respectin' white man or woman's goin' to fetch an' carry fer wages like they do in England. This is America, where we're all as good as one another, equal like the good God made us. I daresay I could find you some *help*, though, if that's what you want."

"It would only be for a week or so, just until we're settled. After that I should think I'll manage on my own." To tell the truth, I was terrified of being left alone to "make do" in the little log house, and when Adam suggested finding someone to help us move in, I leaped at the chance.

Lizzie Fletcher frowned. "I'd lend you Jinnah for a short while, just till you're fixed, but . . ." Jinnah was a freed slave who helped Lizzie at the boardinghouse, an attractive, light-skinned woman from Virginia, the state which had given her its name.

"I wouldn't hear of it, Mrs. Fletcher. You've more than enough work for Jinnah here. But if you know of anyone else who might . . ."

"Help out," Lizzie Fletcher finished for me. "An' I calculate you better start callin' me Lizzie. *Mrs. Fletcher*'s goin' to be a mite in the way if we're to be friends, an' I reckon you may need a friend or two in Independence before you're through."

And that was how I acquired one of the best friends I was ever to know, and through her, for a week, the services of sixteen-year-old Addie Bee.

"Now Addie—is that what they really call you? Addie?"

"My name's *Adeline,* so Ma says, but I just gets *Addie.*"

"Well, then, Addie—if a dollar and a half will suit you—"

"If it's just for the week, I guess so. Wouldn't want to stay on longer since mayhap Ma'll need me back home. Reckon we'll git to killin' a hog soon enough, an' she'll be right homely if I ain't there to boil the blood."

Hitching her cotton skirt more firmly round her waist, the gangling child spat on her hands and proceeded to drag one of our heavy boxes into the middle of the floor before heaving up the lid and digging inside it to see what it contained.

There was already a table in the cabin, massively strong and made so large by the previous owner that he'd had to leave it behind when he went. With the table in its center our largest room would serve as kitchen, parlor and dining room, with the addition of two sturdy wooden chairs and a stool bought from the town's carpenter. The same man had also built a bedstead for us in the interval between two coffins; Adam had strung it with a lattice of rope, and had managed to find a mattress filled with buffalo hair which Lizzie insisted would be even more comfortable than cornhusks.

Aunt Grace had given us bed-linen and rugs which she didn't need, but though the rugs certainly brightened up the little cabin and gave a touch of incongruous luxury to the rough pine floor, I wondered how the sticky lumps of resin which oozed from each split in the wood might affect them.

"They'll just spoil, I calculate," remarked Addie Bee helpfully as she heaved up on end the box which had contained the rugs. On Lizzie's advice I was turning all our boxes and trunks into cup-boards, and putting up shelves on pegs driven into the logs forming the cabin walls.

On her knees, Addie plunged into the next packing-case, and pro-duced a porcelain teapot. She let out a whistle of surprise.

"Well, look at that now! Reckon that'll get broke for sure, Miz Gaunt. I'd jump slick to put that in the loft, if I was you, an' all these little cups an' plates along with it. You're a downright Englisher, sure enough! Little tiny teacups like eggshells, an' a tablecloth with stitchin'. . . . Wait till Ma hears about all this fancy stuff!"

As it happened, Mrs. Bee didn't wait to hear but came to see for herself, and leaned against the doorpost in silence for almost an hour and a half, scrutinizing every item that was taken from our boxes and smoking a short clay pipe which she took from the bosom of her cotton shirt.

Armed with a list Lizzie Fletcher had given me, I'd made a foray to Meadow's store to order a couple of heavy black iron kettles, a Dutch oven and a three-legged skillet which the storeman called a *spider,* all to be sent out later by cart. Surrounded by these items, the hearth looked pleasantly domestic, and I began to feel I'd done quite well in arranging our new home. I surveyed myself in the looking-glass, clad in a simple blouse and skirt, and smiled at my previous fears. Why—there had been no reason to worry! Here I was, a frontierswoman already, with a cabin of my own, a kettle of meat over the fire and dough rising by the hearth. What on earth would Aunt Grace have said if she could have seen me now?

Two days later, reality hit me squarely in the face when Addie Bee went home. There had been meat stewing over my fire, certainly, but only because Addie Bee had "fixed" it. Showing an unexpected skill at baking, she'd also "fixed" Johnny-cake and biscuits almost before I could blink, and when she left for home to help out at the hog-killing I suddenly found how helpless I really was. What possible use was a knowledge of watercolor sketching when there were meals to be got? Where was the point of a neat step in the cotillion when water had to be fetched from the creek? I could have cursed Aunt Grace as I stood there, gazing round my lonely log cabin: Addie Bee, who couldn't have told watercolor paint from quince jelly, would have had everything right in a trice.

Adam had vanished that morning with the long rifle tucked into the crook of his arm, in search of something for the pot. After a couple of hours he returned with two furry corpses, holding them out to me as if they were now entirely my responsibility.

For a moment I stared at the dangling dead creatures, each with a neat patch of blood soaking into its fur where a lead ball had found its target. Two pairs of eyes stared back at me, misted in death, and eight little paws hung pathetically limp.

"What's the matter?" Adam wanted to know.

"I don't know what to do with them."

"Skin them and cook them—what else?"

"Oh, Adam, I couldn't *skin* them! I wouldn't know where to begin. And as for cooking them . . . I suppose I could boil them, or something like that. I've never had to cook a hare before."

"They're jackrabbits."

"Jackrabbits, then. But I can make blancmange, Adam, honestly —and my mother used to bake when I was a child, while I watched her do it."

"And learned precious little, I suppose. Well, we can't afford to keep Addie Bee here forever to cook for us, so you'll just have to learn how to do it in future. It's that, or starve, Rachel. I've cooked for myself often enough in the mountains, but only Indian-style. That'll have to serve for now."

But he made me skin and clean one of the two jackrabbits all the same, once he'd demonstrated how it was done. My stomach heaved as I turned the slippery little body out of its bloody fur jacket, and divided it into pieces. By the time the meat was stewing in one of the iron kettles, I was fighting back tears. How could Adam be so unreasonable?

And he had such odd ideas of what was required. Indian women, he told me, kept a stockpot bubbling all the time, adding each day whatever game came to hand, mixing it with wild cherries, various herbs and roots which they dug up or grew themselves. In an Indian village the meals had no timetable. Everyone ate when they were hungry, and any visitor calling at the lodge was offered food as soon as he arrived. I remembered then that Adam had once had an Indian wife—Tahtokay, whose red stone amulet still lay in a trunk under our bed—and I wondered if he was secretly comparing his two wives, and which one he'd rather have had at that moment.

I struggled on, keeping a pot on the hearth as he wished and trying with increasing desperation to bake respectable bread from a supply of milk I'd found nearby and Lizzie Fletcher's recipe for "milk emptins," a substitute for yeast. I added salt and water as she'd instructed and left the mixture near the fire to ferment, but somehow I never succeeded in catching the result before it putrefied, and the bread I made stank so badly that neither Adam nor I could eat it.

I'd never imagined it could be so hard to keep house: at home in Crow Cove the village girls married their fishermen and seemed to take to housekeeping as chickens take to corn—and yet here I was after three years of expensive education in ladylike ways, quite unable even to keep the fire in my hearth alight from one day to the next.

To make matters worse, little by little Adam was returning to his old way of life, coming and going at all hours of the day and night, always with the long gun across his arm. He never openly criticized my efforts to keep house, but I was sure he felt I'd failed him. And my plans had been so different: all the way from Liverpool I'd treasured an idyllic picture of the two of us together on a rustic porch, bathed in the rosy light of evening, embracing ecstatically, perhaps, as Adam discovered at last that I was the only woman he could ever truly love. Instead of which . . . I began to think his wretched gun spent more time in his arms than I did.

I tried to avoid looking in the mirror now, since all I saw was my sunburned, peeling nose, my untidy hair and my rough hands with their cracked fingernails edged with grime. In Liverpool I'd brushed aside Adam's insistence that he couldn't love me. *He'll come to love me in time,* I thought. *I can make him love me.* But when such a careworn, bungling creature waited for him in our cabin, what reason did he have for spending more time at home?

And the misery went on. When the wind blew from a certain

direction the chimney smoked and I became red-eyed from crouching over my pots. At night I lay on our buffalo-hair mattress as the wind tore at the mud roof and a fine stream of gravel sprinkled down into my face and hair—hair I could hardly bear to wash in the silty sludge which swirled in the water from our stream. Mice had moved into the cabin almost as soon as we did, leaving their droppings in any bag of provisions they managed to chew into, and as if that wasn't bad enough, I woke one night in the small hours to see the silhouette of a rat perched between two of the unchinked logs in our bedroom wall. Adam was quite unperturbed, but since I was afraid of being bitten while I slept, he took to keeping a loaded pistol by the bed, and I would wake in the darkness to the sound of a tremendous explosion whenever he found himself with a clear shot at one of these uninvited visitors.

It was squalid: that was the only word for it—*squalid*. And that thin, loose grit was everywhere. As soon as I brushed a layer of dirt from the floor into the yard outside, the wind seemed to blow it back in again. It must have come under the door or through the cracks between the logs or down the sides of our precious glass windows— I don't know how it came in, except that it did. We ate grit, we drank grit, and we washed in it too. It stung our eyes when we rubbed them and even seemed to fill our lungs, settling into every crease of skin like a fine pencil line. Adam shrugged and ignored it, but I couldn't. I simply never felt clean, and between the dirt, the army of crawling insects which shared the cabin with us and my continued failure at housekeeping, I began to imagine I might even go mad.

Nowadays I never knew when Adam would be at home. At first he disappeared for a day at a time, and then overnight, and after a while for two or three days in succession, hunting or making contact with the assorted groups of people who lived along the upper river. I hated being left alone in the cabin, but I didn't dare to protest. He'd begun to look more like a trapper, too—like the men I'd seen at the river-landing on my first day in Independence, in wool trousers and an old cotton shirt, and a fringed buckskin coat which had been stored with the Hawken rifle in the St. Louis warehouse while he was in England.

I'd never seen anything like that deerskin coat—sewn, Adam said, by a Crow woman armed with no more than a bone awl and thread made from buffalo sinew. All down the front, small metal discs and colored glass beads dangled on lengths of sinew from a pattern of quilling; there were long fringes at its seams, and though by the time I saw it the coat was stained by time and hard use, it must have been magnificent when the skins were white and new. Even now it shrugged off thorns, kept out anything but a deluge, and turned the wind better than anything a human hand could weave.

I thought of my own fumbling embroidery and realized that the Indian tribes were the ones who knew the secret of living in that unforgiving land, a secret I would never learn. I watched Adam closely, and wondered how strongly his old life was calling him. Sometimes now when I spoke to him he answered me absently, and I knew his mind was ranging elsewhere like a boat tugging at its moorings in a strong current, anxious to be off on an urgent tide.

I was that mooring. Adam was tied to me—tied by my helplessness. Without me, he could have gone where he pleased. And the thought gave me no pleasure.

———

On the day that Lizzie Fletcher came to my rescue, Adam and I had at last had an open disagreement. Or rather, Adam lost patience with what he called my extravagance in buying expensive wax candles from Meadow's store when I should have been making my own.

"I don't know *how!*" I wailed at him, overwhelmed by misery.

"Then throw pine chippings on the fire if you want more light," he said crossly, and swung himself up on his big bay gelding to ride off toward the river-landing, leaving me alone for the rest of the day.

When Lizzie arrived in the afternoon on her elderly mule, Mary, I was almost hysterical with misery and resentment. In a rage of frustration, I'd hurled a plateful of my bitter-tasting, greenish biscuits against the log wall of the cabin, too furious at the constant failure of my baking even to pick them up.

"Too much saleratus." Lizzie retrieved one of the rejected biscuits from a corner, and sniffed it suspiciously. "You having problems here, honey? Seems like you are, I'd say. Maybe I ought to have come out this way before now, 'cept that with you two being kinda newly married and all, I thought you'd want to be alone together for a bit before folks started visitin'."

"Oh, Lizzie, I hardly ever see Adam these days! I'm sure he wishes he'd never married such a hopeless fool—everything I do seems to end up a disaster!"

"What nonsense! That husband of yours is too downright sensible to go thinking any such thing. Now, don't you worry yourself about it any more, Rachel, 'cos I'll take you in hand as I would my own daughter, if I'd been blessed with one. Must say, I thought when I saw you, you seemed a mite gently raised to get along out here. But a woman's a woman, after all, an' nothing in creation can hold her down for long. We'll soon turn you into the best little housekeeper west of the Mississippi, you see if we don't."

And that afternoon Lizzie stood over me, issuing instructions, while I produced a batch of amazingly perfect baking. After that, she began to visit the cabin almost every day, and as the weeks passed I learned such miraculous skills as how to melt deer tallow in a kettle over the fire to make candles, how to mix castor oil and whisky as a hairwash, and the deft pouring of muddy creek water from one jug to another until it was clear enough to use.

"You got pork salted down for the winter yet?" she asked me one day in late September. "No? Thought not. Well, you'll need it here, despite what your husband can do with that gun of his. I was fixing to speak to Mrs. Bee about it for myself, but I'll ask her to accommodate you with a hog or two at the same time. I expect she'll have plenty. They're an ungodly family, but they *can* raise hogs, and that's a fact."

The first result of this arrangement was a formal visit from Mrs. Bee, who smoked her pipe at my enormous table and drank strong green tea from the spout of the teapot, declaring "it tasted better so." The second result was an invitation to the marriage of her daughter Addie to one of the town blacksmiths—or rather, to the "frolic" that followed, to which Adam and Lizzie and I accordingly went, and enjoyed ourselves a good deal more than we'd expected.

By the time the last leaves fell from the trees that year I could make a tub of lye soap, start vinegar for pickling, and I'd even cleared part of the overgrown garden behind the cabin, grubbing out tree and shrub roots ready for the rows of potatoes, peas and squashes I meant to grow the following year.

At the far end of the garden a little copse of pine trees sheltered the stable from the worst of the prairie winds, and not long after we'd moved into the cabin I discovered that the trees were the favorite perch of a pair of squirrels. Suddenly I was reminded of Crow Cove and the great, dark forest at the top of the hill, that magical place of my childhood, full of enticing sounds and scents and the rustle of a thousand unseen watchers. These pines were a mere echo of its glories, an untidy fringe of green behind our stable wall, but even they offered a home to a flock of buxom, companionable pigeons, and in season their ripely splayed cones to the sharp teeth of the squirrels.

Gradually the squirrels became accustomed to the sight of me toiling in the garden and would venture down from the branches to fetch some particularly tasty morsel, crouching among the soft needle-litter, a shiny seed clasped in delicate, gray-gloved hands, ready to flee in a second back to the shelter of the pine boughs if I made any sudden movement.

Sometimes I sat down on a mossy stump to watch them, remembering not to stare directly like a waiting cat, but to turn my head a little until they were more confident of my peaceful intentions. And on the day when the bolder of the two accepted a walnut kernel from my hand before scampering, shocked by his own daring, back to the shelter of the pines, I'd have traded every tallow candle and every tub of lye in the world for the old, familiar wonder of it all.

I remember feeling happy—truly happy—as I bent again to my hoe, listening to the roo-rooing of the pigeons as they discussed this latest development.

"It's good to hear you singing again." I heard Adam's voice a short way off.

"Was I singing? I hadn't realized."

Adam had been feeding our two horses in the stable, and I'd forgotten he was within earshot. Now I turned to look at him as he stood in the stable doorway: my beloved Adam, strong, sun-brown and smiling.

"It's a long time since I've heard you sing," he added. "You had me worried for a while, do you know that? Not because there were scores of things you couldn't do—I expected that, and I knew you'd learn it all in time. But you seemed to have lost confidence in yourself. I used to hear you down by the creek, sobbing over some spoiled biscuits you were throwing out for the pigeons, and I'd no idea what to do about it."

"I thought—I thought you'd wish you'd never married me. I thought you'd send me back to Liverpool."

He stared at me in surprise. "Good Heavens, whatever gave you that idea? Send you back to Liverpool—just because your baking was a disaster, and you bought up every candle in the store?"

"I still think tallow candles stink."

"I know they do. And there's still dirt everywhere, and mice in the cornmeal, and rats in the roof. That's just the way it is out here. But you're singing again, Squirrel, which proves none of it matters. Buy every candle in the world if you want, so long as you can still sing about it."

"Do you really mean that? You aren't angry with me anymore?"

"I was never angry with you. Impatient, maybe, I'll admit. And concerned. But never angry."

"Oh, Adam, I wish I believed that."

A look I recognized came into his eyes. "Is Lizzie Fletcher coming out here today?"

"No, she's going to something called a 'quilting' in town."

"Then come here, and let me prove to you I was never angry."

————

After that I really believed that all might be well—that Adam would accept at last that there was a place for me in his life, and that he needed me. As winter loomed ahead I saw a chance for my wish to come true: I was happy in my home, and I knew that in the winter months Adam's journeys would be curtailed by the bad weather and we'd grow closer again in our snowbound, log-walled world.

And then, one day, walking with Lizzie along the main street of town to buy coffee at the store, I thought I saw, striding toward us on the boardwalk, a figure from my past. I was startled, and studied the man closely as he passed. He was wearing a short coat and boots and a fancy waistcoat, and his face was half hidden by a wide-brimmed hat, but there could be no doubt it was one and the same person. His skin was the same bluish-white, his hair as black and his eyes as blue as they'd been in St. John's three years earlier. Even his walk was the same arrogant stride I remembered so well.

But the last person I'd expected to see in the main street of Independence was Francis Ellis.

11

"Francis Ellis?" asked Lizzie with a frown. "I don't recall a *Francis* Ellis. There's a *Frank* Ellis, sure enough, but I don't expect he'd be any friend of yours."

"Perhaps the man I used to know is calling himself Frank these days. Is this Frank Ellis a schoolmaster?"

"A schoolteacher? Well, if that don't beat all! If Frank Ellis is a schoolteacher, honey, I'd hate to think what he's teachin'! No, I'm sure now he can't be the feller you mean. The Frank Ellis I have in mind came here with a woman named Connery about six months ago—much about the time you arrived here yourself. The two of them took over the Trader's House, the big three-story hotel near the square, but from what I hear it ain't much of a hotel anymore. Not the kind of hotel you'd want to stay in, if you get my drift."

"You mean it's a—"

"I mean what I say, Rachel. No more, no less."

Lizzie Fletcher went on folding linen, dividing it into precise rectangles as if she wished the whole world could be pressed and sorted as neatly as her immaculate laundry.

"I've never been inside the door of the Trader's House, so I can't swear to what goes on in the place, an' I certainly don't intend to speculate. But it don't take a genius to see the Frank Ellis I'm talkin' about is nothin' but trouble for this town, and I'd be real surprised to hear you'd ever known a man like him."

"It doesn't sound like the same person, certainly. Except that I'm sure I recognized him in the street a few days ago, when we were on our way to the store."

"Well that only makes it more unlikely. Frank Ellis don't come out much in daylight, I believe, but mostly stays holed up in that hotel of his. Not that I know much about him, understand—or care to know, if it comes to that. I just thank the Lord my poor Asa ain't here anymore to see what this town's become. It's an ungodly place, an' that's the truth. There's far more need of a missionary in Independence than out on the plains saving those poor deluded Indians. Pass me that bar of soap there, Rachel, an' I'll store it with the linen."

Mechanically, I passed the soap, and Lizzie stowed it away at the back of her big wooden cupboard. The subject of Frank Ellis and the Trader's House was closed as far as she was concerned, but I was still puzzled and uneasy. I was sure the man I'd seen in the street was the same Francis Ellis who'd stayed with us in St. John's, charmed me with his facile manners, entranced me with lines of stolen poetry, and . . . The memory of the other things he'd done was still enough to bring a hot flush to my cheeks. I'd never mentioned any of it to Adam. How could I even begin to speak of a time when I'd been so appallingly foolish? The thought of Francis Ellis showing his sly, plausible face in Independence, of all places, was enough to make my newly risen spirits sink once more.

Perhaps he was only passing through. I dimly remembered Andrew MacDonald telling me that his protégé had opened a school in this region, but he'd told me on that wonderful night when Adam Gaunt came back into my life, and I'd hardly heard a word of the news he brought. But I was sure Uncle Andrew had said *teaching*. Francis had been expensively educated until his father's death, and would surely have put that education to use in earning a living. Perhaps, then, he was merely visiting Independence from some other town nearby.

Then I remembered the embroidered silk waistcoat, of a kind I'd last seen worn by the New Orleans gamblers aboard the *Southern Rose*. Would a poorly paid, respectable schoolteacher wear such finery? It didn't seem likely. And to be honest, I couldn't picture Francis, with his taste for the good things in life, spending his days beating Morse's Geography into small heads at a charge of two dollars a term per child.

It began to seem more than possible that the man I'd seen was indeed Frank Ellis, part-owner of the notorious Trader's House. If that was so, it was no longer surprising to find him in the same town. For someone in that sort of business, Independence was a logical place to set up shop. A busy crossroads of the West and likely to become far busier in future, the town was already full of hard-living teamsters and traders looking for entertainment at fancy prices. All

I could hope was that although I'd recognized him, swaggering past
Titus Meadow's store, Francis Ellis hadn't recognized me.

———

I could hardly avoid going into town after that, but whenever we
had to collect provisions or to visit Lizzie Fletcher I tried not to walk
past the flat wooden façade of the Trader's House on the same side
of the street. The roadway was wide, and even if Francis—or Frank
Ellis, as he seemed to prefer—was standing at a window, I'd only be
one more passing figure at such a distance.

But Independence wasn't Liverpool, and it was inevitable in such
a small place that one day we'd come face to face.

Adam and I had ridden into town to buy a new hoe and some
lamp oil at one of the stores and to call on Lizzie on our way home.
I'd become quite a competent rider by then, though not in the manner Aunt Grace would have wished. I'd found it strange at first to
see women riding astride their horses like men, but there were no
sidesaddles to be had in town, even if I'd been accustomed to using
one, and so I'd learned to control my horse from a most unladylike
posture, one leg dangling on each side of the animal, my skirts
bunched up around me and my stockinged calves perfectly visible to
the public gaze.

As luck would have it that day, Frank Ellis was crossing the muddy
street just as we approached, dodging a racing wagon and its team
of sweating mules as he came. He was almost under my horse's nose
when he stopped at last and looked up, and there was nothing at all
I could do to avoid the meeting.

"Why—it's Rachel Dean, surely! Yes it is! Little Rachel Dean from
St. John's! What in the world are you doing in this godforsaken
hole?"

He'd caught the horse's bridle in one hand and was staring up at
me out of those bold eyes of his, just as if we were the oldest of
friends.

What could I do, except get the meeting over with as quickly as
possible?

"Adam, this is Francis Ellis, an acquaintance from St. John's. Francis, I don't believe you've met my husband, Adam Gaunt. Francis is
a schoolmaster," I added maliciously.

"Frank Ellis," he corrected, holding out a hand which Adam ignored, keeping both of his on the reins of his horse.

"And I'm not exactly a schoolmaster anymore."

"Aren't you, Francis?"

"*Frank.*"

"Frank, then. Frank was my brother Edward's tutor," I said quickly to Adam, who was sitting motionless on his horse, regarding Frank Ellis and his silk waistcoat with disfavor. No doubt Adam, with his greater experience of the world, could guess exactly in which department of it Frank Ellis was currently employed.

"I see," he replied without enthusiasm. "And are you living here in Independence these days, Mr. Ellis?"

"Frank," Ellis reminded him. "And yes, as it happens, I've bought a business here in town. There are plenty of opportunities in Independence for a man who's able to take advantage of them, I reckon. And I see no reason why that man shouldn't be me. But Rachel Dean —of all people! I can hardly credit it . . . Rachel Dean!"

"Rachel *Gaunt,*" I said at once, glancing at Adam.

"Oh, I beg your pardon. *Mrs. Gaunt,* of course. Rachel's mother threw me out, you know," he remarked blandly to Adam.

"Indeed? And why was that?"

I held my breath, wondering what would come next.

"I guess I spent too much time in the bars of St. John's," Ellis continued smoothly, "and not enough in the schoolroom. That must've been the reason, don't you think, Rachel?" He grinned up at me, and I was seized by a desire to kick him in the face.

"But I'd better not hold you folks up any longer. Maybe some day soon I'll call on you wherever you're settled, and talk over old times, hey Rachel?" Bold as brass, he waited for the invitation to be confirmed, his hand still on the bridle of my horse.

"Maybe," agreed Adam. "Good day, Mr. Ellis." And he began to turn his horse's head away toward the square.

"Frank," insisted Ellis again. "Just Frank."

With that he let go of my horse at last and I was able to kick it into motion alongside Adam's, though a strange prickling sensation at the back of my neck made me certain Frank Ellis was still watching us ride off.

"How much of a friend is that fellow Ellis?" asked Adam as he helped me down in front of the store.

"He was only a student my mother engaged as Edward's tutor. Andrew MacDonald recommended him, but he didn't last very long with us. I imagine my mother thought he was a bad influence on Edward."

"Do you know what he's doing here now?"

"Not teaching anymore, so he says." I avoided Adam's eye.

"Gambling or running a bar, by the look of him. I'd forget him if I were you, Rachel. Men like that are just troublemakers. Throw him out if he comes to the cabin." He stared back sharply up the street. "Or I will."

———

Oh, how our past comes back to haunt us! I was sure Frank Ellis would find his way out to our cabin sooner or later. He knew I loathed him, and the fact seemed to hold a strange fascination for him, since he waited barely a week before turning up at my door one afternoon when Adam was out with his gun.

"I shan't invite you in," I told him as he stood outside.

"Now, what kind of Western hospitality is that? As I remember, we were pretty good friends, three years ago. Very good friends, I'd say." He stood there on the doorstep with his broad-brimmed hat in his hand, his black hair gleaming like polished ebony and an ingratiating grin on his face.

I noticed he had gold studs in his shirt, and he spoke a good deal more like the owner of an exotic silk waistcoat than a university man.

"I've no intention of discussing the past with you. Whatever happened between us in St. John's is over and done with. You took shameful advantage of me when I was too young to know better, and I wonder you have the impertinence even to speak to me now."

"Hell—you're beginning to sound like your old lady, Rachel. Is that what marriage does to the women of your family?" He fished a cigar from an inner pocket and scraped a match for it on the sole of his shoe, a gesture I'd seen a hundred times on the Mississippi steamboat. It occurred to me that Frank Ellis had missed his vocation in life: he should have been an actor.

"Get out of here, Francis—or Frank, or whatever you call yourself these days. I don't want Adam to come back and find us talking."

"No? Talking's no sin. Or does your fine, upright husband reckon I poison the air just by standing here?" Frank Ellis snorted, and settled himself more firmly before my door. "Just as well he doesn't know about our little . . . *friendship* a few years back."

"What makes you think he doesn't know?"

"Because he would've got down from his horse that day we met in town, and knocked me into the dirt. I hear he's that kind of man, Adam Gaunt. And he didn't do it, so I'm sure he doesn't know. Don't you fret—I'm not going to be the one to tell him, either. I've no desire to get my jaw broken."

He took a couple of paces backward, and surveyed our home.

"Well, I must say, Rachel, I thought your mother had bigger plans for you than to keep house for a skin-hunter. Why—you were her precious daughter! She sure as Hell made it clear she didn't want me to marry you."

"Marry me! Apart from the fact that I was only fifteen years of age, marriage never entered your head, Frank Ellis, and you know it!"

"I'd have found you something better than this, at any rate!" With a contemptuous wave of his hand he indicated the cabin, the stable, and my hard-won vegetable plot. "What kind of a hovel is this for a woman like you? You're working yourself to death here, Rachel. You'll lose your health and your looks, slaving for a family in this backwater. Say what you like about me, but one day I'm going to have a big house and servants—the kind of place you had before you lowered yourself to this."

"This kind of life is all I want, so you can keep your sympathy. Marry me! As if you would! You're a lying rat, Frank, and you always will be."

He shrugged. "I've been called worse. But looking around, I still say you'd have been better off with me, rat or no rat. I'm in a pretty fair way of business now, and it pays a damn sight better than schoolteaching."

"I've heard what kind of business you're in. You and your lady-friend. Miss Connery, I believe?"

"Kate Connery. Crazy Kate. She's my business partner, that's all."

"I'm sure she is."

"Purely business, I assure you. For one thing, I couldn't afford her." The confident grin was back on his face. "For another, I prefer brunettes. Particularly brunettes with brown eyes who like poetry."

That was the last straw. "Get out of here, Frank! I don't want to see you again, or speak to you, or have anything more to do with you. Get on your way into town before Adam comes back and throws you out of the yard! He knew exactly what kind of scum you were as soon as he set eyes on you."

"Oh, did he? A dirty, Injun-loving trapper calling *me* scum? Well,

Rachel my dear, I may be scum in your eyes, but I've heard enough about men like your virtuous husband to know the sort of trash *you've* taken up with!"

And with that Frank Ellis clamped his hat squarely on his head, turned on his heel, and began to walk back to the horse he'd tied under a tree by the roadside. He'd almost reached it when a long shadow materialized out of the bushes and I realized it was Adam, a dark shape under the overhanging branches, the ever-present gun in his right hand.

To my satisfaction I saw Frank Ellis increase his speed toward the waiting horse. As he heaved himself into the saddle, Adam strolled across and stood for a moment by the animal's head. Then he stepped back, and the horse seemed to erupt into motion, carrying my visitor swiftly along the road which led back into town.

"I've told him not to come near you again." Adam lowered the butt of his gun to the ground as he joined me in the doorway. "He seems to have taken me at my word." He glanced back in the direction Frank Ellis had taken. "He's dross, a man like that. And a coward into the bargain. Best forget him, Rachel."

It was an odd thing to say: *forget him,* as if in some way Adam had divined there was something to forget. But he never mentioned Frank Ellis again after that, as if the past was over and done with, and had no claim on the present. The tragedy was that it did have a claim—at least, in Adam's case it did, and that claim became stronger with every day that passed.

―――

Living as we did on the western outskirts of town we had few regular callers except for Lizzie Fletcher, and I was startled one evening by the sound of a pounding knock which set our door shuddering on its hinges. Adam leaped up to open it, and I heard his exclamation of surprise and pleasure when he recognized our visitors.

I'd been sitting by the fire, almost half asleep over a length of calico I was turning into a blouse, and I looked up in astonishment to see two extraordinary figures tramping across my tidy rugs, sniffing the air like animals unused to having a roof over their heads.

One was squat and muscular, the other of medium height, but both of them were clad from head to foot in fringed buckskin turned shiny black with months of grease, and hung about with a small arsenal of weapons. Each man carried a rifle like Adam's which he propped ceremoniously against the wall near the door, just as a city gentleman might leave his hat and cane.

"Rachel, these are old friends of mine. Antoine Bleu—" he indicated the taller man, recently clean-shaven, to judge by the whiteness of his chin against the mahogany tan of the rest of his face, "—and Ed Ballantine. Antoine's half James Bay French and half mountain lion, as you'll hear when he tries to speak English, and Ballantine . . . Well, they say some old she-bear dropped him one day on the Yellowstone, and he's been living among men ever since." Ballantine was the troll, those parts of him still visible beyond his buckskins generously covered in thick black hair which crept like a weed across the backs of his huge hands and curled in tangles to his shoulders. His mouth was lost in a matted beard and his looming brows drowned his eyes in deep pools of shadow.

The two men nodded and mumbled a greeting as Adam herded them further into the room, bringing with them their own bitter, musky smell—a ripeness composed of sweat and woodsmoke, beargrease and horse. What was it Pierre La Fontaine had said? *Good men, but savage beasts, most of them.* And they were exactly like wild creatures, those two, ill at ease in my little house.

"The last time I saw these fellows, they were camped on the Bayou Salade, arguing over whether they should go down to Taos or up to Fort Laramie for supplies and just about to beat one another senseless over it. They've been partners ever since I've known them, and they've never agreed on anything."

Antoine Bleu turned to grin at him.

"This beats the Bayou Salade, I think, Adam! No more mountains for you, eh? And why not?" He spread out his arms in a great Gallic shrug. "Why sleep out in the cold when you have Madame waiting at home for you?"

"Oh, I wouldn't say I've hung up my boots yet, Antoine. Not entirely, anyway. But find a chair and have something to eat."

For once I had reason to bless my stockpot as I watched the two trappers fall upon platefuls of deer meat from the black iron kettle, returning to fill their plates time after time until they could pack no more into their stomachs. Antoine Bleu managed to keep up some kind of conversation while he ate, but Ed Ballantine said nothing at all, shoveling the pieces of bread and gobbets of meat deep into his mouth with his knife, hardly pausing to chew, and then, as his hunger abated, dropping the knife in order to chase the last morsels round the plate with his fingers.

I'd never seen anyone eat like that before, and I could hardly tear my eyes away. When I did, I saw Antoine Bleu watching me with amusement.

"You have to excuse my good friend. *Tonerre*, Ballantine! Do you have to eat like a wolf with his throat cut? You eat faster with eight fingers than I do with ten!"

For the first time I noticed that an area of raw flesh marked the place on the apelike trapper's left hand where two fingers and part of his palm had been cut away—the result, explained Bleu, of a crushed finger which had turned gangrenous. Unusually fastidious, Ballantine had insisted on seeking the help of a proper medical man, and the two trappers were now returning from their expedition out of the mountains, hurrying back to reach Fort Laramie before the first snows of winter made the prairies impassable.

At last Ballantine dropped his empty plate on the table with a grunting bark of satisfaction.

"Good doin's, Ma'am," he mumbled, wiping his mouth on the back of his hand. "Man from St. Louis tol' me Adam here'd got hisself fixed up with a wife, an' I could hardly b'lieve it, but I'll be dogged if I've eaten better since I wintered with the Flatheads two years gone." He gave a great sigh, as if exhausted by the effort of so much conversation. "I got a mouth drier than a Pawnee moccasin, Adam, just a-beggin' for a drink. Don't suppose you got any liquor in this love-nest of yours?"

Adam grinned, and fetched a jar of corn whisky.

Antoine Bleu leaned across toward me. "Ballantine is a pig," he confided, his eyes twinkling among the leathery creases of his face. "But I had to come to the settlements with him on account of he gets into trouble." He glanced across at his companion with affection, and then suddenly slapped him hard on the shoulder. The blow was so enormous that I expected Ed Ballantine to be hurled out of his chair; but he sat on, chuckling and unmoved.

"Don't you pay no heed to Antoine, Ma'am, nohow," he re-marked. "Soon's he heard there was gonna be a lady in the house, darned if he don't go an' shave off his whiskers right away. Trust a Frenchy not t'miss a chance! Beggin' your pardon, o'course, Ma'am."

I made some polite, noncommittal noise, and bent my head

quickly over my sewing before the trappers could see that I was close to laughter. But the laughter faded quickly enough as the three men sat over their whisky and their mountain gossip. It was almost impossible to disentangle the jumbled *patois* of the trappers, but from time to time I realized they were discussing comrades who had "gone under" since Adam had been among them, scalped by Blackfeet or shot by Mexicans, or knifed by another trapper in a drunken brawl at the rendezvous.

Ballantine and Bleu did most of the talking, fueled by the circling whisky jar, while Adam listened, putting the odd question here and there. The mountain dialect virtually barred me from the conversation, but I could tell that to him it was an old and well-remembered song: there was an eager interest in his voice which I'd missed for many weeks past.

All three men had their feet in the gray ash at the edge of the stone hearth, lost now in reminiscence, and I could easily imagine them in the same flame-lit circle in a sheltered valley-head in the mountain wilderness. Antoine Bleu and Ed Ballantine were an unlikely pair of sirens, but I knew their song was casting a powerful spell over Adam nevertheless. When the fire began to burn low he got to his feet at once to fetch more wood from the yard, anxious to prolong the moment and its magic.

With Adam out of the room and Antoine Bleu staring sleepily into the fire, Ed Ballantine suddenly appeared to remember my presence.

"Seein' you there sewin', Ma'am," he observed, "puts me in mind of a Minnetaree squaw I once know'd. That woman was the smartest thing with a needle I ever did see. She could sew beads smaller'n an ant's eye in patterns you wouldn't believe, just for the doin' of it."

"What's a *squaw*, Mr. Ballantine?" I'd heard the word before, and I was curious.

"We-e-ell . . . I'd say a squaw was an Injun's wife, 'cept that it don't always work like it does among white folks. 'Part from the Cheyenne, that is, where the women are kinder partic'ler." The trapper's brow furrowed in concentration. "You take that Minnetaree gal, for instance. I paid her pappy for her in beaver plews, for the winter, an' she was a good girl, or this child wouldn't say so. Then after a bit she went back home with her mirrors an' dress-cloth an' such, an' she weren't my wife no more. But she'd make some Injun buck a dandy missus all the same. They think better've their women for havin' lived with a white man, you see."

I could hardly believe what I'd been told—not what Ballantine
had revealed about the casual coming-and-going of the Indian
women, but the staggering notion that a winter spent with the squat,
shaggy trapper with his rancid smell and gross eating habits could
actually raise the marriageable status of any Indian girl. Ballantine
saw the expression on my face, and mistook it for disapproval.

"They're good women in their own way, most of 'em, though their
families never leave you alone, an' they do talk some if you don't
beat 'em now an' again."

"What's all this you're sayin'?" demanded Antoine Bleu, waking
up.

"Missus Adam was askin' 'bout Injun women, an' I was tellin'
her."

"What the Hell do you know about women at all? You know
less'n a beaver knows about the Holy Bible."

"I was just goin' t'tell the lady . . . the best squaw I ever had was
a Bannock woman, 'cept she brought her mammy an' half her fam'ly
along to keep her company. She was the best by a long way, an' I've
had Crow women, Flathead, Nez Percé—"

"Shut up, Ballantine—"

"—but never a Snake, for some reason. Ain't that queer? I reckon
you'd have to ask Adam 'bout *them*."

Antoine Bleu promptly kicked his friend hard on the shin, and Ed
Ballantine let out an indignant yelp.

"What you say that for? You drunken *crétin! Tête de mule!* Madame, you don' pay no heed, it's liquor talkin'. Ballantine's a born
fool, an' that's a fact."

"Please don't be concerned. I didn't even hear what Mr. Ballantine
said." It was a lie, but it saved any further discussion, and by the
time Adam reappeared, his arms full of cut wood, my head was bent
once more over my sewing as if the conversation had never taken
place. But I'd learned a great deal that evening, nevertheless. Oh, I
knew there had been women in Adam's past—many of them, no
doubt—and Ed Ballantine had told me nothing new. It was the way
in which he'd spoken of Adam that made me realize that these two
trappers knew my husband much better than I did myself. They were
part of his other existence, the wandering years, while I'd been his
wife for less than twelve months. All of a sudden I began to feel as if
I were married to a stranger.

The trappers stayed with us for three days, turning my once-tidy cabin into a mountain camp with their stores and equipment, spending most of their time before the fire, swapping yarns about their own and their comrades' adventures until my head swam with their tales. Ed Ballantine had a particularly revolting story of two Canadian hunters guzzling the barely cooked intestines of a fat cow buffalo, starting at opposite ends of the greasy coil and racing one another to the middle. He told it with a wealth of gestures and sounds and repeated it three or four times during the days he spent with us. Of Indian women, however, he said not another word, and I could only suppose Antoine Bleu had warned him to hold his tongue.

Another thorn in my flesh was that Ballantine in particular chewed tobacco, spitting constantly and, it has to be admitted, accurately—usually into the fire, but occasionally in other directions when the level of whisky rose inside him. The trappers were far from unusual in this. I'd discovered that spitting was a common habit in the country, and though spittoons were provided in most public places, every floor seemed to be disfigured by yellow stains, and it was hard to avoid getting the disgusting mess on one's skirts. I hated having to endure it at my own fireside, along with the stale morning-reek of chalk pipes smoked late the night before.

At last, however, the two men deemed it time to move off across the prairies to Fort Laramie. I stood at my door watching the burly Ed Ballantine haul himself aboard his horse while Adam passed him the rope of the pack-mule loaded with their winter supplies.

"That's a good man." Antoine Bleu, coming out of the house behind me, nodded his head in the direction of the other two.

"Mr. Ballantine? Oh—Adam . . . Yes, I know he is."

"A good man—inside, you know? But *voyageur*, all the same . . ." This defeated me.

"*Voyageur* . . ." Bleu looked round for inspiration. "Go and come . . . like a bird—you understand?" He waved his hands to indicate the swooping flight of some great, soaring eagle.

"Yes," I said sadly. "I do understand."

———

What I understood was that to keep Adam—to keep even part of Adam—I had to let him go wherever he wanted, for as long as it pleased him to be away from me. *Go and come, like a bird*, Antoine Bleu had said, and he knew Adam better than I.

But it was hard to part with him, nevertheless, and each parting was made worse by the dreadful news the trappers had brought from the river. The steamboat *St. Peters,* which had so nearly brought us upriver from St. Louis, had gone on its way to Fort Union carrying a deadly cargo. One of the crew had been infected with smallpox, and when a Mandan Indian at Fort Clark took it into his head to steal the sick man's blanket the disease immediately began to ravage the whole tribe. The Fur Company's new commander at Fort Union, traveling aboard the *St. Peters,* quickly went down with the infection, and his wife along with him; she'd died, poor woman, after giving birth to a daughter.

The Mandan Indians were dying in dozens. Those not yet infected were taking their own lives by swallowing arrows or leaping from high cliffs after killing their wives and children to save them from the disease. And now the Sioux, who'd been raiding the Mandans, were dying too. It was said along the river that the Assiniboins and the Blackfeet had the infection, and the Minnetarees, who'd defied a warning to keep away from the disease-ridden areas. The traders upriver had tried to keep the Indians away from the forts once smallpox was confirmed, but the Indians suspected the white man's trickery and simply stole the goods which were no longer offered for trade. I began to pray for the coming of winter and the snow which would keep Adam at home.

I never enjoyed the lonely days when Adam was away. At night I kept the door firmly barred and one of Adam's pistols ready loaded on a shelf nearby, and though by day I was usually too busy to be really unhappy, I was always pleased to hear the squeal of Mary, Lizzie's mule, in the road beyond our fence, and to know that the preacher's widow had ridden out to visit.

"Lizzie—" I asked her one day, "is there a doctor anywhere in Independence?"

Lizzie put her untidy head on one side and considered my question.

"The feller who owns one of the livery stables is a doctor, of sorts," she offered. "Went to liveryin' when he couldn't make a livin' out've medicine. Plenty people fell sick all right, but they either got better on their own, or they died off too quick for him to make any money out've 'em. 'Sides—folk round here'll dose themselves before they'll go to a doctor. Sulphur, calomel, jalap—that's the kind of doctorin' they stick to. I don't know as I'd trust the man at the livery stable anyhow. If doctors come way out here it's usually owin' to the fact they've killed a few people somewhere else." She gave me a searching look. "Why d'you want a doctor, anyhow? Are you sick? You look fine to me."

"I think I'm going to have a baby."

For weeks I'd longed to confide in someone, and now I poured out my story. Poor Lizzie, who'd borne four infants only to see them die one by one before their second year, promptly confirmed my diagnosis. There was no doubt about it: unless she was very much mistaken, a child was on the way.

"You don't want a doctor, m'dear, you want a midwife, and there's no shortage of those. Heavens, I've attended so many lyin'-ins I've quite lost count. Don't you fret, you'll be all right when your time comes." She twisted up another straggling wisp of hair and trapped it under a pin.

"What does Adam think of the news, then? He'll want a son, I calculate, like the rest of 'em. Daughters all in good time, but a son first."

"He doesn't know. I haven't told him yet."

"Well, you'd best get on with it, then. He'll be a pappy in the spring."

How could I tell Lizzie of my fears? That I hadn't dared to tell Adam another helpless being was about to come into the world to depend on him—to expect love from him, to expect him to be there whenever he was needed, to demand all the things he found so hard to give?

At the same time I resented my cowardice: why should I be afraid to tell my husband our love had resulted in a child? I was going to have a baby—Adam's baby—and yet I couldn't bring myself to say the words.

In the end, it was only when he came in one day from watering the horses to find me collapsed in a chair, suddenly dizzy, that the secret spilled out.

I watched, wide-eyed, for signs of his displeasure—yet he seemed oddly taken with the idea.

"For some reason, I hadn't thought of it," he admitted. "I'd got used to having just the two of us here—you and me. Never saw myself as a father, somehow. By why not, after all?"

For a moment he fell into a thoughtful silence, and I wondered if he'd remembered that other baby—Tahtokay's child—which had hardly lived long enough to draw breath.

"When will it happen?"

"About the end of March, Lizzie reckons."

He nodded. "Good. Then you and the baby can move in with Lizzie Fletcher while I'm gone."

"I don't mind staying here on my own for a few days. You know that."

"This'll be for more than a few days."

My heart sank. This was the moment I'd feared.

"Where are you going, Adam? And how long will you be away?"

"Andrew Drips is taking the Fur Company traders to the rendezvous next summer. Black Harris is going with him, and he's suggested I join them too. It means leaving at the beginning of April, and getting back in September, if all goes well."

"Six months!"

"Probably nearer five, or five and a half, if I don't have to go all the way to St. Louis on the return trip."

"But why do you have to go at all? Is there no one else?"

"There could be trouble from the Hudson's Bay men this time, and there's talk of finding a new site for the rendezvous on the American side of the divide. In any case, I can't afford to turn down what they're offering to pay. We need the money."

To be honest, it was no more than I'd expected. If I'd married a soldier or a sailor I'd have seen even less of my husband, and he'd have gone into even more danger in the line of duty. The annual fur caravan was a highly organized affair, planned with great precision, whatever went on at the rendezvous itself. At least Adam would be at home when our child was born, even if he'd have to leave soon afterward. I kept telling myself how much bleaker the future might have been.

And spring, thank heavens, was months away.

Once the winter blizzards set in, Adam was kept nearer home for a while as I'd predicted. I'd never seen snow like it. Sometimes it snowed for days on end, the fierce, cutting winds driving the snow in great drifts round the house, piling it up against the windows and making the rooms dark even in daytime until I heated a flatiron in the fire and held it against the glass with a thick cloth to melt the outer coating of snow which shaded the light. One night I went to bed with my hair still damp and woke next morning to find my plaits frozen stiff; I discovered that unless our few precious eggs were kept near the fire they were frozen solid; and I even had to thaw out the ink-bottle before I could write a letter to Aunt Grace in Liverpool telling her of our new home and the coming baby. Clothes-washing became impossible, since although I managed to tie what I'd washed securely to the line in the yard it was literally blown to shreds by the wind.

And yet the blizzards could stop suddenly for no apparent reason. Sometimes in the middle of the night an eerie calm would descend and the falling flakes would vanish, leaving the world quite still and sinister as if some catastrophe was about to happen. Adam loved those frozen lulls in the storm, when he could walk outside in the darkness to study the clear black sky with its canopy of stars. I never failed to be amazed by the ease with which he could identify planets and constellations, as if charting his way through the heavens was no harder than following a twisting mountain trail.

It was during one of these strange calms, late on a winter afternoon, when a face suddenly looked in at the window. I screamed: I couldn't help it. I'd been sitting near the window, trying to catch the last of the fading daylight on the tiny gown I was stitching for the baby, and Adam was cleaning his rifle by the fire. All at once, a face stared directly into my own, a face with narrow, wolfish features and two glaring eyes, the entire scalp shaved naked except for a stiff topknot of hair woven with feathers and quills.

All Ed Ballantine's tales of Indian attacks came back to me in a rush. I was certain the cabin was surrounded, and we'd both be massacred before my baby had even come into the world.

Adam leaped to his feet, seized a shotgun he kept for shooting prairie-fowl, and slowly unbarred the door a few cautious inches. He peered through the gap for a moment, and then I saw him swing the door fully open and go out.

"Oh, Adam—be careful!"

He glanced back through the doorway. "Don't be afraid. I know this man." And he vanished outside once more.

My heart thumping against my ribs, I crept to the door and squinted out into the winter gloom. I could hear Adam's voice a short distance away, although I'd no idea what he was saying. After a few seconds I heard another voice, low and guttural, and a conversation which went on for some minutes, though it seemed to contain such long silences that I guessed much of their talk was being carried on in sign-language.

As my eyes became adjusted to the twilight I began to make out two figures in the yard outside. Adam was standing halfway between

the cabin and the road, very dark and broad against the white of the
snow, partly obscuring the slighter, blanket-wrapped form of the
Indian facing him. Now that I could see the whole of the man he
seemed less frightening than before. I'd noticed people of his race in
the streets of St. Louis, and occasionally in one of the stores in
Independence, but they'd always been dressed, more or less, in the
same clothes as their white neighbors. This red man wore fringed
skins similar to Adam's buckskin coat and a meager, store-bought
blanket, but in addition to his ornamented scalplock he had several
glass pendants fixed to each ear, and he was hung about with a
necklace of what looked like the claws of some large animal and
various other bunches of quills and beads. His face was as sharp as
a hatchet, and his bright glance fixed on me at once, standing just
inside the door of the cabin.

Adam must have seen the movement of the Indian's eyes, and
guessed the reason.

"Come and meet our visitor," he instructed over his shoulder.
"His name's Bird That Watches Smoke, but if you call him Watches
Smoke, he'll answer to it. I've traded with him before, northwest of
here."

I had another reason to be nervous. "What about the smallpox?"

"His people haven't been infected so far. He's a Sauk Indian. They
live not far away from here—at least, his band do. But they know
all about the disease, and they won't trade at the forts upriver. He
wants tobacco and he's offering a buffalo robe. Come and see."
Without turning round, Adam held a hand out to me, and in spite of
my misgivings I left the shelter of the house and stumbled through
the crunching snow to join him.

Watches Smoke inspected me keenly from head to foot, his eyes
glittering with interest, the feathers in his scalplock rustling in the
breeze. When he'd completed his scrutiny he said something in his
own language.

"That was *charmed to meet you*," Adam translated.

Without thinking, I returned the greeting, and immediately felt
foolish. Anyone would think this was the most genteel drawing room
instead of a patch of snowy ground on the edge of the American
prairies, and my befeathered visitor a solemn gentleman in a silk hat
and gloves.

Adam sensed my confusion. "No harm in politeness," he remarked. "The fellow's come calling, after all. And brought his wife.
See her under the tree there?"

Once more I peered into the twilight, and eventually made out an indistinct figure mounted on a paint pony and holding the halter of another, waiting silently under a nearby cottonwood.

"What do you think of the buffalo robe?"

Adam signed to Watches Smoke to hold out the tanned hide for me to inspect. It was thick, and warm, and heavy, cured to soft perfection by a Sauk woman—perhaps the woman waiting with the horses under the tree. As soon as I touched it I knew I wanted to have it for our bed, and there remained only its price to be settled.

At last, after what seemed a good deal of argument, the Indian was satisfied with his bargain. The appropriate amount of tobacco was fetched from the store and Watches Smoke strode off to join his wife under the cottonwood, where he leaped gracefully on to his pony, disappearing with the woman through the deep snow into the darkness.

After that Watches Smoke came regularly to the house, usually accompanied by the young woman who would never approach the door but sat astride her pony a little way off, holding the hackamore of her husband's mount and watching all that went on. Gradually I became more accustomed to the Indian's wild appearance, and though he never came inside the cabin, preferring to trade for blankets or knives in the open yard, I learned a word or two of his tongue and some parts of the plains sign-language, and by a process of smiling and nodding conversation of a kind could be carried on.

All the same, I was now glad that I would be staying with Lizzie Fletcher while Adam was away. I was thoroughly alarmed at the idea of Watches Smoke and his silent wife—or some of his friends, perhaps—suddenly appearing at the house and finding me all alone. Goodness only knew what might happen.

And so as winter began to relax its grip, spreading the promise of fresh grass to the prairies again, I carefully rolled up my rugs, put our household goods into boxes and trunks, and made everything ready to transport to Lizzie's cellar for the summer. As the time of my baby's birth drew nearer it seemed sensible to move entirely into the boardinghouse; Adam was often away all day, and Lizzie was well qualified to deal with any emergencies.

After one false alarm which threw the whole house into a frenzy in the middle of the night, Matthew Edward Gaunt finally made his way into the world on the 27th of March, 1838, with a yell which proclaimed him the most important person in the world. And as far as I was concerned, at that moment he was.

"Easier than some I've known," commented Lizzie dryly as she cut the cord.

"Yes?" I was aching, and exhausted.

"Sure. Though he's the most beautiful child I've ever seen, and that's a fact," she declared, as I'm sure she did at every birth she attended.

But by the time the baby arrived, Andrew Drips had been in Lexington for several days buying supplies for his men at Aull's store, and horses and mules from Jem Hicklin. The twenty two-horse carts, forty or so men and a small horse herd finally rolled out of Westport in the first week of April, but Adam gave himself a few more days at home with us before setting out to catch up with it. When he left, it was with last-minute instructions from headquarters in St. Louis that the rendezvous was no longer to be held at Horse Creek, but at the junction of the Popo Agie and Wind rivers, where the two united to become the Bighorn.

"I'm sure Andrew Drips will be pleased to hear *that*," he remarked gloomily. "It looks like being a fine trip in every way. The spring's late this year so the plains'll be wet as Hell, and I hear we've been saddled with a crowd of squabbling greenhorn missionaries to take along. Sorry, Lizzie, I'm sure they're all saints, when you get to know 'em."

"Don't apologize to me, Adam. I've only knowed one saint in my life, an' that was my Asa, God rest him. Now you sit and admire your son for a bit, and tell that little wife of yours what a clever girl she is. Women like to be fussed over at a time like this—ain't that so, Rachel?"

But the problems of the journey ahead had already begun to eclipse the birth of his son in Adam's mind, and by the time he finally rode off I knew he was long gone from me in spirit. At last, with a swift embrace and a touch of his fingers to my face, he vanished toward the wilderness, and I was alone.

———

There was nothing for it after that but to settle down with my baby and wait for Adam's return.

It was hard at first to be without him, and I was grateful to find so much of my time taken up by all the perplexing, confusing discoveries of new motherhood. Frustrated, Matthew could cry himself purple in a few seconds, seeming almost to stop breathing until I became frantic for his life; when his demands were at last satisfied he became benign again, a genial tyrant who burped and cooed in my arms as if nothing could ever upset him. If he remained sleepless, I imagined he was ill: when he slept soundly for hours on end I was certain of it, and I could hardly keep myself from poking him awake to find out what was wrong. "Wait till you have eight of them," Lizzie used to say when I called her yet again to give an opinion on his color, or his breathing, or some mysterious mark which had appeared on his tiny chest. "When there's eight little ones runnin' around you won't make such a fuss, I guarantee."

Gradually, though, I did manage to look beyond the four walls of my room, and I began to enjoy the bustle of town, the general gossip of the boardinghouse and trips to the store on Lizzie's behalf while she took care of little Matthew, a task she adored in spite of her denials.

For many years Independence had been the natural jumping-off point for the well-worn Santa Fe Trail winding down past Fort Dodge toward Mexico, a route carved out by trading caravans loaded with bolts of calico, glass beads, mirrors, cheap razors and cutlery, flashy hair-combs, trinkets and gimcracks of all kinds as well as basic stores like sugar and the universally acceptable whisky. After a successful season, the prizes were brought back—furs, and quantities of Mexican silver and gold.

I always found something of interest as I walked through town— usually the heavy, rumbling wagons of the traders, heralded by the squealing of their mule-teams as they ploughed through the churned mud underfoot and the cursing of the teamsters who urged them on with long whips toward the gathering-point beyond the town.

Independence was growing rich on the Santa Fe trade, and would grow richer in future as the westward tide of humanity began to flow more strongly. The town was ideally placed for the business of channeling travelers in one direction or another, and the grimy bleakness which had dismayed me so much at first sight was principally caused by its distance from all that could be called luxury in that corner of the world, and not from the poverty of its citizens. The people of Independence were used to "gettin' along" on whatever was available. Everything which appeared on the shelves of the stores, from salt to the complete works of Shakespeare, from window glass to flutes (and I'd seen all these things) had to be brought by river from somewhere like St. Louis or Pittsburgh at a cost of nearly a third of the price of the article. Whatever came aboard the steamer was in stock, what failed to come was out of stock, and the customer had to go without.

Lizzie Fletcher was a regular client of Titus Meadow's General Store near the square, a building which boasted the biggest false front and the tallest shop sign in town. I'd always found it a daunting place, but now, armed with Lizzie's neatly written lists, I soon became familiar with its dark and spice-scented interior.

Right at the back, where the highest shelves clung perilously to the board wall, the piled goods disappeared into dusty gloom. Nearer the door, daylight glinted on rows of copper pans and lamp flues and splashed color on the stack of cotton bolts at the end of one of the long side counters. Everything spoke of honest prosperity and solemn endeavor, from the swinging brass scales to the squarely penned price-cards. Even the counters were impressively solid, worn concave in some places by the constant passage of heavy dollars to and fro, and partway down each side counter stood a row of glass cases expensively shipped from St. Louis, the greasy, pawing fingerprints of eager customers polished off almost as soon as they were applied; it was a point of honor in the store.

From this cave of wonders Titus Meadow dispensed his wares: boot-blacking, ladies' fans, coffee, the ever-present chawin' tobacco, a spade or a hoe, worm powder for animals and humans, bacon, crackers, or pairs of boots which very nearly fitted. With two assistants Mr. Meadow ruled over the business of the store from a post of honor next to a massive iron stove in the rear of the room which was also the main trading-post of town gossip.

Titus Meadow himself looked like a man who had once been fat, but had worried himself into thinness. His shoulders were hollow, his jowls had collapsed, and only a round, low-slung belly testified to his former glorious girth. He was a wizened pear in a white apron, fussing round some favored customer, buzzing a tuneless hum which rose in pitch as his agitation mounted.

He even buzzed at me when I visited his flavorsome empire, and I gathered that something about Adam had impressed Titus Meadow at first sight, and that he thought I too was therefore deserving of respect. In fact, not only did I receive his most deferential attention whenever I stopped by for a paper of pins or a few pounds of sugar, but sometimes I was even treated to the highest accolade the store could provide, a regal nod from the angular, brown-clad Mrs. Meadow, the scourge of the time-wasting menfolk who gathered to chew the fat each morning round the welcoming iron stove.

"Well, you look a deal more cheerful these days, an' that's a fact," Lizzie Fletcher observed one afternoon about six weeks after Adam's departure. I was perched on a wooden bench in the kitchen, dragging off my mud-caked boots after walking to Meadow's store for a bobbin of thread. The boots were a fright, but I'd soon ruined two pairs of shoes in the mired streets, and had finally resorted to wearing small-size boys' leather boots under my long skirts. Lizzie Fletcher's remark made me pause for a moment, gripping the second boot by its muddied heel.

"I suppose I am happier, since you mention it. I was tired for a while after Matthew was born, and I hated to see Adam go away. But now I've every reason to be happy. Six weeks have passed already, and I'm forty-two days nearer to having Adam back again! There's your reason, Lizzie!"

Later, though, I wondered if the explanation was quite so simple. I missed Adam badly, of course, and ended every day by wondering how much closer to the rendezvous—and further away from me— he'd traveled. In another couple of months, perhaps, I'd be able to reverse the process, knowing that the passing of each twenty-four hours brought him closer to home. Every day, by that calculation, should bring me a little extra happiness.

But much as I missed him, Adam's absence had given me a chance to prove I could manage on my own. Out at the cabin, the storehouse roof had blown off one stormy night; our second horse, left for me in a livery stable in town, suddenly seemed to be running up colossal charges since Adam was no longer around to query the bill, and something had to be done.

And then there was Frank Ellis. Now that I was living in town I could hardly avoid bumping into him at some time or another and with Adam away, I'd have to cope with the consequences myself.

In the end I managed to deal with all these problems unaided, and the results were no worse than if Adam had been there to make the decisions himself. I persuaded the young son of a nearby farmer to mend the roof of our store, rewarding him with a watercolor sketch of his parents' house for his mother to hang on her wall—and an excellent bargain it proved to be. After that I paid precisely half of our bill at the livery stable, and told the liveryman I was removing my horse to another establishment where the owner knew better than to try to swindle a lone woman.

The problem of Frank Ellis was more complicated. Whatever Adam had said to him that day at the cabin when Frank set off at such a pace back to town, I'd seen no sign of him all winter, and I'd even begun to wonder if perhaps he'd drifted off again to another township where he felt his talents would bring a greater return.

But of course I did meet him one day, quite by chance, as I was crossing the square. I saw him approach from a long way off in his broad-brimmed hat and his fancy waistcoat, and I knew he'd also seen me, since he slowed his pace as if he meant to stop and say something. Taking a deep breath, I doubled my speed, hitched my chin into the air, refused to meet his eyes, and swept past with the majestic air of a grand duchess seeing nothing she chooses to ignore. Frank Ellis didn't exist. I left him to come to terms with this development, and went on my way.

And all the time, in his cradle at Lizzie Fletcher's house, the trusting eyes of my baby son searched out my face, and his tiny fist closed round my finger as if I were his whole world, titanic and infallible. I was far from infallible, Heaven knows, and though I never doubted that for Matthew's sake I would risk the worst the world could offer, sometimes his blind faith in me filled me with dismay.

Guiltily I remembered a time when I'd gazed at Adam in that same helpless way, and I wondered if it had had an equally disquieting effect on him.

Before Matthew was two months old I wrote once more to Aunt Grace in Liverpool, giving news of the birth. For a fleeting second I thought of writing to my mother. Would the passing months have cooled her rage? Would the birth of her first grandchild give her an excuse to patch up our quarrel?

As soon as I'd thought of the idea, I dismissed it. If my mother had hated my marriage to Adam so much, she was unlikely to be pleased that the union had produced an heir. In any case, it was more than likely that Aunt Grace and my mother had come to terms once more; however much they scratched and spat like fighting cats, they never seemed to lose contact, and I didn't expect that Aunt Grace would miss such a good opportunity of upsetting her sister. I could be sure that in due course my mother would be informed of Matthew's arrival.

Matthew's arrival. We had been two, and now already we were three. From having nothing and no one, I now had two human beings who were dearer to me than life itself, and both of them were changing me, subtly but irrevocably, as the months passed by.

In an unlooked-for way my baby son supplied the physical closeness I'd lost with Adam's departure. His steady suck at my breast was a source of continual pleasure: late at night in my bed he would fall asleep, sated, his head surprisingly heavy against me, his tiny fingers settling like gentle starfish on my skin until I could hardly bear to divide his little body from my own. It was as if the cord had never been cut and he was still part of me, my flesh sustaining his. As the weeks grew into months I became confident in motherhood, growing lazy and luxurious, my small breasts swollen and ripe in the service of my son.

Adam came back at last on the nineteenth of September, lean as a bowstring from the hard trail, his skin tanned bronze by the assault of sun and wind. I welcomed him home a different woman from the girl he'd left behind almost six months earlier. Spring had turned to summer. I'd become warm and golden where before I'd been green wood; instinctive and knowing, demanding from him as well as giving. I no longer waited, helpless, for his word: that was my son's role now. I'd proved myself as Adam's wife—and I'd been without him for too long.

In the years that followed, I remembered that winter as the happiest time of our marriage. His wanderlust blunted for a while, Adam was tolerant of domestic routine and amused by his tiny son, and I welcomed each snowfall as another rampart around our blessed hearth and each roaring blast of wind which drowned out the siren-song of the wilderness. In the long nights I lay in Adam's arms once more under the Sauk Indian's buffalo robe, and believed that at last I could make him forget the seductive call of the mountains.

But plans for another odyssey had already been made, though Adam couldn't bring himself to tell me until it was unavoidable. At the Popo Agie River he'd met up with Joe Walker, a man whose name as a pathfinder was already a legend among trappers like Bleu and Ballantine, and an agreement had been made between them.

When he called on us in late winter, I liked Joe Walker at once. Perhaps a year or two older than Adam, he stood an inch or so shorter, but gave an impression of breadth and power where Adam was spare and supple. With his silver-streaked dark beard and twin-kling blue eyes he was a romantic figure, possessed of swashbuckling style and a sly humor of his own which never descended into cruelty. If he hadn't come to take Adam away from me once more, I'd have welcomed him without reservation as a friend. As it was, I watched the two men resentfully while they discussed their plans over our massive table.

When Adam had arrived at the rendezvous that summer he'd found Joe Walker driving a herd of more than a hundred California horses back east where they would find a ready sale. There was good business to be done in trading cattle and horses, and Walker was content to take on a partner whose efficient, hard-headed attitude to life was the same as his own. Eavesdropping on their conversation I discovered that the arrangement had been made as long ago as the previous summer, though Adam hadn't breathed a word of it to me.

After a while, I couldn't bear the hurt of his secrecy anymore.

"May I ask," I broke in, "when you propose to leave, and how long you'll be away? Since no doubt you expect me to be here when you come back?"

I saw Joe Walker's blue eyes sweep questioningly toward Adam.

"We'll leave in a month's time." Adam was defensive. "And we'll be back again in the autumn . . ." His voice dropped to a murmur. ". . . Next year, that is."

"*Next year?*" I thought I'd misheard him. "Do you mean a year and a half from now? Eighteen months?"

Adam nodded, and smoothed the rough map in front of him with his fingers, avoiding my eye. I couldn't believe it. Eighteen months apart—and he'd known for so long without telling me. I stared from Adam to Joe Walker, and then back again to Adam. There was so much I wanted to say yet I'd no idea where to begin. Inevitably, I made a bad choice.

"Take me with you, Adam, please! Surely this time I could go too! I'm sure Mr. Walker here would take his wife with him," I added desperately, though I knew the argument was hardly appropriate. Joe Walker's seasonal "wives" were all Indian women, well used to the hardships of the trail.

"And what about Matthew? You can hardly drag him all the way to California and back. No, Rachel, you can stay with Lizzie as you did before. Once La Fontaine pays me what he owes, there'll be enough money for your room and board, and I'll feel happier know-ing you're safe in town."

I had to bite my lip to keep back the words I longed to say. My home, my family . . . It was all about to dissolve again. I felt myself on the verge of hysteria, but I couldn't bear to give way to tears before the watchful eyes of Joe Walker.

I could be married to a soldier or a sailor, I reminded myself. *If I try to hold Adam back now, I'll lose him for good. I must learn to let him go with good grace.*

Adam clearly felt guilty for not having spoken before. The guilt was there in his voice as he lay in bed that night, listing all the advantages of his horse-trading trip to California.

"There's Matthew's future to consider, and our own. I might even find us some land in Oregon and we could settle out there, just as we once discussed. You don't really enjoy living in this poky little town, do you, with every man-jack of them knowing your business?"

"I don't mind it."

"Well I do. And a few seasons' horse-trading would buy us the freedom to go where we choose. Away from here, and the filth in the streets, and the small-mindedness—"

"How do you know Oregon will be so much better?"

"Because it's vast, and it's almost empty. There are no people creeping over the face of it, leaving their slug-trails behind them."

"There will be—one day."

"Then we'll go somewhere else."

"Oh, Adam, you can't go on forever! Don't you see that?"

"I don't see it at all."

I could tell, by the sound of his voice in the darkness, that he was losing patience with me. He'd made up his mind to go to California, and was inventing reasons to prove it was the best thing for all of us that he should. To argue would only be to sour the atmosphere between us, and I was powerless. But I hadn't forgiven him for keeping me in ignorance of his plans for so long, and with a chilly silence descending over us I turned my back on him and waited despairingly for sleep.

Adam had brought back a horse from the summer rendezvous of which he was particularly proud, a Palouse, as it was called, raised by those master horse-breeders, the Nez Percé Indians, in the strange coloring of its kind—dark bay to the hindquarters, then suddenly white with bold brown spots as if the horse had collided with a paintpot. It was an intelligent, spirited animal, and I longed to have one for myself.

Now Adam promised me, as if it was the price of his freedom, that he would bring me a Palouse of my own when he returned. The bargain became a bitter game between us, standing for all those matters of hurt and betrayal which were beyond discussion. And on that gray morning when he set off once more toward the mountains, and beyond them to California, the spotted horse intruded to the last, a shield behind which Adam could ignore my deep distress.

"Adam—" I'd seen him turn his horse's head at last to the west.

He swung round in the saddle. "Don't worry, I won't forget your pony! Trust me!" And with a final wave he kicked the animal into a gallop, dwindling rapidly to a tiny speck against the limitless landscape.

12

A traveling daguerreotype-maker, one of Morse and Draper's disciples from New York, had arrived in town not long before Adam left, turning out dim, silvery portraits of the wanderers who thronged Independence to be sent home to sweethearts and families. At the door of his tent he'd hung examples of his art: Missouri-farmhands-turned-adventurers, stiff in go-to-meeting clothes before a canvas landscape and a sheaf of trailing vines; dark-eyed Mexicans in spurs and extravagant hats, one foot on a sawn-off log; the occasional solemn couple newly united in matrimony, the bride seated, her husband standing rigidly behind her as if defying her to bolt. These pictures were something entirely new. The pale little ovals seemed like magic to me, preserving their sitters in time-defying chemicals, and on the spur of the moment I begged Adam to have a likeness taken to keep by me while he was away.

I fully expected him to refuse point-blank. Something in his soul recoiled from leaving even such a tiny trace of where he'd been and how he'd looked, but by then I was so near to giving way to utter despair that he went to the picture-tent as I'd asked, and stood—feeling like a fool, he said—before a draped plush curtain while the man fiddled interminably with his plates and lenses.

And I was disappointed by the result; it made Adam look hand-some but commonplace, which he was not. The camera had caught only the outer shell, while the man within had fled.

Nevertheless, it was better than nothing, and I set the picture up like an icon on the shelf in my neat white room at Lizzie Fletcher's house. I held Matthew up to it every day, reminding him that it was the image of his father who would return, all being well, in time to celebrate my twenty-first birthday.

I wasn't the only person made miserable by Adam's absence. Often now I would see Watches Smoke in the main street of Independence, weaving his way through the crowd of passing townsfolk toward one of the stores where he hoped to exchange cured pelts for tobacco or blankets. His appearance no longer alarmed me, but in any case, much of the proud wildness I remembered from our first meeting seemed to have deserted him in the dusty streets of town. His necklace of bear-claws had gone and he'd stopped painting his head with vermilion dye, presumably to make himself more acceptable in the white man's village. His young wife never came with him. No doubt she was waiting patiently somewhere on the outskirts of town, holding the hackamore of her husband's horse. What else could a wife do, but wait?

The snows of winter came at last. Then, with agonizing slowness spring succeeded winter, and with a rush of green to the land, time began to pass more quickly. Matthew had become a voracious explorer, and soon exhausted the possibilities of the yard behind Lizzie's house. His greatest treat—all the more exciting because of its rarity—was the hiring of a one-horse gig from the livery stable to whirl out in style with his mother and Aunt Lizzie to the river-landing to view the steamboat when it called. He was almost two and a half years old, no longer a baby but changing into a strong-willed little boy with ideas entirely of his own, and I was sad that so much of this transformation had taken place without Adam being there to watch it.

Still, when Adam returned in the autumn I could share my memories with him: Matthew trying to capture a buzzard, or scaling Lizzie's wooden fence to see the marvels on the other side—or the dreadful day he vanished from the yard, to be found stumping unconcernedly between the hooves of the horses in the nearby livery stable.

Gradually the picnic days passed, and Adam's return came nearer. I showed Matthew how to count the remaining weeks on his podgy fingers, and his daily attempt to chart his father's return became a hilarious ritual among the other boarders in Lizzie's house. He was a fair child who seemed set to share Adam's coloring, though sometimes I fancied I could also see in my son's gray eyes the same self-absorbed, restless expression which I dreaded so much in Adam's. Then he would smile at me, and I could convince myself I'd imagined the resemblance.

Two months to wait, at the most. Then four weeks, then two . . . perhaps ten more days . . . which passed. Another week, at the most. . . . And then the week had gone by, but still Adam hadn't returned.

I continued to wait, and as the days passed a sense of unreality began to possess me. I knew it was ridiculous to expect a precise arrival date after a difficult eighteen-month journey through mountain and desert—but I did expect it, nevertheless. Adam had promised to come back in September, and he was now almost a month late.

I took to hovering near the front door; I hardly ever went far from the house anymore. And when, on the 10th of November, I caught a glimpse of a tall male form approaching the door, I was there, wrenching it open, almost before the brisk knock could echo through the house. Adam was back at last!

Except that it wasn't Adam, but Joe Walker, feathered hat in hand, waiting somberly on the threshold.

———

I gaped at Joe Walker in disbelief, suddenly seized by a sense of doom. If Joe Walker was back—where was Adam?

From a great distance I heard Lizzie Fletcher's businesslike step on the planked floor behind me and felt her arm round my shoulders, guiding me into the kitchen. Joe Walker followed us through, and as Lizzie pulled out a chair for me by the table in the center of the room I saw him take up an uneasy position with his back to the fire.

"Where's Adam, Joe? Where is he?"

As soon as I asked the question I felt foolish. He'd come to tell me where Adam was—I could see it in his face—and I knew for a certainty from his expression of reluctance and concern, that there was more to tell than a simple story of delays on the trail.

Joe Walker cleared his throat unwillingly.

"To tell you the honest truth, Ma'am, I don't know where he is."

Joe's blue eyes regarded me sympathetically, and I realized he'd wasted no time in coming to find me. He was still travel-stained and weary from the long drive; his buckskins were shiny with long use, and his wide-brimmed hat, which he'd thrown down on the table, made a circle of trail-dust on the spotless wood.

"There ain't much more to say. Adam went off on his own, we arranged to meet up again, an' he never showed up. That's the long an' short of it." He shrugged, as if the whole story was contained in those few words.

"Well, if that don't beat all! That's not much of a tale to bring to a poor girl wonderin' where her husband's got to!" Lizzie burst out indignantly. "Where did all this happen, then? In California? In the mountains? There must be more'n you've told us, I reckon! Here—" From a nearby cupboard Lizzie produced a bottle of whisky and some glasses. "Now I don't doubt we're all in need of some of this. Rachel, you too. You must be dry as a cob, Mr. Walker, an' I calculate you've still a deal of talkin' to do." She passed him a brimming glass. "Now, get this down, and tell us everything you know. *Everything*."

"Please, Joe. Tell me exactly what happened." I felt strangely calm, as though I'd known all along that this time something would keep Adam from coming back to me.

Joe Walker had stationed himself firmly before the warming fire, legs astride, thoughtfully swirling the whisky in his glass.

"We rode on down to California like we planned, an' picked up a herd of pretty good stock. Soon as the weather cleared we started back east with them, travelin' fast as we could, considerin' the size of the herd we were drivin'. We'd just about got within sight of the Sawtooths when for some reason Adam took it into his head to have a look back down the Snake River a ways. I don't know why, an' he never said. Hell—who knows why Adam did anythin'?" He gave me a swift glance. "Anyhow, we fixed to meet up again at Fort Hall an' drive the herd on down toward South Pass. 'Cept he never showed up, like I said." Joe Walker spread his arms wide to indicate his mystification.

"How long did you wait for him? Perhaps he was delayed."

"No, Ma'am, I waited long enough. Adam knew that country like his backyard. If he wanted to be someplace on time, there warn't nothin' to stop him."

"Are you sure he couldn't have got lost?"

"Lost? *Adam?*" Walker gave a snort of laughter, a sudden release of tension. "No, Ma'am, he couldn't have got lost."

"Then something must have happened to him! Why didn't you go and search?" All of a sudden I was outraged at the callousness of this man who was supposed to be Adam's friend. "Do you mean to tell me you sat safely in the fort, waiting, and when he didn't arrive you just started for home without him? He would have gone searching for you, Joe!"

"No, Ma'am, he would not, I can promise you that." Joe Walker sounded hurt. "He wouldn't have gone searching, because there just ain't no sense in it. There's no tellin' where he might have gone. You've never seen the kind of country there is in those parts. Might as well try to find a louse on a bear's belly. Adam knew what he was doin'—an' he didn't want nursemaidin'."

"He was alone?"

Walker nodded. "That's how he wanted it. In any case, we needed all the men to move the stock." He paused, and then shrugged again. "I'm real sorry to have to bring you the news, Rachel, but there's nothin' I can do about it."

"Mr. Walker," interrupted Lizzie, who'd been listening in thoughtful silence, "are you certain that's all you know? 'Cos I wouldn't like to think of poor Rachel here frettin' over what you've said, when there's somethin' you've missed out. You sound to me like a man who knows more'n he's sayin', an' I reckon Rachel has a right to the full story."

"Well . . . When you say *the full story,* Ma'am . . . I've told you everythin' I know for certain—which ain't much, when you string it together. But I did hear somethin' else—just a rumor, mind, an' I can't vouch for the man I got it from. . . . But a Canadian trapper came into Fort Hall while I was there, an' said he'd seen a Crow Injun ridin' a horse which sounded mighty like Adam's. That Palouse of his he was so fond of. Kind of recognizable, that spotted animal."

I couldn't accept this slender evidence as reason for gloom.

"But there must be more than one Palouse in the mountains, surely! And I thought the Crows were friendly."

"So they are, so long as you're watching 'em. That goes for any of the breed. But this one, so the trapper said, had Adam's apishemore under his backside—red, with a white stripe, weren't it?"

This was a real blow. I remembered that saddle-blanket well.

"Perhaps he's been taken captive by the Indians!"

Walker shook his head. "The mountain Injuns don't take captives like that. They either rob you an' leave you alone, or . . . well . . ." His voice tailed off.

"You think he's dead, Joe, don't you?"

"I only go by what I know, Rachel, not what I hear. An' all I know is, he didn't make it to the fort. *Why* he didn't make it is somethin' else."

"He'll come back, Joe. He must come back! All sorts of things could have happened to delay him! Your trapper could be mistaken about the horse, after all . . . And if he's still alive—is it possible for a man to come through the mountains in the winter months?"

"It's possible, yes, but not easy. And a man can't make it without a horse."

"As long as it's possible, I won't give up hope. I'll go on believing Adam's alive, and I'll wait for him to come back."

Joe Walker regarded me in silence for a moment, the fingers of one hand combing his silver-streaked beard. "You do that, Rachel. But I wouldn't wait too long, if I was you."

"But he may be alive. You said yourself that you couldn't be sure."

"Yes, Ma'am."

"But you think I'm wrong, all the same."

"Rachel, he's your husband, an' I reckon you should know. Adam's been a friend of mine for years, but I've no more notion of how his mind works now than on the first day I met him. He had a purpose in goin' off down the Snake like that, but he didn't tell me what it was, nor anyone else. Maybe he *is* alive like you say, an' he had some good reason for not gettin' to Fort Hall when he said. But it's ten to one he met up with some trouble back there—Injuns, or a bear, maybe. You'll have to face the fact, it could be you're a widow now. What'll you do if you don't see him again?"

"Mr. Walker!" exclaimed Lizzie, shocked. "Trust in the Lord, an' He'll surely give us hope."

"Reckon so, Ma'am. Hope don't always put bread on the table, though."

I didn't even dare to consider the possibility that Adam was dead, leaving me alone in this alien land.

"I won't give up hope, Joe, whatever you say. Will you promise me something?"

"Anything I can do."

"If you do hear news of Adam—good or bad—will you write to me? I don't care if it's years from now. Even if he . . . doesn't come back . . . I'll still want to know what really happened. The whole story. Everything you know."

"Sure. If that's what you want."

"You could write to me here. Lizzie will know where to find me."

Walker nodded. "Reckon that's about all, then. I hate to be the one to bring you news like this. There's a bunch of good boys gone under since I started in the mountains, an' that's a fact. But if it means anything, there weren't one of them would've lived any other way, risks or no risks."

He retrieved his hat from the table, and stood, turning the brim between his fingers.

"Ma'am . . . Rachel—"

"Yes?"

"How're you goin' to be fixed for money now? I'll pay you Adam's share of the stock we bought, just as soon as I get paid for it myself, but in the meantime, if you're short—"

"I'll manage. Until Adam gets back. But thank you for asking, all the same."

There was nothing more to say, and Joe Walker took his leave, refusing Lizzie's offer of food. There was relief in the set of his broad back as he strode out of the kitchen, his unpleasant duty done.

It was only after I heard the front door bang shut behind him that the tears came, great hot tears which streamed down my face to splash in patches on my cotton blouse. I'd lived in such terror of losing Adam, as if our happiness had been too great to endure. And yet, in spite of all Joe Walker had said, I still couldn't bring myself to believe that Adam was dead. If there had been a corpse to grieve over, cold and final . . . But without that, how could I believe in his death? For Adam not only *had* life, he *was* life. If he'd died it would have taken far more than the quick snuffing of a candle: the world would know; I would know. I wasn't a widow. Adam would come back.

I returned to waiting, and I waited all winter for that familiar step outside the door, for Adam's voice asking Lizzie where to find me. I stared at faces in the street, and at every horse that passed. And all the time I had to reassure Matthew that his father—the father he couldn't remember—would come back to us both before long. Sometimes, gently, Lizzie would try to talk to me of death and resurrection, and of how I'd be reunited with Adam in a perfect world to come, if not in this one. But I brushed her comfort aside. Adam would return in the flesh, as strong and vital as he'd been on the day he rode off.

In the spring Joe Walker sent some of the money due from the sale of the California horses, and I continued to pay Lizzie for our weekly board. But Matthew needed boots, and my own clothes were becoming threadbare and stained beyond repair by the filth of the winter streets. However carefully I managed our slender budget, our little store of money continued to dwindle, and as soon as the worst of the cold was past I decided to move back to the cabin. Lizzie was horrified, and offered to keep us both for as much as we could afford to pay—or for nothing, until more money came my way. But the more she protested the more determined I became. If Adam came back—*when* Adam came back—he would find me waiting for him at our own fireside, just as if my faith had never wavered for an instant.

It became a point of honor to keep a fire going in the cabin hearth, but at the price of a hard, lonely life on the edge of town. Without Adam to shoot jackrabbits or prairie-fowl for the pot, Matthew and I existed on whatever we could grow or buy cheaply in town. I was given some chickens, which at least supplied eggs and the odd cooked fowl, but for the rest we lived on beans, potatoes and squashes, and the inevitable cornmeal mush. Even Mrs. Bee's salt pork became something for special occasions. My hands grew rough and scarred from chopping firewood, and since I'd sold our one remaining horse as an unjustified luxury, I had to walk into town for provisions, carrying the bags of flour and meal slowly home on my back unless Lizzie insisted on bringing them out to me on the irascible Mary. And at night I sat behind my stoutly barred door and listened to the whoops and yells of drunken teamsters returning to their camp beyond town after an evening's revelry in the barrooms near the square.

The face which looked back at me from the mirror now was thin and burned brown by the sun. My eyes stared out accusingly from great purple hollows and there was a scar on my cheek where a sliver of wood had flown up from the axe to cut me. I looked like a drudge —a wretched, starved drudge—and I wanted so much to look pretty . . . When Adam came back.

Then one evening as darkness fell I heard a knock at the cabin door. It was a strange sound—odd in a way I could hardly define, more of an accidental thump than a summons to open up. Cautiously, I eased the bar from its hooks and opened the door an inch or two. There was no one on the doorstep, and not a soul to be seen in the yard, but as my eye traveled downward it fell on the haunch of a freshly killed deer.

I got such a fright that I almost drew back and slammed the door. Then I realized that the meat was a gift, and the giver was no doubt waiting close by to see how his present was received. I peered out into the dusk. There in the roadway stood a blanket-wrapped figure, only just discernible, black against the blue dimness all around.

"Watches Smoke? Is that you?"

I saw the man in the road nod his head.

"Is this—for me?" I pointed to the venison, and then to myself.

The Indian nodded. "You," he called, and raised his right hand, index finger extended, in the zig-zag movement which I knew was the Plains sign for *alone*.

I was relieved—I admit it—when he turned to go, then as the wind whipped at the skirts of his blanket and I saw how painfully thin he'd become and how sharply his bones stood out under a scant covering of flesh, I felt ashamed of my fears. How could I possibly be afraid of a man in that condition—a man who'd ignored his own great need to bring food for the wife and son of a friend?

"Watches Smoke—wait! Do you—want to eat—here? With us, in the cabin? There's plenty of meat for us all." I beckoned to him and made eating motions, pointing to the house.

The Indian hesitated, his threadbare blanket drawn tightly about him like the rags of his dignity as a giver of gifts. He was hungry— desperately hungry—and I could see him glance down at the meat lying on the muddy step and then stare up at me, suspicion and need struggling against one another in his mind.

I stood back from the door, giving him freedom to enter the house. After several seconds during which his eyes never left my face, weighing my intentions, he walked swiftly up the path toward my open door.

"Watches Smoke," I asked as he reached me, "your squaw—is she here with you?"

His black eyes fixed me fiercely. *"No—squaw."* And with that he passed in front of me and entered the house.

I'd come a long way from the hesitant girl brought as a bride to the cabin a few years before. Thanks to Adam, I could skin a haunch of venison, spit it and have it cooking over the fire within minutes, and this time, with my own hunger lending speed to the knife, the meat was sizzling over the flames before Watches Smoke had time to change his mind. Not that I ever imagined he would. While the venison cooked he crouched, motionless, by the hearth, his eyes fixed on the meat, the firelight dancing dull red on a body even more emaciated than I'd realized when it was shrouded by the old blanket. Two or three strings of cheap glass beads dangled from his neck across the pitiful hollows of his collarbones; his cluster of earrings had gone, and I was sure I could have counted his ribs if he'd stood up. Life for Watches Smoke, too, had become hard.

I wondered where his wife had gone. Back to her own family, perhaps, if her husband had failed to look after her properly—or perhaps she was dead of one of the white man's diseases which were fatal to the Indians.

Watches Smoke clearly knew that Adam hadn't returned, and I wondered how he'd found out. How I wished I could question him in the Indian tongue, in case by some chance he'd heard news of Adam from his own people! Then I realized he'd probably watched the cabin and seen me alone, plodding into town with Matthew or chopping firewood in the yard.

The outermost layer of venison cooked quickly and soon gave forth an irresistible smell. Without a word, Watches Smoke suddenly drew out a long knife, lunged at the meat, hacked off a large piece for himself, and started to chew with noisy relish. Matthew, who'd been careful to sit as far away from the wild red man as he could, watched every move, his eyes almost starting out of his little head with amazement.

I'd been about to fetch a plate and cutlery, but I was so hungry myself—for hunger had imperceptibly become part of our lives— that the sight of Watches Smoke stuffing his mouth with such haste banished any remaining restraint. I, too, fell upon the slowly turning meat with unashamed greed, sawing off a chunk of it for Matthew and another for myself.

Juices from the venison ran down my chin as I crammed the succulent slices into my mouth; the sharp, gamey tang of the meat mingled magically with the reek of wood-smoke where the fire had crisped it, filling my nose and mouth with its wonderful flavor. I thought of Ed Ballantine and his table manners, and my own righteous horror as I'd watched him eat—and I wished him there in the cabin once more so that I could humbly beg his pardon for my presumption.

Next to me, so close that his copper elbow brushed the fringe of my shawl, Watches Smoke tore pieces of the roast apart with impatient fingers before packing them into his mouth, oblivious to everything else. He'd been so hungry—yet instead of keeping the meat for himself, he'd brought it to the cabin. Because Adam had befriended him, and he knew Adam's wife was alone.

I watched Matthew happily gnawing a lump of venison, his fingers shining with grease. Poor little chap, he hadn't eaten so well in weeks. Now he was too busy eating to speak, but sensing my approval, he looked up at me and grinned. It was a feast—a banquet

—a glorious celebration of the end of hunger for the present. Following Watches Smoke's lead, I leaned forward and cut myself some more.

At last Matthew announced himself full to bursting and his eyes began to droop heavily in sleep. Watches Smoke's jaws had slowed, and he was digging with his knife at some persistent scrap lodged between his teeth. All three of us were greasy, and sated, and happy: the red man, the white woman and her child, united in bloated satisfaction.

There was still meat on the bone—oh, the luxury of waste—but diffidence began to descend between us once more with the ending of hunger. Watches Smoke withdrew into his blanket, his face as impassive as ever and only his shining, restless eyes betraying any interest in his strange surroundings. Our brief moment of kinship was over. He was an Indian again and I was white, and I wondered if there was any way I could make him understand how grateful I was for his kindness.

Remembering a half-full jar of whisky I'd discovered earlier that day in the loft, I fetched it down and out of habit poured a good quantity of the stuff into one of my best wineglasses, the nearest container to hand. Watches Smoke watched me intently, and when I handed him the glass, drained the contents without ceremony, holding the delicate goblet out at once to be refilled. He was evidently no stranger to firewater corn whisky, and was well into his second glassful as I carried Matthew into the next room to put him to bed.

When I returned to the fire a few minutes later, Watches Smoke and the whisky jar had both vanished soundlessly into the night, leaving the door wide open. After a moment I realized that my elegant stemmed wineglass had disappeared with him.

————

Unfortunately Watches Smoke wasn't my only unexpected caller. A few days later, a frightening midnight visit by a group of drunken teamsters forced me to accept at last that I must move back to town, where a lone woman and her child could find safer accommodation.

"No more'n I expected," said Lizzie tartly. "This town's goin' all to ruin, for sure. I told you weeks ago I'd be happy to keep you and Matthew on account, and you can pay me when you're able. Help out round the house, if you must. Jinnah's right down magged with all the folk that's comin' an' goin'."

"I couldn't let you do it, Lizzie. I'll happily help out in any way I can, but I must give you something for our board. Independence is so busy now, you could find someone willing to pay almost any price for a room."

"No one I'd care to have in the house, thank you kindly. Anyone payin' so much would expect to be spittin' an' smokin' an' drinkin' liquor, an' I won't tolerate that kind of behavior in my home. *Mrs. Fletcher's place is solemn as a hen-coop*—that's what they say in town, an' it suits me jes' fine. So you sit tight, Rachel, and don't you fret. You'll get through this all right, see if you don't."

In the end we settled on the paltry sum of two dollars a week; it was far less than Lizzie could have asked from a stranger, but it was enough to strain our already slender budget. We needed money to live—and for another project which had begun to take shape in my mind as, little by little, I'd begun to face the awful probability that Adam was gone for good. Without ever admitting it openly, when the spring of 1841 came and Adam didn't appear from the snow-bound mountains as the passes opened, I realized in my heart that I'd never see him again. Adam was surely dead, or he'd have found a way of coming back to me.

And without Adam's return to fasten on, I began to look round for another way forward, for a new horizon on which to fix my sights. Before long, I'd decided to go home—not to St. John's, where I'd been so unhappy, but to Liverpool, to Aunt Grace and Captain Fuller, whose house had been home to me during some of the happiest days of my life.

At the same time I was ashamed of my failure to come to terms with this country which Adam had chosen; I'd wanted so much to make myself part of it, and eventually I might have done so. But hardship had stripped the romance from my eyes. America had taken Adam from me, and given me nothing in exchange. Lizzie Fletcher was the kind of woman this new nation needed, with an abiding faith in the future and a fierce, unquestioning belief in her own contribution to it. I knew I could never match Lizzie's blind optimism, and with Adam gone, I had Matthew's future to think of—all I had left of the man I'd loved.

Always, my thoughts returned to the same theme: money. We needed money to make the long journey to Liverpool—we even needed money to stay where we were, and I had almost none left. It crossed my mind to ask Aunt Grace for help, but pride kept me from putting the words on paper. I'd chosen to follow Adam, and nothing would make me admit it had been a mistake.

Yet Adam had said Pierre La Fontaine still owed him something for his previous trip west. With new hope in my heart I made the long river-journey to St. Louis, leaving Matthew in Lizzie's capable hands, and searched out the Fur King in his warehouse lair.

I came home again with a bare eighteen dollars, hardly enough to pay my fare to the city. There should have been more—much more. I knew it, and I could tell from his deceitful face that Pierre La Fontaine knew it too, but was confident I had no way of proving the debt. "*Hélas,*" he murmured over my hand as he showed me out, "such a sad loss, your husband. But I cannot afford charity, all the same. . . ."

———

"Well, that settles it," said Lizzie firmly as soon as she heard. "No more talk of money. You don't pay me a cent until such time as you got means to do so."

"I'll find a job, Lizzie, and pay you as we arranged. Don't worry —there must be something I can do."

Lizzie grumbled at that, but she could see I'd made up my mind. I fully intended to pay my way at the boardinghouse, and to save up enough money to take Matthew back to England, however I had to manage it. I'd find work somewhere, and after that . . . Well, I was no stranger to scrimping and saving. I'd made my decision—and the chance of a job presented itself so quickly that for once I could believe Lizzie's just and merciful God had not abandoned me.

Passing Titus Meadow's thriving emporium one morning on an errand for Lizzie I noticed a square of white card propped in the right-hand window between a bottle of horse liniment and a cluster of lamp-chimneys. Meadow's General Store, it announced, required an assistant of good appearance who could read a bit and count some. Applicants should inquire within.

Titus Meadow oiled forward as usual when he saw me, though perhaps a little less eagerly these days now that news of Adam's disappearance had spread round town.

"I need a job, Mr. Meadow. The job you're advertising in your window."

At once, the benevolent expression departed from Titus Meadow's face, and he began to wheeze his dismay.

"Oh, Mrs. Gaunt, I don't think we want a lady here. . . . By which I mean, a woman. Certainly not someone like yourself. Wouldn't suit you at all—there's all manner of low types come in here, and you'd have to see to them. It wouldn't suit at all, I reckon. Not at all."

"Mr. Meadow, I've no choice. I must have some work to keep myself and my child, now that I'm alone. I can work hard, I assure you."

Titus Meadow's voice quavered with reluctance, and he looked nervously round the store for support.

"I don't doubt you'd work hard, don't doubt it at all, Mrs. Gaunt. But, you know, there's a deal of *heavy* work to be done sometimes, and you don't look over-strong, if you'll pardon—"

"*Titus!*"

There was a stirring in a shadowed doorway to the rear of the store, and with a rustling of stiff skirts Mrs. Regina Meadow sailed into view, tall and straight as a ship's mast, angular as its spars. At the black iron stove she hove to, and stared at her husband.

"What does Mrs. Gaunt require?"

"Mrs. Gaunt has come about work, my dear. About the card in the window. She wants to work here, and I've told her it's quite out—"

"You're not in black, I see, Mrs. Gaunt."

Regina Meadow turned her pale eyes on me, taking in every detail of my modest gray dress buttoned tightly to the neck where it finished in a dainty piqué collar.

"I don't know for certain that I'm a widow, Mrs. Meadow." The truth was that I'd hesitated once more before taking the final plunge into widowhood, as if my descent into somber black would make Adam utterly, conclusively dead, and I would be the slayer of all hope.

Regina Meadow stalked toward me across the floor and thrust her bony features down toward mine. I could smell the faint, flowery scent of lavender-water which hung about her like a faded bouquet.

"You may depend upon it," she pronounced with finality. "Depend upon it, Mrs. Gaunt—you are a widow."

She straightened her ramrod back once more, and it seemed to me that Death itself had set a skeletal hand on my shoulder, snuffing in its dusky crape any last flicker of faith which remained.

"Titus," continued Mrs. Meadow, "we should remember the teaching of Our Lord toward those in distress. Charity, Titus."

"Of course, my dear."

"Besides, as I recall, the last boy you hired cleared out on a wagon to Santa Fe, and Bobby McGuire sneaked off with five bags of meal after that brawl in the Trader's House. I don't convene such things will happen to Mrs. Gaunt. She is a mother, after all, Titus."

The storekeeper's jowls wobbled unhappily. "But don't forget, there's the stove to feed, an' the sweeping-out, an' the windows to fix—"

"If Mrs. Gaunt wishes to work here, she must carry out the duties which go with the position," concluded Regina Meadow calmly. "Is that agreed, Mrs. Gaunt?"

"Certainly."

"But you must wear black, like a decent woman. Otherwise, what'll people think of you? Mr. Meadow will explain the pay." And with a nod of somber dismissal she set sail again for the dark doorway in the rear of the shop, her husband's eyes solemnly following until that square, chocolate-brown back had disappeared from view.

And with that I became a shop assistant, and the first stage of my grand plan seemed to be under way at last.

13

The wage at the store was as miserly as I'd expected—three dollars a week and a corner of the back shop to sleep in had I been the kind of rootless young fellow they usually employed. Still—it would pay for our lodging at Lizzie's and leave a little over for clothes and other necessities. Perhaps I could find work as a dressmaker in the evenings, and save my earnings toward the cost of the journey to England.

I'd made inquiries in St. Louis about the price of the Atlantic passage, and discovered that even a modest cabin for Matthew and myself would cost around a hundred and forty dollars. Then there was the journey from Independence by river to Pittsburgh and the last link in the chain, from Pittsburgh over the Alleghenies to New York. One way or another, I reckoned I'd need at least two hundred and fifty-five dollars in my purse when I left Independence, allowing for a short wait in New York while I found a vessel ready to sail. I could have saved a fair amount by traveling as a deck passenger on the riverboat instead of in the cabin, but I'd seen the wretched conditions of the creatures traveling amongst the cargo on our way upriver from New Orleans, and I dreaded joining them, a lone woman with only a small boy for an escort.

Two hundred and fifty-five dollars. My anxious arithmetic covered several pieces of paper, but I could see no way of reducing the amount. Some days, when I was tired and dispirited, two hundred and fifty-five dollars might as well have been the moon, I had so little chance of laying my hand on it. Yet I was determined to try, all the same.

For the rest of that summer I toiled behind Titus Meadow's counter, fetching and weighing out, cutting and measuring, cramming swollen and calloused feet into shoes of all sizes, counting out crackers from the tall wooden barrel by the stove, fishing with a hooked pole for the row of buckets swinging above my head, pouring out gallons of stinking oil for lamps, or unrolling calico, flannel and plaid stuffs before the critical eyes of women customers.

One minute I was out with a broom, sweeping the inevitable dirt from the boardwalk down into the rubbish-strewn street before it could blow back through the open doors of the store; next moment, I might be called upon to dispense hairpins to one of the girls from the Trader's House, or louse powder, or coffee, tobacco or flour to a departing teamster, before going out yet again to brush the billowing dust away from my employer's threshold.

I welcomed the work. While I was busy I had no time to think, but as soon as I had a few minutes' leisure, painful memories of Adam came rushing back. The sight of myself each morning in the mirror, clad in solemn black, had done as much as anything to convince me I was now a widow, though a widow without a grave to visit or a corpse to mourn over.

Perhaps it was a morbid preoccupation, but I'd have given a great deal to know the manner of Adam's death, however awful. Not knowing left me prey to dreadful imaginings in the middle of the night, when I'd wake in panic, calling his name. But there was no one to ask—until the day I looked up from polishing one of Titus Meadow's glass cases to find Antoine Bleu standing before the counter, a doleful expression on his normally cheerful face.

"Madame! So I find you here! I go to the cabin, but the fool who lives there now tell me he don' know where you've gone. *Et tonnerre!* Now I find you by luck. I think maybe you go back to England since . . . since Adam isn't here anymore."

He regarded me solemnly enough, but the straggling fur hat whose tails dangled about his ears made him look almost comic. It was a long time since I'd spoken to anyone in the greasy buckskins of the mountains, and I couldn't help feeling a lurch of the heart when I remembered that Antoine had been Adam's friend for many years.

He was gazing round the store now, sniffing the mingled household scents of Titus Meadow's stock, and I felt compelled to ask my question.

"Is there anything you can tell me—anything at all—about what happened to Adam? It would make such a difference, just to know for certain."

Antoine shook his head gloomily. "I never hear of a man disappear so quick. Just one day, and he was gone. Nothing. Not a word. I have even asked some of the Indians, but they don' know." He paused, trying to think of something comforting to say. "Sometimes it happens like that, when a man goes off on his own. Maybe to me, too, one day." He made a face and crossed himself quickly.

"Oh, Antoine, please take care. No more risks—nothing can be worth that."

"It's all I know, Madame. How can I live otherwise?"

"Adam said that to me, once. And you told me he was a—"

"A *voyageur,* Madame."

"Coming and going like a bird."

Antoine nodded. "Free like a bird. An' that's what you must remember now. No more sadness. All free like a bird."

For a moment we stood there in melancholy silence, sharing our loss. But the sound of our voices had roused Titus Meadow out of the back shop to see what was afoot, and I hastily set about fetching the salt and sugar which had brought Antoine Bleu into the store in the first place. A few more minutes under the storekeeper's suspicious eyes were enough to complete the transaction, and though I'd dearly have loved to keep Antoine in the store, simply for the pleasure of hearing him talk about the old days he'd shared with Adam, there was no good reason for him to stay.

"One thing," he murmured softly as he picked up his purchases at last. "You need any help, Madame? You need money for something right away? I don' have much, but if there's anything—"

"Thank you, Antoine, you're a good friend. But this job pays for my keep, and I'll find a way of saving for our passage to England sooner or later."

Titus Meadow was bearing down on us from the back of the store.

"That's good. But don' forget, I was Adam's friend, and I help you if you need it. And Adam's boy also. Don' forget."

And he was gone, with the springy step of a man unused to the hard streets of town.

"That feller try to make you take furs for his provisions?" demanded the storekeeper sourly, glaring out through the open doorway.

"No, he didn't. He never mentioned furs." For once I could be perfectly honest.

"Well, just remember, Mrs. Gaunt, I don't take pelts in trade. Nor eight-cent fowls, if it comes to that. Honey, if it's good, an' salt pork an' some cornmeal. But no pelts. No, sir—no pelts in this store."

And with a final shake of his jowls, Titus Meadow stamped back to his labors behind the pot-bellied stove.

———

I wasn't alone in my duties. Titus Meadow had another counter-hand, a pleasant, freckled youth called Charley who made no secret of the fact that he'd only come to Independence from his Missouri farmstead in order to go further west, and would be off as soon as a means of travel offered itself. In the meantime he slept in the huge storeroom behind the main shop, missing nothing that went on in the store and providing a mine of information on his employer's private life. I knew it was wrong of me to listen to his scandalous confidences, but the more pompous Titus Meadow became, the more tempted I was to let Charley rattle on as he pleased.

"You watch," he told me one morning. "Next time Frank Ellis comes in here, you watch if the Ol' Man don' jump like a jackrabbit, runnin' around as if a coyote had hold of his tail. An' never a sign of his Missus."

"Does—does Frank Ellis come in here often?"

"Too often for the Ol' Man's likin'. And Missus Meadow wouldn't ever let the man in the store if it weren't for ol' Titus. But Titus—he's got hisself a woman across there, an' I calculate he don' care if Frank Ellis buys the whole damn rig."

"Charley, that can't be true! Not Mr. Meadow!"

The boy winked solemnly. "Just you wait. You'll see. Any day now he'll be off 'on business,' dressed fit ter kill, an' when he thinks he's gone far enough down the street, he'll walk across like it just came into his head, an' jump into the Trader's House quicker'n you can spit. I seen 'im do it time after time. So's the whole town, if he only knew it."

Once Titus Meadow's occasional excursions had been pointed out to me, I realized that he did go out with great ceremony perhaps once a week, his thinning hair slicked down with macassar-oil, his best coat drawn tightly over his drooping paunch. He'd pause mag-nificently in the middle of the store, his jowls vibrating in sinful anticipation, and haul out a heavy gold watch with every appearance of a man keeping an important appointment.

"Business meeting," he'd announce in his breathy tenor. "Might be gone a goodish while. Lock up at closing time if I'm not back." With that he'd leave the store at a brisk pace, turn left along the

street and, when sufficiently out of the line of sight, scuttle across it
and double back to the door of the Trader's House.

On these afternoons there was no sign of his wife. Mrs. Meadow
was always safely "at a prayer-meeting," though whether this was
true or merely a front for her injured pride I never discovered. Regina
Meadow was a puzzle. I knew that if it hadn't been for her I'd never
have been given my job at the store, but I found her no less stiff and
forbidding for all that. She'd walk in each morning, spectral in her
brown dress, and slowly survey the place with pale, resentful eyes,
searching for something left undone. If she found anything amiss
she'd draw it to my attention in the same cold, measured tones she'd
used on my first day in the store, and her chill disapproval was
enough to send me scurrying to put things right. I couldn't warm to
her—yet it was hard not to feel some pity for a woman whose
husband made a fool of her in such a public fashion.

Gleefully, Charley pointed out Titus's lady-friend as she passed
along the street one day beyond the open doors of the store. Remembering Lizzie's tight-lipped outrage at the goings-on in the Trader's
House, I expected some glamorous, painted *demi-mondaine* like the
"actresses" I'd occasionally seen boldly taking the air in a Liverpool
park. But Titus Meadow's young lady didn't fit my idea of a whore
in any way but one—the obvious possession of large, heavy breasts
accentuated by a tightly fastened bodice. Her face was pleasant, if
hardly beautiful, her hair assisted (I was sure) to a high degree of
blondness under a tilted straw hat.

But there was no plunging decolletage, no fur and feathers—just
a simple pink dress fitting closely round that astonishing bosom. The
woman—*Meg,* so Charley informed me—could have served behind
the counter of a Liverpool baker's shop without seeming at all out
of place. Once more I found myself feeling unaccountably sorry for
Regina Meadow.

Mrs. Meadow, like Lizzie's women-friends, would have loved to
close down the Trader's House. For one thing, it was so near the
square that no one could avoid passing and repassing it in the course
of a day in town. To make matters worse, it carried on its business
in a cheerfully blatant manner, as if its size and popularity did away
with any need for discretion. The bar was always packed by evening,
and since it was officially a hotel there were even half-a-dozen rooms
to let on the topmost story in which hardy souls had been known to
spend a night. But there were, so Charley informed me darkly, a row

of hot, overfurnished chambers above the long bar in which Meg and her colleagues received their visitors. Not that Charley had ever been further than the mirrored bar, of course—and then only for beer—so he hadn't seen these velvet dens of pleasure with his own eyes . . . But he'd *heard,* nevertheless.

As far as Lizzie's ladies were concerned, Frank Ellis was a monster in human form, and I had good reasons of my own for not wishing to be left alone with him in the store.

One day, however, when the storekeeper was off on one of his mysterious jaunts and Charley had left for the café where he took his meals, I heard the strutting step of Ellis's high-heeled boots approaching the doorway of the store. He walked in, stopped a few paces over the threshold and stared about him with the air of a man who has made a satisfying discovery. The store was empty, and I was alone behind the counter.

"Are you going to speak to me today, or are you still too much of a lady for such things?" Ellis strolled arrogantly toward me, his hands in his trouser pockets, his shoulders punching the air as if he were forcing his way through a crowd.

"I work here, so it follows I must speak to the customers. Whoever they are."

"Well, I guess that's an improvement, at least. I'd begun to think I was invisible, as far as you were concerned."

Ellis reached out, selected a cracker from the barrel, and began to munch it with cool insolence.

"Why don't you tell me what you want? Apart from that cracker."

"*Want?* I want to know what it's like for you to be down in the dirt with the rest of us sinners, Mrs. High-and-Mighty Gaunt! Sweeping up after foul-mouthed teamsters or fetching and carrying for the whole town—maybe you're not so much of a lady after all."

"I may be obliged to see to you as a customer, *Mr. Ellis,* but I don't have to listen to your insults. Now, do you want to buy something, or not?"

Ellis helped himself casually to another cracker, and surveyed me through half-closed eyes.

"D'you know, I can remember when the shopkeepers of St. John's used to think themselves lucky to have your trade, you and your mother. *Yes, Mrs. Dean! Not at all, Miss Dean! Honored to have you in the shop, Miss Dean!* And now look at you! Running errands for that old devil Titus for a few cents a day! And where's your fine skin-hunter now, may I ask? Sitting in some tepee with feathers in his hat and a fat squaw stirring the pot? Or d'you reckon his Indian friends hung him up by his heels in the end, and took his hair for some buck's leggings? Sure—that's what's happened to him! No doubt about it!"

I was shaking—literally shaking—with fury and disgust. But I wasn't going to give Frank Ellis the satisfaction of knowing it.

"What—do—you—want—to—buy?"

He stared into my face.

"Havanas." And as I reached for them he added, "—not the ones on the counter. Titus keeps some others for me on a shelf at the back."

Still shaking, I fetched the stepladder and climbed up where he indicated.

"Next shelf. Yes, that one. At the back."

They were there, as he'd said, wooden boxes of the best Havana cigars, a clandestine supply kept for the owner of the Trader's House by one of his best customers. I carried the box to the counter and watched as Ellis selected a dozen.

"If that's everything . . . *Mr. Ellis* . . ."

"You make it sound like a slap in the face, d'you know that?"

"Do I?" I met his gaze defiantly.

"You may not believe this, Rachel, but I'm prepared to help you now that self-righteous husband of yours—"

"You're speaking of a dead man—remember that."

"Dead and *gone,* at any rate."

"And still worth a thousand of you, Frank Ellis."

"All right—I own a grog-shop! I admit it! But I'm trying, in the only way I know how, to get some of the things you chose to throw away when you came here. Money—position—everything I lost when my father died and I had to give up at Yale. One day I'll go back east a rich man, and no one will care if the money came from liquor, or card-playing, or whores or whatever. It'll buy as much as the profits from money-lending, I daresay."

This reference to my mother's fortune brought me up short. It was more widely known than I'd thought, then, her connection with the notorious Relief Association.

"I don't care how you make your money. I've good reasons of my own for despising you, as well you know."

Ellis raised an eyebrow. "You aren't still angry with me for that business in St. John's? How you women do hold grudges! Well then, I'm prepared to make it up to you now, Rachel. Now you're alone. You have—what do the racing men call it? *Class*. And this place—" He waved a contemptuous hand, encompassing the entire store in the gesture. "Let's say it's hardly the place for you. I'll find you somewhere to live, you and the boy. I'll pay the rent, and—"

"Pay for the cigars, and be on your way, Frank. At once."

"You're way ahead of me, Rachel. You haven't heard the rest."

"I don't need to hear the rest. Pay me for the cigars, and get out. And take your dirty, rotten suggestions with you. I don't want anything to do with you or your money."

He tossed a few dollars down on to the counter, and gathered up the cigars.

"You say that now. But wait till you've been here a bit longer. You'll change your tune."

I was saved from answering by the sound of Charley's whistling in the street outside. Pocketing his cigars without a word, Ellis bowed in a mockery of politeness and strutted smugly out of the store.

———

I'd been unlucky to be alone when he called; the next time Frank Ellis came for cigars all three of us were present, and beyond throwing me a significant glance there was nothing he could do to pursue his unpleasant line of conversation.

Almost before I noticed it, summer became autumn and winter loomed ahead. Somehow or other, store-work and Charley's chatter had filled my lonely days, leaving only the evenings and the nights for aching solitude. I saw less of Matthew now, and though I knew Lizzie looked after him every bit as well as I could myself, I missed his bright little face and fumbling questions even more than I'd expected. And I'd had hardly any inquiries for dressmaking work. No one seemed to want fashionable gowns in town—certainly not the harassed, sun-bonneted wives of dispossessed farmers looking to Oregon Territory and to California for a second chance.

With the decline in the beaver trade, the trappers had begun to work as guides and wagon-masters. Tom Fitzpatrick had set out from Independence in May at the head of a party of seventy emigrants with the intention of pushing through the Rockies to the other side. I'd seen them set out, dogged and unsmiling, on their way to whatever hardships awaited them on the Plains and in the mountains.

But where they'd led, others would surely follow. Sometimes it seemed to me that the whole world was on the move, a westerly tide which was surging from one side of the country to the other—sweeping everyone with it except for me. My face was still set toward the east, yet after days of indecision I spent my slender savings, a ludicrously tiny amount, on warm winter clothes for Matthew, and our journey to England seemed further away than ever.

Only one human being was more wretched than I was that winter, though at least the Christian season of peace and goodwill meant nothing to him—simply another unfathomable festival of the white man's tortured God. As the cold weather set in, Watches Smoke became a common sight around town, bringing pelts which he tried to trade in the stores and saloons, usually for whisky. No one admitted doing business with him, but somehow he always seemed to find the liquor he wanted, and with it a taste for more. Before long he no longer bothered with pelts, but brought an old bow or a ceremonial relic of some kind which he hawked round town in the usual way. From time to time he found a sale: traders on their way to St. Louis knew there was a market back in "civilization" for the trappings of the picturesque western savage, and they paid the Indian with a paltry amount of watered whisky.

Guiltily I remembered our feast of deer meat in the cabin, and the jar of whisky which had vanished with Watches Smoke into the night. But I was sure it hadn't been his first taste of the stuff; he'd drained his glass with the practiced ease of a regular drinker. No doubt my elegant crystal goblet, too, had long since been traded for a few drops of the precious liquid.

Eventually, more emaciated than ever, Watches Smoke was reduced to begging. For an inch of whisky in a filthy tumbler he'd execute a shambling, unsteady Indian dance before a jeering line of men in a bar saloon. He became the butt of jokes, the town buffoon, tottering along the snowy roadway oblivious to catcalls and ribald shouts unless there was the promise of liquor in the offing. Then—uncomprehending—he would join in the general laughter, grinning vacantly and nodding in drunken agreement with whatever obscenity was flung at him. I longed to know what had happened to his shy, gentle squaw. Had she caught a glimpse of their bleak future together, and left her husband to his humiliation?

There was nothing at all I could do to help him, only watch in distress as his inevitable end approached. There were worse deaths, after all, than perishing in the clear air of the mountains, under a wide sky, with the smell of freedom all around.

For some reason Watches Smoke seldom came into Meadow's General Store. Perhaps the huge signboard and the bright clutter of hardware with which Charley almost filled the boardwalk each morning persuaded him he could expect no charity inside. One winter day, however, when I was alone for a few moments in the store —Charley having gone out on an errand—I looked up as a shadow fell across the square of light in the doorway to find Watches Smoke, hideously thin in a tattered blanket and blackened buckskin leggings, swaying on the threshold. His feet were bare in spite of the lacerating cold. He'd either lost his moccasins or traded them away. Slowly, painfully, he limped across the floor toward me, leaving a damp track over the clean-swept boards.

I never had time to utter a word. Titus Meadow, whom I'd imagined safely in the storeroom to the rear, erupted from the shadows behind the iron stove with a shrill screech of rage. His long white apron hampered his forward rush, but his intention was clear. Brandishing the shop broom he charged toward the shrinking Indian, howling curses as he came.

I saw naked fear light up in the drunkard's eyes, bright as the big oil-lamp in Lizzie's window. Flinging an arm before his face, he stumbled out of the store, knocking aside the returning Charley in his blind desperation to escape.

With a snort of triumph, Titus Meadow stamped back to his den. As soon as he'd disappeared, I dug into my purse for a few coins, pushed them into the cash-drawer and snatched a lump of bacon and some crackers from the barrel. Leaving an astonished Charley to look after the store and hugging my booty to my chest, I ran out into the street.

Watches Smoke hadn't gone far. I found him slumped on the icy ground, halfway up the alley between Meadow's store and the barber's shop next door. He looked up blearily as I approached, flinching in anticipation of another attack, until a faint glimmer of recognition dawned in his ravaged face, and he struggled to rise. I held out my offering. It seemed so little, now that I was confronted by his appalling need.

Crouching there in the brown slush of a leaking gutter-pipe, he began to cram the crackers into his mouth with shaking fingers, crumbs raining about him, hardly pausing to chew. The sight was unbearable: it was obscene to stand there, watching his degradation, and I fled back to the warmth of the store, trying to blot out the awful vision, a voice in my head asking again and again *Did Adam suffer so?*

"You're wasting your time," Charley told me at once. "He'll trade the bacon for liquor—see if he don't." Realizing I was in tears, he said no more.

———

I began to feel trapped in the town, that winter of '41—as trapped by my poverty as the would-be Oregon settlers were trapped by the snow. And try as I might to protect him, Matthew had now begun to realize how poor we were. I daresay I worried about him too much—but he was the center of my life now that Adam had gone, and I'd tried so hard to make it up to him for having no father . . . Perhaps we did spoil him a little, Lizzie and I, in spite of our good intentions.

From somewhere back east one of the harness-makers had shipped a parcel of wooden toys—simple things, no more than a monkey which looped and swung at the top of two sliding sticks—but having come expensively all the way from Philadelphia, their price was more than most people could afford.

Instantly he saw one, Matthew wanted it.

"Buy a monkey for me, Mamma."

"I can't, Matthew."

"Buy a monkey, *please.*"

"No, I'm sorry. We can't afford it."

"But I want a monkey!"

A dozen times a day the cry went up—*I want a monkey, Mamma!*—until at last, driven to distraction by my utter inability to give him the toy he longed for, I snapped back, "Well, you'll just have to *want,* won't you!"

As soon as the words were out of my mouth I heard my mother's voice, in the days of our own wretched poverty in St John's: *You'll just have to want, won't you!* I hadn't understood then—any more than Matthew could understand now—that a mother with no more than ten cents to her name can't afford a two-dollar wooden monkey.

"Matthew—come here, darling."

I sat him gently on my knee, his eyes still brimming with tears of desolation.

"You have to understand, Matthew, that since Papa . . . went away, we just can't go out and buy whatever we want. We need food and clothes more than we need toys."

"When Papa comes back, I'll ask him."

"Papa isn't coming back, darling. You know that."

Matthew looked up at me, his lips pressed together in a quivering line, torn between hopelessness and a profound sense of injustice.

"Then I *hate* Papa for going off and leaving us! I'm glad he's dead, if he made us so poor! Why shouldn't I have as much as the others?"

"Matthew! That's a dreadful—" But he'd gone in an instant, squirmed from my grasp and fled to his secret perch in the plum tree to rage at the unfairness of a world where a father he'd never known had nevertheless managed to deprive him of a wilderness of wooden monkeys.

———

All things considered, it was amazing that I had any heart to sing in the mornings as I swept cracker-crumbs and boardwalk litter from the threshold of Meadow's store. Yet I was singing, and swinging my broom to the rhythm, too, on the day which changed my life more than I could have believed.

Lord, we are few, but Thou art near, Nor short Thine arm, nor deaf Thine ear—and then I broke off suddenly as I saw the highly polished boots of Frank Ellis strut toward me across the boardwalk. There was no one else in the store at that moment, and I scuttled quickly back to my post behind the tobacco jars.

Frank Ellis looked round the store.

"Was that you I heard singing just then?"

"I may have been singing, yes."

"D'you sing anything besides religion?" He was eyeing me speculatively, his usual insolence forgotten in the pursuit of some more important objective. I wondered what it could be.

"I sometimes sing other things. A little opera. One or two traditional songs. Why do you want to know?"

Ellis ignored my question. "Have you ever sung on the stage? Or been trained for it?"

"Of course not. Though I did have singing lessons, some years ago."

He nodded. "Thought so. You sing well."

"Thank you. Now, did you come here to listen to my singing, or is there something I can do for you?"

"I think maybe there's something I can do for you."

"If you're going to make any more of your insulting suggestions, you can leave right away, or—"

"Or what? You'll call old Titus out from wherever he's hiding? Go ahead. See where it gets you. He won't throw *me* out, that's for sure. Titus an' I are very old friends."

There was nothing I could say to this. I hadn't the slightest doubt he was right.

"In any case—" He gave a casual shrug. "I've no intention of insulting you, as you put it. This is a business proposition." Ellis scratched the side of his nose thoughtfully. "Though it depends on whether you want to go on working for a few cents a day in this packing crate of a store . . . or earn some real money for a change. Do you want to hear what I have in mind?"

I knew I should close my ears to anything Frank Ellis might have to say, and send him about his business. But the little word *money* had done its work. I hesitated a moment too long, and Ellis made the most of my uncertainty.

"Right now I've got a problem across at the Trader's House. Don't suppose you've ever been in the place, being such a lady, but we like to keep some kind of entertainment going on to amuse the boys while they're drinking. We've had acrobats from Italy, and a juggling infant prodigy—and we had a feller once with a tame bear. But whatever else comes along, we always have a female singer. Always. Because the boys expect it, and when there's a pretty girl on the stage, they don't bother to count what they're drinking." A conspiratorial grin spread over Frank Ellis's face.

"I hired a woman—I *thought* I'd hired her, at any rate—to come up from New Orleans to the Trader's House for the summer. Princess Fatima Farouk, she called herself. Genuine oriental singer and dancer. Except she fell for some trumpeter in Baton Rouge, and I got a letter to say she won't be coming anymore. So here I am, with bills out to say 'Forthcoming Attraction,' and no one to put on the stage."

"My heart bleeds for you."

"Just listen, damn you, and don't get clever. Now, there I was— all at once without my forthcoming attraction—and then suddenly this morning I find someone with a right-down concert-hall voice yodeling hymns to an empty store as if the Second Coming was just around the corner. And I look in to see who it is . . . And it's you, of all people. Mrs. High-and-Mighty Rachel Gaunt!"

"Don't call me that."

"Wasting a good voice on the ears of some Holy Hannahs in Lizzie Fletcher's parlor when you could be across the street, keeping the boys happy for me!"

He finished his tale like a conjuror producing flowers from his hat.

"You aren't serious! I couldn't possibly sing in the Trader's House! I couldn't even be *seen* in the place!"

"Would ten dollars a week change your mind?"

"And in any case, I can't dance."

"There's no trick to it. We'll teach you."

"It's impossible! You're mad!"

"Well, I must say, I'm disappointed in you, Rachel. I thought you had more spunk than those cackling chapel hens. I'd heard you were a woman who did what she thought was right, no matter what anyone else said, whether it was feeding drunk Indians or running off with a trapper. Are you telling me I'm wrong?"

"But—" A vision of ten dollars a week swam before my eyes. In a few months I'd be able to save the fare to England, provided Matthew and I lived in our normal frugal manner. Then I thought of Lizzie Fletcher and her hymn-singing ladies, praying for the destruction of the Trader's House, that lair of Satan, whose welcoming lights beckoned passing sinners into the very mouth of Hell.

Ellis watched me hesitate.

"Twelve dollars, then. And I'm not asking you to mix with the customers. I know you wouldn't want to do that. All you'd have to do is to sing a few songs for them every evening, and then run off home. Where's the harm in that?"

"I know you, Frank Ellis. And I don't trust you. There has to be more to it than you've said."

"Not a thing more. Just sing your songs, take your money, and go back to Lizzie Fletcher's place."

"And that's *all* there is to it? You'll promise me that?"

"That's all I want from you, Rachel." Frank Ellis held his broad-brimmed hat against his chest. "You have my word on that. Besides, I've no inclination to go where I'm obviously not wanted. I'm simply trying to help you out—and myself at the same time, of course. Twelve dollars: what d'you say?"

"It's more than I'm earning here."

Ellis gave a crowing laugh. "I'll say it is! But you'll be worth it to me, if you bring the boys into the bar. There are far too many hotels and saloons setting up in town these days, half of them flea-bitten holes with a plank for a bar and liquor that'd melt your teeth if it wasn't watered down so much. The Trader's House has a reputation for offering the best, an' I mean to keep it. But I need some special entertainment to offer my customers."

I reeled back from the edge.

"No . . . It wouldn't be right. There's Matthew to consider. And Lizzie. Even if I didn't care what people said about me, it wouldn't be fair to them."

"That's no problem. We'll change your name and how you look, and then who's to know? If you don't tell anyone, I certainly won't, and nor will the girls. Who's going to care who the singer is, any-how?"

Ellis paused, and in the brief hush Titus Meadow's steady tread could be heard advancing along the boardwalk outside the store.

"At least give it some thought," Ellis finished quickly. "Will you?"

I shook my head, more in confusion than refusal.

"Will you think about it?" he persisted. "I'll give you two days. Don't turn me down till you've thought how you'd spend the money."

Titus Meadow was almost at the door, and his wheezy breaths whistled like a blacksmith's bellows just outside. Frank Ellis showed no sign of giving up.

"Oh, very well—I'll think about your offer. But I promise you, you're wasting your time."

"I'll be back on Monday." With a cheerful wave to the approach-ing storekeeper, Frank Ellis strode away into the street outside.

"What did he want?" asked Titus Meadow at once, glaring after Ellis's departing back.

"Ribbon," I said maliciously, shocking myself with the glibness of my lie. "Pink ribbon. For one of his girls. *Meg*, could it be?"

"How in the world should I know?" demanded the storekeeper hotly. "*Meg*, indeed! And who is *Meg*, may I ask? *Meg*? I'm sure I've never heard of anyone by that name! No, sir! What d'you take me for?"

He was still blustering indignantly as he wandered off to his usual post by the black iron stove.

———

Several times that evening I almost brought myself to the point of confiding in Lizzie. The very thought of standing on a little gilt stage hung about with lamps and plush curtains (so Charley had described it) warbling some sentimental ballad for the amusement of a roomful of drunken men struck me as ridiculous. If word ever leaked out about my new occupation no respectable woman would speak to me again, and I could imagine their highly honorable husbands looking away from me hastily in the street in case I should greet them as old friends . . .

The trouble was that the more I thought about those enticing twelve dollars—and another twelve after that, and so on for as long as it took me to save the fare to England—the less I cared about the disapproval of those ranks of respectable women. How many of *them* were struggling, as I was, to scrape together the price of freedom from their town?

In the end, I didn't mention Frank Ellis's offer to Lizzie. I knew Lizzie would soon convince me to forget the whole idea, and knowing that saved me from having to speak.

I brooded about Ellis's twelve dollars next day in the store, and Titus Meadow unwittingly helped me to make up my mind. Running to serve two people at once, I managed to spill a few ounces of flour between barrel and scales. Not content with taking me to task for my clumsiness in front of his smirking customers, he scolded me again whenever he had a moment to spare for the rest of the day.

Thoroughly upset, I cut my finger while hacking a plug of chewing tobacco from its great, fruity cake, and my renewed carelessness led to a further lecture. It was plain I could do nothing right: I was ham-fisted, and my incompetence was costing the store a fortune. Titus fully intended to take payment for the spilled flour from my wages, plus something for any tobacco I'd spoiled by bleeding over it. Goodness only knew why he'd given me the job in the first place! So much for taking pity on a poor widow! So much for charity!

All of a sudden my temper snapped.

"Then you know what you can do with your job, Mr. Meadow," I retorted, whipping the strings of my long apron from neck and waist. "You owe me two dollars and forty cents." I held out my hand. "And you can keep the forty cents for the spoiled goods." Titus Meadow gaped at me, his mouth a silent oval of dismay.

A few minutes later I fled from the store, clutching the money in my hand. Without slackening pace I sped through the slushy debris and mire of the street under the very noses of the lead oxen of a

three-span team and flew on winged feet toward the wide doorway
of the Trader's House. I knew that if I once stopped, I was lost. It
had to be done before doubt could set in, before I could think clearly
again.

Oh, what would Adam have said?

In the pounding vault of my mind I heard his voice, as distinct as
if he were at my side. *Do it. If you think you're right, do it, and be
damned to their whispering and pointing. Don't let anyone tell you
how to live your life. Your first duty is to survive. Do it, Rachel. Do
it.*

The voice was so real, so resonant with life that I almost faltered
in my flight down the busy boardwalk. Then all at once I was directly
in front of the Trader's House, where a buzz of conversation and the
rhythmic tinkling of a piano indicated that the bar was drawing
breath for a good night's sinning.

14

Goodness knows what I expected to find on the other side of the double wooden doors of the Trader's House—drunken debauch at the very least, after all the things which Lizzie and her friends had said. Yet it wasn't like that at all.

Certainly it was murky enough for the most rampant orgy. Any light which seeped in from the street gave out just inside the dusty windows, and I had to wait until my eyes became accustomed to the gloom beyond before I could see any more.

To all intents and purposes, the ground floor of the Trader's House was simply a huge barroom stretching back from the street, the lower half of its walls coffee-brown, the upper half papered in striking crimson with a moiré stripe. Two stuffed and mounted buffalo heads stared one another down from opposite sides of the room, one of them wearing a sign on his curling horn which read "NO SPURS UPSTAIRS," giving him the coquettish look of a gypsy with a rose behind her ear.

But if it hadn't been for the flirtatious buffalo and the long bar down one side of the room, the Trader's House might easily have been a mission hall filled with plain tables and chairs. For all its size, less than a dozen people leaned on the solid wooden bar counter, their faces staring back at them from the extravagantly etched and gilded mirror for which the Trader's House was famous: a couple of dusty teamsters, the town carpenter-coffin-maker and one of the barbers, a group of moustachioed men in tight Mexican trousers and huge spurs, a young man in an out-at-elbows coat whose low-crowned hat lay beside him on the counter, and another, older man in black, his fingers flashing gold rings.

The last two had female company, one a redhead and the other a blonde, and if I hadn't known it was a business encounter I'd almost have taken them for sweethearts. But leaving aside the glasses and bottles on the counter, the inside of the Trader's House looked rather less debauched than a board-school social, and about half as enjoyable.

Quite alone, Frank Ellis sat at one of the round wooden tables, chewing the end of a finger, engrossed in the sheet of thick yellow paper spread before him. All of a sudden he glanced up and saw me, rocked his chair back on its hind legs, and tossed down the pen.

"Well—this is a surprise! Are you going to tell me you've made your mind up already?"

"Yes, I have; and I'll take the job. But only on the terms we discussed, Frank. I want that understood."

"Twelve dollars a week. That's what we agreed."

"And we also agreed there'd be no more to it than that. You know what I'm talking about."

Ellis spread his hands wide, the picture of injured innocence.

"I made you a promise, Rachel! What else do you want me to do?"

"Keep it, Frank. That's all."

———

Lizzie was every bit as horrified as I'd expected. For an awful moment I thought she might even tell me to find lodgings elsewhere, and I tried anxiously to reassure her.

"I've made Ellis promise he'll give me a new name and some kind of disguise, so Ada Bullitt and the other ladies will never know it's me. Oh, Lizzie, I *may* still stay here, mayn't I?"

"Stay here? I'd like to see them try to make you go! Of course you can stay, honey. Whatever's makin' you do such a thing as this, I'll allow you got honest reasons." Lizzie patted my hand forgivingly. "It ain't for me to judge other people's actions, Heaven knows, but I reckon you ought to remember your singin' voice was a gift from the Lord, an' it ought to be employed in His business, not windin' up a bunch of drunks in a barroom. It makes me crawl all over to think of it! But I'll surely pray for you, an' ask the Good Lord to keep you out of harm's way."

"I won't have to work there for long, Lizzie. In five or six months I'll have raised enough to take Matthew back to Liverpool. Think of it—just six months! And when you come down to it," I added, as much to convince myself as Lizzie, "all I've agreed to do is *sing*."

"Oh, Rachel," murmured Lizzie uneasily, "they do say the Devil has all the best tunes."

———

Mademoiselle Valentine? Me?" The name had been printed in large red letters on the signboard at the door, but I still couldn't believe it. "THE TOAST OF PARIS," the poster had declared, "The Famous French Chanteuse, brought by special request to sing at the Trader's House."

"Like it?" Ellis wanted to know. And when I didn't answer, he went on, "I'll guarantee you, by the time you step out on that stage tomorrow night, you'll be a proper French singer, with all the fal-lal that goes with it."

"Frank—I don't speak French."

He shrugged. "Neither do those farmboys out front, so who's to know?"

Amazingly enough, Frank Ellis was right. By the time I finally slipped between the gold fringes of his red plush curtains and promenaded out on to the tiny stage, I doubt if even Lizzie would have recognized me as the little widow who'd stood for so many months behind the counter in Titus Meadow's store.

Frank Ellis may have planned my debut, but it was Crazy Kate who worked the transformation. Kate Connery—*Crazy Kate* to friends and enemies alike—was the redhead I'd seen on my first visit to the long barroom of the Trader's House. Summoned by Ellis, she stared hard at me for a few minutes, penciled brows knitted, her jaws moving reflectively on the end of a black cheroot.

"You're pretty enough, honey, I'll say that. But there's somethin' else needed here, if I could just run my eye on it."

She made me sit down, stand up, turn around, stick out my backside and then my chest, hold my arms up, and finally stand with my back to her, squinting over my shoulder, "As if the best-lookin' man in the world just snuck up an' called your name."

As a result of all this, Crazy Kate decided what the *somethin'* was, and I found myself running back to Lizzie's cellar to unearth the dramatic French corsets I'd bought with Aunt Grace years earlier in Liverpool. It was a long time since I'd worn them—they'd never been intended for chopping firewood and hauling creek-water—but now Kate decreed they must be laced on as tightly as was consistent with singing.

"You want a little more up front, dontcha? Give the boys somethin' to look at, that's what you're here for."

As far as I was concerned I was there to sing—and my misgivings turned to near-panic when I was helped into the dress Kate had found for me.

"But this was made for someone half my height! It only comes down to my knees!"

"That's the idea, honey." Cheroot clamped tightly between her teeth, Kate tugged at the hem where fussy pink roses pegged up a row of ridiculous flounces. Suddenly I was a caricature Arcadian shepherdess in blue-and-white satin pulled tight at the waist and cut so low in front that a single sneeze could leave me naked. The skimpy top disappeared into a froth of the same pink roses round my breasts and shoulders, sewn on flesh-colored net so that it seemed from a short way off as if only a scattering of petals covered the most vital places. The general effect was of a garment about to slide off at any moment.

"I can't wear this!" I looked down, horrified at the sight of my white-stockinged knees clearly displayed below the hem. "I might as well be naked!"

"Sure—any time you want, Rachel," agreed Frank Ellis smoothly, strolling into the room without knocking. "If you want to show off your bare arse to the world, you're welcome to do it. That *would* bring them in."

"Doubt it." Crazy Kate surveyed her handiwork critically. "I've seen more meat in a plate of five-cent soup. Just as well the girl that owned this thing was kinda skinny."

"She looks fine to me, Kate." Frank Ellis ran a leisurely eye over the lustrous white flesh swelling out beyond the pink roses of my bodice, but my hasty attempt to pull the dress higher about my breasts only exposed more of my thighs below the hem, and Ellis reached out to knock my hands aside.

"You've got a nice figure, don't hide it. Kate, give her a fan or something to wave around if she's nervous. And for God's sake fix her face."

Kate fixed my face with proper theatrical paint, left behind, like the shepherdess dress, by some long-departed entertainers who'd run up vast debts everywhere and been hustled out of town without their props.

I sat for this ordeal on a hard wooden chair, my face tilted up to catch the lamplight, a cloth tied round my chin, while Kate painted on what she judged to be gypsy features suitable for a real French chanteuse. The smoke from her cheroot made my eyes water, and after a while I began to count the freckles on the bridge of her nose.

"Kate—"

"Keep still!"

"Why do they call you *Crazy* Kate?"

"Stop wrigglin', damn you! You want eyes like a China girl?"

"Well—why, then? You're just about the sanest person here, as far as I can see."

"A good deal saner than Frank Ellis, that's for sure."

"Then why?"

"I killed a man once." Kate squinted down at the effect she'd created. "A long time back, down Orleans way."

"Good gracious!"

"He was a gamblin' man. We'd been married three weeks when he went off with a steamboat pilot's wife whose man was never t'home. I chased after them, an' shot the rat. It was lucky for me, the Creoles understand that kinda thing. They just about cheered me out of the courthouse." Kate applied a last dab of rouge, and stepped back to admire the result. "They tell me you're a widow, Rachel."

"Yes—I am."

"Well, that's somethin' we got in common, then, ain't it."

———

They put me on stage the following night—pushed me out in the fizzing lamplight of the tiny semicircular platform to a dull roar, the howl of a wolfpack in full cry, a predatory baying rising from a hundred throats and a hundred pairs of lungs as the patrons of the Trader's House caught sight of their quarry. Thanks to Frank Ellis I'd been skinned and trussed, thrown like meat to the wolves.

He told them I'd taken Paris by storm, driven an English lord to kill himself, and sung for the crowned heads of Europe, who'd queued to sip champagne from my shoe. And now Mademoiselle Valentine was theirs alone, summoned to the Trader's House expressly for their pleasure.

The stamping rose to a crescendo, and I froze where I stood, not quite in the bright center of the tiny stage. I could see almost nothing beyond the lamps at my feet, but I could smell the musky scent of the crowd and feel the rumbling growl of longing which washed toward me. Terror closed my throat before that mindless, swaying mass: a disembodied hand reached out, scrabbling for my ankle, the fingers open and grasping. But someone had been posted before the stage for just such an eventuality. As I watched, the hand was crushed beneath the base of a bottle, and I heard a yelp of pain as it slipped away.

They couldn't get hold of me, these men, yet the thundering wave of their admiration lapped around me, cheering me, confirming once and for all that the sad little widow who'd toiled in the general store was invisible behind the bewitching French chanteuse.

Experimentally, I flirted a little with my fan—and the drinkers cheered on cue. More confident now, I minced to the edge of the platform and wagged my finger in playful rebuke, drawing more whistles and shouts from the darkness beyond. Ellis had coached me in what to say next, and in a grossly exaggerated French accent borrowed from the villain of a melodrama I'd once seen on the Liverpool stage I duly greeted my audience. On the spur of the moment I blew them an extravagant kiss, and another outbreak of roaring washed up from the bar. I began to relax. This wasn't so hard after all.

Frank Ellis and Crazy Kate between them had chosen my repertoire, a mixture of sentimental ballards and barroom ditties, all of it ridiculously simple to sing. I was surprised to find that the unashamedly mawkish songs were received as well as the rest. Not a glass clinked as I sang of parted lovers and sweethearts gone to seek their fortunes: three-quarters of the men in the room must have left someone behind on a homestead or in a distant town, and the one lone wag who dared to jeer was instantly quelled by his soft-hearted neighbors.

"Let the Frenchy sing, damn you!"

Encouraged, the Frenchy sang the songs she'd been taught—one by one, the sentimental with the bawdy, accompanied by the grizzled piano player on his box-instrument just as she had been by Signor di Angelo's genteel pianist in faraway Liverpool. Elated and euphoric, I plunged without a second's hesitation into my final piece, a song which had shocked me into silence only the day before.

It was the tale of a fly buzzing in a lady's boudoir, settling on one part of her anatomy after another as she tried to swat it down, and it was, as Kate remarked once more, "to give the boys sump'n to look at," being full of explicit gesture. But exhilaration sang in my veins: I was no longer poor Mrs. Gaunt, I was Mademoiselle Valentine, and I could force the whole room to respond to my caprices. I held out my arms to them, quite forgetting to shield my uplifted bosom with my little blue fan, and they roared for more. They were still roaring as I ran back behind the red plush curtains at the end of my act.

Frank Ellis had been standing just behind the stage, watching my performance. As I fled past him, he gave me a curious stare from those sly blue eyes of his, and reached out a hand to hold me back.

"Well, well," he said. "Who'd have guessed it? With a bit of work you could be quite good."

I looked at him in surprise, still floating six feet above the dirty floor of the back quarters of the Trader's House. I thought I'd been magnificent.

"A bit wooden," he went on. "You'll have to move about more. Kate'll show you some dance steps tomorrow. But I've seen worse, all the same. You're quite a little actress, Frenchy."

Lizzie had waited up for me in her thick cotton nightgown, her hair in a fat gray plait over one shoulder.

"Well?" she demanded. "How did it feel?"

"The fires of Hell?" I was still too elated to be serious. "Oh, Lizzie, it was so . . . so . . ." But I couldn't think of words to express the feeling of wild exultation I'd discovered that night.

In the days which followed it occurred to me sometimes that with no difficulty at all I'd become two separate people. Not a soul had recognized me in the Trader's House that night; all they'd seen was some fantastic creature who pranced and kissed her hand to a roomful of men at once. I was able to crouch inside the oh-so-public body of Mademoiselle Valentine, anonymous and inviolate, and Valentine could do or say what she pleased without incriminating me at all.

Life slipped once more into a routine. At last I could spend all day with my son—reading to him, playing with him in the woods, supervising his supper and bedtime. And then, after kissing him goodnight and pretending not to see the reproachful look in Lizzie's eyes, I would set off to become my other self on the stage of the Trader's House.

At last my life had new purpose and direction. Instead of endless, empty years stretching before me, there were now fixed dates—the day on which I hoped to be able to give up my job at the Trader's House, the day by which I reckoned we might have reached New York, the day we might arrive in Liverpool, and so on. I still missed Adam with a longing which went beyond words, a misery which fed on itself, on my empty arms, on the wide solitude of my bed in the small hours of the morning. But the image I treasured of him was dimmer now. Sometimes I looked at the shadowy daguerreotype which took pride of place on the shelf in my bedroom, and caught a glimpse of a man I didn't recognize. Could my worshiping eyes have worn away the likeness?

In an odd way, the raw emotion which flowed over me each evening from the men in the dim, lamplit bar served to fill the emptiness in my life—at least for an hour or two out of each twenty-four. Hidden inside the outrageous Valentine, I was able to hold out my arms to be cherished, curling up like a little cat in the warmth of their welcome, in a love which would cost me nothing.

Gradually I learned my trade, until I could make the most of each gesture and each line of my songs. I'd pause for a second, one dainty finger touching my chin, staring at them over a bare, raised shoulder, my face a caricature of innocent surprise. What had I said? When the men roared their approval, I pretended to pout; now the room erupted in laughter, and I would walk to the edge of the stage to make eyes at the elderly pianist as if he were my only friend in the world. It was the worst, the most elaborate form of flirtation, and I knew it. But if my conscience ever troubled me, week by week I had the satisfaction of watching my savings grow.

A long time before, in one of my rare moods of buoyant confidence, I'd written a letter to Aunt Grace in Liverpool, briefly explaining that I was now a widow, and adding that Matthew and I were set on returning to Liverpool in late summer of 1842. If it wasn't inconvenient, would Aunt Grace put us up for a short while until I could find lodgings for us elsewhere and a means of earning a living?

Now, at last, Aunt Grace's reply reached me after its long journey across land and sea. She was saddened by my news—though I thought I detected a slight hint of I-told-you-so all the same. She'd always thought, she said, that no good would come of running off halfway round the world to live among savages. I pictured the "savages" who held twice-weekly prayer meetings in Lizzie's parlor, and smiled. But at least she was prepared to offer her widowed niece and fatherless grand-nephew a roof over their heads for as long as they needed it—and the next piece of my plan fell into place.

Unfortunately, in Independence another piece was tumbling head-long out of it.

Once or twice it had crossed my mind that Titus Meadow might discover my secret during a visit to his blond lady-friend on the first floor. But even if the storekeeper did find out who was there on stage, masquerading as a French singer, how could he spread the word round town without giving away his own sinful activities in the same building?

I'd reckoned without love. Titus Meadow's affair with Meg had become more than a mere business arrangement; his heart had been captured as completely as any schoolboy's, and in the violence of his love he threw caution to the winds, sneaking out almost every evening to the Trader's House on the basis that if his precious Meg was entertaining him, no one else could be enjoying her services.

I'd never understood how Regina Meadow could shut those pale eyes of hers to what was so obviously going on between her husband and one of the town whores. But at last, so Meg told me later, that long-suffering woman had endured enough. While Titus was discreet she'd borne his behavior with patience, but now the whole town of Independence was sniggering and pointing and nudging with its grimy elbows as Mrs. Meadow swept past, and the time for action had come.

Very late one night, as Titus tiptoed into the darkened house, fumbling his way to bed in the hope that his wife was asleep, Mrs. Meadow rose up, lit a lamp, and tore so many strips off her husband that he was reduced to mere rattling bones when she'd finished.

The Trader's House, she told him, was a den—a lair—an abode of demons and lewd women, a filthy hole where the mouth of Hell puffed forth fire and brimstone to entrap such miserable sinners as he.

But my dear Regina—

No decent human would set foot in the Trader's House. No chaste woman would be seen within its doors, if it was the only structure left standing on the Day of Judgment.

But Regina, my sweet—

No one with whom she, Mrs. Titus Meadow, had the slightest acquaintance would cross its sulphurous threshold, except her despicable, deceiving wretch of a husband. Worm! Betrayer! Dragging his wife's good name in the mud by consorting with a loose woman in that place! Why—she would cut off her right hand before touching a hair on the head of one of the women from the Trader's House!

In that case, Regina, I calculate you'd better fetch a knife, because little, mousy, widowed Mrs. Gaunt is currently parading her undoubted and almost naked charms there before the greedy eyes of a hundred men each night.

Early next morning, Lizzie Fletcher, her hair positively cascading from her wispy knot, received a grim-faced delegation of female boarders, led by Ada Bullitt, the temperance lecturer. Mrs. Gaunt must go—immediately—or they themselves would leave in a body. They couldn't continue to share the same roof—perhaps even the same teacup, God help them—with such a harlot.

Was it possible that Mrs. Fletcher hadn't been aware of her friend's profession? . . . And here I interrupted to save Lizzie's reputation. Of course Mrs. Fletcher hadn't known: the idea was unthinkable. I'd kept my work secret, telling no one. And I glared at Lizzie, daring her to contradict.

There followed a conference on the subject of Matthew, who might already, at four years of age, be tainted by his mother's misdeeds. But here in the end even Miss Bullitt consented to be merciful. Matthew might stay on at Mrs. Fletcher's, but Rachel Gaunt must find shelter elsewhere. And I insisted on going, despite Lizzie's protests that she wasn't going to be dictated to by a bunch of crazy old hens. Why should she pay the price of my sins, after all?

And so, in April, with just over three months' wages still to earn, I moved into one of the vacant hotel rooms on the top floor of the Trader's House. I still sneaked into Lizzie's house by day to spend time with Matthew and to put him to bed each night in his little cot in Lizzie's own room, but I slept at the Trader's House, where Matthew couldn't be with me, and it pained me to think it was now Lizzie who soothed his nightmares instead of his mother. But I refused to be cast down. By the middle of July I'd have him back and we'd be on our way to England at last.

Two things still contrived to upset my peace of mind. The first was that Watches Smoke, who'd somehow managed to survive the winter, occasionally turned up now in the bar of the Trader's House. He was a pitiful sight, filthy and unkempt, his head no longer shaved in tribal fashion, his skeletal frame covered in tattered buckskin trousers and someone's cast-off shirt. For a few minutes he'd be permitted to wander about the bar, his face set in a ghastly smile, offering a few dance-steps for the amusement of the crowd provided someone would buy him a drink. The barkeeper or Frank Ellis usually chased him out after a short while when the customers had grown tired of his antics, but one busy night when everyone's attention was elsewhere he appeared suddenly at the edge of my lamplit stage, his wolfish countenance up-turned, his glittering, fevered eyes fixed upon me.

There was no doubt that he'd recognized me—for paint was no novelty to a red man—and the realization almost made me falter in midverse. We'd both seen better days, the drunken Indian and the French chanteuse. What must he make of me now, the white squaw with the bold eyes and the painted lips?

My second unwelcome discovery was that Frank Ellis was beginning to seek out my company once more. He'd even taken to hovering behind the stage until I finished my performance every night, when he'd try to trap me in conversation before I could run off to the sanctuary of my top-floor room with the stout lock on its door. By day he knew I was busy with my son, but he tried to waylay me before I could leave, offering picnics or drives to the river—all to be shared with Matthew if necessary—and when, inevitably, I refused his invitations, he simply became more persistent than ever. His behavior began to annoy me—and to worry me. To find Frank Ellis, a man accustomed to lying in bed until noon, up and about at seven o'clock with his hair slicked down and a smile on his swarthy face was certainly cause for concern.

At last I decided to have it out with him.

"You gave me your word," I reminded him one day when he'd been particularly pressing. "You promised me this would only be a business arrangement, and that's why I agreed to it. Or was that another of your lies, Frank?"

"It is a business arrangement. An' so far as I can see, it seems to be working pretty well. I don't see you have any cause to complain."

We were standing in the narrow back corridor of the Trader's House, the bleak little passageway running behind the bar and the stage which gave access to both. He'd stopped me on my way to the back door, this time suggesting a drive out in the direction of Sapling

Grove, and as I was already late for my daily walk with Matthew I had even less patience than usual.

"I undertook to sing for your customers, Frank, and you agreed to pay me twelve dollars a week. I've no complaints at all about that. But as I told you before, that's where it ends. I don't want anything to do with you personally, and you gave me your word you'd respect my feelings."

"Did I? Well, maybe I did at that. But what I've got in mind now is to do with business as well, so I don't reckon it counts."

"I don't want to hear it."

"Listening won't cost you anything. Come an' have a drink in the bar."

"Certainly not!"

"Then at least come into the office." He jerked his dark head in the direction of the office door a few feet away.

"No. You can say anything you want to say to me out here."

"As you please."

Ellis glanced up and down the passageway to make sure no one was within earshot. Remembering the narrow back stairs to the upper floors, he walked to the bottom step and peered upward, and then, satisfied that no one was lurking nearby, came back toward me and leaned against the wall where I stood, his head so close to mine that I could feel his hot breath on my ear as he spoke.

"I've been watching you on stage, Rachel. Every night. And you're a sight better than I expected. As a matter of fact, you're damn good. You can do anything with those men out there—you can drive them wild when you want, just by wiggling your backside at them. I'll be honest with you: you've brought good business into the Trader's House, an' I've been having a few thoughts about where we could go from here, you an' me."

"Don't bother, Frank. I'm not going anywhere with you." I made a movement to go, but he pushed me back against the wall.

"Now hear me out. Like I said, I've been watching you a lot lately, Rachel, an' I reckon there's more of your old lady in you than I thought. Your ideas aren't so high-minded after all, are they? You like money just as well as I do—enough to throw your principles aside an' come to work in this place—"

"That was only—"

"You don't have to make excuses to me. Maybe your dear, departed husband believed in putting virtue before dollars in the bank,

but I know you don't. Deep down, you want money as bad as I do
—an' I reckon together we could make a pretty good team. What
d'you say?"

"Never, Frank. That's what I say. I don't know what's put this
idea into your head, but I don't want any part of it."

I saw his eyes narrow in sudden suspicion.

"Maybe you think you could do better on your own—in St. Louis
or New Orleans? Got a taste for the bright lights now, is that it?"
He paused, but before I could answer he went on, "Don't fool yourself, Rachel. You'll never amount to much alone. But with me to
look after you . . . we could both do pretty well."

"I told you, Frank—forget it." For a moment I thought of adding
that far from pursuing a stage career, I'd be leaving the Trader's
House the instant I'd saved two hundred and fifty-five dollars from
my wages . . . Then I thought better of it. I must let Ellis imagine I'd
be there as long as he had work for me. "I don't intend to sing
anywhere but the Trader's House," I assured him truthfully.

"Well, that's better." He looked mollified. "And I guess the Trader's House will do for the time being. We can turn this place into a
little gold mine, you an' me—"

"I thought you had a partner already. What about Kate?"

He snorted. "Kate only has one talent in the world, Rachel, an'
they don't give out medals for it. 'Sides, Kate's got no head for
business. You leave her to me. I reckon I can buy her out of the
Trader's House for next to nothing, an' keep all the profits for ourselves. The considerable profits you're going to make for us,
Ma'm'selle. What about it?"

I was disgusted by his little scheme. But I needed my twelve dollars
for a few more weeks yet.

"You'll have to give me time to think it over," I said evasively.
"I'd no idea I was as good as you say."

"Believe me, you are. Every bit. But take some time to think if you
want. I guess that's fair. Just don't be too long about it."

———

A week passed, and Ellis said no more about his scheme, though
he continued to hover around me as if I were some valuable possession which might slip through his fingers. I don't think he ever
missed one of my performances on the little stage; he was always
there when I came off, staring at me as if he could hardly believe

that Mademoiselle Valentine and Rachel Gaunt were one and the same.

Then one night he intercepted me in the bare corridor behind the stage as I finished my act.

"You're keeping me waiting, you know," he said, blocking my path. "I'm not a patient man. I expected an answer before now."

"I—I haven't really had time to give it much thought."

"Well, think about it now." He'd stationed himself squarely before me, preventing me from reaching the foot of the stairs which led up to my room.

"Frank!" I began to feel anxious, and groped for an excuse to get past him. "How can I possibly discuss anything with you in this rigout? At least let me go upstairs and change." I tried to move past him, but he caught my arm.

"Oh, I don't know . . . You seem fine to me. Yes—I like you just the way you are, Rachel. You look a sight better in this stuff than in that black dress you always wear." The fingers of his free hand brushed the red-dyed marabout feathers which trimmed the bodice of my latest costume and for a few seconds touched naked flesh. I flinched as if they'd been white-hot.

"Hey now, honey—what's all this? Don't get modest with me! I've seen you on stage, don't forget. I know what you're like under all that pious black. Sleeping alone doesn't suit you any more than it suits me, does it?" And this time he trailed a finger quite deliberately across the bare expanse of my breasts.

"Stop that!"

"Now see here—if we're to be partners—"

"We are *not* to be partners. If I was starving in the gutter I wouldn't want to be a partner of yours, Frank Ellis. You wanted a decision, and now you've got it." And with all my strength I pushed him away, slid past him and raced up the stairs to my room, slamming the door and locking it fast behind me.

My breath was coming in great spurts and my heart still hammered from my frantic run upstairs. I collapsed on the bed and stared at the ceiling, trying to will myself to stay calm and collect my thoughts.

The next moment, it seemed, Frank Ellis was in the room with me, the passkey clutched triumphantly in his hand. He was in shirtsleeves now, his collar unbuttoned, but all I saw was the expression of naked greed on his face as he flung himself on top of me on the bed, pinning

me down with his weight, gripping my hair to twist my face round
to his.

"By God, if I'd known in St. John's what you were really like, I'd
have made damn sure your mother never found us!"

"No, Frank! Leave me alone!"

I tried to scream, but he slammed his hand over my mouth, almost
choking me with its pressure. I tried to beat my fists against him, but
my arms were pinned and he was far stronger than I'd ever imagined.
He didn't attempt to kiss me or to disguise in any way that all he
wanted was to possess me, to penetrate me, to degrade me with the
violence of his lust. I felt him forcing my legs apart, further and
further, wedging his knees between mine . . . But my petticoats delayed him, the layers of ridiculous petticoats which had stiffened my
scanty hem. Ellis was groping and tearing at them savagely, his hand
still over my mouth, his weight driving the breath from my body and
preventing me from squirming free . . . And all the time his eyes
stared into mine, shining with triumph.

He twisted for a second to fumble with the buttons of his trousers
—and I saw my chance. In the brief moment that his weight shifted
to one side, I managed to free my right hand. I could only think of
one thing to do, and I did it. I dug my nails—Mademoiselle Valentine's long, crimson nails—deep into the flesh of his cheek, and tore
downward with all my strength.

I felt raveled skin under my fingertips, and a gush of sticky blood
between my fingers as he pulled away with a scream.

Then his blood—Ellis's blood—was running down my arm and
on to the bed-cover. He'd staggered into the middle of the room, his
hands to his face, blood dripping down on to his fancy waistcoat,
his trousers undone and his shirt hanging loose. But there was nothing comic about the look in his eyes. He gave me a glance of pure,
unadulterated hatred and lurched out of the room, leaving a bloody
mark on the doorpost as he went.

I was sobbing and trembling, yet from somewhere I found the
strength to pull a heavy chest of drawers across the door so that it
couldn't be forced open. I sank down on the floor, my back against
the massive piece of furniture, and let my tears flow at last, carving
oily channels through my thick makeup.

I lay there for a very long time, until I had no more tears to shed
and Ellis's blood had dried to a dark, crusted stain on my hand and
arm. Mechanically I pulled myself to my feet, poured water from the

jug into my washbowl, and set about clearing every last particle of Frank Ellis and Mademoiselle Valentine from my face and body.

It was impossible to sleep that night. Instead I sat up at the head of the bed, Adam's pistol, loaded, in my hand, and reviewed the wreckage of my life.

I should leave the Trader's House right away—that was clear—and find some other means of raising the balance of the money I needed. But where could I go? I couldn't ask Lizzie to take me back: Ada Bullitt and the other ladies would never allow it. And in any case, wherever I went I'd have to pay for my lodgings, eating into the money I'd saved with no way of replacing it.

And I had to have that money. Two hundred and fifty-five dollars: it had so nearly been within my grasp.

I let my mind stray back over the scene in my room: there was still a bloodstain on the bed-cover to prove it had been no nightmare, but a desperate battle for my self-respect . . . A battle I'd won. I—Rachel Gaunt, the little widow—had beaten Frank Ellis. I'd shown him I still considered him the same rotten, loathsome creature as ever, and I'd never, ever, submit to him.

The question was—what would Ellis do next? If I showed no sign of leaving the Trader's House, he might well tell me to go. Yet I was useful to him, as he'd admitted himself. I must be bringing in hundreds of dollars in trade, and yet I cost him only twelve dollars a week.

Everything depended on whether pride or greed had a firmer hold on Frank Ellis—and whether I could bear to go on as I was until I had the final few dollars in my hand.

By first light I'd decided what to do. Nothing.

I'd pretend that everything was perfectly normal, and wait for Ellis to make the next move. It would be dangerous, I knew, and though I doubted if he would risk attacking me a second time, I'd make sure I was never alone with him again, and I'd carry Adam's pistol with me no matter where I might be. And as soon as the town opened for business, I'd smuggle Addie Bee's blacksmith husband up the back stairs of the Trader's House to put a new lock on my door.

But as the day wore on it became evident that Frank Ellis had gone to ground. There was no sign of him when I left the Trader's House to go to Lizzie's, and he was nowhere to be seen when I returned that evening to give my performance as usual.

I unlocked my door, turning my own private key in my own private lock, and looked round carefully before committing myself to going inside. Everything was just as I'd left it. My red, marabout-fringed stage dress hung from its hanger on the side of the wardrobe, my makeup was ranged on the dressing table as usual, and nothing seemed to have been touched.

I began to feel more confident then. The room was mine once more, and after a day spent in Matthew's cheerful company my life seemed to have begun to slip back into its proper perspective. But I took Adam's pistol with me all the same as I pattered downstairs to the stage, the barrel tucked into the waistband of my dress, its awkward bulge concealed by trailing feathers. The pistol was loaded and I was probably in the greatest danger of shooting myself by mistake, but as I turned into the cold little passage behind the stage I caught a glimpse of Frank Ellis passing through the door which led out into the barroom. He'd emerged from his lair at last.

I looked nervously for him in his usual place as I finished my last song, but his corner behind the plush curtains was empty, and I heaved a sigh of relief. The passageway, too, was empty, and I fled toward the stairs and the sanctuary of my room before he could emerge from the bar once more.

But as I reached the top of the stairs I realized at once that something was wrong. Lamplight flooded across the corridor from my doorway and the door itself swung wide. My indestructible lock still clung to the doorpost—it was the wood of the door which had given way around it, probably in response to a few heavy kicks.

I hauled out my pistol, and held it before me in both hands as I peered into the room. It seemed empty, but I checked under the bed and inside the wardrobe to be certain, the pistol going first in each case. Why, then, break down the door?

That was when I saw the note, a sheet of white paper propped below the mirror on my dressing table. I laid the pistol down next to my powder-box, picked up the note, and began to read.

You little whore, did you think you could keep me out of here with your fancy lock? I go where I like, and I take what I want—and don't you forget it. Because I know what you are. You're a whore, Rachel, just like the rest, except you don't have the guts to admit it. From now on you're finished in the Trader's House. Pack your bags and get out of here in the morning. And you can spend tonight wondering if I'm going to be back for what I didn't get last night. Sleep well, honey!

I couldn't believe it. I had to read the note twice through before its meaning sank in. Insults—threats—from a man lower than any worm in creation! All of a sudden I was consumed by black rage. Ellis might have snatched away my twelve vital dollars and left me homeless and jobless, but by Heaven, I'd make him take back the things he'd said about me! And he'd apologize for them, right there and then in the bar, in front of his precious customers!

Quite forgetting I still wore the garish paint and feathers of my stage costume, I dashed to the broken door and clattered as quickly down the narrow staircase as my high heels would allow.

The entrance from the narrow passage to the bar emerged just short of the counter itself with its spittoons and pillars, and I was still burning with righteous fury when I threw open the door and stalked defiantly into the crowded room. I saw Frank Ellis at once, exactly where I'd expected to find him, leaning on the bar, a bottle and glass at his elbow. And as he turned his head momentarily, I saw on his cheek the evidence of my own desperate strength—four long, parallel red scars, still raw and bloody from the night before.

He was standing with his back toward me, and as I walked into the room he reached up to touch the scars as if he was in the middle of some jocular explanation, some tale to amuse his cronies. *Just you wait,* I thought, outraged at the idea. *I'll give them the truth instead of your dirty lies.*

It was only when the members of Ellis's circle fell silent, gaping in my direction, that I realized I was still wearing Mademoiselle Valentine's brilliant rouge and flimsy red marabout feathers.

Standing directly in front of Frank Ellis was a huge lout of a man with an entirely bald head whose name, I vaguely recalled, was Kinsella. I'd never heard him called anything else, and even half of his name was enough to produce contempt wherever it was mentioned. He'd arrived in Independence at the start of '41 with the idea of joining the band of settlers Fitzpatrick had led through the mountains to Oregon, but Bartleson and his comrades had rejected him out of hand as a drinker and a troublemaker, and he'd been left behind.

Since then Kinsella had set about repairing his reputation in a hectic career of alcoholic brawls all over town. No doubt that was why Ellis had hesitated to throw the man out of the Trader's House; though Kinsella would certainly have been ejected in the end, he'd have done a lot of damage as he went.

Now he stood, monstrous and swaying, his naked scalp reflected incongruously in the elegant gilt mirror above the bar, a whisky glass hardly a thimble in his massive fingers, his little eyes bulging out of a face like a side of raw meat as he caught sight of me in my ridiculous get-up.

Coming to the bar had been foolish, and as soon as I realized my mistake I turned on my heel and tried to retreat by the way I'd come. But before I could even reach the door Kinsella had knocked aside the other men at the bar and caught up with me in a couple of strides, grabbing me painfully by the arm.

"We-e-e-ell—if it ain't the little Frenchy!" Kinsella bent down and breathed horribly in my face. "I been askin' ol' Frank here if he'd get you down in the bar to drink with me an' the boys, but it seems you're kinda shy, huh? Well now you're here you can come'n be friendly like a good girl, an' see what nice fellers we can be if we're treated good."

I'd no choice. His grip on my arm was as fierce as a vise, and I found myself being dragged by main force toward the group at the bar.

"Ain't this fine, boys? Lookee who's come out to see us." Without letting go of my arm Kinsella commandeered the whisky bottle which stood on the counter, hauled out the cork with his teeth, and poured a large shot into a nearby glass.

"Here." It was a command, not an invitation, and I obediently sipped a little of the pale liquid, feeling it burn a raw trail down my throat. Directly opposite, Frank Ellis glared at me venomously and touched the angry red scars with his fingertips. I could expect no help from him.

The irony was that outside on the street, in my normal black daytime dress, Kinsella would never have dared to lay a finger on me, and every man in the room would have set upon him had he tried it. But dressed as I was, after the performance I'd given . . . To my horror I noticed the other men in the group melting, one by one, into the noisy throng which packed the bar until there were only three of us standing alone. Kinsella, Frank Ellis, and me.

I felt Kinsella let go of my wrist for an instant and tensed myself to run, but before I could slip away he'd slid an arm possessively round my waist, pulling me sharply against his slablike side. He was breathing noisily, peering directly into the deeply cut bodice of my dress with its fluttering feathers, eyeing my all-too-visible breasts with greedy anticipation.

Panicking, I thought of my pistol . . . And remembered with dismay that it must still be lying where I'd left it, next to the powder-box on my dressing table upstairs.

Setting down his glass on the bar, Kinsella attempted to thrust his free hand down where his eyes had been. Furious, I knocked it aside, only to find my lower jaw seized in an iron grip and my face wrenched up toward his.

"You're a regular hellcat, Frenchy, I can see," he grinned. "But I reckon I can fix that." Leaning forward and twisting my head painfully backward, he forced a wet, violent, ugly kiss on my lips. Squirming desperately, I pushed him away with all my strength, only to feel him catch me round the waist once more.

"You *animal!* Let go of me!" I tried to twist out of his grasp, but he only gripped me harder, almost forcing the breath from my body. Out of the corner of my eye I could see Frank Ellis watching intently, his pale skin bluer than ever, the lamplight glistening on a slick of sweat on his upper lip. Beyond Ellis, the barman continued to serve his customers, but slowly, warily, alert for a possible fight in the corner where we stood.

Ellis tried to play for time. "Come on, Kinsella—forget her and have another drink. She's just the singer—she isn't worth the trouble. Here—fill your glass."

"I know what she is!" roared the bald man indignantly. Bending me painfully over the unyielding edge of the bar, he shouted in my face, "I know you're somethin' special! So I reckon you'll cost me a few dollars more'n one of the others, right? But I've got the money, don't you worry! Kinsella's got whatever it takes!" Fishing with his free hand deep in a pocket he produced a fistful of coins and flourished them before my eyes.

"Frank!" I cried, near to hysteria. "For God's sake!"

A slow suspicion simmered in the brain of the hulking Kinsella. I saw his face darken with resentment, and he glared at Frank Ellis.

"Is she your woman?" he demanded wrathfully. A red tide of anger rose above the dirty collar of his shirt to tint the folded skin behind his ears and suffuse his naked scalp with an ominous blush of rage.

I saw Ellis shake his head, a lock of oiled black hair dropping over his brow. He looked at me for a second and then shrugged.

"Not mine, Kinsella. Not at all. She's just one of the girls."

For a moment the lumbering giant continued to glare at him, then all at once he grinned hugely once more and swung me round against him as if I'd been a doll he clasped to his huge gut and barrel chest.

"Well, ain't that fine, little girl? That just leaves you an' me. So what about us goin' upstairs to finish our palaver, huh? I reckon you can be a whole lot nicer to a feller when you choose."

Crushed in his monstrous embrace, I was almost helpless, but terror and disgust gave me a last burst of strength. Pushing myself away from him as fiercely as I could, I gathered all the loathing that was in me at that instant, and fairly spat out my answer.

"Never! Not you—not anyone. But never a filthy pig like you!"

It was strange how quickly that busy, noisy bar fell utterly silent, even the last discordant notes of the piano dying suddenly in the leaden air. Not a glass clinked, not a foot scraped on the boarded floor.

A patch of space in front of the bar had cleared itself miraculously. A few yards away, a solid wall of figures showed where the patrons of the Trader's House had retreated out of harm's way. I could see the lamplight glint on a blonde curl or the taffeta sleeve of a dress where Ellis's girls were watching from the crowd.

Kinsella released me at last, letting me crash back against the bar, limp from his crushing embrace. His eyes stared uncomprehendingly and his mouth moved a little, as if searching for words he'd never known.

Then—hideously loud in the vacuum—someone sniggered at the back of the room. Kinsella's huge, bare head swung round to survey the semicircle of faces, dangerously stupid like a bull in a yard, cornered and goaded to rage. His little eyes glared balefully from one onlooker to the next, searching for the man who'd dared to jeer.

As he turned I saw his hands grope for the belt under his sagging belly and drag from it a heavy five-shot Paterson Colt revolver, its nine-inch barrel a toy in his great paw. A rustling gasp passed through the crowd. Here was unlooked-for drama.

Terrified, I tried to back away from him along the bar, but the movement caught Kinsella's eye and the massive, shining dome of his head swung back toward me, dark with fury, his eyes dilated with barely controlled madness. He'd no idea who'd dared to laugh at him, but at least he was sure of the cause of his humiliation, the uppity whore not four feet away who'd made a fool of him in front of them all.

With his huge thumb he cocked the gun, the click of the hammer and the revolving cylinder like the turning of a lock in the loaded silence. There was a massed rustling and the shuffling of countless feet as the crowd in the bar packed itself ever more tightly against the far wall, close enough to watch the fun without attracting the maniac's attention.

I heard whispering, loud in the silence:

What's up, friend? Some harlot's gonna get a beatin'. Not a harlot —it's the singer. Same thing, ain't it? Shhh. Not our affair, nohow.

Behind me I heard a light step as Frank Ellis moved out of the line of fire.

"Not good enough for you, am I?" demanded Kinsella, his tiny, glittering eyes challenging mine. "Everyone else, but not me, is that it?" He was holding the gun at waist height, but at such close range he couldn't possibly miss.

I tried not to look at the black muzzle of the gun, waiting to punch death into my body. All I could see was Kinsella's contorted face and his wet, shining eyes.

He made a slight movement of the gun barrel in the direction of the ceiling.

"I'll give you one more chance, Frenchy. You comin' upstairs with me?"

His voice seemed to fade as if it came from a very long distance away, and the words meant nothing to me. My mind was suddenly filled with an image of Adam—not the stiff figure in the daguerreotype, but Adam as I'd seen him last, astride his spotted horse in the spring sunshine, scenting freedom, anxious to be off and away to . . . to the future, whatever that might hold. It was Adam's voice I heard. *Trust me,* he'd said. *Trust me.*

Waking from my vision, I faced Kinsella with defiance.

"Go to the Devil!"

In that fleeting instant something swift and dark flashed between us, pushing me off-balance—or it might have been the impact of the lead ball, like a fist smashing into my body in a burst of searing pain, before the crash of the Colt echoed round and round in the dizzy vault of my head and I was only aware of the rough wood of the bar floor pressing uncomfortably against my cheek. The floor was wet, I noticed incongruously, wet with a dark liquid which ran swiftly along the joints between the nearest planks before darting at right angles to find a new parallel channel a few inches away.

I had no desire to move. Except for the dreadful ache slowly eating into my body and the roaring all around me. I'd never felt so languid, so peaceful. I pushed weakly at the many hands which were laying hold of me, turning me, lifting my sagging form in their arms, till the ache became a tidal wave of pain which engulfed me, sucking me down into the welcome oblivion of its soft black chasm.

And as I spun down and down into the void, I heard a disembodied voice far above my head.

"Who was it? Some dumb savage, friend. Some drunken Injun you'd see staggerin' round town, fallin' in the mud as often as not. Well, his luck ran out this time, an' no mistake. Why'd he want to run to the counter just then, anyhow? Loco, Injuns. You can never tell with them."

And then the lights went out for good.

15

They carried me to Crazy Kate's room, afraid to go further before stanching the blood which seeped from my side, staining the red feathers of my bodice a deeper shade of carmine. For several hours I knew only that I'd passed into a world of madness and pain, carried there in the mouth of some great beast against whose gnawing I struggled in vain.

Then gradually the world began to divide itself into light, darkness and shadows; I became aware of a haze of amber lamplight in a dim room and of faces looming above me, their eyes wide pools of concern. Voices spoke to me, their meaning hopelessly lost in a babble of words. Hands smoothed my hair, supported my head so that I could drink from a cup, then laid me gently back on the pillow. At last I slept, sliding gratefully into the absolute peace of unconsciousness.

I've no way of telling for how long I slept—it might have been for minutes or for hours—except that the room was still dark when I woke and lamps were lit nearby. Above my head, garlands of paper flowers twined round the brass rails of a bed, and a lace-edged cloth draped the makeshift wooden table beside it. Even the rough planked door had been concealed behind a cotton hanging, looped back with ribbon to a large nail knocked into the wall nearby.

Kate's room. I'd never crossed its threshold before, but I'd passed the open door several times on my way upstairs, marveling at the determination of women to create comfort—even a kind of beauty —in the barest of circumstances.

I tried to sit up, falling back with a groan as the beast of pain bit deeper into my body, and the sound woke someone dozing in a chair near the window. Crazy Kate, a sleepy mass of tumbled red hair and flounced wrapper, yawned, stretched, and came over to inspect her patient.

"Is it hurtin' bad, darlin'?"

From somewhere among the soiled valances of the bed she produced a whisky bottle and held it up for me to see.

"You want some of this?"

I shook my head, and Kate returned the bottle to the floor, settled herself on the edge of the bed, and lit a cheroot.

"We all thought you were gone for a while there," she remarked somberly. "Doc Dobson had a fine time pickin' around for the lead, did you know that? No—don't suppose you did. Just as well."

I made a feeble attempt to look down past the rise of my ribs, tugging weakly at the sheet which covered me.

"You won't see much, honey, you're all bandaged up. The Doc did a good job though. I stood over him right through, an' he was nearly sober when he done it. I only give him a drink when he finished." She glanced down at the small amount of whisky left in the bottle. "He didn't drink all of that. Most of it went inside you, to clean the wound."

"What did the doctor say?" To my surprise, my voice came out as a whisper. "Where . . . Is it bad?"

"Someplace in the female workin's, he reckoned." The black cheroot in Kate's teeth wagged as she spoke, and a narrow twist of ash cascaded on to the embroidered bed-cover. She brushed it away impatiently. "A man of Doc's education's wasted in a livery stable, don't you think? He's got a real delicate touch with those little knives of his. No horse's going to appreciate that."

There was another thing I had to know. "Kinsella—"

"Bastard's been run out of town," Kate reported matter-of-factly. "It would have been a darn sight better if someone had put a shot into *him*, but none of 'em had the guts. I knew Ellis wouldn't stand, if it came to a showdown. He ran like a rat when the shootin' started. Say—" she added suddenly, "I don't suppose you know how he came by those marks on his face, by any chance?"

She read the answer in my eyes.

"I guessed as much. It's a pity Kinsella didn't use his gun on Ellis while he was shootin' so elegant. Goodness knows where he's got to now."

"Jail . . . Kinsella . . . Arrest . . ."

Kate grunted with contempt. "Do you think a jury in this town would jail him? What for? Killin' an Injun's no crime—and puttin' lead into a woman in the Trader's House ain't much worse. Now—

if you was some Bible-totin', hymn-singin' Holy Hannah, that might be different. But don't you fret. Some of the boys took him off toward the river, an' I expect they've made him wish he ain't done what he did."

I was confused. Something in Kate's account didn't fit my own jumbled memories of events in the bar.

"Indian?" I murmured.

Kate lit another cheroot from the stub of the first.

"He came up out've nowhere, a knife in his hand, just when Kinsella fired. Some drunk Injun, wouldya credit it? But he sure saved your hide, honey. The ball we took out of you went clean through him first. In, an' then out. He didn't have a chance." She frowned for a second. "Maybe you've seen him round town? A thin feller— he did a crazy dance for a shot of whisky."

"Watches Smoke." It took all my energy to whisper the name. "He was called Watches Smoke."

"Yeah?"

Kate pondered this for a moment, then drew her legs up under her and leaned back against the high footboard of the bed. Lost in thought, she watched the swirling smoke-rings from her cheroot twine upward in the lamplight, eddying and looping into the sepia shadows of the ceiling.

"Strange, ain't it," she observed suddenly, "how women are the strong ones? I mean, how they're the ones that survive, in spite of bein' little an' puny?" She thought about it for a moment. "I guess it's because they have to carry the next generation. Nature don't need a man for more'n a few seconds, then he might as well get his fool head shot off. But the women have to go on, an' so they just set their teeth an' get to it." She took another long drag on the stub of the black cheroot.

"But did you ever wonder how it is, if men are so downright dumb, that us women do so much of the hurtin'?"

———

I slept very little for what remained of the night, but nevertheless I felt stronger as the pale dawn displaced the shaded lamps, turning the white lace window-curtains into a dark tracery against the blueing panes.

Morning brought Doc Dobson to check on his patient. A middle-aged man with the watery eyes of a dreamer, reeking of the stable, he carried in his pocket the piece of misshapen lead he'd cut from my body.

"By rights this is yours," he offered, holding it out. "A keepsake for you."

"I'll take it, if you don't want it, honey," Kate put in, seeing me shudder. "See here—I'll put it in this jar by the bed, in case you change your mind."

And then, wonder of wonders, who should appear but Lizzie Fletcher in her Sunday bonnet, striding like my guardian angel through the Valley of the Shadow, scattering demons with every twitch of the hem of her fiery robe. When she realized that the room was Crazy Kate's place of business as well as her living quarters, she sniffed the air as if the very atmosphere were sulphurous and glared at the twinkling beads suspended from the lamp-glasses and at the extravagant bed-cover with its strip of sacking at the bottom to protect it from the customers' boots.

"Don't you fret, honey—we'll fetch you home right away."

Before long, four strong men—strong, sober and religious men— were sent to snatch me on a makeshift blanket stretcher out of the abode of temptation into the healthful climate of Lizzie Fletcher's boardinghouse where a bachelor parson had been summarily turned out to make room for me. Matthew, white-faced and bewildered, was allowed to visit me for a few brief minutes to be assured that all was well. Then, mindful of the doctor-liveryman's instructions that "it won't mend, 'less she lies still for a while," Lizzie took charge of my convalescence.

When Miss Bullitt and the sisterhood protested, she quoted scripture.

"Joy shall be in Heaven over one sinner that repenteth, more than over ninety and nine just persons, which need no repentance. Those were the Lord's words, Ada Bullitt, an' you'd best pay 'em heed. *Rejoice with me; for I have found my sheep which was lost.* And we nearly lost her altogether, poor lamb. But our Savior reached out a hand to her, an' preserved her. Are you sayin' we should do less'n that, Sister?"

Thus Lizzie won the day, and the forces of outraged decency fled in disarray.

For two weeks I was shielded from all visitors except Doc Dobson and poor Matthew, who found it hard to understand why his Mamma couldn't chase him and play with him as she'd been accustomed to do. Day by day, however, my strength returned and my wound began to heal, though the bruised and torn places inside me could still ache by the end of a long afternoon or make me gasp with sharp agony after too sudden a movement.

Confined to my room, I'd no way of knowing that my standing in town had undergone a subtle change in the fortnight since the shooting. In some mysterious way Kinsella's pistol-ball had turned me from an outcast into a near-heroine. As soon as it became known that Frank Ellis had stood by while I was shot down, he became the villain of the piece by popular vote and a great wave of sympathy rallied everyone to my side.

I only understood this, however, when Lizzie at last permitted visitors, and with decidedly pinched lips conducted Crazy Kate to my room.

"I want you to know this ain't my idea," Kate warned me as soon as the usual courtesies were over and Lizzie had withdrawn. "Not the visitin'—I was comin' anyhow to see how you were doin'. But I'm supposed to bring you a message, an' give you this." From a purse in her hand she drew a stack of ten-dollar bills, which she laid on the table next to my chair.

"What on earth is that for, Kate? Have they taken up a collection?"

"Not exactly." Kate took a cheroot out of her purse and looked at it regretfully. "Better not light this in here, huh?"

Regretfully, she restored the cheroot to her purse, apparently grateful for an excuse to delay what she'd come to tell me. Then she moved forward to the very edge of her chair, and stared down at her hands.

"The money is from Frank Ellis, Rachel. . . . Now wait before you yell at me! I told you this warn't my idea; I'm just deliverin' the message, right? Now that's better. Remember, you're sick." Kate waited until I'd calmed down to her satisfaction before going on with her tale.

"Frank came creepin' back the day after the shootin', an' tried to make out nothin' had happened. He put up a bill outside sayin' '*See Where The Shootin' Took Place*,' an' said no one was even to scrub the mark off the floor—thinkin' he could make a lot of money out of the event. But folks in town didn't take kindly to the idea, and women like Regina Meadow were delighted to have somethin' to use against Ellis at last.

"So they tore down his signboard, an' went to have it out with him. An' he told them the whole thing had been a mix-up an' he'd thought you an' Kinsella had an understandin'—"

"*What?*"

"—an' that he had it all figured out to look after you, an' he'd pay Doc Dobson's bill, an'—an' I was downright mad, Rachel, I never heard such a swod o' lies in my life!"

"Kinsella—and me! How could he even suggest it!"

"I'm thankful to say most folks didn't believe it. But they're waitin' to see what you're gonna do, all the same. We had to wait, with you bein' so ill, but now Ellis has sent me round with this—" She indicated the money on the table. "His conscience money. There's two hundred to be goin' on with, an' he says there'll be more if you need it."

Two hundred dollars. More than enough, with what I'd saved, to take us to England. And he owed it to me—by Heaven, he owed me a great deal more than two hundred, and by his own admission I had him over a barrel. But to accept the money was to let Frank Ellis escape. And all the dollars in the world wouldn't make up for what he'd done.

"You can take it straight back to him, Kate! I won't touch his filthy money!"

Kate nodded. "I warned him you wouldn't take it. But he's tryin' to buy himself time in this town, an' he knows if you come out of this like an angel, they'll run him out for sure."

"You tell him—you tell him, Kate—" I was shaking with anger.

"Tell him yourself, if you want. He's waitin' outside in the yard to see you."

"*Out there?*" I pointed to the window.

"Sure. Him an' half the town."

She had to help me out of my chair, but I was determined to reach the window or die in the attempt. And when I looked out through the open casement I could hardly believe that such a crowd of people could have assembled so quietly. They were standing in the road and in the yard, men and women together, in twos and threes and larger groups, staring up at the house, wondering what was going to happen. When they caught sight of me there was a buzz of excitement, and I saw many of them glance away toward the lonely figure of Frank Ellis, waiting uncomfortably before Lizzie's door.

"Ellis!" I called, my voice as firm as I could make it. "Frank Ellis! Come out here where I can see you!"

"Why, Rachel!" he exclaimed smoothly, backing out into the yard and looking up at me, his broad-brimmed hat clutched to his chest. "I'm happy to see you looking so well!" I noticed with satisfaction that the scars from my clawing fingernails were still livid on his cheek.

"If I look well, it's no thanks to you, you miserable coward!"

"That was a misunderstanding, honey! I thought——"

"There was no misunderstanding, Ellis! You ran, and left me to be killed! I pleaded with you for help, and you turned your worthless, misbegotten back on me. And now you're trying to buy me off!"

A low murmuring began to swell through the crowd, and I could see Frank Ellis glance round nervously.

"Rachel, honey—jes' let me come up an' explain——"

"Here's what I think of your explanations, you lying snake!" By now I was leaning on the sill for support, but with the last of my strength I threw the pile of bills out into the yard where they separated and fluttered down, an accusing blizzard of paper, over Ellis and his audience alike.

"I hope you rot in Hell for what you did!" I shouted at him, and drawing back into the room, slammed the casement shut.

Kate caught me as I started to slide, exhausted, to the floor.

"Well, I guess that's told him," she observed complacently. "I always knew you had it in you to be a real woman, Rachel."

———

Lizzie Fletcher didn't put it quite like that.

"I'm surprised at you, Rachel," she told me later, "an' that's a fact! I thought you'd done with makin' a spectacle of yourself before crowds of folk—an' turnin' my yard into a medicine-show into the bargain! I suppose you know Miss Ada Bullitt's gone off to find herself new lodgin's elsewhere?"

"Oh, Lizzie—I'm sorry! I was so angry, I just didn't think."

Lizzie relented at once.

"No, my dear, I don't suppose you did. An' don't you fret. I'd just about had enough of the woman anyhow. It was always *Oh, Mrs. Fletcher, not hominy again, surely!* or *I declare, Mrs. Fletcher, there's a fly in my pitcher!* until I was fixin' to tell her to go at the end of the week anyhow." She paused for a moment. "But Rachel—you sure threw away a lot of money."

"I know I did. But I won't take a cent from Frank Ellis, and not just because he treated me so badly. There was Watches Smoke too. His blood was on those bills even more than mine."

"Well, I guess you did right to give the money back, however you went about it. An' I'm proud of you, Rachel—don't ever think otherwise. You earned your deliverance. An' I expect that man Ellis is goin' to get exactly what he's earned, too."

Lizzie was right. Late that night, almost asleep, I heard the sounds of shouting and revelry begin to drift over from the main street. The noise went on for some time, and then from somewhere just beyond the yard gate I heard the voice of a lone balladeer yelling unfamiliar words to a well-known tune. He was far too drunk to make much sense of the verses, but the chorus came to me clearly where I lay in my bed.

> *He lied to save his hide* (shouted the minstrel),
> *And they shot poor Frenchy down—*
> *So the whole damn population*
> *Ran Frank Ellis out of town.*

So they'd done it after all, and Independence was free of Frank Ellis at last.

———

Next day I heard the whole story from an exultant Lizzie.

The scene in the yard was hardly over, apparently, when Regina Meadow and the chapel sisters called a public meeting to propose that the owner of the Trader's House should be run out of town. For once the menfolk agreed, but before anything could be done Frank Ellis got wind of the plan and had vanished from Independence a bare half-hour ahead of the mob.

"Trouble is—they tell me that woman Kate's got the place now," Lizzie added glumly. "Ellis sold her his half-interest for nothin' at all, simply to get clear in a hurry. I guess things'll go on much the same, when all's said and done."

"Kate isn't so bad, Lizzie. At least she's honest, which is more than you can say for Frank Ellis."

I never regretted flinging Ellis's blood-money back at him—even when my pile of carefully saved dollars refused to come to more than one hundred and forty-five, a hundred and ten dollars short of the money I needed.

"You know a feller called Blue?" Lizzie demanded one morning, interrupting yet another counting-session.

"*Blue?* Not Antoine Bleu—a trapper—with a beard and buck-skins?"

"That's the name all right, but there's no beard, and he ain't in buckskins. Come askin' about you, wonderin' how you're doin'. You want to see him?"

"Oh, please."

Lizzie stood aside to admit Antoine—clean-shaven and, except for the long knife in his belt, dressed like any Missouri farmer in wool trousers and a flannel shirt. But his smile was the same—good-humored and wise—and just at that moment I couldn't think of anyone I would have been happier to see.

"Two minutes, Mr. Blue," Lizzie said firmly. "I won't have her tired."

"*Bien entendu, Madame.* Trust me. I don' come all this way to make her ill."

He'd left Ed Ballantine at Fort Union, so he told us, and made the long journey downriver to see if I was still in Independence. And he knew—he knew the whole story of my months in the Trader's House: someone had told him, I could sense it, though he never mentioned it directly. What must he think of me now, his friend's widow, showing off her body in a barroom for twelve dollars a week?

"So—" he finished his tale as Lizzie rose meaningfully from her chair, "maybe now I'll stay in town until you're well again."

"I couldn't ask you to do that!"

"You don' ask. But I'll do it all the same. I think you need some-one to keep you out of trouble." He grinned wickedly. "I'll come back to see you tomorrow, if that's allow'."

Lizzie followed him to the front door and then returned, regarding me for a moment from the doorway with her head on one side.

"You got more color than I've seen in days, Rachel," she said sagely. "An old friend's better than any dose of medicine, I reckon —especially if he keeps your mind off that money you're always counting." She crossed the room and began to pat cushions back into shape. "Tell me—all that stuff you got stacked in my cellar . . . You plannin' to take the china back to England with you, an' the fancy carpets?"

"Goodness no. I'd almost forgotten about them."

"Then why not sell it all? There's plenty folks round here puttin' down roots, settlin' in. Good stuff like that ain't easy to come by, even now. The china must be worth somethin' on its own, an there ain't hardly any of it broken."

"That's a wonderful idea! But would people want it—from me?"

Lizzie snorted with derision. "You just see if they don't, honey! You just see if they don't!"

———

Lizzie was proved right. Independence was growing wealthy from supplying the needs of a swelling tide of passers-through, but though the town now had money to spend on its own comfort there was little of quality and elegance to buy, and Lizzie's description of my Rockingham tea and dessert services—an unsuitable wedding present from Aunt Grace—soon had the better-off ladies sprinting decorously to the door. I might be a woman of no reputation, but that evidently made no odds when there were bargains to be had. My dusty boxes were soon hauled up from the cellar, and one by one the items which had originally caused Addie Bee such amazement were taken out into the light of day again.

I'd forgotten how beautiful the Rockingham cups really were. The translucent porcelain, garlanded in trailing flowers and gold scrolling on a green ground, had hardly ever been taken from its packing, except in honor of the occasional visitor. Once or twice in the cabin, Lizzie and I, starved of elegance among our cooling candle-molds and tubs of lye, had lovingly laid it all out on the massive kitchen table to spend a sentimental half-hour drinking tea for old times' sake. But Lizzie was right: far better now to turn it into useful dollars for the journey to England.

Within a few days the tea service had gone and the matching dessert plates had vanished to the dinner table of the local justice of the peace, to the great satisfaction of his wife. The oriental rugs were carried off by a horse-trader's lady brought up in St. Louis and used to better things than Independence could provide, and soon my marquetry workbox had followed them along with a little traveling writing-desk fitted out with silver ink-bottles, and the last of Aunt Grace's heavy linen sheets, embroidered at the hems with drawn-thread work.

I'd expected to regret watching them go, those last relics of my life with Adam, but instead I discovered a curious satisfaction in being

rid of them all, as if I were purging my mind at the same time of
memories which could only bring unhappiness.

———

Two hundred and twenty-six dollars. Sitting under my shady tree, I
counted the money again. Two hundred and twenty-six dollars and
fifteen cents. The final total.

Antoine Bleu was lying stretched out in the grass at my feet, his
eyes closed. He'd become a regular visitor without ever seeming
intrusive; he was always there when I needed a friend—kind, self-
mocking and loyal—consoling me on gloomy days when my wound
was painful, teaching Matthew to use a bow and arrow like an
Indian boy, often simply lying quietly nearby in the shade of the old
tree while I sewed or read a book.

"There's something I don' understand—" he'd said to me one day
soon after he arrived. He was lying in the sun-speckled grass, his
eyes closed, and I'd assumed he was asleep.

"What's that, Antoine? What don't you understand?"

"I can't see why you let *those people* tell you what to think."

"Which people do you mean?"

"Those women in town. Why do you believe what they say about
you?"

"When they say I'm no better than a whore?"

"*Justement.*"

"Perhaps it's true."

"I don' think so."

"Why not? Because I was Adam's wife? The wife of your friend?"

"No. I don' care whose wife you were. But I know if those things
were true, you'd have told me. Because you're an honest woman,
Rachel. Simple as that."

I glanced down at him then, half-convinced he was making fun of
me. But there was no hint of amusement in his face. He'd meant
every word, exactly as he said it.

"You and Lizzie—you're the only ones who believe in me."

"Two people is better than nothing, don' you think?"

He reached up and took my hand in his, and I realized with a start
that it was the first time—discounting Doc Dobson and his little
knives—that a man had touched me since Frank Ellis and Kinsella. . . . As soon as I could, I slid my fingers from his grasp.

"What's the matter, *chérie?*"

"Nothing. Nothing at all."

"Then give me your hand again. Like that. So."

Reluctantly, I did as he asked. If I'd refused, I'd have had to explain why even that simple contact, flesh against flesh, made my stomach turn over in panic, and I couldn't have borne it—even for Antoine.

His hand was strong and warm as Adam's had been, and I noticed a long white knife-scar across the knuckles.

"Whatever happened to your hand?" I tried to focus my attention on the scar to silence my wildly beating heart.

"A beaver get angry an' chase me with a knife."

"A likely tale! What really happened to you?"

He looked up at me curiously for a moment, squeezed my fingers gently, then disengaged his hand.

"We both have our secrets, *chérie,* don't we?"

I was selfish enough to take his friendship for granted, obsessed as I was with my own troubles and with my great, overwhelming need to escape from the town of Independence. It had become a fixation with me. Somehow I'd come to believe that if I could only shake the dust of that Missouri township from my shoes, I could also leave behind the contemptible, tarnished creature I saw each morning in my mirror. And that was why, sitting under my tree that day with Antoine stretched out at my feet, I was counting my little store of money for the hundredth time.

"Well?" he demanded at last. "How much you got?"

"Two hundred and twenty-six dollars."

"Is that enough?"

"It depends. Doc Dobson says I shouldn't travel for another four weeks, so I shall owe Lizzie for a month's board. And after that . . . I suppose it might be possible, if I traveled as a deck passenger on the steamboat to Pittsburgh. That way I could save forty dollars."

"So much?" Antoine opened his eyes in astonishment.

"They charge more at low water."

"Ah. But then, a deck passage is not so good. If the boat goes down, you get drown first—if it gets blow up, then you get dead first. Mathieu might fall over the side. An' there are sometimes robbers or drunkards. . . . It's no good for a woman alone, I think."

"That's what Lizzie says. She says I'm crazy even to consider it. But if it's all I can afford, I may just have to make up my mind to take a deck passage. I'm sure it can't be so bad, really."

Antoine considered this in silence for a few minutes, his eyes closed once more.

"You know—maybe it's time I saw this Pittsburgh. I hear it's a beautiful place. Very fine, like the mountains."

I burst out laughing.

"Pittsburgh! Antoine, you'd hate it! Who on earth told you it was beautiful? It's just a big, smoky city, with lots of factories."

"Then I must see it for sure," he said calmly. "Maybe in another month or so. And then we could travel together on the boat, and you wouldn't be alone. *Voilà!* No more problem."

I could hardly believe his kindness.

"But you don't really want to go to Pittsburgh! And I couldn't possibly ask you go all that way, just to look after me! It's generous of you—more than generous—but I won't let you do it."

In the grass, Antoine rolled over on to one elbow and regarded me steadily.

"There's no way you can stop me, *chérie*. If I want to go to this Pittsburgh, I will go. If you ask me to go to all the way to New York with you, I'll do that too, and I will be very happy."

"But—"

"Do you want that? All the way to New York?"

I couldn't help laughing. "Pittsburgh would be far enough, Antoine—if you're determined to come."

"*Complètement*. You think I let you go so far on your own, you and the boy? What for you take me? 'Course I come along." He turned onto his back again, and closed his eyes. " 'Sides—maybe by Pittsburgh I even talk you into stay in the States, *chérie*. That's a good enough reason, *n'est-ce pas?*"

As I'd expected, it was another month before the doctor pronounced me fit to travel and by then I was desperate to begin my journey, to shake off the swelling township, dusty and muddy by seasons, milling with emigrants and their wagons, their oxen and their swarming families, all straining westward as if the Rocky Mountains were the gateway to a promised land. All I knew was that the mountains had taken my husband from me, and I imagined them crouched there across the prairies, magnificent and deadly.

Parting from Lizzie was another matter, and many promises were made and tears shed at her door before at last Matthew and I were whirled away toward the river-landing in Dobson's gig, past the town square and Meadow's store and the Trader's House with its lights burning even at midday, and then out by the temporary camps of the emigrants and a few clusters of newly erected houses, until even these had disappeared and all that lay ahead was the river-landing where Antoine Bleu had promised to wait for us.

We were free. Matthew and I were going home at last. And I refused to let myself think of anything beyond reaching Liverpool and the calm, orderly house in Leghorn Street which lay at the end of our journey.

———

But there were more than two thousand miles to be traveled before we even reached New York, some sixteen hundred miles of it on one riverboat after another, down the Missouri River to St. Louis, part-way down the Mississippi and then round into the Ohio River for the long haul upstream to Pittsburgh where the final section to New York would begin. Since the rivers were particularly low at that time of year only the smaller boats could pass successfully over the bars and rapids, and even they could only carry the minimum of freight. As a result it was less cramped than usual for passengers traveling cheaply, as I was, in the nooks and crannies which remained.

There were no such luxuries as bunks or staterooms on these decks; blankets or a buffalo robe spread in a corner sufficed for a bed and any cooking was done on a big iron stove just aft of the engine compartment where the deck-planks rumbled and shook even more than usual, and passengers queued up to brew coffee or cook bacon as hunger took them. But on warm river nights a cooling breeze caressed the wide decks of our steamer and there was nothing to do but lie and doze in our corner or hang over the guard-rail watching the river water slip by a few feet away, talking of anything that came into our heads.

And Antoine was there as he'd promised. Just . . . *there* . . . until I realized how lost and lonely we'd have been without him. He was perfect company on the long river passage, amusing and serious by turns, and possessed of a lazy, amorous Gallic charm which gradu-ally began to warm away my problems like summer mists.

"I like to see you smile, *chérie*. You have a beautiful smile, now you let me see it sometimes."

"How many girls have you said that to, Antoine? I bet you've long since lost count."

"Plenty women, maybe. But this time it's true."

"Oh—go on with you! I'm thin as a rake, I'm far too pale and my skin's gone dull with too much paint, and my eyes—"

"—make me think of *la Madone*. The Madonna. It's true," he added as I opened my mouth to protest.

"A saloon-singer like me? I hardly think so."

"But you don't sing in a bar anymore, *chérie*. So why not?"

"Because . . . Because of all those men *looking* at me . . . and thinking about me. I feel so . . . dirty. So worthless."

"Listen to me—" Suddenly Antoine took me fiercely by the shoulders. "I don' come all this way with a worthless woman. You understand? I've known plenty of worthless women in my time, an' you are not one of those. I don' want to hear you say that again."

I was so taken aback I just gaped at him in astonishment. Fortunately, he took my silence for assent, released my shoulders, and returned to his contemplation of the evening river.

He was jealously protective of our privacy; shootings were still newsworthy enough in the river towns for word of the incident in the Trader's House to have spread to St. Louis and beyond, and Antoine was careful never to say anything to our fellow passengers which might link me with that infamous saloon. Sometimes it was hard to resist their questions during those days of slow progress up the shallow Ohio River when the quizzing of neighbors on names and family histories became the main pastime on the cargo deck. The most persistent questioner was a round little man from Wheeling who saw Antoine's accent and deeply tanned skin as a challenge to his detective powers.

"Where're you folks trav'lin' from, friend?"

"Downriver," supplied Antoine briefly.

"An' where're you headed?"

"Upriver."

"Oh." The man from Wheeling digested this. "You a farmer someplace?"

"Nope."

"Horse-dealer?"

"Nope."

"Flatboat man?" asked the citizen of Wheeling, becoming desperate.

"Not that either."

"Well then, friend—what *do* you do?"

"I kill things," said Antoine simply, indicating the long knife at his belt. At which point his inquisitor moved hastily away toward his own party nearby, and we were left in peace for the remainder of the journey.

"Ed Ballantine will be wondering what's become of you, Antoine," I teased him one evening as we pulled slowly away from yet another landing.

"Oh, I don' know." Antoine considered the toe of one boot. "He'll just think I'm involved with a woman, Ballantine." He looked up at me suddenly. "An' so I am."

There was no mistaking his meaning. His level blue eyes met mine in mute inquiry.

"Oh, Antoine—" I shook my head, helpless to go on.

"Except that the woman is not involved with *me,* isn't that so, *chérie?*"

"I don't know what to say . . ."

"Then say nothing. *Tu vois comment je t'aime,* but you don't have the same feeling. *Bien.* I understand. Forget I speak. And now we talk about something else."

But I could think of nothing else, and I was miserable.

"You've been so very kind to us . . . You came all this way simply to help me—and you *have* helped, more than you'll ever know—and I've been selfish enough to let you do it—and given you nothing in return."

"*Mais non.* Don't feel like that. You were the wife of my friend, so of course I help you. What are friends for otherwise?" He glanced out across the river, where a widening expanse of water now separated us from the bank. "Except I always hope you change your mind about going to England. But it isn't so."

"No, Antoine. I'm sorry."

"There is somebody waiting for you there? Another man, perhaps?"

"No—just my aunt and her husband. But you see—since Adam . . . died . . . I've had to manage here alone, and I've made such a mess of everything . . . America isn't my country and it never will be, though God knows I've tried hard enough to find a place for myself. England—well, I wasn't born there either, but it's the country I call home. I *understand* it, in a way I'll never understand America."

"In time, maybe. And I would help, if you let me."

I shook my head. I couldn't say anything that didn't sound churlish and ungrateful.

"But if Adam was still here . . ."

"That . . . would be different."

"Ah. For Adam, you would stay here."

"Yes."

"I understand." And he looked away again, across the twilight river, an expression of such profound sadness in his eyes that I felt like a murderer.

Across the deck, in the shadowy corner we'd claimed for our own, I heard Matthew wake and whimper in fright. Some bad dream had disturbed his sleep, some phantom conjured up by the banging of the engines or the crack of the steam exhaust. But after I'd hugged him for a while and soothed him, and wiped away the two great tears which had rolled down his cheeks, he dropped quickly back into a deep sleep, his fears replaced by an expression of profound contentment.

I gazed at him for a few moments. How simple it had been to reassure him, to promise him all would be well and his mother would keep him safe forever! How I wished someone would do the same for me—even if the promise were as hollow as mine had been—enough to banish the fears of one night, until dawn brought back its load of troubles.

I glanced across at Antoine, now only a dark silhouette at the steamer's rail. If some good angel had come to me then and made it possible for me to love that man of kindness and understanding, I'd have welcomed that love with open arms, then and there, on our spread buffalo robes on the hard deck, with the river running blackly beyond. But I didn't love him—and I owed him too much to ask him to share me with a ghost.

With a sigh, I rolled myself up in my blankets and tried to sleep.

We reached Pittsburgh next morning and went straight to the canal wharf, where we found a canal boat almost ready to leave for Harrisburg. I was as relieved to be quickly on our way as poor Antoine was dismayed; I knew he'd expected a day or two's delay in Pittsburgh in the hope of persuading me to stay, and I was afraid I might give in at last to his gentle perseverance.

"This Liverpool must be a hell of a place," he conceded at last, shaking his head in defeat. "You want so much to go back there."

"But you understand why, Antoine. Otherwise—if I stayed for anyone, it would be for you."

"Maybe I come and visit you one day in England, and see if you're ready to come back with me. How's that?"

"That would be perfect," I agreed brightly, knowing as well as he did that it would never happen. "Lizzie will always know where to find me."

A great bustle broke out along the wharf as the passengers and their luggage were finally summoned aboard, and the canal boat made ready to leave. Matthew was tugging at my skirt, anxious to explore our quarters, and there was no more time for goodbyes.

"Thank you, Antoine, for all your kindness! You'll never know how much you've given me." I tried to take his hand, but he pulled me into his arms instead, kissed me fiercely, murmured, "*Au revoir, chérie,*" and walked swiftly away into the smoky, thundering city.

With him went the last of my life in the West. New York lay ahead of us across the mountains, then the broad Atlantic Ocean and at last, after weeks of weary travel by land and sea, England and the city in which rested all my hopes for the future.

Matthew and I were really, truly, on our way to Liverpool.

16

In the late evening of the 25th of August, 1842, our ship hove to at the mouth of the River Mersey. Next morning as we made our way upstream toward the busy dockland and the city I waited eagerly at the rail to point out to Matthew the landmarks I remembered from five years before. "From my girlhood," I'd been about to say; yet I was not quite twenty-three years of age—hardly an old woman, but already a lifetime away from the impulsive child who'd left that same river for New Orleans five years before.

And here we were, Matthew and I, at last within sight of the city I'd described to him so often. To Matthew, New York had been a city of enchantment, of streets teeming with horse-omnibuses and phaetons, of red-brick canyons which shimmered in the summer heat, of churches, parks and bandstands: for my part, I'd rejoiced in the long-lost sight of people in bright, elegant clothes—people who'd never chopped a stick or gutted a jackrabbit in their lives. Ah, New York had been a wonder . . . but here—at last—was Liverpool.

And I began to wonder if perhaps my memory had failed me. I hadn't expected the dreary row of waterfront warehouses to look quite so much like their distant cousins along the East River, with the somber backdrop of tall buildings and church spires behind. I hadn't remembered how hugger-mugger it all was compared with the sprawl of New York, how hemmed-in and cramped after the wide spaces of Broadway.

It would take time to become accustomed once more to such a dense warren of humanity after the open skies of the American West. There had been dust and filth aplenty in the streets of Independence—and people, too, by the time I left—but somehow even the dirt and the discomfort had never seemed so overwhelmingly depressing as it did in this city where every vista seemed closed off by brick walls pocked with little windows, and the streets were mere gullies carved between these masonry cliffs by the irresistible current of scurrying mankind.

Here at last was England, though it seemed strangely shrunken from the ample land I remembered half a decade before. Such a small raft to float such a multitude of people! Right to the edge of the water they jostled and crowded, elbow-to-elbow and knee-to-knee, milling into the small clear spaces which remained, covering the green with paving and cobbles, hewing down trees, enslaving the rivers to spin wheels and grind cogs. Where did one go to draw breath? I could suffocate—drown in the welling tide of humankind . . . Yet somewhere in that flood I must learn to swim for my own and my son's survival. There was no other course open to me.

Leaving instructions for the forwarding of our trunks I found a place for us in one of the first boats ashore. But as our horse cab swung and swayed us through the teeming city toward Leghorn Street, I saw little to raise my spirits.

How had I ever managed to live a bare mile away from these scenes of misery without noticing their existence? The great rubbish-heaps near the docks where incoming vessels dumped the waste from their holds and their galleys must have stood there then, and the ragged, barefoot crew of haggard scavengers who crept over their slopes must have attended them just as busily. The streets must have been every bit as full of beggars—crippled, ulcerated and hollow-eyed—in the days when I passed on my way to the haberdasher's to select my buttons and ribbons. No doubt I'd been careful to walk round the gaping cellar-mouths where whole families existed like sewer-rats, the children picking over the generous gutters outside. Had I been blind in those years of plenty?

There were no beggars in Leghorn Street to shuffle their rag-bound feet past the worthy gateposts of the well-to-do. At least Captain Fuller's tall house looked exactly as I remembered it, solidly bricked and four-square, a haven from the shifting world beyond.

Aunt Grace was at home, and rushed to the hall with great squawks of astonishment when she heard my voice. Her mouth dropped open when she caught sight of my drab, travel-stained black dress, but she recollected herself in time to kiss me soundly on both cheeks and then to do the same to an affronted Matthew. And when Captain Fuller returned in late afternoon and found us chattering by the drawing-room fire which my aunt had insisted on lighting, he hugged me uninhibitedly and swung Matthew, squealing, into the air above his head. Oh, it was wonderful to feel part of a family once more, and to feel there was a home, however temporary, to which we belonged!

Aunt Grace too looked exactly as I remembered her—tall and lugubrious like Lizzie's mule—but the Captain was even rounder and redder than before. And naturally they wanted to know everything which had happened to me since I left. Some of it—the bare outline—I'd put in my few letters to Aunt Grace, but instinct now warned me to take care how I filled in the missing facts. My arrival in Liverpool offered the chance of a new beginning. It was like a second birth: whatever tale I told would be my official history from now on, and if I left out those scandalous months of my life which had made me an outcast in Independence, no one in Liverpool need ever be any the wiser.

So I didn't mention the Trader's House or Mademoiselle Valentine. In any case, it was already becoming hard to believe that Frank Ellis, Crazy Kate and the gilded, lamplit stage had ever existed. But the proof was there if I ever needed it, in a livid scar where Kinsella's shot had ripped into my body and in moments of sudden, unexpected pain as my slowly healing flesh reminded me of my secret past. Who was singing on the little stage now, I wondered, as I sat amid the silver and the porcelain at my aunt's table in Liverpool?

Instead I told them about the cabin, and the mud, and the snow, and about working in the store and staying with Lizzie, and the emigrants setting off for the mountains, and Adam setting off . . . and never returning. And I told them about the steamboats on the rivers, and learning to ride, and the Fur King's palace, and New Orleans—and I made up a tale about being shot by accident at my store counter by a crazy drunk, mad with corn whisky, and they accepted it with all the rest. Aunt Grace sucked her long yellow teeth in disapproval, and declared that people who *would* live in a savage country laid themselves open to a fate of that sort, by which she meant losing a husband, and being shot as well. Goodness only knew, she continued, why poor Mr. Gaunt—God rest his soul—was so bent upon living there in the first place.

"I had thought," remarked Aunt Grace suddenly, "that this might have been the time for your mother to forget her grievances and do something to help you out. I wrote to her, and said as much. But she wouldn't hear of it. 'I told that girl,' she said, 'what would become of her. I told her she'd be left with nothing, but she wouldn't listen. Well, she made her choice. Now let her suffer for it.' "

Captain Fuller shook his head and made a clicking noise of annoyance.

"Hard as nails, my sister-in-law," he observed.

"And I said to her, you may be sure, that your husband had died, not gone off or broken the law as she predicted. But it made no difference. No difference at all. Sometimes I wonder what my sister is made of!" continued Aunt Grace darkly. "Not flesh and blood, but iron, I shouldn't be surprised."

"I expected as much, Aunt Grace. I doubt if my mother will ever forgive me for marrying a man she hated. Not now, anyway, after so long. There was a time—once—when I thought she might change her mind. When Matthew was born, I almost wrote to her—"

"Oh, *I* told her about Matthew! 'You have a grandson now,' I told her. 'A darling baby boy, who's the very image of his father.' " Aunt Grace frowned. "I won't repeat what she said about *that*."

"Then it's just as well I didn't write."

"Just as well, my dear," agreed the Captain. "No reason to cause yourself distress. Besides, you still have your aunt and me, remember. You're welcome in Leghorn Street for as long as you want. And we'll have you afloat again in no time, just see if we don't."

They couldn't have been more hospitable, my aunt and her husband, but all the time I was conscious of the great effort Aunt Grace was making to avoid asking what I proposed to do next. It wasn't so much that she minded having two extra mouths to feed. It was simply that my presence in her home, without a purpose, without a role in life, irritated her like a trailing thread-end, and she longed to have me tied off neatly in some useful occupation.

Her efforts to stay tactfully silent on the matter only made things worse. Forthright by nature, she'd come to a sudden halt as she saw the conversation leading into awkward territory, fall silent for a moment with her mouth ajar, and then attempt laboriously to change the subject. One day I could stand it no longer, and as soon as Captain Fuller had left the house to go into the city, I took the bull by the horns and raised the question myself.

"I had thought I might find a post as a governess with a decent family," I suggested. "After all, thanks to you I can paint a little, and I know something of music. And all those months in the store made me quite good at arithmetic. You'd be amazed how quickly I can count up nails!"

Aunt Grace looked pained. "I'd say nothing at all about that particular talent if I were you, Rachel. I know you've been abroad for a
while, my dear, and *their ways* aren't exactly *our ways*, but I do urge
you to remember that well-brought-up ladies have no need to count
up nails."

"No, Aunt Grace," I murmured obediently, thanking Providence
that my aunt had no idea of the other talents I'd acquired while
abroad.

In any case, Aunt Grace had veered off in another direction.

"And what do you propose to do with Matthew? You can hardly
take him governessing with you."

"I had thought . . . if I paid you for his board and lodging . . . he
might stay here and be a companion to Harry."

Harry, at eight years of age, had begun by hating the idea of a
younger boy about the house, but he'd found in Matthew a willing
slave, and the two were now inseparable when Harry wasn't at his
lessons.

"Paid me?" Aunt Grace's eyebrows rose. "Quite apart from the
fact that I wouldn't hear of such a thing . . . just what were you
proposing to pay me with, may I ask? You don't seem to have
thought this out at all, I fear. If the family's a really good one, they
won't expect to offer you a wage. And if they're willing to pay a
governess a large salary in addition to keeping her, they must have
difficulty in getting young ladies of the right sort. In other words,
you wouldn't want to have anything to do with *them*."

"Oh."

"Yes—*oh*. You'd better think carefully about this, dear, before
you go rushing into something you'll regret."

"Perhaps I could be a nurse, then."

"A *nurse?* Rachel—I think we'd better talk about this another
time, when you're in a better state of mind. It seems to me—" and
here Aunt Grace took a deep breath, putting her hand to her bosom
to still her palpitating heart—"it seems to me that you've got hold
of some very queer notions in the last few years. A nurse, indeed!
You'll be telling me you want to be a shop-girl next, I shouldn't
wonder!"

As that very suggestion had been on the tip of my tongue, it
seemed wise to keep silent and put off any discussion of my future
to another day.

But the more I thought about it, the more I realized how impossible it would be to find work—paying work—which would suit Aunt Grace's notions of what was permissible. If governessing was fraught with problems of caste and nursing was impossibly sordid, then there was little left but shop-work, and that appeared to be beneath my dignity too.

And yet what was I supposed to do? I could hardly live in my aunt's house and take up work which shamed her in the eyes of her friends. The only alternative was to move out with Matthew to modest lodgings somewhere else, and work at whatever job I might find—in a cotton-mill if necessary. Pride was all very well, but we couldn't eat pride or burn it in the grate. The specter of the beggars on the rubbish-heaps rose up before my eyes. Were my son and I to be homeless after all in that swarm of a city?

But before I could even raise the matter of employment again with my aunt, Captain Fuller himself took a hand.

The Captain had now almost given up going to sea—he was "beached" these days, he said—and while I was in America he'd accepted a position with the owners of his ship *Spartacus,* J. G. Oliver & Co., which carried the courtesy title of Commodore and command of a large mahogany desk in the company offices. From this comfortable quarterdeck he supervised the seaworthiness of the Oliver vessels and gravely lectured the senior ship-masters on their passage-times.

Yet in his own house he was amazingly invisible, and I'd come across him hiding in a corner of the drawing room or lurking in the hall as if he had no decent right to be there. He would rise up from his armchair with an apologetic cough, as if he felt awkward and out of place like a piece of new furniture which hadn't yet found its proper position in the house. The Captain had been so often at sea, and for so long at a time, that the household had organized itself to manage without him, and didn't seem to have noticed his permanent return. Six days out of seven he breakfasted early and left for the Oliver offices where his right to rule was unquestioned, leaving Aunt Grace in command of the house in Leghorn Street, just as if he were still at sea.

Because of this, both Aunt Grace and I were startled to discover that Captain Fuller had not only taken aboard my thorny problem, but had worked out a possible solution.

"It's only a suggestion, mind," he warned me, tugging at his spiky gray whiskers. "You mayn't like the idea at all, and I don't suppose

the pay'll be overgenerous, but it's work, certainly, and it's respectable, and I daresay you'd learn the ropes as quick as any other. Long
hours, though, and hard work."

"Hard work never hurt anyone," observed Aunt Grace, who'd
never tried it. "Provided it's respectable work, that is."

"Oh, very respectable, to be sure." Captain Fuller gave me a solemn wink. *If only they knew,* I thought with amusement.

"Respectable enough," the Captain continued, "and useful work
too. Better than governessing someone's spoiled brats, anyhow. It's
clerking, of a sort, though not in the shipping office."

"*Clerking?*" demanded my aunt in dismay. "For Rachel?"

"For the Benevolent Fund, wife! As a Visitor, really, though she'd
have to keep track of the payments too. That's what I meant by
clerking, which you've such a horror of. Sam Coker reminded me
only the other day that someone was needed to do the visiting, now
his wife's too sick to manage it."

"What's the Benevolent Fund?" I was anxious to find out more
before Aunt Grace could think of any further objections.

"It's a fund Jonas Oliver's father set up to make payments to the
widows and families of seamen lost on Oliver ships. Not for the rest
of their lives, you understand, but to tide them over, if there's real
hardship. Sam Coker's in charge of the fund, so you'd be answerable
to him in the first instance."

The Captain paused to make sure I'd taken all this in.

"Sam Coker's manager of the shipping office, you see, and until a
couple of months ago his wife did all the visiting for the Fund—
going to see widows and parents and so on, to find out what needs
doing. A woman's generally better at that kind of thing, so Jonas
Oliver says. You have to decide if they're really in trouble or just
bronzing it to get their hands on some cash. And don't look at me
like that, wife—some of them take up with a new fellow before the
corpse has gone cold, believe me, and another woman can soon tell."
The Captain winked again. "But as I say, Mrs. Coker's got a bad
chest and she's not well enough to do the work anymore. So I said
to myself—*There's a job for our Rachel, if she'll do it!*"

"Well, I think it's out of the question," Aunt Grace put in before
I could reply. "Rachel would have to go into those dreadful courts
by the docks, and talk to those people. . . ."

"I wouldn't mind that—really I wouldn't. It's work, and that's
what's important. Goodness knows, I'm lucky to be offered it! I'm

just amazed there are so many seamen drowned that someone's kept busy all the time."

The Captain nodded gravely. "Oh, there are, my dear. It's a hard, dangerous life at sea, you know. There are more than thirty ships in the Oliver fleet—big ones and little ones—and between the weather and the sea, they often run into trouble from time to time, or the men aboard them have mishaps. At least Oliver's do something for the families—many shipowners don't bother at all. So you'd be doing good work, be assured of that. Sam Coker would give you the list of names, and then you'd call on the people concerned and go back and tell him what you found. Then you'd have to keep a record of payments and receipts and so on in a businesslike fashion. But then, working in a store as you did, you'll be used to that."

He sat back and put his hands on his knees.

"How does that strike you, m'dear? It's probably not quite what you had in mind, I know, but you can always try it, and if you run into shoal water, well—haul off, and you've lost nothing."

"As long as I can earn enough to support Matthew and myself, I don't mind what I do," I assured him. "I think I'd be very happy to work for the Benevolent Fund—and I can't tell you how grateful I am."

"It's still clerking work," sniffed Aunt Grace with a disapproving tilt of her head. "Charity visiting? It's hardly what I'd have wished for you."

"I'm lucky to find anything at all, Aunt Grace. Even if it only pays a little, there may be enough to find cheap lodgings somewhere, and then we'd be off your hands."

"Now, don't you be in such a hurry to sling your berth, Miss," warned the Captain, ignoring his wife's frown. Aunt Grace hated sea-language in the house. "I don't see why you have to go running off like that. This is a barn of a place for the three of us. I'll never know why your aunt wanted to have it at all—a cottage would've done for me. But since we do have all this space, I can't see why you and Matthew shouldn't share it. It's good for Grace to have a young lady like yourself round the house. I know how you women like to talk." And the Captain winked again.

"Tell you what—wait until you see how you go on with the Benevolent Fund, then you can decide. Seems to me you should've learned not to make up your mind in a hurry by now, eh?" He wagged a stern finger at me, but the twinkle in his eye belied his warning tone. "Take your time, m'dear, and range along the coast for a bit. Is that a bargain?"

It was—indeed it was. And in some ways it was the best—and the worst—bargain I ever made.

17

We knew what it was to be poor, Matthew and I, though no doubt Aunt Grace would have called our situation *carefulness* rather than poverty. Yet even in the worst days—the days of the venison feast shared with Watches Smoke in our little cabin—we'd never descended into that utter hopelessness of true destitution which I saw daily in the streets of Liverpool. Our kind of poverty had brought the much-darned stocking, the frayed collar and cuffs, the split shoe which becomes a major catastrophe on a slender budget. Here in the Liverpool cellars people died each day of hunger and watched their children starve before their eyes. Always, the specter of famine haunted the cluttered courts and alleyways near the docks, and in the weeks that followed it became so familiar to me that I never failed to put up a prayer at the end of each day: *God, if you can hear me—spare my son from ever knowing the horror of want.*

But if we hadn't starved, I knew that as long as I lived I'd never forget the sensation of counting the last few cents I had in the world. And so at the end of October I started work for the Benevolent Fund with an evangelical determination to do what I could for my fellow human beings. My bookkeeping experience might be slight, but I was certain I knew hardship when I saw it.

Sam Coker, the manager of the shipping office, was a thin, anxious man in his late forties with a long nose, an invalid wife, and a large brood of children who lined up pan-pipe fashion for Sunday church parade and took it in turns to cause their father concern. The Oliver shipping office was staffed entirely by men, and my appearance on the premises only seemed to increase Sam Coker's store of worries.

He found me a dark corner near his own desk where I was almost invisible, and explained with breathless urgency that I was to call at the office first thing each day to collect my instructions, and then once a week to make up the ledgers of the Benevolent Fund. For a salary of sixty-five pounds a year I was to seek out and report on the families of missing or disabled Oliver crewmen and deal with claims which came by post from other parts of the country. And having told me what I *must* do, Sam Coker spent so long telling me what I *mustn't* do that I began to think that if the Oliver directors hadn't believed firmly in the charitable sense of women, I'd never have been allowed to pass the imposing doors of the office at all.

"I hadn't realized," I remarked later to the Fullers, "how many people are needed to run a shipping line." The size and bustle of the Oliver office had taken me by surprise.

"Well, my dear, if you add up all the clerks and apprentices in the Liverpool office, and the fellows in the counting-house and in the London office, and the agents overseas—not to mention the seamen themselves—you'll have some notion of the Oliver empire." The Captain was comfortably settled by the drawing-room fire, a glass of brandy in his hand, and seemed disposed to talk. "And every one of them dependent on Jonas Oliver for a wage. It's a bad time for shipping, too, with trade falling off everywhere, but so far we've managed to weather the storm. You allow Jonas Oliver—he'll find a way. That's why Oliver's is one of the biggest shipping lines in the country now."

"And the Oliver family first cousins to the queen, the way they carry on," sniffed Aunt Grace. "Despite the fact that old Captain John was hard put to find the price of his sea-boots, not so long ago!"

"Half a century ago, wife!"

"Who was Captain John?" By now I knew when Tom Fuller was about to embark on one of his tales of the old Liverpool ship-masters.

"Captain John Oliver—Jonas Oliver's father. He was a slaver—master of a Guineaman, at the end of last century. Whydah on the African coast, the Middle Passage to the West Indies—" the Captain's hands described the route, "—and then back to Liverpool with sugar and whatnot. That was his trade, except during the French War, when he waited for the Frenchies to do the work for him. They'd ship their slaves from Africa, then he'd help himself to the cargo and sell it at a good profit in Jamaica. He was a shrewd man, Captain John."

"He was a pirate," Aunt Grace put in tartly.

"He knew enough to come ashore for good in 1801, when the talk was all of Abolition. Married Old Pearce's daughter Alice and settled down to raise a family and trade with his ships."

"He wasn't what you call *wealthy,* even then," added Aunt Grace, anxious that I should grasp the humble beginnings of the Oliver clan.

"That's true." The Captain nodded. "The Oliver money only began after the Abolition Bill was passed. There was a rare old panic in Liverpool, I can tell you. All the merchants thought they'd be ruined without the slave trade. Land was going for a song and city property for nothing at all. John Oliver kept his head and bought all he could—and then borrowed to buy more."

"And made a fortune out of it," said Grace sourly. "Enough to marry his high-and-mighty daughter Verity into a baronetcy, and leave young John and Jonas in charge of a thriving business and a fleet of ships."

"Didn't one of his sons die shortly after I came here from Newfoundland?" I vaguely remembered reading an obituary in a newspaper, and my aunt remarking that the dead man had been one of the owners of Captain Fuller's ship.

"That's right, m'dear! Fancy you remembering . . . Yes, that was John, Jonas Oliver's brother. John was the merchant of the family— the ships were always Jonas's concern. Though now, of course, Jonas is sole head of the company."

"Except that George Broadney is an important stockholder by right of his wife, Verity, and he's never done putting in his two pennyworth. Or Verity either, if it comes to that. You've said so yourself, Thomas."

"Maybe I have, but that's no reason for you to go repeating it. Sir George and Lady Broadney are no concern of Rachel's."

This was certainly true, and I'd more than enough to keep me busy without poking my nose into Oliver family squabbles. When Sam Coker handed me the list of possible claimants from the Benevolent Fund which had built up during the two months since his wife had given up her duties, I was appalled by the scale of death and injury which was part and parcel of a seaman's life.

Bosun Kelly had fallen from the mainyard of the *Siciliana,* bursting his ribs like a stove-in birdcage, leaving himself unfit for any kind of work; the *Fort Wolfe* had disappeared on her way from Montreal with timber, depriving the Randell family, the Shaws, the Greys and the Powers of a breadwinner and taking numerous single men to the bottom with her; the *Langdale* had been knocked down in a gale, killing still more men whose relatives had petitioned Oliver's for assistance. All of these embarrassing, persistent people were thrown into my lap to be visited and reported on, and if absolutely necessary, paid.

"We're not supposed to give them a pension, remember," Sam Coker had warned me. "We're just tiding them over for the present. All you have to do is to look into their immediate needs—if they're short of food or coal, and so forth. They'll have to see to themselves sooner or later, and it's misplaced kindness to do too much for them. Mr. Oliver's very insistent on that point."

Mr. Oliver, I soon discovered, was very insistent on a great many points, most of them to do with money. He was said to keep a tight grip on the purse-strings of his shipping empire, and to demand at short notice an account of where every penny had been spent. His careful ways were a byword throughout the office, and to my surprise Captain Fuller, normally so open-handed, entirely approved of them.

"Waste's a sin at sea," he declared. "There's a use for everything, no matter whether it's a rope's-end or a leaking cask."

I thought of the crippled Bosun Kelly, bedridden under frayed blankets, or the beggars swarming over the dockside rubbish-heaps not a quarter of a mile away, and silently agreed with him.

As the novelty of my first few weeks in the Oliver office wore off I became accustomed to the sights and sounds of the place, though I never lost the feeling of being an alien creature in that totally male domain. Always, the principal topic of conversation was the coming and going of Oliver vessels, and in time I too began to recognize the names of the numerous ships and to take an interest in their welfare.

Brunhilde was overdue from New Orleans with a cargo of cotton —but storms had been reported in the Atlantic, and *Brunhilde*'s master was no gambler. The *Nessmore* would leave next day for Buenos Aires to return with her hold full of hides, while *Khandiva* was bound for Calcutta with the chief clerk's son aboard as second mate.

The *Easdale,* the *Severn Valley,* the *Brander*—by Christmas they were more than simply names. They'd become creatures of notorious quirk and character, their passage-times against ships from rival lines giving the whole office cause for celebration or despair. *Khandiva* was lucky—everyone said so—while the *Brander* was a slow old slop-bucket no matter who was on her quarterdeck. *Severn Valley,* the clerks muttered behind their hands, was a man-killer. Two men a trip she did for—or more—and she didn't turn her nose up at officers either.

From my corner I watched the grave-faced ship-masters pace down the corridor to the hallowed Masters' Room, their tall hats held stiffly at their sides like symbols of office. Further down that same corridor was Jonas Oliver's private office and Captain Fuller's more modest apartment, but in many ways the Masters' Room was the holy of holies of the Oliver Line, and the right to enter it admitted a man to an elite brotherhood of the sea, the lonely band of commanders on whose judgment depended the fate of a ship and all those aboard her. Some of the masters were middle-aged, many surprisingly young, but there was an air of consequence and serious purpose about them all, as if life were too important a matter for laughter. Even Captain Fuller, whom I spied occasionally through the glass-paned partition of the main office, wore a solemn expression on company premises which I'd never seen at his own fireside.

It was a long time before I set eyes on my employer, though there was no shortage of gossip about him in the office. The junior clerks, who lived in mortal fear of his reprimand, soon informed me (out of their seniors' hearing) of his temperament (withdrawn), his fortune (considerable) and his marital state (widower). His wife had been a fragile, elfin creature who'd developed consumption soon after the marriage and had died before giving him children. His sister Verity was rumored to have spent the four years since this lady's death lecturing Jonas on the need to marry again and sire an heir. Their brother John had left three daughters, and it was unthinkable that J. G. Oliver & Co. should continue without an Oliver at its helm.

"Who'd 'ave 'im—that's what I'd like to know," remarked a wages clerk one morning, shaking rain-water from his umbrella. I'd met the boy on the narrow staircase as I arrived for work.

"Any woman with a bit of sense, my lad," declared one of the men from the counting-house, turning in at the door just behind us. "Think of all that money! Old Jonas could swaller a sov'reign an' shit it in silver, he could. Half the women in Liverpool would be happy to become Mrs. Jonas Oliver, if he was the Devil himself! I tell you—if I wore skirts, I'd be flashing my eyes at old Jonas, an' no mistake."

"You'd be wasting your time, you," rejoined the wages clerk, shaking drops of water over him. "D'you think 'e'd look at anyone with your taste in whiskers?"

A good-natured chase followed round the ranks of desks, instantly quelled by the arrival of one of the senior clerks.

In spite of the long hours of business the mood in the teeming office was generally cheerful, and I was grateful for the casual banter of the young clerks after my often depressing trips to the more dismal corners of the docklands, seeking out those who'd asked for the help of the Benevolent Fund. Sometimes the petitioners came to me— perhaps an aged mother from the country districts beyond the city, presenting herself in person at the Oliver office after a weary journey to the center of Liverpool, and I'd listen to a stream of fond tales of the missing man before handing over the small amount of money which Sam Coker allowed. Usually there were outstanding wages to be paid, and I would watch the old woman leave once more, wrapped in her coarse woolen shawl, pathetically grateful for her little store of money. It was blood-money, to all intents and purposes —and what would happen when that pittance had gone?

Even in the lowest and most desperate days of my exile I'd lived like a princess compared with some of these. The misery I saw in Liverpool made me ashamed of my own past despair: my sufferings had been so trifling in comparison with these. Now I saw families who'd pawned everything they owned except the rags on their backs, a cup to drink out of, and a knife to cut their bread. One sailor's widow, with two small children to feed, had taken to sewing—not dressmaking, but basic seaming, eighteen hours a day, for the princely sum of two shillings a week; her grate had been cold for a month and the three little bodies were huddled for warmth under the skirts of the thick wool greatcoat she was toiling to finish.

Whatever Jonas Oliver permitted me to give the seamstress, could it ever be enough? How, I wondered, could we possibly "tide her over" until she could "manage" for herself? To the little allowed from the Benevolent Fund I added sixteen shillings of my own. It was all I could afford, and I cried myself to sleep that night, dreaming of the freezing garret and those three emaciated bodies under the half-finished greatcoat.

Sometimes it seemed as if however much I dispensed from the Fund, it was only a drop in the ocean of the city's vast poverty. I became more conscious than ever of my own small comforts, and I was grateful that as Christmas approached Matthew and I could feel part of a family once more and share in the fuss which would fill my aunt's house at the festive season, numbing the loneliness which still gripped me like a physical thirst in unguarded moments.

For I'd only come back to England to escape from memories of Adam. I could admit as much now when I forced myself to be honest, shamed by the sufferings of others into recognizing my own unhappiness for what it was—nothing but self-pity. What right had I to be sorry for myself? I was healthy, I had good friends in Aunt Grace and the Captain, I had a roof over my head, food on the table, and work which paid something, at least; and I had Matthew—my son and Adam's—to love and be loved by in turn.

Determinedly I forced myself to walk once more past the hotel where I'd spent my first night with Adam. And having laid that ghost I found it easier to bear the stray memories which crowded back, seeded by such tiny, inconsequential things as a sound or a smell, or the sight of a tall, broad-shouldered figure walking past the drawing-room windows in Leghorn Street. The drawing room itself, to my great relief, had been redecorated by Aunt Grace in the "Chinese style," and a colossal enameled vase now stood in place of the armchair which Adam had so often occupied on peaceful winter afternoons. So his shade no longer haunted even Leghorn Street, driven out by the fans and lacquered cabinets of an oriental palace.

As I'd expected, Christmas at my aunt's was delightful, thanks to the Captain's constant good humor and his refusal to treat Matthew any differently from his own son. After Christmas I proposed looking for new lodgings once more, but the weather had worsened by then and the Captain wouldn't hear of our moving out until spring. Watching Matthew's happy face as he played with the crowd of expensive toys in Harry's nursery, I realized how much the change to dingy lodgings would distress him when it came.

Matthew had always resented the injustice of a world which bestowed far more on some than on others, and with the curious logic of a child, bitterly blamed his dead father for leaving us to struggle for a living.

"Don't worry, Mamma," he kept assuring me, "I'll make us rich when I'm grown up—just you wait and see. I won't go off and get killed the way Papa did. I'll buy us a house as big as a whole street, and a carriage with six horses like the little one on Harry's windowsill."

"But Matthew," I protested, laughing, "that's the Queen's coach! It's far too grand for us!"

"No, it isn't!" Matthew declared passionately. "Why shouldn't we drive around in a golden coach instead of having to go in smelly omnibuses with lots of other people? I hate being poor and having to wear Harry's old clothes! I hate it, Mamma! Oh, I know we haven't any money now, but I'm going to be rich when I'm old enough, and then I'll have lots of clothes of my own—and as many shoes as I want."

There was a look of grim determination on Matthew's face which disturbed me.

"Money doesn't always bring happiness, Matthew."

"Well, I don't like being poor. I want to try being rich instead."

We were better off than many—we had food, and shelter, and self-respect—but it grieved me that I couldn't give him more; and in a strange way I became infected with his steadfast ambition. I really began to believe that one day—somehow—Matthew would have all the benefits that had been showered on his cousin Harry. Adam was now beyond help, but Matthew had a right to the best I could contrive.

It was fortunate for Nancy Morris that I was in this new, resolute frame of mind when I first came across her.

———

I'd never have known about Nancy and her troubles if it hadn't been for Father O'Hara, whose flock lived in and around the paved courts off Shaw's Alley, in a cluster of shambling tenements and hutches surrounding the flagged yards near Salthouse Dock. I was careful not to visit these places after dark, but in daylight I no longer had any fear of them. Dressing as simply as I did, I looked more like a nun than a prospect for robbery, and I found I could pass where I pleased unmolested, though the accumulated filth of these crowded courts was quite ghastly to see and even worse to smell. I'd gone to Shaw's Alley on the day in question to visit the Kelly family, and in the rubbish-strewn entrance to their court I encountered Father O'Hara, surrounded by children and up to his ankles in old cabbage leaves and mud.

Nancy Morris, he'd said. *I beg you—visit Nancy Morris.*

I found them at last, Nancy and her mother, high up a rotting staircase in a single room under the leaky leads for which they told me they paid one shilling a week. In spite of the bitter cold that day they were huddled before a tiny iron fireplace containing a fire the size of three candles, yet the first thing I noticed was the shining grate —as black and burnished as a piece of glistening coal—and the clean rag-rug on the floor in front of it. The room was almost bare of furniture, but as well-scrubbed as the Morrises could make it, the thin patchwork quilt on the bed immaculate, and their own, much-darned clothes faded with constant washing.

But there was a wanness about the faces of mother and daughter which I recognized with a sinking heart; the blue hollows below their cheekbones spoke only too clearly of meager food and desperation, in spite of the fact that Nancy was obviously far gone with child.

Jack Webb, she said, was the father—Able Seaman Jack Webb of the Oliver vessel *Mount Rose,* lost on the Runnelstone off Land's End seven weeks since, when her master mistook a fogbound Land's End for the Lizard, and ran his ship ashore. Two men only had survived the wreck, and neither of them had been Nancy's Jack.

Now here she was, about to bear his child, a widow *de facto* if not *de jure,* and Mr. High-and-Mighty Oliver not prepared to give her a brass farthing. Nancy had gone to the offices in Water Street for the balance of her lover's wages and had been turned away. What was she to do? She was a country girl by birth—her long-dead father had worked on the land—and she'd loyally come to Liverpool with her man and her invalid mother, and Jack had supported them both.

" 'E never beat me, Ma'am—never once, I swear it. 'E was a good man, till 'e were took, an' we'd 'ave been wed when we 'ad the money. Not like them dirty dockers 'ere abouts." Nancy sniffed. Even in adversity the Morrises were a cut above the dockers of Shaw's Alley.

It was possible, she said, once the baby was born, that she might get a stocking-frame for making cotton hose "at five shillin' a week," but in the meantime she was reduced to what she could make at stocking-seaming, which was a pitiful one shilling and tenpence.

They were behind with the rent—and no wonder—but in spite of that I could see in their faces how little they spent on food. No doubt the room was bare because the pawnshop had seen most of their possessions.

"Per'aps," Nancy ventured hopefully, "I might even get a place in a screw-factory. That's better work, an' regular. But as for now, with the baby comin' an' all . . ." Her voice tailed off, her attempt at optimism fading in the face of colossal hardship. She looked wanly at me for a moment, and then turned away. "I don't want to go on the streets, Ma'am," she whispered. "Not if I can 'elp it. . . ."

For once I wasn't so much saddened by her plight as enraged. Oliver's had refused to pay this woman the money she was due—money earned by the hard toil, by the *death* of the father of her baby. It was insufferable! Still furious, I marched into the Water Street offices and confronted Sam Coker.

"Nancy Morris," I announced, tapping the top of his desk with a peremptory finger. "Jack Webb," I added as Sam Coker looked blank. "The *Mount Rose*. He was a seaman on the *Mount Rose*."

"Yes, I know all about the *Mount Rose*. Piled up off Land's End. Went on the rocks in fog. Who's this man you're asking about?"

"Jack Webb. You must remember the name."

"I'm sure we've dealt with all the dependents from the *Mount Rose*."

"No, you haven't. There's a woman called Nancy Morris in Shaw's Alley who's carrying Webb's child. He was living with her—in what you'd probably call 'an irregular union.' She tells me she came here to collect his wages, and no one would give them to her. I imagine there was some kind of misunderstanding."

"This woman—you say she's not his wife. His *widow*," Sam Coker corrected himself.

"In everything but the eyes of the law."

"Ah well, that would explain it. There's been no misunderstanding, Mrs. Gaunt. The Benevolent Fund is only obliged to make payments to wives or families. And as for the man's wages . . . well, if she wasn't legally his wife . . ."

"But he was supporting her! And her sick mother too! What difference would it make if they'd been properly married?"

"Oh, a great deal of difference, Mrs. Gaunt!" Sam Coker looked shocked. "Surely you must see that!"

"No, I'm afraid I don't see it. I'm satisfied the child is Webb's, and that if he hadn't died on an Oliver ship he'd have looked after it and married the mother."

"I don't see how you can possibly be sure of that." Sam Coker's face assumed a smug expression. "Mrs. Gaunt, I realize that as a lady, you're not used to . . . what goes on in the dockland. Some of these women, they go from one man to the next—ahem—if you see what I mean—"

"Nancy Morris isn't that kind of woman. You told me to go and visit these people to decide which ones are making a genuine claim, and I promise you, the Morrises deserve all the help we can give them. And Jack Webb's wages into the bargain. They could starve without that money."

To my disbelief, Coker shook his head. "No, I'm sorry, Mrs. Gaunt, but under the circumstances, since this girl was never the man Webb's wife, Mr. Oliver wouldn't countenance it."

"Have you asked him?"

"Asked Mr. Oliver?" Coker looked alarmed. "Of course not. I don't need to ask him. I know exactly what he'd say. This kind of casual arrangement—a man and a woman—can hardly be encouraged. No, it's out of the question."

"Oh, is it?" I was beside myself with indignation. There stood Sam Coker, father of Heaven only knew how many helpless infants, quite prepared to see a baby starve to death on a point of principle. "Very well, Mr. Coker—then I shall ask him myself. We'll see what Mr. Oliver has to say."

"But—he's far too busy to be bothered with a trifling matter like this."

"Mr. Coker—" I drew myself up as tall as I could. "Kindly inform Mr. Oliver that Mrs. Rachel Gaunt would like a few minutes of his time."

For a moment Coker hesitated, eyeing me with apprehension. Then fear of the furious female at his desk overcame his dread of his employer, and, hopping down from his high stool, he scuttled away along the corridor toward Jonas Oliver's distant lair.

I took several deep breaths, conscious that I was probably about to commit the ultimate sin—to argue with Jonas Oliver over money. But the sum was so paltry to a man of his wealth! A pound or two would tide the Morrises over the birth of the baby and allow them a few weeks' grace for Nancy to find work. Though I'd have died before begging a favor for myself, I was quite ready to beg for the Morrises.

"They'll spend money on themselves, the Olivers," Aunt Grace had sneered, "but they like to know where every penny goes to, all the same."

Yet I'd heard that although Jonas Oliver was said to inspect every ledger-page in the office, his abiding passion lay elsewhere—in the building of new ships—and much of his time was spent in shipyards

and drawing-offices, discussing refinements which would make
Oliver vessels faster and more beautiful than any afloat. Many an
Oliver ship was identified at sea long before her house-flag was visi-
ble, simply by the purity of her lines and the rake of her masts. The
masters of the company's older vessels, bluff-bowed and slab-sided,
might find it hard to extract the price of a pot of varnish from Jonas
Oliver, but his crack ships never put to sea without a fresh coat of
gilding on their gingerbread-work or a newly painted figurehead.
There was money to be had, all right, if it added to the glory of the
Olivers.

Sam Coker soon returned, his long nose quivering with disapproval.

"He'll see you," he announced tersely. "Just for a few minutes,
mind. And you're to take the Fund ledgers along with you."

With all that I'd been told about Jonas Oliver whirling in my head,
I gathered up two of my enormous ledgers and set off along the shiny
brown corridor which led to his office, my heels clacking on the
wooden floor. Jonas Oliver's door, when I reached it, was paneled,
and I had to peer round the ledgers in order to select a place to
knock. Immediately, a quiet voice instructed me to enter.

His hair was fair—fairer than Adam's, I thought automatically, as
though Adam had become the measure against which all men must
stand. Jonas Oliver's hair was also thinning, I noticed as he failed to
look up at me but continued to scratch in a looping hand on the
page spread out across the desk before him.

I stood in submissive silence for what seemed an eternity; no doubt
he was letting me know my lowly place in the scheme of things, and
I realized I'd gain nothing for the Morrises by irritating my employer.
But the combined weight of the heavy ledgers was becoming too
much for me, and before long, despite my best efforts to prevent it,
one of them slipped to the floor with a bang.

Jonas Oliver glanced up at once, frowning, and I saw a face of
unusual pallor framed in fair whiskers, the mouth small and pink
below a neat, blond moustache. Two unblinking eyes in a pale shade
of blue watched me with disfavor as I looked round for somewhere
to lay the remaining ledger while I rescued the first.

"Leave it—please."

Waving me aside, he rose at once from his buttoned leather chair,
strode round the end of the enormous desk like a knight sallying out
from his keep, swept the offending book from the carpet at his feet

and dumped it with a loud, dusty thud on one corner of the desktop. In silence he held out his hand for its mate, and slapped that down on top of the first.

Then with a couple of side-steps he'd slipped back behind his bastion of a desk, as if in that leather-bound fortress his dignity was assured, and he could meet my eye once more with full authority. For Jonas Oliver was a man of middle height, perhaps thirty-six or thirty-seven years of age, and of unimpressive build, a nondescript emperor to rule over such a far-reaching empire. Yet Jonas behind his monstrous desk was the despot before whom the office trembled . . . and having found him out in this little ruse, I felt a great deal less awed in his presence.

He'd hauled one of the ledgers across the desktop and opened it at random, casting an eye over my painstaking columns of names and figures.

"So you're Mrs. Gaunt," he said abruptly, raising his glance at last from the long ruled page. "I'd expected an older person, for some reason."

This disconcerted me.

"Older?" I heard myself murmur. "Why should you think that?"

"You *are* Captain Fuller's niece, I suppose? Well then; his description of you—as a widow, and so on—made you sound older than I imagine you are."

"My age was never mentioned as a qualification for the position."

"Neither it is. But you must understand, Mrs. Gaunt, that the working of the Benevolent Fund is a very small part of our business here. Very small indeed. And I expect whoever administers it to carry on that work without running to me for help all the time."

This was unfair. "Mr. Oliver, I've held the post since November yet this is the first time I've set eyes on you. And believe me, I wouldn't have done so today if I'd been allowed to do my work unhindered."

"November . . . Indeed?" Jonas Oliver reopened the ledger before him and selected another page. "November . . ." he repeated thoughtfully. "Of course."

No answer seemed to be required to this, and I stood silently at the edge of the mammoth desk while he examined my work, running a pale, tapering finger down the long columns of figures.

I felt free to stare. I'd been led by the junior clerks to expect an elderly man, but though the fair whiskers gave him an appearance of great *gravitas*, I suspected this too was only a device. Everything about Jonas Oliver was just so, from the precise and elegant knot of his cravat to the perfect fit of his formal black dress coat and the strict rhythm beaten out on the desktop by the end of his pen. Nevertheless, I was beginning to wonder if he'd forgotten my existence when he suddenly slapped the ledger shut and treated me to a searching stare.

"And how have I hindered your work, then, Mrs.—ah—Mrs. Gaunt?"

I took a deep breath, and in that pause the clock in the corridor outside began its chime for twelve noon.

"I have an appointment at ten minutes past twelve, Mrs. Gaunt."

As briefly as I could, I described the plight of the Morrises and the company's refusal to hand over the dead man's wages. "Five pounds, six shillings and fourpence. It's so little to you, and it could save those poor women from starvation. And the baby."

"This man—Webb, did you say his name was? He was on the *Mount Rose?*"

"He was, Mr. Oliver."

Jonas Oliver pursed his lips. "A bad loss, the *Mount Rose.*"

"A tragedy for Nancy Morris."

"But she wasn't his wife, you say?"

"His wife, in all but name."

"Impossible, Mrs. Gaunt." He shook his head. "If you were a little older you'd understand the situation. As it is . . . Forgive me, but I can't think of a delicate way to explain this . . . Men like Jack Webb—seamen—have what you're pleased to call "wives in all but name" in every port across the world. Am I to pay out money to every Nancy Morris who presents herself at my door, claiming to have had an understanding with a dead sailor?"

"Mr. Oliver, I'm talking of the man's wages. Money which you owed him! That's hardly charity."

"But suppose we allow this woman to claim the money, and then tomorrow another so-called wife appears? Or even a genuine wife, with a paper to prove it? What are we supposed to do then?"

"That won't happen."

"How can you possibly be sure of that?"

"Because I've spoken to Nancy Morris, and I believe what she says. She's carrying his child. Jack Webb's child."

"Pah! So she says."

"Five pounds, six shillings and fourpence, Mr. Oliver. Which you owed to a dead man. Is that such a risk? You could pay more for a lapdog!"

"Mrs. Gaunt—you're asking me to treat this woman as the seaman's legal wife, and connive at this . . . casual arrangement. A union which had never seen the inside of a church."

"It was Father O'Hara who told me of the Morrises in the first place."

"Yes. Well. I believe the Catholic clergy sometimes take a more lenient view of these things than our own."

I felt my temper rising. "Mr. Oliver, if I were you, I wouldn't turn to the church for support in this! *Faith, hope and charity; but the greatest of these is charity,* so we're told. Charity toward Nancy Morris—faith in my judgment—and hope that God's mercy is more liberal than our own!"

For a moment Jonas Oliver said nothing, but simply stared at me in frigid displeasure. Then he warned, "You're lecturing me, Mrs. Gaunt."

"I beg your pardon. I shouldn't have spoken as I did. Nevertheless, you must help Nancy Morris."

"And why *must* I do this, pray?"

"Mr. Oliver, your company has a reputation for treating its seamen well—by and large—"

"*By and large!*" Indignation brought him upright in his chair. "*By and large!* I hope we're better thought of than that! And are you telling me, Mrs. Gaunt, that the world will think less of Oliver's if we leave this Nancy Whatever-her-name-is to make her own way out of her troubles?"

"No, Mr. Oliver." I paused. "But I shall think less of you."

Our eyes met—mine defiant, Jonas Oliver's pale and angry.

All at once, he pulled out a gold watch, flicked it open and glanced at the dial.

"*By and large,* indeed . . . Mrs. Gaunt, you have made me late for an appointment." Abruptly, he stood up. "Tell Coker I'll authorize the release of the man Webb's wages—and whatever else you think the girl deserves. No, don't thank me, Mrs. Gaunt. Charity, as you pointed out, is our Christian duty. But I trust *you* will think more charitably of us in future." He gave me another hard stare then pushed back his chair, ready for departure.

"There's no need for me to take up any more of your time, Mrs.

Gaunt; I'm sure there's plenty of work for you in the office. You may leave those ledgers with me for the present." He waved a hand in dismissal. "Thank you, Mrs. Gaunt—that will be all."

That contemptuous wave put me back in my place, and no mistake. Yet at least Nancy Morris and her baby were safe—that was something I'd achieved. At the back of my mind, however, was the dreadful suspicion that I'd only confirmed Jonas Oliver's doubts about my suitability for any position of trust. Not only was I alarmingly young, apparently, but I was also far more outspoken than any young woman had a right to be. Like Nancy Morris, I thought grimly, I might soon be existing on the charity of others.

But four or five weeks went by, and no more was said. My encounters with Jonas Oliver were limited to passing him once or twice in the corridor, and on each occasion he inclined his head with military precision and murmured, "Good day, Mrs. Gaunt," as if I were some lady he'd chanced upon in the park. Before I could even return the greeting he'd gone on his way, his pale blue stare already fixed on some distant objective.

It seemed, thank goodness, that my job with the Benevolent Fund —and my sixty-five pounds per annum—were safe. It was a wage, at least, though hardly enough to give me independence from my aunt, and part of me, the part recently sprung into existence, already longed for something better. Depending on my mood, I swung between humble gratitude and soaring ambition, and as Fate would have it, it was on a day of particular optimism, when I could almost believe that our fortunes could do nothing but improve, that my mother chose to reach out a malevolent hand, all the way from St. John's, to show me how hollow my hopes really were.

I'd arrived home that evening to find Aunt Grace flushed and scowling behind the teakettle, clutching three closely written pages on which I recognized my mother's firm hand. My mother applied herself to writing letters with the same grim certainty she brought to conversation, splaying the nib of the pen in her vehemence. The result was a hatching of broad, dark strokes interlaced with finer scores as the words poured rapidly on to the page. My mother's letters were never elegant notes, but bold patterns of complaint or accusation.

I knew the sisters still corresponded, continuing their private quarrels as though the passing years and the Atlantic Ocean didn't exist. Aunt Grace sniped and boasted, my mother jeered and dragged up past embarrassments; Aunt Grace passed on news of my doings, which she knew would annoy her sister, and my mother replied by heaping curses on my head to the great indignation of Aunt Grace. It was a wretched, unsatisfactory correspondence but at least it kept them on speaking terms, and through the agency of my aunt I occasionally heard news of my brothers and sister. Though I longed for a letter of my own from Reuben or either of the others, I knew that my mother would intercept any attempt on my part to make contact.

Aunt Grace raised hot, resentful eyes as I entered the room, speechlessly brandished the swatch of papers, shook her head, and returned to her reading. My heart sank. I didn't wish to know what my mother had written; there'd be nothing but abuse for me.

"Of course I must tell you . . ." My aunt fixed me with uncertain eyes. "She says she doesn't care whether I tell you or not, the heartless monster—but of course you must know." She reached across the table to wrap her bony fingers round my wrist in a gesture of sympathy.

"Sometimes, my dear, I feel my sister is a total stranger to us. How she can behave as she does is beyond me. Perhaps if she devoted more time to studying the Scriptures . . ."

Releasing my wrist, she pushed the letter across the white-work tablecloth with a tiny sigh of baffled resignation. I picked up the pages, and they rustled between my fingers until I steadied my shaking hand against the table-edge.

"Dear Sister—" my mother had begun, "—I send you news which you will not, I think, find surprising. My husband Joseph has been unwell for some time—*you know his condition,* which did not improve. Two nights ago he departed to his Maker, after some little suffering which he bore with more resolution than I had expected. He was able to take leave of his children, and then I sat with him till the End, which found him lucid but entirely prepared. May God grant him his just reward, though I tremble to think what that might be, for he tried me sorely on this Earth."

My father was gone, having taken leave of his children—and I was not of their number. My mother had warned me I was as good as dead to her, and she'd meant what she said.

For a moment I recalled a picture of my father in the early days in the store at Crow Cove, when he was still cheerful and full of pur-

pose. Then the image was superseded by another, the likeness of a
man sprawling drunk in his chair at supper, his theatrical gestures
making the candles flicker, his eyes bleared and unfocused. Beyond
him I could see my mother's set face, filled with disgust. How had it
really been for him at the end, I wondered?

But the letter gave no further clue. "So it has finished," I read next.
"Joseph is dead. Whether or not you tell that girl of his, I do not
care."

But she did care, all the same; she knew Aunt Grace would pass
on the news, and the next passage confirmed it.

"Joseph had it in mind at the end to send her secretly the price of
a small property of his mother's which she left him near Liverpool,
and had written a paper to that effect. But I found where it was
hidden and the paper no longer exists, so Rachel shall never have her
money now. Tell her that, if you will."

How grateful I would have been for that little sum of money! Even
a small amount would have helped me along the road to my longed-
for independence. No doubt it was all my father had left to dispose
of: the house in St. John's and any business capital had long since
been tied up in my mother's name. Perhaps in the end my father had
pitied me as I'd so often pitied him; perhaps he'd tried to make
amends for the bruises he'd sometimes inflicted, and the greater,
darker bruises on my soul. But my mother had prevented his last
kindness, and wanted me to know it.

She'd finished her letter by forbidding my aunt to harbor Matthew
and myself in her home. Grace was to turn us out at once to make
our own way in the world, if she wanted to stay on good terms with
her sister.

"Do you *see* what she's written?" hissed Aunt Grace in my ear,
her indignation mounting. "Her own daughter, to be turned out into
the streets! And she calls me 'foolish,' and even threatens me! With
what, I should like to know!"

She almost snatched the pages out of my hands. "Your poor father
—may he rest in peace—had a hard life, my dear, I'm sure of it. And
if he sought the comfort of strong spirits from time to time . . . well,
we should try to forgive rather than blame. And yet—on his death-
bed—she boasts that she's cheated him of the little legacy he wanted
you to have! Rachel, my dear, I'm sorry for you."

I hardly heard her: I felt sick with shock. Why should my mother
still wish to hurt me after all this time?

Aunt Grace patted me consolingly on the hand.

"I'll write to her today—at once—and tell her I've offered you a place in my home for as long as you need it, my dear. There'll be no more talk of moving out into lodgings. Our home is yours and Matthew's for as long as you wish, and my sister may say what she pleases."

With a saintly expression on her long features, Aunt Grace rose sedately from her chair and, holding the three pages between finger and thumb, sailed off purposefully toward her writing-desk.

———

As one door closes, another opens. It was one of my aunt's favorite sayings, and though several months elapsed between the slamming of the door on my father's legacy and the amazing opening of another leading to financial security, the two incidents are linked in my memory, perhaps because each one involved a letter.

I was fortunate in being kept very busy by the shipping line in the early months of 1843, busy enough to forget my mother's ill-will in the constant procession of tearful widows and crippled seamen who came my way. But no one in the office criticized my work and Jonas Oliver continued to wish me a solemn *good day* on those rare occasions when I encountered him about the building.

Aunt Grace had persuaded the Captain to take a cottage for the month of June at Waterloo, by the seaside, on the grounds that Harry would benefit from daily draughts of ozone and the Captain could commute to the Water Street office just as easily from Waterloo as from Leghorn Street. Matthew was to go with them, and the Captain pressed me to go too, at least for a few days.

"It's time you had a rest from the office," he suggested. "The work's hard, and it isn't always pleasant, I know. Even a week by the sea would set you up, and I'd square it with Oliver's."

But I was quite content to stay peacefully in Leghorn Street for a while with a maid and the daily woman to look after me, and I'd no intention of putting myself in Jonas Oliver's debt. Though he'd never sent for me again I knew he inspected my ledgers regularly, and with those cold blue eyes still fresh in my memory I refused to ask him for favors.

Shortly after arriving in England I'd written to Lizzie Fletcher in order to assure her we were safely in Liverpool, and to let her know we'd be staying in Leghorn Street for some time. I'd heard nothing

in return from Independence, but ten days after the Fullers left for
their Waterloo cottage a bulky packet arrived for me in Leghorn
Street, rather battered from a good deal of handling. It contained
two letters: Lizzie's, in a painstakingly neat hand, folded round another packet assigned to me at "Mrs. Fletcher's House, Independence." After staring at the enclosure for several uneasy minutes, I
decided to read Lizzie's news first.

Independence, it seemed, was bulging at the seams, growing even
faster than before, full to bursting with emigrants and their wagons
now that the mountain trail by South Pass was worn wide by iron-
shod wheels and the pressure of a thousand trudging feet. Booming
Independence was taking a grip on its own future, laying out a
formal grid pattern of streets and suburbs, and even making plans
for a real brick courthouse in the square in the center of town.

Lizzie rattled on, relaying gossip about people and places whose
names were now just a memory to me. Titus Meadow's Meg had
fled overnight with an Army surveyor, and Titus, devastated, had
returned to the thankful arms of his wife. For the present, all was
bliss in Meadow's Store.

No one had seen anything of Frank Ellis, though Crazy Kate was
working hard on the transformation of the Trader's House into a
proper hotel, and was *Miss Kate Connery* to one and all. By chance
Antoine Bleu had passed through Independence just as Lizzie was
writing her letter, conducting a wealthy Scottish aristocrat on a
shooting tour of the Wind River range. Antoine looked well, she
reported, and sent his good wishes—"and a heap of French talk"
which Lizzie "didn't convene to understand." Dear Antoine, I
thought—it was probably just as well.

There was a postscript, hastily written. The second packet had
come to hand just as Lizzie was sealing her own letter, and she'd
enclosed one with the other, adding a few lines in explanation.

I'm told this letter to you is from Mr. Joe Walker, who came with
news of your husband when he was first missing. It was brought here
by a Mr. Harris—a very tall man with strange blue-black marks on
his face, who says you will know him. He stayed to eat with us and
told us all kinds of stories of his life in the mountains, most of which
I guess he made up, they were so very peculiar. But we were all kept
laughing. He said I should tell you the man Ed Ballantine has been
injured by a bear, he is quite bad but not in danger of his life. Mr.
Harris said he was trying to catch the animal with a table fork at the

time, but I reckon he has made this up also, he looked so droll when he said it.

I guess Mr. Walker's letter has more news of your husband, since I remember you asking for this, if it should come to hand. From what Mr. Harris told us, I'm sure Adam is now with the Lord in His Glory, where you will meet him again in God's good time.

So Joe Walker had written at last, and Moses Harris, Adam's comrade of the fur-trail, had delivered the letter to Lizzie Fletcher on his way through Independence. With trembling fingers I undid the fastening and turned the single page the right way up.

Two years back, you asked for an account of your husband's fate, if I should ever learn of it. What follows was told to me by Indians of the Blackfoot tribe on the Green River, and I have no reason to mistrust their story. The bearer of this letter will vouch for what I say.

The old man and his son say they were following deer on the Bighorn when they came across the body of a man in buckskin at the bottom of a high bluff, laid out as if he had fallen. They claimed to have seen him among the fur traders at the rendezvous, a tall man they called Gray-eyes. His neck was broken, but there was no other injury they knew of. The Indians left his body under some rocks where he fell.

From this I take the dead man to be your husband, Adam Gaunt, since I have heard the Blackfeet use that name of him. The Blackfeet say there was a Crow hunting-party nearby at that time, and they reckon the Crows took his horse. You recall I already told you a Crow had been seen with the Palouse mare.

I reckon you always believed something of this kind had happened to Adam, but now you know for certain.

The man who brings you this letter also carries a sum of money due to your husband from the sale of horses, from La Fontaine in St. Louis, and some other debts.

Yr friend,
Jos. Walker.

I bent down to retrieve the slip of paper which had fluttered from the packet as I opened it. It was a bill of exchange drawn on the Bank of England for more than three and a half thousand pounds. Sitting in my chair, the carefully written pages laid out in my lap, I burst into tears.

18

I wanted to go on working for the Benevolent Fund. It seemed callous to turn my back on these widows and fatherless children who desperately needed a champion, simply because my own fortunes had taken a turn for the better.

"Tell Mr. Oliver he needn't pay me," I suggested to the Captain when he broached the subject. "I'd willingly do the work for nothing."

"Rachel, m'dear—how much difference do you think your little wage makes to a company the size of Oliver's? None at all! Yet there might be another young woman in Liverpool very glad to have it— as glad as you were once. And I'm sure you could find plenty of other ways of making yourself useful, if you look around."

Captain Fuller was right, of course, and a few days later I officially informed Sam Coker that due to a change in my circumstances I wished to give up my post with J. G. Oliver & Co.

Aunt Grace was cock-a-hoop at the news, in spite of the fact that Joe Walker's letter at last told me the circumstances of poor Adam's death.

"After all," she crowed, "you've always known Adam Gaunt was dead, so it can hardly come as a surprise to you now. And it's been so awkward, not knowing quite what to tell people . . . You should certainly look upon it as *good* news, dear, since you're thoroughly a widow now, and a widow with a small competence for a change. It's a very comfortable situation, I promise you. As a daughter or a wife you can do nothing at all for yourself, but as a widow—oh, there's many a woman in this city would be pleased to have as much control over her own affairs!" She frowned for a moment, considering what I should do first with my newfound freedom.

"The Captain will lay out the money for you where it will bring good, safe interest. And then you must definitely take a house nearby. Yes—I'm sure that would be best, you shall have the littlest, most charming house we can find for you in this neighborhood, in a *good* street, quiet but not unfashionable . . . Somewhere I shan't mind being seen. I shall look out for something suitable straight away."

By August, with some misgivings, I'd found a small terraced house barely a quarter of a mile from Leghorn Street and a little to the east. My income wouldn't be large—some hundred and thirty pounds per annum—but it would stretch to the employment of a maid-of-all-work and a daily girl at a shilling a week, with the promise of Aunt Grace's groom to help with occasional heavy duties and the use of the Fullers' brougham when it could be spared.

"Quite respectable," pronounced my aunt when my household was complete. "Respectable enough for a single lady living quietly, at any rate, though for goodness' sake tell that girl of yours not to call you *Mum*. If she can't manage *Madam*, then *Ma'am* will have to do. And Rachel, please leave the kitchen work to the servants! What will people think of you, if you're constantly popping in and out of the kitchen to interfere?"

"But I cook far better than Bernadette does!"

"Her name isn't *Bernadette*, surely!" My aunt cast her eyes up to the ceiling.

"Aunt Grace—didn't you mention calling on Mrs. Ripon today? Only I'd hate to make you late . . ."

And away swooped Aunt Grace in the brougham, taking her scolding with her and leaving my little house to settle into comfortable peace once more. Matthew went back to copying his letters on the parlor table, Bernadette applied herself to scrubbing the doorstep, and I returned guiltily to the custard I was making in the kitchen. I felt guilty, certainly, but only for disappointing my aunt. Now that I had a home of my own once more I intended to run it as I pleased, and if five years of living in the American West had molded my ideas of ladylike behavior, then so be it. I couldn't believe Lizzie Fletcher was any less of a lady for laundering her own sheets than Aunt Grace was for not laundering hers.

Nevertheless, my aunt meant well, and I tried to avoid upsetting her too badly. Now that my charity visiting and my clerking duties were behind me, Aunt Grace seemed determined to fit me out with a ready-made circle of acquaintances, "suitable" ladies of stifling domesticity or elderly matrons with spinster daughters of approximately my age, and it was often hard to think of excuses to avoid being dragged out with her on tedious afternoon calls.

"I trust you aren't going to have one of your headaches on Thursday evening," she remarked pointedly one day. "Mrs. Ripon expressly desired me to bring you to hear Charlotte play since I told her how well you sang, and you'll find that Sophia Ripon is acquainted with the very best people in Liverpool. I hope you realize how hard I worked to get you an invitation."

Curiously enough, I did have a headache that evening, but I knew better than to beg off Miss Charlotte Ripon's harp recital. At the appointed time, along with a great crowd of "the very best people," I took my place on a tiny, hard chair in one of the last rows ranged across Mrs. Ripon's cavernous drawing room and prepared to be impressed by the *soirée musicale*.

It all began most successfully. Charlotte Ripon performed with vigor, her proud mamma accompanied her on the pianoforte, those of us on the gilt chairs rushed to applaud, and one or two kind souls even called out "Delightful!" and "Bravo!" at the end of each piece. Miss Charlotte blushed prettily and turned to her harp once more.

As time wore on, however, the audience began to shift uncomfortably in their seats. Miss Charlotte's voice and her playing were in fact only a little above average, the chairs were agonizingly hard, and the concert a good deal too long. I was hugely relieved when supper was announced; the heat in the drawing room had made my headache worse, and when after supper Miss Charlotte indicated that the second half of her repertoire was still to come, I decided I'd prefer to listen to it from a corner near the doorway to the hall where a cool draft filtered into the room and the sound of Charlotte Ripon's voice was muted enough not to intrude on my thoughts.

I'd been standing in this out-of-the-way spot for some minutes when I realized I wasn't alone. Someone else had taken up a similar position a few feet away—a shadowy gentleman of slight build who was leaning against the wall near the tall double doors in an attitude which suggested overwhelming boredom.

Just as I was studying him, the man turned his head and saw me. It was Jonas Oliver, impeccable as ever in a brown dress coat, frilled shirt and crimson waistcoat, the slenderest of gold chains glinting across his shirt-front amid a constellation of diamond studs.

Embarrassed, I looked away at once toward the lighted dais where the harpist continued to pick out her wandering, shapeless melody, but out of the corner of my eye I could see Jonas Oliver staring at me with a puzzled expression on his face, doubtless trying to fathom where he'd met me before.

———

Abruptly, Charlotte Ripon came to the end of her piece, and the audience, taken aback by the unexpected silence, were a second or two late in applauding. Under cover of the hasty hubbub which followed, Jonas Oliver strolled across to me, his satisfied air indicating that he'd established at last who I was.

"Mrs. Gaunt," he announced with one of his stiff little bows. "This is a pleasant surprise. I thought I'd missed you in the office lately."

"You may well have missed me, Mr. Oliver. I left your company three and a half months ago."

"Then I'm sure the loss is ours, Mrs. Gaunt. I seem to remember you as a source of useful advice—*by and large*. Wasn't that your expression?"

For a moment I thought he was still offended by my remark. Then I noticed the merest glint of amusement in his eyes, and realized that in his own austere way, Jonas Oliver was teasing me.

"Mr. Oliver, you must know that when I used those words I had no intention of offending you."

"I'm pleased to hear it. But it's unfortunate that you've left us, all the same. You appeared to . . . *relish* the work so much."

"My circumstances were altered recently—for the better. I've no need to work for a living anymore."

"Then I'm happy to find you leading the kind of life for which you're obviously more fitted. To tell the truth, you always seemed rather out of place in Water Street. The counter clerks were hardly suitable company for a lady of your background."

The applause had subsided, but it seemed that Miss Ripon had been persuaded to play once more. This piece, however, was definitely to be the last. As the rows of uncomfortable chairs shifted and wriggled themselves into position for yet another long wait, Jonas Oliver leaned toward me.

"Are you enjoying the concert, Mrs. Gaunt?"

It was hard to know what to say in reply; perhaps the Olivers and the Ripons were good friends.

"Charlotte Ripon is . . . an *unusual* musician . . ."

"Exactly what I was thinking myself. Most unusual. In fact, I was wondering if she might not sound even better from the hall outside. Would you care to try the effect?"

I had to stifle a giggle. "I'd be charmed, Mr. Oliver."

Careful not to attract attention, I slipped silently through the half-open double doors into the cool, tiled hallway. Just to the right of the drawing-room door stood a high-backed wooden settle; I tiptoed toward it and sat down, and a moment later Jonas Oliver emerged from the drawing room to join me. From there the sound of the harp trickled not unpleasantly into the great vault of the hall, drifting in a ripple of liquid notes toward a distant cupola at the top of the stairs.

"A great improvement," Jonas Oliver remarked dryly after listening for a few seconds. "I must bear in mind for the future that when Charlotte Ripon reaches the concert platform, the best seats will be outside the hall."

"How unkind of you, Mr. Oliver! And we must be back in our places by the end of the performance, before our hostess realizes we've played truant."

"I'll allow you to go back, on one condition." Jonas Oliver's tone was severe.

"And what's that?"

"You must promise me not to shout 'Encore.' I couldn't bear any more of this apology for music."

"Oh, you have my word on that," I assured him, laughing. "But if you dislike the concert so much, why in the world did you come here this evening?"

He glanced back through the drawing-room doorway.

"You may have noticed a thin, yellow-haired woman sitting near the front, next to a man of about my age who's almost asleep. That's Verity, my elder sister, and her husband, George Broadney. Verity and Sophia Ripon are very good friends—which is to say, they kiss when they meet and criticize one another when they're apart. Verity was absolutely determined I should be here tonight."

"Captain Fuller often mentions Lady Broadney. I believe she and Sir George take a close interest in the shipping business."

This time Jonas Oliver regarded me with open amusement. "Is that what Tom Fuller actually said, Mrs. Gaunt, or are you paraphrasing his words? No—don't answer that. Tell me instead, do you have brothers and sisters who plague you with good advice?"

"None in England, I'm afraid," I said, choosing my words carefully. "I seldom see my family. Except for the Fullers, of course."

"And you're a widow, I believe, with a young son. Do you find it lonely here in Liverpool, Mrs. Gaunt, or do you enjoy your freedom?"

"I've learned to accept widowhood, Mr. Oliver, if that's what you mean. The Fullers have been very kind to me, and I've made new friends since coming back to the city. But at the same time, I'm quite content with my own company—and the company of my son."

Jonas Oliver nodded. "I wish my sister could understand that point of view. She prefers to live in the middle of din and confusion, in a perpetual crowd of people, and what's worse, she pushes them constantly in my direction. My wife died some years ago, and unfortunately I have no children."

Any observation I might have made was cut short by the sudden ending of the harp recital next door. Guiltily, we scuttled back to our places just inside the drawing-room entrance and clapped enthusiastically while Miss Charlotte Ripon bowed and blushed on her dais and her mother beamed proudly nearby.

When at last the applause died away I found myself escorted with punctilious correctness toward Lady Verity Broadney and her husband, waiting near the dais to congratulate Sophia Ripon on her daughter's remarkable talent.

"Verity, may I present Mrs. Gaunt? My sister—Lady Broadney."

I noticed that Jonas Oliver gave no reason for our acquaintance, never mentioning my recent employment in the Oliver offices. Verity Broadney inclined her head in a gracious bow, but her eyes were gimlets; in spite of her brother's silence on the matter there was no doubt that by the end of next day Lady Broadney would know all there was to know about Mrs. Rachel Gaunt.

I was sure she'd already guessed the price of my gown to within a sixpence and the exact value of the bracelets at my wrists. George Broadney, on the other hand, seemed less interested in my clothes than what might be inside them, gazing at me with unmistakably lascivious speculation.

And well might he stare, I thought later, examining myself in my bedroom mirror: I'd looked better that evening than I'd done since I left the city six years before. My wound had healed, and with it the most painful of my memories; my skin shone with health once more and my dark hair formed lustrous coils under a little velvet turban.

I'd allowed myself at last to spend something on clothes, and I'd had an evening dress made up in rich dove-gray satin—slight mourning, but in the fashionable style of an open robe—and the low, turned-back collar framed my shoulders to perfection.

Well might George Broadney lick his slack lips and his wife fix me with hard eyes. Little Mrs. Gaunt, released from her high desk in the Oliver office, was the equal of any woman in the room, and if the admiring glances I saw around me were anything to go by, better than equal. And I suspected that Jonas Oliver was aware of it.

Oh, it did wonders for my morale, that recital of Charlotte Ripon's!

But though the encounter with Jonas Oliver had been amusing, I knew it was unlikely to happen again. The fact remained that although I was now socially "acceptable" I'd recently occupied a lowly position in the Oliver office, and I was sure that when she discovered that choice piece of gossip Verity Broadney would take her brother severely to task for presuming to make an introduction at all. Jonas would be told that Mrs. Gaunt was *no one,* and must be strictly ignored in future.

And I couldn't help laughing when I thought of Mademoiselle Valentine and her pink tulle roses. Ignore me, indeed! And to think how I could have livened up their *soirée musicale!*

As I expected, it was some time before I saw Jonas Oliver again, and neither my aunt nor Mrs. Ripon brought the meeting about. By a strange chance it was Nancy Morris who flung us together once more, just as she'd been the cause of my first encounter with Jonas in the Oliver offices.

Nancy had promised faithfully, when our battle with Oliver's was finally won, that after her child was born she'd bring it to visit me. I'd expected her to forget me long before that, but to my surprise, shortly after I moved into my little house she appeared on my door-step carrying the baby in her arms and solemnly presented it to me in the most formal manner. The child was almost five months old by then, a boy named James after his dead father and Albert after the Prince Consort whom Nancy loyally admired, and I was pleased to see that little James Albert and his mother looked plump and prosperous at last.

"You brought us luck, Ma'am, an' I won't forget it," Nancy promised me. "If the babe 'ad been a girl, I was goin' to ask if I could call 'er after you—but I'm pleased it was a boy, all the same. Jack wanted a son, 'e always said. You know 'ow it is."

"Oh, I know how it is, Nancy. But then, I was more fortunate than you. Matthew's father at least saw his son before he died. Poor Jack never had a chance to set eyes on little James Albert."

Nancy nodded silently and drew her shawl closer round the child slumbering peacefully in her arms.

"And how is your mother now, Nancy? Are you still living in Shaw's Alley?"

"Oh, no, Ma'am, we're in a much better way now. Father O'Hara's cook left 'im an 'is 'ousekeeper Mrs. Dobbs bein' so old, she can't be left to do much in the kitchen. I can't cook fancy, but the Father likes things plain anyhow, an' so I've been 'elping out Mrs. Dobbs for five shillin' a week while Mother keeps the baby, an' when I do the silver an' so on in the church I get another few shillin' on top. We've got a cottage now behind Father O'Hara's house. Well—I call it a cottage, but it's no more'n two rooms, really."

"Nancy, that's splendid! No wonder you look so well."

"An' it's all thanks to you, Ma'am, I'm mindful of that."

"It sounds to me as if it's all thanks to Father O'Hara. If it hadn't been for him, I'd never have known about you at all."

"Ah, but it was you worked the miracle, Mrs. Gaunt. I know that in myself."

Nothing would shake Nancy's faith in me, and while it was flattering, it was also rather embarrassing. I wondered how she'd discovered my new address; even if anyone at the Oliver's office knew where I was to be found these days it was unlikely they'd give out the details to a casual inquirer. But Nancy was one of those people who seem to be able to tap into the very bloodstream of a city. I'd last seen her at her lowest, temporarily at bay, her resources drained. Now she was back on her feet once more the whole city was her bailiwick; she seemed personally acquainted with almost all of the people living in the dockside warrens, with their complicated relationships and their family histories—and what she didn't know she could find out in an hour or two of judicious activity. What amazed me was that somehow or other this singularly resourceful woman had decided *I* was a miracle-worker.

It was for that reason she turned to me on the day her friend Eliza Rose died. I asked her later why she hadn't gone to Father O'Hara for help instead of coming all the way to my house and hustling me down to the dank cellar near the docks where Eliza Rose had lived, or rather *existed* with her four children, dying by degrees from a wasting condition which left her almost paralyzed on a bed of rags.

"I knew you'd make it right, Ma'am," she said simply. "That's why I came to you."

There was nothing I could do for Eliza Rose. She must have been dead for more than an hour by the time Nancy and I gingerly negotiated the steep stone steps leading down into the gloom of the cellar to gaze on her waxen features. Sarah, the oldest girl, had sped round to Nancy's cottage early in the afternoon to say that her mother seemed worse than usual; she seemed to be asleep, but she was making strange noises when she breathed. Nancy had taken one look and decided the case was hopeless. All she could do was to call in a neighbor to wait with the dying woman and come running for me to save the Rose children from the workhouse.

"They'll be kept apart otherwise, you see, Ma'am. Sarah'll be sent out to work an' the littl'uns kept separate in the men's an' women's halls, an' they'll likely never see each other again. An' they're such a close family, Ma'am. Young Sarah's looked after 'em since their Ma was took bad an' their Dad went off, an' they look to her as a mother, almost."

I looked round the bleak cellar. The cracked and uneven bricks underfoot were slimy with damp mold; the walls were as bad, and from somewhere overhead I could hear trundling cartwheels and the tramping feet of people passing by in the street, oblivious to the tragedy which had taken place below the cobbles. The Roses had owned little more than a couple of broken stools and a table, an old carving-knife and whatever heap of rags formed the communal bed on which their mother now lay dead. In the center of the table, however, was the only thing of value in the entire dwelling—a blue-and-gold-bordered china plate.

Nancy Morris followed my eyes.

"It's Father O'Hara's. I been bringing them the scraps from the kitchen—only the scraps, mind, the bits Mrs. Dobbs throws away. An' I brought them bread, too, when I could. Eliza Rose an' me come from the same village, until she married that swine of a man."

"The children's father? Where is he now?"

Nancy shrugged. "Who knows? They're better off without 'im, even in the workhouse."

They were all staring at me, wondering with absolute faith how I would contrive to put an end to their suffering. Five pairs of eyes watched me, unblinking, in the dimness of the cellar—not fearful, just curious to know how the miracle would be achieved.

What on earth was I to do? Nothing by myself, that was clear; and I could only think of one person whose influence might be powerful enough to manage something for the Rose children—Jonas Oliver. He wasn't unapproachable—the gleam of amusement I'd seen once or twice in those pale eyes declared as much. But I knew his views on charity were governed by rigid convention, and I'd no idea how I could justify asking him to intervene in the case of Eliza Rose. To Jonas, the workhouse would probably seem the obvious place to take charge of the children.

But while I deliberated they stood silently before me in that dismal cellar, watching me, waiting for me to produce the solution to their wretchedness . . . And I couldn't bring myself to admit there was nothing I could do.

———

This time Jonas Oliver met me at the door of his office as I clattered down the brown-painted corridor, Sam Coker's astonished eyes following me every step of the way.

"Mrs. Gaunt—this is a surprise. A pleasant one, nonetheless." Jonas pulled out a chair for me in front of his desk. "Is this a social call, or do you plan to go into the cotton-importing business now?"

"Mr. Oliver, I assure you I wouldn't have wasted your valuable time on a social call."

"So it's cotton, then, Mrs. Gaunt, is it? Or timber, perhaps, or corn?" His tone was irritatingly light, as if he'd found this the best way of dealing with unexpected female visitors.

"I need your help, Mr. Oliver. That's why I'm here."

"Indeed?"

I waited to see if he would take refuge behind his huge desk—and when he didn't, but simply perched himself on a corner of it, I breathed a sigh of relief. That, at least, was a good sign.

"And how may I help you, Mrs. Gaunt?"

"You can't help *me* directly, Mr. Oliver—though I'd be greatly in your debt if you could help someone else . . . Some other *people*. I worked for the Benevolent Fund long enough to know the responsibility you feel toward seamen's families . . . And my aunt tells me you're a member of the Liverpool Vestry, overseeing poor relief. . . ."

"And since I'm a thoroughly good fellow, you expect me to give you a donation for some good cause, is that it? Well—how much am I to subscribe?"

"I'm afraid it isn't as simple as that."

Jonas Oliver sighed. "Very well, Mrs. Gaunt, you'd better explain what you want."

"Mr. Oliver—have you ever visited one of the cellars in this city? I mean, a cellar where people are living?"

"No, I can't say that I have. I've never needed to visit one. There are proper authorities for that kind of thing."

"That may be so, but I doubt if any city official has ever seen the inside of the cellar I've just come from. Look at my shoes—" I lifted the hem of my skirt, and held out a foot. "Do you see that mold on the toe of my boot?"

Jonas Oliver obediently gazed at my foot.

"That came from the cellar floor where the Rose family live."

"Dear me—most unpleasant. What possessed you to go poking about in that sort of place?"

"Mr. Oliver, it may have been unpleasant for me to visit, but these poor people have to spend their lives in it! And the damp is only a small part of their trouble. As well as being flooded with rain-water and Heaven knows what else, it's so dark down there that when they come up into the street during the day, the light hurts their eyes!"

"Indeed?" His fair eyebrows rose by a fraction.

"Mrs. Rose has been ill for some time, and she finally died this afternoon. I can't tell you what was the matter with her; I should think it's a miracle she survived as long as she did in those conditions. Her husband disappeared a year ago, and there are four children left now—three of them very young, and a girl of thirteen or fourteen who's been looking after the others since her mother was taken ill. That's why I need your help, Mr. Oliver. For the Rose children."

"I see." Jonas Oliver frowned. "Forgive me if I'm a little slow in following your story, Mrs. Gaunt, but this man Rose—was he a seaman on one of our ships?"

"No, Mr. Oliver."

"But he *was* a seaman, I take it?"

"No . . . I believe he was a burglar, in fact. A house-breaker."

"I know what a burglar is, thank you, Mrs. Gaunt." For a moment I thought Jonas Oliver was about to tell me I was dismissed from my position, until he remembered I was no longer in his employment.

"Correct me if I'm wrong, Mrs. Gaunt—but you admit these Rose children have absolutely no connection with J. G. Oliver and Company? No connection of any kind?"

"I'm afraid not."

"Then will you explain to me why I'm expected to help them? Why can't they go to the workhouse in the usual way?"

"Because the workhouse will break up the family—what's left of it. The little ones look on their sister as a second mother, and they're very close. I'm afraid of what will happen if they're kept apart from one another."

"You're being a little overdramatic, Mrs. Gaunt, aren't you? It's always been my impression that children make new friends quite easily. Their affections are rarely very lasting. No doubt they'll adapt to different circumstances."

"With respect, Mr. Oliver—you have no children. You're hardly in a position to know how lasting their affections are! If you did have children of your own, perhaps you'd understand why—"

I fell silent, appalled at what I'd said. His eyes had met mine in that instant—furious, anguished—with a flash of icy fire in their pale depths which told me more than I'd any right to know about his longing for children of his own.

"Forgive me—I'm so sorry," I stammered, helpless to repair the damage.

He rose to his feet without a word and went to stand at the window, staring out at the busy thoroughfare of Water Street. After several silent minutes he turned back to me once more.

"No, Mrs. Gaunt, I'm afraid I can do nothing to help you. You must understand that I have many calls on my charity, and I have to confine it to our own people—Oliver employees and their families. The workhouse is an admirable institution, and I'm sure it will take perfectly good care of these children. Though, as you point out so succinctly, I'm hardly an expert on the subject of child-care."

"Mr. Oliver—please. I realize I've been unforgivably rude. But don't let my bad manners condemn these poor children, I beg of you. If you know of anywhere they could go—together—"

"Nowhere, Mrs. Gaunt, I assure you."

"There must be *somewhere*—some way of keeping them together as a family—"

"I very much doubt it. And now, if that's all I can do for you—"

He crossed the room toward the door with the intention of opening it for me to leave. I rose to my feet.

"Mr. Oliver, I know what you must think of me."

"Do you, Mrs. Gaunt?" He smiled politely.

"And you're quite justified in thinking it."

"How kind of you."

"But I will not abandon those children! *Please* reconsider—"

Jonas Oliver's fingers were on the door-handle.

"Mr. Oliver—at least come with me to see the conditions in which they've been living! Come—now—to see the cellar which is their home!"

"I assure you, that's quite unnecessary. It wouldn't make a jot of difference to my opinion. The workhouse is clearly the place for these children. They'll be fed there and properly clothed—whatever you may think—and I don't need to see this cellar of yours to know the workhouse will be an improvement on it."

I plunged on, regardless of his icy displeasure. What was the point of delicacy after the damage I'd done?

"Mr. Oliver, are you *afraid* of what you'll find there? Would you actually shrink from going to the kind of place I had to visit on behalf of your Benevolent Fund? A woman alone, as I was?"

"Of course not! How can you possibly suggest—"

"Then come with me now. Come back with me to the Rose children, and watch me tell them they must go to the workhouse in the morning. Or tell them yourself, if you're convinced it's such an excellent place."

For an eternity of silence, we stared at one another across the Persian carpet of his office. Then all at once, Jonas Oliver opened the door, and indicated that I should pass through it.

He followed me into the corridor.

"Wilson—my hat, if you please. I'm going out."

———

If the Rose children were impressed by the sudden appearance in their cellar of a gentleman in a dress coat and a silk hat, they never showed it, and I realized they'd calmly expected great wonders to occur as soon as I took a hand in their fate. I'm sure if I'd produced a genie out of a bottle complete with satin turban and curly moustache they'd only have stared at him with the same solemn trust they showed at that moment.

The doorway to the cellar was so low that an adult had to bend almost double to enter it from the foot of the steep stone steps, but as soon as we were inside I realized that Mrs. Rose's body had been removed, and I wondered how Nancy had managed it. This time I was prepared for the squalor—for the moss on the walls, for the tiny barred window stuffed with rags and the rotting boards round the empty grate—but I waited to see what Jonas Oliver would think of this miserable corner of his city.

For several minutes he said nothing, but stood in the center of that dismal space and stared about him at the cracked brick floor, the filthy bed, Father O'Hara's empty plate on the table, and the round, trustful eyes of the four Rose children lined up before the hearth. Then he turned to me and shook his head as if trying to shake the vision from his mind.

"It's appalling. Almost beyond belief. Unfortunately I don't suppose it's any worse than a hundred others." His eyes swept over the place once more. "The mother's dead, you say?"

"She died today. There, in the corner, earlier this afternoon."

"I see. And who is this?"

I beckoned to Nancy. "This is Nancy Morris, Mr. Oliver. Nancy, you've heard of Mr. Jonas Oliver."

Jonas frowned at me for a moment. "Nancy Morris? I've come across that name before, surely."

"The father of Nancy's baby was drowned on the *Mount Rose*. Jack Webb. Perhaps you remember my asking you for—"

"Ah yes. I remember it well, Mrs. Gaunt."

"Mrs. Gaunt saved us all, Sir," Nancy put in quickly, afraid she'd brought down some trouble on my head. "She saved my mother an' me. An' the baby, too."

"She saved you, did she, Mrs.—ah—Mrs. Morris? But then, she's a remarkable lady, Mrs. Gaunt. Given time, she may save us all yet."

He turned away from us, and beckoned to the eldest child.

"You, girl—what's your name?"

"Sarah, Sir," whispered the child, attempting a curtsey.

"And who are these others?"

"That's Robert—he's seven. Stand up, Robert! An' next to him is Jenny. I don' know how old Jenny is, Sir, 'cept she's less'n Robert. An' the littl'un at the end is Pig."

"Pig? That isn't a name, surely."

"It's all she's got, Sir. I never 'eard 'er called nothin' else."

"It's Elizabeth, Sir, after her Ma," supplied Nancy. "*Pig* was just a baby-name."

At the sound of her name the little girl toddled forward, scanned us all suspiciously from the distance of a pace or two, then walked boldly up to Jonas Oliver and thrust her tiny hand in his.

"Hey, Pig!" cried Sarah, scandalized. "Leave the gentleman alone!"

"She'll not do any harm there." Jonas glanced down at the solemn infant in the ragged shift who clung to his hand, sucking her thumb and watching him with avid eyes.

"The problem," he remarked to me over his shoulder, "is where to send them so that they'll stay together."

"Exactly."

He gave me a warning look. "I do realize that this is what you've suggested all along, Mrs. Gaunt. I've come round to your point of view."

"Thank you, Mr. Oliver. I hoped you might."

"The sticking-point is how to achieve it." He thought for a moment, frowning, while the toddler at his side continued to look gravely up at him.

"Now, Sarah—" He turned again to the eldest. "How much do you know about life in the country? Have you ever been out of the city to see the fields and the woods?"

"I was born in the country, Sir. We lived there, me an' Ma, before she got wed to Bob Rose an' we come to live in Liverpool. These three's 'is, Sir, but I ain't."

"I see. Well, I'm afraid there's nothing we can do for your mother anymore, but how would you children like to live in the country from now on? All of you—together."

Sarah's wan face lit up with hope.

"Oh, Sir—that'd be like a dream come true! Fer me, at any rate, since these littl'uns 'ave never seen much but the city. But they'll do as I tell'em, Sir, I promise you. Hey Jenny—hey Robbie—d'ye hear that? We're goin' to the country!"

"I don't see why my sister and her husband shouldn't find a home for these children." Jonas Oliver addressed me over his shoulder once more. "It's about time George Broadney put his hand in his pocket to help his fellow creatures. And if he won't see they're fed and looked after, then I will. Young Sarah seems to be a capable girl. There must be some work she could do on one of his farms in return for the children's keep." From a pocket, he produced three sovereigns. "Sarah—you're to take charge of this money. I expect you to buy some food with it, and something for you all to wear. Will you mind staying here for one more night?"

"They can come back with me, Mr. Oliver, since it's just for a night."

"Very well, Mrs. Morris. I'll see that someone collects them from you tomorrow and takes them to their new home. And—could you perhaps clean them up a little? Lady Broadney has rather strict ideas on cleanliness and they might as well start off in the proper condition."

"I'll see to it, Sir—and thank you for your kindness."

"Oh, don't thank me, Mrs. Morris. Once again, it's all Mrs. Gaunt's doing. She's the one you should thank."

Jonas bent down and gently disengaged the clinging Pig, retrieved his hat from the table where he'd set it down and, with a brief nod at the row of watching children, ducked out through the low doorway toward the stone steps leading up to the street.

"'E's a good'un after all," Nancy hissed at me conspiratorially, with a jerk of her head toward the doorway. "I always thought 'e was a proper swine, but 'e's turned out a good'un after all."

Jonas was waiting for me on the pavement at the entrance to the cellar, where even the foul city air tasted like nectar after the dank filth of that underground den.

"Mr. Oliver—I owe you an apology for everything I've said today." I felt genuinely contrite: he'd done all I'd asked of him, and more. "You've behaved like a true Christian—though I must admit, I did think you might once you saw the children for yourself, and the squalor they were living in."

"Did you indeed, Mrs. Gaunt?" Jonas Oliver stared at me speculatively. "And why should you think that, I wonder?"

"Because I believe you have too kind a heart to see children in such misery without lifting a finger to help." It wasn't quite the truth—but I'd already trespassed too far on his private unhappiness.

"That was shrewd of you, Mrs. Gaunt. You maneuvered me into doing exactly as you wished."

"I did nothing underhand, Mr. Oliver, surely—"

"I never suggested you did. You were entirely—ruthlessly—honest about what you wanted from me. And I've no objection to honesty." Once again, the speculative expression came into Jonas Oliver's eyes.

"Suppose I told you there was a condition attached to my helping those children."

"A condition?" This was something unexpected.

"I'm a businessman, Mrs. Gaunt. I'm accustomed to a return on my investments." He paused. "Let's say I'll find a home for these children on one of George Broadney's farms . . . provided you agree to accompany me to a concert next week. Those are my terms. One concert, in return for the happiness of four children."

"Mr. Oliver, I would be delighted to go to a concert with you."

"Excellent. I'll call for you at seven on Wednesday evening, then, Mrs. Gaunt. And this time—I think we may safely sit *inside* the hall."

19

"There'll be talk, of course," said Aunt Grace as soon as she heard about the concert. "You do realize there's bound to be talk? They'll all wonder who on earth you are, sitting beside the great Jonas Oliver and his friends. He's almost never seen out in town—or if he is, he's usually with those dreadful Broadneys. Verity keeps him on a short leash, I can tell you. If he's taking you to this concert, dear, it's only because his sister doesn't know about it, you may depend on it!"

Nevertheless, I enjoyed the concert—and I enjoyed our visit to the theater the following week, too. As my aunt had predicted, the know-alls in the audience craned their necks to see who'd arrived with Jonas Oliver that night, though the Broadneys occupied the same box and Verity sat sedately between us. Even after the curtain went up I noticed the occasional flash of opera-glasses from the darkened stalls as someone made a closer inspection.

That, however, was as far as the gossip could go; Jonas was a great deal too careful of his family's position in society to be seen in my company in circumstances which might give rise to common tattle. Yet he did continue to spend time with me; we drove in the park in his carriage so that Matthew could sail his model boat on the pond, we drove out one day to the Broadneys' country estate for tea, and to call on the Rose children, and we continued to attend concerts and the theater, always with Oliver acquaintances or with George Broadney and a frosty Verity in attendance so that supper could be taken afterward in absolute propriety.

For a long time I wondered why he enjoyed my company. Why should he choose to be with little, widowed Mrs. Gaunt of all people, when any unmarried daughter of the local gentry would have jumped at the chance of an invitation? It was only when I remembered the huge mahogany desk in his office and the swiftness of his retreat behind it that I began to understand how uneasy his shyness

made him in women's company, and how hard he found it to make
the kind of casual small talk round which a dinner party could
revolve.

Captain Fuller had been quite right when he described John
Oliver, Jonas's dead brother, as the merchant in the partnership, and
Jonas as the shipowner, for Jonas lived solely for his ships. To this
end he was stripping J. G. Oliver & Co. of its trading business,
turning it purely and simply into a shipping line. Sailing ships were
his first love, although as the advantages of steam became increasingly obvious Jonas was able to find a corner of his heart for steamships too, and he could discuss either kind of vessel with the
eagerness of a schoolboy for hours on end.

Because of that, whenever we ran out of something to say we fell
back on ships, the ships of the Oliver fleet whose progress I'd followed through months of office gossip. So the *Khandiva* had been
dismasted in a tropical storm and had limped into port under jury-
rig? Ah, but then she'd always been fortune's darling. And what
about the *Nessmore,* and the plodding *Brander?* They'd done well
enough—but not a patch on the ships which the Oliver line would
build in the future. . . . And Jonas would describe vessels to me
which existed only in his imagination but which he dreamed of
building; he'd lean forward intently in his chair, his pale blue eyes
burning with the zeal of a prophet, a passion in his voice quite
startling in that man of icy control.

It was hardly drawing-room conversation, but then Jonas Oliver
had little interest in politics when they didn't affect the health of the
shipping industry, his taste in books ran to coastal charts and ship
design, and I realized quite early in our friendship that our visits to
the theater were purely a kindness to me, and that he spent most of
the play thinking of cargoes or tonnages.

How many ladies would be thrilled to be told of the island of
Icheboe off the West African coast, 26° South by 15° East, many feet
deep in the accumulated droppings of seabirds? Only a woman who
understood the constant scramble for cargoes, and realized that the
discovery of this stinking treasure of fertilizer would keep Oliver
seamen in work for many difficult months—in short, little Mrs.
Gaunt, familiar with the business of the Oliver office, sympathetic
and practical.

And yet there was more to Jonas Oliver than ships and account-
books. Aunt Grace had called all the Olivers mean, but I came to

understand that to Jonas there was a great difference between company funds, which he treated with scrupulous care, and his own money, with which he was amazingly generous. He'd never have done anything so improper as to make me a personal gift, but instead he lavished presents on Matthew until I became so embarrassed that I finally asked him to stop.

"I beg your pardon," he said stiffly, sitting very upright on a chair in my little parlor. "I'd no wish to offend you." He'd come straight from the office with Uncle Tom Fuller in tow as *chaperon,* to bring us yet another lavishly bound volume.

"Oh, good gracious, I'm not offended, Mr. Oliver! It's just that— well, I can't imagine how much that beautiful Grimms' *Fairy Tales* must have cost, and it's only a few days since you gave him a splendid *Aesop.* . . ."

"Do you mind my giving him books? I thought he enjoyed reading."

"He does, indeed. Very much."

"Then he ought to have something to read, Mrs. Gaunt. And it gives me pleasure to see him happy. Would you deny me that? No, of course you wouldn't, being a sensible young woman. And in any case, I came here today to ask for your permission to carry him off for the afternoon—and you too, if you'll come. The *Celaeno*'s just back from Calcutta, and I thought young Matthew might be interested in coming aboard with me. The *Celaeno* was one of the first ships I ever built, and she's still a beauty, as I'm sure Captain Fuller would agree. I'd enjoy showing her off to you, if you can spare the time."

We both went, Matthew and I, and my son was allowed to stand in the helmsman's place at the ship's wheel where he barely came up to the big brass boss in the center but tugged at the spokes with all his strength. After that he was carried off by a cheerful bosun to be held up to ring the ship's bell by special permission of the *Celaeno*'s captain himself. He returned half an hour later, having toured the entire ship—"And seen where the sailors live, Mamma!"—clutching a fistful of trophies including part of a real shark's fin and a whistle carved from a mutton-bone left over from the galley.

For days afterward he went to sleep clutching the whistle tightly in his hand, having told everyone who'd listen that as soon as he was grown up he'd be off to sea in an Oliver ship, just like his hero, the bosun of the *Celaeno.*

Jonas was pleased and flattered by the success of his treat. I was the one who was uneasy, alarmed by signs of affection on Matthew's part for this kind friend who showered him with expensive gifts and took him to exciting new places. Matthew had liked Jonas from the start with the simple straightforwardness of a child, and we heard "Mr. Oliver says" at least a dozen times a day. I knew there was a great gap in Matthew's life which should have been filled by his father, but while I was grateful to Jonas Oliver for bringing a little male influence into an existence spent largely among women, I worried about the day when Jonas's interest in me would wane, and Matthew and I would be alone once more.

Yet in his own, orderly, decorous manner, Jonas continued to seek my company, and if anything, seemed to spend even more time with me than before.

Shortly before Christmas, cards arrived at Leghorn Street and at my own little house, inviting Captain and Mrs. Fuller and Mrs. Gaunt to a formal dinner at Jonas Oliver's own substantial house on the outskirts of the city. Aunt Grace, as usual, was torn between refusing to go—to show her independence from the Oliver family—and accepting the invitation in order to have a good look at the inside of the Oliver mansion, an almost irresistible attraction. Captain Fuller solved the problem by insisting that we should all go.

"It's Rachel he wants in any case, m'dear," he declared, "not two old fossils like us. And well may you blush, young lady—you know it's true. And I warn you, when Jonas Oliver takes an idea into his head . . . Just look out, that's all. He'll drive on under every stitch of canvas, fair weather or foul, no matter what."

It was the first time anyone had put into words a suspicion which was beginning at last to dawn on me.

———

Yet I knew very little of him, in spite of the time we'd spent together. His likes and dislikes, his fears and his personal ambitions—nothing was ever allowed to break through that austere restraint, and it wasn't until I visited his home for the first time that I realized there was a side to Jonas Oliver the existence of which I'd never even suspected.

He still lived in the mansion his father Captain John Oliver had built twenty-five years before. It was every bit as large and impressive as I'd expected, but even in my wildest imaginings I hadn't allowed for the objects which crowded the walls of several of the elegant rooms—case after case of beautifully displayed and mounted butter-flies. Their jeweled colors blazed from the frames with the brilliance of enamel: iridescent green, shimmering magenta or luminous blue, barred and spotted and fringed with patterns in black and vermilion, like masterpieces from the bench of some supernatural goldsmith.

Beneath each spread-eagled insect was a meticulous card bearing its name—hawk-moth or monarch, swallowtail or burnet, Mourn-ing Cloak, Painted Lady or Emperor—each one pinned alongside others of its family or its country of origin and sealed under a glass cover. The Almighty himself could hardly have been more precise when he brought them into being.

The sheer number of specimens was enough to stun the eye. One case held a regiment of creamy moths, row upon row of them, each one differing from the last in some infinitesimal detail which had qualified it for eternity on the collector's pin.

Several of the smaller boxes held a single specimen. Framed in gold, a pale green Moon Moth from North America stretched the finned tails of its wings like an exotic from the *corps de ballet;* nearby a South American swallowtail flaunted its tropical beauty, modest head and limbs almost hidden by the shimmering shawl of its wings.

I tried hard to imagine the creatures in flight, a flickering cloud of color amid the submarine blue of a rain forest. But try as I might, I couldn't associate those endless ranks of corpses, that perfect mosaic of death, with the fleeting, heart-stopping beauty of a butterfly on the wing. There was simply no connection: the glass cases before me were no more than tombs, while out in the wilds the butterflies rejoiced in life, all the more glorious for the brief, wasteful days of their existence.

"You're surprised, Mrs. Gaunt?" I'd been so deep in thought that I was quite startled when I heard Jonas Oliver's voice at my elbow.

"I don't suppose you expected a dull man of business to have an appreciation of beauty. . . . A love of gracefulness and symmetry, and richness of color? No—I'm sure you didn't. You think of me as a man with a cash-ledger for a mind, Mrs. Gaunt. Nevertheless—I assure you even I know true beauty when I see it before me. And I prize it greatly; I'll go to almost any lengths to possess it." He made a gesture toward the collection of insects, but his eyes never left mine. "Perhaps you'll understand when you know me better—isn't that possible?"

"I—I am truly amazed by your collection, Mr. Oliver," I murmured awkwardly. "And it's true—I've never seen anything like it. Did you find all these butterflies yourself?"

"Some of them, certainly." At last he glanced away toward the rows of cases. "I began the collection as a boy, with the insects I found in the countryside near this city. The British butterflies and moths are in the library, by the way. But these specimens here in the drawing room . . . alas, the majority of them aren't mine, though I did bring back a few myself from overseas. The masters of all our ships know of my interest in these creatures, and if they find some new moth or butterfly for sale in a foreign port they're authorized to buy it for me. Even our agents have been pressed into service."

"Your collection is . . . breathtaking. The longer I look at it, the more I see. Even the tiny white moths—when I study them closely they have their own, individual patterns."

"There you see how Nature squanders her genius! In the ordinary way of things these exquisite colors would simply wither in death and be lost. Yet I can preserve them for all time, for your enjoyment."

"It's sad, though, to think they must die for the privilege."

"Is life such a precious thing? Mrs. Gaunt—I can offer them immortality! Isn't that better than a short, dangerous existence in the open air?"

"I doubt if I'd choose it."

"No?" Jonas Oliver examined the nearest case of sooty moths. "I don't think I'd hesitate for a moment. But then, one must have something worth preserving, even if it's only a name." He lowered his voice so that no one could overhear us. "Now your loveliness, Mrs. Gaunt, deserves to be commemorated—like the best of these."

I looked at the butterfly corpses in their perfect ranks and felt a sudden chill, as if an open door had allowed a draft to enter the room. Fortunately at that moment Verity Broadney, acting as her brother's hostess, began to pair off the throng of guests to go in to dinner, and I was saved from finding an answer.

————

There was no doubt about it. I was being courted, besieged in a perfectly proper but persistent manner by Jonas Oliver. However unlikely it might seem to his family, I was sure he had marriage in mind: a man in search of a mistress would have gone about the process quite differently. Before long Jonas would ask me to be his wife, and I'd have to decide on my answer.

And oh, what a gulf existed between Jonas and Adam! Between Jonas, who believed that rules were vital for the proper functioning of life and would have died before flouting one, and Adam, who simply ignored the existence of any rules; between Jonas, the builder of empires, and Adam, who'd hated the sight of another human footprint in his path! They were like beings from different stars.

What, then, should I say to Jonas Oliver when he asked me to marry him?

The truth was that my ways—my own, private ways, not the games I played for society's sake—were not Oliver ways, and never would be. I'd lived too long in the Outlands to believe in the rituals and rules anymore. And I'd have to tell Jonas, as I'd told Antoine Bleu, that half of my heart had been buried with a dead man, laid under a pile of rocks near a bluff on the Bighorn, and hardly enough of me remained to be a wife to anyone. In all honesty, that would have to be my answer. I couldn't be the wife he wanted.

"Mr. Oliver says—"

Matthew, of course, was devoted to Mr. Oliver. Jonas had even set aside a pony in his stable exclusively for Matthew's use, and told us to call whenever my son wished to ride. Books, microscopes, model sailing ships—and now a pony. Matthew was becoming thoroughly spoiled, and I saw problems ahead when my friendship with Jonas ended as it must, and he paid no attention to us anymore.

My conscience began to torment me. Was it right of me to think only of myself in this? With Jonas Oliver as his stepfather, Matthew's future would be secure and his life happier than I could ever make it on my own. Watching him there on his fat little pony, plodding with a groom at his side down the broad carriage-sweep, I realized how much such a marriage would mean to my son. Would it be such a huge sacrifice, after all? Would it be so hard to be Mrs. Jonas Oliver, to live in comfort for the rest of my days and see Matthew inherit wealth and position?

I began to feel myself enveloped in a large, soft net where my struggles toward freedom were becoming feebler by the day.

And I'd learned to value my freedom. I'd come to enjoy thinking for myself. I could fill my head with my own thoughts as naturally as filling my lungs with air. They might not agree with Aunt Grace's notions, or Verity Broadney's, or Jonas Oliver's, but they were every bit as valid, and I'd tested them in pain and desperation none of them dreamed of. And Jonas had no concept of this. He'd expect me to lean on him, to defer to his judgment in all things, to ornament his home in dainty idleness.

The irony of it all was that Adam, to whom I'd tried to cling, had loathed the responsibility of my dependence on him. I could see that now, when it was too late to make amends. Was I simply about to make the same mistake again, to marry another man who wanted me to be something I wasn't?

There was, of course, another stumbling-block—those parts of my life which I'd tried to leave behind me forever on the other side of the Atlantic. If Jonas asked me to marry him, I'd have to tell him the truth. And after that, I thought grimly, I'd soon know whether Jonas Oliver thought me fit to be his wife.

Strangely enough, it was Verity Broadney who brought matters to a head, without intending to in the very least. Shortly after my appearance at a ball in the Assembly Rooms in Jonas Oliver's party, Lady Broadney took it upon herself to call on me and find out once and for all how things stood between us. Two days after the ball, the huge Broadney carriage waited for almost an entire afternoon outside my little house, while the neighbors peered through their figured muslin curtains, desperate to know what was taking place in my modest parlor.

I'm sure Verity thought she'd managed her visit very cleverly. For a full half-hour she made innocent small talk over the teacups before steering the conversation stealthily round to matters which really concerned her, such as *what,* precisely, my position in the Oliver office had been, and how I'd made her brother's acquaintance in the first place. No doubt Verity intended her questions to be subtle, but I found them increasingly offensive. She was interrogating me, and I felt my cheeks beginning to glow with indignation.

Lady Broadney knew I'd spent some time in America: what had I thought of society in the States? How did it compare with what I'd been used to in Liverpool—assuming, of course, that I had any experience of good society in England. . . .

I grew more and more angry. At last, after a good deal of beating about the bush, Verity came to the business of her visit.

"Mrs. Gaunt," she said sharply, setting down her teacup squarely on the table, "what I require to know—what, indeed, I must know —is whether there exists any kind of *understanding* between you

and my brother. Has he, in a word, made any *promises* to you with
regard to the future?"

"Lady Broadney, I'm sure Mr. Oliver is the correct person to
answer that question. He'll tell you all you need to know."

"No doubt he will, if I ask him. But I had hoped you might save
me the trouble."

"I'm not sure I even understand the question. What promises do
you think your brother might have made to me?"

"Come now, Mrs. Gaunt—you must know exactly what I'm talking about! Jonas has paid you considerable attention in the last few
months—good gracious, you always seem to be together! The whole
of Liverpool is talking about an *attachment* between you."

"Goodness! Are people really saying such things?" I made a great
show of innocent surprise. "And Mr. Oliver has been so very kind."

Verity scowled at me across the tea table and wriggled her feet
until her overboots squeaked.

"You must understand, Mrs. Gaunt, that my brother has a position to keep up in this community. He's head of the company. He's
a councillor. His circumstances must be above reproach."

"Oh, but I'm sure they are, Lady Broadney."

"But don't you see how much damage could be done to his authority if news of a—well—a liaison with a former employee became
public!"

The word *liaison* finally concentrated my mind in a way that hours
of gentle attentiveness from Jonas could never have done. I was
damned—yes, damned—if I was going to allow that smug, yellow-
haired harpy to make her insulting suggestions in my own parlor! *If
that didn't beat all creation!* I had a sudden desire to snatch her
wretched overboots and squash them, one by one, into her mean
little mouth. *And that,* as Antoine would have said, *is a fact, by
jingo.*

"Liaison?" I asked naïvely. "I can't imagine what you mean."

Verity Broadney struggled with her temper.

"Surely a . . . lady . . . of your sensitivity must understand a simple
word like liaison, Mrs. Gaunt! I can hardly make myself plainer! I
believe my brother is infatuated with you. I believe you know that
perfectly well. Therefore I must know if you've managed to lure him
into some entanglement he'll find difficult to break when his—*aber-
ration* is over. For Heaven's sake, Mrs. Gaunt—*has he asked you to
marry him?*"

"To marry him, Lady Broadney? Marriage to Mr. Oliver? Good gracious—it never crossed my mind."

———

In his own good time, at a proper moment, Jonas Oliver asked me to marry him, and I accepted, as I'd decided to long before. He chose a snowy February night for his proposal, in the midst of a sparkling party which seemed to spread itself throughout the brightly lit ground-floor rooms of his house. Shortly after midnight he drew me aside to the library, insisting he'd something important to show me.

The library had been locked, though lamps were lit in the deserted room warming the colors in the portrait of Captain John Oliver above the chimneypiece and illuminating a set of plans spread out on the long table. They were plans for a sailing-ship, and even I could see that this one was to be something out of the ordinary.

"She'll not be as light as Low's *Sea Witch,* you understand—I never thought much of that ship in a seaway—but as you can see, she'll have the same hollow lines. That bow—" Jonas tapped the paper. "That bow is the shape of the future. Perfect. Fast."

"But she'll be beautiful!" By now I was accustomed to picturing a finished vessel from a set of drawings, and I was genuinely awed by the perfection of this one. "When will you start to build her? There won't be another ship to touch her anywhere in the world."

Jonas nodded. "I intend her to be unique. Anywhere she goes, I want men to gaze at her and say, 'That's the finest ship I've ever seen. An *Oliver* ship. *The* Oliver ship.' "

"Oh, they will, I know it! But what will you call her? She must have a name to match her looks."

"What do you think I ought to call her?"

"Oh, my goodness—something like *Sea Nymph* or *Amphitrite,* perhaps. Or name her for a star, or an ancient goddess."

"That isn't quite what I had in mind." Jonas frowned a little, and began to roll up the end of the nearest sheet, forming it into an exact cylinder between his elegant fingers.

"Then what name have you chosen?"

"I hope," announced Jonas with sudden decisiveness, "she'll be called the *Rachel Oliver.* But that depends entirely on you, my dear. What do you think of it for a name?"

I stared at him, stunned. Was my price as a bride as high as that? I tried to collect my scattered wits, and make the confession I'd promised myself—the confession I owed him.

"Oh, Jonas—it's—the most wonderful idea. . . . But are you sure —I mean—you know what people will say—and there are parts of my life in America which are hardly . . . Not that I'm ashamed of what I had to do, but you should know—"

Jonas held up an imperious hand.

"Rachel, my dear, you've told me all this before. Do you imagine I think any less of you because you've had to work in a general store to make a living?" He paused, and to my eternal shame I said nothing.

Taking my silence for an answer, Jonas went on.

"Don't you know what I value in you, even more than your beauty? Your wonderful honesty—the honesty which made you tell me all this when you could easily have said nothing about it. No one in Liverpool will ever find out how you lived in the backwoods of America, I assure you! There—does that set your mind at rest?"

"But—"

"No one will ever know, my darling, I promise you. Let all that be a secret between us." He took me gently by the wrists. "Now, if we've disposed of your little problem . . . Tell me again what you think of my Queen of the Seas—my exquisite *Rachel Oliver*."

"I think . . ." There was no going back. "I think *Rachel Oliver* will be quite perfect, Jonas."

It was enough. With a little smile of satisfaction, Jonas bent forward to imprint a solemn kiss in the center of my forehead.

We were married two months later, in April 1844; I wore pale blue silk almost the color of Jonas's eyes, and a pale blue crêpe bonnet, with the diamond brooch Jonas had given me as a wedding present fastened at my throat. There had only been one slight impediment to the marriage—the singularity of my widowhood, confirmed only by Joe Walker's letter—but Jonas was in no mood to let a small detail stand in his way. In the end I simply signed an affidavit to the effect that my first husband, Adam Gaunt, of the town of Independence, Missouri, in the United States of America and late of Norfolk, England, had met with a fatal accident sometime in August or September of 1840 near the Bighorn River in the western American Territories—and I was free to remarry.

There was no rancor at the wedding. Even Verity had to welcome me into the family as if she could think of nothing more delightful, lining up with the rest to kiss me fleetingly on the cheek and to murmur something in my ear about not taking anything she'd previously said in the wrong spirit. This, I presumed, was as near an apology as I was likely to receive, and a plea for me not to tell Jonas of her interference.

The Broadneys even loaned us their London house in Eaton Square for the first week of our married life. We were due to leave for three weeks in Paris, but Jonas had one or two important appointments in the capital before we sailed, and assumed I'd want to tour the shops while he was occupied with business.

"Remember—" he reminded me briskly the day before our wedding, "you're to buy anything in London that takes your fancy. Clothes—jewelry—anything you see. I expect you to outshine every woman in Paris when we get there. My wife—my very dear wife—will be perfect in every detail."

This touched a nerve, and reminded me that I was running out of time for something I'd meant to say.

"Jonas—"

"Yes, my darling—what else have you thought of? A watch, perhaps? Or a morocco dressing-case? You've only to ask. I can't refuse you anything today."

"It's just something which . . . which you ought to know. Before —well—"

"What on earth's bothering your little head now?"

I paused, disconcerted. In the last few weeks before the wedding I'd begun to notice a subtle change in Jonas's manner toward me. He was still as attentive as ever, still as concerned for my welfare, but there was a new possessiveness in his voice when he made introductions, as if I were some great prize safely netted and ready for a place on his wall. I was halfway to becoming a wife instead of a person in my own right, halfway to being no more than a postscript to my husband, obliged to echo his opinion on every matter with only the most frivolous thoughts to fill my own "little head."

I felt trapped—diminished—but there was no going back now. I pushed aside my doubts and pressed on with what I was bound to say.

"Please listen, Jonas. Sit down here and listen. This is important."

"Oh, very well." With an indulgent sigh, he sat down beside me on the sofa.

"You see—while I was in America I was involved in a shooting. It was an accident, of course. Lots of people have guns there, and they aren't always very careful with them."

"Rachel, you know I don't shoot. You need George Broadney if you want to discuss that sort of thing. He'll shoot anything that'll run away from him."

"No—not sport shooting, Jonas. Pistols. Handguns. A man—a drunk—fired a gun, and wounded me. The point is, it left a scar—rather a bad one. I would have told you about it before, only it was difficult. . . ."

"Yes, I can see that." Jonas sounded irritated. He stared at me as if he'd missed some blemish he ought to have discovered. "I've never noticed a scar."

"Not on my face. On my body. Here." I put a hand to my side.

"Oh, for Heaven's sake—" Jonas was now considerably embarrassed. "I really don't understand why you're worried about that. I'd probably never have known about it *there*. How on earth would I see it? I'll be your husband after tomorrow, Rachel, not an anatomist. Now, can we please talk about something else?"

His embarrassment confused me; and I was even more confused when we arrived at the Broadneys' house in Eaton Square and the housekeeper ushered us upstairs.

"This will be your room, my dear," declared Jonas, indicating a large airy chamber with a half-canopied bed. "Mine isn't quite so large, but it's the one I usually have here."

He crossed to double doors in the far wall and threw them open on another similar room beyond.

"We'll be very comfortable, I'm sure, Mrs. Hatcher. I see you've found us some spring flowers as I asked. Thank you for that. Mrs. Oliver will appreciate them—won't you, darling?"

"Oh, yes," I agreed automatically, still disconcerted by his arrangements. "The flowers are lovely."

"Perfect," pronounced Jonas decisively. "Everything is perfect."

I was still bewildered that night as I prepared for bed, alone in my room once my new maid—appointed on Jonas's instructions—had swept out with my dress and petticoats over her arm.

Time passed. I sat before my dressing-table mirror, my hair left unbraided—for this was, after all, my wedding night—my face scrubbed clean, my prettiest nightgown still showing the folds of its packing.

Eventually, I climbed into bed, and pondered the mystery of my missing bridegroom.

Separate rooms; separate beds. Perhaps this was how all very rich people slept, splendidly alone. The poor, after all, had to cram five, sometimes six people into the same bed, and presumably the rich felt obliged to go to the opposite extreme. Or perhaps it was all for show, another of these rituals which had to be observed for appearances' sake, and the rich took secret delight in lying in one another's arms like the rest of us, when they thought no one could see.

For I desperately wanted Jonas to be there with me, to tell me he loved me even if he didn't really mean it, to hold me tightly while I fell asleep and to be there beside me in the morning when I woke. I'd missed Adam so very much; and it was only after traveling on the riverboat in Antoine's cheerful company that I realized how achingly lonely I'd been, and would be again, with no one.

And there I was—lonely—on my wedding night. What if Jonas never came through to my room? My God, was it possible he'd only married me for form's sake, and preferred to spend his nights with slim-hipped boys? I'd heard of men who'd done just that, who'd passed forty years of marriage without ever laying a finger on their wives. And yet I knew—perhaps better than anyone—how much Jonas Oliver wanted children of his own and there was only one way of getting those. I was sure he'd married me for my proven record. I already had a son, and where there was one child there could be more. So Jonas would come to me in the end, if only to sire an heir.

The minutes passed, and I reassured myself that Jonas wanted me as a man should want his bride of less than twenty-four hours. He'd kissed me briefly in the carriage after the wedding ceremony, briefly and chastely as if I'd been something very precious which he might damage . . . Yet there had been pride of possession in his eyes then, and I'd had no doubt that he wanted me as a woman, as his wife.

It was quite late at night when he opened the double doors and came into the room in his nightshirt. He seemed surprised to find the lamp still lit beside the bed, and promptly turned it out.

"I don't think we need that anymore, do you?" The bed creaked as he climbed into it, and then there was silence.

"Well, it's been a long day for both of us," he remarked suddenly. "Yes—a long day." Silence again. "And I've an early meeting with the Company bankers tomorrow. Boring, but there it is. No way out of it."

"What a pity." I waited for him to kiss me. I began to wonder what he'd do if I kissed him first.

"Yes, it is a pity. I'd have liked to spend the day with you, but I imagine you'll find some way of amusing yourself. And I'll see you at dinner."

"I'll tell you then what I've been up to."

"I'll look forward to that."

This was beyond belief. We'd had the same conversation, or its equivalent, a hundred times before. Now I wanted some declaration of love, of affection at least—something to make me feel valued and cherished in these secret moments together.

"George and Verity have made this house very comfortable, don't you think?" I had the distinct impression Jonas was staring about him in the darkness.

"Yes—they have."

"Of course, they've spent a great deal on it."

"I suppose they must have done."

"No lack of money in the Broadney family."

"No."

At last I heard him turn on his side, toward me.

"You must be tired, my dear, after all the excitement today."

"Not so tired as all that, Jonas. Not now you're here." I'd seen passion in his eyes, genuine passion, when he talked of his ships; now I waited for it again.

I felt him slide across the bed, pulling the sheet out of his way. All at once he was next to me, groping for me, pushing my nightgown up round my thighs. I tried to reach out to him, to be kissed or caressed . . . but I don't think he even noticed, there in the darkness.

"I know you're tired. I'll be as quick as I can, my darling," he whispered—and he was, oh my God, he was—no sooner begun than finished, without reference to me, or what I wanted, or how I felt, as if no more of me existed than the one tiny part which was of use to him. . . . And even then, when I tried to flex my body, to match the runaway rhythm of his desire, to hold and contain it—he thought he'd caused me pain in some way, and begged me to lie still, the better to endure him for a few moments longer.

And two great tears rolled down my cheeks in the darkness, and I wanted to die there in that ridiculous bed where I'd become a *convenience* for this man I'd married, a headless, soulless broodmare for the progeny he wanted so badly.

"I'm sorry, my dear. Perhaps I was a little—eager. But I thought

—since you aren't a virgin . . . Does it still hurt? Would you like me
to stay with you until you're asleep?"

"Please, Jonas—yes." He'd made it sound like the greatest favor
in the world.

He stayed with me until he assumed from my even breathing that
I was soundly asleep, then slipped out of bed and pattered contentedly back to his own room, shutting the double doors with the
utmost care in case he wakened me again. I wanted to rise up in bed
and shout after him *Come back here, light the lamp, and look at the
woman you've married!* But I didn't, of course, because I was Jonas
Oliver's wife, and Jonas's wife would never behave like that. Instead
I lay, wide awake, in my canopied bed and felt emptier and lonelier
than ever before.

———

By next day I'd decided that Jonas wasn't to blame, and that perhaps
I'd been singularly fortunate in finding Adam, that free spirit. Jonas
had never known the fine, sensual adventure of shared desire. It must
be the fault of the other women in his life—in his bed—who'd lain
like martyrs while he serviced them and never expected more. Perhaps—I thought—little by little, I could make him aware of me and
my need of him. He was thoughtless, but not heartless.

Later that very day I learned how the future was to be.

"Good Heavens—Sophie Greenwood!" he exclaimed after dinner,
scanning his copy of *The Times*. "Well, I'm damned! What on earth
is that woman doing in London? Ah—she's appearing in a play at
the King's. That explains it."

"Who's Sophie Greenwood, Jonas?"

Jonas put down his paper for a moment, and frowned.

"Well—you might as well know, since you're one of the family
now and it might save a dreadful *faux pas* at some future date . . .
Sophie Greenwood is an actress, my dear, though not a very good
one. I believe we saw her as Lady Macbeth on one occasion in
Liverpool—the good-looking woman who shouted most of her lines
from the edge of the stage."

"I think I remember her."

"Yes—well—Sophie Greenwood also happens to be George
Broadney's long-standing mistress."

"Jonas!"

"He rents rooms for her near the theater in Liverpool. That's why

I was surprised to see her turning up in London. George doesn't usually like to let her out of his sight. Doesn't trust her."

"Oh, poor Verity!" For a moment I was genuinely sorry for my shrewish sister-in-law. "How awful if she found out!"

"Oh come, Rachel—Verity knows all about Sophie Greenwood! She never mentions the woman, of course, but she knows, all the same. Most wives do, I imagine. And you must bear in mind that my sister has her children to fuss over and her charity committees and so forth, so she's happy enough. Technically, George is committing adultery, but I don't suppose that bothers him. This actress isn't his only *diversion*."

I struggled to reconstruct Lady Macbeth in my mind.

"What on earth does George Broadney see in her?"

Jonas rustled the pages of his *Times*.

"I understand—ah—or rather, George has told me—ah—that the Greenwood woman *enjoys the attentions of men,* if you catch my drift. Sophie Greenwood is . . . quite *avid* for it, I believe. Don't look at me in that peculiar manner, Rachel, it's perfectly true. Some women have a kind of perversion in that direction—degraded women, prostitutes and the like. To my mind, it must turn a woman into some kind of animal, but George seems to find it exciting."

Jonas retired behind his paper once more, and his voice became slightly indistinct.

"However—please remember that I've only told you about this Greenwood person to avoid any kind of embarrassment in future. I don't expect to hear her name on your lips—ever. Is that quite clear, Rachel?"

"Oh, yes, Jonas. It's all absolutely clear."

What was I to do? I tried to tell myself I was no worse off than a nun in her cloister—except that a nun has never known the fleshly pleasures she so willingly gives up. I didn't have that good fortune: I'd expected those moments of delicious intimacy—of fierce, voluptuous enjoyment—as a necessary part of my marriage. Jonas Oliver had expected a saint, a spirit without a body, an unfeeling vessel for his own shame-faced lust . . . and instead he'd chosen me. Sophie Greenwood and I were sisters under the skin—harlots, Jonas would have called us—she in George Broadney's bed and I in my secret heart.

· · ·

But pleasure is not a necessary part of conception. Within six months I was pregnant, and Jonas was over the moon with delight. The pregnancy was an awkward one, and after several early alarms I was forced to spend most of the remaining months in bed. Jonas, however, showered me with gifts—earrings I couldn't wear, furs which only hung in the wardrobe once I'd admired them, and even the promise of a new house of our own at some time in the future, after the baby was born. All I really wanted was to be able to leave my bed and regain possession of my own body once more.

As it turned out, Jonas's daughter struggled into the world almost a month before her time, to be baptized Alice after her paternal grandmother. I was determined no child of mine would ever be called Susannah.

For a while after the birth I was the center of attention, cosseted, praised and visited by all and sundry. Then the excitement died down, and depression and restlessness set in. I was still tired from my confinement, but now, ironically, I had nothing to do, nothing which would fill my days as my work for the Benevolent Fund had done, or the multitude of tasks which had been part of life in the cabin in Independence.

Having cared for Matthew night and day from the first moments of his life, I found it odd to be reduced now to the role of visitor in the highly efficient nursery Jonas had organized for the new baby. The nursery was no affair of mine: it was foreign soil, where my little Alice existed in a starched, meticulously aired world of snowy white cotton and lace-trimmed gowns, ruled over by a fiercely possessive nurse.

Even seven-year-old Matthew had outgrown my care. From now until he was old enough to be sent off to school he'd spend most of his time in the schoolroom with his tutor or in the stables—no doubt picking up an education of a different kind from the grooms.

And now that I had to live in it I found Jonas's house as dark and empty as a mausoleum. I might have been its mistress in name, but an army of servants kept it swept and burnished without any direction from me, as they'd done since Jonas's first wife died. The mansion had been his family home, and it had never occurred to Jonas to move so much as one of the great brocaded chairs in the somber entrance hall. I wandered aimlessly from room to cryptlike room, my melancholy made worse by the endless vista of massed butterfly corpses on every wall.

When I could stand it no longer I reminded Jonas of his promise that we'd have a new house of our own, and to my great surprise I found him firmly in favor of the idea.

"I've been thinking about what we should build," he announced a few days later. "Something more in keeping with our position, perhaps, now that the company's doing so well. A house big enough to hold a decent ball in now and again—with a large, open entrance hall with marble pillars and a stone fireplace like the one at George's place—and a purpose-built stable-yard nearby with an archway over the gate, and brass-mounted stalls for the horses—"

"But Jonas, you *hate* horses!"

"Yes, I know I do—but fortunately Matthew's interested in them, and a gentleman ought to ride. Oh—and a tower. We must have a tower over the archway. With a clock."

I couldn't help laughing. "It sounds as if you're designing a palace, Jonas, not a house! Think how much all that would cost!"

"I'm aware of what it would cost. I've already spoken to an architect about it, and I think we might be able to build what I have in mind for a little over seven thousand pounds."

"Seven thousand! But that's a fortune!"

"To some people, perhaps. But I daresay the Olivers can run to it. Railway shares are paying five percent at the moment, and as long as corn goes on fetching eighty or ninety shillings a quarter, we'll ship as much as we can find."

After that, in my mind, too, a house began to take shape.

"Oh, Jonas, can we have lots of windows? Big, wide windows, to let in plenty of light? Will you ask the architect?"

"The architect will give you whatever you like," he told me indulgently. "So build what you please, and hang the window tax."

We built our house not far from the pleasant, leafy slopes of Mossley Hill to the southeast of the city, and it was almost large enough for a palace, a long, low palazzo with Florentine towers and a broad terrace to one side. On the ground floor there were wide bay windows and on the next story each sash window had an arched top which, I hoped, along with the ornamental balustrade which ran along the edge of the roof to hide the leads, would give the house a little grace to balance its size and solidity.

Built of shining white sandstone and surrounded by a high wall, it was inevitably named the *White House*. I loved it from the first; I loved the way the sunlight poured in through my great windows, and sometimes at night I would walk out on to the terrace for the simple pleasure of seeing my house ablaze with the brilliant gas-lighting Jonas had insisted on having in every room.

The cost of the project was astronomical, yet sometimes Jonas even took me to task for trying to save money on details. I soon discovered that nothing was wasted, in Jonas's mind, which was spent on maintaining the reputation of the Olivers. Far from being niggardly with money, Jonas gave me an entirely free hand to buy furnishings; his only stipulation was that everything must be new and in the latest fashion. George Broadney's old French furniture had been sat on by real French kings and was perfectly acceptable in the house of an ancient and noble family. But the Oliver wealth was only two generations old. Elderly furniture in the Olivers' rooms would only imply that they'd fallen on hard times, and Jonas refused to risk giving any such impression.

With a heavy heart, on Jonas's instructions, I threw out the Chippendale and Sheraton chairs his father had bought and ordered more elaborate versions from Mr. Nixon of Great Portland Street in London. The Olivers could only have the best, though I did manage to squirrel away a beautiful satinwood Sheraton settee for my own private sitting room where I was permitted to do as I pleased.

Stifling my instinct for plainness—born, no doubt, of rough plank floors and unchinked log walls—I clothed my rooms in rose-colored silk, hung velvet curtains and immense Osler chandeliers and covered my ottomans in cabbage-roses. Verity arrived like a medieval pedlar bearing fire-screens and coal urns, pier-glasses and console tables until Jonas was enchanted, and I watched sadly while my huge drawing room filled itself with fashionable clutter. At least I had my own private sanctuary, my little sitting room beyond the library where sunshine sang from my eccentric white and yellow walls even on the dullest days of winter and I could dream my simple dreams untouched by the grandeur of the Olivers.

Even before the White House was complete I'd twice become pregnant again and twice suffered a miscarriage. My duty to give Jonas his longed-for heir began to obsess me, and as soon as we were installed in our magnificent home near Mossley Hill and I discovered I was once more carrying a child, I was so nervous of taking risks that I spent almost the entire pregnancy in bed, hardly stirring for fear of losing the baby.

Once more the child arrived early, and this time the birth was agonizing and difficult. For several days it seemed as if the baby could never survive, but by some miracle, Louise Verity Victoria Oliver strengthened her tiny hold on life to give Jonas a second daughter. I'd prayed so hard for a boy that I felt it must be a judgment on me.

"They're cursed with girls, this generation of Olivers," observed my aunt smugly, bringing a reluctant Harry to view the new baby. "John Oliver had three of them, and now here's Jonas with two. Heaven knows what the old Captain would have said. Still—maybe it'll be a boy next time, my dear. After all, there's Matthew to prove you do know how to produce them."

I didn't tell her what the doctor had said as he left my room after pronouncing little Louise out of danger at last.

"You were lucky this time, Mrs. Oliver. Very lucky indeed." Then he sighed, and shook his head. "But I doubt if you'll ever bear another alive."

The doctor was right. Another miscarriage followed, and then a dead boy, lost at five and a half months. After that there were no more pregnancies.

"To be honest, Mrs. Oliver, I'm surprised you've managed to bear children at all, after the injuries you received in that shooting accident," the doctor confessed. "Whoever was so careless with a gun did you a great disservice. But the creation of life is a wonderful thing. It can defy the worst that human beings will do to confound it. Your two daughters are miracles in themselves, Ma'am—you should count yourself fortunate to have them, and forget any thoughts of bearing more."

After the doctor had gone I stared at myself, naked, in the pierglass in my dressing room, the ugly scar where Kinsella's bullet had entered my body now healed into a livid star on my creamy skin.

If it hadn't been for Watches Smoke, I would be dead, I told myself. If it hadn't been for the Trader's House, and Frank Ellis, and my obsession with leaving Independence, I would never have had to face the bully Kinsella, would never have been shot. And if it hadn't been for Adam Gaunt . . . Why, there was a thought to conjure with.

Late in December 1847, on Sir Robert Peel's recommendation, Jonas became Sir Jonas Oliver, which went a long way toward healing his disappointment at having no male heir. And willy-nilly,

Mademoiselle Valentine was transformed into Lady Oliver, which amused me greatly in those wild moments by myself in the garden, when the hidden, secret Rachel was allowed to be alone with her thoughts.

———

It seemed, for a time, as if Fate had finished with me. My family in St. John's were no more than a memory, only Lizzie's occasional letters reminded me that my years in Independence were more than a dream, and even Adam Gaunt was reduced at last to the face of a long-lost stranger in a tarnished silver frame. Was I happy? I was content, at least, and I counted my blessings.

And then, one spring morning in 1848, Aunt Grace climbed a little stiffly from her brougham in front of my door, her face glowing with the momentous news she had to tell me. The words came bubbling out even before we reached the peace of my sitting room.

"My dear—" she screeched, snatching at my arm, "—you'll never guess what I have to tell you! Prepare yourself!" Then a sudden thought struck her. "Perhaps you should sit down—are you carrying again, child?"

"No, Aunt Grace, no more babies. Just tell me what's happened."

"It's *Reuben!* Yes—*your* Reuben! Your brother, all the way from St. John's, and a great, strapping lad he's turned out to be, too."

"Reuben's come to find me? Oh, Aunt Grace—I can hardly believe it! When did he arrive in Liverpool? What did he say? Why didn't he come here, to the White House?" I besieged her with questions, and she waved me away.

"Now, Rachel—all in good time. And yes, dear, it's true he came to find you . . . True in a way, at any rate. You must remember that your mother . . . Well—you see, Reuben just arrived at the house one day, just came up to Leghorn Street as soon as his ship docked, and he was *there* on the doorstep when Jessie opened the door—and I thought 'Good Heavens, who's this great, sturdy fellow come to visit?' and then he told us who he was—Reuben Dean, my nephew from Newfoundland, and I suppose he does have a *look* of Susannah—"

"But what did he say about *me?* Did he know I was married again, and that I had Matthew and my babies—"

"Rachel, my dear, he never knew you'd been married at all. 'I've come here, he said, *to see where my poor sister died.*' "

Aunt Grace fell silent, and gazed at me with soft, piteous eyes. This time I did sit down, as the world roared in my ears and the room swam dizzily before my eyes.

"Died?" I echoed stupidly. "He thought I was *dead?"*

"And why should he think that? *Well may you ask,"* snapped Aunt Grace indignantly. "He thought you were dead because my sister—my nasty, ill-natured sister—went back to St. John's after your marriage, and told your poor father and Maria and your brothers that you'd fallen ill of scarlet fever here, in Liverpool, and that you'd died—died in her arms, the wretch—shortly after she arrived at your bedside. Oh, she painted a pretty picture of your sufferings —bloated and black with fever, and I don't know all what. Reuben certainly believed it, poor lamb, and of course she kept all my letters locked away in her desk to prevent anyone from finding out the truth, although your father must have discovered it wasn't so. Oh, she's a wicked woman, my sister! I won't *tell* you what the Captain called her."

"And where's Reuben now? What did he say when you told him? Is he coming here to see me?"

"Now wait, Rachel—just wait and I'll tell you everything in my own way. Reuben's ship—he's an officer on the *Maid of Corinth,* by all accounts—his ship put into Liverpool two days ago, and he took the chance of seeking out the aunt he'd never seen and hearing exactly how his beloved sister died—for that was what he called you, my dear. *His beloved sister.* He'd remembered, by good luck, that my husband was a sea-captain, and that his ship was the *Spartacus,* and of course as soon as he asked a few questions in the docks the seafaring folk told him exactly where to find us." My aunt smiled wanly at the memory.

"Oh, he was so shocked to learn of what his mother had done— and so happy, so happy to know you were still alive! He was all for coming here straight away to see you, but the Captain said . . . Thomas said *no,* not all of a sudden like that. You're not as strong as you were, Rachel, with all these confinements, and the shock wouldn't have been good for you. And also, when you remember that Jonas Oliver knows nothing about . . . Well, I presume he knows nothing about . . . how you came to marry Adam, and to quarrel with your mother . . . Well—the Captain felt it'd be bound to come out if Reuben arrived at the White House just like that. And so he sent me here to prepare you—and to tell you that Reuben will be at our house in Leghorn Street this afternoon, so that you can meet him and tell him yourself all your good news!"

How can I describe that meeting? After it was over, all I can remember was weeping tears of joy against Reuben's brass-buttoned coat and marveling at the height and breadth of my almost-twenty-year-old brother, so changed from the gangling child I remembered leaving behind in St. John's.

He'd run off to sea, my tall, gray-eyed brother, when he was barely fifteen—walked to the city in the middle of the night and persuaded the skipper of a topsail schooner in St. John's harbor to sign him on as deckhand and cook. By the time my raging mother learned about Reuben's escape, the *Molly* had passed far beyond the horizon and my brother was free.

"I couldn't stay a day longer in that house," he told me, a frown knotting his sunburned brow. "I never knew what Mother was going to do next. One minute she'd be all over me—almost—well—almost like a lover, if you can imagine that; and then a few moments later she'd be shouting at me for some little thing I was supposed to have done wrong."

Reuben shook his head in perplexity.

"Edward was always her favorite—he's supposed to be taking over the business, and he'd never do anything to spoil his chances. Susan Vinegar—do you remember Susan Vinegar, Rachel?—Susan's like my mother's second self now, spying on everyone and going back to tell tales. And Maria—Maria should've been married years ago, but Mother's never found anyone good enough for her precious daughter. Do you remember how pretty she was? Well, she isn't so pretty now. If she gets a husband now it'll be thanks to Mother's money, I reckon. I know I've spoiled my chances of getting a penny —she's told me as much already—but I don't give a damn. I like the life I'm leading, and it suits me. I'm second mate, Rachel, through my own hard work, and I'm almost qualified for master, though of course I'm too young for a command."

"Reuben—when Papa died . . . What really happened?"

The joyous beam faded from Reuben's face.

"Well, you know how he drank."

"But he wasn't drinking so much when I left St. John's."

"Ah, but then Florence Sutter was there to take his mind off the bottle. I suppose you know they were having an affair?"

"Are you sure? My stars!" It had never occurred to me there might be more to Miss Sutter than simple governess. "Thank Heavens Mamma never knew!"

"Of course she knew! Nothing ever happened in that house without her knowing it, believe me. No doubt she thought Miss Sutter was a convenient way of keeping her husband at home—until Florence became greedy and began to demand furs and jewelry from her lover. There was an almighty row one morning, I remember—all three of them in Mother's study—and the governess was gone by dinnertime.

"After she left Father began to drink again; I don't know how often he was fetched back from town, unconscious with drink. Mother fairly screamed at him sometimes—you could hear her all over the house. And then after a while she went quiet . . . You remember how she did that sometimes, and we all knew that some trouble was brewing? Well, suddenly Father stopped going into town at all, and just stayed at home to drink. And there was always brandy there—as much of it as he wanted, *she* saw to that." Reuben shook his head again, bewildered by the wickedness of it all.

"From that day on, Father was never sober. He started first thing in the morning, sip-sipping from some bottle or other, and it went on all day. Mother almost seemed to encourage him. There were no more rows, and he could have as much as he liked—though strangely enough, he was more decent to me in those last weeks than at any time I can remember."

"He died of it, then?"

"Must have, I reckon. First off, he complained that his back was sore all the time; then he began to spend every day in that big carver in the dining room, staring out at the garden with a glass in his hand and a bottle on the table beside him. Mother used to come in and fill the glass for him, I remember. Then after a bit he took to his bed, and seemed to get thinner and thinner. And the pain was pretty bad, then. I sat with him sometimes, and it was all he could do to keep still. He knew he was dying, all right."

"He tried to send me some money in secret, you know. He must have found out somehow that I was still alive, and he wrote out a kind of will—"

"So that's what it was!" Reuben lifted his hands from his knees in sudden comprehension. "I knew there'd been a row about something. Mother found out he'd been rifling her desk—reading her letters from Aunt Grace, and so on. That must have been how he found out you were still alive, and I suppose he tried to draw up a will then. Mother was almost too angry to speak—and she burned a paper, I remember. She lit it from the candle by his bed and burned it before his eyes . . . Black ash even dropped on the sheet before she'd throw the pieces into the grate. He was in tears, Rachel. She pushed us out of the room, but I could hear him sobbing . . . He died not long afterward. And that was when I decided I had to run away to sea. I tried to live with her, Rachel—it just wasn't possible."

I shook my head in disbelief. Why all the hatred? What compelled my mother to tear her family apart in that way?

"So now you know why I left home," Reuben was saying. "But I can hardly believe what she's done to you. Why did she tell us you were dead? What did you do that was so bad?"

"I married a man she hated, Reuben. That was my crime. I married him without her permission, and she never forgave me."

"But Sir Jonas is absolutely respectable now, surely—"

"It wasn't Jonas. Jonas Oliver is my second husband. Before Jonas I was married to a man named Adam Gaunt, and I went off with him to America."

"Oh." Reuben frowned. "What happened to him?"

"He died in an accident in the Rocky Mountains. Matthew is Adam Gaunt's son."

But of course, Reuben had never met Matthew, or my daughters, or Jonas. Thankfully, when they did meet and I could explain that this great strapping fellow was my brother who'd gone to sea and had come to visit me after years apart, Jonas and Reuben seemed to approve of one another, though even after weeks had passed Reuben still went in awe of the head of the Oliver empire. In the meantime, however, Jonas had discovered that Reuben was a good seaman and a clever navigator, and as a kindness to me, he suggested that Reuben sign on as second mate of the *Rachel Oliver,* where he'd be well placed for future promotion in the Oliver fleet.

And that was how, at the end of 1848, my brother Reuben left Liverpool for New York on a voyage which would end more than a year later by reawakening the ghosts of my past to turn my quiet, comfortable world completely topsy-turvy.

PART THREE
The River

20

Long before the *Rachel Oliver* reached New York, Jonas had changed his plans for her. Across the Atlantic a cry had gone up from beyond the Rocky Mountains, a cry powerful enough to make the carpenter throw down his chisels, the student desert his books and the farmhand leave his plough where it stood.

GOLD! GOLD AT SUTTER'S MILL!

The company agents in New York sent Jonas a copy of the *Daily Tribune* describing the gold fields as "the new El Dorado, where fortune lies abroad upon the surface of the earth as plentiful as the mud in our streets." The advertising columns were crammed full of lectures on the geology of California or the wildlife of its sierras, or simply on the gold, gold, gold which lay about in great nuggets on the surface of the earth and glinted as dust in the rivers.

Almost daily, stories filtered back to the east of tea-caddies full of gold dust and nuggets as big as a man's two fists; why—even a boy could grub up a lifetime's wages from the dirt underfoot in a few short months. Gripped by gold fever, the *Tribune* reported, men were thronging west with pick and shovel, a few spare woolen shirts, a guidebook to the diggings and unbounded hope in their hearts. Some, for Heaven's sake, even took evening dress in anticipation of the high times to come.

I read the newspaper reports with sadness, thinking of those great mountains which for so long had been a barrier crossed only by the hardy and resourceful. Now the westward tide had turned into a torrent, and the torrent into a flood of humankind. The gold-hunters were a different breed from the patiently plodding settlers. These new Argonauts raced overland or crowded into any craft which seemed likely to float its way to the gold fields, desperate to claim their share of the spoils. Before long the Californian soil would be ploughed up with pick and shovel; miners would swarm over the ravaged slopes of the sierras, damming streams and stealing creek-water to wash the precious golden grains from the silt. The Plough-man's furrow would soon run, straight and wide, from the Atlantic Ocean to the shores of the Pacific, and just as Adam had feared, there would no longer be any place for the Hunter.

But even while I brooded over the yellowing pages of the *Tribune*, Jonas had thought of a way of winning some of the Californian wealth for himself. So New York was crowded with men urgently seeking a passage to the gold fields? Here was the *Rachel Oliver*, about to dock at any moment: *ergo,* combine the two and there was a guarantee of instant profit. Rather than leave the roomy Oliver ship waiting at her pier for a cargo, she could be fitted out with tiered bunks, filled to bursting with miners and sent off to California. Jonas wrote at once to the agents, and I resigned myself to many months without my brother, who would twice have rounded Cape Horn before I saw him again.

────────

By midsummer 1849, we reckoned, the *Rachel Oliver* should be safely in San Francisco Bay; but long before that rumors began to reach the Oliver offices in Liverpool that no ship anchoring off the gold-rush coast could count herself wholly out of danger. One mas-ter recently returned from New York brought tales of mass desertion by gold-hungry sailors as soon as the San Francisco shoreline came into plain sight. And these were no mere seamen's yarns—he himself had heard the stories from a steamer captain newly in from the Isthmus with the California mail.

Jonas immediately dismissed any idea of harm coming to the *Rachel Oliver*—at least, always in my hearing.

"Ferris is an excellent commander," he insisted. "A fine man. A religious man. Won't stand any nonsense from his crew. Reuben will be perfectly safe, my dear, and home before you know it. There's absolutely no need to worry."

Then as December approached with no word of the ship's return, we began to notice the name "San Francisco" more often in our newspapers, followed by an account of deserted vessels crowding its anchorage, stranded without men to sail them home. Some ships, added the reports, were rotting where they lay or had been run ashore to be converted into makeshift lodging-houses for the swell-ing population of the city.

Jonas almost exploded at the thought of his fine ship high and dry on the beach, cut up into windows and doorways for the accommodation of grimy miners, but I was now greatly concerned about Reuben, and as the months passed without any news of him, I grew more and more anxious.

At last at the end of April, to our great relief, word came from the Oliver people in New York to say that the *Rachel Oliver* had been sighted by a steamer bound from Panama to New York, and was expected to reach port in a couple of weeks. Instantly Jonas was plunged into a fever of impatience to know what had delayed his ship: within hours, he'd decided to set out for New York on the first available vessel and hear the story at firsthand.

There was no question of my going with him, and so I waited at home to worry about Reuben until such time as Jonas returned or remembered to send me some news.

But Reuben was safe: I learned that much from a brief letter of his own which arrived a fortnight later, though he said little beyond adding that there had been "some trouble" among the crew and that the ship had indeed been stranded at San Francisco. When he returned to Liverpool Jonas too was strangely evasive about whatever had happened aboard the *Rachel Oliver*. All he'd tell me was that the crew had deserted their posts and run off to the gold fields, and that Reuben, left by a series of disasters the senior officer aboard, had somehow managed to scratch up a handful of seamen and sail the vessel home.

Here was astonishing news! My own brother—loyal, earnest Reuben—sailing Jonas's favorite ship through the storms of Cape Horn! It was almost beyond belief, and I was furious at Jonas's refusal to tell me every exciting detail.

"No doubt Reuben will tell you the whole story when the *Rachel* gets in."

Jonas had returned by steamer from New York as soon as he'd satisfied himself that his ship was safe, leaving Reuben to sail the *Rachel Oliver* home. "Your brother's uncommonly pleased with himself, I may say—though the boy has done well, there's no doubt of it."

"Done well? So I should think! By the sound of it, he's singlehandedly saved your ship for you!" How dare Jonas be so grudging!

"Yes, I suppose he did save her . . . Reuben and—ah . . . Well, yes, you're right my dear, Reuben was principally responsible for bringing the vessel back. I don't think anyone would dispute that, and I've told him he may keep command of her for the time being."

"You said he was *principally* responsible. Was there someone else, then?"

"Did I say that? No, no, Reuben is undoubtedly the hero of the hour. You can make as much fuss of him as you please when he comes home." We were having breakfast at the time, and I saw Jonas set his teacup down with deliberation and rise to leave for the office.

"Wait, Jonas, please. How can you tell me you've just made my brother the youngest master in the Oliver fleet, and then disappear off to your office with hardly a word of explanation? Besides—you started to say 'Reuben *and*—' and then you stopped."

"Did I?" As always, Jonas pushed his empty chair symmetrically up to the table.

"Yes, you did." I had no particular reason for pursuing the point, except that I hated the way Jonas was being so secretive about something which concerned my brother. I saw him frown uncomfortably, embarrassed by some memory he didn't want to share. "Who else was involved in this, Jonas?"

"Oh . . ." Jonas drummed his hands on the back of his chair. ". . . Nobody really. Just a rather strange fellow who helped Reuben out in San Francisco. Called himself 'Colonel,' though I'm certain he'd never seen army lines in his life. Disreputable sort of man. Handsome enough manners, but no doubt on the run from the law. You'll see ten of his kind any day in the dock at the Old Bailey."

"Nevertheless, he was kind to my brother?"

"So it seems. Though I'm sure he had his own reasons for getting Reuben out of trouble. He provided a crew, by all accounts, in exchange for a passage to New York."

"Then you actually met the man!"

Jonas began to move toward the door. "He joined us for dinner ashore one night. Reuben seemed to think I ought to thank the fellow —but I got his measure straight away, believe me. A blackguard through and through, just out for what he could get. No doubt he expected a reward."

"But didn't you offer him one? After he'd saved your ship?"

"Offer him money? A man like that? I should think not! Good Heavens, Rachel, sometimes I wonder at you!"

With a great snort of indignation Jonas finally escaped, and I was compelled to bide my time, more curious than ever, until Reuben came back to us.

The lilacs in the most distant corner of the White House grounds had almost shed their heavy, scented blossom by the time Reuben returned. I'd had an arbor built there, a trellised wooden retreat with an arched roof where I could sit alone on sunny days or find a refuge from summer showers. Soon after it was finished, a delicate ivy took the little arbor for its own, clinging lovingly to the arches in living festoons of green, smothering the dainty roof right up to its pointed white finial until the original graceful shape was lost in a tumult of leaves.

This was where I took Reuben just as soon as I could carry him off from the polite formalities of the house.

"Now," I said, "tell me everything. All that's happened to you while I've been here, worrying myself to a shadow. I want to hear every last little bit."

"You already know most of the story, it seems to me."

"I certainly don't! Last time I saw you, you were an insignificant second mate with your buttons still shiny on your new coat, and now you come sailing back from San Francisco *Captain Dean,* a dashing hero—and you just shrug when I ask you how it all came about, as if it was the most natural thing in the world!"

"As Jonas said—I stuck to my duty to the company. And in any case, he rather hinted that I shouldn't alarm you."

"Alarm me? Reuben—I'm your sister, not your maiden aunt. Surely I've a right to know all your adventures?"

"Well . . ." Reuben was clearly torn between pride in his great exploits and Jonas's possible displeasure if he talked about them. "Oh, hang it all!" he burst out. "What harm can it do?"

He leaned forward eagerly on the wooden bench, his eyes shining, and I realized how much he'd wanted to share the story with me all along.

"It was the Captain's fault, really—all the trouble, I mean— though plenty of other ships lost their crews in the same way, goodness knows. Did Jonas tell you Ferris is dead? Well he is—shot with his own pistol when he tried to stop his men running off to join the miners. Yet he drove them to it himself. From the day we left New York he had a bee in his bonnet about this blessed gold rush: he used to preach to us twice a week—ranted at us, passengers and crew alike—about working for the *Devil's wages* and how we were all on a short ride to Hell.

"Day or night, he had both watches on deck; no one was allowed to rest for a moment. If hard work could save the men's souls, then that's what he'd give them. Oh, he sailed the ship like a dream, but by the time we put into Valparaiso for water I reckon he was completely crazy."

"Oh, Reuben, how dreadful! Jonas was so sure Captain Ferris could deal with any trouble—and yet he was the cause of it all!"

"The men had other reasons, too. The miners had been visiting the fo'c'sle, spreading tales of the gold nuggets to be found everywhere at the diggings, and it must have sounded like Paradise after life aboard the *Rachel*. Perhaps if the old Mate had still been with us . . . but he'd fallen from the mainyard two months out of New York and died of his injuries. So when the crew turned on the officers and tried to jump ship, they took us completely by surprise. That's when Ferris was shot—by accident, maybe, or perhaps a settling of old scores. When I went to help him they laid me out with a belaying-pin. Look—you can still see the scar."

Reuben bent his head to show me a curving, purple-white mark at his hairline, and I began to realize how easily I might never have seen him again. To have found my brother after so long, only to lose him in such a way—perhaps Captain Ferris had been right after all, and the Devil's gold brought nothing but disaster.

"You might have been killed, Reuben! And all for a handful of dust!"

"Oh, I don't think so," Reuben said matter-of-factly. "The men had no grudge against me, they just wanted to get ashore as soon as possible and out to the diggings. No—the worst part was that with Ferris and the Mate both gone, I was left in sole charge of the *Rachel Oliver*—my first command, with no crew to sail her."

"No one at all?"

"Just Brodie and Vaughan, the other two mates, and the bosun, the chips and the cook—and a couple of older seamen who had families in Liverpool and stayed on the ship. Eight of us, all told."

"But why didn't you just leave the *Rachel* where she was, and make your own way home? Jonas could hardly have blamed you."

"Do you really think so?" Reuben shot me a disbelieving glance. "Then you don't know Jonas, I fear. I lay there in my bunk, my head throbbing, imagining the lecture I'd get if I came home without the *Rachel Oliver*. *I trusted you, Reuben. . . . I expected better than this of my wife's brother. . . . How could you turn your back on my ship without even trying to save her . . .*" Reuben managed a passable imitation of Jonas at his most pompous, and I was forced to laugh.

"He'd never have said such things! He does try to be fair, you know."

"Maybe he does. But I didn't think it would help my ambitions to be master of my own vessel if I turned up in Liverpool with my tail between my legs, having abandoned the first ship that was well and truly *mine*. A ship named after my sister, too." He reached out to squeeze my hand. "I could hardly leave that to rot in the bay, now could I?

"No—I was determined to bring the *Rachel* back somehow, though I can't say the situation was very encouraging. Yerba Buena Cove was almost full of abandoned ships—brand-new full-riggers, barks, schooners, brigantines—it would have broken your heart to see them all. And every man-jack aboard them run off to the gold fields." He shook his head in amazement at the memory, and for an instant I envied him his adventure. Despite the danger, there'd been challenge—and *life*—in that far-off place in a way I'd long since forgotten.

Fortunately, Reuben was too absorbed in his tale to notice my wistful expression.

"My first thought was to make inquiries ashore, in case any of our own men were still in San Francisco and having second thoughts about what they'd done. There's a beach, you see, about a mile out of town, where the incoming miners all get together. They've built a village out of tents and packing-cases where they wait until they've collected a big enough party to travel out to the diggings in the Sierra.

"In the end I found one or two of our old crew—Fiddick, MacSween, Beale the quartermaster—decent enough men who'd fallen in with the wrong crowd. But they told me they'd made an agreement to stick with the others for safety's sake, and I couldn't persuade them to come back to the ship."

"I hope you had them arrested and charged with mutiny!"

"Arrested? Rachel, you're talking about San Francisco, not Liverpool. A couple of years ago, the place hardly existed: now it's full to bursting with gold-crazed men, and more of them arrive every day —Americans, Chinese, Mexicans, South Sea Islanders . . . Nobody cares where a man came from, or what he did before he got there.

San Francisco's a paradise for gamblers and swindlers and cutthroats of all kinds, believe me."

"How dreadful!" Yet I was anxious to hear more. "Go on with your story, then. If no one was interested in anything but digging for gold, however did you find men to sail the *Rachel Oliver* home?"

Reuben studied his boots, suddenly tongue-tied. "I didn't do it all myself," he admitted at last.

"Ah!" Here was the mystery which had absorbed me for days. "The famous Colonel! Now, I certainly want to hear about *him*. Jonas was so disapproving, the man must be absolutely fascinating."

"I really don't think I should say anything about him."

"Why ever not?"

"Jonas wouldn't like it."

I almost shook him in my frustration. "Oh, Reuben, for goodness' sake! You can't tell *half* a story, and then suddenly refuse to finish it. At least tell me why Jonas loathes this man so much, if he was the means of saving his ship."

"Did Jonas tell you that?" Reuben sounded aggrieved. "It wasn't my fault the two of them fell out. I tried to warn Jonas that the Colonel wasn't exactly what he thought; after all, I'd sailed back with him from San Francisco, and I knew what he was like.

"But Jonas wouldn't listen. He took one look at the Colonel and assumed he held army rank—and before I could stop him, he'd invited the man to have dinner with us at the Astor House. *If you can spare the time from your military duties*—that sort of thing. He even gave him some old copies of *The Times* he'd brought over from England. Insisted he take them."

"And yet Jonas told me the Colonel was a brigand!"

"Ah, yes—that's what he decided later—during dinner, when he began to quiz the Colonel on his army career and discovered his rank was more honorary than real. It happens all the time in California, you see—even the surveyor-general of the district is known as General Smith. Everyone's a major at the very least. And the Colonel just —well—suited the title, I suppose. It seemed to fit him."

"Oh." The more I heard, the more puzzled I became.

"And then, in the course of the meal the whole story came out. I don't know how Jonas imagined the Colonel had helped me to find a crew for the *Rachel*—marched a regiment of marines up the gangplank, perhaps—but when he discovered exactly how it was done

. . . However pleased he was to see his ship back, he didn't want to have anything to do with any *unpleasantness* that might have been involved."

"What sort of unpleasantness?"

"Well . . . persuading men to sign on, if you see what I mean. Usually by getting them drunk or drugging them."

"Kidnapping?" I was horrified. "Just taking ordinary people off the street?"

"Seamen, mostly. I'm afraid it's quite common in the big ports." Reuben sighed, and seemed to decide that the truth had better be told, if only to redeem himself in his sister's eyes.

"You see, when the *Rachel*'s men refused to come back to her, I was at my wit's end. I mean, there were masters with a lifetime's experience stranded in the same port. If they couldn't raise a crew, how was I supposed to manage it? I tried asking here and there—and as often as not, I was told *Go and speak to Colonel Allen. If anyone can find you a crew for your ship, he can.* No one seemed to know much about him, except that he'd been in San Francisco since long before gold was found—and that nothing ever happened in the city without the Colonel getting to hear of it. *Ask for him at the 'Chin Hua,'* they said. *The Gold Blossom. Old Wang Chen will know where to find him.*"

Reuben paused, and I urged him on. "And what was the Gold Blossom? A restaurant of some kind?"

"A gaming-house, principally. Fan-tan tables—that kind of thing." I sensed that he was being evasive.

"And?"

"And there were . . . ah . . . women. Young Chinese girls. In little rooms."

"A brothel? Is that what you mean?"

"Well—yes. And there was another room at the back, lit by a few Chinese lamps, where men were lying on mats on the floor, smoking opium."

"And that's where you found Wang Chen?"

"Wang Chen and the Colonel, though I didn't realize it at first. They were playing backgammon in a corner, with a whisky bottle on the table between them, and a couple of glasses. Heaven knows what I expected to find in that ghastly den—and certainly Wang Chen had a face that'll haunt my dreams till the day I die, though the Colonel himself looked . . . normal, I suppose you'd say. Normal

—and yet he gave the impression of a man who was tired of living."
Reuben shrugged. "I can't describe it any other way."

Something in Reuben's voice told me how much the scene had
affected him, and warned me not to inquire further.

"But the Colonel agreed to help you."

"Hardly! He promised me a crew, all right, but at a price no one
in creation could pay. I don't think he cared whether we did business
or not. At any rate, I called him a robber and stormed out of the
place."

"Oh, Reuben, how brave of you!"

"Brave, perhaps, but not very clever. You see, if I'd only thought
. . . I didn't need a whole crew for the *Rachel*. All I needed was a
scratch crew to sail her as far as Callao, where I could ship more
men for the passage to New York. *That's* the bargain I should've
made with the Colonel. Just for a part-crew." Reuben looked somewhat shame-faced. "The trouble was, I didn't think of that until very
late in the evening, and by that time I'd been in and out of every bar
in San Francisco." He threw up his hands in frustration. "I couldn't
help it, Sis. I thought I'd lost my last chance of saving my ship."

"Well, never mind." I gave his arm a sympathetic squeeze. "Tell
me what happened next."

"When I realized—when I grasped the fact that I could make do
with maybe fifteen or sixteen men—I decided to go back to the Gold
Blossom and try to make my peace with the Colonel. But it was a
hard place to find, and I suppose I was very drunk by then. At any
rate, just when I'd turned down an alleyway which I reckoned ran
down one side of the Chin Hua, two men jumped me—robbers,
armed with knives. I struggled like blazes, of course, and landed
a couple of good blows; but they soon knocked me on my face in
the mud, and one of them was just about to cut my throat—like
this—"

"Reuben!"

"Oh—sorry, Rachel. At any rate, I was sure I was done for, when
a door opened nearby and someone looked out. I heard a voice call,
'What in Heaven's name is going on out here?' followed by great
scuffles and thuds in the darkness; people kept trampling over me
. . . And suddenly there was silence except for the sound of someone
running away and another pair of feet walking slowly toward me."
Reuben clasped his hands between his knees. "Of all people, it was
the Colonel. He'd heard the noise in the alley at the side of the Gold
Blossom, and come out to see what was happening."

"And he'd scared off the robbers! How lucky!"

"Only one of them ran away. The other man was dead, further down the lane, with the Colonel's knife in his heart."

"Oh, gracious Heavens . . ."

"It was his life or mine, Rachel."

"But to kill a man so casually—"

"So expertly, you mean: I never even heard a groan . . ."

"Reuben! How can you say such things!" Yet now I began to understand the awe in which he held the Colonel; I'd even begun to share it myself.

"There's no doubt the man saved my life—though he didn't know I was the robbers' victim, as he was at great pains to point out. *I'd have done the same for any poor fool*—that's what he said, as if he couldn't have cared less. Yet once I'd pulled myself together he took me off to a Mexican bar to sober up on strong coffee, and read me a lecture on drunken sailors who blunder about the back streets, begging to be attacked.

"What with the whisky I'd drunk and the sheer relief of being alive, I remember telling him all about the ship, and about Jonas, and the fact that the *Rachel* was named after my sister, and how I'd found you again after so many years apart . . . I must have bored him silly. But when I'd finished he gave me a strange look, as if something I'd said had brought back an old memory, and then sat silent for a few moments, just staring at the whisky in his glass. Next thing I knew, he'd offered to find me enough men to take the ship safely to Callao, and all for the price of a passage to New York. Would you credit it? That's all he wanted—a passage to New York for himself, bag and baggage. The only condition was that we were to leave San Francisco when it suited him—not a day sooner or later."

I shuddered. "I don't know how you could allow a man like that aboard your ship." Not only did the Colonel have blood on his hands—he was a man *tired of living*. Who would want such a comrade in the storms of Cape Horn?

"I can't say I was particularly happy about it. But he was offering me a chance of saving the vessel, even though he kept us waiting in the bay all through November and December. Believe it or not, it was Christmas Eve when he finally decided to leave. That's when the fire broke out near the Plaza . . . Oh, Rachel, you should have seen the blaze—a great red glow hanging over the city just before dawn, spurts of orange flame everywhere, and a fearful crashing and roar-

ing as the fire leaped from one building to the next. The wooden
houses and the gambling-halls burned like straw, and the paint-
stores were turned into torches . . . And then in the midst of all the
uproar a boat put out from the shore—a big black boat, creeping
toward us like a beetle across the shining water. It was the Colonel,
bringing the men he'd promised—seamen, most of them, as I told
you, though there were a few miners and army deserters among them
—all of them drunk, or drugged by his Chinese friends."

"Do you think it's possible he started the fire himself?"

Reuben shrugged. "Who knows? Though even if he had nothing
to do with it, I'll bet he knew the fire was going to happen. Why else
should he choose that particular day to leave? Not that it made any
difference: we had to sail for Callao at once, before any of the men
in the fo'c'sle could come to their senses."

"And you told Jonas all this over dinner? You must have been
mad! No wonder he was so upset!"

"Good gracious, no—I told him very little of it! But I had to
explain how I'd come by a crew to sail the *Rachel Oliver* to Callao,
and even that was more than enough for Jonas. It wasn't that he
minded picking up a crew in such a disreputable way—it was simply
that the man who'd arranged it all was sitting calmly at his dinner
table, drinking his wine and smoking one of his cigars. A man no
better than a brigand, to Jonas's way of thinking. And Jonas didn't
know the half of it."

Poor Reuben—no wonder he'd been so anxious to confide in me.

"And I'm afraid the evening ended rather badly." Reuben looked
glumly at his boots. "You know how smug Jonas can be sometimes?
It's true, Rachel, even you must admit it—and for some reason he
was at his very worst that night, perhaps because he was so pleased
to have his ship back safe and sound, or perhaps it was just that he
felt particularly virtuous compared to the two sinners sitting across
the table from him. At any rate, he told us a long story about how
the ship was named after his very dear wife, whom he'd married as
a penniless widow after her husband had died adventuring in the
wilds of America—except he made it sound as if the poor man had
done it out of sheer fecklessness—and he made a great drama of
how you'd been left in very poor circumstances, never dreaming that
one day you'd have a queen of the seas named for you—"

"Oh, Reuben, he didn't!" Though even as I spoke I could hear
Jonas's voice in my head, preaching his moral tale.

"He said all that and more, I'm afraid. If he'd claimed to have found you selling matches in the street, it couldn't have sounded worse. Anyway, the Colonel stood it as long as he could, and then he suddenly said his piece and left."

"What did he say, exactly?"

"Not much, when I come to think of it. It was more the way he said it—very soft and cold. *How fortunate Lady Oliver has been to find such a paragon for a husband.*"

"That's all he said?"

"Just that."

"That doesn't sound so awful."

"You didn't hear him say it. Or see the look in his eyes. Jonas was scared to death, I can tell you." Reuben frowned, trying to recapture the moment. "And yet I can't think what upset the Colonel so much. He was just . . . very angry, all of a sudden; there seemed to be a kind of bitterness inside him that could blaze up without any warning."

Something in Reuben's story stirred old memories of my own, for hadn't I known that bitterness myself? No amount of comfortable living among the Olivers would ever heal the scars of those lonely months as an outcast, struggling to survive in the shadow of a growing town—hiding, deceiving, showing one face by day and another by night, and yes—sometimes *tired of living,* for who had a better right to such weariness? We were kindred spirits, Reuben's Colonel and I, the Colonel with his knife and his backgammon board and I with my scarlet feathers. If the Colonel had found a pleasant game of backgammon in a Chinese brothel, then good luck to him.

"Well, I hope your Colonel is a happier man now, wherever he's gone," I observed aloud.

"He's a very rich one, that's certain. You should have seen the gold—" Reuben stopped abruptly, shocked at what he'd been about to say. He seemed embarrassed, and looked away.

"What gold should I have seen?"

"Nothing. I promised I wouldn't tell anyone."

I knew I should have left Reuben to guard his secret, but by now I was in the grip of an overwhelming passion to know everything there was to know about the enigmatic Colonel. I was possessed by it; fascinated; I simply had to find out whatever it was Reuben had promised not to reveal. And to my shame I knew exactly how to make him tell me.

"So the Colonel showed you the spoils of his crimes, did he? And swore you to silence? That was unfair of him, I think."

"It wasn't like that, Rachel, believe me. It's just that—it was all so amazing I said it would be a fine tale to tell Jonas . . . And he flew into a rage and made me promise not to tell a soul. Not a soul."

"Not Jonas, at any rate."

"No one, he said."

"He could hardly have meant your sister, Reuben! In any case—" I took a breath "—I don't think I want to hear any more about your dreadful Colonel and his wickedness. Jonas was obviously quite right: the man was no more than a common swindler."

For a few seconds, Reuben wrestled with his conscience.

"Rachel, if I tell you the story, will you give me your word not to tell Jonas?"

"Of course." The words slid out so easily I was astonished at my deceit.

"Oh, very well then. I can't see what harm it would do." Reuben leaned forward eagerly, his hands on his knees, his eyes bright with conspiracy.

"The bargain I'd made with the Colonel, if you remember, was that I'd carry him to New York along with whatever baggage he wanted to bring."

"I remember that."

"I expected . . . Well, I don't quite know what I expected, and yet when the Colonel's baggage came aboard there was hardly anything of it—just an old valise and some books and other things, less than a fo'c'sle hand might take aboard his next ship. And part of it was downright odd—an old flintlock rifle and two kegs of rifle-balls— two small, heavy wooden kegs, with the lead balls rolling about loose inside. You could hear them rattle as the kegs were set down on deck.

"I had it all carried aft to his cabin, but it puzzled me no end, I can tell you. If the Colonel was afraid of mutiny, then why not bring pistols? Though he had those too, I discovered later . . . But a rifle like that was no good for anything but shooting gulls off the fore-tops'l-yard—and why bring so much lead for it? Did he think we'd be boarded by pirates? And there was something else which bothered me at the time, though I couldn't quite lay my hand on it then.

"But we'd not long rounded Cape Horn when someone sneaked aft and ransacked the officers' accommodation. I was pretty sure it was the steward we'd picked up in Callao, but at any rate, the thief made a thorough search of my cabin—fortunately without finding the money I'd hidden behind some paneling—and then went through the Colonel's quarters in the same way. He'd even splintered the wood at the top of each of the little kegs—you could see the gray rifle-balls rolling around in the space below.

"*No doubt he expected to find gold in those,* the Colonel said. And suddenly it came to me. Two kegs of rifle-balls—but no powder, or none that I'd seen. Yet when I asked the Colonel about it he didn't answer; he just smiled, and touched his finger to his lips, like that." And Reuben made the sign for silence.

"I only found out the truth when we reached New York. The Colonel went off at once in a cab with his valise and his gun and his wooden kegs, and I didn't see him until later in the day, when he came aboard again just before Jonas's dinner. He'd brought four of the lead balls back with him—as a keepsake for me, he said.

"Well, of course I'd no use for the wretched things. I can't remember what nonsense I produced by way of thanks, but the Colonel suddenly began to laugh. *And I thought you'd found me out, Captain Dean!* Without another word he rolled one of the rifle-balls to the brass corner of the desk, and smashed it flat with the ink-well. Absolutely flat, with one blow. And dammit, it was gold—solid gold —an ounce and a half of California's finest, at sixteen dollars to the ounce, covered with two coats of gray paint. The little kegs had been full of them—kegs made up by a Chinese carpenter, with a hollow space in the middle to keep the size and weight right for lead. We'd sailed back with more than fifty-one thousand dollars in gold, sitting there in that cabin for anyone to find. Which was why, the Colonel reckoned, any thief was bound to think it was worthless."

It had been the cunning of the friendless, always on guard.

"And where had it all come from, this gold, do you suppose?"

"Partly from land speculation, he said."

"Is that possible?"

"That's what he told me. That he'd come to California years ago, when San Francisco was still a peaceful little Mexican village, and bought land, intending to settle. Then when gold was discovered, the price of land went up seven times in a year—and the Colonel sold out, and bought more land where he expected people to build. And went on, lot by lot, piling up a fortune. It could be true, I suppose— plenty of other men have done the same."

Reuben frowned, and then added, "What I couldn't understand was why he'd risked carrying so much gold aboard the *Rachel;* I suggested he'd have done better to let the Miners' Bank ship it back east for him, and he admitted he'd done business with them in the past. *But with respect, Captain,* he said, *your ship could have ended up God knows where—and gold speaks every language in the world.*"

I shook my head, filled with conflicting emotions. "What an amazing man."

"*Amazing* is the least of it."

"And dear me, what a tale to tell!"

"But not to Jonas, Rachel. You promised to keep it a secret from Jonas."

"So I will, my dear, depend upon it." And I busied myself with a stray stem of ivy to hide my guilt-flushed face.

21

I took a secret, sinful delight in Reuben's tale of his voyage to the gold fields, and brooded over it for a long time. More than anything it made me realize how empty was my own existence, when I could only live through the adventures of others and through small scraps of news gleaned from reading Jonas's newspapers.

Shortly before Jonas left for New York to meet the *Rachel Oliver* I'd found just such a crumb of interest—a column or two of familiar names in the decorous pages of *The Times*.

DEATH OF THE EARL OF WELLBOROUGH

A gloom has been cast over a large part of the County of Norfolk by the sad news of the death last Friday of the Earl of Wellborough. Taken ill suddenly on the night of Thursday, he passed rapidly into unconsciousness and died peacefully next morning without regaining his senses. In private life as amiable as in public eminent, His Lordship was in his seventy-ninth year, and the memory of his virtue and distinguished character will long remain in the nation's mind. The patent of the peerage bears date 1616, and the title devolves on the Earl's eldest son, Henry, Viscount Ledgate, who was at his bedside during the last melancholy hours and now becomes 9th Earl of Wellborough.

The report went on to list the earl's political and military achievements, his enlightened contribution to farming on the flat lands of East Anglia and his dedication to the welfare of the Church of England. The earl's wife, Lady Catherine, having died many years before, the earl was survived by two sons—his heir and a younger son, Richard—and by two daughters, both well married, one to a lord lieutenant and the other to a duke's heir.

The old hypocrite, I thought, thinking of his third, unacknowledged son, hunted like an animal through the Fens by his bailiffs.

As well as the earl's huge country estates, reported *The Times,* he'd built up a large personal fortune in land within the boundaries of the City of London, most of which was expected to be divided among his children after other, smaller bequests had been made. An obituary by the Prime Minister followed on another page.

I'd no interest in the Prime Minister's platitudes. I thought only of Adam, dead almost ten years before the father he despised, cut off from his family. Would my own mother, too, pursue her hatred to the grave?

———

At least Reuben was home again, if only for a while. His presence in the White House was a welcome diversion from our dull and stuffy existence, and I loved to watch him leave for the Oliver offices in Water Street in his fine new tall hat, the symbol of his promotion to master. His command of the *Rachel Oliver* admitted him at last to the leather-bound Masters' Room, that holy of holies, the youngest captain ever to tread its Turkey carpet.

I envied him his sense of purpose. My own days were all too often empty, or filled with the fiddling social obligations which Verity Broadney insisted on.

There were many maddening things about Verity, but the worst of them was a thin, nasal whine of a voice which reminded me of the sound of chairs being drawn slowly across a wooden floor. A lecture from Verity could sound like the breakup of a prayer-meeting, setting my teeth on edge and making me want to rush for fresh air. Unfortunately, as Jonas's older sister she'd appointed herself the conscience of the family, with unchallenged right of entry to my drawing room whenever she wished.

And as Lady Oliver (though, as Verity pointed out, the wife of a provincial knight hardly ranked alongside a baronet's lady) I was duty-bound to take up a certain position in the city. Verity herself, imbued with this sense of *noblesse oblige,* spent much of her time sniffing into every corner of Liverpool and the districts round about, hunting down deserving objects of her charity and her moral precepts, which she dispensed with equal shrillness at one and the same time.

I knew only too well that her charity stopped short of me. She'd objected strongly to welcoming a jumped-up, fortune-hunting little widow into the Oliver family, and I'd heard—from various gleeful female "friends"—that she'd tried everything she could think of to prevent her brother's marriage.

But the marriage had taken place after all, and Verity had salved her injured feelings by doing her best to turn me into an Oliver. I knew from the start there was nothing to be gained by resistance, so I allowed myself to be co-opted on to the governing boards of poor houses and pauper schools, and to be drawn into endless Church bazaars requiring the embroidery of needle-cases and pen-wipers. At Verity's heels I inspected the workhouse midday meal on appointed Sundays, suffering inwardly for the haggard men and women standing humbly by their plates until the gentry were satisfied and the meal could proceed.

This was charity by committee, with no need ever to come face to face with the desperate families of dead seamen or the starving scavengers of the dockside middens. All the same, it did let me see how much could be done through Oliver money and influence.

And why shouldn't the Oliver family put their profits to good use? As often as not, they were profits wrung from the human cargoes carried in Oliver ships, the poor emigrants drawn by the promise of a better life in the New World if they could only survive the hunger and disease of the outward passage. By far the largest number of these people were Irish, but for every one who reached Liverpool and found a place among the fetid pack in the bowels of an outward-bound ship, two or three more got no further than Prince's Dock. Liverpool was swollen with an Irish invasion—famine-ridden country-folk gulled and preyed on by the low-life of the city, robbed of their pathetic possessions almost as soon as they set foot in the place. Never mind *noblesse oblige*—the Olivers were part of this traffic, and now an Oliver could help make amends.

Leaving Verity to her subscription teas, I toured the free hospitals asking what was needed to improve medical care and the patients' diet. I came away with long lists of food, instruments and linen, and set about hounding the city merchants into providing them. I found premises for free schools and hired teachers for them, and then begged and bullied Jonas's friends into becoming governors and trustees. But when I suggested one day to Verity that a notorious cotton-mill in which George Broadney "had an interest" might benefit from a medical officer, a schoolroom, a lending library and regular brass-band excursions for its workers, even Verity was moved to remark that my enthusiasm for the welfare of the lower orders was becoming a dangerous obsession.

Yet what else did I have to occupy my time? For I had plenty of time on my hands—those same hands which had worked hard in my cabin in Independence, or in Titus Meadow's store or Lizzie Fletcher's kitchen. Now I was mistress of a mansion run by a staff of servants who neither wanted nor needed my interference. If I dared to visit the kitchens, everyone stood stiffly to attention until I'd gone, and I could feel the cook's polite smile change to a resentful scowl as I retreated along the tiled corridor. I discussed menus with her and inspected the weekly accounts—Jonas was most particular on that point—but even these duties were more of a ritual than a necessity.

And yet unlike any of my elegant friends I could have done every household task almost as well as the maids I employed. Sometimes I itched to show a new girl how a rug should be thoroughly beaten or a steel grate cleaned. I often wondered how Verity would react to the news that Lady Oliver had been seen in the stable-yard splitting logs for kindling, or sitting on the kitchen step, plucking a chicken. I doubted very much if Verity was aware that chickens came with feathers in the first place.

Twelve-year-old Matthew was away at school now for months at a time, and even when he came home for the holidays he hardly seemed to need me at all. His indifference was all the more difficult to accept because for so long we'd been everything to one other, Mrs. Gaunt and her son; more than that, he was all I had left of Adam, and for that reason I'd tried to hold on to him for as long as I could. But Matthew had inherited his father's fierce independence, and the boyish battles of school had only encouraged his self-reliance and his swift rejection of any interference from me. Unfortunately it had also given him a swagger and a loudness which I regretted, and an alarming talent for spending money.

Matthew was clever, but lazy too unless a subject happened to interest him. Fortunately, while he'd long since forgotten his ambition to go to sea, the idea of making money from shipping began to fascinate him, and he plagued his stepfather again and again to take him to the docks whenever Oliver vessels were in port, and where even the most senior masters, in Jonas's hearing, called him *Mister Matthew*. I never found out what they called him behind my husband's back.

Jonas was surprised and pleased by Matthew's interest, and willingly took him wherever he asked. And I was happy to see them together: I still felt guilty over my failure to give Jonas a son to inherit his shipping empire, though Jonas always treated Matthew as his own child and never mentioned the lack of an heir of his own blood. I'm sure he found Matthew's company easier to bear than that of his two daughters: Alice and Louise were rampantly, exuberantly female, and though Jonas clearly doted on them both, it was with a vague, benign affection, as if they were creatures too exotic to be romped with and hugged like ordinary mortals.

The girls were both fair, like Jonas, though Alice's fairness was more of a honey-color and her eyes were paler, hazel versions of mine. Louise was a tiny, silver-fair, blue-eyed angel who charmed everyone she met and held even her stiffly starched nanny in the palm of her little hand. I loved them both dearly, and longed for the day when they'd be old enough to be companionable, released from a world of airing-cupboards and bread and butter in which I was only a tolerated visitor. Until then, we shared nursery teas and bedtime kisses, and walked in the garden scuffing the autumn leaves with our boots until Nanny scolded us all for risking a chill in our hatless heads.

Jonas couldn't imagine any woman wanting more. He went on being sensible and benevolent and fond of me in his own arid way, but for most of the time I knew his mind was elsewhere. Any part of his day not filled by Oliver shipping business was taken up with his butterflies, and not only those—for Jonas had moved on from setting and framing butterflies to the smelly complexities of taxidermy, and his workshop next to the billiard room was a horrid gallery of bones and skins and tortured wire armatures ready for the remains of some small animal he'd acquired.

He brought his first attempt very proudly for me to admire—a red squirrel perched on a sawn log—and through gritted teeth I assured him it was remarkably lifelike. In truth, the squirrel seemed to have an air of surprise not inconsistent with having seven inches of tempered iron wire thrust through its backside and up toward its nose and I wished devoutly that Jonas had left the poor dead animal alone . . . though of course I said nothing remotely so disloyal.

After the success of the squirrel a positive mania seemed to grip him, and a small army of kittens and bullfinches and newts followed the squirrel into eternal preservation, staring rigidly out of tall glass cases as if scared stiff by their first glimpse of the hereafter.

One particular tableau turned my stomach even more than the rest

—which was unfortunate, since it was Jonas's favorite. Under a glass dome the size of a hatbox three ginger kittens stood frozen in bizarre jollity, one playing a tiny fiddle, one tootling a silver flute, and the third beating a minute drum. To add to the horror, each one, prancing on his hind paws, was dressed in a waistcoat and pantaloons and sported a jaunty cap with a feather. The little mouths of the fiddler and the drummer gaped open to show rows of baby-sharp teeth round a plaster tongue. Six little eyes, wide and glassy, seemed to follow me accusingly past the table in the hall where they scraped their silent melody—a dead-march, despite the mad grins, for three infant lives, drowned by a whistling stable-boy in a bucket of foul water.

It made me think of my own dead babies, and feel sick.

After that I found myself looking at Jonas's hands, at his long, slender fingers which had always seemed so beautifully impractical, and shuddering at his touch. What poor, soft corpse had they disemboweled that day before they were laid on me?

In the White House the ranks of butterflies had been confined to the library where they covered the walls with a mosaic of crucified color. It was a room I avoided. The squirrel was there on his branch, and a pheasant and a hare shot by George Broadney at Jonas's request, and even to sit on the buttoned settee made me feel like an Egyptian princess in her tomb, escorted to the hereafter by an army of tiny dead things slaughtered for her comfort.

First Adam, and now Jonas. Why did the hands which touched me always have to deal in death? Adam for profit, Jonas for amusement —neither of them giving it a second thought.

It surprised me how seldom I thought of Adam nowadays. Even with Matthew before me—slighter than Adam, but so alike in the gray eyes and sun-tawny hair—it was hard to conjure up a clear picture of his father anymore. I still kept his daguerreotype likeness along with the red stone amulet in the bottom drawer of my dressing table next to a box of fans, and from time to time I'd discover it there while I was dressing for a ball or for the theater. Then I'd gaze in perplexity at its silvery surface, trying hard to recognize the somber stranger who stared back at me over the years.

And so I settled by degrees into the White House near Mossley Hill with my carriages, my lapdog, my children and my husband, my lady's-maid, the children's nanny and the nursery-maids, the butler and the footmen, the housemaids, kitchen-maid and cook, the grooms and the stable-boys and all the squabbling hordes without whom it was impossible to live a civilized life. And every so often, alone by the fire in my sitting room, I remembered gorging myself on the haunch of venison Watches Smoke had brought, holding the meat in my fingers until grease dripped from my elbows, excited, sated and desperately grateful. And I wondered which life was the real one, and which fire had burned brighter in my hearth.

———

"You need a change of air," Jonas remarked at the beginning of April 1851. "You've been doing too much of this charity work, I shouldn't wonder. You'll wear yourself out, you know—I think I'll suggest to Verity that she ought to leave you in peace for a bit, and not go adding your name to all her blessed committees."

"I don't mind, Jonas. It gives me something to do. And you spend just as much time on company business."

"That's quite different. Men are fitted for that kind of thing, and women aren't. It's a scientific fact. Anyway, here's something for you to think about for a while—what do you say to the idea of going to London for the opening of the Exhibition?"

"Oh, Jonas—I'd love to be there! I knew you and George would be going to the opening ceremony, certainly, but I never thought of being there myself—though I'd hoped to see the Exhibition before it was all over. . . ."

"This jaunt was George's idea, as a matter of fact. He's very keen that we should all go—Verity and their two eldest girls, and you and Matthew."

"And what about Alice? She'd adore it—I'm sure she would."

"I think not, Rachel. Alice is a little young for this kind of thing. She'd only get bored and make a fuss. And Louise is *certainly* too young. No—Matthew will come with us, of course, but not the girls. I know you'll miss them, my dear, but at least you'll have Matthew for company. I'll write to his headmaster today."

George Broadney had planned everything, it seemed. He and Jonas had both been involved for some time in subcommittees with grand titles: I'd seen documents headed "The Great Exhibition of the Industry of all Nations" on Jonas's desk in the library and plans of the huge glass building which was to house it, and I knew that Jonas had been involved with a model of Liverpool Docks which was to be shown off there. I couldn't imagine what George Broadney's role might be, though—unless there was to be an exhibit entitled "The Development of the Sporting Gun"—and I longed to ask Jonas if Sophie Greenwood or whoever had succeeded her in George's affections would also be in London at the time.

The Queen was to open the exhibition at noon on Thursday the 1st of May, and by Wednesday evening our party had assembled for dinner at the Broadneys' house in Eaton Square. Jonas, Matthew and I were by no means the only house guests, and Verity had filled her dinner table that night with quite a crowd—no doubt in order to impress her provincial relatives with her glittering London circle.

The dowager Duchess of something-or-other sat in the place of honor on George's right and an elderly French diplomat at Verity's side. Other lesser grandees were scattered round the table, but I noticed that Verity had taken great care to seat Jonas next to a round-eyed young woman called Lettice Wyre whose husband had already sailed out to his uncle's merchant house in Melbourne, Australia. Lettice was to join him in another two months.

"Cyril is such an ambitious man," I heard her confide over the quail cutlets. "What he really wants is to set up in business for himself. But I'm sure, Sir Jonas, I've no need to tell you how stifling it can be for a man of real ability to be starved of a chance to make his mark. Thank you—I'll take a very little wine." Lettice allowed Jonas to fill her glass to the brim.

"Everyone in London says you are quite the shrewdest man in the shipping business. Oh, they do—you mustn't be modest." And Lettice laid her little hand reproachfully on Jonas's sleeve. "And so I wondered—what would you advise poor Cyril to do in the circumstances? I told him," she rushed on without giving Jonas a chance to reply, "that he ought to become agent for a large British shipping line—a line which everyone in the world knows of and respects. And particularly, a line with a far-seeing, progressive man at its head, who would notice Cyril's talents and use them to the full. Don't you agree, Sir Jonas?"

I heard no more until the ham escalopes had been cleared away. With particular malice Verity had placed me between a deaf cavalry major and a Russian who spoke very little English yet seemed determined to explain some complex engineering project of his own which was on show at the Crystal Palace. As a result I'd no chance of eavesdropping until the Russian, satisfied he'd converted me to his new aqueduct system, turned his attention to the eldest Broadney

girl, seated on his left. I glanced through the floral decorations to
where Lettice Wyre was still besieging Jonas, her great doe eyes
eating him up, her fingers accidentally brushing his as she reached
out for her wineglass.

"I'm sure if you'd only consider it, dear Sir Jonas—making Cyril
the Oliver's agent in Melbourne, I mean—you'd see what an excellent idea it would be. I'd be so very, very grateful if you'd even think
it over."

I heard Jonas murmur that he'd certainly consider the possibility,
although the Oliver Line had a perfectly efficient agent in Melbourne
as things were.

"But you'll do your best for us—for *me*—won't you?" sighed
Lettice, opening her shining eyes wider than ever. "I'd do anything
in my power to make sure you didn't regret the decision . . . Anything at all . . ."

"WOOL, LADY OLIVER—" roared the deaf major suddenly in
my ear. "DO YOU KNOW THAT WOOL NEXT THE SKIN IS A
SOVEREIGN REMEDY AGAINST RHEUMATICS? NO—I
DIDN'T THINK YOU WOULD. NEITHER DOES MY QUACK
OF A DOCTOR! MERINO—ALPACA—CAMEL, EVEN—
THEY'RE ALL EXCELLENT. IT'S THE OIL, Y'KNOW. WHY, I
REMEMBER ONCE IN AFGHANISTAN . . ." And off he went on
some shouted reminiscence which effectively drowned out Lettice
Wyre's maneuverings until it was time to leave the gentlemen to their
brandy and cigars.

———

The men of the house-party sat up late that night after the ladies had
gone to bed. As usual, Jonas and I had been given the same adjoining
rooms we'd occupied on the first night of our marriage. The Olivers
set great store by tradition—the room next to mine was always
known as *Sir Jonas's Room* (he wouldn't have had a moment's rest
in any other) and a bottle of his favorite boot-blacking was kept
ready in the butler's pantry for his periodic visits to the capital.

I was known to have an eccentric passion for fresh air, and as I
got ready for bed that night I noticed that the bedroom window had
been left open by the exact inch and a half I preferred, although I
knew how Verity cursed the smuts which flew through it to spoil her
curtains. The connecting door to Jonas's room was shut, since he
was still downstairs, but I was sure that as soon as he came to bed it

would be opened precisely halfway and left like that—as a symbol of . . . well, as a symbol of something important to Jonas, at any rate.

I'd almost fallen asleep by the time I heard the soft click of a door-handle, and I assumed Jonas was preparing for bed in the next room. Then I heard an unexpected sound—the *chink* of glasses, and a faint thud as a heavy object was set down on the table beside the bed. Startled, I struggled to sit up—to find George Broadney, a quilted satin dressing-gown wrapped round his ample girth, about to dump himself down on the edge of my bed.

"George!" I hissed indignantly. "What on earth do you think you're doing here?"

"You don't have to whisper, my lovely. Jonas isn't in there, you know." He stopped untwisting the wire from the cork of a chilled champagne bottle long enough to gesture toward the door between the two rooms. It was still closed.

"Can't call on a lady without bringing a gift." George's voice was thick with brandy. "Now, just you try some of this. This stuff's special. I keep it locked up at the back of the cellar—and I have the only key to the door. Only very beautiful ladies are allowed to taste this." He poured the liquid into the two glasses he'd brought, where it fizzed gaily and released its bubbles in a shining stream.

"George—get out of here. You're hopelessly drunk! What will people think when you come calling on me at this time of night? Jonas could come upstairs at any minute."

"Oh, no, he won't," sniggered George, looking owlish and put-ting a fat forefinger to the side of his nose. "Because I know where Jonas is—and somehow I don't think he'll bother us for a very long time."

I began to be alarmed.

"What do you mean, you know where Jonas is? He's still down-stairs in the drawing room, where I left him."

"Not at all, my chuck. . . . Don't you believe it! Jonas isn't down-stairs anymore—he's *upstairs* with Lettice Wyre. And I don't imag-ine they're discussing the weather in Melbourne!" George sniggered again, and then stared at me.

"Oh, come, Rachel, you must've seen the way she was all over him at dinner. Wiggling her little body at him and offering him anything he wanted, if only he'd give the Oliver's agency to dear Cyril. . . . Dammit—that's the right sort of wife for the Cyrils of this world! While her husband's off earning a crust, she's back here selling herself for the old man's future. But if I know Jonas, he's a sight too smart for little Lettice. If he steers the right course he can have the girl *and* do what he likes with the agency. You aren't drinking, Rachel." With a grin, George attempted to push a glass into my hand.

"I don't believe any of this nonsense! Jonas would never do a thing like that! He has no interest at all in Lettice Wyre."

George leaned closer. "Why not? Because he bores you silly in bed?"

"George—get out of my room this minute before I ring for the maid! And don't think I won't do it, simply to avoid a scandal. It may be your house, but this is my room and you've no business being here. Take your bottle and your lies and get out."

But George Broadney was staring at me, his mouth ajar.

"By God, Rachel, I can see why Jonas married you! When there's color in your cheeks like that. . . . Verity always says she can never understand what Jonas saw in you, but I can understand it, all right! You're the kind of woman every man dreams of finding—and a damn sight too much of a woman for Jonas Oliver, I'd say. Why do you think I went to all the trouble of arranging this visit? Because I reckoned you'd be a regular hellion between the sheets—when you found yourself with a real man instead of that stuffed-shirt brother-in-law of mine—"

"Don't be so disgusting, George—"

"Come on, now, Rachel, you don't have to be prudish with old George. I've had enough of that sort of thing from Verity. *Disgusting* was her favorite word for anything I ever wanted to do: every time I laid a hand on her she whined *Don't be so disgusting, George.* I'd never have married her, if it hadn't been for her Oliver stock."

George took a long draft of his champagne. "All the Olivers are like that. Their mother was a mealy-mouthed old bitch, and she passed it on to the children. I imagine Jonas must be just about as exciting in bed as a plank of wood—am I right, Rachel?"

Leaning forward suddenly, George slipped a hand inside my nightgown and touched me as I hadn't been touched for years. Angrily, I pulled his hand away.

"Jonas is your brother-in-law, for Heaven's sake, and your friend—and your business partner. Do you want me to tell him what you've been up to?"

"Oh, Rachel, Rachel—why should the saintly Jonas have all the fun?"

George untied the sash of his dressing-gown and let it fall open. Underneath, he was stark naked.

"Now my darling—do you see what just sitting here on the bed next to you does to me? I promise you—we could have a perfect night together while Jonas is off with that Wyre woman. In fact, I'm sure this'll only be the first of many. . . . Because once you've tried it you're bound to want more. . . ."

He pulled me against him and began to kiss my lips and then my throat, unbuttoning my nightgown until he could pull it down off my shoulders. I could hardly believe what was happening—I was horror-struck, and every bit as confused and upset as George had intended me to be about the idea of Jonas in bed somewhere with Lettice Wyre.

George was sure that the urge to get even with Jonas together with his own amorous skills would make him irresistible as a lover. Nothing I'd said had had the least effect on him, and now he was within a groping hand's-breadth of getting what he wanted. I couldn't even scream without waking the house.

Trying frantically to ward off George's pawing, my hand touched salvation. On the table beside the bed was the bottle of priceless champagne, its icy sides beaded with chill moisture; gripping it firmly, I emptied the whole lot in a freezing stream straight into his lap.

For a moment he clung to me in mute shock. Then he let out a stifled gasp of anguish and pulled away, staring in disbelief. The bed-cover was soaked—his dressing-gown and the carpet too—and his plans for the night had clearly received a setback.

I giggled. I couldn't help it, even though I knew he'd be furious. For several seconds he said nothing. Then he got to his feet and pulled his damp dressing-gown primly around him.

"Good God, Rachel, that was Bollinger '46. You didn't have to be quite so dramatic."

———

My memories of the Great Exhibition are inseparable from my memories of that night—and the continuing suspicion and bewilderment of the days that followed. Had Jonas really been with Lettice Wyre, or hadn't he? Certainly the door between our two rooms was open as usual when I woke in the morning, but though after George left

I'd lain awake for another hour or two, waiting for Jonas to come to bed, tiredness overtook me in the end and I'd no idea what time he appeared.

Over breakfast I watched them both closely. At the far end of the table Lettice was picking at her eggs, dark circles under her eyes. Jonas too looked weary, I thought, and I began to wonder if George Broadney had told me the truth.

"I hope I didn't disturb you when I came to bed last night," Jonas whispered to me at last. "I was very late, I'm afraid. That blasted Russian was desperate to explain to me how his aqueduct worked— the fellow you were sitting next to at dinner. Something to do with reversing the flow of a river with some sort of pump. But really, his English was so awful that I couldn't understand half of it. The brandy didn't help, either."

"Do you know—" shrilled Verity from the other side of the table, "I think we must have a champagne-drinking ghost in this house. I almost tripped over an empty bottle and two glasses left outside my door last night. Someone must have been having a little party, I think."

I looked down hastily at my plate. It had been the only way of getting rid of the evidence of George's visit. Thank goodness champagne didn't leave a stain on carpets.

But had Jonas really been cornered by the Russian engineer? Or had he simply invented a plausible excuse for his absence? George Broadney had been very sure we wouldn't be disturbed, and I couldn't believe even he would risk being discovered *in flagrante* by his wife's brother. All day long the questions tormented me, and yet somehow I couldn't believe it of Jonas—upright, pompous Jonas, apologetic, hasty, fumbling Jonas—the fastidiously honorable man I'd married.

We were hustled to our places in the Crystal Palace by eleven. The old Duke of Wellington was there, limping heavily, and Palmerston, and Paxton the designer—and shortly after twelve the Queen herself arrived in pink satin and gold with Prince Albert in a field marshal's uniform, the Prince of Wales in highland dress and the Princess Royal in white lace with a wreath of flowers in her hair.

"Look at them," hissed Verity acidly in my ear. "Like refugees from a costume party."

But my attention wandered during Prince Albert's speech—lofty rhetoric about the commissioners of the Exhibition and the blessings of Divine Providence—and I hardly heard the Queen's reply in her tiny voice, or the Archbishop of Canterbury's long prayer. It was only the sound of the *Hallelujah Chorus* which brought me to my senses while the royal procession formed up and walked the length of the nave and back. At last, after the Queen had left, we were finally free of our hard chairs and at liberty to tour the exhibition.

In the next two weeks we went again and again to the huge glass palace with its transepts and galleries and vaulted halls enclosing whole trees within their arches. My mind was still in a whirl, but even if I'd been as steady as a judge, the sheer size of the exhibition would have ensured that I remembered it only as a vivid hotchpotch of images. Jonas was beside himself with excitement, desperate to see his Liverpool dock model in its place of honor, with its tiny warehouses and cranes and its minute ships—a satisfying proportion of them flying the Oliver house flag at their mastheads.

But there were endless galleries of similar objects from all over the world, carved in wood or bone or woven from grass or cabbage-leaves: telescopes, steam-engines, ivory thrones and walnut pianos, beds which hurled the sleeper to the floor at a preset time; iron fountains and porphyry vases—everything which could be cut from stone or slate or molded in glass or gutta-percha. . . . And not far from the perfect brilliance of the Koh-i-Noor diamond in its golden cage, a statue which caught and held my eye, *The Wounded Indian* by Stephenson of Boston—the shaven-headed savage, mortally hurt, gazing sadly at the arrow which had impaled him. I lingered in front of it after the others had walked on. The Indian looked so thin and tired. . . . Had Watches Smoke known of the bullet which killed him, I wondered, as he bled to death on the dusty floor of the Trader's House?

Each Saturday—five-shilling day, the grandest of the week—we went back once more, and not far from the main door of the Crystal Palace I found the ultimate irony, children begging in rags from the crowd of exhibition-goers. It would have made an excellent sculpture for the Main Avenue—*Destitution holding out its hand to Invention.*

A policeman soon chased the children away, but not before I'd managed to slip a sovereign into a grubby palm.

"You'll only encourage them," Jonas remarked virtuously. "They'll get used to having something for nothing. Rewards should be earned, after all."

Had Lettice Wyre earned her reward, I wondered? And I had to bite back the retort which rose to my lips.

Later that day I stood in front of the fur companies' exhibit in the Western Nave, not far from the lighthouse lamp and the telescope, hung all over with beaver furs and buffalo-robe railway-rugs, and wolf pelts and bear-skin foot-muffs—as limp and sad as they'd ever looked piled up on our cabin floor . . . and horror of horrors, on the furrier's stand next door, a whole suit made of white egret-feathers which had cost the death of Heaven knows how many little birds. Adam, hunter though he was, would surely never have countenanced that. And suddenly I was thinking of Adam again, riding off toward the mountains like a hawk released from its cage. Oh, Adam, why did you have to leave me behind in a world full of George Broadneys and Lettice Wyres, and suits made of slaughtered birds? If only . . . Oh, if only . . .

So much would have been different.

22

One morning in the autumn of that year our nearest neighbor, old Admiral Keane, was found dead on his bedroom floor by the valet who'd come to wake him. Within weeks his executors had put his house, Westwood Park, up for sale—curtains, carpets, pictures, books, table-linen and all. It was even rumored that the Admiral's spectacles were still on the night-table next to his bed.

I was saddened by the old man's death. The Admiral had been one of Nelson's lieutenants at Trafalgar, and he often told me how he'd seen the great man's corpse folded into its cask of rum for the homeward passage. In later years he'd spent long enough on the Mediterranean station to develop a passion for the soft, fleshy fruit of the region, and soon after buying Westwood Park he'd commissioned a series of hothouses—then a great luxury—to provide a supply of fruit for his retirement.

Admiral Keane had never married ("Never saw the need, m'dear . . .") and since I knew how lonely he was in that great barn of a house, I used to visit him whenever I could and listen to his stories of the old wooden-walls of Nelson's navy. In return he sent me huge baskets of peaches, figs and nectarines, warm and ripe from his garden of glass.

Westwood Park itself had started life at the beginning of the previous century as a modest country manor house, only to suffer from the alternating neglect or architectural whimsy of its later owners. As the city advanced toward it, the manorial land was sold off, leaving only four or five acres of parkland and the area immediately surrounding the house, where a formal garden had been laboriously cut out of rough heathland only to be returned to romantic lakes and lawns as the fashion changed.

Over the years the house had been enlarged and a classical portico added to its rustic gables; yet time had mellowed every new outcrop of raw stone, and the Admiral had had the good sense to leave his house alone to mature like a fine wine into the sum of its diverse elements. Westwood Park couldn't have been more different from the modern, Italianate splendor of the White House, but I was fond of its creeper-whiskered face just as I might be of an old and undemanding friend.

A rutted lane ran between the Admiral's parkland and our own grounds toward the open countryside beyond, with the White House wall on one side of it and an iron palisade on the other, through which a little gate led into the Admiral's shrubbery. It had been a useful short-cut; and for weeks while Westwood Park remained empty I found it hard to pass the gate in the lane without automatically turning my steps toward the old house to call on the Admiral. It was Verity Broadney, that tireless gleaner of information, who brought me the first tidings of our new neighbor.

"It seems, my dear, you've seen the navy set sail only to have the army march in."

"Whatever do you mean, Verity?"

My sister-in-law was a bright green splash on the sofa opposite, thin where Jonas was slight, pinched where he was thin, her vivid yellow hair a frizzy, frenzied version of his as if all the jangling energy in her body was trying to crackle out of the top of her head.

Now she leaned significantly toward me.

"Flaxman the banker tells me the house has been bought by a Colonel Someone—and for no small price, either, since there were several parties interested and the Colonel was determined to have it. I daresay the White House must already be worth a great deal more than Jonas laid out for it." Verity looked smug for a moment, and then frowned. "You should be pleased at my news, Rachel. You might have had to live next door to some uncouth grocer who's made his fortune in tea. The very worst people seem able to afford anything they want these days."

"Oh, but you've disappointed me, Verity. . . . Is that really the best neighbor you can find for us? A dull old colonel—and no doubt his dumpy, managing wife? And I'd expected a prince of the blood royal at the very least!"

Verity scowled and wriggled in her seat. "Be frivolous about it if you like, Rachel, but one can't be too careful about one's neighbors these days. It's quite different for us, of course, because we aren't in town; but Jonas *would* stay in Liverpool, and as I warned him at the time, money doesn't necessarily mean respectability anymore, and quite frightful people will try to call if they're given the least encouragement. For Jonas's sake you really must take care."

As usual, Verity managed to imply that while my reputation might not suffer from living among doubtful characters, my husband's certainly would.

"Well, Verity, I don't imagine you've anything to fear on that score. Any colonel who isn't off campaigning with his regiment must be old and fat and perfectly proper. I expect he has gout and long gray whiskers, and an elderly wife with a swarm of little dogs." The King Charles spaniel curled up at my feet lifted her dainty head at the word *dogs* and gazed up at me inquiringly. "At least they'll be company for poor Lottie. Do you know, I think she misses old Admiral Keane?"

Two months passed, and I became vaguely aware that the Colonel and his household had moved into Westwood Park, but mindful of Verity's warning, I avoided paying even a courtesy call until I could find out what manner of family had moved into the Admiral's house.

Verity had been busily at work, trawling for information, and on the night of a ball given by the Broadneys for their eldest daughter, as soon as decency allowed, Verity, splendid in tarlatan and diamonds, sidled across to whisper in my ear.

"I must speak to you! Such news—you'll never believe it, I promise! Come to the morning room in five minutes."

Greatly wondering, I did as I'd been told, and found my sister-in-law fairly quivering with agitation.

"You haven't called, have you?" she cried theatrically, seizing me by the elbow. "Only tell me you haven't called!"

"Called? Where should I call, for goodness' sake? Verity, please let go of my arm—you're crushing my gown."

"Called at Westwood Park! Where else?"

"No, of course not. You were so anxious that I shouldn't call until I'd heard more about the family. . . ."

"Well, that's a mercy!" Verity plopped down on to a chair with a great rustling of petticoats, and fanned herself with a fashion journal from the table. "I was afraid I might be too late."

"But you advised me months ago to avoid my new neighbors at

first, until we knew what sort of people they were. I've done exactly as you asked, surely."

"I *know* you have, Rachel dear. At least, I know that *now*. But sometimes . . . Sometimes I don't believe you even listen to my advice, let alone follow it. And I do worry so much about Jonas."

I let the remark pass.

"So you disapprove of the Colonel and his family, then?"

"Disapprove? Just wait till I tell you what I've heard!" Verity's diamond earrings shivered, and she lowered her voice dramatically. "You'll remember, my dear, that I warned you to beware of your new neighbors, and you laughed at me—oh, yes, you did, don't deny it. But I was right!"

"But Verity, you're always right! And now you're going to tell me this Colonel of yours is so depraved as to wear a straw hat to church and go to the races in an omnibus!"

"Worse than that—much worse! Though I daresay if he ever crossed the threshold of a church—which I doubt—he might well have the effrontery to wear something unsuitable."

"Goodness, whatever has the old fellow been up to?"

"Old! He's not *old!* A little older than you or I, perhaps, but that's hardly decrepit. . . ." Verity's steely glare dared me to disagree.

"His name's Allen. Colonel Allen. That's all I know about him, except that he's not English, I believe, but American—which is bad to start with."

With a wave of her elegantly gloved hand Verity banished the United States from social acceptability.

"Furthermore, so my London friends tell me, he has no wife, and spends his time either traveling abroad, or hob-nobbing with artists and scandalous people like that."

"But Verity," I suggested innocently, "even the Queen paints. Quite well, I believe."

"You're being deliberately foolish," said Verity severely. "Her Majesty may *paint,* but nobody would dare to call her an *artist.* It's an entirely different thing. Artists are—well—disreputable people. Everybody knows that."

"I don't see why that should follow." Verity's small-mindedness was annoying me even more than usual. "Why should artists be so disreputable?"

"For one thing, they paint people with no clothes on," declared Verity triumphantly. "And no decent person does *that.*"

"Well, I can't see why the Colonel's habits should matter to us in the White House, even if he fills Westwood Park with naked ladies. It sounds as if he'll find us far too dull to bother with."

Verity shrieked with alarm at the idea. "Good Heavens, Rachel—what are you thinking of? I hope you'll take *great* care to avoid the man! It would be impossible to have him as an acquaintance under the circumstances. Who knows what liberties he'd take? You can't possibly risk being introduced to him, Rachel—think of poor Jonas."

"I'm sure you can trust me to do what's best for Jonas."

Verity pursed her lips and said no more on the subject.

But Jonas, I discovered, had already made inquiries of his own.

"I believe I've met the man, Rachel—in New York—and I didn't take to him at all. Verity's wrong about his being American. He's English, I seem to remember, but no more of a colonel than I am, and a pretty villainous sort of fellow altogether. He's wealthy, certainly, but I doubt if his money was honestly come by. No—it's quite out of the question for us to have anything to do with him. I've warned Reuben to stay well out of his way."

Something struck a chord in my memory. Could this be Reuben's Colonel from San Francisco?

"How did you come to meet him, Jonas?"

"I don't see why that should matter."

"Oh . . . no reason—except that he doesn't sound like the kind of man you normally do business with. . . ." I tried to keep the curiosity out of my voice.

"I should think not! No—he's that peculiar fellow Reuben brought back from San Francisco, I'm sure of it. Absolutely not the kind of person we want to know."

"I understand that, Jonas."

"I don't want the servants mixing with the household at Westwood Park either. No gossiping in the lane, or anything of that sort."

"No, Jonas. I'll speak to Stevens about it."

"I can't think what's prompted the man to buy an ugly old house like Westwood Park in the first place. There can't be much to interest him round here. I just hope he takes the hint, and keeps away from *us,* that's all."

"Let's hope so, Jonas."

But I was fascinated all the same.

Jonas needn't have been concerned. To my secret disappointment Colonel Allen turned out to be no more anxious to make the acquaintance of his neighbors than we were to make his. But from gossip which came my way over the teacups of my afternoon callers I learned that some of what Verity had said of the Colonel did appear to be true. There was no Mrs. Allen, and a housekeeper ran the household at Westwood Park—this had been certified by the butcher and the coal-merchant—but although nothing had been seen of the notorious artists and their naked models, Verity's tales from London were enough to make sure that the Colonel would never be received, even if he wished it, in Liverpool's better circles.

Considering George Broadney's reputation, I found Verity's sanctimonious eye-rolling downright hypocritical. Why should George be allowed to go his own, lecherous way, simply because he was a baronet? No hostess banned the Broadneys from her dinner table because of George's scandals—and George was a married man with numerous children. The Colonel's worst crime seemed to be having painters as friends—what harm could that do to anyone else?

I was sick to death of the society hens who clucked in my drawing room, sniggering over their tea-cakes, and I secretly wished the Colonel well.

"I haven't set eyes on him," Reuben confessed when I tackled him on the subject, "though Jonas is sure it's the same man. I can't imagine what he's doing here in Liverpool. Jonas has made it very clear I'm to keep my distance—not that I've any desire to make his acquaintance again, believe me. That sort of man brings trouble wherever he goes."

Aunt Grace had a theory of her own.

"*Allen?*" she exclaimed. "*Allen* with an 'e'? But that's a family name, Rachel—surely you know that. I was a Miss Allen before I was married, and so was your mother. And now this man—*Allen*, you say. . . ." She halted, her mouth ajar. "Why, bless me if it won't be Isabella's boy—Cousin Arthur's son, that went off to the army, oh, ten years ago now. . . . Gracious yes, I'm certain of it, he went out to Kabul as a corporal with the infantry in '42, and now he's home again, and a *colonel* too!"

"That's rather a fast promotion, isn't it, Aunt Grace? From corporal to colonel in ten years?"

"But so many officers have been killed, my dear! *Someone* has to be promoted—and after all, he is an *Allen*. I shall write to Arthur directly, but depend upon it—it's Isabella's boy home again, you'll see."

"I'm sure you're right, Aunt Grace."

Christmas came and went, and the usual round of Oliver merrymaking subsided once more into the sleet and ice of February. The main road from the city became a treacherous slick of frost, its ruts and potholes crusted with frozen mud which made even a carriage-journey an adventure of straining horses and skidding wheels.

One icy afternoon, Vickers, my personal maid, taking Lottie for her daily ramble, tripped and badly twisted her ankle in a dark corner just outside the gates of Westwood Park. Fortunately she was seen from the lodge, rescued by Colonel Allen's lodge-keeper, and carried at once to his master's house. Before long a gratified Vickers found herself settled in an armchair in a ground-floor room which had once been the Admiral's study, being soothed with good brandy while her swollen ankle was examined and then bandaged by the Colonel's housekeeper herself.

"With her own hands, my lady," Vickers recalled later for my benefit. "And very neatly, too, as you can see. I'm sure I couldn't improve on it myself."

Hardly anything, it seemed, had escaped Vickers's penetrating eye.

"She's called Mrs. Gibson—the housekeeper, I mean. . . . At least, I think that's what the groom called her when he brought me in. A middle-aged woman, my lady, and *quite* respectable, whatever people may say."

Vickers rattled on, flushed with the excitement of having penetrated the lair of wickedness next door, and I didn't attempt to stop her. To tell the truth, I was dying to know what changes Colonel Allen had made in the house of my old friend the Admiral.

"Westwood Park seems very little altered, my lady—though of course I was only inside it once or twice, when I took calf's-foot jelly to Admiral Keane. The Colonel seems to have kept most of the furnishings just as they were, and the pictures too. It's not at all up-to-date." She cast a smug glance round my pretty sitting room, in its sunny and impractical colors of white and gold.

"And"—Vickers returned to her tale—"I did see *him*—Colonel Allen—though only for a moment, at the door." Vickers had been sent home in the Colonel's carriage, her ankle propped up on a cushion, and was captivated by this courtesy.

"He isn't a handsome man, in the way Sir Jonas is handsome," she simpered, "but very tall and distinguished. He'd been out riding, and came back just as I was leaving—all muddy, in a greatcoat and boots. And I really can't say he looked much like—well, what people insist he *is*—though I daresay—"

At that point I sent her off to bed and ordered a hot poultice for the twisted ankle. Then I sat down to write a note to the Colonel, thanking him for his kindness to my maid. Whatever Jonas and Verity might say, it would have been grossly impolite to do nothing at all, and within minutes the note had been signed, folded and sent off to Colonel Allen at Westwood Park.

Shortly after ten o'clock next morning a basket was delivered for Lady Oliver containing the biggest mass of scented white and yellow flowers I had ever seen. Delicate white Cape irises and brilliant sunshine-yellow star-shaped jonquils filled it to the brim, their fragrance bringing spring to the rooms they passed through in spite of the grim grayness beyond the windows. There was no note with the flowers —only the information that they'd been cut on the Colonel's instructions from the Westwood Park hothouses, and no thanks were required.

Here was a difficulty. The flowers had been cut; they could hardly be sent back. If accepting them was awkward, to return them would be highly offensive, and in view of the Colonel's kindness to Vickers, quite out of the question. I began to suspect Colonel Allen was perfectly aware of my dilemma, and had refused any thanks in order to spare me the embarrassment of a reply. The matter was to rest there.

And so I put aside my doubts, and the irises and jonquils filled three large vases in my own white and gold sitting room, where their heady perfume lingered long after the blooms themselves had faded.

Nothing was heard from Westwood Park for several months after that. The house might easily have been empty for all I saw of my new neighbor, but of course I'd already been told by the all-knowing Verity that Colonel Allen spent much of his time traveling abroad.

While the branches were still bare of leaves there was one place on the east terrace of the White House, outside the breakfast-room windows, from where the pitched gables of Westwood Park were just visible beyond a tracery of twigs. Often, when the girls and I were out throwing a ball for Lottie on the terrace, well wrapped up against the wind, I'd glance curiously across at the zig-zag outline of the mossy old roof, gray against the clouds, a fortress in its forest. Then, with the coming of summer, a tide of green lapped to the treetops and Westwood Park was all but submerged by it, though by that time Lottie and I had already abandoned the terrace in favor of exploring further afield.

———

In early July 1852 a letter arrived from a firm of London lawyers, explaining that Colonel Allen was to be abroad for two months and would be pleased if Lady Oliver could make use of the contents of the Westwood Park hothouses in his absence. There was an abundance of soft fruit, the letter continued, which would be at its best while the Colonel was away, and he'd regard it as a kindness if Lady Oliver would save this bounty from going to waste. His gardeners would be instructed to call each day for orders.

We grew a little fruit of our own at the White House, certainly, but nothing compared with the magnificent harvest of figs, nectarines, melons, oranges and grapes which Admiral Keane had established at Westwood Park. It seemed almost criminal to refuse so much glorious fruit—but I guessed what Jonas would think of it even before I'd asked him. Jonas consulted Verity, who in addition to being an expert on social niceties was made bilious by fresh fruit. True to form, Verity decreed without hesitation that the offer must be declined. *Must be declined.*

"But it isn't as if the Colonel will be at home!" I wailed miserably when Jonas told me what Verity had dictated. "I'd never have to meet him, or speak to him . . . and besides—I'd send Mrs. Locke to decide what she needed for the kitchen, or simply order it from the Colonel's gardeners! Wouldn't that do?"

"That isn't the point, my dear," Jonas insisted patiently. We'd had the same argument several times in the past week, and I knew there was a dead barn-owl in his workshop awaiting attention.

"Then what *is* the point, Jonas? I must be very stupid, since I can't see it at all."

"In that case, you'll just have to trust me to know what's best. Verity's absolutely right. If you accept the Colonel's offer you'll put us in his debt, however much he claims to be in *ours.* Suppose he then presumes to call on us? Or what if, by some chance, you find

yourself at the theater in the next box to the fellow? Can you refuse
to greet him as a friend after accepting his oranges and what-have-
you? Surely, Rachel, it's better to make it plain now that we intend
to have nothing to do with him? Someone of his reputation. . . . If
it's the fruit you regret, my dear, I'll find you as much fruit as you
want elsewhere. Shiploads of it. Now—shall we declare the matter
settled?"

And Jonas rose to his feet and left the room, which was his usual
way of putting an end to any dispute.

It wasn't entirely the waste of fruit which disappointed me. As July
passed into August I found myself thinking more and more of the
long line of hothouses Paxton had built for the Admiral—three-
quarter span against the south-facing wall of the kitchen-garden—
and the tall, free-standing orangery and vinery with their arched
gable windows, and the cool house, full of pelargoniums and chry-
santhemums. On summer days, when his rheumatism wasn't too
painful, Admiral Keane had often taken me on a stately tour of
inspection, his ranks of gardeners springing stiffly to attention, each
man in front of his own particular responsibility.

I'd loved the lofty, white-painted hothouses, their glass roofs supported by the slenderest of ornamental iron brackets and curlicues.
The sounds of the outside world were dulled in their steamy brightness: rain and wind were of no account there, and they offered the
delicious childhood thrill of standing under a downpour, entirely dry
and safe in the shelter of a thousand panes of pattering, streaming
glass.

At the White House we'd built a conservatory beyond the dining
room and lean-to glass-houses on the back of the coach-house wall,
but none of it approached the grandeur of the glass at Westwood
Park, where the fruit trees were so long established that the borders
were congested with their roots and the houses themselves enmeshed
in their woody embrace.

As it happened, Lottie's favorite walk led up the narrow lane
which separated the two properties, a right-of-way used mainly by
light carts and travelers on horseback, its banks overgrown with
docks, foxgloves, and the dry, sinewy stems of cow parsley. Often in
the afternoons I'd stroll along one of the two parallel ruts of beaten
earth which formed the highway while Lottie snuffled industriously

through the long grass. At the end of the White House wall we'd turn into the rear gate of our property and walk slowly up the drive, both of us spinning out the last minutes of our ramble; the spaniel knew as well as I did that our freedom had ended for the day.

Halfway along the lane was the narrow iron gate in the paling which bounded the grounds of Westwood Park, a side entrance leading through a fringe of trees to a shrubbery running the length of the drive. In the Admiral's day the gate had always stood open, but since the property had changed hands it had been kept locked, its hinges and its iron handle moist with new oil.

Then one afternoon, on a day so warm I'd seriously considered staying in the shade of the conservatory and leaving Lottie to amuse herself on the terrace, I found the iron gate in the lane standing ajar as it had done in the past. Curious, I gave it a push, and it swung fully open on its oily hinges without so much as a squeak, disclosing the familiar view through the trees and bushes which bordered the drive, across the lawn and the wild garden beyond it to where the white arches of the orangery were perfectly duplicated in the dark mirror of the lake.

It was a paradise of green and white . . . until a fish rose suddenly to a fly, the reflected image exploded into a myriad tiny splinters of color and swelling ripples put an end to its tranquility. I stood at the open gate, as refreshed as if I'd been offered a glass of cool water on my way along the dusty lane.

Lottie, joyously scenting former pleasures, promptly scuttled through the open gateway and began to root among the trees beyond. Irritably, I called her back, but the spaniel had become suddenly deaf among the new and exciting smells which rose up from the leaf-mold and demanded to be followed to their source.

The dog trundled, nose-down, toward the shrubbery, and I took a few steps after her. I called again, only to catch sight of her plump rear waddling through the laurels and laburnums in the direction of the carriage-sweep.

The drive was deserted, a heat haze hovering over its hard-packed surface. Away to my left, where the drive curved round toward the front of the house, there wasn't a soul to be seen, and the few windows at the end of the creeper-covered mansion which were visible from where I stood had their blinds drawn or their shutters closed.

Directly across the drive, a formal lawn descended in leisurely terraces toward the lake—clipped to the plush smoothness of green carpeting, but empty of human presence. The lake and the long grass around it were just as silent. Only the breath of a breeze stirred the whispering reeds at the water's edge as a moorhen slid out of their shelter, drawing a rippling vee in his wake.

Lottie halted, and turned inquiring eyes toward me.

All at once, I made up my mind. Picking up my skirts, I sped across the shadow-dappled drive to the lowest corner of the lawn, the heels of my satin boots sinking into the turf and slowing my progress. Avoiding the long grasses of the wild garden I passed between the lawn and the lake, Lottie at my heels, and rounded the dense clump of rhododendron bushes shielding the orangery.

The orangery door was locked—a bitter disappointment.

Why this new obsession with latches and locks which had never troubled the Admiral? Beyond the glass panes I could see among the thick foliage of the orange trees the shining globes of the ripening fruit, warming from the most vivid of greens to their own full glowing color. I longed to walk the length of that vaulted glass-house once more, my feet ringing on the concrete path, my lungs full of its hot citrus smell—but the orangery had been put out of bounds to me. Jonas and Verity had seen to that.

Beyond the orangery was the walled garden, one half of its double wooden gates standing open. I peered inside, searching the regimented strawberry beds and vegetable plots for any sign of life. Low box hedges lined the gravel paths, as precisely clipped as they'd been in the Admiral's day, and along the wall to my left was the line of hothouses whose produce I'd been forced to refuse. Now, on impulse, I tried the door at the nearer end, expecting it to be locked like the orangery. To my surprise, it opened at once.

Without any hesitation I stepped inside, Lottie scuttling anxiously at my heels before the door could swing shut on her beloved mistress.

———

The thick, humid, blanketing warmth of the hothouse enveloped and absorbed me. The concrete path was damp where the gardeners had drenched it, drawing water from huge tanks to slake the border soil and the gritty paving. Now the dampness rose in a steamy mist, prickling the roots of my hair and settling on my skin like drizzle. It smelled of succulence and honey and the sugary sweetness of hot earth before it dries; its familiar tang caught at the back of my throat, cloyingly airless, as if I were drowning in syrup.

The first house held peaches, espaliered on wires or trained in fans against the whitewashed brickwork of the rear wall. The large leaves matted the wall, curling and green, splayed out around the bursting, fuzzy fruit, except where the gardeners had been at work, tying back the leaves to turn the peaches to the sun. The trees were at all stages of ripeness; some of the peaches were bicolored, damson-red on one side mottling to white-gold on the other, while nearby the branches were loaded with soft orbs of the deepest crimson.

A few yards beyond, a tree had already finished its unwanted harvest. Chocolate-brown, squashy, rotten fruit lay around it on the soil, plush with gray mold, stinking of old jam; above it clung others, ready to disintegrate at a touch, waiting only to plump into the earth alongside their wasted sisters.

And I had caused the waste. I was seized by delicious guilt, half-intoxicated by fumes from the fermenting peaches moldering into sweet putrefaction all around. The Colonel, far away on his travels, had been powerless to halt his harvest. His trees would load their branches with fruit while there was moisture and sunlight: they could no more hold back or measure their abundance than they could weep for the ruin of their labor.

When Nature herself was prodigal, why should mere mortals hold back?

I reached out toward the lapping green, and disengaged a peach. It dropped, warm and downy, perfectly filling the hollow of my fingers. The thin skin parted between my teeth as if it had been about to burst from tightness, releasing a flood of blood-warm juice which trickled down my chin. How could such pleasure amount to a sin? He who created the peach had designed it for just that purpose. Surely the sin lay in refusing His gift?

The peach, gaping to reveal its brown seed, wrinkled like a human brain, was staining the glove on my right hand. Taking another bite, I wandered on through the miasma of rotting fruit toward the next section of the hothouses, and on to the next after that. Nectarines, melons and second-crop figs all clustered ripe on their branches or lay where they'd dropped into the moist soil of the bed below. In the melon-house each fruit hung snugly from the roof in its own special net, like a colony of plump, mottled bodies in tiny hammocks.

The heat was intense, the sunlight made blinding by the white-painted wall at the rear. The paving scratched beneath my soles as I walked, almost drowning the muffled twittering of birds on the roof-ridge and the humming of a giant bumblebee which blundered from one trellised stem to the next, drunk on the scent of honey hanging in the air like incense. It was a world of succulence and plenty, of luscious flesh which begged to be touched, of warmth and sated senses and ungrudged sweetness. No wonder Jonas and Verity, those dry puritans, had kept it from me.

The sugary wetness of the stolen peach had soaked my glove as a punishment for my disobedience. It was high time I removed myself from the Colonel's garden.

There was a gap in the middle of the line of hothouses where a gate divided the boundary wall. Beyond it against the panes of the next house I could see tall columnar tomato plants, their trusses of juicy red glowing like hot coals amid the dark green leaves; but the door at this end of the row of fruit-houses was locked, and there was nothing for it but to go back the way I'd come, back through that perfumed glass cloister with its abundant harvest wasting on the ground.

I'd almost reached the final door leading out into the walled garden when a shadow fell across it, startling me. *Suppose Colonel Allen has returned unexpectedly,* I thought in panic, and then scolded myself for my silliness. I very much doubted if the Colonel ever set foot in his hothouses; and besides, he was safely abroad.

The young man who'd opened the glass-house door—a gardener, from the dirt on his hands and his bare forearms—stared at me in surprise which turned quickly to suspicion.

"Can I help you, Ma'am?" He made it sound less like an offer of assistance than a demand to know why I was there.

I quickly explained who I was, holding my juice-stained glove out of sight against my skirts.

"I often walk my dog in the lane between our two houses, and this time, because your gate was unlocked, she came in. She was accustomed to run through here when Westwood Park was Admiral Keane's, I'm afraid."

Lottie, at my feet, stared up adoringly, her eyes bulging with devotion, the very image of absolute obedience.

"Yes, m'lady." The gardener sounded unconvinced. I hoped he couldn't be certain the hothouse door had been securely closed.

But the incident shook me out of my daydream. By the time I'd retraced my steps past the reedy border of the lake, across the drive and through the shrubbery to the side gate, I'd shrunk back into my decorous everyday self, oh-so-respectable Lady Oliver. Thankfully,

there was no need for anyone at the White House to find out where
I'd been, and if the gardener's boy ever told his superior and the
story found its way to Colonel Allen, what could he believe of me,
except that I'd gone in pursuit of my dog?

———

Silly nonsense, Aunt Grace called it, when I told her of the Colonel's
offer and my reasons for turning it down. Aunt Grace still called on
me at the White House from time to time, but although I knew how
much she enjoyed whirling in her brougham up the curving carriage-
sweep to our front door, just to be in the territory of the mighty
Olivers always put her on the defensive. Aunt Grace had never altered her opinion that it was her own husband, Captain Thomas
Fuller, whose single-handed efforts kept the Oliver ships at sea and
saved the company from insolvency. It was all very well for her niece
to be married to Sir Jonas Oliver and to enjoy his wealth and position, but that wouldn't blind Aunt Grace to the family's shortcom-
ings, the greatest of which was overweening pride. And now that
same pride had driven them to fling their new neighbor's generosity
back in his face.

"*Pride goeth before destruction, and an haughty spirit before a
fall,*" she repeated solemnly. "The Olivers had better watch their
step, that's all. As the Captain would say, they think no small beer
of themselves, your husband and his sister. And who was Lady Verity's father, in any case, but a slaver before he set up in business? A
sea-captain and a slaver."

"Aunt Grace! Please . . ."

My aunt held up a hand to indicate that she would say no more
. . . and then thought better of it, and added in a loud hiss, "All I
mean is that the Olivers have no cause to set themselves up as
saints."

"I'm sure Verity and Jonas did what they thought was best."
Whatever my private opinion might be, I felt bound to defend the
Olivers. "It would be dreadful to be beholden to a man like that,
surely."

Aunt Grace pursed her lips. Since the Colonel had turned out not
to be a long-lost relative after all, she was torn between condemning
Jonas and Verity's mean-spirited behavior and defending the notorious owner of Westwood Park.

"I daresay he was only trying to be a good neighbor," she ven-

tured. "Besides—didn't you tell me this . . . Colonel Allen . . . has
spent many years in America? Well—there you are! You know perfectly well the Americans have all sorts of ideas different from our
own. We ought to make allowances for this gentleman if he's spent
a great deal of time among them. Indeed we should." Before I could
remind my aunt of her often-aired views on *respectability*, she
quickly changed the subject.

"And speaking of America, do you know your mother is poorly?"

I hadn't known, and I wasn't sure what to say. I knew Aunt Grace
still exchanged letters with my mother and had often suggested a
reconciliation between us, only to be told in no uncertain terms what
she could do with her peace-making. But my aunt still clung to the
hope of a reunion, and doggedly sent news of each of us to the other
—news which was received with very little enthusiasm at either end.

"I had a letter from Susannah only the other day," my aunt was
saying, "not from St. John's, but from New York, of all places. It
seems she's been there for months now. Edward's remained behind
in Newfoundland, but Maria's there with her while she consults a
doctor she's heard highly spoken of. She says the doctors in Newfoundland have no idea of their trade." My aunt paused, and
frowned at me. "You don't ask what her trouble is, I see."

"I'm sure you'll tell me, whether I ask or not."

"Really, Rachel—what am I to do with the pair of you? Very well,
I'll save you the trouble of asking. Your mother complains that she
can't sleep at night, and that sometimes her spirits are very low and
she constantly mislays things. *Oho, is that all your trouble?* I wrote
to her. *Wait till you have my palpitations and my rheumatic knees!*
What's a few hours' sleep, after all, when you can't get to your feet
after a prayer in church?" Aunt Grace folded her hands primly. "Not
that I imagine that would bother your mother. She was always an
ungodly creature."

"And you were only trying to be sympathetic."

"Exactly! And I've told her if she's as ill as she thinks, she should
come to London to see Professor Pickstone, who did so much for the
late King, so they say. Melancholia is his particular study."

"Good Heavens, I hope she won't do anything of the kind!" The
idea of my mother arriving in England was utterly horrifying.

"Oh, never fear—your mother has no intention of setting foot in
this country again. She's told me as much time after time. She claims
that England brought her nothing but ill-luck, or some such non-

sense. And as you've cause to know, when your mother makes up her mind about something, the dead will walk again before she changes it."

If Aunt Grace was right, then surely I was perfectly safe.

23

Throughout October the White House was in turmoil. Louise, my delicate five-year-old angel, caught whooping-cough, and the entire household revolved for a month round the room where she lay coughing and vomiting while relays of nurses helped me tend her day and night.

The doctor came and went, grave-faced, and prescribed belladonna and potassium. We feared pneumonia had developed; that Louise had become convulsive; that at the very least her ears were affected. But my blond, fragile daughter was made of sterner stuff than any of us realized. Little by little she began to recover, though for many weeks afterward the occasional fit of coughing would seize her and the dreadful, sucking whoop of her indrawn breath would echo through the house.

Jonas was concerned about Louise, but detached. What angered me most was that he never seemed to grasp the serious danger to his daughter—or if he did, he had absolute faith in his wife and the doctor to make her well again. Even when I was at my most desperate, red-eyed from worry and lack of sleep, Jonas would listen patiently to my bulletins on Louise's health, nodding as if to say *Well, well; how vexing* . . . and I could see from his eyes that his thoughts were elsewhere, wrestling with matters which had nothing to do with the present crisis. Almost hysterical with exhaustion, I discovered a great well of anger inside me, a surge of black rage and resentment that anything in the world should be judged more important than my child's life. Even after the danger was past and I was able to sleep again the memory of that anger remained, smoldering like live coals among the ashes. And I hadn't forgotten Lettice Wyre.

One early November evening Jonas cleared his throat with particular vigor between the removal of the roast from the dinner table and the arrival of pudding. I recognized that solemn throat-clearing; it usually meant that some important announcement was on its way.

"There's something I've been meaning to speak to you about, my dear," he began gravely as soon as the servants had left the room. "I'd have mentioned it before now, but you were taken up—very properly taken up—with poor little Louise."

Ignoring the expression on my face, he pressed on with his grand announcement.

"Now, however, it's high time you gave some thought to it too. The days are passing."

I waited to find out what this important matter might be that had taken up so much of his attention.

It was a new ship—or so it appeared at first—but this time a vessel so different and so revolutionary that even I could appreciate the excitement surrounding it.

The Oliver Line already owned six steamships, of which two—the *Abercorn* and the *Zetland*—were on the North Atlantic run, both fitted with low-compression, single-expansion engines driving paddlewheels at each side. They'd proved to be reliable ships, but it had soon become clear that in heavy seas one paddlewheel or the other was constantly out of the water, putting a dangerous strain on the engine.

The answer, Jonas had decided, was screw-propulsion. His great dream was of a ship fitted with an iron propeller, built entirely of iron, a ship driven by a far greater head of steam passing through not one but two cylinders at high and low pressure, saving a third of the fuel used by a vessel such as the *Abercorn*. A Scotsman, John Elder, had been working for some time on an engine of this kind, and Jonas was eager to put his invention to the test in an Oliver ship.

Building work had already begun in a Birkenhead yard—in some secrecy, since this was to be a ship like no other. The plans spread out on the library table showed a monster of four thousand tons with a bridge amidships like the *Abercorn* but without the clumsy paddleboxes which gave that ship her waddling gait. As a great concession Jonas had rigged her as a four-masted bark, though he was confident the sails would never be set between ports.

"She's a steamer, pure and simple." He tapped the plans with an elegant finger. "Don't be misled by the masts. Sooner or later we have to put our faith in steam, whatever the Jeremiahs may say, and build a ship with no other means of propulsion. I'd have taken the masts out of this one long ago, only I'd never raise the money to build her if word got out.

"Passengers like to see masts and yards on a ship. For some reason it gives them confidence in the vessel, even if they never see a sail set." He shook his head for a moment over the folly of sea-travelers.

"Cunard's managed to convince the government he needs a mail contract to make steamers pay on the North Atlantic—don't ask me how he did it, but the fact remains that he's got his money, and he and Collins have put their heads together to fix the cargo rates between Liverpool and New York, so now they think they're both sitting pretty. But *this* ship'll teach them a sharp lesson: just look at the amount of space we'll have in the hold and on the passenger decks without all that paddlewheel machinery! At seven guineas a ton, she'll make a handsome profit without a penny from the mails."

He spun round to face me, his face glowing with pride and excitement.

"*Altair*—that's what I'm going to call her. *Altair,* after the eagle star, because she'll be the Star of the Seas."

"Won't Cunard or Collins start building screw steamers as soon as they know about this one?"

Jonas shook his head.

"Not by a long way. Cunard's directors are a cautious lot. They'll wait to see if the *Altair* blows her boilers before they'll try to build anything like her. And Collins has ploughed every cent into his ships already—and he's shaking them to pieces trying to set records for the crossing. No—we'll be able to pick and choose our trade for a good few years. We might even be able to take over the mail contract when Cunard's time runs out."

"Well, it's certainly very exciting, Jonas." I was bemused by the figures of tonnages and steam-pressures he'd thrown at me. "But I don't see how I can help you with your new ship. You did say I should turn my mind to it, and of course I'll be pleased to do anything I can—but I can't imagine what."

"Ah—yes." All of a sudden, Jonas looked a little anxious. "Perhaps I should have told you about this earlier. You see—Prince Albert is making a private visit to the Chorleighs at Asterholm at the end of this month, and old Chorleigh—who's one of our stockholders, remember—has given him some fanciful tale about our plans for the new steamship. Well, you know how quickly the prince takes up any novel engineering project. The long and the short of it is that he wants to visit the yard to see the whole thing for himself."

"Oh, Jonas! How proud you must be!"

"Yes, I am, of course," admitted Jonas warily. "It's a great honor. But the point is, my dear . . . He's coming on here for dinner afterward. To the White House. Perhaps I should have mentioned it before."

———————

It's amazing how much can be achieved in three weeks. Such a starching of linen and caps and aprons went on that the laundry room was permanently enveloped in a fog of the stuff; the drawing-room wallpaper, which had barely hung a year, was "breaded," just in case; a perfect sea of vinegar-and-water flowed over chairs and tables, followed by a vat of paraffin oil and considerable elbow-grease; the dining table itself was fed with beeswax until it shone like a mirror, only to be hidden by a damask cloth of dazzling whiteness over another of green to give the correct tint. As the great day approached, lobsters were ordered, and delivered, and inspected, and sent back, and reordered, and reinspected, and grudgingly kept. Chickens arrived in flocks, salmon in shoals, and enough sugar was poured into jellies and pastries to strip the West Indies of cane.

And all the time I was nagged and chivvied by Verity Broadney in a white heat of jealousy that the honor had fallen to me.

"What shall you serve your soup in?" Verity had demanded to know. "You'll certainly need something very large. . . . Why—I know! You shall have my tureen! Of course you shall, Rachel *dear*. The Broadney tureen: it's big enough for an army. There—that's decided."

Verity treasured her large silver soup-tureen, ample enough for a hip-bath, made in the Russian style like an Aladdin's lamp, with upward-curving handles and a rampant bird on the lid. I knew what she was thinking: if Lady Broadney had been upstaged as hostess, at least her massive tureen would claim a share of the credit for the evening's success. *Poor thing—she was quite lost until I lent her My Tureen. . . .*

There was no point in taking the problem to Jonas. If the tureen had boasted a steam-engine and funnels instead of its hideous gad-rooning he might have taken an interest. Unfortunately, as things were, I knew the disgusting thing was doomed to squat on my elegant serving table however hard I might try to give it back.

Time fled. The servants were briefed, the kitchen exhorted, the grooms and the gardeners mustered. The table was laid and finger-glasses set out, only to be rejected—except for one—on Verity's instructions. Since the days of the secret Jacobite toast to "the King over the water" it seemed that only royalty might swill the fingertips if royalty were present in case any guest should hold his wineglass over his finger-glass at the crucial moment. I was humbly grateful for being rescued from this gaffe, and afterward tried hard not to resent the Russian tureen.

If I was the general of my little army, I realized what I needed was an efficient aide-de-camp, and since Reuben was at home for a short while I sent him off to Father O'Hara's house to ask Nancy Morris if she'd help me out in my hour of need. After Mrs. Dobbs's retirement Nancy had succeeded to the post of housekeeper, and ran the priest's household with amazing efficiency. The tradesmen who'd shamelessly cheated poor Father O'Hara in Mrs. Dobbs's day didn't dare to pad their bills by so much as a penny now that Nancy was in charge. She was a good-looking young woman of twenty-seven now that she'd had the chance of a few years of solid food and a steady wage. We'd never lost touch, and from time to time she visited me to tell me how little James Albert and the rescued Rose children were faring.

"That man Webb"—Reuben remarked over luncheon, "—the father of Nancy's child—he was on a ship called the *Mount Rose* that was wrecked off Land's End, you know."

"His ship was wrecked on the Runnelstone, as a matter of fact. I first met Nancy shortly after Jack Webb was drowned, when Oliver's refused to pay her his outstanding wages. In those days she and her mother were in a pretty desperate state."

"I'm surprised to hear that—she seems such a capable woman. You'd think she'd easily have found work somewhere."

"She was about to have the baby any minute, Reuben."

"Oh . . . I see." Reuben looked faintly pink.

"You must have had a long talk with Nancy, it seems to me."

"The Mate of my old ship *Maid of Corinth* had sailed as third officer in the *Mount Rose,* and I'd heard quite a bit about her from him." Pensively, Reuben traced the pattern on his plate with the point of his knife. "Handsome-looking woman," he added irrelevantly.

I finally ran Jonas to earth in the library, and presented him with the finished menu. Turtle soup with slices of lemon would be followed by turbot in lobster sauce, then salt-marsh mutton, rich wild duck, and cold dishes of pigeon, ham and quails in the manner of Provence, the Basques and—if the truth be told—Mossley Hill, *aux fines herbes*, *sur canapés* and *au cresson*, chased down by strawed potatoes and *salad à la Victoria*. On the heels of that would come *gelées de fraise au Champagne* and *bonne bouchées à la Torque*.

"It isn't champagne and claret you need with this," remarked Jonas sourly, "so much as a good indigestion remedy. Give him a glass of Tokay as a stomachic, poor fellow, or he'll never sleep."

"Very well, then—tell me what can be left out."

"Nothing! Nothing! Stuff the man like a capon if you must. I'm sure he's used to it."

Jonas, of course, would have been happy to give the Prince Consort bread and cheese if it meant having a few more minutes to dazzle him with the wonders of his new venture. The *Altair* had already become Jonas's grand obsession; as the date of the visit drew nearer I'd found him more unapproachable than ever, completely absorbed in a world of cylinder-jackets and scum-pans, throttle-valves and gauge-cocks, shut in the library with huge folded sheets of designs for hours on end, utterly oblivious to the passing of mealtimes until violent hunger gripped him and he emerged from his sanctuary, shouting indignantly for food.

As luck would have it, the only real contact I had with him during those weeks was a serious row on the subject of Matthew. For once, I knew Jonas's entire attention was focused on what I was saying—but only, in the end, to disagree with me.

From the first days of our marriage it had been a great relief to discover how easily Matthew had accepted Jonas as a stepfather. If anything, he seemed delighted with his wealthy stepfamily, reveling in the attention of our numerous servants, the generous size of the White House and an apparently limitless wardrobe. Before long he even announced to us that he no longer wished to be known as Matthew Gaunt, but in future as Matthew Oliver. Since he'd no memories at all of his real father, he wanted nothing further to do with his name.

Jonas was charmed, and I felt bound to give my blessing. I'd tried loyally to create a lasting image of Adam Gaunt for his son to treasure, but I had to accept now that I'd failed. It was true that Adam had died before Matthew was old enough to remember him, but at the same time I couldn't rid myself of an uneasy feeling that Matthew's fondness for the Oliver name had more to do with the family's wealth and position than with any real affection for Jonas. I was uncomfortably aware of a calculating side to Matthew which I didn't altogether admire, though I understood the loathing for the days of our early poverty which had brought it about.

Matters came to a head at the worst possible time. Three days before the Prince's visit, Jonas received a letter from Matthew's headmaster asking for the boy to be fetched home, where he was to stay until the school term resumed after Christmas. The charge was flagrant drunkenness.

Half an hour later, before Jonas could even issue instructions, Matthew himself appeared in high good humor on a hired livery horse, having dismissed himself from school and made his own way home, leaving impudent directions for his trunk to be sent on after him.

The boy was four months short of his fifteenth birthday, and I was appalled at the idea of his racketing about the countryside on a rawboned mare with scarred knees and a mad light in her eye. I was even more appalled by the accusation of drunkenness which had brought it about. I'd never forgotten how drink had gradually destroyed my father, starting in the warmth of good fellowship and ending as a secret vice. Was Joseph Dean's grandson about to set off down the same painful road?

Matthew was cheerfully unrepentant.

"Smashed the teapot like a good'un, this last time," he told me proudly. "Famously drunk, I was, down at the ol' Bush. Slantindicular when I got back to school, and then all Hell broke loose. The Doctor was all set to thrash me, then he remembered it wasn't the first time I'd skipped off classes, and he sent me down instead. Still —you know what they say about the barber's cat, Mater—"

"I don't want to know what they say."

"—'all piss and wind.' And that's the Doctor for you," Matthew finished triumphantly, standing with his backside to the fire burning in my little sitting room, the tails of his coat tucked up, his hands thrust arrogantly into his pockets. There was a smugness and a cocksureness about him which, I realized guiltily, Adam would never have tolerated for a moment.

"I won't have language like that under this roof, Matthew," I said

sternly, but Matthew just grinned and shrugged, and began to whistle a barroom ditty.

"What your stepfather will say to all this, I dread to think."

I hoped devoutly that this time the strait-laced Jonas would give
Matthew what he badly needed—a good dressing-down. I recognized a strength of character in Matthew which my father had never
possessed, but his growing taste for drink made me sick with worry.
Perhaps if his allowance were cut or he were forbidden to ride for a
bit, he might come to his senses.

Yet to my amazement Jonas simply laughed at Matthew's account
of his crazy ride home across several counties, and capped it with
some story of his own father's wild youth.

"Damn a horse if I go back to school, anyhow," muttered Matthew rebelliously. "Latin and history won't be much use for what I
want to do in future. I want to work for the shipping line with you,
Sir. And Greek verbs don't build ships!"

"No, but arithmetic does—and geometry," Jonas pointed out
mildly. "Just you come and look at the plans I'm working on now,
my boy, and you'll see what I mean. I know there are still sailmakers
who can look up at a yard and then cut out a sail for it on the
strength of what their eyes tell them, but those days are nearly done.
Ship-building's entering the age of science at last. If you can't count,
you can't build a steamship. No, Matthew, you'll have to go back to
school for a year or two yet, and then we'll see. And don't worry,
I'll square it with the Doctor."

And that had been the end of the matter, until I raised it again as
we were preparing for bed that night. I was sitting in front of my
dressing-table mirror, brushing my hair, and as soon as Vickers had
left I called through the half-open door to Jonas in the next room.

"I do wish you'd been harder on Matthew, Jonas. He's turning
into a drunken lout, and now he seems to think you approve of his
escapades."

"I may not have given him a whipping, my dear, but I wouldn't
exactly call that approving of what he did."

"But *drinking*, Jonas! At his age! *Drinking*, and whatever else that
might lead to! Suppose he only goes off and does it again?"

"Of course he'll do it again. He's just a boy, Rachel. He'll grow
up quickly enough one of these days."

I could hardly believe this was Jonas talking. I paused, shocked,
the brush buried in my hair.

"I must say, I'm surprised to hear that from you. Did you go drinking in back-street barrooms before you were even fifteen?"

"Something of the sort, no doubt," said Jonas easily. "Before I learned that it wasn't worth a sore head the next morning. As Matthew will learn, I'm sure, if he's given time."

"Jonas, this isn't like you at all! Will you be so lenient with Alice and Louise when they're old enough to go out and enjoy themselves?"

"Of course not!" Jonas's astonishment floated through to me. "You can't seriously suggest there's any similarity between the sort of conduct you expect from your daughters, and this little spot of mischief Matthew's got into! Oh, I can understand how hard it is for you to let go of him. . . . There you were, left a widow with a son to bring up on your own. Matthew was all you had—you were bound to worry about him—bound to be overprotective. All I'm saying is that it's time to use a looser rein on the boy. Give him the freedom he wants. . . ."

I was already across the room, staring at him from the doorway.

"Overprotective, did you say? What on earth do you mean?"

"You've molly-coddled the lad. Tied him to your apron strings. It's perfectly obvious to me that his behavior is just a reaction against your possessiveness. Now he's free of you, he's trying his wings."

Jonas was in his dressing room, his back to the door, absorbed in retrieving shirt-studs and dropping them one by one into a small tortoiseshell box. Even the set of his shoulders looked smug and self-satisfied.

"*Molly-coddled* him?"

"Made him a mother's boy. Suffocated him. That sort of thing. And don't imagine I'm not concerned about him. I've given the matter a great deal of thought lately, and I've decided that since he seems to be so interested in the shipping business, and since we've no son of our own, Matthew will be the one to take over the company from me one day. Now I can't have a milksop running the Oliver Line, can I? Just because his mother can't bear to let him out of her sight?"

My explosive howl of rage brought Jonas running out of his dressing room to face me.

"How dare you tell me all those days of working, of saving every cent to feed and clothe my son and bring him back with me from America, have made him a milksop! How dare you! You and Verity —you've never known what it was like to be short of money! When did you last have to decide between buying a few pounds of flour or a pair of shoes?"

Jonas opened his mouth to answer, but I was too quick for him.

"Of course I cared for my son, and worried myself sick about him! Do you call that being possessive? Was I supposed to turn him out on the streets to fend for himself? Would that have prevented him from becoming a *milksop,* do you think?"

"Rachel, this is nonsense! I didn't mean—"

"You self-righteous, pompous hypocrite—"

"Keep your voice down!"

In truth, the business of Matthew's drinking was merely an excuse for a long-due venting of feelings which I'd tried valiantly to hold in check. Now that the dam had burst, the depth of my rage exhausted and frightened me. In my fury, I came close to revealing the real extent of my sacrifices on Matthew's behalf—the ghost of Mademoiselle Valentine waited at my elbow—but at the last minute I drew back from that fatal precipice. Slamming shut the door between our two bedrooms with a final, furious exclamation, I fell across my bed, suddenly drained of strength.

———

The door wasn't locked, but Jonas made no attempt to open it. I could hear him moving about his room and the final creak as he climbed into bed, and then there was silence. If I'd expected him to sue for peace I was to be disappointed.

Next day Jonas had gone from the house before I came downstairs. He'd left word that he wouldn't be home at midday, and I ate luncheon alone with Matthew in the breakfast room.

By evening, as I dressed for dinner, I was beginning to wonder if Jonas intended to humiliate me by not appearing for the meal, when the door between our two bedrooms opened and he came in without knocking. In one hand he held a flat, leather-covered box.

He regarded me in silence from a few feet away, then cleared his throat ceremoniously.

"Now Rachel, I haven't come to lecture you. You know that's not my way. But there's one thing I must say before we go any further; your behavior last night was quite dreadful. I'm sure you know that now. Some of the things you said to me were very hurtful, but on reflection I realize you didn't mean them."

"No, Jonas. I'm truly sorry," I lied.

Jonas pursed his small pink lips, and frowned.

"D'you know, for a while I couldn't imagine what had come over you. *This isn't my Rachel,* I said to myself. *We don't have arguments like this.* Because one of the things I've always admired in you, my dear, is your willingness to be guided. You're always happy to take advice from someone with more experience of life. And in this case —about Matthew—I was in the right, and you were quite wrong to disagree with me."

"Yes, Jonas," I admitted mechanically.

"Good. I thought you'd see the sense of my words when you'd had some time to think them over. And I've been giving some thought to the problem of Matthew's drinking too," he conceded handsomely. "I think it's time I took a greater interest in the boy— took him in hand, perhaps. Shaped his energies toward a goal. Let him see the responsibility which lies ahead of him. Then, when the time comes for him to run the company, we'll all be proud of him."

I nodded in weary silence.

"Of course, I realized in the end what was the matter with you. You're overtired. You've had a great deal of extra worry over this dinner for the Prince, and I've been too busy to notice. It was wrong of me to place such a burden on you. I should have asked Verity to take charge: she has a natural talent for that sort of thing." Jonas laid a soft white hand on my shoulder, and slipped the leather case into my lap. "So we'll say no more about it, shall we? Now—open the box and see what you find. I was going to give you these tomorrow night, to wear for the Prince's dinner, but you might as well have them now, my dear. I hope they give you pleasure."

Listlessly, I undid the clasp of the case. I was tired, as Jonas had said—too tired to challenge his account of our quarrel. What, after all, would I gain by it? And perhaps everything would still work out for the best in the end. Matthew, who'd never be shamed into mending his ways, might be persuaded to do so with the glittering bribe of the Oliver Line before his eyes.

I raised the lid of the leather case. Lying on a bed of black velvet were a necklet and two bracelets of magnificent pearls, exquisitely matched for size and color, double rows fastened with great bosses of diamonds—a large clasp for the necklet and smaller ones for the bracelets, winking and glittering as I tilted the case, sparkling with vermilion fire in the gaslight. Even knowing what I did of the great wealth of the Olivers, I was stunned by the gift.

"Well?" demanded Jonas above my head. "Will they suit what you've chosen to wear for the Prince?"

"Perfectly."

"There—you see, my dear! I was right to choose pearls for you. When you've more time to think about it, you'll find I'm usually right." And Jonas bent forward, and kissed me lightly on the forehead.

———

In the greatest haste, I'd ordered a dress in sea-green silk faille, its deeply cut neckline rich in lace and ribbon, the skirt and elaborate overskirt very full over the obligatory horsehair petticoat and several more. On the evening of the dinner Vickers helped me to dress, lacing the long corsets I only consented to wear in the evening, and finally fastening Jonas's pearls round my neck and wrists where they glowed with opaline tints of rose and green.

Examining my reflection in the mirror, I cursed the current fashion for excessively low necklines. My shoulders were too thin to be so naked. The Queen had made the style fashionable, but then, the Queen had plump, rounded little shoulders and well-covered arms on which it looked well.

For a moment the image in the mirror reminded me of another green dress, sixteen years earlier, in which I'd run down to dinner in my aunt's house to find Adam Gaunt waiting unexpectedly in the drawing room. It was an eerie moment of recollection, and I wondered why on earth I should suddenly remember that night—unless there was something familiar in the blue-gray shadows where the bodice was gathered, or in the fullness of the skirt. . . .

That well-loved gown had been so much simpler than the one in which Lady Oliver would greet the Prince Consort. And there were other differences. . . . Nowadays, brushing my hair at night, I'd sometimes find a single strong strand of silver threaded through my dark waves; now there was a thin line like a pencil-stroke under each eye, more obvious when I was tired, no doubt the first of many which would mark the passing years.

Diane de Poitiers, beautiful mistress of a French king, was said never to have let herself laugh or cry in case a stray crease rooted itself in her skin. In that case, I thought, perhaps after all I'd reach old age with the rosy smoothness of youth. Jonas might still succeed in preserving me in my glass case at the White House, where life had slipped into a serene round of polite society and well-upholstered living.

I touched the pearls at my neck. No argument was to be allowed to disturb the smooth surface of our existence. Jonas knew best, and under his ordered regime there was nothing to cry for anymore—and precious little to laugh about. Eternal beauty was the reward. Given time, I might even grow accustomed to being shown off on my pin.

As I'd promised, I slipped upstairs to the nursery to let the girls see me in my finery before the first of my guests arrived.

The visit to the shipyard had gone well. I could tell as much as soon as Jonas stepped lightly out of the Prince's carriage at the front door of the White House, still talking excitedly to his distinguished guest, his hands describing in the air the great sweeping arcs of his steamship's hull.

The Prince Consort was slighter than I'd expected, though of course I'd only seen him close to on the day I'd been presented at Court, standing by the side of the queen, who was short enough to make any man look tall. Jonas and the prince were well matched, Prince Albert as dark as Jonas was fair, both looking pale and over-worked but chatting with an intense and enthusiastic absorption about a subject close to both their hearts.

Prince Albert was all nose and moustache, I decided as I curtseyed before him. He was thirty-two, the same age as I was, though he looked a good deal older, the pale dome of his head framed in carefully combed strands of hair and the whiskers which flourished round his jaws. I saw his heavy brows draw closer as I was presented by the Earl of Chorleigh but his expression cleared at once, and I was surprised at the sudden youthfulness a smile brought to his normally rather severe features.

"Your husband is a clever man, Lady Oliver," he told me. "This new ship of his will show that Britain can lead the world in carrying cargo and passengers at economic prices. It's a most exciting idea. You must be very proud of Sir Jonas."

"Oh, I am, Sir." What else could I say, with the double rows of Jonas's pearls looping my neck and wrists like priceless fetters, my reward for acknowledging my husband's worth and his right to know what was best for us all?

The dinner was faultless. I knew from Jonas's approving glances in my direction and from Verity's distant smirk that I'd passed the test and upheld the Oliver name. Dish after dish was conveyed soundlessly from the kitchen by servants threatened with frightful reprisals if so much as a silver dish-cover was allowed to crash to the floor. Not a shoe squeaked, sauces were handed impeccably, wine was offered and poured, desserts came and went, the prince's wishes being paramount in everything. Just before the brandy and cigars were brought I led the ladies through to the drawing room to drink coffee, beginning to feel I might relax at last after the rigors of battle.

I was deep in a conversation about fox-hounds with the middle-aged, genial countess of Chorleigh when a footman appeared at my elbow with a silver tray, a white envelope framed in its center. On the envelope were the words *Lady Oliver, The White House* in an unknown hand.

"I believe it's urgent, my lady," William informed me in a low voice.

"Then open it, my dear," boomed Lady Chorleigh. "Open it, for goodness' sake."

I excused myself, and opened the note. At the top of a single sheet of thick paper was the address of Westwood Park.

"Dear Lady Oliver," it began, "Mr. Matthew Oliver met with an accident in town this evening, and was brought to this house by Colonel Allen, who happened to come across him in the street. His condition is not dangerous, but the Colonel felt it wise all the same to have him examined by a doctor. We are advised that he should rest with us here until tomorrow at least. Please do not be unduly concerned. Everything has been done for his comfort, and your son is perfectly safe."

The note was signed *C. E. Gibson, Housekeeper.*

For several seconds I stared at the paper in my hand, numb with shock and incomprehension. Matthew was at Aunt Grace Fuller's house, surely, safely in Leghorn Street, spending the evening with young Harry. There must be a mistake: Colonel Allen could hardly know Matthew by sight—perhaps he'd taken some other young man for my son in the half-light of a city street.

And I couldn't imagine why Matthew should have been in the city at all. Why hadn't he been with Harry and Aunt Grace? I'd welcomed his new friendship with his eighteen-year-old kinsman—according to Aunt Grace, Harry was a paragon among sons, devout, studious, and ready to take his mother's advice in everything. I'd hoped Matthew might adopt Harry for a model, and I'd gladly consented to his spending the evening at his great-aunt's house. It was inconceivable that he should now be lying, injured, in a strange bed, while his mother poured coffee for her guests not quarter of a mile distant.

"Not bad news, I hope," rumbled Lady Chorleigh at my side.

I showed her the note.

"Oh, but you must go at once! Of course you must go. The Prince will insist, I'm sure of it. We must send word to him in the dining room. You can take our carriage, since it's just at your door. Yes, indeed you must, and I'll play hostess till you return. No, my dear, not another word! Westwood Park is hardly a step away, is it not?"

Prince Albert professed himself most concerned. Lady Oliver must on no account stand on ceremony: he knew only too well the devotion of a mother for her children. There was nothing else for it—she must go at once to her son's bedside.

I was grateful for his kindness. Jonas, adrift among the stars aboard his steamship, agreed that I should do as I thought best—go, stay, whatever I thought proper now that His Royal Highness had given his permission. He was sure I was fretting over nothing, but I might as well set my mind at rest. . . . The fact that I was bound for Westwood Park, that den of immorality, seemed to have slipped his mind. If I wished to go, then I should go as soon as I pleased. And Jonas returned to the dining room, where the smoke of many cigars had already launched the *Altair,* her sisters and her successors, like so many wraiths upon the mellow air.

Wrapped in a voluminous velvet burnouse, I was bundled—alone, since there was no one to go with me—into the Chorleighs' great dress-coach for the short ride to Westwood Park. The carriage smelled of mustiness and the countess's eau-de-cologne, and jolted abominably. In spite of the fur rug over my knees I shivered in the darkness, watching the black, skeletal trees pass one by one across the dim blue rectangle of each window.

It was all so unreal. Behind me was my own brightly lit home, where my husband was entertaining the Prince Consort. Yet here was his gracious hostess, clattering off in the opposite direction, unescorted, in a borrowed carriage, hastening through the night toward the somber gables of Westwood Park.

The wet branches of winter shrubs and trees lashed the windows as the swaying coach turned into my neighbor's gates only to begin its headlong flight once more. Beyond the windows, the tree-lined drive was in utter blackness. There was nothing to be seen of the graceful orangery or the lake, or the walled garden with its lavish, seductive glass-houses. My hand moved involuntarily across the fur rug, as though hiding a stain on my glove. . . . Did the hothouses still smell of honey, swallowed up in the winter darkness?

I shivered again, my apprehension not solely for my injured son.

24

They were expecting me at Westwood Park. The Chorleighs' groom had hardly leaped from the carriage-box to open my door and release the two narrow folding steps when the great oak door of the house swung open and the figure of a woman stood on the lighted threshold.

"Please come this way, Lady Oliver." Straight, gray-haired and dressed in severe black, she waited for me just inside the pillared entrance.

"Mrs. Gibson?"

"That is correct."

"Thank you for your note, and for all you've done for Matthew. But I had to come—I had to see for myself—"

"Of course. I quite understand."

With a gesture, she invited me to go before her into the hall, and to my astonishment I realized it was exactly—in every detail—as Admiral Keane had left it. In an alcove to the right of the front door a barograph in a glass case and a bronze bust of Lord Nelson stood on a mahogany secretaire as they'd always done. Directly opposite was the same huge canvas massively framed in gilt, depicting a British warship holding off two French vessels simultaneously, a subject dear to the Admiral's heart.

Even the walls were the same gloomy blue-green I remembered, and directly ahead at the end of the hall the ponderous stone staircase with its iron balustrade rose, uncarpeted, toward the upper regions of the house exactly as before. If Admiral Keane himself had come limping out of his study to greet me, his stick tapping on the black and white tiled floor and his breath whistling in his throat, I wouldn't have been at all surprised.

"Colonel Allen regrets that he cannot receive you himself," said the housekeeper in flat, precise tones, "but he has instructed me to offer you any assistance within our power at Westwood Park. I imagine you'd like to see your son straight away. If you'll come with me, I'll take you to him."

At her signal, a footman came forward to take my velvet wrap, then Mrs. Gibson led the way up the great staircase, her back very straight in her plain black dress. Hurrying after her, I felt hopelessly encumbered by my extravagant skirts, and for a moment I wished Verity had been with me to appreciate the ridiculousness of the situation. Here was the house whose very name made her shiver with horror: this was Westwood Park, that lair of wickedness—and yet it was respectable Lady Oliver, hostess to a prince, who was hurrying up the stairs with her shoulders as bare as a harem-girl's and her naked bosom festooned with pearls.

At the top of the staircase a corridor ran parallel to the southern frontage of the house, with rooms opening off it at intervals. Mrs. Gibson crossed noiselessly to where a narrow strip of light crept under one of the doors; without knocking, she silently turned the handle and stood back to let me walk past her into the room.

Heavy shutters were closed over the windows, locking out the frosty night. The light I'd glimpsed beneath the door came almost entirely from a fire burning brightly behind its brass fender on the opposite wall, but between the tall windows a single candle flickered on a table by the head of a big, canopied bed, picking out the gold threads in its ancient hangings. As I entered, a maid who'd been sitting on a chair near the bed rose, bobbed, and quietly left the room.

Just beyond her chair a thin form, still and pale, lay under the brocaded bed-cover, hardly seeming to disturb the geometric regularity of its pattern. Matthew's skin was the color of buttermilk, whiter than the glossy linen pillows under his head. His eyes were closed, the lids bluish, and just above them a thick cotton bandage was wound two or three times round his head. He lay so quietly that I waited until I'd seen him breathe before I could be sure of his being alive at all. Yet his breath, when it came, was a long, sonorous indrawing of air followed by a gusty exhalation. Matthew, utterly oblivious to his surroundings, was snoring.

I was taken aback. Matthew looked so small, there in the giant bed, and all at once very young. The bandage round his temples had made my heart leap—yet he was clearly asleep, not unconscious.

"You see how he is, Lady Oliver." The housekeeper was standing next to me. "There's no danger, as I told you. But the doctor said he should stay with us tonight. Tomorrow he can go home."

"But his injury . . . his head . . . You said there'd been an accident."

"You must understand, he was very—muddy—when Colonel Allen brought him here. And there was some blood on his head. Just here." She indicated the place. "I think someone must have hit him."

"*Hit him?*" The question came out more loudly than I intended.

Mrs. Gibson touched a finger to her lips. "Better not wake him. Though I daresay it wouldn't be easy."

"I don't understand any of this! Who could have hit him? Where was Matthew when the Colonel found him?"

"I'm afraid he was involved in a fight, near the docks. By good luck Colonel Allen was passing in his carriage when the young man was arrested by the constables. The Colonel recognized him as your son, and spoke to the men who were holding him. I believe he gave them some money. At any rate, they released him into the Colonel's charge, and Colonel Allen brought him back here. He was afraid you might be shocked by your son's appearance—there was a lot of blood on his face, though the wound was only slight.

"As I told you, someone must have struck him on the head—perhaps a constable, or one of the men he was fighting. Or he may have fallen to the ground—who knows?" The housekeeper's eyes met mine for a brief second, then flicked away again, leaving the faint ghost of a smile. "The young man was . . . confused . . . so the Colonel said. He kept falling down in the roadway. He was very dirty when he arrived here."

"Falling down?" I stared at her, uncomprehending. Then all of a sudden I recognized the smell which had met me as I came into the room. Cheap brandy. I bent low over Matthew, and sniffed. His breath reeked of the stuff. Matthew had been drinking—heavily—and in the course of it had become involved in a fight in some filthy dockland tavern.

A wave of shame swept over me. My drunken, sottish son was sleeping off his spree in a comfortable bed in Westwood Park instead of in some dismal cell, thanks only to Colonel Allen's presence of mind. This neighbor whom we hadn't considered good enough to offer us fruit from his garden had nevertheless gone out of his way to rescue a brandy-sodden boy from a dockside gutter, had brought him to his home, called a doctor for him, put him to bed and no doubt made him fit for his mother's inspection into the bargain. Whoever the man might be, however he might choose to live, we had scant right to his kindness.

"He was in Paradise Street, Lady Oliver."

Mrs. Gibson said no more, but her meaning was clear. Paradise Street near the docks was no place for a boy of Matthew's age to be wandering. Its bars and brothels and its squalid, flea-ridden lodging-houses drew the seafaring community like a magnet. The street was famous across the world for its bizarre entertainments, its knife-fights and its accommodating women, celebrated in song wherever seamen hoisted sails or tramped round a capstan.

But how on earth had Matthew found his way there? And where was the pious, studious Harry Fuller? I could almost have shaken Matthew awake in my furious determination to have an answer.

Mrs. Gibson was bending over Matthew's still body, examining his bandage.

"The bleeding has stopped," she reported after a moment. "It was a long cut, but not deep. I'm afraid his head will be twice as sore tomorrow, though, because of it."

"It's no more than he deserves, the wretched boy." Now that I was sure Matthew was in no danger, my anxiety boiled over into anger. "Who knows what might have happened to him if Colonel Allen hadn't passed by at that moment? Sir Jonas and I are most particularly grateful to him. I'd like to thank the Colonel in person, if I could."

"I'm sorry, Lady Oliver, but that isn't possible."

"Then I'll write tomorrow, and thank him for his kindness. Matthew has caused him a great deal of trouble. My son's behavior was quite unpardonable, and you may be sure I shall get to the bottom of it when he's able to give an account of himself."

"You needn't be too concerned, Lady Oliver. The Colonel wasn't much put out."

"But it should never have happened."

Mrs. Gibson smiled again. "Young men have a great deal to learn, and a sore head can be a valuable lesson. That's the Colonel's opinion."

"Then I hope Colonel Allen is right. But I fear it may take more than that to curb Matthew's taste for adventure."

I think I must have sighed then, tired and perplexed as I was. The day had been so long, filled with anxiety about the Prince's dinner—and now Matthew's deceit and his drinking. . . .

"All this must have come as a shock to you," Mrs. Gibson suggested kindly. "I'll leave you for a while with your son. Ring when you wish to go, and I'll come for you again." With a rustle of her black skirts the housekeeper vanished tactfully from the room, closing the door behind her with the faintest of clicks.

———

I was grateful for those few moments of peace.

Not four feet away, Matthew, the cause of all my worry and shame, snored on, quite unaware of my mortification. At least now, perhaps, Jonas would take some notice of my anxiety. This was no schoolboy prank, something to be laughed off as youthful high spirits. This time, Matthew had lied to me about spending the evening in Leghorn Street, and had deliberately set off for a night's drinking in a dockside tavern. Every time I looked at his pale face on the pillow, my father's wasted ghost seemed to hover over Matthew's head.

Even now I suspected Jonas would punish Matthew for a crime far more serious in his eyes than simply being found, fighting drunk, in Paradise Street. Matthew had been rescued from the police by a man his stepfather considered beneath contempt; he'd succeeded in entangling the Olivers with the *wrong sort* of people. No doubt Jonas would have overlooked this drunken spree, too, had Matthew been in the company of one of the Earl of Chorleigh's sons. . . . *Boys will be boys, after all, my dear.* But to leave his stepfather indebted to the notorious Colonel Allen—that, I suspected, would cost Matthew dear.

It was all so petty and ridiculous. And now, presumably, the Prince Consort's visit had set the final, golden seal on the Olivers' place in society, justifying all the day-to-day maneuvering and scrambling for position which went on. And here was Matthew, undermining all their efforts, contriving a pleasant surprise for Jonas over breakfast next day. So be it—if the ensuing row served to shock Matthew into mending his ways, perhaps it was all to the good.

I sat down on the cane-seated chair near the head of the bed and examined Matthew's boyish features, relaxed and softened in sleep. There was nothing more to be done for him at present, and I knew I ought to return to the White House to resume my place as hostess. . . . Yet no one would miss me—not really. Besides, my absence would give the ladies free rein to criticize the decoration of my drawing room, which would add greatly to the gaiety of the occasion. Prince Albert, no less, had approved my truancy. There was no need to hurry back.

It was pleasant to have a few moments of quiet, after the turmoil of my own house. Here, in this plain room full of the Admiral's old-fashioned furniture, everything was peaceful and straightforward.

I let my eyes wander from the bed to the spaces beyond, to the white wainscot, the simple washstand with its floral jug and basin, the upright chairs and the plain white marble chimney-piece where a tall mirror reached almost to the cornice. To an eye accustomed to the solidity of modern furniture the room seemed spartan indeed, its walls hung with a couple of Dutch seascapes and some engravings framed in black-bordered glass in the style of years long past. The entire contents of the room had belonged to the Admiral; now they'd been taken over, just as they stood, by the mysterious Colonel Allen, reprobate and rescuer of drunken boys.

Westwood Park said nothing at all about its new owner. It was almost as if the Colonel were merely passing through the house— making a temporary camp for himself, leaving every room just as he'd found it. If he was indeed Reuben's strange outcast from San Francisco, no doubt Colonel Allen would vanish again one day, and nothing would remain to prove he'd ever existed.

I am clean forgotten, as a dead man out of mind. It had been one of Adam's sayings, a scrap of text from the Prayerbook. I'd remembered it often after his death. Why on earth had it come back to me now?

Perhaps the Colonel was right. Perhaps this was the best way to live one's life, as a bird or a butterfly might live it—briefly part of the throbbing, breathing world and then gone, leaving no trace except a tiny, moldering contribution to the rampant fertility of the soil, engendering more birds, more butterflies. . . .

Instead, for me, there was the plodding ceremonial of the White House, which rolled along, its wheels greased by soft soap and plate powder, browning and blacking, laundry-blue and cod-liver oil. Was human life really insupportable without the piano-tuner and the morning governess, the umbrella-mender, the man who reblocked silk hats and the gardener's boy who led the old cob in his great leather boots round and round the lawns, dragging the mowing-machine? Oh for saleratus bread once more, and bacon in the skillet. . . . Oh to be a bird or a bright, fleeting butterfly!

. . .

Across the room, another door, identical to the one by which I'd entered, stood ajar. No doubt there was a dressing room beyond it, which in turn communicated with the corridor outside.

Then—surely—my eyes began to play me false in the half-light.

For a second I fancied I'd seen the gap between door and doorframe widen a fraction. Perhaps a draft from the corridor had nudged it open: the Admiral's old house had always been dark and chilly, even in midsummer.

The door stirred again, and this time I was sure I'd seen a human hand in the opening, the fingers curled round the inner handle.

Someone was watching me. My first thought was to ring for a maid or the housekeeper: yet even if the bell was answered at once, minutes might pass before anyone reached me.

I rose to my feet, jerking my skirts clear of the chair-legs. Keeping my eyes fixed on the treacherous strip of shadow across the room, I began to move backward toward the door through which I'd come, one hand groping behind for any unseen obstacle. The heel of my slipper caught in a petticoat-hem and with a gasp of fear I tore it free. Glancing quickly over my shoulder, I saw I was nearly at the door, and turned to make a final dash for safety.

"Wait!"

It wasn't a plea, but a command.

"Don't go, Rachel. Not yet."

All at once the dressing-room door opened wide, revealing the figure of a tall man in evening dress, entirely in black except for his white shirt-front, his face in shadow.

"I didn't mean to frighten you," he said softly.

There was something familiar and yet unfamiliar in the voice. And my given name instead of *Lady Oliver*. I hesitated, one hand still stretched out toward the door, poised for flight. At the same time my eyes strained to pierce the gloom beyond the huge bed and its elaborate hangings.

"Colonel Allen . . ."

"If you like. That's what they call me here. Though you of all people should know better."

The blood began to pound a tattoo in my ears—a mad dance of horror and joy, spinning round and round, a lunatic rhythm which whirled faster and faster in my head until I thought *This—this is madness!*

"Who are you?" My voice was shrill with panic. In the vast bed Matthew stirred uneasily. The stranger across the room took two steps toward me, and the firelight illuminated his face. It was the face of a devil . . . with the features of Adam Gaunt.

"No! Get back! You're a ghost . . . I've conjured you up . . . out of my wicked imaginings. You've come to punish me—no—don't come near me!" In desperation I began to gabble: "Our Father . . . which art in Heaven . . . Hallowed be—"

"Rachel!" The devil became suddenly impatient. "Stop that! I'm no phantom! Look—here—"

". . . *Thy Kingdom come . . . Thy will be done . . .*"

The devil crossed the room in three strides, gripped me by my naked shoulders and shook me viciously.

"Stop that! D'you hear me? Stop that!"

". . . *Give us . . . give us . . .* Oh, God forgive me, I've forgotten. . . ." I was sobbing now; all I knew was that I had to finish the prayer to banish this evil, tormenting spirit back to the shadows from which he'd come.

"That's enough! Do you still think I'm a ghost?" Releasing my shoulders, he gripped one of my hands in his own. I felt it burn as if I'd touched fire.

"Flesh and blood, Rachel. As real as you are."

The room began to sway—or perhaps it was I who swayed.

"Not a ghost? . . . Not dead, then?"

"No—never dead." He held me by the shoulders again, as if sheer physical contact would convince me of his living reality. "Do you understand, Rachel?"

I shook my head. And oh—I met his eyes at last, and was helpless to look away. Adam—alive, and standing before me; it was too enormous a truth to be encompassed. . . . I opened my mouth to speak, but no sound emerged. Instead, I felt my knees begin to buckle and give way. My head was filled now with the roaring tumult of a cataract, sweeping away the frail bridge between perception and understanding; I felt an overwhelming need to sit on the floor, which was solid, and real, and welcoming. Suddenly a dead weight, I began to slide from the grasp of the devil who held me, my fingers trailing helplessly down the black Saxony cloth of his coat, tearing loose a button as I fell.

The floor was as comforting as I'd hoped, the carpet silky and warm against my cheek. Feet tramped across the room; bells rang;

doors opened and shut; and all the time I lay, clinging tightly to my precious corner of reality, the Admiral's Persian carpet.

Low voices in the air discussed me, then—reluctantly—I allowed myself to be lifted into a chair. The acrid fumes of smelling-salts were thrust under my nose, dragging me back to sensibility. *No—please—let me lie here . . . where I'm safe. . . .*

After a while I was gently raised to my feet, and people—unknown people—half-carried me down the long stone staircase and across the hall.

The velvet wrap was placed carefully round my shoulders once more, and a gust of freezing air from the open door revived me enough to scramble almost without assistance into the Chorleighs' waiting carriage. Someone—the housekeeper, perhaps—climbed in after me, taking the opposite seat, and the carriage rolled out into the darkness.

Vickers put me to bed in the White House, and let it be known in the drawing room that Lady Oliver had returned in a state of collapse, overcome with nervous exhaustion and anxiety over her son's condition.

Somewhere downstairs the Prince Consort and his party took their leave, expressing their concern for Lady Oliver's health and that of her son. Carriages drew up at the door, and rumbled away again. Cheerful voices floated up to my window, a concerto of incomprehensible cries like the chorus of Bedlam, distorted by distance, all unreal. Long after the last of the din had died away Jonas came softly in to see me, smelling of cigar-smoke and whistling under his breath. He bent over the bed, frowning a little and not entirely steady on his feet. I closed my eyes and pretended to be asleep.

Only when I was sure the entire household had gone to bed did I relax the fingers of my right hand, which had remained clasped with the desperate strength of the drowning round a single, black, silk-covered button.

25

One thing was certain: ghosts have no use for buttons, especially large, expensive buttons covered in black silk, with a metal eye at the back whereby a tailor might sew them on. The button I'd torn from the walking dead still trailed its raveled length of silk thread and a tiny patch of fine wool cloth which had come away with it. I'd spoiled the coat, without a doubt—though the weight and grandeur of the button made it clear that its owner wouldn't go in shirtsleeves because of that. Oh, a woman can tell a great deal from a button.

So Adam Gaunt was alive after all . . . though for the next seven days I kept to my bed, seeing hardly anyone, as if somehow in that sanctuary of feather pillows and embroidered sheets I could pretend that nothing had changed, and that my world was still the safe, familiar, comfortably tedious place I'd left in the Chorleighs' carriage for the journey to Westwood Park.

By the third day even Jonas had become concerned about me. He'd never known me to be ill, yet now I lay haggard and hollow-eyed in my darkened room, refusing the most tempting dishes the kitchen could provide. In spite of my protests he called in Dr. Jefferson, who pronounced me feverish from a chill caught on the night of my ride to Westwood Park and warned that only my naturally strong constitution was keeping pneumonia at bay.

That put an end to my solitude. On the doctor's orders hot, towel-wrapped bricks were laid against my feet and cloths wrung out in ice-water pressed to my forehead. My pulse was taken every hour and bowl after bowl of thin gruel brought to my bedside until I could have howled out loud to be left alone. And through it all poor Lottie haunted my room, her huge moist eyes fixed on me in silent anguish as she lay curled up beside the bed.

My supposed illness at least saved me from Jonas's questions. Using my weakness as an excuse, I'd given him only a brief account of my reception at Westwood Park, claiming I'd spoken to no one but the housekeeper, and seen only a couple of servants besides. As things had turned out, I said, Matthew had been more drunk than injured, but he'd lied to me about visiting Aunt Grace, and this time his breach of trust must be punished.

Jonas accepted my story with relief. I'd deliberately underplayed Adam's part in Matthew's rescue, and Jonas was able to decide that the debt to our mysterious neighbor was slight. The Olivers could decently continue to be as standoffish as ever.

Matthew himself returned in the middle of the following afternoon, still pale, and considerably chastened. Called to my bedside to apologize, he seemed utterly crestfallen and very anxious to go off to his own room as soon as possible. There was no hint of his usual swaggering bravado; whatever his rescuer had said to him before he left Westwood Park, it had knocked all the arrogance from Matthew at a single stroke, leaving him utterly deflated. For a moment I was almost sorry for him, and resentful that a mere neighbor should have dared to lecture my son. Then the real truth of the situation burst upon me. Who, after all, had more right to reprimand Matthew than his own father?

What shreds of Matthew's self-respect were left, Jonas proceeded to destroy, though as far as I could tell, his principal concern seemed to be that the matter might have found its way into the newspapers, dragging the Oliver name in the mud of Paradise Street.

Matthew had said little in his own defense, but one astonishing fact which emerged from the interview in the library was that the expedition to Paradise Street had been the original idea of Harry Fuller. Harry had known of a bar—Mother Beckett's, a reeking hole at the mouth of a rubbish-strewn alleyway—where he'd already struck up a promising friendship with a young woman called Annie who collected pots from the tables. Annie had been there when they arrived, and so delighted to see Harry Fuller that she'd summoned a friend to keep Matthew company.

The evening at Mother Beckett's had gone along as merrily as a marriage-bell until a friend of this friend—male, more than a head taller than Matthew and armed with a wicked-looking knife—had claimed her back for himself. The entire clientele of the tavern had willingly joined in the resulting brawl, and the whole broiling, punching ruckus had spilled through the doorway into the street outside, where Matthew, reeling about on the edge of the melee, had first been picked up by the police and then rescued from them by the timely intervention of Colonel Allen.

Jonas came out of the library and made his way directly to Leghorn Street to seek out young Harry. There followed an interview quite as unpleasant as Matthew's had been, involving Harry, a furious and dumbfounded Captain Fuller, and a sobbing Grace, with Jonas putting an unanswerable case for the prosecution.

I learned all this at second-hand as I lay miserably on my pillows, hoping for some miracle to undo the events of that night.

But seven days passed, and no miracle occurred. Hidden among the drift of snowy pillows, the black, silk-covered button continued to bear witness to the flesh-and-blood existence of a man I'd long believed dead. In spite of everything—in spite of Joe Walker's letter, in spite of the years which had passed in silence and emptiness— Adam Gaunt still lived.

There could only be one explanation: I hadn't waited long enough for him to come back. I'd only given him two years to return, and then I'd turned my back on him for my own selfish reasons. And what were two years in such a wilderness? As I'd feared, Adam had been taken captive by Indians, or had been stranded somewhere without a horse, injured, perhaps, and unable to leave the mountains —and I'd waited a bare two years. I should have had more faith; I should have listened to the voices in my head which promised me he hadn't died. Good Heavens, had I not loved him enough after all? And then Joe Walker's letter had misled me; it hadn't been Adam, but some other poor man, lying broken at the foot of that bluff on the Bighorn. Perhaps Adam had come back to Independence and found me gone . . . ? And by the time he'd learned I was in England I'd married again and his son was calling another man "Papa." Tears poured down my cheeks when I realized the catastrophe I'd brought about: "*The crisis*," reported Dr. Jefferson, feeling for my racing pulse and solemnly clicking his teeth.

If only the doctor could have given me a cure for the guilt I felt, and for the pain I'd inflicted on Adam! For seven days I lay racked by misery, appalled at what I'd done. Yet questions persisted in my mind. Why had Adam been unable to get in touch with me for so long? Surely Lizzie Fletcher would have known if he'd returned to Independence, looking for me—she could have told him at once where I'd gone. . . . And why San Francisco, of all places?

The questions churned round and round in my mind, blotting out everything else. Shock and shame crowded out sensible thought. All that was certain was that Adam Gaunt was alive, alive, alive . . . and I'd failed him.

Yet somehow even accepting that dreadful fact seemed to make a difference. Gradually my strength began to return, until at last I was well enough to lie in the afternoons on a day-bed in my sitting room, pushed into the bay of the windows overlooking the wintry, sleet-spattered terrace. There I stayed for hours at a time, Lottie at my feet, a book unread on my lap, staring out toward the tall, bare trees which just failed to hide the gables of Westwood Park.

———

Christmas 1852 was nearly upon us. As usual, our celebrations at the White House involved the Broadneys and their family, Aunt Grace Fuller, the Captain and a somewhat subdued Harry, Ellen Oliver, the widow of Jonas's brother John, and a host of minor Oliver relations and hangers-on. I'd counted on Reuben's company to take my mind off my troubles, and I was disappointed to discover that he wouldn't be with us after all. The *Rachel Oliver* was due to reach New York on the 22nd or the 23rd of December, and Reuben had told me rather shamefacedly before he sailed that he'd been invited to spend Christmas Day there with our mother, who was now established in an elegant house near Washington Square.

I knew he hadn't written to her for a long time—not since the day he found out that she'd lied to them all about my death. But Aunt Grace had filled his ears with tales of her sister's illness, and had found him a more sympathetic listener than I'd ever been.

All of a sudden Reuben began to feel guilty for having stayed away from his mother for so many years; and the longer he avoided her, the guiltier he became. Now her illness had made him conscience-stricken—but even then, painfully honest as usual, he'd refused to return to her side on the basis of a lie. Instead, he wrote to her at last, describing our meeting and asking for an explanation of her deceit. To his surprise, he'd been invited to call and receive the explanation in person when he was next in New York—and immediately decided our mother must be even more ill than Aunt Grace imagined.

I wasn't so easily convinced, but I was too wrapped up in my own misery to give it much thought. I was only sorry Reuben would be away when I needed him most.

It began to look as if we'd see very little of Matthew either. Matthew, who considered himself too much of a man-about-town for the sentimental festivities of Christmas, had found a new outlet for his energies on the hunting-field, but for the sake of Jonas and the girls I made a great effort to pull myself out of my depression and join in all the ritual of the festive season, the picture of a loyal wife and devoted mother. I played my part to the hilt, startling Verity Broadney with my sudden, heart-warming enthusiasm for my Oliver in-laws. Verity immediately became convinced I'd been dangerously ill after all: what else but the chill touch of death on my shoulder could have produced such zeal for life or such a delight in the company of others?

And, indeed, Verity was almost right—there was indeed a ghost stalking to and fro on the fringe of my decent, contented family, ready to shatter our peace into a thousand atoms.

All through Christmas and the days that followed I clutched my husband and children to me, glorying in every tiny, inconsequential detail of our lives—walks in the frosty lanes with the girls, Lottie skipping ahead of us through the stiff grass, the ritual of nursery tea on those days when even Jonas could be persuaded to share the bread and butter and sesame cake, carol-singing in church, Christmas presents laboriously wrapped in secret and piled round the tree —every single second of it precious beyond imagining.

As a family we lined up to distribute gifts to the servants—dress-lengths to the maids, money to the menservants, and, if they were married, a cured ham or a joint of beef to take home. The house was decorated with swags of evergreens, and on Christmas morning, before everyone assembled for church, Jonas solemnly kissed me under the mistletoe in the hall. I'd known he would do it; he did the same thing every year. Yet for once even that time-worn seasonal habit was solid, and sensible, and comforting to me in my secret distress.

Then suddenly the organized cheerfulness of Christmas was over. Winter set in with a will, Matthew was sent reluctantly back to school, the girls spent much of the day in the care of their governess, and Jonas returned to his workshop to gaze at the most recent designs for the *Altair* over the heads of two martens he was mounting on a twisted conifer branch. One by one, the companions of my lonely hours slipped out of my clutching fingers until I was left alone with my thoughts once more.

I'd neither seen nor heard anything of Adam Gaunt since the night of Matthew's adventure, though I knew instinctively he was still in Westwood Park, waiting for me to make a move. And time was running out. Adam's patience was infinite, I knew, but if he believed I was trying to ignore him, to pretend he didn't exist, he'd soon take matters into his own hands, and the whole dreadful mess might become public property.

A day came at last when I realized I couldn't delay any longer. Returning in the carriage one afternoon from a meeting of the Ladies' Committee for Poor Relief, I happened to glance along the lane which separated the White House gardens from the grounds of Westwood Park as we passed its junction with the main road. In the distance, no more than a dark silhouette against the frosty landscape, a solitary horseman rode in from the open country beyond. I'd no need of closer scrutiny. The rider was Adam Gaunt, his bearing in the saddle as unmistakable as the day I saw him ride off for the last time on his spotted Palouse.

After dinner that night, pleading a headache, I went upstairs to my bedroom and laid out on my dressing table three objects taken from a deep lower drawer. In many ways, they were the story of my life with Adam—first, the ancient, inlaid red stone amulet he'd given me in Crow Cove; next, the daguerreotype portrait made shortly before he left for California; and lastly the big black button which had finally convinced me he was still alive. There they lay on the polished mahogany—three parts of a conundrum, never adding up to the answer I needed.

Why was Adam in Liverpool? Why had he gone to such trouble to buy Westwood Park? He knew I'd long since given him up for dead—that I'd made another life for myself—and yet in spite of all that he'd come to seek me out. But *why?*

Always, I came back to the same conclusion. He'd come to punish me for my disloyalty. I couldn't imagine what else he might want with me.

Though if that were true why had he kept himself hidden? Even now, I'd only discovered his presence at Westwood Park by a mere accident. And there had been the gift of sweet flowers and the offer of fruit. . . . I could still feel the sticky dampness of that stolen peach soaking into my palm, and the fumes of the fermenting fruit filling

my head like strong wine. The peach had been honeyed . . . tender
. . . and it had belonged to Adam. Even from a thousand miles away
he'd managed to seduce my senses that day in the drunken heat of
his hothouses. The cloying, luscious memory was still on my lips.
What kind of punishment was that?

And what was done could not be undone. For good or ill I'd
buried the man I'd loved, and chosen a new road. Adam and I were
strangers now. If he wanted me to beg his forgiveness, I'd do it: there
was no doubt I'd carry the guilt of my betrayal until my dying day.
But then he must go—back to his mountains or wherever he'd come
from—anywhere, provided it was many, many miles away from me
and from my family. That was what I had to tell him. To go, leaving
me to the magnificent tedium of my life among the Olivers.

I still hoped I might not have to meet him again to say it.

For two successive days I tried to put my feelings into a letter, only
to feed page after page to the glowing grate in my sitting room as
the words refused to arrange themselves in the proper order. *On
your honor, as a gentleman,* I wrote—and then remembered that
Adam had always had his own ideas of right and wrong . . . *out of
pity and decency,* then . . . *out of the love we once shared. . . .* My
hand began to shake so badly that the pen made a blot on the page.

No, there was only one honest way to settle the matter between
us—as I think I'd always known. I'd have to meet Adam once more,
and make my appeal to him when I could watch his face and judge
the effect of my words. It was the only way I could be sure he'd leave
me in peace for the rest of our two cursed lives.

It wouldn't be easy to find an opportunity. Lady Oliver could
hardly drive in her furs up to the front door of Westwood Park like
a dowager paying a call—and Jonas would have a seizure if he heard
I'd received Colonel Allen at the White House. And yet to attempt a
secret meeting would only start whispers of scandal; I could imagine
the tattle in the servants' hall, soon to become common gossip all
over town. How often had I heard the first hints of my friends'
indiscretions in the same way? *Can you believe it—Lady Oliver has
been seeing Colonel Allen in secret. . . .* Vickers would tell Mrs.
Locke and the cook would tell the house-maid, the house-maid
would repeat it to the groom who'd pass it on to the Broadneys'
groom as they waited one night outside the theater, and before I
could draw breath it would have dropped like a stone into Verity's
lap. And Verity would certainly tell Jonas.

In my carriage I was surrounded by grooms and coachmen; in the garden there were gardeners and odd-job men; footmen and the sharp-eyed Vickers always knew when I left the house and when I returned. My day was made up of such an inflexible routine that I was hardly ever alone, hardly ever free from the attentive eyes of my warders. In the hallway, even the kitten-orchestra stared at me accusingly as I passed. And all the time I could feel Adam counting the passing days, and waiting for me to act.

Then just when I was at my wits' end, Jonas presented me with the opportunity I needed.

It seemed that while I'd been confronting the ruin of my life, Jonas had been wrestling with the problem of propeller-shaft vibration, which had plagued experimental screw-driven ships to the point of shaking them apart at the stern where the shaft passed out through the hull. Recently Jonas had heard of tests being carried out using the hard and oily wood *lignum vitae* as a buffer between shaft and hull, where it seemed to absorb much of the troublesome vibration. Now he was desperate to go and see for himself if the wood could be used in the design of the *Altair*. There was no time to lose; he made plans to stay in London for a week, leaving by train the following Thursday.

My heart leaped. This meant that Jonas would be away from home on a Sunday, the only day in the week when the watching eyes around me would be fewer.

As in most households, on Sunday afternoon almost all of our servants were given liberty from three o'clock until half-past nine or ten at night, leaving a single nursery-maid upstairs to supervise the girls' afternoon nap, a couple of grooms in the stable, and a solitary footman snoring by the pantry fire to answer bells or make up fires. To allow the kitchen staff an afternoon off, Jonas and I usually ate a cold supper left ready by Mrs. Locke in the dining room.

It was the best chance I'd ever have. If I arranged to meet Adam in the walled garden at Westwood Park I'd have no need to go into the house, and on a cold, frosty Sunday the garden itself would be deserted. I scribbled a note, sealed it, and called a footman.

"A letter was delivered here today which should have gone to Westwood Park," I told him. "I've explained the circumstances to Colonel Allen, and enclosed the letter. You needn't wait for an answer," I added as an afterthought. Adam couldn't refuse to meet me, for there'd be no other opportunity.

The week dragged by, and on Thursday Jonas left in the carriage for the railway station. For days he'd spoken of nothing but *lignum vitae,* and when he kissed me briefly on the cheek, I had the distinct impression he was kissing the cold iron side of the *Altair.*

For another two days I was on edge, bored and fretful.

Then on Sunday afternoon my plans almost foundered. I'd expected my maid Vickers to go off with the others at three o'clock—most of the servants were taking the train to nearby Southport Sands to view the vast corpse of a whale stranded there a few days earlier, and I didn't think she'd want to miss the jaunt. But Vickers apparently felt that dead whales smacked too much of a sideshow for a Sunday outing. Instead, she'd agreed to go with a woman friend to a Reading Evening at the Congregationalist chapel—but not until four-fifteen. Now she'd decided to fill the idle hour by repairing the torn braid on one of my morning-gowns, and had settled herself comfortably in my dressing room surrounded by her papers of pins and spools of thread, at a window which commanded an excellent view of the front drive. Horrified by this new turn of events, I searched desperately for an excuse to leave the house alone.

"Matthew's mare hasn't been out of the stable for days," I declared on a sudden inspiration. "We both need some exercise, and there may not be such a good day again for a while. Yes—I shall definitely go out for a short ride this afternoon."

It was all I could think of—and I saw Vickers's eyebrows lift in silent surprise. Well—her face informed me—if Lady Oliver thought it was proper for a lady to ride on a Sunday afternoon, then no doubt she should know best. Perhaps there were special rules for the gentry; it was whispered that Prince Albert himself had been seen playing chess on the Lord's Day.

Tight-lipped, she helped me into the simple dark blue skirt and short coat of my riding-habit and handed me the veiled silk hat, half the height of a gentleman's, which went with it. The expression of it's-not-my-place-to-say-anything was still on her face as I left the house by the front door and walked purposefully round toward the stable-yard in the rear.

As soon as I was sure I couldn't be seen from the front windows I left the broad carriage-sweep for the screen of shrubs beyond it and, ignoring the stables, pushed my way through the densest bushes until

I reached the back gate. There I turned into the lane dividing the two properties, and walked quickly along it to the little iron gate in the palisade, hoping against hope that no one would pass who might wonder what a lady in riding-dress was doing afoot on that frosty afternoon.

I'd asked Adam in my note to make sure the gate was left unlocked. Now I noticed that a slick of new oil ran from its hinges, tracing a glossy line down its black paint before dripping into a dark, greasy patch on the earth below. The way was prepared: the gate opened easily at the first touch, sending a little shiver up my spine and dispelling the last doubts from my mind.

Adam would be there, then. Waiting for me.

26

The wooden gate beyond the orangery leading into the walled garden opened as easily as the gate in the palisade, scraping across its stone threshold on tiny, trapped pieces of gravel. I stepped through the archway, my eyes anxiously sweeping the cultivated slope of the garden as I closed the gate behind me, leaning back on its weathered boards until the latch clicked softly into place. With the gate shut, the four-square, mellow brick boundary was unbroken once more—a rampart enclosing a private world and shutting out another.

Adam was sitting on a stone seat in the middle of the walled rectangle, his back to the higher ground on which the glass-houses stood and to the gate through which I'd entered. At first I thought he hadn't heard me come in, but as I made my way quickly along the red-graveled paths between the stiffly frosted box-hedges, I saw him turn his head at last to watch my progress.

He must have been waiting there for some time, stretched out across the massive, lichenous seat with its crouched-lion supports, hatless, his hands thrust deep into the pockets of a black greatcoat he hadn't bothered to fasten. I wondered how long he'd been there —thinking, and waiting for me to arrive. If he shared any of the awkwardness and unease I felt, there was no sign of it.

He rose slowly to his feet as I approached the final turn in the path, still regarding me gravely. It was hard to go on under that unblinking scrutiny, and I stopped for a moment to tuck the veil of my riding-hat more securely under my chin. The gesture gave me confidence, though when I started toward him once more I found he'd already turned back to his view of the southernmost wall of the garden and the frozen, geometric beds between.

He didn't look at me again until I came to a halt only a few feet away from him.

"You're very punctual, Lady Oliver."

He consulted a heavy gold watch, then slipped it away again. *Lady Oliver*. The name sounded stranger than ever as he pronounced it.

"This is the only seat I can offer you, since you won't come to my house." He indicated the stone bench with its chained lions. "Where have you left your horse?"

"I don't have a horse. I came on foot." All of a sudden, I felt foolish. "I had to find an excuse for leaving the house."

To cover my embarrassment I made an elaborate show of brushing a scattering of dry leaves from the stone seat before sitting down at its nearest end.

"An excuse?" Adam's eyebrows rose. "Does he have you watched, then?"

"Of course not."

"Not even when he's in London?"

I stared at him, startled. "How did you know Jonas was in London?"

Adam shrugged, and sat down in his former place on the stone bench.

"I've very little to do here, except mind other people's business. And the Olivers lead such public lives, after all. Sir Jonas has gone to London, I'm told, to see an engineer about this wonderful steamship the whole of Liverpool is talking about. The *Altair*. . . . Like the star. . . . They're calling it the *Hot-Air*. Did you know that?"

I kept my eyes on the toes of my boots, warm with annoyance behind my veil. I hadn't heard Jonas's ship called the *Hot-Air*, and it irked me to find out in this way.

Adam was watching me again. "You didn't know," he concluded. "Well, why should you? No doubt as a loyal wife you've absolute faith in your husband's schemes."

"Naturally," I snapped back at him. "The *Altair* will make the whole world take notice. You'll see."

"And as a loyal wife, you waited until Jonas had set off for London, pretended you were going riding, and came out to see me here."

"You make it sound like some kind of sordid rendezvous."

"Do I? But I take it Jonas doesn't know, all the same."

"Jonas . . . Jonas spends most of his time on business as it is. I saw no point in giving him extra worries."

"No indeed."

I searched Adam's face for any hint of sarcasm, but his expression was flint-hard, yielding nothing.

"Well—since this isn't to be a sordid rendezvous, and since you were the one to arrange the meeting, you'd better tell me what it's all about. What's this important announcement you've come to make?"

I stared at him in disbelief. This was incredible. How could he sit there so calmly, with the world-weary air of a banker considering a loan, when such a gulf yawned between us, such a span of empty years and unanswered questions? I don't know what I'd expected—but never in my wildest dreams had I imagined us arguing over a half-built *ship*. Thrown off-balance, I allowed a long moment of silence to pass while I tried to recapture the words I'd rehearsed with such care.

"You look well, at any rate," he remarked more gently. "At least, I assume you do, behind that veil. This life must suit you."

"It does," I said quickly. "I'm quite content."

"Ah. . . ." It was almost a sigh. "Well, as I say—you look well on it."

"And you look . . . different."

It was no more than the truth, now that I was able to study his face more closely. The years hadn't dealt harshly with him, though there was silver now in the tawny, grass-gold hair and a web of fine creases at the corners of his eyes. But he'd changed, nevertheless: something was missing that I'd loved and feared in days gone by—not of the flesh, but of the spirit within, like the candle enclosed by a lamp.

The answer came to me as I studied him. A bright flame of purpose had withered and died out in Adam Gaunt, the burning light in a face set toward some distant horizon, not to be deflected. There was weariness now where that nomad passion had been, fatigue in his voice, and hard, uncompromising lines round his mouth.

Yet his eyes were the same. I'd forgotten those restless, compelling gray eyes, moody as the sea. They were moving slowly across my face now, searching behind my veil for the underlying meaning of my words.

"*Different?*" His voice caressed the syllables. "*Different?* In what way, I wonder? Older, certainly. Time changes us all."

"Time hasn't changed you so much, Adam. . . . But something else has."

He looked away again, and settled himself deeper into his greatcoat.

"Perhaps you're seeing me at last as I really am, without all those silly, romantic notions that used to fill your head. How old were you then? Sixteen—seventeen? Neither a girl nor yet a woman, and dreaming of a hero who'd come and carry you off." He shook his head ruefully. "I was never the hero you wanted. And now you can see that too."

I checked myself on the point of blurting out a denial.

"Are we to sit here all afternoon?" Adam demanded suddenly, hunching the greatcoat up around his shoulders.

"Why—do you feel cold?" The brightness was already fading from the frosty sun.

"I've been colder. But usually to better purpose. So far you've told me you're devoted to your life among the mighty Olivers, and you find me changed for the worse. What next, I wonder?"

"Adam—" Involuntarily, my gloved hands lifted toward him in a tiny, desperate gesture. "It wasn't easy for me to come here today. Can you imagine how I felt when I realized you were still alive?"

"No doubt I completely spoiled your Christmas." He picked savagely at a stray thread on his coat until it snapped in his fingers and was tossed down on the path. "Is that what you've come to tell me? That I've upset your peaceful, respectable existence?"

"You've every right to be angry with me, Adam. I know that. I've treated you shamelessly, though as Heaven's my witness, I never meant to. But I should have realized—in spite of what everyone told me—that you weren't dead—that you'd come back to find me. I should never have left Independence so soon."

Now that I'd started, the words came tumbling out. "I don't blame you for wanting to punish me in some way. . . . I can only ask you to forgive me—"

"Forgive you? *Punish* you?" There was incomprehension in his voice. "Is that why you think I came here? To punish you for something? Rachel—what on earth are you talking about?"

"Because I didn't wait for you . . . Because I took Matthew and came back to England . . . And married Jonas . . . Don't you hate me for it?"

He stared at me incredulously.

"Rachel, have you spent the last two months blaming yourself for failing me in some way? For not waiting forever in Independence until I came back?"

"Of course I have. Adam, I feel like a criminal—"

"Oh, my God, what a shambles!" Adam gave a sigh of pure weariness, and closed his eyes for a second. "I was so sure you'd realize what had happened. It seemed so obvious. Yet you went on believing in me to the end. . . . And you still don't understand, do you?"

"What is there to understand?"

"Rachel . . . It wouldn't have made any difference if you'd stayed in Independence until Doomsday. I've never gone back there. I never intended to go back there. The longer I stayed away, the more impossible it became to go back. Do you understand now?"

All at once the full significance of his words exploded in my mind. I'd endured weeks of shame and self-reproach—tormented myself with my guilt—and now I discovered I wasn't the betrayer after all. I was blameless: Adam—the man I'd loved and trusted—had cold-bloodedly betrayed me. Realization turned to disbelief—disbelief to outrage, anger, pain sharper than any physical wound. My heart thumped crazily behind my ribs, and I had to force myself to speak calmly.

"Are you actually telling me you could have come back at any time, but you chose not to? There was nothing to stop you? No accident? You weren't captured, or injured in any way?"

"Not in any way."

"You deliberately turned your back on us—on your wife and son? Just turned your back, and rode away without another thought?"

"It didn't seem like that at the time, but yes, I suppose that's what I did."

"Adam . . . !" The word burst from me like a howl of accusation.

"Go on—call me what you like. . . . You can't say anything I haven't said to myself a thousand times. I don't expect you to forgive me. I don't even expect you to understand why I did it."

"By God, you're right! I don't understand how you could do such a thing. Not for a moment! I loved you, Adam—didn't you know that?"

"I knew it."

"And didn't that make any difference at all? Or if you'd grown tired of me—what about Matthew? Had you no feelings for your son?"

"Of course I hadn't 'grown tired of you'! Though . . . it was hard to be *needed* so much. Maybe that had something to do with it."

"But in common humanity, couldn't you have told me that? I'd never have held you against your will."

"Wouldn't you?" It was a cry from the heart, and for a moment I was unsure.

"I—I don't think I would have. But at least we could have done *something*—made some arrangement . . . but just to abandon us like that . . . How could you do it?"

Distractedly, he ran a hand through his hair. "I felt it might all be for the best in the end. There was money to tide you over—at least there would have been, if that wretch La Fontaine had paid what he owed. I thought you'd probably come back to England, to your aunt. . . ."

"Adam—" I shook my head, unable to find words for what I thought of him.

"At least I've told you the truth now. I could have let you go on blaming yourself, thinking I'd spent the last twelve years searching for you, only to find you'd taken up with another man."

"Goodness knows why you bothered, after all this time! If you could live with yourself after abandoning a woman and a tiny baby in the wilderness, what difference would one more lie have made?"

"Very little, it's true. But I wanted you to know the truth all the same."

He was leaning forward now, staring down at the frost-glazed path, comfortless, unresisting, patiently accepting the worst I could say of him.

"If you only knew what I went through after you left . . . The loneliness—the misery—the struggle I had to keep going—"

"I do know. Most of the story, at any rate."

"How do you know? Who told you?"

Adam smiled faintly. "I ran into Antoine Bleu one day in Sacramento. I'd last seen him—oh, years back, before I left Independence. 'Hello, Antoine'—I said—'It's good to see you again.' I think I even held out my hand. He took one look—and then he hit me. Harder than I would have believed possible. I thought he was going to kill me." He ran a rueful finger along his jaw. "He almost knocked my head off."

"I'm pleased to hear it. It's no more than you deserved."

"When he'd calmed down a bit he called me every insulting name he could think of. And then he told me what had happened to you after I left—all about your job in the store, and the Trader's House, and the shooting." Adam glanced gravely across at me. "Antoine loved you, you know."

"He wanted me to stay in America with him."

"You should have stayed. He's a good man. I doubt if you'd ever have had two cents to rub together, but you'd have been a great deal happier than you are now."

"How dare you tell me what I should have done! You gave up any right to interfere in my life long ago."

"Still—I'd like to see you happy."

"Do you honestly expect me to believe that? When you made me more wretched than you'll ever be able to imagine?"

I waited for him to speak, but he simply shook his head as if there were no point in trying to explain.

"And now I realize you never gave a single thought for me or for Matthew, it's a good deal easier to tell you what I came to say." I took a deep breath and launched into the speech I'd prepared, but now with a vastly different emotion behind the words.

"All I want from you is to *go away*. Do you hear me, Adam? I don't know why you've come back here after all this time—and I don't care—but if you're going to try to ruin the life I have now, I won't let you do it. That's all I have to say to you. *Go away*."

"Short, and to the point." For several seconds Adam said no more, but stared out toward the distant horizon, his hands thrust deep into his greatcoat pockets, his face expressionless.

"What makes you think I've come to ruin your life, Rachel?" he asked at last.

"Why else would you be here in Liverpool? Spying on me—living secretly in this house? If you haven't come here to destroy me for good this time, then why have you come?"

"Why indeed?" he said softly. "You'll never know how often I've asked myself the same question." There was desolation in his voice now, as if I'd banished a last, small shred of hope. Slowly—reluctantly—I felt the great tide of my anger begin to ebb away.

"I don't want to quarrel with you, Adam. There's nothing to be gained by raking up the past with questions and accusations. But if you owe me anything at all for those empty years—do as I ask, I beg you. Don't spoil everything for us now—for Matthew and me. Whatever reason you had for coming back—forget it, and go."

For a second I almost yielded to the impulse to lay a hand on his arm, to prove it wasn't vengeance but anxiety which drove me. Then at the last moment my courage failed me, and I turned the gesture into a mere twist of the fingers.

"Why not go back to America? You'd be happier there, I'm sure."

He considered this for a moment. "As a matter of fact, though you may find this hard to believe, I never meant you to know I was here in the first place."

"Never—at all?"

"Never."

That, at least, would explain the mystery of his long silence.

"I . . . can believe what you say."

"Thank you for that. It happens to be true. This business with Matthew . . . I acted without thinking. He was as drunk as a lord and covered in filth from the gutter, and a couple of thick-headed constables were just about to haul him off to the city jail. I suppose I should have left them to it and let Jonas bail him out next morning. But Devil take it, Rachel—Matthew is my son, after all! How could I leave him in the middle of a tavern brawl, with his head broken by some roaring madman?"

"*Your son?*" The words fell oddly on my ears. "You've come rather late to fatherhood, surely! You may have sired the boy, but Jonas has been more of a father to him than you ever were!"

"Then Jonas has done a poor job, it seems to me." Adam sounded stung by my retort. "Matthew's turning into a selfish, arrogant little swine who hasn't had his backside kicked as often as he should."

"Oh, that's excellent! Jonas tells me I've made a milksop of my son, and now you say I haven't beaten him enough. Apparently I'm to blame for all his faults! Is that why you came back to Liverpool, Adam? To find Matthew again, and see what I'd made of him?"

"No. Not exactly. . . . Though perhaps it was high time I did."

Overhead, the sky began to darken ominously, and a cold, sleety rain started to fall with drenching suddenness. Adam rose to his feet, and held out a hand to help me.

"Come—we can talk indoors."

Pointedly, I ignored his hand. "There's no need. I've said all I came to say, and it's time I went home."

"You'll be drenched before you reach the gate. Come up to the house, and out of this rain."

"Not to the house! I won't go into your house!"

He looked round, perplexed.

"Up here, then." Taking my arm, he began to hustle me along the frost-hardened path and up the slope to the nearest of the glass-houses, propelling me into its welcome warmth while the cheated downpour rattled a tattoo on the panes above us.

———

Inside the glass-house it was no longer tropically humid but temperate, hoarding the heat of the thin winter sunshine long after the sun itself had fled. The air was soft and mellow, faintly censed with sweetness, a honeyed echo of the peach harvest which had been left to dissolve unwanted on the ground.

"You know your way about these places, I believe." A few feet behind me, Adam brushed the wet from the shoulders of his great-coat.

"Your gardener told you he'd found me here?"

"You and that ridiculous dog of yours."

There was no point in attempting an excuse—and, besides, it no longer mattered. I felt like a child caught in some mischief, relieved at being found out, at having passed the dreaded moment of discovery.

"You didn't have to smuggle yourself into the garden, you know. I offered you anything you wanted—peaches, nectarines, figs—anything at all. And I was in Italy at the time: you were quite safe from meeting me. Why wouldn't you take it?"

"Jonas made me refuse," I told him frankly. "He said we mustn't put ourselves in your debt. Since you were—well . . ."

"Contemptible? Corrupt? What else did he say? *Faithless?* Oh, it's no more than the truth."

"I'm sorry, Adam." I began to wish I hadn't tried to explain. The ban which Jonas had imposed now seemed so petty and vindictive—and it distressed me to have had a part in it. I glanced helplessly round the sleet-washed glass-house, noticing only that the fanned ribs of the trees trained against the white-painted wall seemed thin and sad after the lushness of summer. But the faint scent of that past magnificence, lingering in the still air, called up a memory.

"I took one of your peaches that day. And ate it. Here—in this glass-house."

He looked at me curiously. "Did you, now? In spite of Jonas and his high-flown principles? Well, well . . . I'm delighted to hear it. I hope your peach was as fine as you expected."

I could still remember the guilty pleasure of that seductive juice squirting into my mouth through skin stretched to bursting with fecund ripeness, and the secret, folded stone like a brain within, mother of peaches and future pleasure.

"It was . . . splendid."

And I remembered then how Adam could listen to my words, not with hearing alone, but with his whole body, weighing and sifting my response, reading the thought that gave it birth as clearly as I understood it myself. It was an unnerving ability. Nowadays in the White House I often had to repeat a sentence before Jonas even noticed I'd spoken.

Adam was leaning back against one of the white-painted pillars which supported the glass roof above our heads.

"So you don't obey Jonas Oliver in *everything* after all," he remarked thoughtfully. "That's encouraging. I couldn't believe you'd changed so much, Rachel. Grown wiser, perhaps, but not become a creature of the Olivers."

I knew I ought to feel offended. Yet all I felt at that moment was beguilingly warm. My breath was creating an uncomfortable dampness behind my veil, and on impulse I took off my silk hat, laying it with my gloves on the cover of a nearby water-tank.

I became aware of Adam studying my face anew, and I began to regret taking off my veil. There was nothing secret in his interest; he examined me quite openly, content that I should be aware of it. His gaze was as intimate as a fingertip passing lightly over my bare skin, tracing a path across downy cheek and warm lips with leisured and hypnotic freedom.

Dismayed, I realized that something subtle had altered between us. Out in the open air, on the stone bench, there had been limitless space all around. Now, shut up in that hothouse, imprisoned by the rain sluicing down the glass roof and walls, we were cut off from the rest of the world, thrown into a sensuous closeness I'd never intended.

In my confusion I tried to turn the conversation to something trivial, and hit on the downpour still dousing the building with its furious squalls.

"What an amount of water!" I exclaimed. "Just imagine—if this were Noah's flood once more, drowning the whole world in rain, and we two were the only ones saved. . . . Just because we'd taken shelter here."

"Alone—just you and I?" Adam regarded me with amusement. "I

don't suppose that would be too hard a fate. I think I could almost bear it. . . . The question is—could you?"

Too late, I saw the trap I'd set for myself, and tried to make light of it.

"Oh, if the flood washed away my rose-beds and my croquet lawn I'm sure I could never survive it." He was watching my face intently, and I longed passionately for the refuge of my veil.

"You were never a good liar, Rachel. Your words tell me one thing, and your eyes another. Not ten minutes ago you gave me to understand I could go to the Devil for all you cared. And yet—now —I believe you do care a little, in spite of all your denials."

"Nonsense. You only see what you want to see." I bent my head quickly over a potted camellia, its fat buds tight with intricately folded petals.

"Yet since I think you may be more interested than you pretend. . . . Will you let me tell you now where I've been all these years?"

"I don't want to hear about it. Why should I care where you wandered off to after you abandoned me?" My voice echoed sharply in the empty spaces of the glass-house; among the plants, my burning face was shielded from his gaze. "I suppose you're going to tell me your tale anyway—though I promise you, you're wasting your time."

"I'll take that risk." Adam leaned back against the pillar, a wild forest god amid a green host of camellias.

"Before I start—don't think I'm trying to make excuses for myself. I don't expect you to forgive me, after the way I treated you. But since you've found out I'm alive . . . Well, I'd like you to hear the rest. When I've done, you can judge me as you please."

What choice did I have? The horizontally slatting rain drummed on the rows of panes around us, filling any silence with its insistent rattle. Just as I'd foretold, the winter flood had washed away the world beyond, leaving only the two of us, marooned in a half-lit ark of streaming crystal. It was no longer possible to escape.

"Tell me one thing first. . . . Tell me about the letter I had from Joe Walker, confirming you were dead. Did Joe really believe you'd died? Or was that letter just a pack of lies from beginning to end?"

"I made him write it."

"Oh, Adam . . ." The pain of it made me catch my breath. "If you only knew how many tears I wept over that letter! And all for nothing! How could Joe Walker do such a thing? I always thought he was an honest man!"

"Don't blame Joe. I was the one who thought of the scheme in the first place. I convinced him you were far better off without me, and in the end he agreed to write a letter making me officially dead, and send it off to Independence."

"I suppose I should at least be grateful for the money you sent me. It meant a great deal to me at the time."

"It was everything I could lay my hands on. Every cent."

"That was honest, at least. But I'd rather have had you back, alive and well, than all the money in the world. Even then."

"But shortly after that you married Jonas Oliver." Adam regarded me thoughtfully.

"Go on with your story. Tell me where you really were when my heart was breaking for you. And tell me why, Adam—*why?*"

I heard a sigh—a long, whistling breath which seemed to weave itself into the dismal wind outside like a forlorn, endless whisper.

"Why, indeed . . . If I could only tell you that! I can't even tell you why I went off down the Snake River that first day—unless it was because I knew there was still a little piece of the Shoshone country I hadn't set eyes on before.

"You've never been alone in the mountains, so you don't know what it's like, just pushing through that great silence, listening to your own thoughts whispering back to you from the pines. It's like —walking through a door and into eternity. All at once you might as well be a willow tree in the valley, or a sage bush. . . . There's sunup and sundown, and day and night, but no Tuesdays and Fridays anymore. And when I did get round to thinking of you—you seemed as far away as the nearest star, like something I'd imagined, surrounded by your flour-bags and your calico in the cabin in Independence." Adam stared out through the streaming glass as if the image was still before him.

"When was I supposed to meet Joe Walker? Heaven knows. But once that day was past . . . well, one day late was as bad as fifty, fifty no better than a hundred. After that I stopped counting the days altogether.

"I spent the winter in a Shoshone village, but just as I was about to go on my way in the warmer weather fever broke out in the camp. Everyone caught it—including me—but it was the old people and the children who died. The rest of us did what we could, but it was little enough. . . . The children suffered more than anyone, because they didn't understand what was wrong.

"There was a little boy—a little fat, laughing baby, maybe a year old . . . His mother took the fever, and the baby died in my arms the following night. There wasn't a single thing I could do about it. I guess that finally brought me back to reality—thinking of Matthew, and what you might be going through without me.

"As soon as I could leave the Shoshone, I made for a place on the Merced River Joe Walker and I had found years before, though we never thought much of it at the time—neither of us being inclined to dig for gold when the price of beaver was so high. Of course, after so many years it took me a while to find the exact outcrop of rock marking the spot, but I recognized it in the end, and there was still gold glinting in the riverbed, just as I remembered. I got a pick axe and other tools from one of the rancheros, and I worked there entirely alone for the rest of the summer—and for the season after that. I think it was the hardest work I've ever done. When I reckoned I had enough I changed the gold for cash in Santa Fe, a little at a time, and set off back east as far as St. Louis. And all the way, I met settlers in wagons, heading for Oregon and California." Adam shook his head in disbelief.

"That's when I persuaded Joe to write the letter—after I'd wrung every last cent of my money out of that French sewer-rat La Fontaine, and turned it all into a bill of exchange for Lizzie Fletcher to send on to wherever you were staying in England. I knew I could never make it up to you for what I'd done, but I reckoned that the money was better than nothing.

"After that I went west again, ahead of the emigrants, as far west as I could go, until I reached a little place called Yerba Buena, right on the edge of the ocean. It was just a peaceful Mexican settlement in those days. And then—dammit if they didn't find gold on Sutter's land, and suddenly the whole world began to pour into town. Before you could turn round it was *San Francisco,* the gold-rush city. All I wanted was to get away, to find somewhere clean and unspoiled. But now there was nowhere left for me to go."

At last it all made sense—Reuben's mysterious "Colonel," Jonas's brigand, and our oddly reclusive neighbor.

"And in the end you sailed to New York aboard the *Rachel Oliver.*"

Adam turned to look at me quizzically. "Reuben told you how he escaped from San Francisco? And I suppose that stuffed-shirt husband of yours said he'd met the wicked 'Colonel Allen' in New York."

"Why 'Colonel Allen,' of all things? *Allen* was my grandfather's name."

"Ah . . . that must have been where I heard it. I'd buried Adam Gaunt, you see, but I still needed a name, and *Allen* was the first to come into my head. Villainous Colonel Allen, living by his wits. . . . They didn't think much of me, either of them—although I rescued your brother from a couple of murderous ruffians and found him a crew for his blessed ship. *Your* ship, come to think of it."

"Are you asking me to believe you helped him because of me?"

"I can't think why else I did it."

"But how could you have known he was my brother? *Dean* is a common enough name, surely."

"I didn't know at first. But then, after I'd dragged him out of the mire in that alley, he was so pathetically grateful he insisted on telling me his whole life story. There was no way of stopping him."

"So that's how you found out I was in Liverpool."

"In Liverpool—and *Lady Oliver*. Reuben's very proud of the fact that his ship is named after his sister. And then, of course, the great Jonas Oliver was waiting for us on the quayside."

"He invited you to dinner."

"And took a great dislike to me—as I did to him," Adam added defiantly. "So I knew exactly where to find you after that—though I still had no intention of coming back to England in those days. None at all." He glanced across at me again to make sure I believed him. "I was only relieved you'd managed to make a new life for yourself after the mess I'd left behind.

"Then I discovered my father had died—oddly enough, his death was reported in one of the newspapers Jonas brought to New York with him. I wrote to an old friend in Norfolk, who told me the lawyers had started to search for me under the terms of my father's will. They'd no idea where to look, of course, but they were bound to make a show of it, at least. In spite of everything the old devil had left me some property in London and a house in Norfolk—provided I could be found to claim it. It's just about the only decent thing he ever did.

"The family had everything neatly divided between them when I appeared on the scene, and they weren't at all pleased. Brother Henry

—half-brother Henry—has got the title now, pompous oaf that he is, and he's made me promise to keep the whole affair quiet for the sake of the old man's reputation. Officially, I'm passed off as some kind of distant cousin, but I know Henry's hoping I'll leave the country again for good." Adam gave another weary sigh. "The two of you seem to agree on that. And just when I've run out of places to go."

———

That was the end of the story. There was nothing more to say, nothing to prevent the profound silence which rushed in to enfold us both—Adam motionless against his white iron pillar, while I'd come to rest on the edge of the big water-tank amid the wintering camellias and hydrangeas.

The silence lingered. Beyond the mass of leaves the rain formed blurred cascades on the darkening glass like a pall of ruched indigo velvet, and the falling dusk cast a soft gloom within the glass-house, muting every color to a degree of gray. But the downpour had slackened, and no longer drummed urgently on the roof. Now the rain blended with the gentle dimness below, whispering slyly against the sloping panes, dissolving judgment, diluting reason.

In that rustling twilight I discovered that I did after all care what had befallen Adam in the long years of absence. What he'd done to me was, as he'd said himself, beyond forgiveness. Yet time had dulled the pain; and my notions of what was right and wrong, just and unjust, seemed to have dimmed with the fading daylight, leaving only colorless shades of necessity.

"You haven't said anything." I realized he'd been waiting for my verdict.

"What do you expect me to say?"

"God knows. Tell me I'm a blackguard and a scoundrel—something like that, I suppose."

I shook my head.

"What good would it do? It wouldn't even be fair. I haven't forgotten that I was the one who wanted our marriage so badly—though Heaven knows, you did your best to warn me. And you were right. You are what you are. You've always followed some star of your own, Adam, and there was nothing anyone could do about that. Not even you."

"That's generous of you."

"None of us is perfect. What was it you used to say? 'Everyone has his own weakness—it's just that we don't see the load on our own backs'?"

"*Suus cuique attributus est error*. . . . You're right, it was from Catullus. How strange that you should remember."

"Oh, I remember everything, Adam. All of it—the good times, and the bad. I've tried not to think about the past, but it's there all the same."

Adam pushed himself free of the pillar then, with a fierceness which startled me.

"Am I insane, Rachel? You know me as well as anyone. Do you think there's some madness in me, to make me abandon a wife and child, all for the sake of an empty hillside and a breath of clear air?"

"The madness of eagles, perhaps." It was harder than ever now to have him so near in that shadowy space, no longer dispirited but vigorous, impassioned, filled with a dream of freedom. "Does it still drive you on, this madness?"

"There are no empty hillsides anymore. There's nowhere left to go."

But even as he said it, I knew I was still bound to send him away. Homeless, purposeless, he must go, and soon. Now it was more necessary than ever.

"Why did you have to come back here, Adam? To Liverpool—to this house?"

"It was time to come back."

He took a step toward me, and I retreated swiftly round the corner of the tank.

"But why now? Because there are no empty hillsides anymore? No more distant horizons waiting for you?"

"Partly because of that. But mostly because for the first time in my life I know what it is I've been searching for. And I haven't quite given up hope of grasping it."

"But you've spent your whole life wondering what was over the next ridge . . . and the next. . . . Has it really made you happy?"

He was standing near me now, absently brushing the young leaves of the hydrangeas with his fingertips, just as he'd once loved to run those same fingers through my unbound hair.

"Made me happy?" He said it as if he'd never considered the idea before. "No, I can't say it's made me happy. I seem to have destroyed whatever happiness I had along the way, and found nothing but disappointment over every new ridge I crossed. Yet it's a hard road ahead if I have to give up the search and make the best of what I have now." He gave me a curious glance. "Is that what you're doing, Rachel—making the best of what you have?"

"Isn't that what we all do?" I said quickly. "And I've been very fortunate—I know that. I'm learning to be content with my life."

"How very pious! That sounded just like Jonas Oliver or his whey-faced sister. The Rachel I remember would have scorned to settle for such half-measures. Aren't there ever times when you long to dance on their dinner table and sing one of your beer-hall songs?"

"Of course not!"

Adam burst out laughing, and for a dreadful, delirious moment I thought he was going to reach out to take me in his arms. "My poor Rachel, I always said you were a bad liar. Remember, I know you better than anyone else—perhaps better than you know yourself. I don't believe they've turned you into a strait-laced, prissy, drawing-room lady yet. You don't belong in their pettifogging world any more than I do."

"Then where *do* I belong? Tell me that if you can."

"Oh, you belong in the wilderness with wretches like me. You've seen too much and lived too hard a life not to know what's important and what isn't. When you've stared hunger in the face, you don't care whether the milk goes into the teacups before the tea, or the other way round. You know it doesn't matter a damn, and that's why you'll never be another Verity Broadney. You've told me as much today, in everything you've said."

It was no more than the truth, and I couldn't deny it.

"Not that I needed you to tell me. I realized as much a long time ago."

"That night in November, when you rescued Matthew from Paradise Street?"

"Long before that."

"But you only came to Westwood Park a year ago."

"That's true. But I'm not talking about here, in Liverpool. Do you remember visiting the Great Exhibition in London in '51? You were there with Jonas and the Broadneys, and Matthew."

A memory of kaleidoscopic confusion stirred in my mind—of great glass halls and telescopes and steam-engines, and crowds of people . . . and of George Broadney and his bottle of champagne . . .

and of Jonas, and Lettice Wyre, and the suspicions which still lurked, unresolved, in my heart.

Adam's voice drew me back to our softly shadowed corner of the fruit-house.

"I saw you there one Saturday, standing in the nave between the lighthouse lamp and the telescope, looking across at the buffalo robes on the fur exhibit."

"I was thinking of you, and those winter days in the cabin. . . . But were you really there all the time?"

"I made sure you didn't see me, though once I was almost near enough to touch you. When you stopped in front of a case of stuffed animals got up like humans—"

"That dreadful German thing! Full of weasels drinking tea, and rats playing the piano! Oh, it was all so pathetic. . . . Jonas was looking at them, not I."

"That's true. You had your back to it all, and you were standing, quite alone, watching the crowds pass by. I can see you now—just watching, and thinking. And wondering what made them so different from you."

He was barely a pace away from me now, his long, lean, well-remembered body half-hidden in the mass of dusky leaves.

"I came across you by pure chance. I walked round a case of fans and there you were—so much like your old self but very solemn and dignified, with Jonas beside you. I moved back into the crowd so that you wouldn't see me, but afterward I followed you for a bit. . . . And I began to realize that try as you might, you'd never be quite like the others."

"Oh, dear . . . Was it so obvious?"

"Only to me." He paused. "But then, I know you so very well."

His eyes told me it was still true: but there was more . . . a plaintive tenderness I'd never seen in all our time together. Before I could answer, he went on softly:

"And besides—I fell in love with you, that day at the Exhibition, between the telescope and the lighthouse lamp, with hundreds of people walking round about . . . For the first time in my life, I fell in love. It was like finding a missing part of myself. I wanted to rush over and take you in my arms in front of them all. . . ." He smiled gently. "Strange, isn't it, to fall in love with one's own wife?"

"No, Adam—you mustn't say it. . . . It can't be true."

"It is true—unfortunately for me. That's why I came back to Liverpool and bought this house—because all of a sudden I had somewhere to go, somewhere to exist that had a meaning for me. I've already told you I never intended to intrude on your life. You'd never have known I was here, if it hadn't been for Matthew."

"Oh, Adam—it's too late for us now. You should have gone away and forgotten me."

"I wanted to be sure your new life was making you happy. That was all. When I met Jonas Oliver in New York. . . . Well, I thought you deserved better, that's all. But I had to see for myself. All I wanted was to know there was nothing more I could give you, and then to leave again. And if you can tell me now—honestly—that you're living the life you've always longed for . . . That church-parade with the Olivers makes you shiver with pleasure, and Jonas Oliver—that cold fish—drives you to ecstasy—"

"I've tried to tell you I'm content, Adam—" Before I knew it, he'd stepped forward and taken my hands in his own, gripping them so firmly I couldn't snatch them away, holding me there against him while he destroyed my dearly won tranquility, piece by precious piece.

"*Content?*" he demanded. "What good is that, for Heaven's sake? A parrot's *content* in his cage because he's forgotten the free forest. Set him loose where he belongs, and watch him fly. . . . *Content* isn't enough."

"It has to be enough! At least I can hold contentment in my hands —feel it—know it's there—rely on it. Jonas and the Olivers may not set my blood on fire the way you did—yes, I admit it—but at least they'll be there tomorrow, and the next day, and the day after that. Because once before, years ago, I thought I could be truly, blissfully happy for the rest of my life. I was your wife, and I was stupid enough to think you loved me. But we both know the worth of that love now, don't we? I'll settle for contentment, Adam, sooner than your kind of love."

"Never mind what you *thought!* Do you ever—ever—remember my saying I loved you, then?" He held me fiercely, challenging me to answer, and then almost at once answered for me. "No—you don't. Because I never told you anything of the sort. Whatever else I did, I was honest with you about that—however badly you wanted to hear the words."

"I must go home now, at once." I struggled to free myself from his clasp, desperate to escape to my safe, polite world where his agonizing truth could not follow.

"Listen to me, for God's sake!" He'd pulled me closer still, sliding his arms about me, crushing me against him as if touch alone must convince me of his words. "I cared about you in those days —of course I did—because you were young and helpless, and you'd no one to turn to. But you're not helpless anymore. There's a strength about you that's all your own. You don't need anyone to lean on—Jonas, or me. . . . Not even me." He gave a wintry smile which touched my heart. "Maybe that's why I love you so much now."

"Don't say that, Adam, please—I can't bear it."

"And you still love me."

"No! That's not true!"

Gently, he tilted my face upward, forcing me to meet his eyes.

"You still love me, Rachel."

"Even if I did, what difference would it make? I can't have you! So it's wrong even to think about it."

"You've no choice—since I won't give you up. I mean it, Rachel. You're the end of all my wanderings: only you can give me peace, and I'll pay any price for that."

I could bear it no longer—standing there with him, knowing . . . *knowing* that as long as he lived, he could enslave me with a touch —with a smile. I cursed myself for ever risking another meeting. I should have written a letter—sent him away—kept him at arm's length, and with him all the dangerous, intoxicating memories of the past.

He'd relaxed his hold on me—confident, no doubt, of his prisoner. In that instant I stepped away from him, snatching my hat and gloves from the lid of the water-tank.

"Move aside, Adam—you can't stop me from leaving. I must have been mad to come here at all. If Jonas ever finds out—"

"To Hell with Jonas!" Adam seized my hat and flung it into a corner among the plant-pots. "I don't give a damn what Jonas thinks! You're all I care about. I *need* you, Rachel—and I can make you happy again."

"For the last time, Adam—I *am* happy. I love my husband and my children, and there's no place for you in my life. *No place*—do you understand? This is the last time I'll ever see your face or speak to you."

"You're wrong. Because I'll stay here at Westwood Park until I've made you accept the truth."

"If I have to, Adam, I'll tell Jonas who you really are and why you're here. I'll tell him everything, and he'll find a way of forcing you to leave the city. He has powerful friends, I warn you."

"He'd be foolish to try it."

Suddenly Adam looked so grim that I was frightened.

"What do you mean?"

"Simply that you're my wife, Rachel, and I won't leave you again. Not now that I know you still love me."

"I *was* your wife—once. Many years ago. Now Jonas Oliver is my husband."

"I very much doubt it."

"What on earth do you mean? Why shouldn't Jonas be—" For a long moment, I gaped at him in horror. "Oh, no . . . Oh, Adam—no . . . It isn't possible! Our marriage was perfectly legal. I signed a paper to say that you were dead!"

"Then you've added perjury to bigamy, I'm afraid."

"But I can't still be your wife! Not after all this time."

"I think a court of law would insist that you are."

"A court of law!"

"If it comes to that. If Jonas wants to make a fight of it."

"I can't believe what you're saying!"

"I've told you I won't give you up. You're still my wife, and if I have to, I'll go to court to prove it."

"But you know Jonas would never countenance such a thing!"

"You mean the Olivers couldn't bear the scandal of it."

"I could never make Jonas stand up in court and ask a judge to confirm that he's married! It would kill him. The Oliver family—the good name of the family—means everything in the world to him."

"More than his wife?" Adam waited incredulously for an answer. "Are you telling me that Jonas Oliver would run away from a lawsuit to prove the worth of his marriage, sooner than risk seeing his name in the newspapers? He'd give up his wife sooner than his reputation?" Adam stared at me for a long moment. "And you still say this man loves you?"

"But what if a court decided the marriage was invalid? That you and I were still . . . Oh, God in Heaven, my poor little girls! Alice and Louise would be—"

"Would be bastards. That's true. But I daresay they'd survive it. I had to, after all."

"No—I couldn't bear it! The whole of Liverpool laughing and pointing at us! Jonas would die of shame."

"Then he'd better not risk putting it to the test. Because I assure you that in the eyes of the law you're my wife and not Jonas Oliver's —always provided the man who married us knew his business, and I see no reason to doubt that."

Adam meant every word of it. I could see the determination in his face.

"I'm sorry, Rachel," he said more gently. "I thought you'd have realized how things stand."

"Why do you want to hurt me like this? Didn't I suffer enough all those years ago?"

"You could have hated me for what I did. You *should* have hated me for it. But you don't. You love me as much as I love you—and because of that I'm not going to do as you ask. I won't give you up, and I won't go away. You're my wife, Rachel, by right of law—and because you belong with me."

I couldn't trust myself to speak. I could only shake my head, more in bewilderment than denial.

Adam bent to retrieve my hat and dusted the flakes of dry soil from it with his fingers.

"If you still don't believe me, I'll prove it to you. Now—before you put this damned veil on again."

He reached out for me, and I realized he was going to pull me to him and kiss me, there and then. . . . A kiss I could have died for . . . lied, deceived and betrayed for. . . . The cruelest kiss of all—and Adam knew it.

He must have seen the sudden terror which flashed into my eyes, because he halted, a hand's-breadth from disaster. I couldn't have run from him. It had been hard enough standing so close, knowing I could never have him. But if he'd kissed me . . . I tried not to think what I might have done.

"I can wait," he said, handing me the hat. "Though not forever. But I will give you time to think. I have to go to Paris on business next week, and I'll be abroad for a while. We'll meet again when I get back, and decide what's to be done."

I shook my head again, miserably. "There's nothing to be done. Someone will be hurt, whatever happens."

"Oh, there's always a solution. There has to be. Come on—I'll see you safely to your gate. It's dark enough now for no one to notice us."

But as I drew near to him in the doorway he reached out and slid a hand gently into the nape of my neck, irresistibly caressing, winding his fingers languorously into my hair, tilting my face up toward his once more.

"Trust me, Rachel. I know I've told you that before, but this time I mean it. This time it's forever. I promise you—when all this is over, we'll be together again. So there's no need for that dismal face. Look —even the rain's stopped for us."

27

Jonas returned on Monday evening, far too full of the wonders of *lignum vitae* to notice anything amiss with me. He was utterly triumphant: the *Altair* would now be perfect in every way, and he'd hardly taken off his overcoat before he'd begun to lecture me on the marvelous properties of the wood of the Guiacum tree and its mysterious self-lubrication. To celebrate the march of science he spent a good part of that night in my bed, still harping on horsepower and steam-governors. If he'd deliberately set out to remind me of the yawning gulf which existed between Adam and himself, he couldn't have made it more plain.

And Adam wanted me—wanted *me,* as Jonas never had—and the knowledge was like a heady draft of wine to my senses. Yet in more rational moments when I succeeded in looking at my situation without emotion, I was soon brought back to earth. *I won't give you up,* Adam had said: but the decision wasn't his to make.

If it turned out that I was legally Lady Oliver after all, Jonas would be entitled to recapture his runaway wife and lock her up in his home for as long as he pleased, until he consented to divorce me as an adulteress. Even if Adam was right and I was still his lawful wife, in the eyes of the world I would have deceived and deserted Jonas, shaming him beyond measure. Either way, I'd never see Alice and Louise again—that was certain. Verity would make sure they grew up to think of their mother as a brazenly corrupt and cold-hearted woman who'd walked out of their lives without so much as a backward glance.

And I couldn't bring myself to do such a thing. I loved my self-possessed Oliver daughters, though I seldom felt I understood them —and I even loved Jonas too, in a strange, almost maternal way. I expect Adam would have told me some of that love was guilt—guilt I felt for the unjust way I'd suspected him of spending the night in

London with Lettice Wyre—for even that ghost had now been laid
to rest.

"Blasted Melbourne agent's gone off to join the opposition,"
Jonas had muttered one night over dinner, carefully wiping his
mouth on his napkin. "Never liked the fellow, myself. Signed his
name all over the page like some ham actor."

"Who was that, Jonas?" I asked cautiously.

"Cobbold. In Melbourne."

"Not . . . Cyril Wyre, then?"

"*Wyre?* Who on earth's Cyril Wyre?"

"We met his wife in London, at Verity's dinner, the night before
the Exhibition. Don't you remember? *Lettice,* her name was."

"*Lettice Wyre?*" Jonas looked genuinely puzzled. "What a peculiar name . . . No, I don't remember her. I never remember any of
these fly-by-night friends of Verity's—you should know that by
now."

I did know. And I knew Jonas well enough by then to be certain
that in spite of George Broadney's scurrilous tales, nothing had taken
place that night between my husband and little Lettice. However
swift his love-making, Jonas would certainly have remembered the
lady's name.

No—Jonas was neither a lover nor a philanderer. I'd married him
knowing what he was, and what he could never be. He hadn't
changed a jot since then—neither for better nor worse. What right
did I have to tell him now that it wasn't enough?

I had chosen my path: now I was bound to follow it. And knowing
that saved me from having to answer all the questions of trust and
blame and broken promises—and freedom, and love . . . Because although I found myself longing once more for the sheer physical bliss
of Adam's presence, I was now Jonas Oliver's wife—and that was
how I'd have to remain. When Adam returned from Paris, that was
the answer I'd give him. Perhaps then he'd realize the hopelessness
of the situation and leave me in peace at last.

And yet in the weeks that followed it was Jonas who began to
draw further and further away from me, despite all my good intentions. Now that work on the *Altair* was well advanced I seemed to
see less of him than ever, and even when he was briefly at home he
hardly appeared to notice my presence. Whole mealtimes often
passed entirely in silence, while Jonas filled his mouth automatically
from his plate and his mind wrestled with some new problem con-
cerning his all-absorbing steamship.

Most days he haunted the shipyard across the river in Birkenhead, superintending every tiny part of the work until the journeymen and their apprentices were nearly driven mad by his persistence. When I reproached him with ignoring the girls for days on end, he promised us an outing together—but even that turned out to be a visit to the shipyard to show off the latest row of iron plates to his mystified daughters. Fortunately, Alice and Louise were already well used to their father's obsession, and strolled composedly in the shadow of the growing hull of "Papa's ship," their white-gloved hands folded demurely across their skirts, listening politely while Jonas held forth on the theory of steam-propulsion.

"Not that I expect them to be scholars," he reminded me later. "Too much book-learning's unbecoming in a woman. I hate these bluestocking wives who are always interrupting their husbands to push in some nonsense they've read in a tuppeny-ha'penny volume as if it was holy writ.

"Besides—they'll ruin their eyesight, peering at books all day. They'd be far better off following the excellent example of their Mamma, and making home and family their entire world. You've never wished for more than that—why should they?"

How could you possibly know what I wish for, Jonas? The question formed itself silently in my mind. *And how shocked you'd be if you did know, my dear . . .*

———

At last even Jonas began to feel guilty about the amount of time he was spending in the shipyard and away from his home and family. But there could be no question of cutting down the hours he lavished on the *Altair;* instead he instructed Reuben, conveniently at home just then, to make sure I wasn't allowed to mope indoors in his absence.

"Take your sister to the park—take her to the theater, if it's decent —and generally keep her occupied, my boy. I entrust her to you: stop her from fretting, that's all."

To my dismay, Reuben took his duties very seriously. The mere sight of me reading alone in my sitting room was enough to send him into vigorous action, and much as I loved my brother, I had to admit there were times when he could be immensely irritating. Life to Reuben was an earnest business. He'd no small talk whatsoever: he'd pounce on any silly little remark I might make in passing and treat it as if it had been a sermon on the human condition. And he'd never give up an argument. He had a maddening way of fastening himself on to the rump of a subject like one of those fighting bull-terriers which sink their teeth into an opponent and then can't release their jaws. Long after a topic was dead Reuben continued to worry it and shake it like a rat, until I could have screamed with frustration.

To make matters worse, ever since he'd spent Christmas in New York with Maria and our mother he'd made it his self-appointed duty to bring us together again, and my refusal even to consider the possibility weighed heavily on his mind.

"It's so unlike you, Sis," he complained whenever the matter was raised between us. "Until now I'd have sworn you were the most sensible, reasonable creature in the world. But on this one point . . . You're acting like a selfish child, and I can't understand it."

"I've told you often enough, Reuben—I never wanted to quarrel with Mamma. I'd happily have made it up with her years ago, if she hadn't insisted she didn't want to see me or hear from me. Ask Aunt Grace. She'll tell you the truth of it."

"I *know* the truth of it, Rachel! You've no idea how many questions Mother asked me about you—what the White House was like, and Jonas, and the girls . . ."

"And Matthew? Did she ask about Matthew?"

"I really can't remember."

"No—because I'm sure she has no interest in Matthew. He's Adam's son, after all."

"There you go—taking offense over nothing. You're the one who's keeping up the quarrel! I'm convinced Mother sincerely regrets all the bitterness and the hard words. She's changed, you know. And her health isn't what it was. I was quite amazed to see her at Christmas, even though Maria had already warned me of her headaches and her strange moods."

"What strange moods?" I was suspicious at once. My mother could act a part to perfection when it suited her.

"Well . . ." Reuben's brow furrowed. "It's hard to describe. Sometimes she seemed overwrought—nervous—almost feverish—speaking so quickly no one could understand a word of it, and laughing suddenly about nothing at all. And then at other moments you could say something to her, and it was just as if she hadn't heard. She'd frown and shake her head, but say nothing. She's quite ill, I'm sure —or something dreadful's preying on her mind."

"Guilt, I shouldn't wonder. Guilt for the way she's treated us all."

"How can you be so cruel, Rachel? Try to see the situation from Mother's point of view. Until now she's always been too busy with business affairs to make any close friends. Her family was all she had —though I admit she was never one to show her feelings—"

"I'm glad you admit that, at least!"

"—and now she sees her children going off on their own, one by one . . . and she's simply an unhappy, ageing woman frightened by the prospect of being alone. *That*'s why I believe that if you'd only write a letter—to prove you still care about her—"

"No, Reuben. It wouldn't do any good, I promise you."

"How can you be so sure? Just a letter, at least—what harm would that do? I'm sure if you begged her pardon for running off with that man—"

"I will *not* beg her pardon! I'm not ashamed of what I did! I love —I *loved* Adam," I corrected myself in panic, "and that's what she couldn't forgive. I won't waste a single second on making excuses for myself."

"But—"

"No, Reuben. And that's an end to it."

Yet Reuben would not be convinced. For days afterward, instead of trying to cheer me up as Jonas had instructed, he'd lapse into spells of glum silence broken by huge, whistling sighs. I had more than enough to disturb me already, and the sight of Reuben sitting by the fire, one large hand clamped on each knee as if the whole weight of the world was bearing down on his shoulders, almost drove me to distraction.

At Christmas Jonas had bought me a slick red pony-phaeton and a clever little mare I could easily manage myself; now the dainty carriage became my salvation. Whenever Reuben was at his most trying, I'd suggest a drive to the park, an outing which never failed to raise my spirits as we cracked briskly round the perimeter circuit behind the bobbing back of the pony. With Reuben as my escort there was no need for a groom—and, indeed, no room for one in the phaeton once Reuben and I were installed and Lottie had scrambled into her place behind us. Then the three of us would whirl off down the White House carriage-sweep, the pony's hooves clacking brightly on the frosted ground, the harness jingling, the phaeton a flash of crimson in the thin late-winter sunshine as we set off for the park.

Once there we'd let Lottie down for a while to run beside the carriage. She loved to race the tall, spinning red wheels, ears streaming out behind her head, eyes shining with the effort of running, until we stopped at last to allow her to sniff among the bushes and indulge her passion for rolling among the drifts of crackling brown leaves which still littered the grass. But as winter slackened its grip the park became busier, especially on fine Sunday afternoons, and our headlong carriage-ride became more circumspect among the romping children and strolling families.

"I daren't let Lottie out alone in such a crowd," I said to Reuben one day. "She might easily wander off and become lost. Would you mind taking her for a short walk instead? Just across the grass beyond the bandstand there, as far as the fountain. She ought to have a little exercise before we go home. I'll be perfectly safe here in the phaeton until you come back."

"I can't possibly leave you here alone! Suppose the pony shies and bolts off with you?" Reuben, with a seafarer's mistrust of horses, was certain the animals spent their entire lives treacherously waiting for a chance to cause an accident.

"This pony couldn't run away if she tried," I assured him, laughing. "She's far too lazy. I promise you, I won't come to any harm in the short time you'll be away. Look—she's much more interested in cropping the grass. Now off you go—Lottie's dying to roll under the trees."

To be honest, I was longing for a few moments alone with my thoughts. Reuben had spent almost every second that day reproaching me with my refusal to write to our mother, driving me almost demented with his persistence. He seemed to have swallowed her tale of woe without a murmur; somehow she'd managed to convince him she'd long since forgiven me for whatever wrong I was supposed to have done her, and that now only my willfulness was keeping us apart.

I had to admire her cleverness. With subtle skill she'd played on Reuben's lofty notions of what was right and just: no mother and daughter ought to be estranged—it was wicked and unnatural—and my stubborn hostility was breaking my invalid mother's heart. Reuben had promptly decided his mother was a saint—and I was a lost soul. The prospect of endless weeks of scolding stretched before me, and I began to long for the day when Reuben would once again be called away to sea.

Oh, I was certain my mother's mind hadn't changed toward me.

And if Reuben's lectures had made me doubt that for an instant. . . . The proof was only a couple of paces away from me at that very moment.

————

"Well, well . . . Rachel Dean! Or should I say *Lady Oliver?* Since you look near as dammit a real lady in that turn-out."

He was standing at the wheel of the phaeton, one small hand on the side of the bright little carriage of which I was so proud. I'd recognized that insolent drawl of his before I even turned my head: it was a voice I'd hoped never to hear again—and even as I turned, part of me still clung to the belief that I might be mistaken, for why should Frank Ellis, of all people, be walking in a sunny Liverpool park on that idyllic afternoon?

He was thinner than I remembered, and his hair was pure white now, a thick, pale mass where once it had been blue-black. Yet he was still a dark man with black brows and eyes like blue marbles, and the same slaty-blue cast to his pallid face, all the more vivid now against the startlingly white hair. Yet for all the whiteness of his skin, one place stood out more livid still—a patch on his left cheek where four gleaming, parallel scars showed where my frantic fingernails had marked him.

He saw my glance, and touched the place automatically.

"In case I ever forget."

I stared at him in silence: I could hardly believe he was really standing there in his cheap, worn coat and low-crowned hat. And yet there was no doubt it was the same man—older, embittered, stripped of his tawdry grandeur along with his fancy silk waistcoat.

"I'd heard a rumor you were dead."

"Then you heard wrong. Though it'd suit you down to the ground if I was, I reckon."

"I didn't wish you dead. Only never to see you again."

"Now what kind of a welcome is that?" Ellis leaned comfortably on the side of the phaeton. "Specially when I've come so far to see you."

"If you've come here to see me, then you've wasted your time, Frank. I've nothing to say to you."

"Maybe not. But you'll speak to me, all the same—here and now, or somewhere else. I've been following you, Rachel. Waiting for my chance."

I looked around for Reuben, but he was nowhere to be seen. For a moment I wondered if I should try to drive off suddenly in order to dislodge Frank Ellis from the side of the carriage. Then something he said made me hesitate.

"Go ahead. Drive off, if you want. It's all the same to me, Rachel. You'll listen to me sooner or later."

"Don't threaten me, Frank. I'm not afraid of you."

"So you say." Ellis's opaque blue eyes stared into mine. "But you don't know why I'm here, yet."

"I don't care why you're here."

"Now, is that any way to talk to an old friend? Since I *am* an old friend, ain't I?"

Ellis paused for a moment, waiting for me to respond.

"Still not interested, Rachel? Well, it doesn't signify. I'll have my say whether you're interested or not . . . Since I've had plenty of time to think about you and me, and the past . . . You know New York at all? You know what I mean by *the Tombs?*"

Who could forget the Tombs? I could still remember passing through the cold shadow of the prison walls and shuddering at the thought of the wretches shut up in the sunless cells behind the rows of tiny window-slits.

"You were sent to the Tombs?"

"I was." He continued to stare at me. "Good name, isn't it? They call it *the Tombs* because so many prisoners hang themselves in their cells before the law has the pleasure of stringing them up in the prison yard. . . . Even death's better than lying in that stinking half-dark behind an iron door, listening to the rats running around and knowing that if you did somehow manage to put an end to it all, they'd have you three-quarters eaten before anyone'd find you."

"No doubt you deserved to be there."

"No one deserves to be in that place!" Ellis's face flushed in swift anger, and his hands gripped the side of the carriage, the knuckles standing out like knots. I glanced anxiously in the direction in which Reuben had vanished with Lottie, and Ellis followed my eyes.

"You'd better hope he doesn't come back till I've had my say, Rachel—otherwise things could get pretty bad for you."

"Cheap threats, Frank! I don't know how you managed to find me here, but—"

"A certain lady told me where you'd gone—a lady who went to a lot of trouble to get me out of jail, though she was just about the last person in the world, excepting yourself, I would have expected to help me."

A sudden chill gathered round my heart.

"Who was this . . . person?"

"Why, Lady Oliver . . . I do believe I've got your attention at last . . ." The sickening grin I remembered so well had spread itself across Frank Ellis's features. "That kind lady . . . was your own very loving mother—who else?"

Who else, indeed? I bit my lip, hoping my agitation wouldn't show.

"Lucky for me she was living in New York by then. And one morning she happened to see a report in the *Tribune* about a little . . . misunderstanding . . . I'd got into, over a young woman and a certain sum of money—as a result of which the lady was considerably upset, and called in the law to stop me leaving town. Which was how I came to be in the Tombs, awaiting trial. But your mother thought she recognized the name. *John Francis Ellis,* the *Tribune* said, *has been sent to the Tombs.* And shortly after that, damned if I didn't have a visit from Mrs. Dean, coming to see if I was the same fellow she'd thrown out of her house all those years before for making up to her daughter."

Ellis grinned smugly again.

"You know—I had your mother figgered all wrong. Now I know her better I can see we're pretty much alike, Mrs. Dean and me. When there's something we want, we go straight for it, both of us. Your mother went off to see the lawyers and the judge—and even the lady in the case—and she was very persuasive, it seems. Just as soon as she'd paid off what was owing they agreed to drop all the charges. And then it was *Step this way, Mr. Ellis, you're a free man today. . . . Mr. Ellis,* mind you. There I was, out in the sunshine, nobody's hand on my shoulder—except your mother's, of course."

"Why should my mother want to help you?"

"That's what I asked myself. *What does she want from me?* Because as you know, she doesn't part with a cent for nothing." Ellis paused for a moment, sliding his hands carefully along the rail of the phaeton.

"But once she told me—well, it all began to make sense. You see, by then I'd shown her this . . ."

Ellis fished in his pocket and drew out a folded, yellowing scrap of paper, jerking it back as I reached out to take it from him.

"Look—but don't touch."

It was a quarter-column from the *St. Louis Gazette*, luridly reporting the wounding by gunfire of a saloon-singer in Independence —an Englishwoman who called herself *Mademoiselle Valentine*, but whose real name was Rachel Gaunt . . . I had no need to read the last few lines. The shooting had brought me a fame I'd never wanted.

"I told your mother the whole story, Rachel—all those things that happened after you came to work for me." Absently, Ellis fingered his scarred cheek. "She loved the bit about the shooting best of all. She made me tell it over and over again.

"That's when she got me out of the Tombs. *We're going to England, Frank Ellis*, she said. *We both have unfinished business with my daughter*. And she was right—we do have a score to settle, you and me. Since you were the one who as good as sent me to the Tombs in the first place."

"Nothing was ever *your* fault, was it, Frank?" I exclaimed bitterly. "If you weren't a liar and a cheat—"

Without a word, and watching me intently, Ellis began to whistle the tune I'd last heard under my bedroom window in Independence, the night the mob marched and danced down the main street into the early hours.

"Don't tell me you've forgotten it, Rachel," he finished softly. ". . . *And the whole damn population . . . Ran Frank Ellis out of town* . . . That's the song they were singing the night they threw me out of Independence. The night Kate cheated me out of my fair share of the Trader's House—and all because of you."

"You got no more than you deserved!"

"That isn't the way I see it. You raised that whole town against me! And why? Because I called you what you were—no better than a cheap whore, except you hadn't the honesty to admit it."

Seized by sudden rage, I lifted the carriage-whip to strike him— and then, just in time, remembered the crowds of curious passersby. I let my hand fall uselessly back to my lap.

"Sensible. Unless you want to make a public show of yourself."

"Say your piece, and have done, Frank. Has my mother sent you to blackmail me with that piece of paper? Is that it?"

Ellis laughed unpleasantly, and shook his head.

"Your mother's a rich woman, in case you've forgotten. There's nothing you could give her she'd waste a second on. No—blackmail isn't her game."

"Then . . . what?"

Ellis leaned toward me until his face almost touched mine.

"She says . . . she's going to finish you, Rachel. She'll send you back to the gutter where you belong. Not all at once, but little by little, when you've had some time to think about it and find out what misery really is . . . That was her message: one day you'll wake up, and there'll be none of this—" Ellis's gesture took in the phaeton and the cheerful families in the park. "It's all she's come to England for. To see you ruined once and for all."

I could feel the blood drain from my face until it was as pale as Ellis's own. With absolute certainty, I knew my mother had meant every word: she wouldn't rest now until my life, my home and everything I held dear lay in ruins before her.

All the same, I was damned if I was going to give Frank Ellis the satisfaction of seeing my fear. I took refuge in a bold lie.

"And that's your evidence? That old newspaper story? Good Heavens, my husband knew all that before we were married."

"I don't believe you, Rachel. If he'd known, he'd certainly never have married you. Not Jonas Oliver."

"Very well then—all I have to do is tell him everything now, and you'll have nothing to use against me."

"I guess you might tell him, at that . . . and maybe he'd be prepared to overlook it after all this time. But what about your smart friends—and your husband's high-and-mighty family? Are you proposing to tell them too? And what about the rest of the city? Somehow I can't quite see Sir Jonas Oliver being happy at the whole of Liverpool knowing his wife had once waggled her backside in a barroom for a few dollars a week. And worse than that, maybe, the way I'd tell it."

"No one would believe you for a moment. No newspaper would print it."

But even as I spoke, an infinitely more dismaying thought occurred to me. What if—

"And after that—" Ellis continued heavily, "—well, there's plenty to tell them about you and that Indian-lover you married, isn't there?"

"Adam?" Sick dread flooded the pit of my stomach as the very disaster I'd imagined became reality. The worst had happened. Somehow my mother must have discovered that Adam was still alive and in Liverpool. Now she had a weapon which could destroy us all —Adam, Jonas and my innocent children along with me.

"No!" I blurted out in wild panic. "I won't let her do it! Adam will find her, and make her leave us alone! I'll tell him what you've said, and—"

Suddenly Frank Ellis was staring at me—his mouth hanging open —staring as if a ghost stood at my shoulder.

"*Adam will find her?*" he said slowly. "Adam *Gaunt,* do you mean? Why, I believe you do . . ."

Speechless with horror, I realized what I'd done.

"Well, well . . . Adam Gaunt, still alive after all this time . . . Because he is still alive, isn't he?" With the swiftness of a cat, Ellis pursued his quarry. "Still alive—and somewhere close enough for you to see him regularly . . ." He watched my face intently. "Or somewhere he can see you . . . Which means Liverpool. Yes . . . I reckon I can guess what happened . . . Adam Gaunt came back to find you—back to this city . . . and if I'm not mistaken, he's here now."

"You'll get no information from me." I looked round desperately for Reuben.

"I don't need anything from you, Rachel. It's written in your face, plain as day. Who'd have believed it! And how very cozy for you!"

"You're raving, Ellis. How can any man come back from the dead?"

"Except that he wasn't dead, was he? Lost—gone—wandered off somewhere in the mountains, but *not dead.*"

"So you say." I was grasping at straws now. "Yet look at me! Here I am, driving in the park, not a care in the world—do I look like a woman whose dead husband has returned to her?"

Once more, Ellis put his face close to mine.

"Yes," he said. "You do."

Then he leaned away again. "At least, that's what I'm going to tell your mother when I see her. I reckon she'll be *very* interested in that piece of information, don't you?"

I knew only too well what my mother could do with that final, damning, devastating piece of evidence which I—in my fatal terror —had given her. I was finally at her mercy; yet the worst of it was the thought of those other innocent souls who would be dragged down with me. Something had to be done—even if it was only a prayer for them to be spared.

"I must see my mother. I must talk to her, and make her understand how many others she'll hurt besides me, people who've never done her any harm."

"You won't change her mind, I can promise you that."

"Nevertheless, I must see her."

"She doesn't want to see you. That's why she sent me here instead."

"But she can't be far away. I don't believe she'd let you out of her sight for more than half a day. Where is she, Frank?"

Ellis grinned. "Somewhere you'll never find her."

"Then give her this message. Tell her I want to speak to her. Say I'll meet her anywhere she wishes—" I hesitated. "Tell her I beg her to see me."

"Ten to one she won't want to meet you."

"Make her understand, Frank. It isn't for me—it's for Jonas and my children. Only for a few minutes, that's all."

"I can see it's important to you." Ellis ran his hands admiringly along the lacquered side of the phaeton. "Maybe I need a little encouragement to make sure the message gets delivered . . . You being such a rich woman nowadays."

"So you meant to blackmail me after all!"

"No . . . those weren't my instructions. It's just something that . . . occurred to me . . . when I realized how much store you set by getting word to your mother."

"I've nothing to give you. I've no money with me."

"What about that, then?" Ellis pointed to a diamond and ruby brooch at my throat, an Oliver heirloom. "That must be worth something."

Instinctively, my fingers flew to cover the glittering stones.

"How do I know you'll deliver the message?"

"You'll get an answer, one way or another. That's how you'll know."

In the distance I caught sight of Reuben's substantial figure advancing toward us, Lottie dragging him along on the end of her lead.

"When can I expect an answer?"

Ellis shrugged, and held out his hand. "You'll just have to be patient."

Nearer now, Reuben approached with his measured tread.

What choice did I have? In silence I unfastened the brooch and gave it to him.

"I must see her, Frank. Remember that."

Ellis regarded me for a second, a curious half-smile on his face. Then without another word he turned on his heel and walked quickly away amongst the afternoon strollers.

"Who on earth was that rough-looking fellow?" inquired Reuben as he reached the carriage and hoisted Lottie into her place.

"He . . . remembered me from a visit to the workhouse," I told him, my face bent low over Lottie's silky head. "He wanted to thank me for finding him work—that was all."

"Did he, indeed . . . Well, it only goes to show I should never have left you. He might easily have been a thief, or a murderer, or anything."

———

I don't think I spoke a single word on the way home, lost in my own dismal thoughts as I was. By the time Reuben had helped me down from the phaeton at the door of the White House, I'd almost decided to tell Jonas the whole sorry tale. I had no doubt my life would be changed forever if I did—right or wrong, Jonas would never forgive me for dragging such a scandal into his home—but it seemed the only way of lessening the damage my mother might cause. Perhaps I owed him that opportunity, at least.

To my surprise, I found Uncle Tom Fuller waiting in the hall as I went in, hat in hand and a somber expression on his face.

"Uncle Tom! I didn't expect to see you here today! Is Jonas with you?"

"He's in the library, my dear, looking for some engine-plan or other. There's been a bit of bother with the *Altair*—pretty serious bother, in fact—and we're needed in Birkenhead right away. We'll only be here for a few minutes. Good day to you, Reuben," he added as Reuben tramped in behind me.

"But what's happened? I thought everything was going so well."

Tom Fuller frowned, and shook his head. "Boiler problem in the engine-works. It seems they fired up the first boiler this afternoon to give it a test, and as soon as the steam pressure rose high enough, the whole thing exploded. I don't know much more about it just yet —except there's three men dead and another two badly scalded. Even the shed the blessed thing was in has collapsed. We'll have to dig it out before we can tell what's gone wrong."

Just at that moment, Jonas erupted into the hall, dragging on his overcoat as he ran. He thrust a sheaf of plans at Tom Fuller.

"I've never liked that design from the first," he announced as if there had been no break at all in their conversation. "I've always thought it was a mistake to put the safety valves straight on to the steam-chest in that way. It's bound to weaken the boiler where it counts most. Hello, Rachel," he added as an afterthought. "Don't keep dinner for me—I'll send out for something at the yard." Grabbing the Captain by the arm, he hustled him toward the door. "On the other hand," I heard him continue, "I wouldn't trust those fellows not to leave a rivet-bag jammed in a pipe when they finished it off. If I find that's the cause, the man that did it will never work again. I'll make sure of that."

And to all intents and purposes, that was the last I saw of Jonas for three days. He almost lived at the shipyard, hovering over the damaged entrails of his beloved steamship like a lover pining for his ailing mistress. When I did see him, he was plunged in such deep dejection that I couldn't bear to add my mother's threats to his burden of woe. In any case, I doubt if he'd even have listened.

For the present I'd have to go into battle on my own.

My diamond brooch brought me an answer sooner than I'd expected. One week to the day that I'd encountered Frank Ellis in the park, a note arrived, delivered by hand, so the footman informed me —"Came in a carriage, m'lady. Not to wait for an answer, so he said."

On the outside was a single line in a hand I had good reason to recognize. *Lady Oliver, The White House.*

Inside there was very little more—but it was the answer I'd hoped for. *St. Veronica's Chapel. Tuesday. Three-thirty.* And that was all.

"Do you know St. Veronica's Chapel, William?" I asked the footman later as he made up the drawing-room fire. "I've never heard of it, but then, there are so many churches in the city now . . ."

"St. Veronica's, m'lady?" The tall footman paused, coal-shovel in hand, stooping before the grate. "The old convent, do you mean?"

"I'm not sure."

"There used to be a convent of that name down Moorfields way, 'cos I remember the nuns going about there when I was a child. The Convent of St. Veronica of Jerusalem, it was called—though it's been closed up this ten years past. I suppose it must have had a chapel of some sort, m'lady, though more'n that I can't say."

The old convent was there, just as he'd described it, through an archway off a dingy cul-de-sac which had once been a main highway, before the growing city overwhelmed it. All the same, I sent my groom striding through the Tuesday afternoon drizzle to knock on the chapel door, half-disbelieving that my mother could have chosen such a place for our meeting.

Everything about it spoke of neglect, from the sooty, bird-splashed niches above its doorway to the skewed slabs of its steps, forced apart by fierce clumps of nettles. Had a mere ten years been enough to work such destruction, I wondered . . . ? And what childhood memory of dark monastic robes and calm, pale faces had prompted my mother to select such a place for her purpose?

The groom returned to the carriage, picking his way fastidiously across the moss-covered flags of the courtyard.

"No answer at all, m'lady," he reported, "though the door isn't locked. I gave the handle a turn, an' it pushed open quite easylike."

"I see." Somewhere inside me—in spite of everything—I'd treasured a hope that this gloomy, dispiriting back-street chapel would turn out to be locked fast, beyond doubt the wrong place for my mother's appointed meeting. But the door stood ajar, left unlocked by some private arrangement so that she and I could meet alone, unwatched by servants or the prying eyes of passersby.

"Wait here for me."

Eight or nine steps were enough to cross the rain-soaked courtyard to the door, which swung open to my touch, releasing a rush of chill, stale air faintly censed with plaster-dust and dry mold.

The inner walls of the chapel had been white; everything else lay under a thick carpet of dust, gray as rough felt in the meager light from the windows.

I waited. No one spoke. No one moved, or coughed, or even seemed to breathe in that empty space in the heart of the city. There was no one at all in that place—no one but me, standing foolish and fearful between the ranks of silent choir-stalls, wondering whether my mother had planned this humiliation as the first of my private torments.

"So you came."

I whirled about, searching for the source of the voice.

"Stay where you are. I can see you perfectly well."

It was *her* voice—my mother's voice—drier and harsher than I remembered it, though perhaps mellowed in my mind by passing years. I could hear her—but she was nowhere to be seen. Unless . . .

A carved screen to one side of the altar steps, half-hidden in shadow, concealed a door by which the nuns must have entered from the convent for their daily offices. I was certain now that my mother stood behind the grating, watching my confusion. I took a step toward her.

"Stay where you are, I said! You asked for this meeting, not I. There's nothing more I have to say to you."

I waited, motionless.

"Why won't you let me see your face?"

"Because I don't choose to." There was silence for a few seconds, then the voice continued. "Someone's shown you how to do your hair, at any rate, though you still have no figure to speak of. You were always a scraggy little brat. God knows what that man sees in you."

"I see there's no point in politeness."

"None whatsoever. Why should we lie to one another? I only came here out of curiosity, to see what barefaced bigamy had done for you. Bigamy—and adultery as well, most like. Are you sleeping with him, too, now he's come back for you?" High in the rafters, the word *you—you—you* echoed to and fro like a malediction.

"If you mean Adam—I've told him I won't see him again. He'll have to live his own life, far away from me."

"How noble of you! A great sacrifice, I'm sure."

"It was . . . a sacrifice."

"Indeed? In spite of the fact that he left you penniless to shift for yourself and your child while he went off on some adventure of his own? Since I assume that's what he did. He left you—just as I said he would." *Would—would—would* . . . Above our heads, the word repeated itself again and again.

"I understand why he went away. Though it's too late for us now. The past is over and done with."

"Then you still love him, in spite of everything?"

"Yes, God help me. In spite of all he's done, I'll always love Adam."

"And Jonas—the brilliant shipbuilder? What about Jonas?"

"Jonas too, in a different way."

"And Reuben, that great lump of dullness? And your children?"

"Of course."

"Heavens above! What a mess you are! Dealing yourself out in little parcels to all and sundry—caring for them, worrying about them—your husband, your brother, your lover, your children . . .

You do a great deal too much loving, if you ask me. Well—see where it's got you now."

"I can't understand what I've done to make you hate me so much!"

"Can't you? Oh, I think you'll understand—one day. When there's nothing left of your hopes and your plans . . . and your precious *love*."

"What do you mean to do to me?"

"I mean to show the whole of Liverpool what a trollop it has been touching its cap to. By the time the newspapers have done with you, the Olivers will throw you out in the gutter where you belong—a pauper—a bigamist—a woman with no name but *harlot*."

"And Jonas? And the children? What have they done to deserve that?"

"Nothing at all. But why should I care about them?"

"You have no conscience about harming them?"

"None whatever."

"Then I shall tell Jonas the whole story. Everything. And if he wants to divorce me after that, well then—"

"Then what?"

"Then . . . I shall just have to accept it."

"You'll go crawling back to Adam Gaunt—that's what you were going to say, wasn't it!"

"No—I've told you." *You—you—you* . . . the vaulted ceiling challenged my lie.

"What rubbish! You say you love him—yet you expect me to believe you wouldn't run back to him if the Olivers threw you out?" From behind the screen I heard a snort of derision. "A fine story! No —I know exactly what's in your mind, Miss . . . And I promise you, I'll never allow it to happen. Do you hear me? *Never*. If I think there's the smallest chance of you and that man being . . . together again . . . I'll prevent it."

"How could you stop us!" Anger made me throw caution to the winds. "A woman of no reputation—a man who's already an outcast—what more could you do to keep us apart?"

"I could kill him." The voice was as thin and dry as a knife-edge. "And I will, if I think it's necessary."

"Murder? Even you would never—no, it's impossible!"

"Impossible? Oh, no . . . it's quite possible, my dear. Why don't you think it over, and see whether your great love is worth the risk.

I'll give you plenty of time to think—and to wonder when I'll choose to tell your little secrets to the world . . . Now be off with you. You've begun to bore me. Go home, Rachel, while you still have a home to go to."

"I can't believe you mean to do this to me."

"Wait and see, if you don't believe it. By the way—I assume this is yours." Something clattered across the stone flags at my feet: the diamond and ruby brooch Frank Ellis had demanded from me in the park. As I glanced down at it in surprise, from somewhere behind the screen I heard the squeal of a long-disused door-handle.

"Wait!" I began to run toward the screen. *Wait—wait—wait . . .* cried the rafters. In the shadows, a door slammed, and a key grated in a rusty lock. By the time I reached the darkness of the screen, I was alone.

———

I had to speak to Jonas. It was the only course open to me—to confess how I'd deceived him, knowingly and unknowingly, and hope that he could find some way of averting the disaster my mother had planned for us. Yet time and again, when I'd made up my mind to tell him the whole sordid story, something intervened to prevent it. *Plenty of time,* my mother had said. *I'll give you plenty of time—* which was my excuse for waiting until I'd found the best moment to speak.

Yet no good moment ever presented itself. How could I begin to tell Jonas of the dreadful, degrading scandal I was about to bring to the Oliver name when he was already in a frenzy of gloom and impatience over the constant delays to the *Altair?*

From odd remarks Jonas made I gathered that the steamship had begun to swallow money at an alarming rate. Little more than half-built, she'd already outstripped her final budget, and the disaster of the exploding boiler had slowed down building work even further. The boilers were being redesigned—and until there were boilers to be installed, various other parts couldn't be constructed around and above them. Eaten up by worry and driven half-mad with frustration, Jonas began to pace about the house in the middle of the night, unable to sleep. At last, for want of something to occupy his attention, he returned to the sanctuary of his workroom where the limp remains of a flamingo were laid out on the bench, ready to be stuffed and mounted.

Brooding on his bad luck, he seemed to have lost interest in the day-to-day running of the shipping line, leaving more and more of the routine work to Captain Fuller. For days he mooned over the dead flamingo where it lay on the bench, brainless and eyeless, the ridged skin slit behind its head like a pink worsted sock, waiting for a bath of arsenical soap to protect it against moths.

But however Jonas lingered over it, the flamingo was soon stiff on its iron wires while the *Altair* still languished on her slipway in Birkenhead, silent and forlorn.

Jonas began to idle, filling his time by drying a clutch of vivid green-and-red caterpillars, each one threaded on a piece of straw in a pie-dish in the bread-oven. It was unfortunate that he didn't see fit to warn Mrs. Locke beforehand, but at least there was a leg of cold mutton in the larder to take the place of the *fricassée* which the poor woman threw all over the kitchen floor.

With the shipyard still at a standstill, Jonas found a new outlet for his energy at home. His dearly bought knowledge of boilers and pipes made him determined to install a hot-water system in the White House, fed by a huge copper boiler behind the kitchen range. For three weeks we were forced to endure dirt and disturbance while Jonas's redundant shipwrights thrust their piping through walls and ceilings on its way to the dressing rooms on the first floor, and Mrs. Locke flatly refused to approach her black iron range now that the death-dealing boiler lurked behind it, giving out ominous gurgles as its contents seethed and bubbled.

All at once the White House—the peaceful, well-regulated center of my life—had become a vision of Hell, the crater of a heaving, puffing volcano. My refuge from the world had become a jungle of thumping plumbing and dribbling joints which clanked and groaned in the night. My home had been plunged into clamor and turmoil, just as my whole life was beset by the ghosts of my past—first Adam, and now Frank Ellis and my unrelenting mother. I began to feel as if I'd no control over any of it: it was a mad, bad dream from which— one day—I should surely wake up, though now I struggled and fought against it in vain. Adam—Jonas—*Altair*—Frank Ellis—my mother . . . It all went round and round in my head, each problem chasing the tail of the one before like the animals on the red stone amulet . . . What was I to do? How could I stop that endless pursuit, halt the wheel which spun faster and faster?

And then one day, amid all the dust and confusion of Jonas's alterations, Lottie disappeared. I wasn't surprised to find her gone. All my little spaniel's favorite corners had been filled with clanging water-pipes. Whenever she lay down in the sunshine for a nap someone chased her away into another room or threw her out into the garden. There was no peace to be found in the White House any more: I knew exactly how she felt.

All that day we searched for her, high and low. The gardeners hunted through the shrubbery and the vegetable garden, the grooms searched the carriages in the coach-house and among the straw in the stable, the housemaids and the footmen looked into every cupboard and under every bed, but all without success. I even made Jonas's carpenters and plumbers search the holes they'd made in the walls in case poor Lottie had taken refuge behind the plaster and been unable to escape.

Then, after dark, the truant returned, trotting through the yard to the kitchen door as if nothing had happened, looking fat and sleek and utterly pleased with herself. The housekeeper brought her to me in my little sitting room, where the spaniel curled up at once in front of the fire as if nothing had happened. To my surprise she wasn't even hungry, which was most unlike her.

"Where have you been all day, Lottie?" I asked her, hoisting her on to my lap. "I've been very worried about you. Though I don't suppose you care at all . . . Have you found yourself a gentleman-friend, I wonder? Is that it? Are you walking out with some handsome fellow who's barked at you from the gate? Because I promise you, you'll find nothing but unhappiness there."

Lottie's big eyes stared up at me in mute devotion, and she licked my fingers with her pink tongue.

"Oh, you want to be friends now, do you? All the same—you must never go wandering off like that again, Lottie. You're a naughty dog."

My fingers had strayed to her silky ears, knowing how much she liked me to scratch her gently there, in a hard-to-reach place under her collar. For the first time I noticed there was a length of thin twine wound two or three times round the smooth leather, tied there in order to keep something in place inside Lottie's collar—a single sheet of paper, folded over and over.

To my horror, I realized it was a letter from Adam. So that was where my faithless dog had been! And as for Adam—how dare he take such a risk! He couldn't have chosen a more reckless way of communicating with me. When I'd read what he'd written, I felt sick at the thought of his note falling by chance into Jonas's hands or being discovered by one of the servants.

> As you see [he'd begun], I'm home again—and I can even bring myself to think of it as *home* since you're such a short distance away.
>
> Paris is no place for an exile—even one with business to keep him occupied. Still—next time I go there you'll be with me, and then it will be the most gloriously romantic city in the world. Or if not Paris, what about Rome, or Naples, or the castles of the Rhine? The choice is yours, my love; I've no preference in the matter, as long as you and I are together.
>
> I promised to give you time alone—and I've kept my word. Now you must do as your heart tells you—and I know as well as you do what that is. Come and tell me so, darling, as soon as you can.
>
> If it's hard for you to leave the house, you'll find me exercising my horses every A.M. in the country beyond the hill. I generally return at noon by way of the lane.
>
> Only believe I love you, and you'll find it easier than you think to do what must be done.

———

For two days I brooded over the note which had come to me in such a foolhardy manner. Adam was so confident—so certain I loved him . . . yet I'd already made up my mind that I couldn't risk meeting him again, even to put an end to his dreams. I'd learned my lesson once before, in the seductive sweetness of the glass-houses at Westwood Park, when he'd thrown my emotions into chaos and nearly —so nearly—beguiled my reason. No—I wouldn't be so foolish again.

But even while I was steeling myself to compose a short, final note which would somehow convince Adam that he'd nothing to gain by staying at Westwood Park, the day came when Jonas at last swung out one of his swiveling brass taps—hidden behind a panel in my dressing room—to send clouds of pure steam billowing into a tin bath dragged across the floor to stand beneath it. Jonas was enchanted: I was almost hysterical with fright. No one could have lived in the neighborhood of that scalding stream: was it just for this farcical moment that my house had been turned upside-down?

Next morning the boiler exploded, drowning the kitchen in superheated water and sending the servants fleeing with shrieks of terror. In his shirtsleeves, Jonas took charge of the devastation, striding through the rising steam like a second Vulcan, shouting orders to all and sundry, alternately scolding and exhorting, as if the chaos he'd caused filled him with as much zest as the launch of a dozen steamships. At half-past eleven Mrs. Locke gave in her notice, saying she preferred a place where the water-closets froze reassuringly solid each winter and tin baths were carried downstairs to be emptied into a drain in the yard in the proper manner. That was a world she could understand.

I could bear no more. With tears of vexation hot in my eyes, I left Jonas to his battlefield in the kitchen quarters, wrapped myself in a thick woolen shawl, and went out with Lottie to the peace and quiet of the garden. Without thinking, I automatically followed the track of our favorite afternoon walk—down the carriage-sweep to the front gate, into the lane, and along it toward the rear of the White House. I'd forgotten what Adam had said about his morning routine —at least, I swear it was the last thing on my mind at that moment —and yet when Lottie and I reached the end of the lane to turn homeward along the White House wall, there was a horseman close by in the rough coat and weatherworn, wide-brimmed hat of a fair-ground horse-coper; it was Adam, riding in from the countryside beyond, tall, strong, wild as a hawk—Adam in his own element, just as I'd left Jonas in his.

As soon as he saw me, he swung himself down from the saddle and strode toward me over the turf, his horse plodding obediently after him.

"I knew you'd come!"

"No, Adam—it isn't what you think." As he tried to catch me in his arms, I pulled back and drew my shawl more closely around me. "I didn't mean to come here today. Today, or any other day, for that matter. I wouldn't have come, if there'd been anywhere else for me to go."

"You don't mean that."

"Please don't come any nearer. You should never have sent me that note—"

To my disgust, Lottie had immediately scuttled over to Adam's feet and now rolled voluptuously on her back, her mouth open and her paws beating a delirious tattoo in the air. I felt miserable with resentment—and yes, stupidly jealous.

"I see you've even managed to seduce my dog," I said bitterly. "Lottie, come here at once!"

The dog ignored me completely, and Adam rewarded her by gently scratching her chest while she arched her back in wanton pleasure.

"You're a good, honest animal, Lottie," he told her. "You know what you want, and you aren't too much of a lady to admit it. You could teach your mistress a thing or two, if I'm not mistaken."

This was too much.

"Lottie! Come here and lie down, you bad dog!"

"Come and fetch her, why don't you?" He'd straightened up: he was standing over the squirming animal in his long boots and his broad-brimmed hat, regarding me with an expression of such frustrated tenderness that I longed to throw myself into his arms and beg him to make all my nightmares disappear.

But I kept my distance—and then at last Adam realized how close I was to tears. I leaned against the stout stone wall of the White House and pressed my hands against my eyes, willing myself not to give way and weep like a fool. At once Adam became concerned, and his genuine anxiety was almost my final undoing.

"Rachel, what's the matter? Is it Jonas? What's happened? Has Jonas hurt you in some way?"

I shook my head. "It isn't Jonas's fault. Not really." And once I'd started to explain about the delays to the *Altair,* and Jonas's frantic boredom and the steam-pipes . . . the disasters of the day poured out in a great stream of woe.

Adam shook his head, helpless to offer comfort.

"Jonas doesn't seem to have much luck with boilers, does he?"

"Oh, Adam—how can you joke about it?"

"Because I don't have a house knee-deep in hot water. But cheer up—you'll soon have the cleanest housemaids in Liverpool."

"It *isn't* a laughing matter." I was smiling now in spite of myself.

"Nonsense! It's the most entertaining thing that's happened for months! Jonas can't get his confounded ship afloat to save himself, so he floods his house instead, petrifies his servants, drives his wife to despair . . . I expect I'll die laughing," he finished savagely, aiming a vicious kick at a nearby boulder. "And what I cannot fathom . . . Cannot—for the life of me—understand . . . is *why* you insist on staying with this maniac who seems bent on blowing up his home and everyone in it. If it's so hellish with Jonas, then leave him to his steam-pipes and his roast caterpillars, and come away with me! I've asked you often enough, God knows!"

"I know that, Adam. But I can't. I just can't. Especially not now when Jonas needs me so much. He's desperately unhappy about the *Altair*—and I'm about to make things a hundred times worse as it is."

"Worse than all that? What on earth's happened now?"

"Oh, Heavens, you might as well know . . . My mother is here— in Liverpool. Actually here, in this city. She found that creature, Frank Ellis, in prison in New York, and brought him here to use against me. He spoke to me—in the park one day—and showed me a newspaper story he's kept, reporting the shooting in Independence . . . But it's worse than that, Adam—"

"Go on." Impatiently, Adam pushed aside the soft nose of his horse, which was nudging his coat-pocket for sugar.

"She *knows*. She knows—because of something stupid I said— that you're still alive, and somewhere in the city. She means to tell Jonas and everyone that I had a living husband when I married again —that my marriage to Jonas is bigamous—that the girls were born out of wedlock . . . I went to see her, Adam—I was desperate—but she wouldn't listen to me. She'll do exactly what she says, I'm sure of it."

"At least then it would all be out in the open—there'd be no more pretense." Seeing my face, he added, "But I know you don't want that. When did all this happen?"

"Just over a month ago now."

"God in Heaven, Rachel! How could you be so stupid? Why didn't you come to me straight away, instead of torturing yourself like this? I'd have stopped Susannah's nonsense soon enough."

"But you weren't here! You were in Paris. And in any case . . . I didn't want to ask you for help."

"Why not? Can't you get it through your head that I *love* you? All you had to do was ask."

"How could I possibly ask you to help me—when I can't give you anything in return? Because I can't, Adam . . . If you help me, it'll only be to go on as I am—as Jonas Oliver's wife. Whatever you think of me—weak, stupid, stubborn, whatever . . . I can't go away with you. You must give up any thought of it."

For a second or two he stared at me, saying nothing. Then he shook his head, as if refusing to accept what I'd said.

"How can you make any decisions, when you're in this state? Wait until you can think more calmly. I promise I won't press you to make up your mind."

"I've already made up my mind, Adam. There are the girls . . . and Jonas needs me too much. I can't turn my back on him now."

"*I* need you, Rachel! Have you forgotten that? What's Jonas Oliver done to deserve you? Why should he have everything he's ever wanted from life?"

I couldn't believe what I'd heard. "You can't be jealous of Jonas —he has so little!"

"He has you, and that's all that matters to me."

"Oh, Adam, he doesn't even have me, if you want the truth! What Jonas has is a wife—the wife he wanted—just as he has the house he wanted, and the piano he wanted, and all the rest. I simply belong in his home, like his clock or his teakettle, and I'm not sure I'm any more useful than either of those. I pretend to manage the house, but I don't really. It would still run like clockwork without me."

"Then for Heaven's sake leave him, and come away with me! You've said yourself that Jonas wouldn't notice."

"I never said that. Jonas needs me there to complete his family— to stand beside him in church—to entertain his friends. I'm part of the Oliver monument—one of the stones Jonas has built into it. If I died, Jonas would be a widower again, and I daresay he'd survive it and find another wife. But if I ran off and left him, the whole tottering nonsense would crumble. People would laugh at him—Sir Jonas Oliver, imagine it! They'd see him for what he is: an ordinary man who wants to build a big, important ship as a memorial to himself. An ordinary man who can't keep his wife at home. It would destroy him, Adam. How could I do that?"

"And what do you get in return? Have you thought of that?"

"Enough to keep most women happy! A big house full of servants, and carriages and horses, and plenty of people to say *Yes, Lady Oliver, whatever you please* . . . Thousands of women would be perfectly content."

"But not you."

"I was content—almost. If you hadn't come back, I would have learned to be content. And I will again—when you go. Oh, Adam, you should be sorry for Jonas, not jealous of him."

But Adam was staring bleakly above my head, to where the white stone balustrade of the White House was visible above the encircling wall. For a moment I wondered if he'd even heard me.

"All my life," he said suddenly, "I've been running away from the Jonas Olivers of this world. All my life!" His eyes swept down, wintry gray, to encompass me at last. "Do you really believe Jonas has so little? It's men like Jonas, burrowing and building and trading, breaking the sod with their ploughs, digging the coal, cutting down trees to make cities—those are the men who'll inherit the earth, not wanderers like me.

"I've seen Jonas and his kind at work everywhere. It's always the same. Even before the grass can spring up from the footsteps of the first, the men coming behind have beaten a path . . . Then wagons roll over it, and the path becomes a highway . . . and the animals and the men of my sort are driven before their wheels. And you tell me Jonas has so little! Jonas has everything! He has the *future!*" Adam made a gesture of futility. "But he won't have you. Not you as well. I don't care what you think you've decided, Rachel—I'll stay near you, and watch over you, and wait for you to come to your senses. You're all I have left in this world which Jonas Oliver and his kind have made—and I won't give you up."

"Oh, Adam . . . You'll make my life impossible . . ."

"You're wrong—and one day you'll realize you need me as much as I need you. In the meantime I'll find out where your mother is hiding, and force her to leave you alone. This business has gone on long enough."

"How will you find her?" I could hardly believe the catastrophe I dreaded might be so easily dealt with.

"There are men in this city who make a good living from finding people who think they're well hidden. Those men will find her, wherever she is. And Ellis too."

"You don't know what she's like. She won't listen to you."

"I think she will. Leave Susannah to me. She's plagued your life for long enough."

"Adam—you won't do anything rash—" There was a light in his eye that frightened me.

"Go back to the White House and hold Jonas Oliver's hand, if that's where you think you belong. I don't know how long it'll take me to make amends for the past, Rachel—the rest of my life, perhaps —but one way or another, I'll do it. I'll make you see that we belong together. Let Jonas have his steamship and his page in the history books, if that's what he wants. All I ask is today and tomorrow— provided I have you. And from what you've told me, I reckon even Jonas might regard that as a fair bargain."

In the secret, disloyal depths of my soul, I suspected he was right.

28

Adam had been so confident of finding my mother and her odious go-between that I almost began to believe the most immediate danger was past. For the first time in weeks I woke each morning without fear of what the day might bring, and I'd already turned my attention to other problems when a blackmailer of a more genteel, more subtle kind decided to pay me a visit.

This new conspirator was my sister-in-law, who called to take tea in my drawing room but swiftly drew the conversation round to the matter uppermost on her mind.

"Not to put too fine a point upon it, my dear—some of us are extremely concerned."

Tall as a candle in acid-green silk foulard trimmed with fierce yellow zig-zag braid, Verity laid her teacup solemnly down on the table, adjusted its handle to precisely the proper angle, sighed, and composed her features into an expression of sisterly concern. Like a fir tree swaying in a gale, she inclined regally toward me and continued in low, conspiratorial tones, "Jonas is spending far too much time on that ship of his."

This was particularly unfair. Jonas had driven himself remorselessly in order to keep up the pace of work on the *Altair*—work which would eventually benefit the shipping line and its stockholders.

"What exactly do you mean, Verity? Spending too much of his own time on it, perhaps?"

"Too much of the company's time, Rachel dear. And too much of his own, I daresay, since he hardly looks well on it. This *Altair* has become an obsession with him! I tremble to think of the money he's spent on it. . . . And goodness only knows if the vessel will ever see the water. George is quite skeptical, you know—though of course he'd never say so to anyone else. He's an exceptionally loyal man, dear George."

"Such a comfort to you, Verity," I agreed, thinking of Sophie Greenwood and the other inhabitants of George's "little place" near the theater. "But I can't believe you think Jonas is neglecting company business for the building of the *Altair*."

"Well . . . that was rather what—"

"Verity, I'm surprised at you, I really am! How can you criticize your own brother like this? I should have thought you and George would have been the first to support him. Loyal as you both are," I added maliciously.

"Now don't misunderstand me, Rachel. Jonas works very hard, it's true, and I know he's built Oliver's into a major shipping line in the last few years—and we're all very grateful to him. It's just that . . . recently . . . his ideas of what's best for the company are a little different from those of the other stockholders."

"Such as George."

"George among others, Rachel dear. The Earl of Chorleigh told me only the other day how concerned he was to hear that work had stopped again in the shipyard."

"Well, you can rest easy on that point, Verity, since everything's back to normal again in the yard. Jonas is there at this very moment. Something to do with the clearance of the pistons, whatever that is. And he's had an idea for steam-heating the whole ship."

"Now, that's *exactly* my point, Rachel! *Another* of Jonas's ideas! Good gracious, this whole ship was something Jonas dreamed up on a quiet day in the office, no more than that—a notion—a whim— and when he first discussed it with the stockholders there was a firm limit on what it was going to cost. But now he's spent *thousands* more than he promised, and the ship isn't anything like finished. Never mind steam-heating—can anyone guarantee the ship will even *sail?* And some people are saying—"

"George is saying—"

"Various people who know their business are saying . . . that Jonas has missed several valuable cargo contracts because his whole attention is given to this wretched steamship. No one at the office can even find him these days to make decisions because he's always in Birkenhead, fiddling with the plans of the *Altair*. The company has managed to limp along like this until now, but it's beginning to affect profits."

"But think how Oliver's will pull ahead of the others when the *Altair*'s finished and carrying mail to New York! There won't be a

ship to touch her." How often had I heard those same words from
Jonas?

"*If* she's ever finished! George says Jonas has more chance of
flying to the moon than making a profit from a ship the size of the
Altair."

Verity's hand flew to her mouth as she realized the extent of her
indiscretion.

"Though I expect he was joking," she added quickly. "In any case,
that doesn't alter the facts. If Jonas goes on spending so much time
and money on his steamship, Oliver's will be overtaken by all the
other shipping lines. Papa created J. G. Oliver & Company from
nothing at all, simply by taking every chance that offered—and
Jonas used to do the same. Nobody grudges him his little . . . exper-
iments . . . provided he goes on making the company profitable.
That's all."

"Then why don't you speak to Jonas about it? Tell him what
you've told me. Or let George speak to him."

Thoughtfully, Verity picked up her teacup again, and swirled the
tea round its delicate, gilt bone-china bowl.

"George says a wife carries most influence with her husband," she
pronounced. "George says a good wife is a counsellor and solace to
her husband, and an ornament to his home. He says—"

"—that I'm the one who must speak to Jonas." I couldn't bear
any more of George Broadney's hypocritical cant. "I quite understand."

I now knew exactly what was afoot. George and Verity must
have conferred in secret with the other stockholders, convinced that
good Oliver business was being sacrificed to the building of the
Altair. George Broadney in particular had no faith in the new
steamship. All he wanted was the biggest profit which could be
squeezed out of the company fleet as it stood. Let Jonas buy a
new ship here and there—reliable sailers with plenty of room for
emigrants or profitable cargoes, or even the odd flyer to keep
him amused. But he wasn't to squander good money on anything so new and untried. Good Heavens, no! Let someone else
take the risks! When the system was a proven success—well, that
was the time to invest in it. And Jonas must be made to realize
this . . . or . . . George and Verity would try to force him to do
as they wished. Worst of all—they'd fixed on me to deliver the
warning.

"Will you do it, then? Will you speak to him?" Verity's mean little mouth stayed half-open as she waited for my answer.

"Do you mean, will I tell Jonas he must give up the *Altair* and stay at his desk in the office in future?"

"Of course not, you goose! Nothing so awful!" Verity leaned across and playfully slapped my hand with her own skinny fingers. "My dear—I'm sure you know exactly how to handle my brother. . . . For instance—since it's perfectly obvious to us all that he's wearing himself out with this steamship nonsense, why don't you suggest he gives up the *Altair* for the time being, and confines himself to company matters? For the good of his health, of course. Perhaps Dr. Jefferson would recommend it . . . if you had a little talk with him first."

"Do you really expect Jonas to call a halt to the building of the *Altair,* and leave her to rust in the yard?"

"He could always sell the hull as it stands. Someone might convert the design to sail. In any case—at least Oliver's wouldn't be spending any more money on her."

"Verity—Jonas would *die* sooner than give up the *Altair!*"

"Nonsense, Rachel! Don't dramatize! I'm absolutely sure you can make him see reason."

"And if I can't?"

Verity smoothed her green and yellow skirts. "Well then, George must try, that's all. But I think it would come better from you."

I never even made the attempt. The very idea of trying to part Jonas from his grand design was so ludicrous that the more I thought of it, the more determined I was to let George and Verity Broadney do their own dirty work. If they wanted to engineer a stockholders' revolt against Jonas's running of the company, then they were welcome to try. If the stockholders were forced to take sides, I was sure even the Earl of Chorleigh had more faith in Jonas than in George Broadney.

But George and Verity spread their net wide. Even Matthew, home from school for Easter, had taken to riding out to the Broadneys' rolling acres whenever he found life at home more boring than usual. Through his exploits on the hunting-field he'd struck up an unexpected friendship with George, who was heard to say that no one who'd ever seen Matthew on a horse could be under any illusion that Jonas was his natural father. Jonas loathed horses, and rode, according to George, "like a monkey on a perch," while Matthew might have been born in the saddle. This talent had brought him George's wholehearted approval, while Matthew unashamedly liked what he saw of life as a landed aristocrat.

"It's all very well, building ships and sending them off all over the place like the Governor does," he remarked to me one day in a rare moment of plain speaking, "but it's *trade*, isn't it, when all's said and done."

"I'm sure your stepfather would call it *commerce*, Matthew."

"Same thing, by another name! It's still a far cry from living on your own estates like George Broadney."

"Sir George Broadney inherited his wealth from his father and his grandfather. The Olivers worked hard for their money, and some people would say that was a more honest way of coming by it."

"I don't see why. When *I* have control of the company, I'll buy myself a big house in the country and spend most of my time there. That's if there's anything left of Oliver's by then."

"What on earth do you mean, Matthew?"

"George Broadney says Jonas is running the shipping line into the ground over this steamship of his. The banks are beginning to jib at the size of the debt, apparently, and Jonas has been talking about raising money on his own account to finish the job."

"Matthew, if you can't call your stepfather *Papa*, then at least call him *Sir* Jonas, please."

"Well, he ain't my father, is he?" Matthew retorted quickly. "And if all you can do is haul me over the coals for taking his name in vain, then I'm sorry I spoke out at all. I only thought you ought to know what's in the wind. George Broadney says we could lose the lot on the *Altair*, easy as damn it. Oliver's name is mud on 'Change, you know."

"I'd no idea . . . Oh, poor Jonas!"

"Poor *us*, you mean!" replied my worldly son. "I want something left of the company when it comes to me, don't forget. And how will you enjoy being the talk of all the ladies' tea-fights in the city, eh? Not much, I'll bet! *Poor, dear Rachel*," he mimicked Verity's nasal whine, "*how clever you are with last year's gowns! I'd never have guessed, if I hadn't seen them a thousand times before.*"

"Matthew! That's a dreadful thing to say!" But it was true enough. George and Verity would be cushioned by the Broadney wealth from the failure of the shipping line, but Jonas could be ruined outright. And if that happened, I could expect no quarter from Verity.

"I'm sure things aren't as bad as you think. Your stepfather hasn't mentioned a word of this to me."

"No—but then he wouldn't, would he? Yet I know for a fact that he spoke to Ellen Oliver about it months ago, and advised her to sell the best part of her Oliver stock. She only has ten percent left now."

This was more alarming. When he died, old Captain John Oliver had left forty percent of the company to each of his two sons, and the remaining twenty to Verity. Ellen Oliver, the widow of Jonas's brother John, had inherited her husband's shares, and I knew that some time before, Jonas had advised her to sell part of her holding to the earl of Chorleigh in order to spread her investments more widely. Now, it seemed, he was worried enough about the present state of the company to urge her to reduce her involvement still further. And yet while Ellen distanced herself from the uneasy finances of the shipping line, Jonas—according to Matthew—was about to stake his entire future on the fate of the *Altair*.

"The Governor's off his coconut, if you ask me."

"Off his *what?* I do wish you'd speak plain English sometimes, instead of these peculiar expressions you seem to have picked up."

"Off his *coconut,* Mater! Off the hooks! *Touched!*" Matthew tapped his forehead and rolled his eyes. "Or should I say *coker-nut,* as they call it in the ring?"

"Oh, Matthew—not prize-fights again! Not these awful brawls in public-house yards, with everyone betting on who'll be killed first! It's so barbaric—what would your stepfather say?"

"The men aren't forced to fight, Mater. They're handsomely paid if they win—and I usually come off a few pounds richer, too," Matthew added smugly. "The Preston Hammer made me twenty guineas at Aintree last week—and haven't you just said how honest it is to work for your money instead of inheriting it?"

"I didn't mean winning it at prize-fights—or at horse-races, for that matter. I suppose that's what you were doing at Aintree?"

"Going to the dogs, Mater, in my own way. Though you'd be surprised who you see at the races. Your wicked Colonel, for one."

"Colonel Allen, do you mean? Our neighbor?"

"The fellow who scraped me out of the mud of Paradise Street just before Christmas and then read me such a lecture next day when I'd a head on me like one of Jonas's steam-pistons."

"Do you often see the Colonel at Aintree?" I tried not to sound too curious, yet I was interested all the same. I'd often wondered what Adam had found to absorb his restless energy since he'd imprisoned himself in Liverpool.

"I've met him there plenty of times. He's not such a bad cove when you know him better—and my hat, he knows a good horse when he sees one. Told me he'd raced against Indian ponies in America, years ago. What d'you think of that?" Matthew was obviously impressed. I wondered what else Adam had told him.

Before I could ask, Matthew remembered something.

"Come to think of it—I was supposed to give you a message from the Colonel, only I forgot all about it till now."

"What message? Matthew—how could you be so careless!"

"Didn't seem important, I suppose. Something to do with an animal. Oh, yes—you aren't to worry about the fox anymore."

"What fox? There must be more to it than that!" I could hardly contain my annoyance. Adam had clearly sent me a message, but goodness only knew what he'd tried to tell me.

"Something about a fox, at any rate," Matthew repeated nonchalantly. "Though I didn't know there was a fox about. Why didn't you ask me to deal with it?"

"A fox?" For a few seconds I was puzzled. Then suddenly Adam's message began to make sense. The fox which concerned us both was my mother.

"Oh—I remember now . . . I thought we'd had a fox near the house, and I was worried for Lottie. What *exactly* did the Colonel say, Matthew? Try to remember, please."

"He said . . ." Matthew frowned with the effort of concentration. "He said to tell you the fox got wind of the hunters and cleared off before he could catch it—but he reckons it knows better than to come back here again. I hope he's wrong," Matthew added. "The Hunt might get the brute next season."

So my mother had fled, driven off by Adam's hired detectives, and no doubt Frank Ellis had been swallowed up in the crowd like a rat in a flooded gutter. Adam seemed to think that was an end to the matter; I only wished I could be as certain as he was.

"Did Colonel Allen say anything about leaving Westwood Park?" I asked casually, fishing for any information Matthew might have picked up.

"Leaving?" Matthew looked surprised. "Why should you think that?"

"Oh . . . I heard a rumor of some kind."

"Well, that surprises me, I must say. George Broadney—"

"*Sir* George, Matthew—"

"*Uncle* George told me he reckons the Colonel's bought himself an interest in one or two companies in the city—and that doesn't sound like a man who's about to clear off, does it? The Colonel must be rich as old boots, though, whatever the Governor thinks of him. Have you seen the horses he keeps?" Matthew whistled in admiration.

"I daresay I was mistaken, then."

"He did mention he'd not be racing for a bit, though. Off to Norfolk, I think he said. Perhaps that's what you heard."

"I believe he has a house in Norfolk."

"You seem to be taking a great interest in your disreputable neighbor, all of a sudden." Matthew gave me a keen stare unnervingly like Adam's. "I thought he *wasn't our sort* . . . Isn't that what Jonas says? Doesn't come up to scratch, and all that sort of thing?"

"*Sir* Jonas, Matthew—I'm tired of telling you."

"*Step*papa." Matthew made a face. "How will that do?" Then a thought occurred to him. "Hey, Mater—I say! Do you reckon if Jonas went bankrupt they'd take away his knighthood, and make him plain *Mister* again? What a rum go that'd be, and no mistake!"

———

In the middle of April Jonas went to London for four days in order to confer with his bankers, and took a room at his club. Under normal circumstances he'd have stayed at the Broadneys' London house in Eaton Square, but a distinct chill had set in between the two families as work continued in fits and starts on the *Altair* and more money was syphoned off from slender company profits to pay for it.

Tired of waiting for me to tackle Jonas on the subject, George Broadney had spoken out at last, with exactly the results I'd predicted.

"Look how long it took to finish the *Great Britain*," George had pointed out, "and what a financial disaster *that's* been! Never out of dry dock—sold off for a song—and now they've put such tiddling engines in her she'll be under sail most of the way to Australia.

"But see here, Jonas—put paddles on the *Altair,* and by God, we'll call it quits. Forget this double-compound-screw-propeller what-have-you, stick a common or garden steamkettle below her decks, and she'll be finished in a trice! Rachel can break the bottle, and we'll have a slap-up send-off when she goes into the water. Won't that do just as well?"

Without waiting for an answer, George breezed on.

"Think what Oliver's could do with the money, Jonas! We should be buying more of these big soft-wood ships from America for the Australian run. Bring 'em over here, copper 'em and give 'em decent copper fastenings—"

"And they'll still fall apart in a few years," Jonas retorted sourly.

"Maybe they will, but by that time, they'll have paid for themselves several times over! Think about it, Jonas . . . Baines is buying American from Donald MacKay and Wilson of White Star's ordering from Jackson in Boston! And what are we doing? Oliver's is still tinkering around with this damned steamship of yours. Burn coal? It can burn money, I'll give you that! But if you won't give up the *Altair,* at least consider paddles for her, and let's be done with the thing. Paddles, Jonas—*paddles!* For all our sakes—"

"*Paddles!*" Jonas roared at me later. "He wants me to fit my beautiful ship with *Paddles!* I'd sooner drag her out to sea and sink her!" He gave a disgusted snort. "I'm damned if I'm going to let George Broadney bully me into doing what he wants. I'm off to talk to the bankers in London next week, and we'll see what he has to say about that!"

I realized how serious things had become when Jonas set off in a blaze of good cheer, unnaturally hearty, making weak jokes about the extravagant gifts he would have to bring home from the Regent Street shops to keep his lonely wife content.

I was worried, certainly, but not lonely. Jonas would be home before long, and soon Reuben would be ashore again for a while. And Adam . . . I'd no idea whether Adam had returned from Norfolk or not, but much as I longed to know, I was determined not to make any effort to find out. Jonas needed me, just as I'd told Adam that day on the heath. He was plainly making himself ill with anxiety over the *Altair,* and I was bound to keep the vows I'd made when I'd married him. *For better, for worse, in sickness and in health . . . Forsaking all others . . .* That was what I'd promised, and that was what I intended to do.

A few days later Jonas returned home, utterly worn out but relieved. From casual remarks he made—since it never crossed his mind to explain his financial affairs to me—I gathered that the bankers had reluctantly agreed to extend the company's credit to pay for the completion of the *Altair,* though at a vast rate of interest and with extra collateral which was to be Jonas's personal responsibility.

" 'Look here—' I said to them," Jonas reported in an expansive moment, " 'd'you suppose I'm not good for the money?' And when I showed them the last letter I had from the Prince Consort, and told them how much we stand to earn with this ship—and the others we'll build after her—well, they sat up and took notice, I can tell you."

Jonas sniffed with satisfaction at the memory. "Oh, they grumbled a bit, certainly—said they'd rather be building railways for the Maharajahs, or some such nonsense—but they put up the money all the same. So just you wait, my girl! We'll make George Broadney and that penny-pinching sister of mine sneer on the other side of their faces! We'll see what they have to say when the *Altair'*s carrying the New York mails at a good thirteen knots, wind or no wind, and hardly tilting the brandy on the saloon table!"

All the same, Jonas was exhausted—worn out in a way I'd never seen him before—and I began to suspect that only a fever of will-power, like a fire consuming him from within, drove him back to his labors in the shipyard.

I was worried enough to bring Matthew home early from school that term—and the mere fact that Jonas, a stickler for education, never protested at all made me more concerned than ever.

Matthew noticed the change in his stepfather as soon as he returned. For a couple of days he said nothing, but I saw him carefully watching Jonas in the evenings when he dragged himself home, haggard and exhausted, to eat a perfunctory dinner before retiring almost at once to bed.

"The Governor's working himself to death," Matthew finally announced one night after Jonas had excused himself and gone upstairs.

"He's very tired, that's true. Perhaps once the ship is finished, I'll be able to persuade him to rest."

"That could be too late, Mother dear. From the look of things, it's time I took more of an interest in the company. Since I'm apparently to run it once Jonas gives up."

"But that won't be for a very long time, Matthew!" I reproached him.

"I wonder." He glanced toward the door through which Jonas had gone. "I wonder."

———

I'd vaguely hoped Matthew might be able to help Jonas in some way, though knowing him as I did, I hardly expected the work of the shipping line to hold his attention for long—especially now that such attractions as horse-racing or rough shooting over George Broadney's land competed for his time. But I was wrong. With sudden single-mindedness, Matthew set himself to learn about every aspect of the business. Uncle Tom Fuller reported that during the day Matthew haunted his office, pestering him for details of ships and cargoes; over dinner in the evenings he besieged Jonas with questions until I felt obliged to call a halt for poor Jonas's sake; and at all hours he visited the docks, sometimes on an errand for Captain Fuller, but often just strolling along the quayside, taking in every detail of the vessels loading or unloading there.

He spoke to anyone who'd answer his questions, and I was alarmed to hear that he'd taken to visiting dockside bars again, or the "Slaughterhouse" in Fenwick Street, where the Water Street clerks took refuge at the end of their working day. But all Matthew would say when I confronted him with this was that he could learn as much about shipping and seafaring over a mug of ale as he'd learn in a year before the mast. He certainly never came home drunk again: whatever he got up to in the taverns of Dale Street and the dockside lanes, it didn't appear to have any effect on him. And because he'd begun to seem older than his years, and because I'd seen exactly the same determined expression on his father's face, I held my peace, and let him go his own way.

One day, however, he came home with a disturbing tale.

He'd set off that morning for Prince's Dock to call on Captain Crowe of the *Fearnmore,* just home after a stormy passage across the Atlantic, and at first he'd been too intent on scanning the ship's hull and spars for signs of weather-damage to notice a dark-painted, four-square, two-horse double brougham drawn up on the quayside nearby, its pleated moire curtains almost fully closed.

But the carriage was still there when he came back on deck with the ship's master, his business completed; and since he was forced to pass close beside it on his way back toward the end of Water Street, it was inevitable that he should glance up at its blank window when he drew level.

As he turned his head, the wine-colored curtain whispered open, and an elderly woman peered out at him over the lowered pane. The face was white and powdered, he recalled later, a spot of livid rouge on each cheekbone only drawing attention to the blue-gray shadow below and the loops of dark hair, stranded with silver, visible under the bonnet-brim.

It had been the woman's eyes which startled him, blue and fever-bright in the lifeless painted face.

The apparition raised a black-gloved hand, curled like a bird's foot, to attract his attention.

"Young man! A moment, if you please."

Matthew halted beside the carriage. "Ma'am?"

"Thank you. I shan't detain you for long. Would I be correct in assuming you are Matthew Oliver, Lady Oliver's son?"

"That's my name, Ma'am, certainly." Matthew tried to identify the strange, nasal inflexion in the woman's voice.

"And how is your respected mother?"

"She's well, thank you."

"And your stepfather, Sir Jonas?"

"Well enough, Ma'am. They're both in good health."

The woman paused, as if considering this. "And your mother is *happy*, I hope?" she inquired suddenly.

"Perfectly happy, Ma'am, as far as one can judge the happiness of others," replied Matthew, wondering what wealthy lunatic had fastened upon him, and how he could manage to shake her off. Inches away, the bright eyes devoured his face, and the narrow, bloodless lips twisted into a bleak smile.

"You're right, of course, Mr. Oliver. How can one ever be sure what goes on in the mind of another person? You're fortunate in having learned that lesson so young."

"I daresay I am, Ma'am." Matthew glanced round, searching for an excuse to escape from the odd conversation.

"But then, you were left fatherless at such an early age. I don't suppose you even remember your own father, Mr. Oliver."

"Not at all, Ma'am."

"Nor how he looked?"

"No, Ma'am—not even that."

"So if he were to approach you in the street today, you wouldn't know him at all?"

"I don't imagine I would." The conversation seemed to be becoming stranger than ever. "But my father's been dead for thirteen years, after all. I think of myself as an Oliver now."

"Ah—the Olivers . . . Such an irreproachable family. Never a breath of scandal . . . Your family are an example to us all, Mr. Oliver."

"You're very kind." Perhaps the woman was some kind of religious fanatic, obsessed with the sanctity of the home.

"Yes, an example to us all . . . in a world where fine old families have often been ruined by the most degrading wickedness. I should hate to see such a thing happen to the Olivers—I should indeed. . . . But I'm keeping you from an appointment," the thin voice continued. "You have business elsewhere."

"I'm afraid so, Ma'am. But if you're a friend of my mother's— may I tell her who was inquiring for her?"

"A friend?" The powdered mask twisted into another faint smile. "Oh—not a *friend*, Mr. Oliver . . . Merely an old acquaintance, I'd say. No, don't trouble yourself on my account. I've enjoyed our meeting. Goodbye."

Three short raps followed inside the carriage, three taps of a cane-handle on the side of the vehicle. The coachman took up the reins, the horses wheeled in a slow circle amid the dockside clutter, and the carriage rolled away in the direction from which it had come, its claret-colored curtains tightly closed once more.

Matthew, who generally kept his own counsel about people and events, was puzzled enough to tell me later about the mystery woman in the curtained carriage.

"Devilish odd, I'd say," he concluded, standing astride the hearth-rug in my dainty sitting room. Ignoring my protests, he pushed the sleeping Lottie ruthlessly off her chair and sat down, while the dog stalked stiffly away to scratch in a corner.

"Yes, devilish odd. I mean—goodish horses, a two-hundred-guinea four-wheeler . . . Yet more paint on her than a tugboat's funnel . . . Quite a collision with the rouge-pot—that sort of thing. And very taken up with you and Jonas—an *old acquaintance,* she said. Seems to me you've some pretty queer friends these days."

"Except that I can't think who she might have been."

Yet I did know, all the same. It could only have been my mother,

Susannah Dean, in that darkened carriage: who else could have had any reason to accost Matthew on the quayside and question him about the state of his mother's marriage? Matthew, though slighter than Adam, bore the stamp of his father's features; he'd come ashore from an Oliver ship, escorted to the gangway by the master himself. He wouldn't have been hard to recognize.

There was no doubt about it—the fox had returned, determined to finish her ruinous work. Adam's searching detectives had hardly caused her to falter for an instant.

"No doubt your mysterious lady sits on one of Verity Broadney's committees," I told Matthew as steadily as I could. "A wealthy lady, though a little odd, perhaps."

But my voice trembled nevertheless, and I hoped devoutly that Matthew hadn't noticed.

29

On the sixth of May word came to us that the fine Oliver ship *Greenhallow*, already overdue, had been wrecked on a barren headland in the Falkland Islands, with her master and every man aboard her reported drowned.

The loss of a ship was no rare occurrence, but Captain Weir had been one of the company's most experienced masters and a popular man; his ship was only four years old, and hadn't yet earned her price. There would be an insurance payment, certainly, but it wouldn't compensate for the blow to Oliver morale. A deep pall of gloom hung over the company offices, and Jonas trailed some of it back with him to the White House each day.

Then a week later, despite my frantic efforts, poor Lottie became ill and died in a remarkably short space of time, her head in my lap, her brown eyes gazing up in piteous appeal. I was utterly bereft—Lottie had been my faithful little companion for so long—and to make matters worse, Jonas tried to cheer me up by offering to mount the dead spaniel in one of his horrid *tableaux*. He'd always thought Lottie a beauty, he confessed: she would be a taxidermal *tour de force*—unless, perhaps, I'd prefer her preserved as if curled up, asleep, to lie all day at the end of my bed.

The very idea sickened me, and as soon as I could, I instructed one of the gardeners to bury Lottie's poor little corpse without ceremony among the rhododendron bushes behind the coach-house.

As if that wasn't enough, Jonas began to complain of headaches, a sore throat, and constant pains in his legs and arms. Assuming he'd caught a chill on his trip to London, I dosed him with Revalenta and tried to insist he go to bed, but he ignored my pleas, setting off for the shipyard as usual to talk to the shipwrights about the progress of the *Altair*.

A few days later he was startled by a stream of blood from his nose, and a feverish flush which seemed to be worse by evening. Cold shivers gave way to sweating; he described it as standing under a shower of cold water which turned in an instant to parching heat.

"It's only a bad cold," Jonas kept repeating, but I'd begun to be afraid for him. I sent for Dr. Jefferson, who pronounced Jonas's pulse slow and asked if his tongue felt sore. It didn't—not that day, at any rate, but by the next, Jonas's cheeks were flushed, eating was painful, and a few red spots had begun to appear on his chest. The doctor came again, and this time drew me aside, whispering the dread words *typhoid fever*—most likely a souvenir of the London filth.

Suddenly the house was filled with hush-voiced nurses as Jonas slid into a delirium which alternated with periods of fevered restlessness when he kept trying to get out of bed despite being too weak to manage it.

Then one bright morning he rallied, and the doctor expressed the hope that the crisis had passed. Next day, however, he didn't seem to recognize me as I hovered by his bed, and spent the whole morning murmuring about the people and places of his childhood.

Gradually he sank lower, but still clung determinedly to life. Little by little his spells of lucid understanding were eclipsed by long hours of trancelike quiet, and at last Dr. Jefferson emerged from the sickroom shaking his head. It was only a matter of time.

During the days that followed I kept watch by Jonas's side, hardly stirring from the room in case he wakened and found me gone. Overcome by exhaustion, I dozed in an armchair by the bed, rousing with a start whenever Jonas cried out or a nurse passed by with her reverential tread. All my meals were now brought up to the sickroom, though I'd no interest in food and sent them back downstairs untouched.

Gradually I ceased to be aware of the coming of darkness or the rosy tint of dawn beyond the shaded windows. I slipped gently into Jonas's twilight world where the laws of time hung suspended and the only measure of the passing hours was the slow, steady decline of the weakened body in the wide white bed.

George Broadney called from time to time with Verity, who sobbed a little and left again quickly, unable to stand the silent, shadowy sickroom for more than a few minutes at a time. Jonas, she whispered to me tearfully, had always been so dear to her (she'd already transferred him to the past tense) that she couldn't bear the sight of him in this last extremity. Big, ugly, salty drops rolled down her long cheeks to splash into the wilderness of silk roses on her bosom.

While Jonas still breathed I waited beside him, thinking of the years we'd shared, and how near I'd come to leaving his home in spite of them. To think of committing a sin, so the Bible warns us, is as bad as the sin itself: then I was guilty of running off with Adam a thousand times in my mind. How often in my dreams had I known again the exultant pleasure of his body next to mine! Though I'd stopped short of the final physical act—how often had I committed adultery with him in my heart? And in my sleepless, delirious mind, when I questioned the unjust fate which was about to rob Jonas of his greatest triumph, it began to seem to me that it was I, with my secret sins, who'd brought him to that state.

On the last day of his life he was conscious for a short space of time in midmorning and tried to smile weakly at Matthew and the girls when I brought them to his bedside. After they'd gone he managed to touch my fingers with a faint pressure as if to console me, while his dry lips struggled to form a word. There were tears running down my face as I bent my head close to his to catch this last, ultimate endearment.

For a moment all I could hear was a hissing sound, repeated twice, and then, quite distinctly—the name *Altair.*

There was nothing for me, as if all along he'd known that my thoughts, my hopes—my love—were given elsewhere. This was all he wanted from me, at the end—to reassure him that although he wouldn't live to see it, the *Altair* would sail one day.

For perhaps an hour after that I sat beside him, stroking his thin, transparent hand, and talking to him of his beloved ship.

"We'll see it through, my dear," I promised. "Don't worry. Matthew and I will look after your steamship. She'll be the most splendid vessel the Mersey has ever seen. Everyone will come to the launch— I daresay Prince Albert will come, and perhaps even the Queen herself. Can you imagine the flags and the cheering? And the band playing, and all the men from the yard throwing their caps in the air as your ship—*your ship,* Jonas—slides down the slipway at last . . . Oh, it'll be a fine sight!"

And I went on, quietly describing the scene which unfolded in my mind's eye as I spoke, a vision which until then had been Jonas's alone.

"And we'll fill her with the best Welsh coal . . . I know they'll need more wood to light it, but we can't have filthy soot fouling those fine white decks, and spoiling the elegant clothes of the saloon passengers . . . And she'll be so beautiful that everywhere she goes, the wharves will be black with people come to see her. *That's Jonas Oliver's ship,* they'll say. *The* Altair—*that's her. The finest ship afloat, Jonas Oliver's masterpiece.*"

I glanced down at last. Jonas lay with his eyes wide open, staring at something above his head, beyond the ceiling of the room, beyond even the roof-leads of the house. His expression was one of profound satisfaction, as if a long-standing mystery had at last been explained, a thorny problem overcome. He looked oddly young, and he was no longer breathing.

───────

As soon as I'd gently broken the news to the children, I sent for the Broadneys. Within an hour, Verity, whose horror at her brother's illness had suddenly transformed itself into decorous grief at his death, arrived to take charge. Shooing me into my white and yellow sitting room with instructions to rest on the day-bed, she and George set about making preparations for a thirteen-hundred-pound Oliver funeral.

From remarks she made during those moments when she condescended to consult me about something, I gathered that the Olivers sent family members to the grave with the same expensive fanfare which attended the launch of their ships on the sea. Jonas was to plunge down the slipway to the hereafter in the presence of the greatest in the land, and the whole of Liverpool was to know it.

I was humbly aware of being the least significant figure in the parade. Let the Broadneys get on with counting their carriages and arguing over the order of the pallbearers; the performance was theirs from beginning to end. Wrapping myself in a shawl, I took the two girls, red-eyed and bewildered, for a walk in a distant part of the White House gardens. Matthew was nowhere to be found.

Next morning, several hours before Verity could be expected to arrive, I carried out a plan I'd made during the long, sleepless night. Quite alone, I made my way with a firm step to the workroom at the rear of the house which had been Jonas's personal sanctum and which I'd hardly ever entered.

The room was whitewashed and monastic, almost half-filled by a

long, heavy bench so immense it had had to be built where it stood.
On its scarred surface the jars and tools and tufts of chopped flax
lay just where Jonas had left them such a short while before: the box
of scalpels exactly parallel to the little iron vise, the scissors alongside
and the tall reels of black thread ranged behind, a pair of hammers
next to them, neatly laid out as if their hafts were still warm from
his hand.

There was a curious intimacy about the room. It had never been
intended for my eyes, and as I forced myself further into this secret
place the hot shame of an accidental voyeur began to flush my
cheeks. But Jonas's passion had been for cold embalmer's instruments—for the slitting, scraping, draining surgery of corpses, not for
any rampant pasteboard copulation. It was death, not life, which
absorbed him.

And now you must understand it all, I thought, eye-to-blank-
socket with the skeleton of a rabbit waiting on tempered wires to
clatter toward me. At its feet lay the narrow skulls of assorted ro-
dents, marshaled in order of size, and on the shelves behind, among
the jars of isinglass and beeswax and oil of petroleum, a starfish
hung stranded on a plank, pinned out like a brittle, five-pointed
crucifixion.

Jonas had kept another trophy here, and after a few moments of
searching I found it—a thick glass jar containing the preserved fetus
of a roe-deer, all sickly, creamy yellow, miraculously folded in on
itself just as it had been drawn from its slaughtered mother, floating,
head downward, in its transparent womb.

Just in time I kept my hands from the jar, remembering that whenever it was disturbed the beautiful sleeper inside would bob solemnly
up and down. Jonas had set it in motion for me once, enchanted by
the slow dance of the pale, steeping fawn. The liquor was cloudy
now with white flecks; the fawn was dissolving into a broth of itself,
escaping at last into its own cloudy essence from the poking of nosy
footmen and feather-dusting housemaids.

On the floor was more debris—wooden boxes of bones, a bright
black and white monkey-skin rolled up like a discarded coat, sacks
of plaster of Paris and red ocher, pots of gum arabic and resin and a
bag of the ubiquitous chopped flax which served Jonas's creatures
for flesh and blood. More trays of butterflies hung on the walls. A
barn-owl which had been one of Jonas's first ventures perched, one-
footed, on a log in the corner; through some mishap its second leg

had fallen off, and Jonas had never found time to replace it. Now the owl glared balefully across the room, waiting for a deliverance which would never come.

In the corner below the owl was an iron vat with a flat wooden cover. Curious, I removed the cover, and half-a-dozen drowned, furry backs bounced up at me from the stinking pool inside. I slammed the lid shut at once and leaned on it, fighting down the urge to vomit. The room was a charnel-house, a freakshow: even the greenish cast of its white walls merged in some way with the pungent smell of chemicals and collective decay which hung about it. A great anger began to possess me when I thought of such a canker of a room existing in the very heart of my home, spreading its fetid stench along the passageway toward my wholesome family hearth. It was a shameful, furtive part of Jonas's life, and I was determined no one else should see it.

Abruptly, I summoned a manservant.

"I want this room cleared. Now—this morning. Take everything in it to the end of the kitchen garden and burn it—and I mean *everything*. If I hear that one single item has been carried away from the bonfire, that man will be dismissed at once."

The footman gaped at me, round-eyed.

"Do you understand me? Very well, then—get on with it. Tell the gardeners to help you, but do it now, right away. And when you've finished, leave all the windows open, have the floor washed down, and the walls. Try to get rid of that smell."

The kitten-orchestra eyed me accusingly from their glass case in the hall.

"And take this away too. I don't want to see it again."

After that I shut myself in my sunny sitting room for the rest of the morning while a bizarre procession of animal remains made its way to the farthest end of the garden, and the contents of Jonas's morgue were given a decent cremation.

By the time Verity's carriage rumbled up to the front door, the whitewashed room had been emptied and only a plume of reeking smoke smudging the sky above the kitchen garden remained as a sign of what had occurred.

———

Verity swept in, a black-clad angel of death. Jonas was to be buried on Thursday in the Oliver plot in St. James's cemetery and his name added to the elaborate monument which already marked the site. Everyone who might come had been invited; carriages had been numbered, the clergy mustered and the order of service discussed. Jonas was to have a veritable army of pallbearers and a stream of family mourners crammed into the first half-dozen carriages, their own vehicles trailing empty at the rear of the procession. Liverpool's most magnificent hearse had been reserved for the occasion, a dusky monster of gilded skulls and ebony cherubs pulled by four coal-black horses, its glass windows tastefully etched with wreaths of roses.

How fitting, I thought, that Jonas should travel to the grave behind glass! I couldn't forget the sleeping, dissolving fawn in its glass jar, and I wondered irreverently if Jonas, too, would bob up and down to the black-feathered jig of the ponies.

Luncheon passed, but Verity didn't leave. Instead she installed herself in my sitting room like one of the black crows which perched on our garden wall and in a subtle, deliberate, tearful manner, set about kidnapping Jonas. I knew she'd never considered me good enough for her brilliant brother: now in death she was determined to repossess him, to snatch him back among the Olivers and shrink me to a fleeting, eccentric episode in his life. And after all that had happened I was too weary to stand up to her, to claim my rights as a wife. All the time my crimes lay bottled up inside me, and in silence I meditated on my guilt.

Yet what had Verity ever done to help Jonas in those last, difficult months? All she and her greedy husband had ever done was to carp and complain, to plot against Jonas behind his back and threaten to take the company from him if their pound of flesh fell an ounce short of their due. Poor Jonas . . . His sister and brother-in-law stood to gain as much as anyone from his hard work, yet they'd turned on him before the end. All he'd asked of us was faith . . .

I tried not to think of the horrors I'd found in his workshop. From the start I'd hated the soft, dismembered bodies, the rolling enamel eyes, the bittersweet smell of the chemicals he used.

"I comfort myself he's with Dora at last." Vaguely, I heard Verity's voice from the sofa opposite. "He missed her so dreadfully, you know, after she died. They'd only been married three years, and she was almost always ailing. But I don't believe he was ever happy again, after he lost her." Verity treated me to a pitying smile. "Not truly happy. You understand that, Rachel, I'm sure."

I didn't know what I understood anymore. Perhaps Verity was

right after all—though I'd tried, God knows, to keep the vows I'd made . . . The vision of Jonas in his last hours filled my mind, refusing to give place to happier memories. He'd lain so still, his skin transparently white, his eyes searching for something beyond my head . . . and the soft, breathing name of the *Altair* on his lips. *Altair* —not *Rachel*. A heartless monster of iron and wood—not the guilty wife who sat, a tearful hypocrite, by his side.

If only Verity would leave me alone! Her pale, accusing eyes, so like Jonas's own, watched me across the hearth, seeking out the raw places of my spirit for her well-planted barbs. I was exhausted and miserable, and so distraught that when a footman came to the door I almost started with fright.

"Colonel Allen of Westwood Park, m'lady. Called to convey his condolences, if Lady Oliver's well enough to receive him."

"The effrontery of the man!" shrieked Verity indignantly. "Who does he think he is, I should like to know? Tell him to leave a card like the others, if he must."

All I could think of was that Adam had come to gloat over the sequence of catastrophes he'd set off.

"No—wait." I halted the servant. "Show the Colonel into the drawing room and ask him to wait for a moment. I'll see him."

I would see him. For wasn't Adam the cause of it all? All the pain and the betrayal, the hopelessness and the guilt?

"This won't take long," I told Verity as I went to the door. "Don't be concerned."

But it wasn't the conduct of an Oliver widow. Verity's scowl said as much, and more.

———

The table in the hall seemed unnaturally bare as I passed it. And then I remembered the kittens with their baleful stare and their silent melody, now no more than ashes in the kitchen garden. *What tune will you play for me now, wherever you are? Shall I dance on Jonas's grave, as Adam wishes?*

He was standing at the far end of the drawing room, staring out of the wide center window across the lawn and the shrubs beyond. His black silk hat and cane lay on the ottoman nearby; a gentleman making a short, official call. Yet the sight of those alien things, so casually laid on my braided cushions—in Jonas's house—somehow dissolved the last shreds of my reason.

"What do you want here?"

He'd turned to meet me—but now he stopped, his head slightly tilted, frowning a little—taken aback by the hostility in my voice.

"I thought—"

"What did you think, Adam? That with Jonas gone you'd only to crook your finger and I'd come running? Was that it?"

"Rachel—"

"He's only been dead a day! Couldn't you wait for us to bury him before you came to see what you could carry off?"

"That's unfair," he said quietly. "Perhaps it is . . . soon . . . But I thought you might need me."

"No you didn't. You saw your way clear at last to what you wanted. And you couldn't bear to wait."

"Rachel, what on earth's come over you? If I've come too soon— if you want me to leave you alone until after the funeral, then say so, and I'll go off and observe the decencies for as long as you please. Perhaps I have been hasty, but only because I was worried about you."

"Were you, Adam? I'm beginning to wonder if you've ever spared a thought for anyone but yourself! Did you ever think of Jonas, in all your schemes? Did you ever feel any guilt for what you might do to him?"

"Jonas had more luck than most. He didn't need my pity."

"Do you call it luck to be struck down as he was, without ever seeing his steamship finished? Was Jonas lucky, do you think, to choose a wife who loved a *dead man* more than she loved him?"

"Jonas never knew that."

"How can you be so sure?"

"Because it's true. And in any case, even if I'd never existed and you'd been madly in love with him—you told me yourself you were never more than a small part of *his* life. *Like his clock or his tea-kettle,* you said."

"I know what I said! And I thought it was Jonas's fault—when all the time I was the one to blame. I gave him so little."

"I don't believe that for a minute."

"Believe what you like, but it's true. I can see that now—now that it's too late. Even while he was working himself to death, I was dreaming of lying in another man's arms. I let him die—"

"His illness wasn't your fault, Rachel! You can't blame yourself for that."

"Can't I? Even though when I should have been worrying about Jonas I was thinking of you? And now he's dead—and you tell me not to blame myself?"

"You might say that now, but once this is all over and you've had a chance to rest, you'll realize how loyal you were to Jonas. Far more loyal than I wanted you to be." Adam reached out for me, trying to take me in his arms. But I wouldn't allow it. I was determined to deny myself that comfort.

"No," I insisted. "I can't forgive myself. And I can't forgive you, Adam. If you hadn't followed me here—filled my head with longing for you—made me think I had a right to hurt everyone else in pursuit of my own selfish desires . . . Then Jonas might never have died."

"Rachel—typhoid fever doesn't care about love or hate—it simply strikes where it can. You had no part in Jonas's death, I promise you."

"I won't listen to any more of your promises! How I wish you'd never come back from the dead! You should have gone on—on and on, just as you said—running forever. You're a lost soul, Adam—there's a curse hanging over you which brings pain to everyone you touch. You wander the world like some death-dealing phantom, looking for someone to set you free.

"Well, I won't be your salvation! I don't ever—ever—want to see you again on this earth. Go back to the grave where you belong, and I hope you find some comfort there! I wish to God it had been you, and not poor Jonas, who died!"

Adam stared at me, horror-struck, and it seemed as if his face had suddenly become that of an old man, as if my words had broken a spell and revealed him as he really was—old as time, old as sin itself.

Then without a word he snatched up his hat and cane, turned on his heel, and left the room. I heard the front door bang like a thunderclap behind him.

————

Afterward I felt light-headed, absolved.

The bizarre pageant of mourning went on around me with its black crape and jet bugles, its black bonnets smelling of camphor, its whispers and sly, sidelong glances, but I was no longer part of it. I'd made my reparation; I'd given up all that was dearest to me, atoned for my sins, and now the slow, stately, sable dance could bow and posture on its way unhindered.

Even the house had become unfamiliar, with its crape-hung mirrors and drawn blinds; I was a stranger in a strange place where a fair-haired man lay in his brass-mounted coffin in a darkened room and was no longer my concern. Verity had made that quite clear. In death the Olivers had cast me out at last.

Matthew's sharp irreverence might have shaken me out of my dismal mood, but Matthew had gone to ground in some corner of his own, and was nowhere to be found. Even Reuben's earnest conversation would have been a relief—but apart from a brief call on the afternoon of Jonas's death I hadn't seen him at all. The Broadneys were always in the White House now, and that was enough to keep Reuben away. He generally avoided the house in any case when Matthew was home from school: Reuben found Matthew arrogant and too clever by half, while Matthew had perfected a cruel parody of his new uncle's most earnest remarks. No—I wouldn't see Reuben again until the funeral.

I certainly didn't expect him to call on the afternoon before it, with Verity and George firmly installed behind lowered blinds in the drawing room—George irritable and hot in an overtight black dress coat and Verity even blacker than before, rattling with jet. Without consulting me, Verity had invited Bishop Caxton to join us for tea; the bishop was to conduct the service next day, and Verity was determined to see it proceed as she wished.

For my part, I was only praying that it wouldn't rain. Though it was now the first of June we'd had several days of heavy showers, and I'd never forgotten driving one wet afternoon past the gates of St. James's cemetery as a funeral procession arrived. The rain had drenched the black-clad column winding its laborious way into the graveyard past lank, dripping shrubs under a sky as somber as widow's weeds. The cemetery had once been a quarry, and that creeping host had seemed to descend into the mouth of Hell itself with their jolting burden under its sodden pall. I hoped, desperately, that the sun would shine on us next day.

And I wished the Broadneys would go and leave me alone.

"A sad loss," the Bishop intoned for the hundredth time, solemnly stirring the cup which rested on his black paunch. "Ah yes—a sad loss. But the ways of the Lord are not for us to understand. Who knows why poor Sir Jonas was taken?"

"Perhaps God's building a steamship," I heard George mutter under his breath.

"But you've shown great fortitude in your grief, Lady Oliver," the Bishop continued. "Though, of course, the support of Sir George and Lady Broadney must be a wonderful consolation." Bishop Caxton favored Verity with a fleeting smile. "You've no family of your own, I believe?"

A few moments previously I'd heard the sound of wheels on the carriage-sweep beyond the open windows as a vehicle of some kind drew up in front of the house. Now the slamming of a door came to us clearly in the drawing room followed by the squeak of axles as the cab—for so it sounded—prepared to move off. Then an altercation seemed to break out between driver and passenger, until finally the man drove away, giving vent to his feelings in a shrill voice which no one in the room could ignore—a stream of pithy remarks on tight-fisted gents who tipped a man sixpence after dragging him all the way to a bloody mansion at Mossley-bloody-Hill.

"I have a brother, Bishop. I think he may just have arrived."

I was right: it was Reuben, filling the doorway, dismayed to find that I had company. Presented to the Bishop, he sat down awkwardly on the edge of an embroidered chair, clearly nursing the hope that my visitors would depart before long, leaving him alone with me.

"Captain Dean is a *seafarer*, Bishop," Verity announced coldly.

"Ah—*They that go down to the sea in ships; and occupy their business in great waters. These men see the works of the Lord: and his wonders in the deep.* You're a privileged man, Captain Dean. You've looked upon the face of the Almighty."

"Oh . . . I suppose I have," murmured Reuben uncomfortably, and at the other side of the room I heard George give a scornful snort.

"Easier than looking a cabbie in the face after tipping him sixpence."

"George . . ." murmured Verity, pretending to be scandalized.

Reuben glanced up, startled, and then realized too late that his run-in with the cabbie had been perfectly audible to us all.

"The man was a blackguard," he muttered defensively. "Talking to me like that! Never mind his sixpence—I should have dragged him off his cab and thrashed the living daylights out of him."

Verity retired with a sniff behind her bonnet-brim.

"Reuben—" I said quickly, "perhaps you're being a little hard on the man. Mossley Hill is quite a long way from the docks."

"No, no—Reuben's quite right!" George put in. "Keel-haul the lubber, Captain. Flog him round the fleet. Make him walk the plank. That's the way you do it aboard ship, ain't it?"

Reuben's eyes rolled toward me as I passed him a teacup, mutely appealing for help.

"Excellent cake," remarked the Bishop blandly, in the manner of a man pouring oil on troubled waters.

"One of my poor brother's favorites." Verity turned her back on Reuben and rewarded the Bishop with a watery smile. "I gave Mrs. Locke the recipe when Jonas and Rachel were married, so that he should always have it." She fluttered a black-bordered handkerchief.

"A sad loss," repeated the Bishop automatically. "Ah yes—"

"More tea, Bishop?" I couldn't bear any more of this. "William— bring the Bishop's cup."

As the footman padded across to the Bishop's chair, I noticed that Reuben was on his feet again.

"Why Reuben, you're not leaving us already? You've only just arrived."

"No, no—I'm not going yet." Reuben's eyes flicked nervously across to where Verity and the Bishop were now deep in conversation while George Broadney sulkily examined one of Jonas's books which he'd found on a side-table. Reuben began to sidle self-consciously toward me.

"Look here," he said in a low voice, "—I know it's a bad time and all that, but there's something I have to ask you. It's very important."

"Come back tomorrow evening, then, after the funeral. Or on Friday, if you prefer. You can talk to your heart's content on Friday."

"Tomorrow evening's too late, Rachel—" Reuben glanced round anxiously. "Can't I speak to you alone for a few moments? Now— this afternoon?"

"Not this afternoon, my dear! It would hardly be polite to leave the Bishop and the Broadneys to look after themselves, would it?"

"This evening, then."

"It looks as if Verity and George will stay to dinner."

"Then how can I . . . Oh, for God's sake, Rachel! This is dreadfully important!"

I could see he was upset—but the last thing I wanted at that moment was to become involved with Reuben's problems.

"More cake, Bishop? And Reuben, I can't imagine what's so important it can't wait until after the funeral. Please leave it until tomorrow."

Reuben's voice became despairing.

"Rachel," he hissed, "if I say to you—*I know the truth!* I know why you've been so desperately unhappy lately!"

"Whatever did you expect, when Jonas was so ill!"

"No, no—it's nothing to do with Jonas." Reuben glanced round again, and licked his lips. "I know . . . you were being threatened. Blackmailed. About your past. Now do you see?"

"What do you know about that?" I whispered, appalled. "Who told you?"

"So it's true! You *were* threatened. I could hardly believe it at first."

"If you'll only come back tomorrow evening, Reuben, I'll explain everything."

"I just wanted to hear from you that it was true. That this blackmailing swine had really threatened you—"

"Tomorrow evening, Reuben!" Somehow or other, Reuben must have discovered the truth about Frank Ellis's errand that day in the park, and I knew he'd demand to know exactly what had taken place.

"Did I hear you say *swine*, Captain Dean?" boomed the Bishop from a short way off. "Is that you still coming down hard on cab-men?"

"Please go and sit down, Reuben," I whispered quickly. "I don't know where you heard this story, but I'll explain everything tomorrow, I promise."

"I simply couldn't believe it." Reuben seemed stunned by his discovery. "And that man, of all people." He paused, and bit his lip. "When Mother told me—"

"Mother!" For a moment, alarm and dismay made me forget to whisper. During the dreadful days of Jonas's illness, I'd completely forgotten our mother, waiting in the shadows to cause her mischief. "Where is she now? What on earth did she say to you?"

Beyond us, the Bishop's voice was still booming across the room.

"Oh, I admit some cab-men are a pretty rum lot, Captain Dean, but you mustn't take it to heart. Remember, the Bible assures us there's hope for us all. *Swine* they may be—but I daresay we'll cast out their devils one day! In fact, I'm about to set up a Mission to

Cab-men like the Mariners' Floating Church in George's Dock. You must know the place, Captain—but I'll wager you don't know its history, do you?"

"Not . . . particularly," admitted Reuben from his post beside my chair.

"Oh, it's quite a tale! Come and sit next to me here, why don't you, and I'll tell you a thing or two about that old ship."

"Reuben, please go and talk to the Bishop," I hissed, "and take no notice of whatever Mamma has told you. I *promise* I'll explain everything to you tomorrow." Even as I spoke, I realized that poor Jonas's death had robbed my mother of her most potent weapon. "And don't worry," I added, "it's all over now."

"It'll all be over tomorrow—that's true," murmured Reuben gloomily, reluctant to leave my chair. For another moment or two he shifted unhappily from foot to foot, moving aside at the last minute to let the footman pass.

"I might be *dead* by this time tomorrow!" he blurted out at last in a stage-whisper. "*That's* the point!"

"What mischief have you got yourself into, for Heaven's sake?" I was now thoroughly alarmed; I could sense my mother's remorseless hatred at work again though I'd no idea how Reuben had become involved in it all. But there was Jonas's funeral to see to before anything else could be done; I owed him that, at least. "Reuben— you're to do nothing—nothing at all—without telling me, do you hear?"

"Rachel, my dear," came Verity's crystal tones from a few yards away, "I think we have *done with tea*—if Captain Dean has no objection, that is?"

The pace of Reuben's nervous jig increased. Under cover of the general disturbance as tea was cleared away, he crouched by my ear.

"Rachel, it's vital I speak to you now. Will you please leave these people for a moment, and come with me into the hall?"

I glanced wildly over my shoulder. Reuben's expression was set, his gray eyes alive with a passionate determination I couldn't fathom. If he'd only wait until next day . . .

"Can we get back to the business in hand?" Verity called across the room. "We really must decide whether George should be a pall-bearer, or walk before the coffin. I thought he might have given the eulogy, but the dear Earl of Chorleigh has agreed to do that, which is excellent. He always looks so well in church, don't you think?"

"Oh, absolutely, Lady Broadney," agreed the Bishop, replete with tea and cake. "Quite the patrician. Quite the patriarch." He folded his hands comfortably across his stomach, and settled himself in his armchair to give the matter his full attention.

"Rachel—" Reuben whispered again.

"Not now, Reuben, please! If you'll only give me another day, and I'll be free of these people . . . Come back tomorrow evening. Promise you'll come."

All at once Reuben seemed to make up his mind.

"Goodbye, Rachel," he murmured, taking my hand in his for a long moment. "I can see it's no use my staying. But if you don't— see me—tomorrow evening . . . Well, it was for your sake—that's all."

And he was gone before I could even ask what he'd meant.

30

The funeral was as correct, as impressive and as public as Verity could have wished.

The Oliver family monument lay on the east side of the cemetery, beyond Huskisson's domed temple but a little short of the clifflike quarry wall already pitted with tablets and niches. The Olivers had edged their plot with stone and filled it with more stone, chiefly a great pedestal covered in names and dates and biblical texts, supporting a group of figures weeping around an urn, their carved draperies swathing the long list of vanished Olivers.

A gentle decay and a wealth of gray, lichenous growth had already begun to soften the absurdities of the monument, and rank grass had risen up tactfully about it, only to be clipped back on Verity's instructions, ready for the new burial.

"*In the midst of life we are in death,*" intoned the Bishop with professional gravity, his voice echoing thinly back from the cliff-face where a clutch of sparrows suddenly spattered away toward the city.

I would have escaped with them if I could: high over the somber ring surrounding the grave—over Aunt Grace's black silk bonnet, over the bowed heads of the civic dignitaries, over the line of Oliver relatives, the ruddy-faced shipmasters, and at the back, a handful of clerks from the Water Street office granted time off from their desks to pay their last respects.

Reuben—strangely—was nowhere to be seen, but Matthew stood at my elbow, his eyes fixed on the polished toe-caps of the Bishop's shoes and a thoughtful expression on his face. I wondered what was in his mind—and where he'd been for the past few days. Matthew was becoming more like his father than ever—self-contained, detached, elusive—impatient of any constraint.

I found myself remembering how much Adam had loathed cemeteries, with their narrow plots and circumspect paths. The great mausoleum in Norfolk where his father's family were buried had disgusted him, its moldering lead coffins shut up behind iron grilles.

"Heaven knows why anyone would want to finish up in there, away from the sunshine and the wind," he'd said when he described it to me. "I suppose they put great men's corpses into these pillared kennels to prevent any noble dust from going to grow fodder for cattle—as if that was a dishonorable end in some way. When my time comes you can put me in the corner of a field," he'd added lightly. "Near a horse-trough, in case I get bored."

"The days of man are but as grass: for he flourisheth as a flower of the field. For as soon as the wind goeth over it it is gone: and the place thereof shall know it no more."

Distantly, I heard the measured tread of the burial service proceed on its way, and against its peaceful inevitability my thoughts became rational at last.

It had been so hard to think of Adam dead. But not Jonas; Jonas had always known that one day he'd occupy this spot among the Olivers—as if he'd been destined for it from the day of his birth and his life had merely been a brief period of light amid the comforting darkness.

"For as much as it hath pleased Almighty God . . . to take unto himself the soul of our dear brother here . . ."

Who was it told me that Jonas had been "called to God"—as if his twopenny turn on the boating-pond had run out at last? Death not as a judgment but as an ending . . . as if we're all given our allotted time afloat before the call comes from the shore.

". . . earth to earth, ashes to ashes, dust to dust . . ."

There, in the hush of the graveyard, I began to return to sanity. Even in the great pit of St. James's cemetery, the sun shone around us and the cheeping sparrows returned one by one to the shrubs on the quarry-face. *In the midst of death we are in life. . . .* And Jonas had not died for any sins of mine.

The weeping figures on the Oliver monument gazed down sadly at the pile of earth which temporarily disfigured their plot. Soon the grass would grow again, and Jonas's daughters would come to lay their little handfuls of flowers on the weather-worn stone. For good or ill, Jonas was already a memory; his daughters and his wife had lives of their own to lead.

". . . In the land of the living . . . Give me peace . . ."

Wasn't that exactly what Adam had asked of me?

At last the Bishop's melodious voice died away, and he closed his prayerbook. In twos and threes the black-clad figures began to turn away from the graveside, those nearest sending stray clods of earth down upon the coffin-lid as they went.

"Thank you, dear Bishop," I heard Verity murmur, laying her hand fleetingly on the Bishop's white lawn sleeve. "That was deeply, deeply moving. You'll join us all shortly at the White House, I hope?"

This was the final act; the last, necessary homage to death—the vast buffet of cold meats and salmon, stuffed veal, celery salad, whiting and watercress, potted beef sandwiches, fruit tarts, cold cabinet pudding and pancakes which waited in the dining room at the White House to console those whom Verity had particularly favored.

As I turned to leave the graveside where the cemetery-men were already waiting with their spades, Verity touched my arm.

"There," she said, pointing to the patch of trodden ground where the soil lay heaped next to Jonas's grave. "I've asked them to keep that place for you. . . . Next to Jonas—and Dora, of course. I thought it might comfort you to know."

———

By six in the evening they'd gone, all of them, even Verity and George in their huge carriage with the Broadney mailed fist on its doors. For the first time in—oh, so long—I was left alone in my solitude. Now there were no nurses, no doctors, no priests, no Broadneys—and no Jonas.

In the end, in spite of all Verity could do, there'd been an indecent amount of sunshine for the funeral—and now the lawn beyond the drawing-room windows was splashed with the long shadows of evening in the golden, wasting summer light. And that light had entered my soul at last, banishing the grim clouds of sickness and death. Jonas had gone; I was my own woman again—and my mother's power over me was broken.

"Reuben! Where on earth—"

He'd come barging into the drawing room before anyone had a chance to announce him—Reuben, striding across the bright carpet, flushed, intent, his mouth set in a hard, resolute line.

"Rachel—thank God you're alone at last! I thought those wretched people would never go. You'd think they'd nothing better to do than drink tea and gossip! I had to wait until the last one had left before I could risk seeing you at all."

"But where have you been? Why weren't you in church? And what do you mean—you had to *risk* coming here?" Vague memories of our snatched conversation the day before began to return to me, and I laid hold of his wrists, almost ready to shake him in my impatience.

"There's no time for questions, Rachel. I don't have very long. The police will be looking for me by now."

"*The police!* Oh, Reuben—what have you done?"

"Just listen to me, please, Sis." Reuben pulled me down beside him on the ottoman, keeping hold of my hand. "I have to go away for a while. Now. At once. There's a little place down the coast where they'll hide me until I can find another ship—I'll send word when I'm safely there—"

I shook my head, bewildered.

"But I had to see you before I went," Reuben continued. "I wanted to tell you myself that it was all over—that you were free at last—"

"What in Heaven's name are you talking about, Reuben? Why should you have to run away from the police? When I missed you at the funeral—"

"Oh, blow the funeral! I tried to tell you yesterday I'd other business which couldn't wait—except that you wouldn't listen!" Reuben took a deep breath. "Rachel—I've killed the man who was tormenting you. Today, while you were all at the cemetery."

"You've *killed* him? Reuben, do you know what you're saying? If there's been an accident of some kind—" I couldn't believe Reuben had simply murdered Frank Ellis in cold blood.

"An accident? Oh, no, I meant to kill him! I swore I would, unless he promised to leave you alone, the blackmailing monster. . . . I've no regrets, Rachel," Reuben added firmly. "I did it for your sake."

I could hardly take in what he was saying. Why, oh why, hadn't he waited until I could tell him that Jonas's death had made his sacrifice unnecessary? Yet his next words threw me into confusion once more.

"When Mother told me how I'd been the means of bringing him here—how he'd only found you through me, and then tricked me into letting him aboard the ship . . . Oh, Rachel, how could I refuse to help you?"

"But how—"

"And the fellow admitted—he *admitted* he'd only come to Liverpool to find you. And when I demanded that he leave you alone in future—he simply refused, straight off. Told me it was none of my business, the scoundrel, standing there cool as you please, even when I aimed the gun at his chest and warned him to defend himself. He never moved—although I know for a fact that he's always armed— or he always was, when I knew him. But all he said was 'Reuben Dean, for your sister's sake I won't harm you. Give me that gun and we'll talk sensibly about this.' " Reuben shook his head. "I was so angry to hear him speak of you in that way—so *angry*—I'd have shot him a thousand times over."

I felt the hands which held mine convulse at the memory, as if the smoking gun still lay between Reuben's fingers.

"Reuben—" I whispered in growing dread, "who was the man Mother sent you to shoot? Tell me, for God's sake!"

"He went down like a slaughtered ox," Reuben continued heed-lessly, "down on the carpet, right next the hearth. I must have hit him square in the heart—I was so near I could hardly miss—"

"Whom have you killed? Tell me!"

Reuben stared at me in surprise. "The man who was threatening you. The blackmailer. The man who called himself Colonel Allen. At Westwood Park."

My shrill scream of anguish genuinely frightened him. He tried to wrench my fingers from his coat, as if he were afraid I'd do him an injury with my bare hands.

"Rachel! For Heaven's sake! What's come over you? The man is *dead* now—he can't harm you anymore. You're free of him forever! Don't you understand?"

"I can't—I can't believe what you've done . . ."

"Don't tell me you're weeping for that criminal's sake! Good Heavens, the man was half-mad! Do you know what he said when I challenged him? 'Do you play backgammon by any chance, Captain Dean?' Well, I said *no*—I couldn't help it—and he said, 'That's unfortunate, I can't find anyone here who plays as well as Wang Chen.' Those were his words, Rachel—as I stood before him with a gun aimed at his heart. Would you credit it? If he thought I wouldn't shoot—well, he was wrong, that's all."

Reuben stared at me, wild-eyed, and I tried desperately to make sense of all he'd told me.

"Are you sure—absolutely sure—that he's dead?"

"I was sure enough at the time—though I didn't wait to examine him, of course. He fell forward when I fired, and lay still . . . and there was a lot of blood. I ran out of the house straight away, but I'm as sure as I can be that he's dead."

"But not absolutely sure." I grasped at the last particle of hope.

"Not *absolutely* . . . But I've seen dead men before, Rachel, and I'm certain that if he didn't die then, he'd be dead before very long. Where the devil are you going?"

I was already halfway to the drawing-room door.

"I'm going to Westwood Park."

"But—why? I don't understand why you're making such a fuss about a dead blackmailer."

"God help you, Reuben—that man was my husband."

———

It was Mrs. Gibson herself who answered the door, a long white apron over her dress. If she was surprised to see a distraught, disheveled woman on her doorstep, alone and dressed entirely in black, she didn't show it in any way.

"Please come in, Lady Oliver," was all she said, as if I were paying the most formal of calls.

I'd forgotten the profound silence of Westwood Park, but it crowded in on me as I walked into the hall. Even in the Admiral's day the old house had been filled with a thick, absorbent hush which doused the chimes of the clocks and swallowed up their slow, dusty ticking. Now as I walked into that high-ceilinged hallway I felt the silence hang like dense curtains around me, and I remembered that in city streets, when an important man was dying, straw was laid outside the house to deaden the sound of passing traffic.

"Mrs. Gibson—forgive me for calling like this, but I heard—I heard there had been an accident . . . I wondered . . ."

She didn't help me; she simply stared at me out of her birdlike eyes—wondering, I suppose, how I knew what had happened.

"That's true. There was an accident—yes. Just after two o'clock."

"And Colonel Allen—?"

"Colonel Allen . . . was shot."

"But is he—" I couldn't even pronounce the word. She must have thought me the most awful fool.

"The Colonel was wounded. But he's still alive. The doctor was with him for most of the afternoon."

"Oh, thank God he isn't dead!"

"Perhaps you ought to sit down for a moment, Lady Oliver."

"Is he well enough to see me? Just for a few minutes?"

Mrs. Gibson looked doubtful. "The doctor said he shouldn't be disturbed."

"Please—just for a few minutes, no more."

Mrs. Gibson gave me an odd look; I don't imagine she was accustomed to frantic women arriving unannounced at her door—let alone a woman who'd just buried her husband, and who until that moment had treated Westwood Park as if it were inhabited by lepers.

"I'll go upstairs and find out," she conceded after a moment. "I'm afraid I must ask you to wait in the hall. We don't often entertain here." She indicated the half-open door of the principal drawing room, where the shrouded shapes of furniture stood in the perpetual gloom of closed shutters.

"I really think you ought to sit down, Lady Oliver. I may be gone a while."

I sat down on the slippery cushion of an old settle, and found myself grateful for the respite. I tried to focus my attention on the great canvas of naval warfare which hung opposite, but there were too many tiny figures flying broken through the flare of gunfire to have a calming effect on my mind. Instead I concentrated on counting the black and white tiles on the hall floor, row by row from the doorway, fighting down the impulse to lift my eyes to the vaulted stairwell up which Mrs. Gibson had vanished.

I'd reached four hundred and eighty-seven tiles by the time I heard her footsteps descending the first few stone stairs.

"If you'd care to come up—" she said, and turned at once to go back the way she'd come.

————

Adam was lying in the center of the bed, propped up against a pile of pillows, his skin almost as pale as the strips of cotton bandage which ran diagonally across his chest and left shoulder. In the shaded evening light his face seemed very drawn and drained of color, though there was nothing dull or lifeless about his eyes. They fastened on me the instant I entered the room and followed me—sharp and searching—as I stepped slowly forward.

All at once I was a seven-year-old child again, creeping nervously into the Widow Creran's room in Crow Cove under the gaze of the shipwrecked man. Adam had looked at me then with those same, savage, slate-gray eyes—and I'd known the same turmoil of the senses which possessed me now.

For several seconds neither of us spoke, and I cursed myself for not having had the wisdom to go back to the White House as soon as I knew Reuben hadn't committed murder after all.

Adam's voice intruded on my thoughts.

"Once upon a time," he said softly, "you brought me a sick seabird. Do you remember, Rachel?"

"How did you know I was thinking of that?"

"From your face, when you came into the room. So like a child. . . . Afraid of what you might find. Not sure, even now."

"I was afraid you were dead. Reuben was so certain."

"Ah . . . Reuben . . . Ready to murder for his sister. And here you are in black, believing yourself free of me at last."

"You know why I'm in black. Jonas . . . was buried this morning."

"Of course. I'd forgotten." Adam shifted uncomfortably against his pillows. "You shouldn't wear black. It makes you look pale. You can wear scarlet for me, when I go."

"But you aren't—I mean—Mrs. Gibson said—"

"I'm not dying, if that's what you're asking. Not yet, at any rate, so the doctor says." He glanced up at me defiantly. "Is that what you came for? To report to your precious brother how well he'd succeeded?"

"Adam—I didn't want you dead."

The eyes searched my face once more.

"That isn't what you said four days ago. *I wish it was you who'd died, and not Jonas.* Those were your words."

"I shouldn't have said those things."

"You said what you thought—and maybe you were right. Maybe I am to blame for everything that's happened. Reuben seems to think so."

"I never dreamed Reuben would do something like this. Don't you think I'd have stopped him, if I'd guessed? This wasn't my doing, Adam, I promise you."

He stared up at me for a moment.

"No," he said after a pause, "I suppose Reuben's quite mad enough to dream this up for himself. And he very nearly succeeded."

He tried to reach out to a small table beside the bed, found the effort too painful, and gestured toward it instead.

"You'll have to come closer."

The tabletop was cluttered with ointment jars and rolled bandages, but among them lay a rectangular silver cigar-case chased
with a pattern of spiraling ferns and curved to fit snugly in an inside
coat-pocket. Jonas had owned a case just like it—except that this
one, I could see, had been dented with terrific force, scored and
creased along its curved side by something which had careered crazily across it before spinning off at a wild angle.

"It would have stopped a ball," Adam observed morosely, "but
these conical bullets are the very devil. Thanks to Reuben I've a
crater in my chest, a couple of split ribs and a large hole in my
shoulder where the lead was cut out."

I gaped at him.

"And that's all? There's nothing more?" I found myself almost
laughing from sheer relief.

"Isn't that enough?"

"If it's no worse than that . . . Adam, I thought you were dead!
When Reuben told me what he'd done—"

"So he rushed back to boast about it to you, did he? I imagine he's
very proud of himself."

I shook my head. "Not now. He's in a dreadful state. He's gone
into hiding, though knowing Reuben, he's quite likely to give himself
up to the police."

"Tell him not to be so stupid! He mustn't go near the police. They
don't know anything about it."

Profound relief swept over me.

"Oh, Adam, thank you! Thank you for Reuben's sake! I thought
—we both thought—someone was bound to have called them."

"Mrs. Gibson was all for it, but I managed to stop her. What good
would it have done? Reuben isn't a murderer: he only came here
because of you. How would it have looked in the law-courts, when
the whole story was dragged out, thanks to your idiot brother?"

I'd noticed a pocket-pistol among the other things by the bed, and
I remembered what Reuben had said about Adam being constantly
armed.

"Adam . . . Reuben told me you never even tried to defend yourself. He couldn't understand why you just stood there and let him
shoot. . . ."

"*Let him?* What could I have done about it?"

"You had a pistol of your own, didn't you? You could have shot
Reuben before he had a chance to fire."

"Are you telling me I should have shot down your brother?"

"Of course not. But I know you could have killed him if you'd wanted to."

"Perhaps I didn't want to, then."

"Not even to save your own life?"

Adam seemed about to answer, then looked away and shrugged. I saw him wince in sudden, renewed pain, and it occurred to me then that he hadn't cared. To shoot or be shot, it had made no difference.

In the land of the living . . . Give me peace . . .

"Adam—I was wrong. About Jonas, and you and me. What we . . . talked about . . . made no difference to his death."

Adam turned his head and looked suspiciously up at me.

"I mean it. You were right. Even if you'd never come back— Jonas would still have died when he did. I was . . . upset. You understand."

There was more I wanted to say, but somehow the words wouldn't form themselves into sensible patterns. I simply stood there beside the bed, twisting the fringe of my shawl between my fingers.

It was a long time before Adam spoke. When he did, I sensed that some great decision had been made.

"Sit down, Rachel. Here—on the edge of the bed." I hesitated for a moment, and then did as he asked. "You're ruining that shawl. Give me your hand instead."

I was surprised by the strength of his grasp.

"What will Mrs. Gibson say if she finds us like this?"

"You're comforting a sick man—what else?" His fingers wound themselves round mine, warm and insistent, and I felt the old, familiar excitement kindle inside me.

"Don't, Adam, please."

"Why not? Don't turn away from me like that. Let me see your face."

"No."

There was silence in the room except for the hissing of the lamp. I was sure Adam must be able to hear the hammering of my heart.

"Rachel—"

"No. Don't say anything."

"What mustn't I say?"

"Anything at all. Please, Adam . . ." His fingers were still caressing mine with a gentle, sensuous pressure I'd never forgotten. ". . . When you do that I can't even think."

"Do you have to think?"

"Yes, I do. For a while, at least."

"Is there anything I can do to help you make up your mind?"

I shook my head.

"Then at least explain to Reuben about us. Tell him I'm not trying to harm you. All I want is to be with you—to be as we once were; *you're* the unwilling one."

"That wasn't why he came here. He had no idea we'd been married, or any of the rest."

"Then why the Devil did he want to shoot me?"

"He was sent to do it. He was told you'd come to Liverpool to blackmail me—to make my life wretched, because of something in my past. And he thought he owed it to me to put an end to your threats—because he was the one who'd brought you back from San Francisco in the first place."

"But the whole thing's ridiculous! Who could have made him believe nonsense like that?"

"My mother can make Reuben believe anything she likes."

Adam stared at me. "Susannah's back in Liverpool?"

"She spoke to Matthew at the docks one day. She didn't give him her name, but as soon as he told me about the peculiar questions she'd asked, I realized who it must have been. And she once warned me she'd kill you sooner than see us together again, though I thought she was only trying to frighten me. I suppose when Jonas died she was afraid . . . Though I never believed she'd really want either of us *dead!*"

"Not you," Adam said slowly. "Just me." His hand gripped mine more tightly. "You could have run off with any other man in the world, and she wouldn't have cared. But instead, you married me. She was angry with you—insanely jealous . . . but she hates me. That's what's behind all this."

"I'm sure she hates both of us."

"No. Just me."

"But—"

"You know why."

"I don't know anything of the kind."

I tried to snatch my hand away and stand up, but he was holding me too firmly, and pulled me back.

"We've never talked about it, Rachel—but you *know*, don't you."

"I can't think what you mean." Memories flooded back to me all of a sudden as if a dam had burst in my mind, releasing a twisting, turning torrent of scenes and words I'd tried to keep shut away. . . .

"Don't say it, Adam—please. . . ."

Through the eyes of a seven-year-old child I watched them once more—Adam and my mother, standing together in the garden as I'd glimpsed them one day from the little window on the stairs, Adam with one hand on the overhanging branch of an apple tree and my mother sliding past him on the narrow path, moving sinuously against his body, hip to thigh like a parading she-cat.

"Face it, Rachel. . . . We can't pretend it didn't happen."

Now, though I struggled against it, my woman's mind made sense of what the child had seen, of the memories I'd refused to acknowledge for so long. Now that I'd grasped the key, door after door flew open on sudden, unguarded gestures, on subtle signals and shared glances which had meant nothing to the watching child but now shouted their secret. Of course they'd been lovers—Adam and my mother—while my drunken father softened his brain and dreamed of clocks he couldn't sell. Of course they'd been lovers! Confined in that locked-in, sea-smothered place—those two—what else could have occurred?

"*No!* It can't be true! I can't bear it to be true!"

"But you must have realized. Not at the time, of course, but later."

"Do you think I'd ever have . . . *touched* you . . . if I'd known? If I'd known you'd been my mother's lover?"

"You never asked me."

"You never told me!"

"Dammit—when was I supposed to tell you? On our first night together, in that dingy hotel room? *By the way, my dear, I've bedded your mother too—more than once, in fact.*"

"At least it would have been the truth!"

"And what would you have done, if I'd told you that night? Run back to your aunt and told her you'd made a mistake? That you'd changed your mind?"

"I don't know. . . ."

"And after that, what was the use? It was too late to go back."

Adam fell back against his pillows, exhausted by the effort of talking, and released my hand at last. Immediately, I stood up.

"Oh, Adam—why did you have to tell me now?"

"I didn't tell you. I forced you to admit something you already knew." When I shook my head, he said it again. "You already knew it, Rachel. But you wouldn't face it. And now you understand why your mother tried to have me killed." With an effort, he leaned forward and reached for my hand again, but I kept it beyond his reach.

"The truth, Rachel. It's the only way. And the truth is that Susannah and I were lovers—for most of those few months I was in Crow Cove. It happened; and then it was over. Just a passing affair between two restless, uncaring people, neither of whom gave a damn for the other, except in that one respect. . . . You could have struck us together and lit a fire from the sparks."

"I don't want to hear about it."

"I'm trying to be honest with you."

"It's too late for that, Adam."

All I knew was that my mother had won again: once more she'd thrust that sweet, inviting body of hers between us, lying where I'd lain, loving where I'd loved. . . . Long before me, she'd gloried in his strength and their shared passion—and he'd never dared breathe a word of it to me.

"It meant nothing, Rachel—not a thing. Not until she discovered you and I were together. . . . That's when the hating began."

"You and I were never together," I retorted bitterly. "Never for a single moment. *Together* means trust—and I was a fool ever to trust you, wasn't I?"

I'd spent my whole life avoiding it, and now I could think of nothing but those two—Adam and my mother—savoring their secret explosion of lust while I, childish and besotted, played with my animals in the yard. *You could have struck us together and lit a fire from the sparks.* What more was there to say?

"Goodbye, Adam."

I turned, and began to walk across the room.

"Rachel! Wait—please!" Adam's voice was hoarse with strain. As I reached the door I heard a movement behind me as if he were trying to drag himself to his feet to prevent me from leaving. But I didn't turn back: I didn't dare look into his face again. It was enough to hear him calling my name as I banged the door shut behind me.

31

"Where on earth have you been?"

From the drawing-room windows Matthew had seen me arrive back, hot and disheveled, at the front door.

"You look like a woman who's just missed her train."

"I went out for a walk. It's still quite warm outside—warm enough to make me uncomfortable in this heavy black dress."

"And your eyes are all red."

"Matthew, we've just buried your stepfather, in case you've forgotten. I'm not in the mood for any more of your questions."

"As you please." But he followed me upstairs all the same, right to the door of my room.

"Mater—"

"What is it now, Matthew?"

"When did you ever go out for a walk without gloves or a hat?"

"Well, I—" I searched round for an excuse. "I told you—it's a warm evening." I began to shut my bedroom door, but he put his hand over the lock.

"There's something else. Why haven't we seen anything of dear Uncle Reuben today? I'd have expected him to be with his precious sister at a time like this."

"Perhaps he's ill."

"Perhaps. Though I could have sworn I heard his voice in the drawing room earlier this evening."

"Matthew, I don't care what you think you heard. I'm very tired, and I'm going to bed early. Now, will you please let me close this door?"

"Very well." Slowly, Matthew took his hand from the lock. "But I'm not stupid, Mater. There's something going on round here that no one's seen fit to tell me about—yet. I smell a large rat, and I reckon its name is *Reuben Dean*. But if you aren't going to tell me what's up, then I'll just have to find out for myself, won't I?"

And with that, he took hold of the outer handle of my door and closed it firmly behind him. I even heard him whistle as he walked off down the passage toward the stairs.

He was right, of course. The whole miserable tale was going to come out now, if only because Reuben had been drawn into it by my mother's insensate jealousy. Reuben, poor misguided creature, would demand to know every last detail, and once Reuben knew . . . Well, Reuben was incapable of keeping a secret. Other people's confidences itched in his mind like flea-bites until he could pass them on; his face alone would make it clear there was something to hide.

And Matthew . . . In all honesty, Matthew had a right to know the truth. Adam Gaunt—whatever else he might be—was still the boy's father. In the past Matthew had never asked me much about his father's family; he found the Olivers more to his taste than a long-dead nobody, and while Jonas lived I'd been able to justify my silence. But now . . . it began to seem as if I owed Matthew a father.

But I didn't owe Adam a son. I owed Adam *nothing*—nothing at all. I couldn't rid myself of the image of Adam and my mother . . . together . . . laughing at me, no doubt, as I innocently imagined Adam my own particular friend, the keeper of my secrets, my confederate against the selfish world of my parents. What had he whispered to her as she lay in his arms in the darkness, the two of them entwined, surfeited with love, in that old bed with the pine posts and the goose-feather mattress? Did he amuse her with stories of the little fears and longings I'd confided to him during the day?

I felt sick to my stomach when I thought of how foolish I'd been.

Mother and daughter—double voluptuaries: and he'd betrayed us both.

————

I sent for Reuben next day—and by great ill-luck almost the first person he encountered when he arrived at the White House was Matthew, sprawled on a stone bench on the flagged terrace which ran along the east side of the building. It was another hot June day and, in an effort to restore some sort of normality to our lives, I'd had tea brought out to us where we sat: the habits of Jonas Oliver's household died hard. Fortunately, the girls weren't at home. I'd sent them off with their governess to sketch plants in the Botanical Gardens—the only providential part of the whole episode.

Matthew had been lying so still on the stone seat, a straw hat tilted over his face, that I was sure he must be asleep. Yet as soon as Reuben rounded the corner of the house, his coat slung over one shoulder and his footsteps loud on the paving, I saw Matthew remove the hat and sit up.

"Well, well—" he called unpleasantly. "The prodigal returns!"

"Matthew, be quiet!"

"It's true, ain't it? Uncle Rube's been hiding like a rat in a hole, if I'm not much mistaken. Otherwise, why didn't he show at the funeral? Hey there, Uncle—did the press gang get you, or what?"

"Hello, Rachel." Reuben dropped into a chair and eyed Matthew with displeasure. "Hello, Matthew."

"Is that all?"

"What d'you mean—*is that all?* What more did you expect?"

"Just *hello,* when you've vanished off the face of the earth for two whole days?" I saw Matthew's eyes glitter. "Or did no one invite you to the funeral, Uncle? Verity noticed you weren't there, you can be sure of that."

Reuben glanced across at me. "I had my reasons."

"And they're none of your business, Matthew."

"Secrets again? My word, I'm getting sick of all the whispering that goes on in this house."

"As it happens, I've one or two things to discuss with Reuben." I rose to my feet. "We'll go indoors to my sitting room."

"Oh, no, you don't!" exclaimed Matthew, swinging his feet to the ground and staring up at me. "I told you I'd had enough of being left out of whatever's going on. Don't you think I notice all the plotting and the mysterious comings and goings? Well, you aren't fobbing me off with this *Mother-knows-best* nonsense anymore. One or other of you is going to tell me what's been happening. Now which of you is it to be? Mater? Or you—*Uncle?*"

Reuben, on his feet now, glanced at me again and then turned back to Matthew.

"Very well—I'll give you an answer. I shot a man, if you must know. I shot him, but as it turned out I didn't kill him, though I had to go away for a bit in case the police found out and came to look for me. Does that satisfy you?"

"Well, Uncle—you do amaze me. . . ." For a moment Matthew looked genuinely surprised. "Fancy that! I wouldn't have thought you'd have been able to hit a barn door with a sledgehammer. Of course, you didn't manage to kill the fellow, did you. . . ."

"No, thank God," I put in. "Reuben was in quite enough trouble as it was. Now, if you've found out what you wanted to know, perhaps you'll let us go indoors."

"Who was it, Uncle? Who did you shoot? One of your sailors? Or someone's husband, perhaps?"

"Stop calling me *uncle* in that offensive tone, will you?" Reuben was already on edge, and now he was becoming visibly annoyed.

"All right then—*Reuben*—I'll ask you again. Who did you shoot? No one capable of shooting back, I'll wager!"

"Why, you little worm—" Gripping the sides of the stone table, Reuben leaned across it until he loomed above Matthew, knocking over the cream jug as he did so. I watched helplessly as a lake of cream poured across the lichenous slab to drip thickly on to the paving.

"Are you calling me a coward?"

"Pay no attention, Reuben—Matthew's just trying to provoke you."

"Don't meddle in this, Mater." Matthew was glaring back, undaunted by Reuben's height and bulk. "*He* said the word 'coward,' not me. What did you do, Reuben—shoot this fellow in the back?"

"*Ask him!*" hissed Reuben in a fury. "Go on—*ask him!* There's his house—not quarter of a mile away! Why don't you go and ask him if I shot him in the back?"

"Reuben!" I pleaded desperately.

"*The Colonel?* You shot the Colonel?"

"I did."

"But what the Devil for?" Matthew was quite indignant. "What has he ever done to you?"

Reuben swung round to face me. "Are you going to tell him?"

"Well—yes. But not now! Not like this!"

"Tell me what?" Matthew was staring from one of us to the other. Then sudden suspicion crossed his face. "Hey, Mater—you haven't been having an affair with the Colonel, have you? Well, by all the saints—you're a sly one, you are! Piping your eye for dear, dead Jonas, and all the time you were carrying on with the wicked next door neighbor! No wonder he asked all those questions about you—"

Moving more quickly than I would have believed possible, Reuben bounded round the table and hoisted Matthew almost off his feet by the lapels of his coat.

"Listen to me—*Nephew*"—he said between gritted teeth —"and you might just learn something. But if you don't keep that dirty, slanderous tongue of yours quiet, I'll ram it straight down your gullet!"

"Reuben! For Heaven's sake! Put him down at once!"

"Do you know, Matthew," Reuben was saying in a horribly soft voice, "it always puzzled me how a decent, kindly woman like my sister could have given birth to a poisonous little weasel like you. Strange, isn't it? I could never quite understand it myself . . . until now. But, you see, I've done a fair bit of thinking in the last couple of days—" Reuben looked across at me briefly, and I could see the anger in his eyes, "—and I reckon I might have some interesting news for you."

"No, Reuben—please!"

"When she heard what I'd done—that I'd shot this man in West-wood Park—and never mind *why* for the moment . . . your mother said a fascinating thing. She said *That man is my husband*. . . . Yes, she did. It's no good looking at her, Matthew—look at me when I'm speaking to you. . . ."

Like a rabbit transfixed by a snake, Matthew obediently turned his head.

"That's better. . . . Now, when I thought about what she'd said— and it wasn't for an hour or two, I admit, because I don't think quite as fast as you do—" he gave Matthew a vicious shake "—but when I thought about it, the idea occurred to me that if the man I shot— and I don't regret it, because he's a cold, corrupt individual at the best of times—but if he really was, by some chance, your mother's first husband . . . then you, my fine friend . . . my clever little friend . . . must be *his son*. In other words, your precious 'Colonel' is your real father. What do you think of that—*Nephew?*"

At last Reuben let go of Matthew's coat. "Though in my opinion it would explain a great deal." He looked across at me again. "But, of course, only your mother can tell you the truth of it. If she *will* tell you, that is."

I stared back at him, appalled—not by what he'd said and done, but by how much he'd changed in those few moments. All of a sudden he'd sloughed off the dogged, blundering Reuben I'd known ever since he came to Liverpool; all his smug self-righteousness had vanished, taking with it every trace of my honest, well-meaning younger brother. In his place I saw a tall, bitter, gray-eyed man made savage by resentment and the suspicion that he'd been unfairly used. And the thought formed in my mind: *Is this the little clockmaker's son? Where in all this cold fury is the puny seed of Joseph Dean?*

There was only one person who could give me an answer to that.

Without protest, Reuben told me where I'd find her. This time there would be no derelict chapel—no hidden eyes watching me from behind a screen: we'd speak face to face, on equal terms—and this time I had nothing to lose.

The carriage pulled up with a jolt before a solid, unexceptional front-age in Prince's Park, a house showing so little sign of life that at first I imagined I'd come to the wrong place.

It was Susan Vinegar who opened the door. She'd no idea who I was, and stared at me sourly as if she expected to be dunned for some charitable contribution.

"Well?"

I could hardly believe this was the same bustling, inquisitive young woman I remembered from my childhood. Susan's wiry fair hair had dulled to the color of damp straw, dragged back from her bony temples into a loose bundle at the back of her head. As she reached out to take the card I offered, she kept her other arm pressed close across her body, hugging her thin chest while her eyes, hooded and suspicious, tried to read the purpose of the call in my face.

The card was taken, and deciphered, and frowned over before Susan looked up sharply with an intake of breath. There was nothing but hostility in that fierce, narrow glare, and I saw her move instinctively to bar the doorway with her own angular body in its worsted dress.

"So it's you, is it?" She held out the card with an abrupt gesture. "She won't see you. Should've saved yourself the drive. You might as well go back where you came from."

"She'll see me. She has no choice."

My eyes met Susan's own, and stared her down. I saw her hesitate, and then glance behind me at a pony-trap which had just halted by the gate.

"Who are those two in the dog-cart?"

"One is a gardener. The other does odd jobs in my stables."

"Why are they here?"

"They'll make sure no one leaves this house until I've finished what I came for."

Without another word the door was slammed in my face, and for several minutes I studied its multicolored glass panes, imagining my coachman and the other men waiting by the carriage exchanging significant glances behind my back.

But with Jonas gone, it no longer mattered. Indeed, the White House servants had been given plenty to gossip about in the past couple of days. Not a face had appeared at the dining-room windows during Reuben's fierce row with Matthew on the terrace, but I was sure that even though none of the footmen or housemaids could have been near enough to hear what was said, they'd certainly know there had been a falling-out between Lady Oliver's son and her sea-captain brother. Even after I'd dragged them both off to the library, sworn them to secrecy and given them a brief account of my marriage to Adam, his supposed death and his reappearance, the bad blood remained. Reuben announced sulkily that he'd be off to sea in a few days in any case, and that until then—while Matthew was still at home—I'd find him in the docks, aboard the *Rachel Oliver*. He was sorry, but there it was.

While all this was going on Matthew had fallen into a sullen silence, and for a few moments after Reuben left I thought he, too, was going to make an unpleasant scene.

Then he looked up at me shrewdly.

"So the Colonel's my father, eh?"

"Yes, Matthew, he is."

Matthew shrugged. "Well, it's certainly a great improvement on a penniless bear-skinner—and a dead one, at that."

"Go and tell him that, why don't you?" I retorted, losing my temper. "Matthew—he's your *father*. Your own flesh and blood. Doesn't that mean anything to you?"

"Oh, sure." Matthew's eyes suddenly blazed with cold fire. "It means just about as much as it meant to him—when he went off to his precious mountains and left us to scrape a living among other people's left-overs!" He turned away, frowning, and stared out through the library windows for several moments. Then he seemed to come to a decision of some kind, and turned back toward me.

"Still—what's done is done, as they say. Tell me something, Mater . . . Does he have any other children, this Adam Gaunt?"

"I . . . I don't believe so."

"I'm the only one."

"As far as I know."

"Ah."

"What do you mean, *ah?*"

"Westwood Park must be worth a bit," said Matthew reflectively. And with that he went out into the garden to meditate on this new turn of events.

———

As swiftly as it had banged shut the glass-paned door was wrenched open once more, and a scowling Susan Vinegar peered out.

"You'd better come inside."

Yet she hardly moved from the threshold and I had to push past her into the meager hall, noticing as I did so that the gap in Susan's front teeth was, if anything, worse than before.

She scrambled quickly after me as I strode past the massive, brass-pegged coat-stand and along a carpet runner which disappeared into gloomy infinity.

"Where is she? In the drawing room?" The look on my face and my determined presence in the hall seemed suddenly to have unnerved Susan Vinegar.

"In the drawing room."

"Show me."

Hastily, she scuttled upstairs as I followed at her heels.

Someone had tried to make the house "modern," but had only succeeded in making it even more dismal than before. A blotchy blue paper covered the walls above a cocoa-brown dado; the skirtings were stained to the color of Brown Windsor soup and the doors painted to imitate wood-grain. I thought of the spacious house my mother had built on the outskirts of St. John's, and reflected that if she'd wanted to hide herself away in this busy city, she'd chosen the most perfect concealment. I'd never have thought of looking for her in this house—nor in any of the thousands like it.

At the top of the stairs Susan Vinegar threw open a door and, without bothering to announce me, directed me into the room with an ungracious jerk of her head. I set my shoulders and marched forward into the shadows beyond.

———

The blinds were drawn, muting the sunshine to a twilight dimness, and for a moment I felt as if I'd stumbled into an auction-hall, a musty lumber-room full of other people's unwanted belongings—tottering bamboo tables, lumpen armchairs, Parian fruit-sellers on the chimney-piece. . . . "To let furnished," as I was sure the advertisement must have put it, depressing as a railway waiting-room in midwinter.

The room appeared to be empty. Then a movement near the hearth drew my eyes to a day-bed covered with a huge paisley shawl.

"I expect I've Reuben to thank for this." My mother's voice came sharply to me across the room, querulous and bitter. "Am I right? Did he tell you where to find me? But of course he did. That boy has never learned to hold his tongue."

I'd remembered my mother as a pretty woman, right up to the time I'd been put on a ship for Liverpool and consigned to Aunt Grace's care. She'd still looked handsome on the day she arrived in Liverpool herself to try to prevent my marriage to Adam. The damage must have been done since then.

Now she was powdered, as Matthew had said, but shriveled and witchlike under the rich folds of her dress. Her hair was barely streaked with silver, but already the firm fullness of her body seemed to have shrunk back on the bone as if the juices of life had gone out of her. Only her eyes were alive, watching me cross the room with a look of malignant distaste.

"Lady Oliver and her gardener—and her odd-job man. Where are your policemen, Lady Oliver? Where are your detectives? What's the matter? Am I not to be hauled off to jail, then?"

"It's no more than you deserve! You should be locked up for the rest of your life for what you did."

"But I haven't been arrested. . . . Which means dear Reuben has kept silent about my part in it all. Well, well . . . I *am* surprised."

Somehow, I managed to keep my temper. "The police know nothing about the shooting. Nothing at all."

"Ah! That explains why there wasn't a word in the newspapers!" My mother sounded disappointed. "So Lady Oliver and her powerful friends can even hide a murder when it suits them."

"A murder?" Meanly, I savored the moment. "But there was no murder, Mother. *No murder*—do you hear? Adam is still alive, no thanks to you."

"What? Impossible!" For the first time I saw her disconcerted, her fingers clenching and unclenching in her lap while her great, loose rings rattled an agitated tattoo of their own. "I was sure he must be dead!"

"Fortunately, Reuben only fired once before he ran off. Adam was wounded, but that was all."

My mother turned her head convulsively. "Worse than useless! I *willed* him dead. What more could I do, but hold the gun myself?"

She sat hunched on the day-bed, staring blankly at some vision I couldn't share. I wondered what she saw. . . . Adam lying in his own blood at her feet? Or some hoarded moment of passion from those stolen months at Crow Cove . . .

I had to fight down an impulse to seize her by the shoulders and shake her.

"*Why* did you do it? That's what I can't understand!"

"I had every right to wish him dead! More reason than you know."

"Because you and he were lovers once, until you drove him away? Is that what you mean?"

"Yes—we were lovers!" She flung the words at me defiantly—and for a fleeting second I recognized the woman Adam had desired. "So he's told you at last, has he? For I'm certain you didn't know when he married you."

"I've known for . . . a while."

"Liar! I can see it in your face! He kept it secret from you all this time! Oh, you're a poor, besotted fool, Rachel. See what your precious *love* does for you? It robs you of the little sense you were born with. Anyone else would have guessed that a man like Adam Gaunt—"

"*Be silent!* I don't want to discuss it."

To my surprise my mother stopped speaking at once, staring at me as if something quite new and startling had occurred.

"But there is one thing I must know," I added more quietly. "Something only you can tell me."

She continued to regard me in suspicious silence.

"Reuben was born the year after Adam stayed with us in Crow Cove. Is he really Joseph Dean's son, as you let us all believe, or . . . is he Adam's?"

"If you know so much, you can find that out for yourself."

"Give me an answer! If you slept with Adam, no doubt you had other lovers too. Who was Reuben's father?"

"That's my business. If it upsets you not to know, then so much the better." My mother licked her dry lips. "And now, if you aren't going to hand me over to the police, go away and leave me alone."

I saw her eyes flick to one side, to a small table almost covered by a silver tray on which lay a green glass apothecary's bottle, a glass carafe and tumbler, and a silver spoon.

"What's the matter?"

"Nothing. Nothing at all."

Again, I followed her eyes to the table.

"What's in that bottle?"

"Medicine."

"What kind of medicine?"

"For my headaches."

"Revalenta? Ipecac?"

"Yes. Ipecac. Or Revalenta. I forget."

Once more her eyes slid irresistibly to the bottle on its silver tray. Then all of a sudden she made a lunge toward the table and darted out a hand—but I was quicker. I was amazed how little strength it took to push her withered body away from me, down again on the day-bed, where she sat glaring up at me with hot, angry eyes.

I took the stopper out of the bottle, and sniffed the brownish liquid inside. It had a bitter, pungent smell.

"This is laudanum. Tincture of opium."

The sight of the little flask in my hand seemed to agitate her.

"I told you—it's for my headaches. I was just about to take some when you came."

I sniffed the bottle again. "I keep some laudanum at home. But this is stronger."

My mother waved an impatient hand. "Susan gets it made up for me. I have a recipe of my own. Now let me have the bottle. I feel a headache coming on."

"How long have you been taking laudanum?"

"For years now."

"Every day?"

"Possibly. I forget."

"And how much do you take at a time?"

She avoided my eyes. "Enough. Give me the bottle."

On the point of giving it to her, I thought better of it.

"Not yet."

She fell back sullenly against the paisley shawl, burying her fingers in the weave to stop the loud, insistent rattle of her rings, all the time watching the precious flask of liquid in my hand.

"Now, Mother—are you ready to answer my question?"

"Go to the Devil."

"I'll ask you again. *Who was Reuben's father?*"

"I won't tell you. Give me the bottle!" Involuntarily, her hands flew to her temples, hiding the desperation in her eyes. "Can't you see I'm in pain?"

"Then I'm sorry for you. But I daresay it's no worse than the pain you've given to others over the years." I moved across until I stood next to the tiled hearth, and held out the bottle between finger and thumb. My mother made a reckless attempt to grab it, but I simply held it above her head, tantalizingly out of reach. "Do that again, and I might drop your medicine on the tiles."

"No!"

"In fact, if you don't answer my question, I may do it anyway." I seemed to hear my own voice from a long way off—fierce, implacable, vengeful—and not myself. . . . Surely not myself.

"And if I tell you—you'll let me have it back?"

"Very well."

For a few seconds she hesitated, and I wondered if she meant to defy me to the last. Then she made a tiny, dismissive gesture with her hand, no more than a twist of the fingers.

"You know it all anyway. Yes, Adam Gaunt is Reuben's father. He'd left Newfoundland before I realized I was carrying his child."

It meant nothing, Adam had said, yet between them they'd created a new life. And now my mother's crime seemed doubly dreadful.

"I can hardly believe it: you sent your son to murder his father. . . ."

"Is that so shocking—when *you* ran off with your mother's lover? You've nothing to be proud of, Rachel—and now give me that bottle. You promised."

"And if Adam had killed Reuben before he had a chance to fire? What then?"

She shrugged fleetingly, her eyes fixed on the laudanum. "Then he'd have shot his own son, wouldn't he?"

"My God, you're disgusting! You're beyond hope." Revolted, I gave her the bottle, and watched her tip a few drops from it into the silver spoon. The first spoonful was followed by another, though her hand trembled so much that a tea-colored pool formed on the tray below.

I found a bell and rang it. Instantly, the door banged open and Susan Vinegar appeared, a gray column of malevolence. She was with us so quickly that I wondered if she'd been listening outside in the passage.

I pointed to my mother, slumped again on the day-bed, her head resting on the heel of one hand, the green glass bottle still clasped tightly in the other.

"How long has this been going on, Susan?"

"Never you mind. It's just her medicine."

"Nonsense! It's laudanum. Look at her—she can hardly live without it!"

"She's no worse than hundreds of others. Maybe she does take a bit, now and then—but it does her no harm, that stuff or the rest."

"What *rest?* What else is she taking, for Heaven's sake?"

"I've told you. It's none of your business. You leave her to me. We'll do all right, me and Mrs. Dean."

"*Fetch it!*" I took hold of Susan Vinegar by her narrow, hunched shoulder, and twisted her round to face me. "Whatever else she's been taking—fetch it this minute!"

Susan glanced down at my mother. "Shall I do it, Mrs. Dean dear?"

But my mother remained silent, caught up for the present in a world of her own. Susan Vinegar hesitated, then with another swift glance at her employer opened a drawer in a bureau nearby and produced a small package tightly wrapped in red waxed paper. Inside was a lump of brown gum with a bittersweet smell.

"Turkish opium made up with honey," she said, holding it out. "Tastes better than the lozenges, so Mrs. Dean always says. The druggist mixes it up for me."

"Susan?" On the day-bed, my mother was stirring. "Susan? What have you got there? What are you two whispering about?"

"Nothing, Mrs. Dean. Don't you worry."

"I can't bear all these questions."

"I'm sorry for that, Mother, since I haven't finished what I came here to say to you."

"Throw her out, Susan. Make her go away."

"I can't, Ma'am! She's got men front and back, guarding the house. I daren't stir out of doors for them."

My mother rose unsteadily to her feet, her eyes bright with resentment.

"Do you think you can keep me locked up like a rat in a trap?"

"That's exactly what I intend to do, since it seems to be the only way of stopping your vicious, murderous obsession."

"You can't guard me all the time. I'll find a way out, you'll see."

I shook my head. "It's too late for that now. But if it gives you any satisfaction, you've got what you always wanted—you've made me realize Adam and I have no future together. I trusted him once, but I was wrong, many times over. And there's no love without trust. I've already told him I won't see him again."

"That's easy for you to say! But has he agreed to leave you alone? No—I don't believe it. He's gone through too much for you. . . . He'll never let you go like that." She stared at me for a moment, and then sighed, uncomprehending. "Why *you*, Rachel? That's what I never understood. Why *you*?"

Slowly, I pushed her down again on the day-bed.

"No more of this. All the lies and the hating, and all the hurt you've caused. It stops *now*. Today."

"How can you possibly stop me? You can't keep me here forever!"

"I can—and I will. In my desk at home I have a sworn statement from Reuben, describing exactly how you tricked him into shooting down an innocent man. With that, and the evidence of this stuff—" I held out the red waxed package—"I could have a magistrate sign a committal order tomorrow, and you'd be shut up in an asylum by nightfall."

"Oh, Ma'am!" wailed Susan Vinegar in anguish, "not in one of those places!"

"Behind bars—locked up with the maniacs—yes."

"You wouldn't dare!" My mother gaped at me in disbelief.

"Wouldn't I?"

"By God, you've changed, Rachel . . ."

"You should know. You changed me."

"You never used to be so hard . . ."

"Then you'll know I mean what I say. Instead of an asylum, from now on you'll stay in this house, day in, day out. I'll send people to look after you—but don't be under any illusions—they'll be working for me. You won't leave the house unless I permit it, and then only under guard. Also, you'll sign a paper giving Edward complete control of your money and your property. Everything."

Behind me, I heard Susan Vinegar begin to sob. "Susan can stay with you—though if I ever suspect she's up to some mischief, out she goes instantly, without wages or character, and she can make the best of it on her own."

"This is a life sentence."

"In effect. Though it's better than prison, where you deserve to be. Now listen to me: my doctor will call on you tomorrow, and you'll oblige me by answering any questions he asks. Because you are sick—I can see that now: you've a canker of hate inside you which has eaten up everything else."

She never answered me—lost in despairing thoughts of her own.

"I'll visit you from time to time, to see if there's anything you need."

Her eyes flashed up at that.

"As my jailer, you mean!"

"If you like. Just as you were mine—once."

Susan came with me as far as the hall, and opened the front door to reveal the broad back of Simms, the odd-job man, who turned at once and removed his cap.

"No one out or in, m'lady," he reported. "Not a soul."

"You'll effectively be imprisoned with her, Susan," I pointed out. "You're sure that's what you want?"

"I want to stay with Mrs. Dean," she said at once. "She's all I have, now. You wouldn't really send her to one of those asylum places, would you? A mad-hospital, I mean?"

"If it becomes necessary, yes I will. But you could help to prevent it, Susan, by keeping a close watch on her. I know you're good at that."

Susan hesitated, and then made up her mind.

"Don't you worry, Miss Rachel—if it's for her own sake, I'll see she keeps away from any harm. I will, truly. You can depend on me."

———

Chronic opium poisoning, Dr. Jefferson reported. And there was more. He found signs of mental degeneration due to the effects of the drug. My mother's memory was unreliable; she suffered from tremors of the limbs; she'd been unable to put the tips of her forefingers together when he asked her to, or to walk along a line in the carpet. And the doctor added the words *persecution mania*—though whether that had preceded her opium habit or been caused by it, he was unable to say.

In the days that followed, I arranged for nurses to be in the house at all times, strong, impassive women well used to the care of the wealthy demented who'd otherwise be an embarrassment to their families. The doors were guarded day and night, and my mother was watched at all times—just as she'd once set Theo the fisherman to watch over my father.

Awake, Susan was with her and her nurses were nearby. Even while she slept, a nurse was by her side. And she ate or drank only what had been prescribed for her by Dr. Jefferson. After consulting his colleagues the doctor decided it would be impossible to withdraw the opium completely—and perhaps not even desirable. Laudanum, in controlled amounts, kept her subdued: without it, he couldn't predict what might happen. And so my mother was to continue an opium-eater to the end of her days. Deranged, imprisoned, loveless and an opium-eater.

No criminal court would have spared her: yet in my heart I felt she'd been right—I'd done nothing to be proud of.

32

I'd grown to hate the *Altair,* in spite of my promise to Jonas that I'd do my best to see her afloat. For what was the *Altair* to me? What were any of them to me, for that matter? Adam, Reuben, Matthew, my mother—but especially Adam. Especially Adam.

Perhaps that was one of the things which drew me to the *Altair* as soon as I saw her. Jonas Oliver's wife and Jonas Oliver's ship: we were well matched, when you came to think about it, both of us high and dry and forsaken, promised much but left with nothing.

The White House had become a silent place once the last of the crape was removed from the mirrors and the queue of formal visitors had come to an end. Reuben had gone off to sea again without giving me another chance to speak to him; Matthew had withdrawn even further into a world of his own and in any case would soon be away at school once more. I realized then the extent to which the house had always revolved around Jonas—Jonas arriving from the office or the shipyard, Jonas rushing off again, pausing to snatch a meal, commanding silence while he worked in the library, announcing bedtime, decreeing who was or was not to be invited to dinner. . . .

What was it Aunt Grace had once said to me? *As a daughter or a wife you can do nothing for yourself, but as a widow—oh, there's many a woman in this city would be pleased to have as much control over her own affairs!* And here I was—independent . . . when for years I'd hardly ordered so much as a coal-box for the house without letting Jonas see the bill for it. I felt like a bear let out of his cage after a lifetime of captivity, turning my great head from side to side —sniffing the air—wondering what in the world to make of my new freedom. And a little afraid of what I might find.

But the past was behind me. Whenever I caught myself brooding —mooning over things which might have been—I forced my thoughts sharply back to the present and the future. And it was in the future that I rediscovered the *Altair.*

I'd taken to coming downstairs late in the morning. Alice and Louise had hardly let me out of their sight since Jonas's death, and now came to have breakfast with me each day in my room, Louise chattering about anything which popped into her little head and Alice rushing immediately to my dressing table to try on three necklaces at once.

All of a sudden, the ice was broken. By some strange process the removal of Jonas's disapproving presence seemed to have banished years of restraint, and I found myself close to my daughters at last. Suddenly they were no longer self-possessed young ladies but real children, anxious for the reassurance of their mother's presence, sharing their secrets, letting me into the private world of the nursery and the schoolroom. I'd almost given up hope of such moments, and I was determined not to waste them now.

So it was quite late when I made my way downstairs one morning three or four weeks after the funeral to hear raised voices in the hall. Captain Fuller had obviously just arrived, but he and Matthew had already found something to disagree about.

"I don't think you should bother the Old Lady with any of this," Matthew was saying. "She's hardly well enough yet to make decisions—and in any case, she doesn't know one end of a ship from the other."

I halted, halfway down the stairs.

"Sir Jonas arranged for your mother to act for you until you came of age," rumbled Uncle Tom doggedly. "So no matter what you happen to think, she has to have her say."

"But the Governor didn't mean her to have anything to do with the shipping line! That's ridiculous! How was he to know he'd die before I was twenty-one? You can be sure if he *had* known he'd have left someone else in charge. Anyone but my mother."

"The fact remains, she has to be consulted."

"Consulted about what, Uncle Tom?" I walked down the last few steps to the hall.

"Oh, blow it—" I heard Matthew mutter.

"About the *Altair*, my dear. And what's to become of her. I know it's an awkward time for you, but—well, if you don't give some thought to it now, you may never have another chance."

We went into the library, all three of us. Somehow it seemed the proper place to discuss business. Jonas's lawyer had already told me that under the terms of his will I was to administer his forty percent share of the company until Matthew came of age, but beyond being considerably surprised I hadn't given much thought to what that might entail.

"Sir George Broadney has asked me if I'll manage the day-to-day business of the shipping line," Tom Fuller began formally. "I told him I'd be happy to do it, if that suited you too."

"I think that's an excellent idea. Jonas had absolute faith in your judgment—he often told me so. And I hope you'll go on with Oliver's after Matthew's old enough to take up some of Jonas's duties. Heaven knows, he'll still only be twenty-one. It isn't much of an age for such a responsibility."

"Alexander the Great was only twenty when he led the Greeks against the Barbarians, Mater," Matthew put in. "See the usefulness of a classical education?"

"The fact remains, Matthew—you've at least another year of that education to go before you even start working in the office."

"Another year of school? But that's ridiculous! Do you really want me cramming Latin verbs when I could be learning about the shipping business here in Liverpool? Learning from people like the Captain," he added craftily.

"None of your soft soap, young man. Your stepfather was absolutely set on another year of school for you, and well you know it," Tom Fuller reminded him. "Besides—education's never wasted. I wish I'd had more before I went off to sea."

Matthew's face promised rebellion. He'd retreated even further into his own thoughts since the day of his quarrel with Reuben when he'd discovered "Colonel Allen's" true identity; I knew he blamed me for keeping secret something which so closely concerned him, but at the same time he found it hard to admit Adam to any part of his life. Adam and I—we'd each failed him in our own way, and now he'd retreated into that cold mistrust of the world at large which armored him against further pain. It irked him to be sent back to school, and for a moment I thought he was going to break his word to me and blurt out some rude retort about seeing what his *real* father had to say. But he didn't.

"If you send me back to school, I'll run away," he promised instead.

"You will not—" I started to say; and then I remembered that if he was anything like Adam, he probably would.

"We'll go into all that later, Matthew. In the meantime, I want to

have a private talk with Captain Fuller. I'm sure you can find something to do elsewhere."

"*More* secrets?" demanded Matthew, giving me a defiant look.
"Well, as it happens, I know exactly what the Captain's come about.
George told me, days ago. George *discussed* it with me, as a matter
of fact."

"*Sir* George, Matthew. And he had no business discussing anything with you before speaking to me."

"Ah, but he knows we see eye-to-eye on the Governor's steamship," retorted Matthew. "I may only be fifteen, but George Broadney says I've a good head on my shoulders, and I've learned plenty
about the business already. Enough to know it's time to throw up
the sponge on the *Altair,* at any rate. If you take my advice, you'll
turn her into cooking-pots as soon as you can."

"OUT!" roared Tom Fuller suddenly, in a voice which had cast
fear into mutinous seamen from the Mersey to Shanghai. "And don't
let me hear you speak to your mother like that again!"

Amazingly, Matthew went.

"Is he right, Uncle Tom? Is George Broadney trying to cancel the
Altair again?"

"Both the Broadneys, I'm afraid. Him and her. They've already
talked it over with the Earl of Chorleigh and Ellen Oliver, and they
seem pretty sure of themselves. If Jonas had still been here, he
could've held them off, but now . . ."

"Do my wishes make any difference?"

"Well, of course they do. Until Matthew's twenty-one, you control forty percent of the company. They're obliged to take notice
of what you want. Or they have to listen, at least." The Captain
thoughtfully unrolled a sheet of engine-plans which lay on the
table. "The point is—have you any notion of what it is you *do*
want?"

"I promised Jonas before he died that I'd see the *Altair* launched
and in service."

Tom Fuller gave a low whistle. "That was a brave promise. You
may have a hard time keeping it."

"I didn't think of that. I just wanted Jonas to die believing it would
all happen as he wanted."

"I reckon you did the right thing, my dear. But do you still feel
bound by that promise?"

"I don't know. It's so hard. I've Matthew's future to think about, and I sometimes wonder—when I hear people talk—whether Jonas was really right about the *Altair*."

The Captain let the plans curl up into their roll, and leaned back reflectively in his chair.

"I won't pretend I haven't asked myself the same question often enough in the past. But remember—even though I'm no lover of steam-engines, I can still see that steam's the way ahead for all of us, more's the pity. Passengers will always choose steam now if they can afford it, and our cargo ships, too, will be steamers one day. Though the *Altair*'s no ordinary steamship. Nearly everything about her is new and untried, from these engines—"he tapped the tightly rolled plan "—down to the size and shape of her hull."

"Still—I've found in the past that Jonas Oliver generally knew what he was about. I reckon if Jonas thought the *Altair* was worth all the money and effort he put into her, then he'll probably be proved right. But that's only a hunch, mind, I'm no expert on steam-ships."

"So you do think the *Altair* should go ahead . . . Is that why you came here this morning? To tell me to fight for Jonas's ship?"

"No, my dear, I came because I don't see why anyone should tell you what to do—not young Matthew, not George Broadney, nor me either. I'm an old man now, and it won't make much difference to me whether *Altair*'s launched or not. But the Broadneys are quite sure they'll get their own way now Jonas isn't here to stick up for his ship—and I just wanted you to have a chance to say your piece before it's too late."

"But I don't know the first thing about steamships, Uncle Tom!"

"If you don't know more than that fat baronet, then I'm a Dutchman! What else has Jonas been talking about for the past eighteen months, if not steam-engines?"

"That's true, I suppose."

"Well, then. Some of it's bound to have rubbed off on you. And anything else you want to know, the men at the yard will tell you. Go over there. Talk to the shipwrights. Talk to the carpenters and the riveters. Look at the ship. And when you've finished that, I'll tell you what I know about the North Atlantic trade."

"I doubt if I'll understand much of what I hear."

"Of course you will. And Jonas thought as much, or he wouldn't have left you in control of that stock, whatever young Matthew says. There's nothing magic about steam-engines. They're great, oily, noisy machines—but they aren't magic. *Sail* now—that's magic. It'd take you a lifetime to learn about sail . . . But not steam-engines."

I had to laugh at that. "You're a die-hard sailing-ship man, Uncle Tom!"

"I'm an old shell-back, my dear, and I'm too old to change now. That's why the company needs someone like Matthew to run it in the future. Shipping's going to change faster than you can blink in the next twenty or thirty years, and that makes it a young man's game. Matthew'll never shilly-shally or want for a decision, you can be sure of that. He mayn't always be right—but then, another year or two will do a great deal for his judgment. He'll be good for Oliver's, I reckon, and I'll do my best to keep things going until then." Tom Fuller stared at the tabletop for a moment, and then glanced up at me. "But this *Altair* business is something you must decide for yourself. D'you hear me? Go and see her, and decide whether she should live or die. If you let the Broadneys make up your mind for you, you'll regret it."

———

It was like visiting my husband's mistress and unexpectedly finding her a beauty.

I hadn't been near the shipyard for months—perversely, the more time Jonas spent there, the less I wanted to view the ship which was absorbing so much of his life. Besides, I remembered her as an ugly, shapeless trough, a hulk composed of jagged rows of iron plates and spidery ribs which seemed to bear no resemblance at all to the glorious vessel Jonas had described so often.

Now, to my surprise, I saw a gigantic ship standing on the slipway, amazingly complete to my inexperienced eye.

"But she has a flat bottom!" I exclaimed to the yard foreman. "Where's her keel?"

"She doesn't need a great keel on her, m'lady. Not this ship. You'll find she'll go to wind'ard like a collier and carry fifteen hundred tons of cargo as she goes, easy as you like." The foreman stopped, embarrassed by his enthusiasm.

"Please go on, Mr. Wesley. I mean to learn all I can about the *Altair*."

"About the *Altair*, m'lady?"

"Most certainly. That's why I've come here today."

"Oh." The foreman scratched his head. "Well then—I suppose you'd best start with her hull." He leaned over to slap the ship's side with paternal affection. "Y'see, the thing about iron is that you can build an iron hull far stronger than a wooden ship, but with considerably more space inside. These plates at the side here are no thicker than your finger, but they're as strong as six inches of wood. To save weight, those ones higher up are thinner, and the ones down on her bottom—beg pardon, Lady Oliver—are the thickest. To make her even stronger, she has a kind of second hull inside, and we've double-ribbed her round the engines, as you'll see when you go aboard."

"I think I understand all that. Go on, please."

"Well, there's six transverse bulkheads in her—walls, you might say, running from side to side—so she's like a row of herring-boxes, each one watertight and cut off from the next. Very safe, you see." He looked anxiously at me, wondering if his lecture was being wasted. "And where the propeller-shaft passes through the hull there's a collar of *lignum vitae*. Now *lignum vitae*, m'lady, is—"

"—the wood of the Guiacum tree. Now, I do know all about *lignum vitae*, Mr. Wesley. Can we go aboard, do you think?"

It was amazing to discover how much I did know. Little by little, Jonas's reports on the progress of the *Altair* must have seeped into my subconscious mind until I almost felt I was on familiar territory. There in the belly of the ship were the huge boilers he'd described to me, and the two cylinders for each engine—one high pressure, one low—and the system of gear-wheels which transmitted the drive to the propeller-shaft. It was all surprisingly logical when I could see it there in front of me, waiting to throw its thundering power behind this monster of the sea.

"You're building her with the engines in? Is that normal? I thought they were usually put in after the launch."

"Often, m'lady, it's true. But then, no one's built a ship quite like this before. Sir Jonas decided to do it this way to save as much time as possible. Since there'd been delays, you understand. Sometimes I think if he could've steamed her off the blessed slipway he'd have done it! That is—" The foreman stopped again, abashed.

"Oh, I'm sure you're right, Mr. Wesley. If there had been a way of building her with wings, my husband would have found it."

Convinced at last that I meant what I said, Mr. Wesley made his tour thorough. By the time I'd taken in the full wonder of the *Altair*'s engines and inspected her coal-boxes and the vast, empty space which would one day be filled by cabins and saloons, I couldn't believe the ship had anything more in store for me. And yet when I emerged into full daylight on the mesh of narrow catwalks and transverse iron beams which would support her broad foredeck, the sheer size of the ship amazed me once more. *Altair* was a giantess—more than twice as long as the old *Rachel Oliver,* towering as high as my own house over her slipway, as broad . . . oh, I can't even remember how broad they told me she was, except that I found myself strolling —strolling—from one side to the other as if I were on a country walk.

Her lower masts were already in place, enormous stumps made of the interlocking timbers of a host of trees. I'd already seen one of her anchors and some chain lying in the yard, built to the same massive, titanic scale. It seemed impossible that this army of ants crawling over her could have given birth to such a leviathan—impossible that she'd been created solely to transport more of these willful, ambitious ants across an ocean.

I stood on that half-built foredeck, the salt breeze whipping my skirts, and tried to replace the drab sheds and roaring furnaces of the shipyard with the gray-green expanse of the sea. She'd walk upon the water, this ship, taking the waves in her giant stride. She'd never have to claw across the ocean for every mile as the sailing ships did: *Altair* would set her face toward New York, and go there as she pleased.

Jonas had been right. He'd shrunk the world. He'd built a ship for the United States of America—colossal, proud and self-assured. Already I could almost feel the great heartbeat of her engines beneath the desert of scrubbed teak which would soon cover her naked iron deck-beams. *Altair* was no longer a half-built figment of one man's imagination. She existed; it was beyond anyone's power to recall her. If Jonas Oliver hadn't built her she'd surely have sprung into being without his help. All that remained was to let her prove herself in the element for which she'd been created.

———

"What you're asking, in fact, Lady Oliver, is *who controls the remaining fifteen percent* . . . Is that correct?" Walter Lightbody eyed me over the top of his gold-rimmed spectacles, and rustled the sheaf of papers on the desk in front of him. "It isn't an easy question to answer, I'm afraid."

Messrs. Lightbody & Moore had been the Oliver lawyers for as long as anyone could remember. Walter Lightbody, the present senior partner, had been a contemporary of Jonas's elder brother John, just as his father had been a friend of Captain Oliver's, and I knew that after Jonas, Walter Lightbody probably knew more than anyone about the history of J. G. Oliver & Co.

"You'll understand, Mr. Lightbody, that I'm anxious to find out exactly where I stand before this meeting takes place."

"Of course. And you're perfectly entitled to the information, I assure you. I take it you know how the Oliver's stock is divided up at present?"

"I think so. I hold forty percent during Matthew's minority, the Broadneys have twenty, the earl of Chorleigh has fifteen, and Ellen Oliver another ten. Is that correct?"

"It is." Walter Lightbody glanced down again at the paper in his hand. "That accounts for eighty-five percent of the stock. Most of it is in family hands, as you say, which means that the ownership of the other fifteen only becomes important if the major shareholders disagree." He looked up at me cautiously. "Do you foresee a possible disagreement, Lady Oliver?"

"Mr. Lightbody, my husband trusted you implicitly, I know."

"I'm proud to say that he did."

"Then for his sake, I'm asking you to help me now. You may already know that Sir George Broadney is determined to cancel the building of the *Altair* as soon as possible, and I've heard he's managed to persuade Lord Chorleigh and Ellen Oliver to support him. That gives him a total of forty-five percent of company stock. But, you see, I don't believe that *Altair* should be abandoned—not just out of loyalty to my husband, but because I've examined the financial position, I've looked at the ship, and I've talked to the builders." I saw the lawyer's eyebrows lift a fraction higher. "I believe that for very little further expense we'll gain a profitable asset."

"I see. You've taken a great deal of trouble over this, Lady Oliver."

"Yes, I have—and I'm convinced that the long-term good of the company lies with the *Altair*. Unfortunately I only control forty percent of the stock, and George Broadney could still force a vote in order to get his way. That's why I have to know who owns the last fifteen percent."

Walter Lightbody nodded sagely, then removed his spectacles and held them carefully in his fingertips, the lenses suspended a hair's-breadth above his paper-strewn desk. For a moment or two he swung them there, intent on maintaining the same precise distance at each swing.

"To be honest, Lady Oliver, it's a slightly . . . odd . . . situation." He pursed his lips for a second. "In fact, it's a situation I find distinctly embarrassing, since I'm partly responsible for its coming about. Though there was actually no problem until quite recently, when the situation which *emerged* proved to be at variance with the situation which we had postulated—"

"Which situation, Mr. Lightbody?"

"Ah. Have I lost you already, Lady Oliver?"

"Completely, Mr. Lightbody."

"Then how can I explain it? Well, now—as I'm sure you know, an old established company like Oliver's—a private company where most of the shares are in family hands—chooses its stockholders with great care. Lord Chorleigh, for instance. The Earl was the first person outside the family to be entrusted with Oliver stock. Then, when Sir Jonas felt that his brother's widow ought to sell more of her own holding, we looked round for another possible stockholder who would have Oliver's interests at heart. That is why we chose Arthur Parrish."

"I'm sure I've heard my husband mention the name."

"Arthur Parrish & Company. It's a well-known Liverpool concern. The firm was built up on small steamers in the coasting trade and tugboats here in the Mersey. Arthur Parrish—the *first* Arthur—worked for old Captain John for many years before he started up on his own account, and Oliver's have been one of Parrish's major customers ever since—towage and lightering and so on. So when it came to disposing of more of Mrs. Oliver's shares, Sir Jonas—and I myself—thought they'd be in good hands with Arthur Parrish—linking the companies together, you see. And, of course, Parrish was a steam man through and through. The *Atlas*—do you know the boat? She's the most powerful tug in the river, and one of the biggest in the country. Arthur Parrish launched her just before he died."

"Arthur Parrish is dead?" My dreams of a possible ally vanished into thin air.

"He died last year. Heart failure, it was. Very sudden. Very sad, believe me. A straighter man never shook hands on a bargain."

"Then who owns Parrish's now?"

"Well may you ask! Until a couple of months ago, I'd have said *young* Arthur Parrish owned it—or what was left of it after the bailiffs had had their way. His poor father would have died of shame to see what young Arthur had done to the business in a few months. It went to his head, you see, and he fell in with a very racy crowd. Spending money he didn't have—and he started off with a fair amount, I can tell you." Walter Lightbody tut-tutted at the young man's profligacy. "Soon everything was mortgages and debts and writs nailed to masts . . . The duns never away from the door and the bank calling in its loans. It was quite disgraceful."

"And what happened?" I was impatient to hear the end of the tale.

"Someone bought up all Parrish's debts. Or most of them, at any rate, and persuaded the bank to extend credit again. There's a manager running the company now—a man called Jackson, who seems thoroughly competent. Arthur Parrish is still nominally a director, but he isn't allowed to make any decisions these days. He's only a name on the brass plate. Whoever paid off the debts is the real owner."

"But why should the Oliver stock be caught up in all this?"

"Ah—indeed. In normal circumstances young Parrish would have inherited it from his father, and there wouldn't have been a problem. There's provision, you see, for Oliver stock to be passed from one generation to the next by inheritance though it can't be sold in the usual way. Unfortunately, the original financial arrangement with Parrish's father made the Oliver shares temporarily a *company* asset instead of a *personal* one—there was some difficulty in finding enough capital at short notice. But the arrangement was only ever supposed to be for a short while, except that old Parrish died before things could be put on a proper footing.

"Then who on earth owns the stock now?"

"Whoever owns Arthur Parrish & Company. And before you ask, I've no idea who that might be. Everything is done through lawyers and nominees. It's most unsatisfactory from the Oliver point of view, there's no doubt about that. Just before he died, Sir Jonas asked me to look into the matter—but I'm afraid I still have no answer for you."

"Then what can I do? That fifteen percent is my only chance of saving the *Altair*."

"And the meeting is in a week's time. Dear me, Lady Oliver—I doubt if we can solve the mystery in a week." Walter Lightbody blinked at me sympathetically. Without his spectacles, he looked strangely owlish and helpless.

"But I must do something!"

"You could write a letter. That would be better than nothing. Write, and I'll forward it to the lawyers who act for the owners of Parrish's. I presume they'll pass it on, together with the notice of the meeting."

"You only *presume* it?"

"What else can I do, dear lady? In the absence of fact, *presumption* is surely all we have left."

———

I didn't share Walter Lightbody's confidence. Six days passed, and though I kept in daily touch with him, there was no answer to my letter. At least, I thought, if the mysterious stockholder came in person to the meeting, I'd still have a chance to put my case. Then it occurred to me that it might well have been George Broadney, with his boundless wealth, who'd rescued Parrish's, acquiring useful Oliver stock as he did so. If that was the case, then the *Altair* was lost—and I was sure this was indeed what had happened when in the end only George Broadney, the earl of Chorleigh, Walter Lightbody and I gathered for the meeting in the big room with the Persian carpet which had been Jonas's personal sanctum.

Everything had been prepared. Jonas's massive mahogany desk had been pushed back into a corner and a round table set up in the middle of the floor with a chair for each of us. There was paper for making notes, pens and an inkstand, the afternoon sun had been shut out beyond half-drawn blinds, and at the lawyer's elbow sat Sam Coker, ready to write down every word that was said.

As we took our seats round the table I realized that my letter— putting every argument I could think of in support of the *Altair*— must have been a complete waste of time. If George Broadney was really the owner of the last vital fifteen percent, all I could do now was to try to persuade Lord Chorleigh that George was wrong, and Jonas's beloved steamship deserved a chance after all.

But George was determined not to give me the opportunity. As soon as Walter Lightbody opened the meeting and briefly summarized the matter under discussion, he went into the attack.

"I'm sorry you felt you had to be here, Rachel. It must be painful for you to sit in this room again and hear Jonas's affairs bandied about in such a manner. Verity had the good sense to stay away."

"But then, George, you look after Verity's interests so well," I said sweetly, "whereas I have Matthew's future to consider."

"I'm sure you can trust me to look out for Matthew as well." George stared at me defiantly across the table. "This meeting's no more than a formality, in any case. We all know what has to be done."

"About the *Altair,* do you mean, George? I was under the impression we'd come to *discuss* the matter . . . or am I mistaken?"

"It's rather late in the day for discussions, Rachel. I know you're sentimentally attached to the steamship—as you're bound to be, after the time Jonas spent on it. But that's exactly the reason I hoped you wouldn't come to this meeting. It's high time we all put our loyalty to Jonas on one side, and looked at the *Altair* from a sensible point of view. A company like Oliver's doesn't make money by building experimental ships, no matter how much Jonas wanted to try out his clever ideas. I'm sorry if I'm being blunt, Rachel—" George had seen the Earl of Chorleigh lift a hand in protest, "—but those are the facts. For once, Jonas's fancy notions ran away with his common sense. Verity agrees with me—and Ellen, too. They've trusted Lord Chorleigh and myself to do the right thing—to scrap the *Altair* and sell her off for what we can get. Then we can put the company back on a sound financial footing."

"But the *Altair* will do that once she's in service. Jonas was certain of it."

"What George is saying, my dear—" the Earl leaned forward and patted my hand comfortingly—"is that much as we admired and esteemed Jonas—and he was a fine man, we all agree on that—this steamship of his was far too risky a project for Oliver's to begin on their own. Oh, I know I was all for it at first. But believe me—now that George has shown me the plans and estimates—"

"I've examined them all for myself, Lord Chorleigh." Out of the corner of my eye I saw Walter Lightbody smile behind his hand. "And I've made a detailed survey of the ship as she stands, and talked to the people at the yard. If we get more shipwrights to work on her, *Altair* could be launched in six weeks' time. Her engines are already installed. Even fitting-out shouldn't take long."

"And when did you acquire all this expert knowledge, may I ask?" George butted in.

"Since Jonas left me to administer Matthew's inheritance. I made it my business to find out all I could about the *Altair* and her prospects."

"And what conclusions did you come to after burning all this midnight oil?" George could barely keep the sneer out of his voice.

"I believe Jonas was right. The *Altair* will beat any ship afloat, for speed, for comfort—and for profit."

"I've never heard such balderdash! If *that's* all your investigations have proved, then you've obviously wasted your time. You should have stayed at home with your sewing and your tea-parties and let those of us with some grasp of business decide what's best for the company. Even young Matthew would have talked more sense, dammit!"

"Come now, Broadney!" Lord Chorleigh protested. "Remember where you are!"

"Well, it's nothing but the truth," George Broadney muttered sullenly. "You and I have made up our minds what needs to be done, Ellen's agreed to abide by anything I say, and all we're doing here is wasting our time listening to the same old argument over again." He broke off at the sound of a knock at the door. Sam Coker rose to his feet and tiptoed across to open it, returning with a folded and sealed piece of paper in his hand.

"What the devil is it, Coker? I thought you'd told the people in the office we weren't to be disturbed."

"Mr. Lightbody's clerk, Sir George. With a note for Lady Oliver." Sam Coker sidled over to my chair, ceremoniously handed me the paper, and then tiptoed back at once to his own place at the other side of the table.

"As I was saying before we were interrupted," George continued irritably, "I can't see that this meeting is any more than a formality. It was only called to put the decision of the majority of stockholders properly in the minutes and to instruct Captain Fuller to carry out our wishes with regard to the *Altair*—namely, to sell her off as she stands or break her up. Now, I realize this is rather out of the usual run of the Captain's responsibilities, so I'd be prepared to take charge of the disposal of the steamship, with an undertaking to get as much for her hull and her engines as I can. As it happens, I've already been approached by . . . a third party . . . and there may be others interested too. Do I take it that everyone's happy to leave the arrangements to me?"

"I don't agree to that."

"No, Rachel, I didn't think you would. But we've already heard your point of view, so I think it's time you gave up gracefully."

"I believe we're entitled to vote on it, George."

"I beg your pardon?" The baronet, who'd turned to speak to Walter Lightbody, swung round to stare at me. "*Vote?* Why the Devil should we need to vote on this?"

"You're speaking to a lady, Broadney," the Earl reminded him sharply. "And as I remember the articles of the company, anyone's entitled to call a vote at any time."

"That's true, certainly," agreed Walter Lightbody, his eyes glinting behind his gold spectacles. "It's in the articles."

"But for goodness' sake, Rachel, there's no point in voting! You know perfectly well Lord Chorleigh has fifteen percent and I have twenty, plus Ellen's ten. That's forty-five percent against your forty. And when I spoke to Arthur Parrish a few days ago, he assured me the Parrish shares would vote with me too if it came to an argument. We all know you wanted to do your best for Jonas—and so you have—but now it's time to go home and forget about the *Altair*."

"I don't think so, George." I laid the paper which Coker had given me flat on the table, smoothed out its folds, and slid it across to him. "That letter gives me authority to vote the Parrish stock as I see fit. Mr. Lightbody will explain to you why Arthur Parrish isn't in control of his company anymore—or of the Oliver stock his father bought. The new owner seems to agree with me that the *Altair* should be given her chance."

"Let me see that!" George Broadney scanned it furiously, and then passed it to the Earl.

"Chester, Chester & Brooks," Lord Chorleigh read aloud. "Perfectly respectable firm of lawyers. Old Mrs. Chester was a Mackintosh," he added as if that settled the matter. "I thought you'd sorted all this out with young Parrish, Broadney?"

"So I had. At least, I thought I had. What I want to know is—if Parrish doesn't have the final say on his Oliver stock, then *who has?* These lawyer fellows?"

"They're only nominees. They only act for the real owner," Walter Lightbody explained quickly.

"Then who *is* the owner?"

"I've no idea," the lawyer admitted. "Not yet, at any rate."

"Do you mean to tell me that some—perfect *stranger* owns fifteen percent of our company, and you can't tell me who he is?"

"That seems to sum up the situation, Sir George."

George Broadney made a sound like a distant explosion.

"Then perhaps Lady Oliver can tell us who's been meddling in Oliver business at her invitation."

"I've no more idea than you, George. I tried to find out, but it was impossible. In the end, I wrote to the lawyers, enclosing plans of the *Altair* and explaining why I thought she ought to be completed. This letter is the result."

The Earl of Chorleigh had been drumming his fingers on the table.

"Well, d'you know, Broadney, I can't say I'm too upset by this turn of events. It did rather seem like stabbing Jonas in the back, after all his hard work . . . ah . . . if you see what I mean. Lady Oliver's right. Jonas had tremendous faith in this blessed steamship of his. Maybe it's time we had some faith in it too. Faith, Broadney—that's what we need." He stroked his whiskers thoughtfully. "And besides, it was going to be deuced hard explaining to Prince Albert why we'd killed the thing off. He keeps asking how the building work's coming along. I daresay we can ask him to launch it now, hey?"

"To blazes with—" I heard George begin, before thinking better of it and lapsing into resentful silence.

———

I'd started well—I had to admit that. In one giant leap I'd graduated from overseeing the weekly kitchen accounts to forcing a decision which George Broadney claimed could bankrupt a shipping line. Little Rachel Oliver—or Rachel Dean, or Rachel Gaunt, or whatever I'd been in my various incarnations . . . but *Rachel,* certainly. *Me.* I alone had saved the *Altair*.

Or not quite alone, as I was destined to discover.

I'd begun to spend more time in the Oliver offices in Water Street. It was still the cheerful, bustling place I remembered from my days with the Benevolent Fund, and now there was the added excitement of planning the fitting-out of the *Altair* which would begin immediately after her launch.

That was where Walter Lightbody found me one morning when he arrived, bursting with achievement.

"Excellent, Lady Oliver! Just the person I was hoping to see—and here you are, in the office. Good morning, Captain Fuller. Good morning, Coker. I have the most remarkable news for you!"

"I'm delighted to hear it, Mr. Lightbody. I'm always ready for good news."

"Well, here it is! I've solved our great mystery! I've discovered at last who owns Arthur Parrish & Company—and of course, fifteen percent of our Oliver stock as well." He cleared his throat in preparation for the announcement. "It's a man called Allen—a Colonel Allen—who I believe is a neighbor of yours, Lady Oliver. How strange that you never knew!"

"Whoever he is, he certainly did you proud over that *Altair* business," remarked Tom Fuller. "Without his say-so she'd never have left the shipyard."

Sam Coker had been scratching busily on a sheet of paper.

"Now that we know who the gentleman is, I'd better send him an official invitation to the launch."

"No," I said at once. "Don't invite him. Leave him off the list." And as they all turned to stare at me: "I don't want that man anywhere near my ship."

33

I'd gone to the forest which began at the top of the slope behind our house at Crow Cove. From a distance the trees formed a dark, impenetrable wall, but at the end of the shrubby track which passed our gate was a narrow, wedge-shaped gap in the dense vegetation marking the start of the woodland—my secret doorway to the forest.

The tops of the trees, some of them forty feet above my head, caught the sun like a thick green thatch of branches, but nearer the ground where the beaten path died out the shadows were bluer and colder. From this point, however, I'd established my own markers, and I pressed on into the ranks of trees until they began to thin a little round my special, private glade where the ferny carpet was dappled a livid yellow-green by filtered light from above, and the air was gorged with the scent of pine-needles.

All at once I knew I wasn't alone. Someone was nearby, keeping a parallel course to my own through the trees. I stopped and listened, straining every sense for a sign of the stranger's presence: but there was nothing—not the brush of a leaf or the faintest snap of a twig underfoot. A pigeon whirred over my head, shattering the silence and making the stillness which followed even more profound than before.

Nervously I inspected the indigo shadows surrounding the glade on all sides. Here and there a branch fanned gently in a little sigh of wind or a bird scuffled through the leaf-litter, but there was nothing at all to suggest another human presence.

I pushed on, disconcerted, tackling the undergrowth where the patches of sunlight were strongest. Now I was reluctant to strike out into the blue-green gloom beyond, feeling safer in the bright shallows than in the depths of that leafy ocean.

Once more I halted suddenly, thinking that at last I'd heard an alien sound: but again utter silence closed round me as I waited. Yet someone was definitely there. It wasn't the silence of a void, but an inhabited stillness containing a living, breathing, *watching* human being. How could anyone move so quietly through the forest? However carefully I laid down each foot, wrapping my skirts about me, an explosion of sound seemed to accompany every step I took.

And all the time I could feel eyes upon me, noting every tiny movement I made. I didn't dare to stop again, and before I realized it, I'd pressed further into the forest than I'd ever gone before, no longer confident of finding my way back.

Bursting through a thick screen of bushes blocking my path I found myself on the bank of a stream which gushed into sight between two gloomy, lichenous boulders. The water sped busily past, dimpling over its stony bed as if it were in no doubt of its way home and had urgent reasons for getting there, though I didn't recognize the stream or the boulders which flanked it—or even some of the close-knit bushes enclosing me on all sides.

Summoning all my self-control, I tried to make a sensible effort to save myself. There were two possibilities—to follow the stream until it left the forest, however far that might be, or to turn my back on the water and walk out of the trees again the way I'd come. I chose the second course and set off once more with determination, the trickling noise of the stream dwindling behind me as I went.

After only a few minutes the noise had disappeared entirely and I was no longer sure of my direction. Somewhere in the leafy shadow which surrounded me I knew, with a certainty which lifted the hair at the nape of my neck, that someone was keeping pace with me, following with the tireless step of the hunter.

Panic squeezed my throat like strangling fingers, and I plunged blindly into the nearest clump of bushes, heedless of direction. My hands flew up to protect my face as I pushed into the closely woven thicket, horror numbing my mind and draining the strength from my legs. Long, curved thorns clawed at my arms, leaving trails of blood across my bare skin; unseen branches whipped and slashed, catching my ankles and making me fall; I scrambled upright, only to trip once more. The soles of my boots slipped on the wet leaves underfoot, plunging me into a hidden ditch, filling my fingers with fragrant leaf-mold. Somehow I scrabbled wretchedly out of the hole, gasping painfully for breath, and forced myself to go on. But I was done for, almost at breaking point, floundering heedlessly through a universe of spinning green. . . . I made one more blind, despairing lunge through the encircling branches . . . and felt my wrist seized in a powerful grasp, my own impetus turning me, slamming me hard into an unyielding body.

Without that hold on me, I'd certainly have fallen. Each breath was agony, and the forest swirled about me like a blue-green tide, sucking at my skirts and threatening to drown me in its immensity.

"Lady Oliver! Lady Oliver, Madam—"

I opened my eyes to see Vickers bending over me, touching me gently on the shoulder and indicating the little teatray she'd set down on the table beside my bed.

"It's seven o'clock, my lady. You told me to call you at seven, do you remember? So you'd have plenty of time to get ready."

I struggled to sit up, still sleep-laden and disorientated, and Vickers leaned over to plump up the pillows behind me.

"You must have been dreaming, my lady." She stopped plumping and straightened the sheet. "I expect you were still worrying about the launch of the *Altair* when you went to sleep last night. I always say worry's the surest way to a restless night. Shall I open the curtains now!"

"Oh—yes. Thank you, Vickers."

The curtains rattled briskly along their rails, and suddenly the greenish gloom of the bedroom gave way to sunlight, banishing the forest and its ghosts. But my heart still pounded from my desperate flight through the trees, and as Vickers drew my bath in the dressing room next door, I sipped my tea and tried to come to terms with my dream.

I knew who the hidden watcher had been. I'd known from the first, but in the curious way of dreams the knowledge had only been released in the last, waking second when I glimpsed the face of the hunter and knew it was Adam.

"Did you decide on the short gloves or the long, my lady?" Vickers appeared in the dressing-room doorway, one pair of black gloves in either hand. Behind her, I could hear water spurting from Jonas's patent tap into the metal tub.

"Long gloves, I think." In honor of Prince Albert I'd decided to leave off full mourning for the day and wear instead a dress of flounced black silk, the black bodice discreetly trimmed with jet beading. It was now almost three months since I'd worn a bonnet without widow's crape, and it amazed me how much better I looked in the elegant confection the milliner had made up from French satin and black ribbon, with dainty quilling just inside the brim. All the same, Adam had been right. Black made me look pale.

And when I thought of that, I remembered my terror in the forest. Adam was still at Westwood Park, I knew, his wounds almost completely healed. Matthew, who'd made a point of trying out every horse in his father's stable until he was forcibly returned to school, had kept me informed of Adam's progress but had given me no hint of what his father intended to do next. Perhaps that was what had really hounded me through the dream-forest: uneasiness at having him so near at hand, watching and thinking.

At any rate, I wasn't going to let him spoil that day, of all days. I'd stood by my decision not to have him invited to the launch of the *Altair*—not, as Verity imagined, to keep his disreputable presence as far away from Prince Albert as possible, but because the *Altair* was too precious for me to bear him near her. In the last few weeks I'd begun to feel as if I were waiting there myself, poised on that slipway. When the ship slid out at last into the gray water of the Mersey, part of me would go with her; most people in the watching crowd would see no more than a giant ship—but Adam would guess the truth. I couldn't bear to think of him standing there, sensing my innermost hopes and fears for the *Altair*, profaning my ship through me.

"Your bath's ready now, my lady. I'll tell Wilson to bring up breakfast for yourself and the young ladies in half an hour, shall I? And I'll put your pocket-watch just *there*, where you can see it. We can't have you late for the Prince—that would never do."

———

Thanks to Vickers, I reached the shipyard almost an hour before the Prince was due. Already there was a milling crowd about the gates, marshaled by an army of policemen into leaving a passage for carriages to get through. They peered eagerly into mine as I passed, but all they saw was one small, rather anxious woman and her two excited daughters—not much of a return on their vigilance.

I'd already had an opportunity to speak to the Prince the previous evening. Once again, he was staying with the Earl of Chorleigh at Asterholm, and the Earl and Countess had given a dinner in his honor for those of us most closely involved with the steamship. Late in the evening, after the gentlemen had joined us in the Gold Salon, the Earl drew me aside.

"Something for you to think of, my dear," he murmured, glancing round to see who might be close enough to overhear. Satisfied we'd found a secure corner between a huge gilt console-table and a window-bay, he announced in a low voice, "I've been talking to His Royal Highness. He seems pretty sure we'll soon be drawn into this business with the Tsar—probably to the extent of a war, if Nicholas is as hell-bent on annexing Turkey as he seems. The Sultan's shaking in his shoes as it is. Says the Tsar's definitely got his eye on Constantinople, and won't be bought off. Been there myself," he added, shaking his head. "Can't think what's possessed the man."

"The Prince thinks we'll declare war on Russia?"

"Britain—and probably France, too. The Frogs have never forgotten Moscow, you see. And the Prince reckons it'd be deuced awkward for us if Tsar Nicholas reaches the Mediterranean. Palmerston's all for pitching into the Russians, and apparently even Balmoral's full of Clarendon's people, nagging about a war."

"What would that mean to Oliver's?"

"*Ships,* my dear. That's the point. If we have to send troops out to the Black Sea, they'll need ships to transport them. And the Admiralty will want *steamships* to do it. Now, who has just built the biggest steamship afloat, eh?"

"Not the *Altair!*"

"*Altair!* Exactly! If Oliver's put in for a mail contract for the *Altair,* the government will make it a condition that she serves as a trooper whenever they need her. Bound to!"

"But she isn't even in service yet! She has to be fitted out first."

"Ah, yes—but we aren't at war yet, are we? I reckon the war and the *Altair* ought to be ready at just about the same time."

"But we need her for the North Atlantic run!"

"You can forget the North Atlantic for a while. If she goes trooping she won't see New York until the government releases her, and that'll depend on the length of the war. Still—I suppose Cunard'll lose a few of their ships, too. That ought to make it even."

"No! We haven't built the *Altair* just to see the government run off with her! Maybe she will have to serve as a troopship for a while —but not until she's proved herself across the Atlantic. I mean to show Cunard and Collins and all the others what an Oliver ship can do!"

The Earl's whiskers bristled with approval.

"Good girl," he said. "Just what I thought myself. Better get to it, then, hadn't you?"

But if a war was looming in Eastern Europe, no hint of it dampened the carnival atmosphere in the shipyard next day. Every rooftop and ledge had been taken over by jostling, waving onlookers, exchanging shouts with their friends down below in the yard or barracking the squads of police who were trying to keep order. One of the largest sheds had been scrubbed out, decorated with flags and bunting, and spread with carpets on which the dignitaries could walk. As we waited there for the Prince Consort to arrive I relayed the Earl's warning to Captain Fuller.

"If we can send her for sea-trials by the end of November, she'll go into service the following month. That means her fitting-out must be done at breakneck speed, but there's no help for it. I don't care how many men we have to hire—three hundred or four if need be, working day and night—but she must leave for New York on the 1st of December."

"In service by December of this year, do you mean—_1853?_ We'll never have her ready by then, surely!" The Captain looked at me as if I'd lost my wits. "Oh, I understand why you want to move so fast —but I can't see how it can be done."

"It has to be done. We've no choice in the matter. _Altair_ must cross the Atlantic while she's still the biggest and newest ship in the world. Once she's made a reputation for herself we can take the cream of the North Atlantic trade for ourselves. But if she doesn't go into service for another two or three years because she's been carrying troops and supplies to the Black Sea, she'll just be another large ship—nothing out of the ordinary. It's a question of _prestige,_ Uncle Tom. Isn't that what the shipping business is all about?"

Tom Fuller grinned.

"Jonas taught you more than I thought."

"Oh, I didn't learn that from Jonas. That's just woman's intuition. We've built a wonderful ship, but we have to capitalize on her while she's still a novelty. I want everyone to know that Oliver's _Altair_ is the only way to cross the Atlantic."

"I'm sure you're right. But whether she can be ready as soon as you think is another story."

"Tell the yard to hire as many men as they need. If George Broadney complains, say I authorized it, and he can bring his complaints to me." I looked round the gaily decorated shed. "Where is George, in any case?"

"Out on the platform, keeping watch over his bottle, I should think. It was bad enough having to hand over some of his best champagne to launch your ship, but he'll go clean off his head if anyone drinks it before it's served its purpose."

As the Captain had suggested, I found George and Verity out on the little platform which had been erected close up under the steamship's soaring bow. From that vantage-point the *Altair* seemed to stretch away forever toward the waiting river, poised in her great wooden cradle to slide down the launching-ways whenever word was given to release her. Her rows of plates had long since disappeared behind several coats of dark green paint; a smart white boot-top ran from bow to stern, and above our heads an elaborate iron star, covered in gilding, had been bolted to the point of her bow, swathed for the day's ceremonial in red, white and blue bunting.

"We just wanted to make sure of our seats," Verity told me acidly. "One never knows, these days. We might have found ourselves hidden away in the back row." The expression on her face informed me plainly that if she and George had found themselves anywhere but at the center of events, I'd certainly have been blamed for it.

"You needn't have been concerned, Verity. You and George have seats next to the earl of Chorleigh, as you see. Right in the front row, with Prince Albert."

Verity inclined her head in cold acknowledgment.

If anyone had a right to feel aggrieved, I reflected, it was Adam. In all justice, it was a gross insult to have left him out of the proceedings when he was actually one of the owners of the ship, but even though I knew how unfair I'd been, I didn't regret my decision one bit. *Altair* was mine—mine alone. If it hadn't been for me there wouldn't have been a launching: *Altair* would never have stood there, waiting to be sent to the sea. And *Altair* was the future . . . the colossus . . . the world-shrinker. . . . My head almost swam as I stood there at the edge of the platform. I could have reached out and kissed her rough iron side.

"I suppose all this paraphernalia's going to work," muttered George Broadney sourly, strolling across to where I stood. "I mean, she will go into the water, will she?"

"Well, of course she'll go in! She's so heavy, nothing in the world will stop her once she starts off toward the river. The men spent all yesterday slopping tallow and soft soap on the bilgeways so that she'll slide off smoothly."

"On the *what?*"

"The bilgeways, George. Mr. Wesley told me exactly how the launch is managed. Those pieces of timber—*dog-shores,* they're called—are all that's holding her in position. As soon as the Prince breaks the bottle the wedges underneath will be knocked out, and the *Altair* will go down the slipway into the river. Those great heaps of chain down below us are bolted to the back of the wooden cradle to slow her down."

George had long since lost interest, and had reached out to investigate the bottle of champagne dangling on the end of its cord, ready to smash on the *Altair*'s stem.

"It was good of you to offer us your champagne," I told him sweetly. "I know how highly you prize it."

"While you have a talent for wasting it." George turned the bottle so that the label was uppermost. "That's better. *Bollinger '46.* Don't think I've forgotten what you did with the last bottle—and now you propose to pour this one all over your blessed steamship."

"Not *me,* George . . . Prince Albert. Do you want him to look at the label and pronounce it a bad year? What would he think of us at Oliver's?"

"He'd realize we've spent so much on this damn ship that we can hardly afford to launch her! That's what he'd think—and he'd be right."

With a grunt of disgust, George Broadney turned his back on the *Altair* and stamped off toward his wife, who'd begun to signal by frantic waves and coo-ees that the Prince Consort's carriage had been sighted at the gates.

―――――

Yet in the end it wasn't Prince Albert who launched the *Altair.* Certainly, he made a speech—praising the far-sightedness and enterprise of J. G. Oliver & Co., the skill of the British craftsmen who'd built the giant steamship, and the brilliance of Sir Jonas Oliver, who'd died so tragically before seeing his dream vessel completed. But as the heaving sea of faces below us strained to see what was happening, the Prince turned to me.

"Now you must launch the ship, Lady Oliver," he announced in his punctilious English. "That is what Sir Jonas would have wished, I'm sure."

He took me by the arm and gently led me forward to the edge of the platform.

I knew the words by heart; hadn't I waited for months to hear them spoken? Standing as straight as I could, I spoke the ritual phrases. *I name this ship Altair. . . . May God bless her and all who sail in her.*

At my side, Captain Fuller passed me the bottle.

"Handsomely, now—"

Nothing remained but to hurl that baptism of champagne with all my strength at the *Altair*'s massive iron bow, adding a prayer of my own as I did so. Above the crash of the bottle and the spatter of precious liquor down the *Altair*'s green paint, I heard Mr. Wesley's cry of "Down dog-sh-o-oore!" from somewhere below, the smack of heavy mauls on the wooden wedges . . . and for a few awful seconds, nothing seemed to happen.

Then with dreadful slowness the space between our platform and the steamship's stem began to increase . . . inch by inch, then foot by foot, as the *Altair*'s weight started to bear her down the ways to the river.

A great roar burst from the massed throats of the crowd which had crammed into the yard right up to the edge of the slipway. Heads bobbed and weaved; flags fluttered; small children shouted from their fathers' shoulders; somewhere beside us the band struck up "Rule Britannia"; the very air suddenly seemed to be full of ringing bells, shrieking whistles and a hysterical crescendo of cheering.

It was at that very moment I saw him, down at the edge of the slipway among the waving caps of the shipyard workers. That shining white head was too bright to ignore—the sun seemed to single it out for me on that brilliant late summer morning—and besides, he was staring up at me, his pale face turned away from the rapidly moving ship just as all the others were turned toward it. He was too far off for me to gauge his expression, but he was standing rigidly, his arms at his sides, his entire attention focused in my direction while the huge cradle with its iron burden ground steadily past his shoulder. The *Altair* was gathering speed now, her stern already in the first lapping of the tide, but Frank Ellis seemed to take no notice, too absorbed in his passion of resentment to be aware of what was going on a few feet away.

I'm certain he never even saw the chains—ton upon ton of looped and shackled links which trailed behind the cradle to check its speed. As the *Altair* slid faster, the chains took up the slack and began to tumble in her wake, twisting and writhing among the blocks of the slipway like mighty toys, puffing rusty dust into the air as they roared behind the ship.

As the *Altair* took to the water the crowd pressed forward, craning to see her afloat. I saw Frank Ellis caught unawares by the surge, tottering for a moment on the very edge of the slipway, arms flailing, suddenly realizing his danger. His mouth opened wide as he toppled into the slithering toils of chain—but his scream was lost in the general uproar, just as his white head disappeared in a welter of dust and thrashing foam below the vessel's bow. Enormous baulks of timber bobbed to the surface as the *Altair* floated free, wallowing in the cross-swells set up by her entry into the water. Ropes snaked out from her bow to the waiting tugs. Faces crowded her rail; small boats sculled out perilously close to her side; but there was no sign of a pale face among the black waves in her lee, no trace of shining silver hair among the floating debris of the launch.

"Excellent, Lady Oliver." At my elbow, Prince Albert surveyed the scene with a satisfaction which indicated he'd seen nothing of the accident. "A most handsome vessel. You must send her to the Thames once she's fitted out—I'm certain the Queen would enjoy going aboard her."

With difficulty I dragged my attention back to the ship. She did, indeed, look handsome: no longer an awkward, stranded mass of iron plates and timber supports, she lay majestically in the river, showing off the elegant proportions Jonas had created for her.

"It's an interesting ceremony, with the wine, is it not?" the Prince remarked thoughtfully. "A ceremony of very ancient origin, I believe. Sacrificial in nature. Quite barbaric. There are still many parts of the world, you know, where ships are baptized with blood." Seeing my face, he added at once, "The customs of deluded savages, I assure you, Lady Oliver. Hardly appropriate when we have such a splendid example of civilized achievement before us. Isn't that so, Lord Chorleigh?"

"Eh? Oh, just what I was thinking myself, Sir. Exactly what I was thinking myself."

———

Hardly anyone else seemed to have seen what had happened. All eyes had been concentrated on the *Altair* as she slid into the water, and it was a full fifteen minutes before word filtered up from the yard that a man had been pulled into the river by the drag-chains.

"You were quite right, my dear," Captain Fuller muttered in my ear as we left for the celebratory banquet. "Some poor devil has been killed, sure enough. It's bad luck—but it sometimes happens at these affairs."

"No one must mention it in front of the Prince. That's important."

"Aye, aye, Ma'am. I'll see to it. Perhaps when we get the chains up out of the river again the dead man'll come up with 'em, and we'll find out who he was. Doesn't seem to have been one of the fellows from the yard, at any rate. I couldn't find a soul who recognized him. In fact it all happened so fast I could hardly find anyone who'd seen him go."

They retrieved Frank Ellis's body later that afternoon, and discovered his name from a receipted bill in his coat-pocket.

"No one's come asking for him yet," Captain Fuller reported next day, "and the police don't seem to know him, though I must say, from his clothes I thought he might be an acquaintance of theirs. A bird of passage, I reckon."

"Why should you think that?"

"He'd hands like a lady—no sign of calluses or scars, such as a working man would have—but at the same time he'd a ready-made coat and trousers, which hardly sounds like a gentleman. No ink on his fingers, so he can't have been somebody's clerk—and when did you ever know a shopman not to have a bit of twine, or French chalk or the stub of a crayon in his pocket?"

"I'd no idea you were such a detective, Uncle Tom."

"When you've been master of a ship for a bit, you get an eye for the odd queer cove, believe me. And that was one of 'em."

"Did he. . . . Did he have anything in his pockets at all?"

"A cheap watch. A handkerchief. About a guinea in small change. A pen-knife, too, as I remember, and a couple of scraps of paper with writing on 'em, though the water had made the ink run so's you couldn't read anything. Oh, and a wad of newspaper—turned to pulp by the seawater. Nothing to give any clue as to who he might be, beyond that receipt with the name *Ellis*."

I let out my breath in a long sigh of relief.

"If no one claims the body, Oliver's will pay for the funeral, Uncle Tom."

"There's no need for that, surely. The parish will bury him, if no one else does."

"I'd like it done properly, all the same. Since it happened at the launch of our ship."

"As you please." The Captain made a note on a piece of paper. "You know they've started fitting-out work on the *Altair,* I suppose?"

"I'm delighted to hear it. I might even go and take a look at her this afternoon. Just to see how she's shaping."

"I don't imagine there'll be much to see yet. They've only just started, after all."

"Still. . . . It would set my mind at rest. As long as I know she's a little nearer being finished."

"Oh, Rachel—" Tom Fuller smiled, and shook his head. "I can see you're going to be worse than Jonas ever was over this blasted steamship."

––––––––

I daresay he was right. But I'd set my heart on seeing the *Altair* off for New York on the first day of December, and I was determined that nothing would stop her being ready for her sea-trials a fortnight before that. In fact, I was so certain she'd not only be ready but would pass those trials with flying colors, that Oliver's began to advertise her maiden voyage with all the fanfare and high-flown description Tom Fuller and I could invent.

None of it, in all honesty, was an exaggeration. As our vast army of carpenters, cabinet-makers, shipwrights, riggers, sailmakers, glaziers, instrument-makers and the rest swarmed over the *Altair,* her echoing hull—empty but for the shining engines which crouched in her belly—was gradually transformed into a thing of genuine wonder. Jonas had designed her with a spar-deck above the deck saloon in her stern, which not only provided passengers with a covered promenade area in poor weather, but also gave the helmsman a safer, raised position from which to steer. Below this in the stern of the ship were the first-class cabins, the music room and the smoking room, and forward of that the second-class saloon and cabins. On the deck below were more cabins, the first- and second-class dining saloons and the steerage accommodation, and below this again, any space not occupied by coal-boxes or engines was turned over to cargo. Right in the bow was a fo'c'sle for the crew, while the quarters of the officers, the stewards, the baker and the cooks were generally amidships on the first two decks.

None of this was particularly revolutionary. What marked out the *Altair* from the common run of shipping was the sheer spaciousness of her accommodation, the height between the decks and the easy comfort of her cabins. Huge glass domes had been let into the upper deck to light the areas below, each one decorated with colored panes and protected by a wire grille from the fury of the sea. The saloons were paneled in glowing New World woods and decorated with historic scenes of exploration. Every door-handle was shining brass, as were the lamps in their gimbals, the curtain-rails and rings for each bed, the companionway-rails, and even the coat-pegs and the racks which would hold the plates and glasses in the dining saloons; and throughout the ship everything which wasn't brass was either of polished mahogany, Italian marble, or the finest porcelain, from the marble-topped tables in the smoking room to the chamberpots in each cabin with the *J. G. O.* monogram printed on the side.

I'd long since lost count of the amount of leather the upholsterers had used, or the bales of chintz and velvet plush. To save time, everything which could possibly be assembled ashore was brought aboard ready-made. Carpet-layers were due to move into the first-class saloon as soon as *Altair* returned from her sea-trials, and huge stocks of blankets and bed-linen, dinner-plates, cutlery, glasses, copper kettles and cooking-pots were already waiting in a dockside warehouse.

By dint of superhuman effort, the *Altair* left on time for her trials in the Irish Sea. Captain Graham of the *Zetland* had been given charge of her and a hand-picked team of officers and engineers culled from the other Oliver steamers. Although it was November the weather was calm, and I saw her off from a tug at the bar of the river with a light heart. She looked every inch a star of the sea—regal and imperturbable, the Eighth Wonder of the World. I looked forward eagerly to her return to the Mersey, once she'd proved herself the thoroughbred she undoubtedly was.

We expected her back on the morning of the 22nd of November, and I was preparing to leave for the harbor to welcome her home when a cab clattered at breakneck speed up the White House drive and skidded to a halt at the door. Sam Coker himself clambered down and was ushered into the library, his face ashen and his spectacles askew.

"Captain Fuller sent me, m'lady. He says could you come down to Water Street right away, because there's been bad news. I'm afraid it's the *Altair*, Lady Oliver. . . . We've heard she's aground."

34

The early morning mist had given way to dismal drizzle by the time I reached the Oliver offices. Inside, it was strangely quiet. No one spoke above a whisper; for once, every head was bent over a desk and every eye avoided mine as I walked through the general office toward the door leading to Captain Fuller's private room. In the hush, my footsteps rang out like drumbeats on the endless wooden floor—an urgent tattoo which only confirmed what the lowliest clerk already knew: that a disaster of some kind had overtaken the *Altair*.

The steamship's Third Mate had brought the news, and had been told to wait in Tom Fuller's office, mud-stained and crestfallen, until I arrived.

"She's on Hilbre Island, m'lady, at the mouth of the Dee." Prompted by the Captain, he pointed out the spot on a chart spread across the desk.

"Five o'clock this morning, she went aground, and Cap'n Graham sent me ashore as soon as we saw it was the top of the tide an' the ship couldn't get herself off. I managed to reach Hoylake across the mud-banks an' begged a ride to Birkenhead on a farm wagon. Cap'n Graham told me to come straight here, an' not to speak a word of it to anyone but Cap'n Fuller or yourself, m'lady. Most partic'ler he was, on that point."

"So I should think," confirmed Tom Fuller severely. "The less anyone knows about this the better, until she's afloat again. The news will spread soon enough as it is, and the last thing we want is to turn the *Altair* into a sideshow. Now—" he fixed the man with a steely glare—"I want you to repeat to Lady Oliver all that you told me about the ship's present state. Never mind how she came to be there. We'll investigate that later. What we need to know now is exactly how she lies."

"Well, Cap'n . . ." The *Altair*'s Third Mate frowned, and picked up the inkstand from Captain Fuller's desk. "Like I said, she's on Hilbre Island, as well as we can judge. You know how much fog there was in the bay this morning, and at first we thought it was Little Hilbre. But there's about 'alf a mile of grass and bushes on her topsides, so we decided it must be t'other one after all."

Leaning forward, he sailed the inkstand across the desk toward a tray of correspondence.

"I'd say she was lying . . . *so* . . . m'lady, up against the island, with her head to seaward, just as the tide swung us round when it pushed us on." The inkstand swung through a graceful arc, coming to rest alongside the tray. "Cap'n Graham reckons she has rock under her stern, though the bottom thereabouts is mostly sand. We put a couple of anchors out soon's we knew where we'd struck, but with the tide turning the ship was too fast aground to haul herself off. Trouble is, with these big tides just now, the ebb goes at a fair old rate, and there's quite a scouring set up under her keel. Cap'n Graham's worried that another tide'll make it worse, an' she'll most likely hog an' break her back."

Seeing my puzzled expression, Tom Fuller explained.

"*Scouring* is when the firm sand washes out from under the ship's hull, leaving part of it without any support. If *Altair*'s sitting between rock and sand she could end up with nothing but air under her keel at some point. And she wasn't built to take that kind of strain."

"So we have to refloat her as soon as possible."

"It certainly sounds like that."

"Beg pardon, Cap'n, but Cap'n Graham reckons there could be dirty weather tonight. He said he didn't like the look of the sky, now the fog's lifted."

"I was thinking that myself," agreed Tom Fuller. "I reckon it'll blow up from the west later on, and we'll want the ship safely back in the river before it gets bad. She could well be making a fair bit of water by now—never mind damage to her propeller or her rudder when she struck. We don't want her dodging round the Irish Sea in the middle of a wild night in that condition."

"Perhaps her steering had already broken down before she went aground," I suggested. "That might account for the stranding."

"No, m'lady, she handled well enough. It's my belief the main compass was at fault—an' that fancy doo-dad that counts the dead-reckoning."

"But her compasses were the finest we could buy! Nothing should
have gone wrong with them."

"Not on an ordinary sailing-ship, m'lady. But you have to remember the *Altair*'s got more iron in her than a dozen foundries; we
allowed for deviation, right enough, but I reckon we should've allowed more. That's just my suspicion, of course," he added. "Cap'n
Graham may account for it diff'rent."

"I'll look forward to that," observed Tom Fuller dryly. "In the
meantime, we must decide how to refloat his ship."

"Will a tug be able to haul her off, do you think?"

"A big enough tug could do it, I imagine. But it'll take a powerful
boat to heave four thousand tons of steamship off a sandbank at the
first attempt. We can't afford to make any mistake with it, or we
could leave *Altair* in worse straits than she is at the moment." Tom
Fuller pulled thoughtfully at his whiskers for a few seconds, then
banged his fist on the desk.

"*Atlas* could do it! She's the only tugboat I know with enough
power to move the *Altair*. Old Arthur Parrish built her just
before—"

"I know who owns the *Atlas*." I cut him short. "And we can't use
her. You'll have to think of another boat."

"But—"

"I won't call out the *Atlas,* and that's all there is to it."

I saw Tom Fuller glance sideways at the popping eyes and open
mouth of the *Altair*'s young officer.

"You, lad—go and tell Mr. Coker I said to send out for some
breakfast for you. But don't leave the office. I'll need you shortly."

The man's grimy face brightened, and with a swift salute he left
the room.

"Now, Rachel—you'd better tell me what on earth's the matter
with the *Atlas*. She's a fine boat, and I reckon she's probably the
only vessel likely to get the *Altair* out of this bit of trouble. You'd
better have a good reason for not wanting to charter her."

"I have. An excellent reason. But I can't explain it to you."

The Captain's expression became ominously grim.

"Yet to my knowledge you've never even set eyes on the boat! I
take it you've some objection to her new owner, then—this Colonel
fellow who's bought out Parrish's."

"I don't want to discuss it, Uncle Tom. We simply can't charter
the *Atlas,* that's all."

"Can't—or won't?"

"If you put it like that . . . No, I won't charter the vessel."

It was the first time I'd seen Captain Fuller really angry. His face, usually so full of good humor, darkened with annoyance, and his voice became the furious bark which had once sent Matthew scuttling for cover.

"Well, I hope you know what you're doing, that's all! I've no idea what's behind this nonsense of yours, Rachel, but I warn you—it had better be something pretty important, because you could lose your ship as a result of it. Do you hear me? You could lose the ship!" He glared at me across the desk, and before I could speak he was ready with another broadside.

"D'you know, in the last couple of months I'd have backed your judgment against anyone's. I'd have sworn you had more downright good sense than George Broadney or any of them—but now I'm beginning to wonder. You don't seem to have taken aboard the first rule of the sea! *The safety of your ship comes before everything,* woman—and I mean *everything.*"

I heard the tread of heavy footsteps advancing down the corridor. All of a sudden the door banged open and George Broadney's booming voice filled the room.

"So this is where you're hiding, the two of you! Whispering in a corner like a couple of thieves! What the Devil d'you mean by not sending for me, Fuller, as soon as you heard the news? If it wasn't for that fellow Coker's presence of mind I daresay I'd never have heard a word of this until it was too late."

"Good morning, George."

"Oh, *good morning,* Rachel! Though a little late, don't you think? I ought to have been consulted from the very first, as you're well aware. Still, I daresay it *could* still be a good morning for all of us—and for Oliver's—provided I'm in time to stop you from doing something foolish."

"There's no conspiracy, George. We've only been deciding how we're to refloat the *Altair.*" With an effort, I kept my voice even. "So there was no need for you to come racing to the office like this. Coker had no business sending for you without the Captain's instructions."

"Oh, but he did have instructions—*my* instructions! I told him to send for me at once if something like this ever happened." He paused, and a sarcastic grin spread over his face. "I couldn't very well leave you to shoulder the burden alone, could I?"

"Everything's under control, George. I expect we'll have *Altair*

afloat again by this evening." Out of the corner of my eye I saw
Captain Fuller's warning glare, and carefully avoided it.

"Aha! Then I can see you definitely do need my advice! As I
expected, you've both rushed to rescue this blasted ship without a
second's thought about what's best for the company."

"I presumed—and correct me if I'm wrong, George—but I *presumed* that refloating the Oliver flagship *was* the best thing for the
company!"

"Maybe . . . and maybe not."

Abruptly, his tone changed. "Rachel, I think we should discuss
this alone for a moment."

"But why? Surely the Captain knows more about refloating
stranded ships than either of us."

"*Alone,* Rachel."

"If it's so important to you." I glanced, mystified, at Captain
Fuller. "I don't suppose this will take long, Uncle Tom. We'll go
along to Jonas's room."

Tom Fuller said nothing, but watched us go, a scowl of mistrust
on his face.

———

To my surprise George Broadney suddenly seemed to make a major
effort to be conciliatory.

"I know we've had our differences in the past, Rachel," he began,
pulling out a chair for me, "and you've made it quite clear we're
never going to be friends. But I can assure you of this—I sincerely
want the best for Oliver's. As part-owner of the company, I naturally
want to see it do well."

"Don't sit there, please, George. That was Jonas's chair."

Choking back an angry retort, he moved to an uncomfortable
upright chair in front of the desk.

"Will that do? Thank you. Now, the point I was about to make is
that you'd do well to remember that you and Matthew hold precisely
twice as much Oliver stock as I do. So if the company makes money
for me, you and your son will do twice as well."

"I'm aware of that, George."

"Splendid. I'd forgotten how good you were at counting shares."
He paused, heavily ironic. "I was simply trying to make you see that
you ought to listen carefully to what I have to say."

"I'm prepared to listen to what *anyone* has to say, I promise you.

But you'd better be quick about it. Whatever happens, we must get the *Altair* off on the next tide."

"That's exactly what I want you to consider, Rachel. Ask yourself this for a moment—are you sure you *want* to refloat the *Altair?*"

"What a stupid question! Of course I want to refloat the ship!"

"Are you sure?" George regarded me quizzically for a few seconds until I began to think that brandy had addled his brain at last. "Are you really sure you want to send the *Altair* back to sea? Even though it might be far better for the company to leave her where she is for a bit?"

I gaped at him speechlessly, unable to take in what he'd said.

"Look at it this way . . . Oliver's has just built the biggest, newest, cleverest steamship in the world, and thanks to Prince Albert, everyone knows about it and reckons that Oliver's is a fearless, forward-looking company, innovator of steam navigation and so forth. *Altair*'s given us a lot of prestige, Rachel, I'll admit that. Our smaller steamers are doing good business as a result. But you don't believe the *Altair* will run at a profit, any more than I do. She'll be like those great Collins' ships—never out of dry dock for one thing or another. Damn it all—here she is, still on her sea-trials, and in trouble already. Her future will be nothing but one long repair bill, just as I always said."

He paused significantly, one fat finger in the air.

"So . . . we could say the *Altair* has done as much for us as we could expect. And now she's even done us a favor by going aground on this wretched island. Don't you see—this is probably the best chance we'll ever have of getting rid of her! We won't have to sell her off for what we can get like the old *Great Britain*. The insurers will pay us her full cost, and we can use the money to buy big softwood sailing-ships for the emigrant trade." He leaned forward to emphasize his point.

"Forget New York! *Australia*'s the place where there's money to be made. Pack 'em in—ship 'em out. And none of this nonsense about competitive fares and a sailing every second Monday that you have on the Atlantic run."

He came to a halt and sat back in his chair, an expectant smile on his face. "Now, that's something you didn't think of, isn't it!"

He was absolutely right. I was stunned by the brazen cynicism of his scheme.

"Are you honestly suggesting we leave the ship where she is, high and dry, just a few hours' sailing from the Mersey?"

"More or less, yes."

"And what do you propose to tell the Lloyd's agent, may I ask, when he wants to know why we did nothing to rescue her? Do you really expect the underwriters to pay us if there's even a *hint* of negligence involved?"

"Oh, I don't mean *do nothing . . .*" George raised a hand in mild protest. "Just *don't do anything in a hurry.* The local Lloyd's man isn't back from Ireland yet, is he? Well, then—why not wait until he arrives? Wouldn't want to do anything without his advice, would we? We could begin to think about refloating her . . . tomorrow, perhaps. Or even the day after. Once another tide or two have done their work. From what that mate fellow says, she's in danger of breaking her back where she lies—and even if she floats off on her own at high tide, there's every chance she might get into more trouble in the Irish Sea. Besides—" George fixed me with a sly stare— "remember how big she is. It might be hard to find a tug powerful enough to pull her off the sand in the first place. It isn't something we could rush into, even if we wanted to."

"And in the meantime we hope she becomes a total loss?"

"Did I say that?" George grinned innocently.

"George . . ."

"Mmmmm?"

"I think that's . . . the most *despicable* scheme I've ever heard in my life! It's downright evil! Never mind that you're asking me to swindle the insurers—there are sixty-five men aboard that ship! Sixty-five officers and crew! Have you forgotten them? Or don't they come into your calculations?"

"Oh, don't be so confounded righteous, Rachel! Don't you think this kind of thing happens all the time? Do you honestly imagine that every ship which goes to the bottom of the sea founders of its own accord?" He gave a snort of exasperation. "Oh, don't be so naïve! This is *business,* not a charity tea-party. And in business . . . well . . . you have to bend the rules from time to time. Everybody does it—otherwise they wouldn't stand the competition for five minutes. Your precious Jonas was no saint, I assure you!"

"Really, George? Are you going to tell me that old lie about Jonas and Lettice Wyre again? The lie you tried to trick me with three years ago?" I saw George hesitate, and pushed home my advantage.

"Perhaps you're right, and there are shipowners so corrupt they'd see men drown in order to make a pound or two. But if there's one thing I'm sure of in this world, it's that Jonas wouldn't have listened to your rotten scheme for a second. He'd have gone out there with the biggest tug he could find, and got his ship back afloat. Abandon the *Altair,* and hope she breaks up or founders? It's the most contemptible suggestion I've ever heard. Stand aside, George!"

I was already on my feet, and now I marched straight past him to the door. In the corridor outside I found Captain Fuller, evidently on his way to look for me.

"Rachel, I must have a decision. High tide's something after five o'clock this evening."

"I know, Uncle Tom. And we've wasted enough time already, thanks to George Broadney. He suggested—oh, I can't even bear to repeat what he said!"

"You don't have to tell me. I know exactly what's in his mind. I've known plenty of ships put to sea before now with a wrecker aboard, paid by the owners to knock holes in the hull when the vessel was far enough from land. Devil take the crew—it's far better for the owners than repairing a worn-out vessel. Oh, I can imagine George Broadney's little scheme, all right."

I was still borne along on a wave of indignation.

"Nothing's going to happen to the *Altair* if I can help it. We'll refloat her this evening, on the next tide."

Tom Fuller looked at me suspiciously.

"Refloat her, no matter what?"

"No matter what."

"Then we must have the *Atlas.* Whoever owns her, she's still the only vessel for the job."

I hesitated, but only for an instant.

"Very well, then. We've no choice. Get the *Atlas.*"

We left the Mersey aboard the *Atlas* at a little before two o'clock.

From the first, I'd been determined to go out with her to rescue my ship; nothing in the world would have kept me from being there —neither the dismally slatting rain which now engulfed the river nor Captain Fuller's insistence that the deck of a tugboat was no place for a woman.

"This isn't a pleasure-trip, you know," he warned me. "None of this once-round-the-lighthouse caper, and make for home if you feel sick."

"I've never been seasick."

"Then you'll probably get in everyone's way, running about and interfering."

"I won't interfere. And you might as well save your breath, because I'm coming anyway. Where shall I meet you?"

"*Atlas* will wait for us at the pier-head, if you're determined to come. But don't ever complain I didn't warn you."

I'd have gone mad if I'd had to wait at home for the rest of the day, wondering how my ship was faring. And after all, what did it matter who owned the *Atlas?* I was hiring the boat, not its owner; Adam would probably know nothing about the rescue mission until the tug was safely back in the Mersey.

"I'll be at the pier-head, Uncle Tom."

The Captain handed me into my carriage with a philosophical sigh, and stood for a moment in the Water Street rain watching me race off to the White House.

Stubborn I might be—but I did realize I couldn't stand on the deck of a tugboat in horsehair petticoats and hooped crinoline cloth. Fortunately, for some reason—sentiment, perhaps—I'd preserved one of the plain wool skirts I'd worn in Independence at the bottom of an old trunk, folded up with pieces of camphor. Vickers fetched it from the box-room with some distaste, but I was beyond caring what she thought anymore: I was going out to save my ship, and if Vickers considered me hopelessly eccentric for setting off in stout boots and a workaday skirt and jacket with Jonas's great boat-cloak thrown round it all—then so be it.

At the last moment, I discovered the jacket didn't fasten where I wished, and flew to the bottom drawer of my dressing table for a brooch I thought would hold it. I'd just picked up the brooch when I saw, half-hidden behind a box of fans, the old Indian amulet which Adam had given me at Crow Cove, and I couldn't resist taking it in my hand again. I'd forgotten how exquisite it was—how smooth and perfect to the touch, how fascinating its endless procession of animal-spirits. Perhaps it might even bring the *Altair* some luck. Without another thought I thrust it deep into the pocket of my skirt.

By the time I reached the docks the rain had redoubled its force, drumming on the roof of the carriage as we sped toward the pier-head, and spurting up from the horses' hooves to spatter among the axles and springs. In the streets people ran for shelter in shop doorways, skipping the puddles in their haste, holding parcels or pieces of sacking over their heads as they went.

Yet even through the downpour I had to admit that the *Atlas* made an impressive sight. Her paddle-boxes stood out on each side like massive shoulders; her funnel rose, thick and black, above the muscular bulk of her superstructure; all her weight was thrown forward toward the bow to punch and thrust her way through the water with her broad, flat tail spread out as a counterbalance behind. *Atlas* wasn't without grace—but it was the powerful, controlled grace of a prize-fighter, whirling on nimble toes to land a driving blow. As soon as I saw her I knew Tom Fuller had been right. This was the vessel which would refloat the *Altair* if anything could.

Captain Fuller was waiting for me on the quayside in an oilskin hat and coat; behind him a crewman stood ready to cast the tug off from the pier as soon as we were aboard. The *Altair*'s Third Mate was there, deep in earnest conversation on the bridge, and on deck half-a-dozen men were flaking down huge coils of towing-cable or lashing coir fenders securely for the journey to the Dee.

Only one figure stood unmoving in that scene of activity. I should have known him by that uncanny stillness alone, but it was his hat I recognized first—the low-crowned, wide-brimmed horse-coper's hat Adam had worn on the day I found him riding home by way of the lane. Now it was shiny with rainwater, casting a deep shadow over that part of his face not concealed by the upturned collar of his greatcoat. No doubt he was gloating over his little victory, I thought, as he came forward to help me scramble down across paddle-box and bulwarks. Coldly, I ignored his assistance, slithering instead to a furious and undignified standstill almost at his feet.

"And when did you become part of a tugboat's crew?" I demanded hotly. "You've no business aboard this boat, Adam, and you know it."

"On the contrary. As her owner, I've every right to be here."

"But Oliver's has chartered her—and as the charterer, I've a right to insist you stay behind." I tried to keep my voice down, anxious not to make a scene.

"To Hell with your rights, Rachel! The *Atlas* is my boat, and I happen to own fifteen percent of the *Altair* too—something you seem to forget when it suits you."

"If I'd known you intended to be here—"

"What would you have done? Stayed at home? You can still go ashore if you want, you know. Captain Dawes can easily put you back on the quay. In fact, he'd probably be delighted to do it."

But before I could think of a valid reason for compelling him to stay in Liverpool the *Atlas* shook herself free of the pier-head, churned the water alongside to a foam with her mighty paddles, and turned her head toward the mouth of the river. As soon as we were underway Captain Fuller came along the deck toward me accompanied by a small, ruddy-faced man whose formal black cap had been crammed over a mass of gray hair.

"This is Captain William Dawes, master of the *Atlas*." Tom Fuller indicated his companion. "I've given him a rough account of our present trouble, but we'll have to see exactly how the steamship lies before we can decide what's to be done."

"Do you know the Dee at all, Captain Dawes?"

The tug-master's bushy gray brows arched in delight.

"Why, bless you, m'lady, I know the Dee all right. I was born in Connah's Quay, upriver there toward Chester—my father sailed the ketch *Margaret* out of Flint, see. My elder brother has her now, but I used to go along as deckhand, and many's the time I've lain wind-bound in Wildroads, waiting for a change in the weather—and that's not a couple of miles from the Hilbres."

"The *Altair* seems to be aground on Hilbre Island itself. That's the nearest to the sea, isn't it?"

"It is, m'lady. But from what Cap'n Fuller tells me, you'll want her afloat before a bad swell or another tide can push her further on."

"Do you think the *Atlas* can do it?"

"Oh, *Atlas* can do just about anything, Lady Oliver. She's a reg'lar little wonder, this boat. You ask the Colonel there." I realized to my annoyance that Adam had joined us, and was standing at my shoulder. Opposite me, Tom Fuller was regarding him intently, and I had no choice but to make an introduction. Tom Fuller continued to frown.

"Forgive me, Colonel, but haven't I met you somewhere before? Can't place the occasion, but I'm convinced we've met."

For a split second Adam's eyes met mine. Then he said easily, "I'm sure I've often passed you in the docks, Captain. I've been trying to learn more about Parrish's business in the last few weeks, so no doubt you've seen me loitering on the wharf, trying to tell the difference between a collier and a man o'war."

"The collier's the one with the shot-holes, Colonel," grinned Captain Dawes, and the tension dissolved—outwardly, at least. As the *Atlas* threshed her way downriver toward the Rock Channel and the distant river-bar, I could think of nothing to ease the disquiet in my mind.

———

The *Atlas* had a small fo'c'sle for her crew tucked between her two paddle-boxes and under the bridge, a hot, cramped cubby-hole near her laboring boiler, bisected by the base of her funnel and smelling strongly of sweat and cooked vegetables. In that tiny space were bunks and living room for eight men: the Captain lived in what amounted to a cupboard toward the bow.

Apart from the helmsman and firemen there was little for anyone to do until we neared the mouth of the Dee, and a kettle was boiled for tea in the fo'c'sle. But after a few minutes of the fetid warmth in that small compartment I decided I preferred to be out on deck where the persistent rain had dwindled once more to drizzle. Before long Adam came out to join me.

"Forgive me, m'lady," he copied Tom Fuller's inquisitorial bark, "but haven't I met you somewhere before? Didn't you once have a small log cabin on the outskirts of Independence, Missouri?"

"That isn't funny, Adam."

"No—I don't suppose it is. But it's the best I can manage at short notice. I didn't expect you to come along on this jaunt."

"Why not? Surely you guessed I'd want to see the *Altair* for myself."

"I expected you to send one of your Oliver lackeys to take charge. And then all of a sudden, there you were, looking just like the Rachel I used to know years ago, before the priggish Lady Oliver came and carried her off. It must be those clothes you're wearing."

"Priggish?"

"Sure—*priggish*. Self-righteous. Smug. Narrow-minded."

"I know what priggish means. And if you're trying to say that I live by some kind of *standards* . . . then yes, you're right. I'm quite happy to be priggish, as you call it."

"While I have no standards at all. Is that what you're implying?"

"I'll do better than imply it, Adam. I'll tell you outright, if that's what you want. It's taken me a long time to see you as you are—a man without any notion of truth or loyalty or decency . . . But I know it now, and I'm not afraid to say so."

We were standing by the fo'c'sle door in the lee of the bridge, and Adam had turned to face me, his back against the planked bulkhead.

"I've told you before—you invented a hero for yourself, and now you've knocked him down. I warned you from the start I was no knight-errant."

"I should have listened to you, then, shouldn't I?"

"Yes, you should. You'd have spared us both a great deal of unhappiness."

He fell silent and turned to look over his shoulder through the rails of the open bridge to where the gray waters of Liverpool Bay were beginning to open up before us. For a long time he stared out over the blunt bow of the tug, and then a thought struck him.

"Are you really on this ridiculous committee to save the souls of Liverpool cab-men? This *Mission to Hackney Drivers,* or whatever it's called."

"Well . . . yes, I am. How did you know?"

"Matthew told me, but I thought he was joking. I've never heard such nonsense in my life. Why on earth do you want to peddle tea and biblical texts to cab-men?"

"They're human beings, and therefore capable of improvement." I took refuge in Bishop Caxton's words.

"Precisely. Human beings—not angels. Normal, sinful human beings, whose worst crime is beating their horses and overcharging their customers."

"Everyone can benefit from a good example." Or so the Bishop had said.

"Rachel—you used to care about *people,* not good examples or 'improvement'! Never in my wildest dreams did I think you'd become a plaster saint, driving around in your comfortable carriage, telling the deserving poor how to improve their lives. What right have you got to tell other people how to live? Since when did you have a monopoly on virtue?"

"I've never claimed anything of the kind."

"You don't have to claim it! You're just . . . so *sure* of your own high-minded morality. I don't suppose you'd bother with a dirty sinner like Ed Ballantine nowadays! And what about Watches Smoke, Rachel? What would you do with him now? Preach at him? Sober him up with a sermon?"

"I don't know why you're attacking me like this!"

"Because I can't bear all this sanctimonious rubbish you've begun to parrot. You sound like one of those terrible women of Lizzie Fletcher's, with their pious expressions and their nasty minds."

I had a sudden vision of Lizzie's female boarders arriving in a mean-spirited group to demand that the wicked Mrs. Gaunt remove her unwholesome presence from the house. Poor little Matthew had almost shared my fate, an accomplice to his mother's misdeeds.

"But I'm nothing like those women! Oh, Adam, that's quite unfair!"

"Is it?" He looked moodily down the deck. "I don't know what you're like anymore. I used to know—and seeing you dressed like that again, with a scarf round your head and a sensible skirt instead of those ludicrous yards of material . . . I began to wonder if maybe, somewhere inside you, there is still the barefoot girl who kept a toad under a stone at Crow Cove . . . Or the woman I remember plucking chickens on the cabin-step at Independence and singing in her garden with her hands raw from digging."

He glanced up at me again.

"Do you remember any of that?"

"You know I do." In the pocket of my skirt the Indian amulet hung heavy against my thigh, round and sleek and perplexing.

"Do you think about it, ever?"

"Not if I can help it."

"Why not? It's part of you."

"It's over and done with. Gone. And I wish it had never happened," I added more savagely than I intended.

"Ah . . . I see."

Why did Adam always make me feel as if I were in the wrong—as if I were the one who was being unreasonable?

"You needn't concern yourself anymore about my mother," I said meanly, rebuilding my defenses. "Reuben showed me where to find her, and I've made sure she can't hurt any of us again."

"I know. Matthew told me what you'd done."

"There was no other way. Though I daresay Aunt Grace will accuse me of heartlessness—when I can bring myself to tell her. I suppose that's what you think too—that I've treated a sick woman very cruelly."

"Why should I think that?"

"Because . . . well, you *know* why."

"Rachel, I've told you this before: Susannah meant nothing to me —ever. And she did her damnedest to have me killed, don't forget.

She was even prepared to risk Reuben's death to be rid of me. If you hadn't found a way of putting a stop to her scheming and her hatred, I'd have been forced to do something myself."

"Hate—and love," I murmured softly. "Two sides of the same coin."

"Did she say that?"

"Not in so many words. But to hate as passionately as she did . . . it was a kind of love—the only love she knew how to give. Sometimes I wonder—" I stopped there, biting back the rest of the sentence; I hadn't intended to speak of the anxiety which had haunted me since that first visit to the house in Prince's Park.

"What do you wonder?"

"I sometimes wonder if—because Matthew is her grandson, after all—if he hasn't inherited some of her coldness . . ."

"There's nothing the matter with Matthew."

"Oh, I might have known you'd approve of his selfishness!"

"I like Matthew, it's true—and how many fathers can say that of their sons? I thought at first he was a spoiled brat, but now I've got to know him, I don't believe he's as selfish as he tries to pretend."

"You've become an expert on Matthew, I see."

"I'm trying to spend some time with him, certainly."

"Jonas always treated Matthew as his own son," I said with deliberate cruelty. "He was very good to him."

"Trying to give him some of your Oliver *standards,* I suppose."

"More than he could expect from his real father!"

"At least I won't teach him cant and hypocrisy."

"No—you'll teach him how honorable it is to leave his wife and child and go off into the wide world whenever the mood takes him, I suppose."

"We've talked about that, Matthew and I. I think he understands why it happened."

"Oh, does he? How very convenient for you!" I was almost beside myself with indignation. "Then perhaps you might also like to explain to Matthew how you come to have another son—an older son you didn't even wait long enough to acknowledge!"

"What's all this? What are you talking about?"

"I'm talking about Reuben. Reuben—your son, after your . . . adventure with my mother!"

He stared at me for a long moment.

"Did Susannah tell you this?"

"Not at first—but I made her tell me the whole story."

"Then I don't believe it for a second. It's pure spite—or an opium dream, no more than that."

He frowned, considering the possibility.

"No, I can't believe it. Susannah was twisting the knife, trying to hurt you."

"She did hurt me."

"But for Heaven's sake, I was only in Crow Cove for—what—two or three months?"

"How long do you think it takes?" I asked acidly. "And I expect you provided plenty of opportunity."

He avoided my eye.

"No, Adam, there's no doubt about it. You only have to look at Reuben to see he isn't Joseph Dean's son."

"Reuben—*mine?*" Adam looked at me incredulously. "But he's . . . he's even more priggish than the Olivers, if that's possible. How can you believe he's my son?"

"Because he is yours, I promise you. He was born in May '28, the year after you left Crow Cove—and now I come to think of it, his eyes were yours from the start. Even when he was a little child they had that same unsettled color and exactly the same expression, as if his mind was wandering somewhere far away."

"I know it's *possible*." Adam glanced at me sideways. "Physically, it's possible he's mine. But, for Heaven's sake—we aren't alike in any way."

"What were you like at Reuben's age, Adam? What made you run away from home?"

"Anger. A sense of wanting to be my own man."

"And weren't you ever afraid of what you'd find—and too proud to admit it?"

"Frequently."

"Well, then. Reuben's taken some hard knocks recently, and he's still struggling to make sense of it all. I hate to think what he'll do when I tell him Joseph Dean wasn't his real father, but you were."

"He doesn't know?"

"He's been away at sea almost all the time since Jonas died. He did come back to Liverpool briefly—just for a few days—but somehow it was so awkward . . . I couldn't bring myself to make him more miserable. How could I tell him that the man he shot—a man he thinks of as a murdering outlaw—is his own father?"

"You're right. He despises me enough already," Adam smiled bleakly. "That's something you have in common, isn't it?"

"The next time he comes home I'll try to explain to him . . ."

"How he came to be conceived?"

"I suppose so."

He looked at me defiantly. "That will be an interesting case for his precious *standards,* I should think."

Adam stalked away from me down to the far end of the deck, where he stood for a while, motionless, contemplating the vessel's marbled wake where it diminished like a wavering slug-trail, back toward the city.

———

It was just after four when we finally caught sight of the *Altair* in the gathering dusk. The tide was making again and the mudbanks were covered; *Altair* was so upright in the water that if it hadn't been for the scrubby island lying just astern of her, she might almost have been steaming out of the mouth of the River Dee into Liverpool Bay. Yet even from a distance there was something about her which proclaimed her a dead ship. Until then, in spite of her huge bulk, I'd always been aware of a little movement about her, an infinitesimal rising and falling even in sheltered waters which marked her affinity with the sea. Now she was motionless, as rooted to the land as a pier or a tree, unable to respond to the tide which flooded about her.

After another twenty minutes' steaming we were almost under her bow, close enough to hear the cheer which went up from the cluster of faces at her rail.

"By the holy jumping mother of Moses," breathed Captain Dawes. "The tide must have pushed her straight over the bank."

"As long as the *Atlas* doesn't go aground beside her." I was horrified to see how near the tugboat was lying.

"No fear of that, m'lady. I could float the *Atlas* in a teaspoon." Captain Dawes spat into the sea to illustrate his point. "The bottom falls away steeply here, just about where we are. It's a deep channel, see. Even the *Altair*'s got several fathoms just a cable or two beyond her bow."

Wherever her bow may have been, the steamship's stern was firmly grounded on the end of a rocky underwater ridge whose visible peaks were the two Hilbre islands and another tiny outcrop further inshore. I could easily imagine the turbulent waters which swirled under her hull, sucking away the sand on which she rested and making the job of refloating her more urgent by the hour.

In the bow of the *Atlas* Captain Dawes and Tom Fuller were holding a shouted consultation with Captain Graham, leaning over the steamship's rail.

"What do you think?" I asked as the two men returned to the bridge.

"One thing's for sure," Tom Fuller remarked gloomily. "If we can't get the *Altair* off tonight, we'll have to open some seams in her hull in order to hold her steady. Unless she does the job for us, of course, which is always possible."

"Make holes in the ship?" I couldn't believe what I'd heard. The Captain seemed to have pronounced a death sentence on the *Altair*.

"If we let some water into her hull she'll settle better into the sand. It might stop this blasted scouring until we can deal with her properly."

"But how can we ever refloat her if she's holed and full of water? It could take months—if we manage it at all. Oh, Uncle Tom, we *must* get her off tonight!"

"I reckon," came a familiar voice behind me, "we ought to concentrate on what we're going to do in the next hour or so. If we don't succeed in pulling the ship free we'll have plenty of time then to talk about turning her into a colander."

"Quite right, Colonel," agreed Captain Dawes, rubbing his hands. "You tell 'em. Wait till we've given old *Atlas* a chance to show what she can do. She's like a woman, m'lady," he added, turning to me. "She don't show at her best till she's up against it. Now, your Cap'n Graham seems to think the two anchors he's got out are holding, so with his anchor-winches an' our own eighty horses hauling away, I reckon we'll have your ship safely tucked up in the Mersey long before the weather turns nasty."

As Captain Dawes clambered aft to supervise the passing of a heavy cable aboard the *Altair*, I realized that the light breeze which had fanned my cheek as we crossed the bay had begun to freshen.

"Come into the fo'c'sle. There's nothing we can do out here."

"No, Adam. I want to stay where I can see the *Altair*."

"Then stand over here out of the way. They'll need those bollards to tie off the cable." Adam took my arm and drew me next to him in the lee of the fo'c'sle.

"She looks so awful, stuck on that wretched island. I couldn't bear it, if we have to leave her there."

"We'll get her off, don't worry. Come Hell or high water, you'll have your ship back—since she's so important to you."

"She is important to me."

"She must be . . . if you were prepared to swallow your pride and come to me for help. Considering you didn't see fit to invite me to the launch. I wouldn't have embarrassed you by being there, but it would have been pleasant to be asked. By the way—" he added as an afterthought, "don't say anything about me to Reuben. I'll tell him the whole story myself."

"Is that wise?"

"It's honest, at least. Anything else would be the coward's way out."

"But why?"

"I've been thinking it over. I don't want to make the same mistakes with Reuben that my father made with me. I never felt I belonged anywhere at all. I grew up with no home and no roots—and I don't want that for Reuben."

"You're a curious man, Adam. If I live to be thousand I don't think I'll ever understand what makes you do the things you do."

"That's something we agree on, then. Except that on recent form I've a pretty poor chance of reaching a thousand."

———

We were forced to find another refuge when the double cable, as thick as a man's arm, was made fast aboard the tug. But there was no undue haste about the preparations, proceeding now by the light of big oil lamps. The tugboat's crew knew their work and went about it with methodical skill, the seamen handling their ropes, the sweating engineers looking to the boiler and pistons, and the black-smeared firemen, weary from stoking their greedy furnaces, clambering out on deck from time to time to empty their lungs of choking coal-dust and find out how the rescue was progressing.

We were to wait until the stand of the tide, the short interval between flood and ebb when the water level round the *Altair* was at its highest. Aboard the *Atlas* we waited in a fever of impatience. I even found myself biting my fingernails, something I hadn't done since I was a child and had had bitter aloes smeared on them by my horrified nurse.

At last the three captains decided between them that the right moment had come. The wind had risen to a squally blast, driving gusts of rain over us from the direction of the darkening bay as the powerful paddles of the tug began to churn the water on either side. I saw the twin anchor-cables leading from the *Altair*'s bow grow stiff and tight, and then our own great tow-rope stretch out, rigid as an iron bar when it took up the strain, creaking and squealing round its bollards as it became taut.

Captain Dawes peered anxiously astern from the bridge, wiping the rain from his eyes.

"Nothing yet," he called out. "Nothing I can see, anyhow. I'll give her a bit more power."

Alongside the tug, the paddles threshed more wildly. Black smoke belched from her funnel, and in the failing light I could see showers of glowing sparks whistling skyward.

"Go forward into the bow." Adam gave me a push. "Just in case the boiler blows."

"I could give her more, Colonel, if you don't care about your engines," Captain Dawes shouted down from the bridge.

"Maximum revolutions, if you please, Captain. Let's get this steamship moving."

"Right you are, Colonel! Stand by down there, you men!"

The tow-rope was singing now, making a cracking, squealing melody of its own as its sinews were stretched and strained. The remains of my fingernails dug into my palms as I clenched my fists fiercely under my rain-soaked cloak. Aboard the *Atlas* no one said a word except for Captain Dawes on the bridge, who kept up a constant muttered litany of his own.

"Come on, you cow!" I heard him repeat to himself over and over again. "Come *on!* Do you want to sit there till you rot?" But the only answer was the thundering cacophony of the engine, a threshing of water and the fearful thrumming of the rope.

Then somewhere astern I heard a faint, ragged cheer.

"She's moving!" yelled a jubilant voice. "I'll swear she's moving!"

On the bridge, I saw Captain Dawes and Tom Fuller shaking hands like the oldest of friends, their faces wreathed in grins. Around us, everyone was slapping backs and punching one another in the ribs from sheer high spirits, waving and shouting to the men aboard the *Altair,* leaping up and down, howling with excitement and delight. Somehow I found myself hugging Adam from sheer relief, before I realized what I was doing and hastily drew away.

But it was hard to be angry, with the *Altair* following docilely behind us like an outsize dog, gathering up her anchors as she came. All the same, I was cross with myself, and crosser when I noticed Adam watching me, a quizzical expression on his face.

"Well, my dear, what did you think of that?" Captain Fuller leaned over the bridge-rail. "Full marks to the *Atlas,* eh? For a while there I thought the *Altair* wasn't going to budge for us, but that last heave did the trick. Next thing's to find out how much she's damaged, and get her home to the Mersey as fast as we can."

It was fully dark by the time a damage report was assembled. By now black, freezing rain was blasting over the tug which pitched and rolled in a nasty short sea. Somewhere in the darkness astern was the *Altair:* every so often, when the clouds parted to reveal the pale disc of the moon, I caught a reassuring glimpse of white paintwork and the bright gold star at her bow.

She was making water, Captain Graham reported—but chiefly in number three compartment which had taken most of the strain, and at a rate of no more than a few inches an hour. Constant pumping was containing the leak, and given time might even gain on it. Provided no more rivets were lost on the way to Liverpool, the captain judged his ship was unlikely to sink.

"She's steering, apparently," Tom Fuller reported, "but it sounds as if she lost pieces from a couple of propeller-blades when she struck. I've told him we'll tow him in."

"Can't she make Liverpool under her own power?"

"Bob Graham says she ought to—at half-speed, maybe—but it's probably safer to tow."

"I don't want the *Altair* arriving in Liverpool under tow."

"As long as she gets there, what does it matter?"

"It matters a great deal. If she's towed in, all the people who said she'd never get beyond Liverpool Bay will think they've been proved right. If she can possibly reach Liverpool under her own power, she has to do it."

"It's an extra risk."

"Then take off any of her crew who aren't particularly needed. *Atlas* can stay near us in case anything goes wrong." The tug pitched violently, and I grabbed a nearby stanchion for support.

"The way it's blowing up now, it might not be easy to get a tow-rope aboard."

"We've had luck on our side so far. I have a feeling it'll last till we reach the river."

"Woman's intuition again, Rachel?" Captain Fuller had to shout to make himself heard.

"Definitely. Don't worry, Uncle Tom. We'll be quite safe."

"*We?* And who is *we,* may I ask?"

"I'm going aboard the *Altair.* I'll sail back with her."

"You will not! If anyone goes aboard, it'll be me. And that's an order."

"I'm sorry, Uncle Tom. You may be Commodore, but you don't give me orders. You stay with the tug, and I'll go aboard the *Altair.*"

"Dammit, Rachel—I'm your uncle, and you'll do as I tell you. If Jonas was here, he'd soon stop all this nonsense."

"But Jonas isn't here anymore. And as a widow I can do as I please. You ask Aunt Grace. She was the one who told me that." All of a sudden I felt elated. Deep inside me, the bold, brazen Mademoiselle Valentine stirred again, shook her saucy red feathers and dared me to do my worst. "I'll be all right—I promise."

"So widows can do as they please, can they?" Adam reappeared from the shadows below the bridge.

"You tell her, Colonel, since she won't listen to me," growled Tom Fuller. "Tell her she can't sail back aboard the steamship."

"Oh, I doubt if she'll listen to me, Captain. Except . . . I wonder how she's proposing to climb aboard. There's no gangway out here, after all."

"There'll be a rope ladder, won't there? It's only a matter of twelve feet or so. Not even that."

"At sea? In the darkness? And can you climb a rope ladder?"

"Of course. We had one in the apple tree at Crow Cove, and I could go up it in seconds."

"It's out of the question," growled Tom Fuller. "It's far too dangerous. Make her understand that, Colonel."

"I can't make her do anything." Adam was looking directly at me. "But if she's determined to go aboard the steamship, then I'm going too."

"No, Adam, it's different for me," I objected, quite forgetting that Tom Fuller was within earshot. "I'm the owner. It would look as if I'd no confidence in her if I didn't go aboard."

"You're *part*-owner. And so am I." Adam's eyes glittered in a brief flare of moonlight. "Besides—I've no intention of missing the fun."

I recognized that look of determination.

"Oh, very well. Come aboard, then, if you must," I heard Mademoiselle Valentine declare.

He'd have come with me anyway, whether I minded or not. Nothing in the world would have kept Adam from an adventure he'd set his heart on. Who should know that better than I?

———

Many hands stretched down to haul me up toward the deck as soon as I'd climbed high enough on the ladder, my skirt looped up into my waistband. I saw the men exchange amused glances, but I didn't care. I'd done just as I'd said—reached up from the bulwarks of the *Atlas* to catch the dangling ladder at the precise moment when the tug was poised on top of a wave. I'd got myself aboard the *Altair*, which was all that mattered to me, and now I could look down from her rail on the rolling deck of the tug I'd just left.

"Maybe Dawes and his boat did get us off," Captain Graham admitted grudgingly, "but I'm blowed if I'll let him tow us back to Liverpool. *Altair* can make her own way perfectly well, provided the leaks in her hull don't start gaining on the pumps, and we ought to make five or six knots in spite of our broken propeller-blades. It's minor damage—nothing to a ship like this. Even at that speed we'll still reach the Mersey bar with plenty of water to spare. Let Dawes look to his own boat, that's all."

"What about the sails, Captain? You could use those, surely."

"Sails, Lady Oliver?" Captain Graham looked affronted. "Those are only for an *emergency*. This is a steamship, Ma'am, and I intend to keep her that way."

"I have the distinct impression we aren't needed here," Adam suggested after Captain Graham had stamped back to his bridge.

He stared into the darkness at the shiny, wet deck and dripping rigging as a few oil-skinned crewmen ran past, heads bent, through rain which gleamed like amber rods in the light of the lamps on the shrouds and deckhouses.

"So this is your wonderful *Altair* . . . *Our* wonderful *Altair*," he corrected himself. "Fitted with every possible luxury, constantly supplied with distilled fresh water—comfortable—commodious—speedy—"

Adam held his arms wide and slowly revolved, taking in the whole depressing scene. "Who could ask for more?"

I couldn't help laughing. "We make a pretty poor showing ourselves, you know. I'm not surprised Captain Graham was less than impressed. In that hat you look more like a bargee than a ship-owner." Rain-water was sluicing off the wide brim of Adam's hat and splashing down on to the shoulders of his greatcoat, where it disappeared at once into the sodden fabric.

"You're hardly a fashion-plate yourself, Lady Oliver. And I don't suppose you did much for your reputation by shinning up that ladder the way you did."

"I told you I could climb a rope ladder."

"And you were right. You went up it like an organ-grinder's monkey. Wait till Lady Verity hears about that."

"Oh, to Hell with Verity." At that moment I meant every word of it. "To Hell with George, too—and the Ripons, and the rest of their awful friends. Devil take the lot of them!"

Oh, I was more than a match for them all, standing on the broad deck of my ship, my wet cloak flapping in the wind but my heart alight with triumph. Above my head, the plume of smoke which had risen steadily from the *Altair*'s twin funnels ever since we left the Dee had suddenly become illuminated from below by a dull red glow. As I waited, the rumble of massive engines began to spread through the ship like the pulse of her life-blood: subtly, the idle rise and fall of her deck steadied to a more purposeful motion as her damaged propeller began to turn.

"We're under way, Adam! Can you feel it? We're bound for Liverpool!"

He'd come across to stand beside me.

"Did I hear you say *to Hell with Verity?*"

"Yes, to Hell with them all! Do you realize—we've saved the ship! They wanted to leave her to break up—but we've saved her in spite of them!" I spread my arms and whirled round on the streaming deck.

Adam was regarding me with a puzzled expression.

"I wish I knew why this ship has suddenly become so important to you. Is it because of Jonas?"

"Jonas? No, of course not. It's because she's *mine!* I fought for her: I even launched her! If it wasn't for me, she wouldn't be here—and she's a marvel!" I seized his hand, and began to pull him along the deck. "Come and see for yourself! Come on!"

There were no lights anywhere in the accommodation, but I knew there'd be a lamp swinging from a brass hook just inside the door of the deck saloon, and I took charge of it, holding it high so that Adam could see the comfortable plush-upholstered seats which ran down each side under the windows, the crimson damask curtains and the satinwood paneling.

"The deck saloon and smoking room," I said. "Those tables are made of Brocatelli marble, I'll have you know. Down this way now."

I dragged him down a brass-railed companionway, stumbling on the dark and unfamiliar stairs.

"This is the library—" I threw open a door. "Or it will be, once the books are on the shelves." The lamp cast a pool of light over tall, glasspaned cupboards and rosewood writing-desks before I moved on. "This is the music room. I had the organ shipped all the way from New York."

At the back of the compartment the carved and gilded organ flashed mysteriously in the lamplight, its rows of vertical pipes gleaming like bared teeth behind the fretwork bars. It looked monstrous and unfamiliar in the semidarkness, a minotaur at the heart of the labyrinthine vessel, and for a moment I was grateful for Adam's reassuring presence just behind me. When he spoke, he was close enough for me to feel the warmth of his breath at my ear.

"Feed him a nice, juicy saloon passenger from time to time, and he'll stay quite tame."

"Idiot!" Once again he'd sensed exactly what was in my mind. "You aren't taking this seriously at all."

I was conscious of Adam being a fraction of a second late in moving aside for me, making me squeeze past him in the doorway.

"Now, down this way—" I hurried through a paneled lobby. "Down this way is the second-class saloon, and the second cabins beyond that."

I led the way carefully through the blackness of the saloon, the lamplight flashing on polished wood and iron columns as I passed. I'd never been aboard the *Altair* at night before: there had always been daylight filtering down from the glass domes on the upper deck to make sense of her maze of saloons and cabins. Now the columns and pillars between the decks multiplied themselves into a moving forest of shadows: looping bronze dolphins twined round the unlit lamps like hungry ivies and an undergrowth of benches and tables thrust out carved limbs to catch an unwary foot.

Adam's light tread followed me down the black hole of another companionway to the dining saloon below.

"This is the second-class dining room. The steerage accommodation is through there. . . . And across the lobby here is the first-class dining room."

"Everyone in his place, I see."

For some reason the sound of his voice startled me in the gloom.

"Now up here—" I mounted another flight of pitch-black steps, clinging to my lamp. "Here we're almost back where we started. Through that door is the first-class saloon. The Grand Saloon."

"I hope they let us in, dressed like this," Adam remarked dryly out of the darkness.

I opened the door and stood aside to let Adam follow—and a cold, rigid hand touched my cheek.

"Oh, my God!"

"What is it?"

For a moment I'd cringed back against him. Now I held the lamp high again to find a life-size bronze female figure standing guard by the saloon door, a pen in her outflung hand.

"That's *Poetry,* by the look of her. Her friend *Music* is on the other side." Adam examined the two bronze women staring disdainfully down at us from their plinths.

"And from the expression on their faces, they've found us out. They know we're out of our class here. We're nothing but imposters —a couple of vagabonds in their Grand Saloon."

"There are other vagabonds all round the walls, then. Look— Columbus . . . Cortez . . . Magellan . . ." I brandished the lamp, and a hundred mirrors flashed in the darkness, making the old explorers stamp and posture like the spirits of some flickering grotto. And there beside me stood Adam, the wizard of that crowded cavern, the lamplight gleaming in those hawk eyes of his. Fascinated, I swung the lamp again. This time it went out, leaving us in total darkness.

"Give it to me. I have some matches here." I felt Adam's hands gently enclosing mine as he reached for the smoking, reeking lamp.

"There's a table here somewhere. I'll put it on that." I held out a tentative hand, feeling ahead in the blackness. My thigh collided painfully with the edge of the table and Adam, following, came up against me, instinctively catching me in his arms.

"Adam—don't—please."

But he kissed me all the same, as if possession had given him a perfect right. And I dropped the lamp.

"Oh, no—now the lamp's broken. I heard it roll away somewhere across the floor."

"We don't need it now. I have everything I want right here."

"Adam—"

And he kissed me again, slowly and lingeringly, until I felt a tingling warmth spread through me from my toes to the roots of my hair. Then he released me—let me stand alone in the pitch darkness as if to say *there you are—see how you fare without me.* And though I couldn't see him I could sense him there, separated from me by the smallest of distances, touching without touching . . . and thin ropes of desire twined up through my body from my belly to my breasts, squeezing the breath from my lungs. I heard my own voice, strangely hoarse.

"There might be—another lamp . . . Down at the end there. Through the door."

"What's down there?"

"There are two cabins made into one in the stern; a stateroom and a sleeping cabin. Jonas . . . planned it that way, in case we ever wanted to travel aboard her. I think there should be a spare lamp in there."

He took my hand in his, and pulled me behind him as he felt his way toward the end of the long saloon. I began to wonder if he could even see in the dark, his step was so sure. Within a minute or two his fingers skimmed hollow wooden panels as he groped for a door-handle; I heard the click of a latch and saw an ever-widening gray strip as the door was opened.

The *Altair*'s stern windows were a line of slanting, moonlit rectangles on the far side of the stateroom. Somewhere below us I could hear an uneven rumble as the damaged propeller beat its way through the night sea, carrying us steadily back to Liverpool. And amid the pale shapes of the room the polished chimney of a lamp gleamed from a table in the middle of the floor.

"There's the lamp—" I exclaimed, grateful for an excuse to snatch my hand out of his. "Adam—" For he hadn't let go, but simply gripped my hand more tightly. "Adam—the lamp is there on the table, as I thought."

"What's through this door?" He tried the handle of the inner door, and inevitably I was carried through it with him, hearing the snap of the closing latch behind us.

I didn't need lamplight or moonlight to know what was there: elegant zebrawood paneling concealing cupboards and lockers, a washstand fitted with fine floral porcelain basins, an upholstered day-bed under the windows—and a wide damask-curtained bunk, too substantial to be called anything but a bed, against the opposite wall.

"The lamp—" I protested feebly.

"Later."

And I was in his arms again, still deluding myself that I could call a halt to it all at any moment . . . that in a second or two I would exert my will and cry *enough*. . . . Except that I wanted it to happen: I wanted to feel his fingers moving in the warm curve at the nape of my neck, spreading there amongst my damp curls, seductive and compelling.

"You're soaked to the skin," he said softly into my hair.

"So are you."

"We make a fine pair." Gently, he unwound my sodden scarf and released the clasp of my boat-cloak, which slipped to the floor, heavy with damp.

It was easier now to reach up and wind my arms about him, pulling his lips down to mine, and it was a homecoming after exile. All the anger and betrayal flowed out of me: all the hard words and bitter secrets had been spent, leaving only the two of us, as it had been in the very beginning.

"What if the ship sinks, Adam—"

He kissed me again, as if he hadn't heard.

"What if—" I tried once more.

"Let it sink," he murmured, his lips moving against mine.

His hand slid once more behind my head, and in an explosion of pins the tight, dark coil of my hair spilled down over my shoulders. Strands of it wrapped themselves about him as he kissed my eyes, the soft hollows below my ears and the crevices of my throat. All at once I knew a great need to feel Adam against me, inside me, until I was utterly engulfed by him, glutted and overwhelmed. My soaking skirt, damp petticoats and all my defenses of linen and lace somehow slid piecemeal to the shadows of the floor until I could feel the warmth of his hands against my naked skin, sliding in blissful freedom over the mounds and valleys of my body, plundering tenderly and insistently until I cried out with the unbearable, forgotten wonder of it all.

There were blankets on the bed and nothing more, but we had made love on rough, prickling blankets often enough in the past. Now the current of his desire carried us both inexorably along, and I found myself responding to its shallows and deeps with joyful familiarity. I could withhold nothing—and in any case, with Adam, half-measures were impossible. He knew me too well, anticipating every tremor which ran through me, gentle and ruthless by turns until longing was replaced by a glorious satiety which roared, exulting through my veins as I clung to him, drowning in the breaking waves of bliss.

And afterward I lay listening to the steady, slowing beat of his heart, reveling in the warmth of his body next to mine—not as a refuge now or a retreat, but because I had chosen . . . and he stroked my cheek with a gentle finger.

"I love you, Rachel. I've told you that before, and I'll say it as often as I have to until you believe me. *I love you.*"

"And I love you." Suddenly I could say it again.

"I think you do. But I wish I thought you loved me enough." He let a curling strand of my hair trickle through his fingers. "What if I asked you to give up the White House and all this, and come back to America with me?"

Disconcerted, I looked for a way of escape.

"What time is it, Adam? We must be in the river by now."

He reached out and groped for his watch on the floor, twisting his head in an effort to read the faint Roman figures of the dial.

"I'd say we're better than halfway home."

"We'll make Liverpool after all."

"So we will. But you haven't answered my question."

"About America? But what about Matthew, and Louise, and Alice? This is their home."

"They could come with us. They'd probably enjoy America."

"Oh, Adam, it isn't as easy as that." I heard him sigh in the darkness. "It isn't, I promise you."

"You mean you don't want it to be."

"Matthew will inherit Jonas's share of the company in a few years. It's a wonderful opportunity for him—and in the meantime—"

"It's all yours, as near as makes no difference. That's the difficulty, isn't it?"

"You make it sound so petty. It's just that . . . for the first time in my life I've found a *purpose* of my own. I can go forward—not as the woman someone else expects me to be, but as *me* . . . doing something for myself . . . making something happen . . . And does it matter so much to you where we live? Must you go back to America?"

I was horribly aware that something was going wrong, that the world was rushing in once more to claim us both and pull us in opposite directions. Yet not an hour before, it had all seemed so beautifully simple.

"Could plain *Mrs. Gaunt* control J. G. Oliver & Co., do you think?"

"Well . . . I don't see why not . . . Except that I've become so accustomed to being *Lady Oliver* . . . and, of course, now I'm a widow—"

"If you are legally a widow."

"But in a strange way it's quite useful to be a widow . . . because . . ."

"Because widows can do what they please. I know. I heard you say it."

―――――――

We lit the lamp, dressed, and made our way out on deck to stand at the rail just beyond the blank windows of the smoking room, watching the Rock and then the piers of the Birkenhead shore slide past in the chilly darkness. Overhead, clouds like rags of gray hodden trailed across the starlit face of the sky, dousing whole clusters of lights in their passage and skimming the bright disc of the moon itself.

"Isn't that your Hunter up there, striding through the sky?"

"Yes, that's Orion, with his long knife and his dogs and his flint axe." Adam squinted up at the cloud-streaked sky, where the constellation hung suspended before us. "There was an old flint-mine near my home in Norfolk, where the ancient hunters had quarried flints for their axes and arrowheads. I often used to go there, to climb down into the grassy hollows which had been their mine-shafts . . . and I'd imagine the old hunters wading as I did through the Fens, thigh-deep and silent, stalking the waterfowl. Somehow I've always pictured Orion as one of those fierce, wild ones."

"Do you remember telling me a long time ago the story of the Hunter and the Ploughman who follows at his heels, on and on through the sky?" I was still staring up at the starry firmament. "Where should I look for your Ploughman?"

"You won't see him at this time of year. He doesn't rise until just before dawn. Besides, he's an important man these days." Adam withdrew his gaze from the heavens. "The Ploughman has a silk hat and a frock coat now, and a pocket full of architects' plans. He's come a long way in the world, though I doubt if his heart has changed at all."

"I should think the Ploughman has long since overtaken your poor old Hunter, Adam. We have steamships and railways now instead of flint axes."

"I suppose you're going to tell me that's progress."

"Of course it is! Look around you—can you honestly tell me you've ever seen anything more wonderful than the *Altair?*"

"The sun rising over the mountains. The birth of a foal. A redwood growing from a single seed."

"Oh, you're just being difficult. You know I didn't mean that sort of thing."

"Yet I can remember when you would have agreed with me."

"That was a long time ago, when I was young. Everyone thinks like that when they're young, but as they grow older they see things differently."

"Tell me some of this new wisdom of yours, then."

"It isn't easy to explain."

"Try."

"Well . . . Do you remember what Prince Albert wrote in the catalogue of the Great Exhibition in '51? I can remember it exactly. *The progress of the human race resulting from the labor of all men ought to be the final object of the exertion of each individual. In promoting this end we are carrying out the will of the great and blessed God.* Jonas kept the catalogue till he died, with that passage underlined."

"I recall reading it, yes."

"Well, you see, until I read those lines again I never understood how Jonas felt about this ship—why he was even prepared to work himself to death to see the *Altair* built. It always seemed such a waste to me. But now I do understand."

I searched for the words to express what was in my heart at that moment.

"To be a human being is to be . . . such a small, puny part of Creation. And yet human beings built this ship—a huge machine powerful enough to shrink an ocean. If we can do that, we can do anything: level mountains, flood the deserts, fly to the stars—anything at all. One day there'll be no mysteries anymore—nothing we can't control or can't make use of. Even the weakest man will be able to hold the world in the palm of his hand, because of the work of people like Jonas Oliver. I want to be part of that march forward,

Adam. It's the most exciting thing I know. *Altair* is only a beginning: we'll build more steamships after her—bigger and faster than this one—"

Adam was regarding me with something like sadness.

"Rachel—I don't want to live in a world where there are no more mysteries. I don't happen to believe it was all put there for our benefit."

I couldn't understand why he stubbornly refused to share my vision. Not an hour before we'd been as one—as close as any two separate beings could be—and yet now . . .

In the pocket of my skirt my hand encountered the Indian amulet once more—subtly, treacherously smooth, an endless riddle like love itself. The amulet had begun it all, so many years earlier at Crow Cove—Tahtokay's amulet which had fatally bound Adam and myself in its charmed circle. All of a sudden I hated it passionately.

"There are your mysteries, Adam!" I held the amulet out to him. "Animal-spirits bringing rain or curing diseases—primitive, harmful beliefs held by deluded people. But one day they'll be gone—exploded—as completely as this." Without thinking, I drew back my hand and hurled the amulet far out into the river.

Adam watched it disappear without a word, leaning on the *Altair*'s rail and staring out over the dark waters of the Mersey where the red stone amulet was already spinning and tumbling its magical way to the river-bed.

At last he turned round, troubled and unsmiling.

"No—it isn't my world, Rachel, this bright new dream of yours. Not the greedy, arrogant, breakneck place you want to make of it with your steamships and your *standards*. You said to me once, *you are what you are,* and it's true. It's too late for me to change, even if I wanted to." He looked out again over the midnight river. "I love you—more than I ever did—but it's the old Rachel I love, not what you've turned yourself into. So for both our sakes it would be better if I went a long way away from here—back to America, probably— and left you to go on with this mission you seem to have inherited from the Olivers. You obviously have everything you want here. There's nothing you need from me."

I could have wept at his stubbornness—but I wouldn't beg. I'd done it once before, and I couldn't plead with him again. If Adam felt he must return to his wilderness, he'd have to go alone. That was all there was to say.

Epilogue

December 2, 1853.

Yesterday at noon the steamship *Altair* left Liverpool for New York, cheered on her way by the hooting of pleasure-boats in the river and a band playing nautical airs on the dockside.

After her stranding she'd gone straight into the Queen's Graving Dock to be inspected by marine surveyors and the underwriters' agents and to have the damaged plates on her hull replaced and her spare propeller fitted. Fortunately there was no need to delay her maiden voyage, and by a curious contradiction the story of her stranding and subsequent rescue only seemed to give her a reputation as an indestructible ship. Before long every place was taken for her first Atlantic crossing, and 1,300 tons of cargo packed into her hold. Even the cabin and stateroom Jonas had intended for our own use had been filled—by an immensely wealthy American lady called Mrs. Vanderdecken, so Captain Fuller informed me round-eyed, a lady who'd insisted on having the best accommodation aboard.

I suppose I should have been flattered, but I couldn't summon up much interest in Mrs. Vanderdecken. With a cruelty which surprised me, Adam had chosen the maiden voyage of the *Altair* as a means of returning to the wild parts of America which he loved.

Then, as luck would have it, Tom Fuller picked yesterday morning to be at his most demanding. By eleven o'clock I'd already spent two tedious hours in the office, examining charters and contracts which he insisted I see, though for the life of me I couldn't understand why he wanted my views on the perfectly sensible decisions he'd already made. At five minutes past eleven he glanced at the clock, and reached for his hat.

"It's time we left for the docks, my dear. The *Altair* sails at half-past twelve, and we ought to be there to see her off."

"She sails at twelve, surely."

"No, no—twelve-thirty. Captain Graham and I were discussing it only last night. Can't think where you heard it was to be twelve noon."

"In that case we've plenty of time to get there. I can finish drafting this letter."

"Nonsense—you've done more than enough for one morning. We'd best be on our way. It wouldn't do for Lady Oliver to arrive after the ship had left, after all. What would Jonas have said?"

"As long as she sails on time, Uncle Tom, it really doesn't matter whether I'm there or not. I shall stand on the dockside and wave goodbye, and that will be my duty done."

"But you'll go aboard, I hope, to wish Captain Graham a safe passage."

"Can't he come to the bottom of the gangway?"

"I should think not! He'll certainly expect to welcome you aboard."

"I don't remember much of a welcome when I went aboard on the night of the stranding."

"But this is quite different."

"I'd rather not go aboard, all the same."

"But you must. It's tradition," Tom Fuller insisted. "The owner always goes aboard to see the vessel off."

"I've never heard of it, then."

"It's tradition as far as Oliver's is concerned, I promise you. Captain John always did it, and Jonas too. You can't let the *Altair* go off without shaking the Captain's hand. That would be very bad luck."

I had to give in. It was sheer superstition, but I knew I'd never hear the end of it if I blighted the steamship's good fortune on her maiden voyage.

We set off for Wellington Dock, where the *Altair* waited with bunting slung between her masts, smoke rising from her giant funnels and her main gangway still stretching down to the quayside. Once aboard, we went straight to the bridge; I was determined to finish the formalities as quickly as possible and leave the ship at once. Adam and I had said all there was to say to one another. I didn't want to risk an emotional leave-taking at the last moment.

My goodbyes on the bridge were soon completed. Captain Graham showed me a chart of the North Atlantic with his course to New York drawn out in pencil, I solemnly wished him Godspeed and fine weather, and we shook hands on the exchange.

I was just about to go ashore again when Tom Fuller materialized at my elbow.

"There's one more thing," he told me apologetically.

"What now? Surely it's time I left the ship."

"Oh, you've a good half-hour yet, my dear. It's only ten minutes to twelve. And you could do Captain Graham a great service, if you'd spare ten minutes to call on Mrs. Vanderdecken in her cabin. She asked most particularly to see you, and poor Bob Graham tells me she's nearly driven him to distraction with her demands. If you'd only say a few words to her it would convince her she's being taken care of, and perhaps keep her quiet for a while. The Captain says she's more trouble than all the rest put together. Ten minutes, my dear—no more than that."

All along the crowded upper deck, I looked anxiously for Adam's tall figure waiting to catch a last glimpse of the city. If there had been any sign of him, I think I'd have turned and fled back to the safety of the wharf—but fortunately he didn't seem to have been caught up in the nostalgia of the moment, and he was nowhere to be seen. I didn't find him in the Grand Saloon either, thank goodness, and I reached the door of Mrs. Vanderdecken's quarters without any embarrassing incident.

Her stateroom door was ajar when I reached it. I knocked, and when there was no reply, pushed it open and went in. The cabin was empty—not just of Mrs. Vanderdecken and her maid, but also of any of the usual paraphernalia of embarkation; coats and gloves laid over chairs, hatboxes and trunks on the floor. The stateroom was now lavishly and immaculately furnished down to a great urn of flowers on the table, but there was no sign whatever of its occupant.

I began to feel angry. However wealthy this American lady might be, and however many servants might normally wait at her beck and call, I wasn't one of their number. If she'd asked to see me, the least she might have done was to be there when I arrived. Crossly, I went over to the door of the sleeping cabin and knocked again. Once more there was no answer: the awkward Mrs. Vanderdecken was nowhere to be found.

So be it: the American woman would have to remain Captain Graham's problem. As I turned sharply away from the door of the sleeping cabin I heard behind me a distinct *click* as the stateroom door swung shut. Well, I thought grimly, Mrs. Vanderdecken has returned too late. It was high time for me to go ashore.

Except that it wasn't Mrs. Vanderdecken—or any lady, in fact—who had entered at that moment. It was Adam Gaunt.

My first, instinctive reaction was one of indignation, followed immediately by panic.

"I must go ashore, Adam. Please move away from the door. We've long since said our farewells, and I won't risk delaying the *Altair* for anything in the world."

He didn't move. "You haven't delayed her. Listen."

A long, rumbling shudder was passing through the ship, and from the dockside I could hear the swell of frantic cheering. I'd been so preoccupied with my missing American that I hadn't heard the thundering paddles of the tugs as they took the *Altair* in tow. On deck the noise would have been unmistakable. There in the stern it was muted to the rumble of distant thunder.

I listened to the sounds of the ship's departure in disbelief.

"We're sailing early! There was half an hour to go before she left —Tom Fuller said so . . . I must go to the bridge . . ."

"It's twelve noon, Rachel. Surely you knew when the *Altair* was due to sail?"

"*Twelve!* But that's what I thought—and Uncle Tom told me it had been changed to twelve-thirty." Suddenly all the peculiarities began to make sense: my uncle's insistence that I come aboard before the ship sailed, the switching of sailing times, the mysterious summons from our American passenger.

"And where is Mrs. Vanderdecken, this lady who was so anxious to speak to me before we sailed? Or should I ask *who is she?*"

"There's no Mrs. Vanderdecken. This cabin was kept for you. It was always intended for you, after all. I thought you might have . . . memories of it."

"Adam, how *could* you!" The last thing I wanted was to be reminded of our night together aboard the steamship, when everything had suddenly been perfect, and then just as suddenly catastrophic. "Still—there's a simple solution. I'll go ashore with the pilot at the Northwest lightship."

"Of course. I'd forgotten you were so handy with a rope ladder." Adam nodded sagely. "It'll make a fine story for the passengers to spread round New York—the owner of the world's biggest ship finding herself stranded aboard and having to climb over the side to go home in the pilot-boat. Is that what you want?"

"Of course not. . . . But this is no better than kidnapping."

"Nonsense. This is your ship, as you keep telling me. Order Captain Graham to turn round and take you back, if you wish. He'd do it, I'm sure. But be ready to read about it in *The Times* tomorrow." He waited for the implications of this to sink in. "On the other hand . . . you could stay aboard all the way to New York."

"But I've no luggage! Nothing! How can I possibly stay aboard? And what about the girls, and Matthew? Who's to look after them?"

"Your trunks are through there, in the other cabin. Your aunt and that Vickers woman packed them this morning and sent them aboard."

"I might have known Aunt Grace would have something to do with such a hare-brained scheme!"

Adam grinned. "You don't imagine Captain Fuller thought of it on his own, do you? No, it was your aunt's idea in the first place, after the Captain had told her he'd seen us together on the *Atlas*. Apparently you were indiscreet enough to mention my name in his hearing. At any rate, your maid is already aboard and your aunt's quite happy to take charge of the White House until you get back."

It suddenly became vital for me to sit down, and I sank on to an upholstered bench below the stern windows, my legs unsteady. Adam watched me for a moment as if afraid I would bolt; then he relented, and sat down beside me, taking my hands in his.

"It was a cheap trick, I admit. But your aunt always had a highly romantic imagination."

"You should have known better than to listen to her."

"Oh, I considered telling her to mind her own business, believe me. I was sure you and I were finished with one another as soon as I saw you throw the amulet into the river."

"I wish I hadn't done that now."

"Well then, maybe there's hope for us after all. At least if we travel together to New York we'll be able to talk it all over without Reuben and Matthew and stranded ships interfering."

"I don't see what we have to talk about, Adam. You said yourself that we live in different worlds nowadays. I didn't succeed in living in yours, and you won't even try to live in mine. I can't go back to a log cabin—not now."

"Have I asked you to?" His eyes searched my face with unnerving persistence. "None of us can go back into the past. I'm not stupid enough to think I can stop the world turning, however much I'll always hate the sight of railway tracks carving up the wilderness."

"And you own a steam-tug yourself. What about the *Atlas?*"

"I've thought of that. I'm going to turn Parrish's over to Reuben, *Atlas* and all."

"Matthew will go mad!"

"It'll be good for him. And Reuben needs an anchor."

"And what about you, Adam? Do you need an anchor?"

"I need you, Rachel. As an anchor, as a lover, as a friend—as a conscience, if you like. And you need me to take the pins out of your hair and all that pious claptrap out of your head—and to run off with you from time to time in the most scandalous fashion. So I'll make a bargain with you. I want you to stay aboard with me until New York—at the speed the *Altair* can cross the Atlantic, you could still be back in Liverpool in time for Christmas. But tomorrow afternoon a boat will go ashore at Queenstown with the last of the mail. If I haven't managed to convince you by then that there's a middle way for us—that we can make a future together somewhere between the wilderness and your blessed shipping line—then you can go ashore there and I won't lift a finger to stop you. You'll be back in Liverpool in a couple of days, and I'll go on alone to New York. And that will be the finish of it, I promise you. No letters—no more reappearances. Now, that seems a pretty fair bargain."

"I only have to stay until Queenstown?"

"Only until then."

"Just one night aboard the ship?"

"One single night."

"That seems . . . fair."

A small boat has just left the *Altair,* bound for Queenstown harbor with the last of the passengers' mail. I'm not aboard her. Instead I'm watching from the steamship's rail as the launch hops and slithers over the waves toward the distant harbor entrance.

"How would you like to be married in New York?" Adam asked this morning, lazily drawing a long strand of hair from my eyelashes as I struggled to wake.

"I thought we *were* married. Isn't that what you always said?"

"Well, in that case we must have a second honeymoon. Let's sail out to San Francisco and travel back through the mountains. You always wanted to see the Rocky Mountains." Adam was lying stretched out beside me like a toppled, gilded statue, his voice as drowsy as a summer bee, the scars of the bullet which had nearly killed him still livid on his skin. "You'll have to go back to calling yourself Mrs. Gaunt."

"What—not *Mrs. Allen,* Colonel?"

"Not *Mrs. Allen,* please. Just *Mrs. Gaunt*—my wife—once and for all. Until there are no more stars and no more mysteries."

Which in Adam's world means forever. And yet . . . I don't suppose it will be easy, being Adam Gaunt's wife again. . . . For one thing, I've become so accustomed to being his widow. And a widow, as Aunt Grace always said, can do as she pleases . . .

ABOUT THE AUTHOR

ALISON MCLEAY lives with her husband and son in Fife, Scotland, near the sea whose moods and mysteries form the background of *Passage Home*. This is her first novel.